JUNIOR

PEARS

ENCYCLOPAEDIA

THIRTY-THIRD EDITION

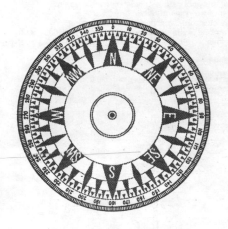

EDITED BY EDWARD BLISHEN

PELHAM BOOKS
Published by the Penguin Group
Penguin Books Ltd, 27 Wrights Lane, London W8 5TZ, England
Viking Penguin, a division of Penguin Books USA Inc
375 Hudson Street, New York, New York 10014, USA
Penguin Books Australia Ltd, Ringwood, Victoria, Australia
Penguin Books Canada Ltd, 10 Alcorn Avenue, Suite 300, Toronto, Ontario,
    Canada M4V 3B2
Penguin Books (NZ) Ltd, 182–190 Wairau Road, Auckland 10, New Zealand

Penguin Books Ltd, Registered Offices: Harmondsworth, Middlesex, England

This edition first published 1993

Printed in England by Clays Ltd, St Ives plc

A CIP catalogue record for this book is available from the British Library.
0 7207 2025 7

Photograph credits for cover

Front cover:

Background: *Cathy Morley*
Jaguar: *Jaguar Cars Ltd*
Sally Gunnell: © *Sporting Pictures*
Map of Europe: © *Royal Geographical Society*

ABOUT THIS BOOK

It's a fact—I've just become aware of it—that, given that I was made of rather longer-lasting stuff than I am, I might have been editor of JUNIOR PEARS for 462 years instead of the mere 33 years I've held the position: but I could not have been its editor a year longer than that. At the very earliest, this annual volume might have burst upon the world in 1531. The reason is to be found on page 607 of the *Shorter Oxford Dictionary* (which isn't particularly short: it's called that because it *is* shorter than the vast *Oxford Dictionary* itself). Go to this short-but-not-very-short dictionary or to the enormous set of volumes it was reduced from (they're likely to be in the local library) whenever you want to find out when a word was first used. And as far as the scholars who worked on this great dictionary were able to find out, the first use of the word 'encyclopaedia' occurred in that year, 1531. So, earlier, it wouldn't have been around for JUNIOR PEARS to use. It came, they say, from the Latin *encyclopaedia*: and that came from the pseudo-Greek (that is, it wasn't the real Greek, but a kind of made-up Greek—I imagine it was the Romans who made it up), ἐγκνκλοπαιλεία. And *that* stands for ἐγκίκλιος παιδ ία, which means circular or complete education. So you said 'encyclopaedia' if you wanted to refer to the whole circle of learning—imagining that all the things it's possible to know were holding hands and forming a great ring. By 1644 the word had settled down to mean a book not absolutely unlike this one, though much more ambitious: 'a work', says the dictionary, 'containing information on all branches of knowledge, usually arranged alphabetically.'*

The tree of learning had fewer branches then than it has now, and far fewer leaves. Those distant smallish woods and forests of knowledge have become an immense jungle. JUNIOR PEARS, like any encyclopaedia today, has to be rather more modest than its 17th century forerunners. And indeed it wears its grand title cautiously. This is, in fact, an encyclopaedia in a sense in which the word was first used in 1801: it's a *specialised* encyclopaedia, for a particular audience. It's for young people, and is intended to provide information on the main topics in which, as we judge, young people are likely to be interested. Partly we hope it will be found a helpful handbook by students: thus the sections on history, geography, and so on. But no young reader is simply a schoolboy, or a schoolgirl, or a student: and though we hope your schooling is so wide-based that sections on sport and ships, and railways and music, may often have some bearing on what you're studying, still these and other similar sections are there mainly to supply information about out-of-school or out-of-college activities.

---

*If we go back rather earlier, to the time of the Celts, we find their priests thought it a sin to set down anything they knew in writing. For editing, or reading, JUNIOR PEARS, you and I might, about the year 250 BC, say, have been in serious trouble.

But if our basic purpose is to provide information, we've never wanted the book to be merely a bulging collection of facts. We've tried to make it pleasant to read as well as easy to consult: here, for example, are all the main facts about motor-cars, but imbedded in a history of the motor-car, and an account of the workings and makings of the motor-car,[1] that form, we hope, more than a dry assemblage of information.

Nevertheless, we've tried to bear in mind that you ought to be able to track down as quickly as possible any single piece of information for which you have some desperate need: therefore each section is arranged so that it yields any particular fact as easily as possible. The list of contents on the title-pages of some sections will be found useful; and other sections, which lend themselves to such treatment, are in dictionary form.

But, of course, a single-volume encyclopaedia is not and could not be a substitute for deeper reading. You can learn from JUNIOR PEARS that two hundred years ago, exactly, in 1793, Louis XVI was executed, and the Reign of Terror began. But to find out what brought the French king to the scaffold, and what sort of man he was, and what exactly the Reign of Terror was, and why it began and how it ended . . . to learn about the marvellous *detail* of the events to which we can give only a line, you must look to the historians. This is one kind of book—aiming to give the gleaming bare bones of information. For the flesh you must look to other sorts of book to which we provide pointers here and there in our lists of 'Further Reading'.

Now and then, alas, a reader fails to find the bone he is after, or finds something amiss with the bone itself. If this happens to you, write to me about it. Complaints or comments of any kind—addressed to 27 Wrights Lane, Kensington, London W8 5TZ—will be taken into account in next year's revision.

Behind certain changes in this 33rd edition lie the very helpful suggestions made by many readers. On the whole, I'd be glad if you wouldn't ask me to carry out extensive research on some subject or other: I'd have to be twenty men to provide such a service. And now and then I've had the mean suspicion that I was being asked to do someone's homework. ('Please tell me everything about the French Revolution and let me have it, with maps, diagrams and time-charts, by next Monday at the latest.') But simpler inquiries, and certainly any criticism you wish to make, will be most welcome. A book like this ought to be shaped not only by a body of contributors but also by a body of readers, and all of us who are responsible for JUNIOR PEARS will welcome your collaboration.

---

[1] It may be worth giving our usual warning that this section, as well as the section on computers, has been found so useful by some parents that the true owners of the book have been deprived of it. *Keep it in a safe place.*

CONTENTS

THE WORLD

1: ITS HISTORY

A DIARY OF WORLD EVENTS

The story of man, who first appeared on the Earth a little less than a million years ago, can be traced back only about 6,000 years. For earlier times there are no written records (nor have archaeologists made discoveries) to help the historian to form an accurate or detailed picture of human activity.

This diary is planned not only to be referred to if you are hurriedly searching for a particular event (or revising a particular period) but also to be read as a story. And a hair-raising story it is, with its empires rising and falling, its barbarian Franks and Goths and Vandals becoming the French and Germans and Italians of today, and the uneasy groupings of nations against one another becoming the enormous anxious grouping of our own time, modified by the extraordinary events of 1989 and 1990. Read the diary through, and consider what a tiny pinch of time these 6,000 years are when measured against the total life of our planet. And remember, as you read, that the diary doesn't cease to be written simply because we have had to break off at 1993 to put it in this book. This diary is now your diary; History is your history.

The first reference to any historical figure in this account is printed in black type. So that if you are interested in, say, Napoleon, and come across his name in ordinary type, you will know that you are somewhere in the middle of his story, and must look back to **Napoleon** in order to find its beginning. The names of battles are printed in small capitals, like this: WATERLOO.

Some of the most important events of all, the passing of great Acts of Parliament and achievements of exploration and discovery, are omitted because they are dealt with separately elsewhere in this section.

B.C.

4000–3000 First settlements in the river valleys of the Nile in Egypt, the Tigris and Euphrates in Mesopotamia, the Indus in India and the Yellow River in China.

By 2000 Chinese civilisation, oldest in the world, covers practically the whole of China.

In the Indus valley the Dravidians have established an orderly system of government; they are often invaded, but out of the give and take of ideas between conquerors and conquered, Hinduism begins to emerge. In Mesopotamia the Sumerians have invented a form of writing (cuneiform), divided the circle into 360°, a degree into 60 minutes and a minute into 60 seconds, and discovered how to extract copper and make bronze. Their knowledge lives on despite their absorption into the Babylonian Empire, whose best-known king, **Hammurabi**, extends the authority of Babylon as far as Syria and codifies his country's laws.

The Great Pyramids

In the Nile valley the Egyptians have already built the Great Pyramids at Gizeh and the Sphinx (2600) and divided time into solar years.

The spread of knowledge from Egypt has helped to create the Minoan civilisation in Crete (named after the legendary king **Minos** (see DICTIONARY OF MYTHOLOGY), whose magnificent palace at Knossos was discovered in 1900).

In Britain the great stone circles at Stonehenge and Avebury are still used for religious worship.

1800–1700 First use in Egypt of papyrus, an early form of paper. Nile valley overrun by Hyksos ('princes of the desert').

The Babylonian empire is overrun by the Hittites; but there is conflict, lasting several centuries, between these and other invading tribes based on Babylon, Nineveh and other cities.

1580 Hyksos driven out of Egypt. Founding of the 'New Kingdom', under which Egypt is to be at her greatest.

1400 Moses leads the Israelites out of Egypt. Knossos destroyed by earthquake or enemies, and Cretan civilisation at an end.

1300–1200 Hittites, now controlling all Mesopotamia, discover how to smelt iron, equip their troops with iron weapons, and clash with Egypt. Neither wins, and both empires begin to crumble.

1180 Siege of Troy: one of the wars by which the ancestors of the ancient Greeks settled themselves round the Aegean, and the only one of which an account survives (in Homer's *Iliad*).

c. **1060–***c.* **970** David king of Israel.

c. **970–***c.* **940** Solomon king of Israel. He uses his enormous wealth, gained through trade, to build the Temple at Jerusalem.

800 The Phoenicians, whose cities of Tyre and Sidon are nearly 1,000 years old, found Carthage.

776 First Olympiad.

753 Rome founded.

750–550 Greek city states emerge on Greek mainland and around the coasts of Mediterranean and Black Sea.

691 Assyrians (already lords of Mesopotamia, Syria, Palestine, Arabia) conquer Egypt.

660 First Mikado in Japan.

612 Chaldeans conquer Assyrians and establish second Babylonian Empire.

597 **Nebuchadnezzar**, mightiest Chaldean emperor, captures Jerusalem and carries off the Jews into captivity.

594 **Solon** lays the foundations of Athenian democracy.

560 **Buddha** born.

551 **Confucius** born.

539–525 **Cyrus**, king of Persia, makes himself master of Asia Minor, captures Babylon, founds the Persian empire and allows the Jews to return to Jerusalem.

525 **Cambyses**, Cyrus's successor, conquers Egypt.

510 Rome becomes a republic.

490 Athens has helped Greek cities on the coast of Asia Minor to revolt—unsuccessfully—against their Persian overlords, **Darius** I of Persia lands a force in Greece to punish Athens; is beaten at MARATHON.

480 **Xerxes** makes a second attempt to crush Greece; exterminates a Spartan army under **Leonidas** at THERMOPYLAE and occupies Athens; but the Persian fleet is destroyed at SALAMIS.

479 Persians defeated at PLAETAEA.

461 **Pericles** becomes the most important person in Athenian politics. Under his leadership Greek civilisation, free of the Persian menace, has its 'golden age'; it is now that the Parthenon is built (447–438). But removal of the Persian danger leads to quarrelling among the Greek city states.

The Parthenon

431–404 Peloponnesian War between Athens and Sparta, ending with the capture of Athens.

390 Gauls capture Rome except for the Capitol, but Romans regain the city by paying a huge ransom.

359 **Philip** becomes king of Macedonia; sets out to make himself overlord of quarrelsome Greek cities.

338 Philip defeats combined armies of Athens and Thebes, becomes master of Greece.

336 Philip assassinated; succeeded by his son, **Alexander the Great**.

333 Alexander defeats **Darius III** of Persia and conquers Egypt, where he founds Alexandria.

327 Alexander extends his empire as far as the Indus.

323 Alexander dies; his empire is divided among his generals.

280 **Pyrrhus**, king of Epirus, aids Greek cities in S. Italy against Rome; defeats the Romans twice but himself suffers heavy losses (hence the term 'Pyrrhic victories', meaning victories won at great cost).

275 Defeating Pyrrhus, Rome becomes mistress of S. Italy, and thus comes into conflict with Carthage.

264 First Punic War between Rome and Carthage for control of Sicily.

260 Roman sea victory at MYLAE.

256 Roman landing near Carthage repulsed.

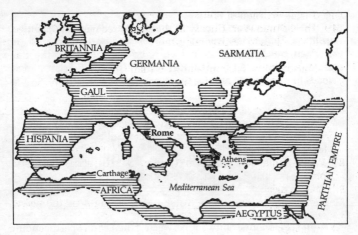

The Roman Empire at its furthest extent

246 Great Wall of China built.

241 Remainder of Carthaginian fleet defeated; Carthage sues for peace and loses control of Sicily.

238 Carthage sets out to create new empire in Spain.

225 Gauls invade Roman territory and are defeated. To prevent this happening again, Rome extends her frontiers northwards by conquering Cisalpine Gaul (modern Lombardy); is now mistress of all Italy.

219 Second Punic War. A 26-year-old Carthaginian general, **Hannibal**, crosses the Alps into Italy, where he is unbeaten for 15 years.

217 Hannibal destroys a Roman army at LAKE TRASIMENE.

216 Hannibal destroys a second Roman army at CANNAE, but is unable to capture Rome itself.

210–206 Roman army wipes out Carthaginian forces in Spain and conquers the country.

204 Romans cross from Spain to Africa.

202 Hannibal returns to Africa to save Carthage, but is defeated at ZAMA.

201 Carthage surrenders her fleet and hands Spain over to Rome.

166 Tartar invasion of China.

149 Third Punic War. Uneasy at the steady recovery of Carthage, Rome resolves to destroy her rival.

146 Carthage destroyed.

102 **Marius** drives back invading German tribes.

91 Revolt of Italian cities belonging to Rome but with no say in government.

89 All Italians become Roman citizens.

88 Civil war in Rome between plebeians (people's party), led by Marius, and patricians (nobles), under **Sulla**. Sulla wins and Marius escapes to Africa.

87 While Sulla is fighting in Greece, Marius seizes power in Rome.

86 Marius dies.

82 Sulla returns, massacres his enemies, strengthens the power of the Senate, becomes dictator.

78 Sulla dies.

73 **Spartacus** leads revolt of 60,000 slaves.

71 **Crassus** crushes Spartacus revolt.

70 Crassus and **Pompey** reduce power of the Senate.

66–62 Pompey captures Jerusalem, conquers Syria and advances to the Euphrates.

60 Pompey, Crassus and **Caesar** divide the government of Rome's dominions, becoming the First Triumvirate (rule of three men). Caesar begins conquest of Gaul.

55 Caesar's first visit to Britain.

53 Crassus defeated and killed by Parthians.

51 Caesar completes conquest of Gaul.

49 Caesar crosses the Rubicon, boundary of his own command, to overthrow Pompey, now his only rival.

48 Caesar defeats Pompey at PHARSALUS. Pompey escapes to Egypt and is murdered.

44 Caesar is murdered.

43 **Octavian**, Caesar's nephew, **Antony** and **Lepidus** form Second Triumvirate.

42 Octavian and Antony defeat **Brutus** and **Cassius**, chief plotters against Caesar. The government of Rome's dominions is divided, Octavian taking the West, Antony the East (which he rules from Egypt with **Cleopatra**) and Lepidus, Carthaginian Africa.

31 Octavian defeats Antony and Cleopatra at ACTIUM.

30 Deaths of Antony and Cleopatra.
27 Octavian, now known as Augustus, becomes first Roman emperor.
4 True date of birth of Jesus.

A.D.

14 Augustus dies.
30 Jesus crucified.
43 Emperor **Claudius** sends force to conquer Britain. The South is soon subdued, despite resistance from **Caractacus**, who is captured and sent to Rome. The Romans work their way northwards.
61 **Boadicea**, queen of the Iceni, revolts against Romans, burns their settlement at London; but her army is annihilated and she takes poison.
68 Nero, last emperor of the house of Augustus, commits suicide.
70 Emperor **Titus** captures and destroys Jerusalem, drives the Jews from the Holy Land.
79 Pompeii and Herculaneum destroyed in eruption of Vesuvius.
82 **Agricola**, governor of Britain, attempts conquest of Scotland.
93 **Trajan** adds Dacia (modern Rumania) and Mesopotamia to Roman empire, now at its largest.
117 **Hadrian** tries to keep barbarians out of Roman territories by building permanent fortifications, including 70-mile-long wall (Hadrian's Wall) from Tyne to Solway.
164–80 Plagues ravage Roman and Chinese empires.
180 Century of war and disorder begins for Rome, during which a succession of generals, many not even Roman by birth, are made emperors by troops in their pay. Perpetual invasions by Franks, Goths, Parthians, Vandals and Huns.
226 **Artaxerxes** founds new dynasty in Persia.
284 **Diocletian**, last Roman emperor to persecute Christians, re-organises the empire with two joint emperors and two sub-ordinate emperors.
312 **Constantine** defeats his joint emperor, **Maxentius**, and becomes sole emperor in West.
313 Constantine legalises Christianity; later makes it State religion.

324 Constantine defeats emperor in the East, becomes sole ruler of Roman world.

328 To celebrate victory, Constantine founds 'new Rome' by enlarging ancient Greek city of Byzantium, calls it Constantinople.

330 Constantine moves capital to Constantinople.

337 Constantine dies, and empire is again ruled by succession of joint (and rival) emperors.

379 **Theodosius the Great**, emperor in the East, drives Goths from Greece and Italy.

382 Theodosius makes peace with Goths.

394 Theodosius becomes last sole emperor of Roman world.

395 Theodosius dies; division of empire into West and East becomes final.

407 As barbarians pour into Western empire, Roman legions are withdrawn from Britain in last attempt to defend Rome. Britain is left easy prey to Angles and Saxons.

410 Visigoths under **Alaric** plunder Rome. Waves of barbarians sweep into Spain, Portugal, Italy, Gaul and North Africa.

434 **Attila** becomes king of the Huns, Mongolians whose invasion of Europe is death-blow for Western empire.

449 **Hengist** and **Horsa**, Jutish chiefs, invade England, set up kingdom in Kent.

451 Invading Gaul, Attila is defeated by army of Goths and Romans at CHALONS.

452 Attila invades Italy; is persuaded by **Pope Leo I** to spare Rome.

453 Attila dies.

455 Vandals sack Rome. In next twenty years ten different emperors rule.

476 Last Roman emperor deposed; Western empire ends.

482 **Clovis**, king of Salian Franks, makes himself first king of Frankland (France), with Paris as his capital.

496 Clovis baptised; Franks become Christians.

527 **Justinian**, whose codification of Roman law is basis for much later Western law, becomes emperor in Constantinople. Attempting re-conquest of Western Empire, he recovers North Africa, S.E. Spain and Italy.

536 **Belisarius**, Justinian's famous general, captures Rome.

565 Justinian dies.

568 Lombards invade Italy, settle in the north.

570 Birth of **Mohammed**.

590 **Gregory the Great** becomes Pope; declares Rome supreme centre of the Church.

597 **St Augustine** lands in England, baptises **Ethelbert**, king of Kent.

601 St Augustine becomes first archbishop of Canterbury.

c. **616** Mohammed proclaims himself the apostle of Allah.

618 Great T'ang dynasty founded in China.

628 Mohammed writes to all rulers of the earth, demanding that they acknowledge the One True God, Allah, and serve Him.

632 Mohammed dies; his friend **Abu Bakr**, first Caliph ('successor'), leads Arabs out of the desert to achieve Mohammed's aim of making the world submit to Islam.

637 Arabs defeat Persians at KARDESSIA. Soon after, Mesopotamia, Syria, Palestine and Egypt fall to them.

638 Jerusalem surrenders to Arabs.

641 Arabs capture Alexandria. Its famous library is destroyed.

643 The Arabs defeat armies of the Eastern empire at YARMAK.

669 Arabs unsuccessfully attack Constantinople from sea.

711 Having conquered East and North Africa, Arabs cross into Spain.

720 Spain subdued, the Arabs (with the Moors) invade France.

732 **Charles Martel** drives Arabs out of France.

751 **Pepin**, son of Charles Martel, crowned King of the Franks, founding Carolingian dynasty.

762 Baghdad founded; becomes capital of Arab empire.

768 Pepin dies; his kingdom divided between his son Charles (later known as **Charlemagne**) and **Carloman**.

771 Carloman dies and Charlemagne takes possession of his lands. From then onwards Charlemagne enlarges his dominions until his power reaches from the Pyrenees to the river Elbe in Germany, and from the Atlantic to the Danube and Tiber.

786 **Haroun-al-Raschid** becomes Caliph at Baghdad; under him Arab empire is at its greatest.

800 Charlemagne crowned in Rome emperor of the Holy Roman Empire.

802 **Egbert** king of Wessex, one of seven Anglo-Saxon kingdoms fighting for supremacy in England. Others are Northumbria, Mercia, Kent, Sussex, Essex and E. Anglia.

809 Haroun-al-Raschid dies; beginning of 200 years of chaos and civil war in Arab empire.

814 Charlemagne dies.

829 Egbert unites England for first time under one king.

840 Frankish empire is divided between Charlemagne's sons and grandsons, whose quarrels lead to its breaking up.

871 **Alfred the Great** king of Wessex, practically the only part of England not in Danish hands.

878 Alfred defeats Danes, compels them by Treaty of Wedmore to stay in their settlements in N.E. England and become Christians.

900 Alfred dies.

919 **Henry I** king of Germany; completes the separation of the Frankish empire into Germany and France.

987 **Louis V**, last Carolingian king of France, dies, and is succeeded by **Hugh Capet**, first modern French king.

1013 **Sweyn** of Denmark conquers England, is accepted as king.

1015 **Canute**, Sweyn's son, defeats **Edmund Ironside**, son of last Anglo-Saxon king, and divides realm with him.

1016 Edmund dies; Canute becomes sole king.

1042 **Edward the Confessor** returns to England as king from Normandy, where he has been living at the court of the Norman

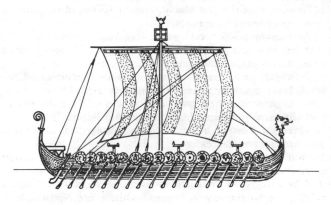

Viking Ship

duke. Leaves government to **Earl Godwin**, devotes himself to religion.

1054 Eastern Orthodox Church breaks with Church of Rome.

1065 Westminster Abbey, rebuilt by Edward the Confessor, consecrated.

1066 Edward the Confessor dies; **Harold**, son of Earl Godwin, elected king. **William** of Normandy invades England and kills Harold at HASTINGS.

1071 Seljuk Turks, having seized Baghdad, sweep across Asia Minor and take fortress of Niceaea opposite Constantinople.

1075 Turks take Jerusalem and Holy Places.

1086 Domesday Book, a survey of England, completed.

1095 **Pope Urban II** summons Christian nations to First Crusade.

1098 Crusaders take Antioch.

1099 Crusaders take Jerusalem.

1135 England plunged in civil war when **Stephen**, grandson of William the Conqueror, allows himself to be elected king although he had previously recognised **Mathilda**, Henry I's daughter, as heir to throne.

1149 Second Crusade ends in failure.

1153 Stephen acknowledges Mathilda's son as his heir.

1164 **Henry II** tries to bring English clergy into the power of the royal courts and clashes with **Thomas à Becket**, his chancellor and Archbishop of Canterbury, who flees to France.

1170 Becket returns, but the quarrel breaks out afresh, and he is murdered in Canterbury Cathedral.

1174 **Saladin** proclaimed caliph; launches a holy war of all Muslims against Christians.

1187 Saladin recaptures Jerusalem.

1189 Third Crusade, under **Philip Augustus** of France and **Richard I**, fails to retake Jerusalem. Siege of Acre.

1191 Crusaders capture ACRE.

1192 Richard concludes armistice with Saladin.

1202 Fourth Crusade; Constantinople captured.

1206 Mogul empire founded in India.

1215 **King John** is forced at Runnymede to accept Magna Carta, which lays it down that no freeman may be imprisoned or punished except by law of the land.

1218–21 Fifth Crusade captures Damietta, in Egypt, but loses it again.

1228–29 Sixth Crusade recovers Jerusalem by negotiation.

1264 Henry III, whose misrule has caused barons to revolt, is taken prisoner at LEWES by **Simon de Montfort**.

1265 De Montfort summons first Parliament in which towns are represented; is defeated and killed at EVESHAM.

1273 Rudolf of Hapsburg, founder of dynasty that is to reign in Austria until 1918, elected Holy Roman Emperor.

1280 Kublai Khan emperor of China; encourages trade and teaches religious tolerance. Visited by **Marco Polo**.

1282 Edward I completes conquest of Wales.

1291 Acre, last Christian stronghold in Syria, is lost.

1295 Edward I summons Model Parliament, so called because for the first time King, Lords and Commons meet.

1296 Edward I attempts to annex Scotland.

1297 Sir William Wallace defeats Edward at STIRLING.

1298 Edward defeats Wallace at FALKIRK.

1301 Edward makes his son Prince of Wales.

1304 Wallace captured and executed, but **Robert Bruce** raises another revolt against Edward.

1306 Robert Bruce crowned king of Scotland.

1309 Papacy falls into French control; residence of the Popes moved to Avignon.

1314 Edward II defeated at BANNOCKBURN by Robert Bruce.

1328 Robert Bruce recognised by England as king of Scotland.

1337 Outbreak of 'Hundred Years' War' between England and France. Causes: a conflict of commercial interests and Edward III's claim to French throne.

1340 English defeat French by sea at SLUYS.

1346 Edward III defeats French at CRECY.

1347 Edward captures Calais.

1348–49 Black Death, the bubonic plague, reaches England, killing nearly one half of the population, and causing acute shortage of labour and social unrest.

1356 Edward, the Black Prince, defeats French at POITIERS.

1369 French renew the war; reconquer province after province.

1372 English fleet destroyed. Impoverished by war, weakened by quarrels between Black Prince and his brother, **John of Gaunt**, England loses French possessions except Bordeaux and Calais.

1378 Rival Popes elected in Rome and Avignon.

1381 Heavily taxed, tied to the land as serfs, the peasants revolt under **Wat Tyler**. Tyler is murdered and the rising crushed, but from this time serfdom gradually declines.

1384 Death of **John Wycliffe**, who has attacked abuses in the Church of Rome and ordered a translation of the Bible into English.

1385 Scots invade England; **Richard II** takes Edinburgh.

1388 Scots again invade; are victorious at OTTERBURN.

1397 Richard II executes or banishes leaders of the barons. Among those banished is **Henry, Duke of Hereford**, John of Gaunt's son and heir.

1399 John of Gaunt dies; Richard II confiscates his estates. Henry, Duke of Hereford, returns to England to lead revolt of the nobles. Parliament deposes Richard and accepts Henry as king—the first to speak English (grown out of Norman French and Anglo-Saxon) as his mother-tongue.

1400 Welsh revolt under **Owen Glendower**.

1403 Scots defeated at HOMILDON HILL. Henry IV crushes revolt at SHREWSBURY.

1415 **Henry V** renews war against France, captures HARFLEUR and is victorious at AGINCOURT.

1420 Henry V recognised by French king as his heir; marries French princess.

1422 Henry dies. French refuse to recognise his one-year-old son, **Henry VI**, as king of France; Henry V's brother continues war.

1429 English overcome all French resistance except in ORLEANS; they besiege the town, but are driven off by an army led by **Joan of Arc**.

1431 Joan of Arc, captured by the English, is burned at the stake; but French advance continues.

1445 **Johann Gutenberg**, first European printer, sets up business in Mainz.

1453 The Eastern empire is at an end when Constantinople falls to the Ottoman Turks, who sweep into Greece and across to the Danube.

1455 Disastrous end of Hundred Years' War has made the English government unpopular, and the **Duke of York** (white rose) claims the throne from Henry VI, a Lancastrian (red rose). So begin Wars of the Roses. Yorkists win at ST ALBANS, but are then defeated; York flees to Ireland.

1460 York returns, is victorious at NORTHAMPTON, but is defeated and killed at WAKEFIELD.

1461 Edward, York's son, proclaimed king in London as **Edward IV.** Defeats the Lancastrians at TOWTON; Henry VI is captured and imprisoned.

1464 Lancastrians defeated at HEXHAM.

1470 Yorkist **Earl of Warwick**, the 'Kingmaker', quarrels with Edward IV, frees Henry VI. Edward flees to Flanders.

1471 Edward returns, defeats and kills Warwick at BARNET and routs Lancastrians at TEWKESBURY.

1476 **Caxton** sets up as printer.

1478 Inquisition begins in Spain.

1483 Edward IV succeeded by 12-year-old son, **Edward V.** Richard, Duke of Gloucester, Protector of the Realm, has himself proclaimed king as **Richard III.** Edward V and his brother are murdered in the Tower.

1485 Henry Tudor, Earl of Richmond, lands in England and defeats Richard III at BOSWORTH. As **Henry VII**, he founds the line of Tudors, breaks the power of the nobles and establishes strong central government.

1492 **Ferdinand** of Aragon and **Isabella** of Castile, whose marriage unites Spain for the first time, finally free the country from the Moors by capturing GRANADA. Columbus sails for the New World in his flagship the *Santa Maria*.

1513 **James IV** of Scotland invades England, is defeated at FLODDEN.

1517 **Martin Luther**, founder of Protestantism, nails to church door at Wittenberg his condemnation of many practices of the Church of Rome.

1519 **Cortes** conquers Mexico.

1520 Luther publicly burns the Papal Bull excommunicating him, and refuses to go back on his teachings. Protestantism spreads; is adopted in Sweden in 1527, in Denmark in 1536. In Switzerland it is established by **Calvin**, whose followers in France, the Huguenots, wage bitter wars with the Catholics between 1562 and 1598. In Scotland the Reformation, as this great movement is called, triumphs by 1560, largely owing to teaching of Calvin's disciple, **John Knox**.

1526 **Baber**, Moslem warrior king, captures Delhi.

1528 Conquest of Peru.

The *Santa Maria* 1492

1529 The Ottoman Sultan, **Suleiman** the Magnificent, having taken Belgrade, the island of Rhodes and Budapest, attempts to storm Vienna but is beaten back.

Cardinal Wolsey, **Henry VIII**'s chief minister, fails to persuade the Pope to grant Henry a divorce from **Catherine of Aragon**, and Henry dismisses him.

1533 **Archbishop Cranmer** dissolves Henry's marriage and crowns **Anne Boleyn** as queen.

1534 Henry VIII, though no Protestant, repudiates authority of the Pope, proclaims himself head of the Church and dissolves the monasteries, confiscating their wealth.

1536 Death of Catherine of Aragon; execution of Anne Boleyn in the Tower of London. Henry marries **Jane Seymour**.

1538 Henry VIII excommunicated.

1540 Henry marries **Anne of Cleves**; later in the year marries **Catherine Howard**.

1542 Catherine Howard executed; Henry marries **Catherine Parr**.

The Tower of London

1547 Ten-year-old **Edward VI** succeeds Henry VIII.

1549 & 1553 First Prayer Books in English are issued by Cranmer.

1553 Mary, Henry VIII's daughter and a Catholic, becomes Queen. **Lady Jane Grey**, to whom Edward VI had bequeathed the crown to avoid return to Catholicism, is also proclaimed Queen, but is arrested and executed. Cranmer is burnt at the stake and succeeded by a Catholic Archbishop of Canterbury. Supremacy of Pope again acknowledged. Persecution of Protestants marking Mary's reign wins her the nickname of 'Bloody Mary'.

1558 Calais, last French possession still in English hands, falls.

Elizabeth succeeds Mary and repudiates authority of the Pope. To spare England the bitter religious wars with which Europe is being ravaged, she begins working out a religious compromise, in which the Protestant doctrines of the Church of England are mixed with many Catholic elements in its ritual.

1568 Mary Queen of Scots, Catholic and heir to Elizabeth, forced to flee to England; imprisoned by Elizabeth.

1571 Fleet of the Christian League, led by Spain, defeats Turkish fleet at LEPANTO and destroys Moslem sea power in Mediterranean.

1585 Elizabeth lands English army in Netherlands to support Dutch in their revolt against Spanish rule, and this brings into the open the undeclared war England has been fighting with **Philip of Spain** as a result of trade rivalry and religious differences.

1586 Battle of ZUTPHEN; **Sir Philip Sidney** slain.

1587 Mary Queen of Scots executed.
   Drake attacks Cadiz.
1588 Philip of Spain sends Great Armada against England; it is
   destroyed by the English fleet under **Howard of Effingham**,
   Drake, **Hawkins** and **Frobisher**.
1603 Elizabeth dies; James VI of Scotland becomes king as **James
   I**. His High Church views displease the Puritans, and the
   powerful new merchant class is offended by his insistence on
   the Divine Right of Kings.
1605 Gunpowder Plot, a Catholic conspiracy to blow up James
   and his Parliament, is discovered.
1609 Holland frees herself from Spain; is soon to be a great
   power, leading the world in trade, art and science and founding
   an empire in East and West Indies.
1618 Outbreak of the Thirty Years' War, last attempt of the
   Catholics to stamp out the Reformation in Europe. The Catholics
   are at first successful, but the tide turns against them when in
   1629 **Gustavus Adolphus** of Sweden comes in on the Protestant
   side.
1620 Pilgrim Fathers sail from Plymouth in the *Mayflower* to
   found the first colony in New England.

The *Mayflower* 1620

1628 Parliament refuse to vote **Charles I** any money until he has accepted their Petition of Right, which declares taxation without consent of Parliament and imprisonment without trial illegal.

1629 Charles dissolves Parliament, imprisoning its leaders. He reigns without Parliament for the next eleven years, raising money by means regarded as illegal, and suppressing all opposition by special royal courts.

1632 Gustavus Adolphus wins the battle of LUTZEN but is slain.

1640 England invaded by Scots; Charles I obliged to recall Parliament to raise money for the war. The 'Short' Parliament insists on airing its grievances before voting money, and is dismissed. Charles has to summon new Parliament and this (the 'Long' Parliament lasting until 1660) sets out to make personal government by a monarch impossible.

1641 Irish rebel against English.

1642 Charles I goes to House of Commons to arrest his enemies, finds them gone. Slips out of London and the Civil War begins. First battle, at EDGEHILL, is indecisive.

1644 Royalists defeated at MARSTON MOOR by **Cromwell**.

1645 Cromwell wins decisive victory at NASEBY.

1646 Charles surrenders to Scots.

1647 The Scots, having made alliance with Parliamentarians, hand Charles over.

A Royalist   A Parliamentarian

1648 Scots, uneasy about their alliance and encouraged by Charles, invade England, are defeated by Cromwell at PRESTON. Thirty Years' War ends without victor.

1649 Charles I executed. England, calling itself a Commonwealth, becomes a republic. Cromwell ruthlessly restores English rule in Ireland.

1650 Charles I's son, later **Charles II**, lands in Scotland, is crowned King of Scotland.

1651 Prince Charles invades England, is defeated by Cromwell at WORCESTER, and escapes to the continent.

1652–54 Trade rivalry between English and Dutch leads to war. Cromwell's navy, commanded by admirals like **Robert Blake**, holds its own against the mighty Dutch fleet.

1653 Cromwell becomes Lord Protector.

1655 Cromwell seizes Jamaica from Spain.

1658 Cromwell dies; is succeeded by his son, **Richard Cromwell**.

1659 Richard Cromwell resigns.

1660 **General Monk**, Commonwealth commander in Scotland, occupies London and invites Princes Charles to return as Charles II.

1664 War between Britain and Holland; British capture New Amsterdam and rename it New York.

1665 Great Plague of London.

1666 Great Fire of London.

1667 Dutch fleet sails up the Medway and destroys British squadron. Britain makes peace but keeps New York.

1670 Charles II makes secret Treaty of Dover with **Louis XIV** of France, promising to declare himself a Catholic, restore Catholicism in England and support Louis against the Dutch; in return Louis agrees to help Charles with money and, if necessary, troops.

1672 Charles suspends all laws against Catholics, and joins with France in attacking Holland. The Dutch, under **William of Orange**, hold up the French by piercing the dykes; the Dutch admiral **De Ruyter** puts the Anglo-French fleet out of action in SOUTHWOLD BAY.

1673 Charles II forced to summon Parliament to ask for money; is compelled to accept Test Act excluding all Catholics from office and to end war with Holland.

1678 **Titus Oates** announces 'Popish plot' to restore Catholicism in England. Attempt is made to exclude from the succession Charles's brother, **James**, a Catholic convert.

1681 William Penn establishes colony of Pennsylvania as refuge for persecuted Quakers.

1683 Turks make final effort to carry Islam into the heart of Europe; are defeated at VIENNA.

1685 Charles II dies; James, though a Catholic, becomes king as James II. **Monmouth**, illegitimate son of Charles II and a Protestant, tries to seize the throne, but is defeated at SEDGEMOOR and executed.

1688 William of Orange, married to **Mary**, James's Protestant daughter, is invited to come over with an army to save the English constitution and Church. William lands at Torbay, and James II flees to France.

1689 The Crown is accepted by William and Mary after they have agreed to the Bill of Rights, limiting royal power. James II lands in Ireland to lead an Irish rising.

1690 William defeats James and the Irish at the battle of the BOYNE.

1701 Parliament passes the Act of Settlement confining the succession to Protestants.

Louis XIV uses a dispute over the succession to the Spanish throne to resume his plan to make France strongest European power. William forms Britain, Holland and Austria into 'Grand Alliance' to stop him.

1702 William dies; succeeded by **Anne**.

1704 Marlborough's victory at BLENHEIM saves Vienna from the French.

1704 Admiral Rooke captures Gibraltar.

1706 Marlborough defeats French at RAMILLIES.

1707 Act of Union between England and Scotland.

1708 Marlborough defeats French at OUDENARDE.

1709 Marlborough victorious at MALPLAQUET.

1710 Replacement of Whigs by Tories, who want to end the war, leads to Marlborough's downfall.

1713 War ends. Britain receives Newfoundland and Hudson Bay territory from France; Gibraltar and Minorca from Spain.

1714 Anne dies and Elector of Hanover becomes king as **George I**. He cannot speak English and has no interest in English affairs; his reign helps to make Parliament even more powerful, leads to the modern pattern of government by a cabinet of ministers.

1715 The 'Old Pretender', son of James II, lands in Scotland to find his supporters have already been defeated.

1720 A financial crisis, the 'South Sea Bubble', produced by wild speculation, ruins thousands.

1721 Sir Robert Walpole becomes first Prime Minister.

1739 Walpole, though anxious to preserve peace, is forced into war with Spain (the 'War of Jenkins' Ear').

1740 Hapsburg emperor, Charles VI, dies. The European powers have agreed to accept his daughter, Maria Theresa, as his heir; but France, Spain and Prussia ignore the arrangement. Prussia attacks Austria; France invades Germany. Britain and Holland enter this War of the Austrian Succession on Maria Theresa's side.

1743 George II defeats French at DETTINGEN—the last time a British king is personally in command in a battle.

1745 French defeat Austro-English army at FONTENOY. Prince Charles Edward, the 'Young Pretender', lands in Scotland and wins victory at PRESTONPANS. He invades England, but finds little support; his army returns to Scotland.

1746 The Jacobites (Charles Edward's followers) defeated at CULLODEN; the 'Young Pretender' escapes to the continent.

1748 War of the Austrian Succession ends. Prussia under Frederick the Great has emerged as the strongest power in N. Germany; Britain has proved herself superior at sea over the French, with whom she continues a struggle for supremacy in India and America.

1756 Seven Years' War breaks out. Maria Theresa, helped by France and Russia, seeks to win back Silesia from Frederick of Prussia, who is supported by Britain under the elder Pitt. The Nawab of Bengal captures Calcutta; locks 140 British men and women into small military guardroom—the 'Black Hole of Calcutta'—where most suffocate. In America French capture Fort Oswego, main British trading centre on Great Lakes.

1757 Clive defeats Nawab of Bengal at PLASSEY.

1758 Fort Oswego recaptured; British take Fort Duquesne, renaming it Pittsburgh in honour of Pitt.

1759 French defeated at MINDEN; in America General Wolfe is slain capturing QUEBEC. There are British naval victories at LAGOS and QUIBERON BAY.

1760 French defeated in India, leaving British supreme. George II succeeded by his grandson, George III, first Hanoverian king to speak English and to regard himself as king of England rather than Elector of Hanover.

1761 George brings about downfall of Pitt.

1763 Seven Years' War ends, leaving Britain with her conquests in India and America.

1773 'Boston Tea Party' brings to a head the long quarrel between George III and American colonists. Colonists maintain they should not be taxed without their consent. When Britain imposes tax on tea, a group of colonists, disguised as Indians, board ships in Boston and throw their cargoes into the harbour.

1775 First shots exchanged between colonists and British troops at Lexington. **George Washington** made American Commander-in-Chief. **James Watt**, pioneer of the Industrial Revolution, completes his first full-size improved steam engine.

1776 The 13 American colonies issue Declaration of Independence (July 4).

1777 **General Burgoyne**, marching from Canada to New York, forced to surrender at SARATOGA. France and Spain declare war on Britain.

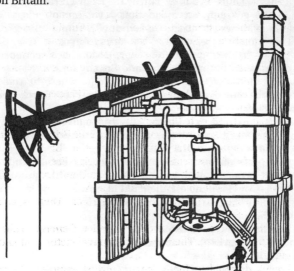

Early Watt's Pumping Engine

1781 British army under **General Cornwallis** forced to surrender at YORKTOWN, Virginia.

1783 Britain recognises American independence.

1788 Founding Fathers draw up American constitution.

1789 George Washington first US President. French Revolution breaks out. Faced with bankruptcy, **Louis XVI** is compelled to summon the States-General (French Parliament) for first time since 1614. States-General turns itself into National Assembly, determined to abolish absolute power of king, and proclaims principles of Liberty, Equality, Fraternity. Louis calls in soldiers; people of Paris retaliate by storming Bastille prison (July 14).

1791 Louis XVI flees, but is caught and brought back to Paris.

1792 Austria and Prussia, wishing to restore Louis, make war on France; Louis is deposed and imprisoned, France becoming republic. Extreme revolutionaries (the Jacobins) gain control.

1793 French occupy Austrian Netherlands (now Belgium); Britain joins in war against France with Holland, Spain, Austria and Prussia. Louis XVI is executed; Reign of Terror begins. In Britain the government, afraid that revolutionary ideas will spread, suppresses all societies in favour of reform.

1794 Execution of **Robespierre** ends Reign of Terror.

1795 Prussia has withdrawn from war, Holland been conquered and Spain defeated; only Austria and Britain are left. **Napoleon Bonaparte** becomes French C.-in-C. in Italy, where he rapidly masters the Austrians. Britain takes Cape of Good Hope, formerly Dutch.

1797 Napoleon threatens Vienna; Austria makes peace. **Jarvis** and **Nelson** defeat Spanish fleet at CAPE ST VINCENT; **Duncan** the Dutch fleet at CAMPERDOWN.

1798 Bonaparte eludes a British fleet under Nelson, lands in Egypt and defeats Mameluke Turks in BATTLE OF THE PYRAMIDS. Nelson destroys French fleet anchored in Aboukir Bay, in BATTLE OF THE NILE. Bonaparte advances into Syria, is stopped by **Sir Sidney Smith** at ACRE.

1799 Britain, Turkey, Austria and Russia combine against France. Bonaparte abandons army in Egypt and returns to France, where he makes himself First Consul.

1800 Bonaparte defeats Austrians at MARENGO. Ireland made part of United Kingdom.

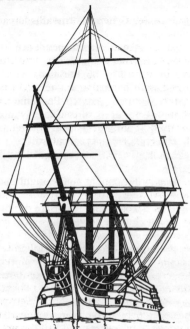

The *Victory*, Nelson's flagship

1801 Austria sues for peace. Russia has withdrawn from war and, with Denmark, Sweden and Prussia, has taken measures against Britain for searching neutral ships to ensure that they do not carry cargoes useful to France. Nelson smashes Danish fleet at COPENHAGEN.

1802 Peace returns for a time. Britain restores Cape of Good Hope to Dutch, but keeps Ceylon (formerly Dutch) and Trinidad (formerly Spanish). Bonaparte made First Consul for life.

1803 War between Britain and France renewed, with Spain on France's side. Bonaparte sells Louisiana to the USA.

1804 Bonaparte becomes Emperor Napoleon.

1805 Younger Pitt builds alliance against Napoleon with Austria and Russia. Napoleon gathers army at Boulogne to invade England. Nelson defeats French and Spanish fleets at TRAFALGAR.

Napoleon defeats Austrians and Russians at AUSTERLITZ. Pitt dies.

1806 Austria again sues for peace; **Francis II** drops title of Holy Roman Emperor, becomes Emperor of Austria. Napoleon crushes Prussia at JENA; is master of Germany.

1807 Napoleon defeats Russians at EYLAU and FRIEDLAND; forms an alliance with Russia at Tilsit. Britain now his only enemy; he seeks to ruin her by excluding British goods from Europe. Britain replies by blockading all countries under Napoleon's control; forces surrender of the Danish fleet by bombardment of Copenhagen. Napoleon occupies Portugal, which has thriving trade with Britain.

1808 Napoleon makes brother Joseph king of Spain. Spain and Portugal revolt; Peninsular War begins.

1809 Sir Arthur Wellesley (later Duke of Wellington) defeats French at TALAVERA. Austria re-enters war; is defeated at WAGRAM and again sues for peace.

1812 Napoleon invades Russia; occupies Moscow after battle of BORODINO, but the Russians burn the city and he is forced to retreat in winter, his 'Grande Armée' being destroyed. Wellington defeats French at SALAMANCA; occupies Madrid.

Dispute arising out of Britain's insistence on searching neutral ships leads to war between Britain and US. Britain occupies and burns Washington.

1813 Prussia and Austria drive Napoleon from Germany. Wellington defeats French at VITORIA; drives them out of Spain.

1814 Britain and America make peace.

Austria, Russia and Prussia invade France, occupy Paris; Wellington marches into S. France. Napoleon abdicates, is banished to Elba. Bourbon dynasty restored.

1815 Napoleon escapes, resumes power, but is defeated at WATERLOO. Banished to St Helena. **Louis XVIII** returns to Paris.

1819 At 'Peterloo Massacre' in Manchester cavalry charge an open-air meeting of supporters of parliamentary reform.

1821 Greeks revolt against Turkish rule. Death of Napoleon.

1822 The poet **Lord Byron** is among many volunteers who go to Greece to help her in her war of independence.

1823 Spain tries to regain her American colonies; Britain recognises their independence, threatens to use British navy to prevent interference from Spain. **President Monroe** of the USA issues what is known as the 'Monroe Doctrine', saying that any interference by European powers on the American continent would be regarded as unfriendly to the USA.

1827 British, French and Russian fleets destroy the Turkish fleet at NAVARINO, making it impossible for the Turks to put down the Greeks.

1829 Greece becomes independent kingdom.

1830 Charles X of France, who has tried to re-establish absolute monarchy, is driven from the throne and replaced by **Louis-Philippe**. Belgians revolt against Dutch rule and become independent. Unrest in Italy and Germany; in Britain the struggle for parliamentary reform becomes intense.

1832 Great Reform Bill is passed (see HISTORIC ACTS OF PARLIAMENT).

1833 Slavery abolished throughout British Empire.

1835–36 Boers undertake their 'Great Trek' to escape from British rule in the Cape; set up republic in Transvaal.

1837 Queen Victoria ascends the throne.

1846 Faced with famine in Ireland, **Sir Robert Peel** repeals Corn Laws (see HISTORIC ACTS OF PARLIAMENT).

1848 A year of unrest: revolt against Austrian rule by Hungarians, Czechs and Italians; Rome declared a republic; Sicily and Naples rise against their King. All these revolts suppressed. The crown of a unified Germany offered to **Frederick William IV** of Prussia, but as a believer in Divine Right of Kings he refuses because crown is offered by representatives of the people. He is forced to give his own subjects a constitution. Louis-Philippe of France deposed; republic proclaimed. In Britain the Chartists demand the vote for all.

1851 Great Exhibition in London.

1852 Louis-Napoleon makes himself French emperor as Napoleon III.

1853 Britain, seeing her position in India threatened by Russian ambitions, and France, under Napoleon III, who wants to strengthen his power by military triumphs, declare war on Russia. Anglo-French and Turkish force landed in the Crimea to capture Sevastopol. In the battles of BALACLAVA and INKERMANN, the Russians fail to drive out allied force. The harsh winter exposes the inefficiency of the British army, especially of its medical services, which **Florence Nightingale** does her best to remedy.

Paxton's Crystal Palace, home of the Great Exhibition of 1851

1855 Sardinia, wanting French and British support in the struggle to unite all Italy, joins war against Russia. Russians abandon SEVASTOPOL.

1856 Crimean War ends.

1857 Indian Mutiny breaks out. Delhi seized by rebels, besieged and captured by the British; Lucknow defended by British garrison. Last Mogul emperor is deposed and British Crown takes over administration of India from East India Company.

1859 Sardinia, under **Victor Emmanuel II**, and France declare war on Austria; defeat her at MAGENTA and SOLFERINO. Sardinia receives Lombardy, gives Nice and Savoy to France.

1860 **Garibaldi** overthrows Kingdom of the Two Sicilies (Naples and Sicily), which, with four remaining Italian duchies, are annexed by Sardinia.

    Abraham Lincoln elected US President. Eleven southern states, wishing to maintain State rights against the central government, particularly on the issue of Negro slavery, claim the right to break away from the Union. Lincoln denies this right; American Civil War breaks out.

1861 Victor Emmanuel proclaimed first king of a United Italy.

1862 **Bismarck**, foreign minister of Prussia, sets out to unify Germany.

1863 **General Robert E. Lee**, commander of Southern forces in the American Civil War, defeated at GETTYSBURG. Lincoln proclaims abolition of slavery.

1864 **Maximilian of Hapsburg** made emperor of Mexico by

Napoleon III. Mexican republicans, under **Juarez**, bitterly oppose him.

1865 General Lee surrenders to **General Grant** and American Civil War is over. Abraham Lincoln assassinated.

1866 USA insists that French troops be withdrawn from Mexico. Maximilian shot.

In brief campaign against Austria, ending in overwhelming victory at SADOWA, Prussia smashes Austria's influence over Germany and insists that Venetia be handed over to Italy.

1867 Canada becomes Dominion.

1869 Suez Canal opened.

1870 Napoleon III declares war on Prussia. French army surrounded at METZ and another, with Napoleon in command, surrenders at SEDAN. Napoleon's Empire collapses; is followed by Third Republic.

1871 United Germany proclaimed with king of Prussia as Emperor. France forced to give Alsace-Lorraine to Germany.

1872 Voting becomes secret in Britain.

1875 **Disraeli** wins control of Suez Canal for Britain by buying shares of the Khedive of Egypt. The Khedive's misrule has made Egypt bankrupt, and Britain and France have to pour money into the country to save it from collapse.

1877 Queen Victoria becomes Empress of India. Russia comes to aid of Serbs, Montenegrans, Rumanians and Bulgarians, risen against Turkish rule. Turks defeated; only under threat from Britain and Austria does Russia stop the war.

1878 Bulgaria established as a separate principality under Turkey; Serbia and Montenegro become independent kingdoms; and Bosnia and Herzogovina, both with largely Serbian populations, pass into Austrian hands, thus causing bad blood between Serbia and Austria. Britain receives Cyprus.

1881 At MAJUBA HILL Boers defeat British force trying to occupy Transvaal. Transvaal is recognised as independent republic under British authority.

France occupies Tunis as part of her policy of creating an empire for herself in Africa and Indo-China. Following discovery of the interior of Africa by **Livingstone** and others, 'scramble for Africa' becomes intense.

1882 Britain occupies Egypt and is drawn into the affairs of the Sudan, where **Mohammed Ahmed** has proclaimed himself

Mahdi (Messiah) and declared a holy war against Egypt and all non-Moslems.

1884 Germany joins in 'scramble for Africa', acquiring S.W. Africa, Cameroons, Togoland and Tanganyika.

1885 General Gordon, sent to evacuate British and Egyptian garrisons in the Sudan, killed in Khartoum by Mahdi's forces.

1886 Royal Niger Company formed to open up interior of Nigeria.

1888 British Africa Company secures what is now Kenya and takes over Uganda.

William II becomes German emperor.

1890 Cecil Rhodes, founder of Rhodesia, who hopes to see British territory extend from the Cape to Cairo, becomes Prime Minister of Cape Colony.

In Germany William II drops Bismarck as Chancellor; the German drive to 'win a place in the sun' becomes fiercer.

1896 Jameson's raid into the Transvaal in support of the British there, whose lives the Boers are making difficult, is a failure. Rhodes, suspected of backing Jameson, has to resign as Prime Minister of Cape Colony.

Italy, having established herself in Eritrea as part of the 'scramble for Africa', tries to conquer Ethiopia; is defeated at ADOWA.

1898 British General **Kitchener**, having defeated the Mahdi's forces at OMDURMAN and recaptured Khartoum, encounters a French force at Fashoda. The 'Fashoda incident' brings Britain and France close to war; but France, fearing the growing strength of Germany, gives in.

Grievances of British settlers in the Boer republic lead to the Boer War, beginning with a series of British defeats.

1900 Lord Roberts wipes out main Boer forces, but Boer guerilla units continue war.

Failure of the Boxer rising in China (a revolt against European and Japanese interference in Chinese affairs) speeds the collapse of Chinese imperial rule.

1901 Queen Victoria dies.

Australia becomes self-governing dominion.

1902 Boer War ends; Boer republics annexed by British Crown.

1903 The American brothers, **Orville** and **Wilbur Wright**, make

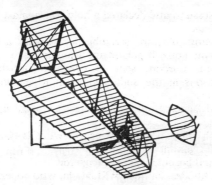

Wright Brothers' biplane 1907–8

first controlled and sustained flight in powered heavier-than-air machine.

1904 'Entente Cordiale' ('warm understanding') established between Britain and France.

Russia which, after completion of the Trans-Siberian Railway, has extended her influence into Manchuria and Korea, clashes with Japan, which is trying to secure for herself as much of the decaying Chinese empire as she can. Japan declares war on Russia, and in a series of brilliant land and sea victories crushes Russia's Far Eastern forces.

1905 Russia forced to make peace and evacuate Manchuria.

1906 In Britain Liberals win great electoral victory and embark on sweeping programme of social reform.

1907 New Zealand becomes dominion.

Alliance between Britain and France extended to include Russia. There are now two great power blocs in Europe— Germany and Austria on one hand, Britain, France and Russia on the other. Tension increases, and the powers begin an armaments race.

1908 Austria annexes Bosnia and Herzogovina, offending Serbia and Russia, since both provinces have largely Serb (or Slav) populations.

1910 Union of S. Africa formed of Cape of Good Hope, Natal, Orange Free State and Transvaal; becomes a dominion.

1911 In Britain the powers of the House of Lords are sharply cut.

Italy, seeking colonies, makes war on Turkey in order to seize Tripoli.

Germany tries to prevent French penetration of Morocco by sending a warship to Agadir. Backed by Britain, France refuses to give way.

1912–13 Two Balkan wars result in the expulsion of Turkey from Europe.

British government introduces an Irish Home Rule Bill which nearly leads to civil war in Ireland.

Tripoli is yielded to Italy.

1914 Assassination of the heir to the Austrian throne at Sarajevo triggers off First World War.

The Germans sweep through neutral Belgium; are halted only a few miles from Paris. The Allies force the Germans back in the battle of the MARNE; by October the struggle has settled down into trench warfare. Russians invade East Prussia, are stopped by **Hindenburg**'s victory at TANNENBERG.

1915 Both sides make costly attempts to break through, without success.

On the eastern front the Germans push the Russians further back.

Turkey, fighting on Germany's side, tries to cut the Suez Canal, but fails. The British fail to open communications with Russia through the Black Sea by forcing the Dardanelles and landing troops on the Gallipoli peninsula.

Italy enters the war on the Allied side. Germans announce that their U-boats will sink all merchant ships in British waters.

1916 Trench warfare continues; huge losses on both sides. British and German fleets meet off JUTLAND; the Germans are so battered that they remain in port for the rest of the war.

Following the sinking of the *Lusitania* with many Americans on board, the Germans are forced to abandon their unrestricted submarine campaign. The Arabs, aided by **T. E. Lawrence**, revolt against Turkish rule. In Britain **Lloyd George** becomes Prime Minister.

1917 Anti-war feeling in Russia leads to overthrow of the Czar; but the provisional government's attempt to continue the war enables **Lenin** and the Bolsheviks to seize power.

The Germans renew unrestricted submarine warfare, and in April the USA declares war.

British and French troops are sent to Italy after the Germans and Austrians have broken through the Italian front at CAPO-RETTO.

General Allenby captures Jerusalem.

1918 Germans launch their final offensive, but fail to break through. Allies counter-attack under **Marshal Foch** and force Germans to sue for armistice in November. William II, the Kaiser, abdicates; Germany becomes republic. Hapsburg monarchy in Austria comes to an end.

1919 Under peace treaties France regains Alsace-Lorraine; Germany loses the 'Polish Corridor' to the new Polish republic; Austria and Hungary are separated; Serbia is enlarged and becomes Yugoslavia; Czechoslovakia is created; the Ottoman empire is broken up, leaving only Turkey itself, which becomes a republic; a League of Nations is created, but its founder, **President Wilson**, fails to persuade his own country, the USA, to become a member; Germany's colonies become League of Nation's mandates; and Germany has limits set on the size of her armed forces.

The British fire on an unarmed crowd in Amritsar, in India, with many deaths.

1921 Ireland, with the exception of Northern Ireland, which remains linked to the UK, is made a dominion after nearly three years of disturbances.

1922 **Kemal Ataturk** seizes power in Turkey, sets out to modernise his country.

Mussolini becomes head of the Italian government, establishes Fascism.

1924 Lenin, having established Communist rule in Russia despite famine and foreign intervention, dies; **Stalin** emerges as his successor and sets out to make Russia a great industrial power.

In Britain **Ramsay MacDonald** forms the short-lived first Labour government.

1926 General Strike in Britain collapses after six weeks.

1929 World-wide economic crisis causes millions to be thrown out of work in the USA and Europe. In Germany **Hitler**'s National Socialist ('Nazi') party makes large gains.

1931 In Britain the second Labour government is replaced by a largely conservative National Government.

In Spain the monarchy collapses and a republic is established.

Japan invades China, sets up a puppet regime in Manchuria. China appeals unsuccessfully to the League of Nations, from which Japan resigns.

1933 **Franklin D. Roosevelt** becomes US President and launches his 'New Deal' of social and economic reform to help America out of the Great Depression. Hitler is appointed Chancellor and makes himself dictator of Germany.

1935 Hitler denounces the terms of the Versailles Treaty limiting the size of the German armed forces.

Mussolini invades and conquers Ethiopia, which appeals in vain to the League of Nations. Mussolini leaves the League.

1936 Military rising against the left-wing government in Spain leads to the outbreak of the Spanish Civil War. Germans and Italians fight openly on Franco's side, and the government receives aid from Russia.

1938 Hitler occupies Austria and claims the Sudetenland in Czechoslovakia. Under the Munich Agreement, signed by Britain, France, Germany and Italy, the Sudetenland is given to Germany; the new frontiers of Czechoslovakia are guaranteed.

1939 The Spanish Civil War ends with the surrender of Madrid; Fascist dictatorship established under **General Franco**. Hitler seizes the rest of Czechoslovakia. Mussolini seizes Albania.

Hitler makes a pact with Stalin and invades and crushes Poland, which is divided between Germany and Russia. Britain and France declare war; the Second World War has begun.

Russia makes war on Finland (in order to bring the approaches to Leningrad under her control), but her armies are beaten in the winter campaign.

1940 Russians break through; Finland sues for peace. Hitler occupies Norway and Denmark. In Britain **Chamberlain** is brought down, and **Winston Churchill** forms a coalition government. Sweeping through Holland, Belgium and Luxembourg, Hitler crushes France, which sues for armistice. Free French under **General de Gaulle** continue to fight from Britain. Britain, having extricated her army from France at Dunkirk, fights on alone. Hitler's plan to invade Britain collapses when his air force (the Luftwaffe) fails to win control of the air in the Battle of Britain; but the Luftwaffe continues its effort to smash Britain by 'blitz' bombing.

Italy enters war on German side, attacks Greece. British

troops begin the capture of Italian colonies in E. Africa; reconquer Ethiopia.

1941 Hitler conquers Yugoslavia and Greece; in June, attacks
Russia. Germans sweep to gates of Moscow and Leningrad, are
caught by the winter. German force under **Rommel** arrives to
strengthen Italians in N. Africa and becomes a dangerous
threat to Egypt, the Suez Canal and Britain's position in the
Middle East.

In December Japan attacks the US Pacific Fleet at Pearl
Harbor, bringing the USA into the war, and invades Malaya,
Siam, the Philippines, Burma and Indonesia. Hong Kong falls.

1942 In Russia the Germans conquer the Ukraine and pene-
trate deep into the Caucasus, but winter sets in again, and a
German army of over 300,000 is trapped and wiped out at
STALINGRAD.

In Africa Rommel defeats the British and gets within 60 miles
of Alexandria, but in the battle of ALAMEIN **Montgomery** defeats
him decisively. An Anglo-American force under **Eisenhower**
takes French N. Africa. Singapore falls, and by May the Japanese
are masters of S.E. Asia, but their advance in the Central and
S.W. Pacific is halted by American naval and air victories in
the CORAL SEA and off MIDWAY.

The Americans begin to roll back the Japanese across the
Pacific, capturing Guadalcanal in 1943, the Gilbert, Marshall
and Mariana Islands in 1943 and 1944, the Philippines in 1944
and Iwo-Jima and Okinawa in 1945.

1943 German forces sent against Eisenhower in Africa, together
with what remains of Rommel's force—altogether over a quarter of a million men—are forced to surrender.

The Allies invade Italy, but the Germans put up stiff resistance, and the Allied advance becomes a long, bitter push up
the mountainous Italian peninsula, lasting until the end of the
war. Mussolini is deposed and imprisoned; Italy joins the Allies.
With Hitler's help, Mussolini escapes.

1944 Russians push Germans out of Russia and advance into
Europe.

The Western allies, under Eisenhower, land in Normandy and
sweep across France almost to the Rhine. A group of German
officers attempt to assassinate Hitler, without success.

The British foil a Japanese attempt to invade India from

Burma and launch a drive for the reconquest of Burma, Malaya and Singapore: completed successfully in 1945.

1945 The Allies cross the Rhine; the Russians invade Germany from the East. Hitler commits suicide as the Russians take Berlin. Germany surrenders. Japan surrenders after atom bombs have been dropped on Hiroshima and Nagasaki. It is discovered that Hitler's Final Solution has led to the murder of 6,000,000 Jews—the Holocaust.

In Britain the Labour party wins an overwhelming victory and sets out on a programme of social reforms designed to produce the 'welfare state' and to give self-government to non-white colonial peoples.

The United Nations organisation is formed.

1947 India, Pakistan and Ceylon become independent. **General Marshall**, US Secretary of State, pledges American aid for Europe's recovery provided the European nations unite in a co-operative effort. With help given under this Marshall Plan living standards in nearly the whole of Western Europe rise within three years well above those of before the war. Russia and countries under her control boycott the Plan.

1948 Burma becomes independent. Communists take over government in Czechoslovakia. There is now an 'iron curtain' between east and west. The Russians try to squeeze the Western Allies out of Berlin by cutting road and rail communications. The Allies supply Berlin by airlift until the blockade is lifted.

The state of Israel is proclaimed.

1949 The USA, Canada, Britain, France and eight other W. European countries join together for mutual defence in the North Atlantic Treaty Organisation (NATO). Chinese Nationalists, under **Chiang-Kai-Shek**, are driven from Chinese mainland and take refuge in Formosa; Communist Chinese People's Republic is set up in China.

1950 N. Korea, under communist control, invades S. Korea. United Nations Security Council (from which the Russian delegate happens to be absent) calls upon its members to stop the aggressor; and American, British and other UN forces land just in time to save Korea from being overrun. The communists are driven back into N. Korea, but as they near the Chinese frontiers the Chinese intervene to drive the UN forces back into S. Korea.

United Nations Building, New York

1951 In Britain the Conservatives under Churchill defeat Labour.

1952 In Egypt **King Farouk** is forced to abdicate by **General Neguib**.

Elizabeth II succeeds her father, George VI.

1953 General Eisenhower becomes first Republican president for twenty years.

Stalin dies; there is a struggle for power inside Russia.

In Egypt Neguib is replaced by **Nasser**.

Korean War ends.

1954 After seven years of war between French and communists in French Indo-China, an armistice is arranged. At the Geneva Conference, French rule in Indo-China is ended, and Laos, Cambodia and Vietnam become independent; but N. Vietnam is left under communist control.

1955 Heads of government of the USA, Russia, Britain and France hold a 'summit' meeting at Geneva, and tension is temporarily eased.

1956 **Kruschev** denounces Stalin's methods in a speech at the 20th Congress of the Soviet Communist party. His speech causes the downfall of the Stalinist government in Poland; and in

Hungary it leads to a popular uprising, put down by Russian tanks.

In Egypt Nasser seizes the Suez Canal. Goaded by the aggressive attitude of the Arabs, who refuse to recognise her, Israel invades Egypt and advances on the Suez Canal. Britain and France demand an immediate cease-fire and, when their demand is disregarded, land at Port Said. Their action is condemned by the United Nations, who order the Anglo-French forces to withdraw. This they do.

1957 Ghana and Malaya become independent.

Russia launches into space the first man-made satellite, Sputnik I.

1958 In France, on the brink of civil war as a result of the disobedience of the Algerian settlers and sections of the army, de Gaulle is returned to power, remodels the constitution, and gives independence within the French community to France's colonies.

1959 Macmillan visits Kruschev in Moscow, and Kruschev becomes the first Soviet head of government to visit the USA.

In Cuba **Fidel Castro** ends the **Batista** regime.

1960 Belgian Congo given independence; sinks almost immediately into chaos. UN intervenes, but disagreement between the great powers and the African nations hampers its work.

Nigeria becomes independent.

67 black South Africans are shot dead by police in Sharpeville.

1961 John F. Kennedy, the youngest candidate ever to be elected to the White House, is installed as President of the USA.

Man's first flight into space is made by **Major Yuri Gagarin**, Soviet airman, who circles the earth at 25,000 miles an hour before landing safely in Russia.

South Africa leaves the Commonwealth because of the opposition of the African and Asian Commonwealth countries to her racial policies.

In Algeria extremists among the European settlers and French Army make two attempts to seize power, but President de Gaulle reasserts his authority on both occasions and continues his efforts to reach a settlement with the Algerian Arabs.

World tension mounts when the Communist East German authorities build a wall across Berlin to stop the flow of East German refugees to West Berlin.

Dag Hammarskjoeld, the UN Secretary-General, is killed in an air crash in Africa, and is succeeded by a Burmese, **U Thant**.

1962 **Colonel John Glenn**, American astronaut, successfully circles the earth three times in his Mercury space capsule.

Two Russian astronauts, **Major Nicolaev** and **Colonel Popovich**, are launched into space, the former orbiting the earth for $94\frac{1}{2}$ hours and the second for 71 hours.

France and the Algerian Arabs sign a cease-fire, and Algeria becomes an independent country.

Jamaica, Trinidad and Tanganyika become independent.

The world's first communications satellite, Telstar, is launched.

The Soviet Union establishes atomic missile bases in Fidel Castro's Cuba, President Kennedy orders Cuba to be blockaded, and the world seems to be on the brink of nuclear war. War is avoided when Kruschev orders the dismantling of the missile bases.

1963 UN military forces seize the main towns in Katanga, **President Tshombe's** secessionist province in the Congo, thus breaking the power of the biggest of the many separatist governments which have been defying the authority of the Central Congolese Government since independence in 1960.

Signing of Test Ban Treaty in Moscow between USA, Russia and Britain marks easing of East–West tension.

Kenya and Zanzibar become independent members of Commonwealth.

Harold Macmillan resigns for health reasons and is succeeded by Lord Home who relinquishes his peerage to become **Sir Alec Douglas-Home**.

President Kennedy is assassinated. His Vice-President, **Lyndon B. Johnson**, takes over.

1964 Kruschev falls from power. As Secretary General of the Russian Communist Party he is succeeded by **Brezhnev**.

Labour Party narrowly defeats Conservatives in General Election. **Harold Wilson** becomes Prime Minister.

Lyndon B. Johnson, the Democratic candidate, wins a landslide victory in US presidential election.

1965 Sir Winston Churchill dies and is given a State funeral.

Russian **Colonel Leonov** becomes first man to 'walk' in space, American **Major White** the second.

The Government of **Mr Smith** in Rhodesia, a British colony, declares independence and is condemned as 'illegal'.

1966 Mrs Gandhi, Nehru's daughter, becomes India's first woman Prime Minister after **Mr Shastri**'s death.

Nigeria's unity is shaken by a series of military coups in which many of the country's leaders are killed. A colonel in his thirties, **Yakubu Gowon**, emerges as Head of State.

President Nkrumah of Ghana is deposed by a military coup while on a visit to China.

The fighting in Vietnam between the Communist Vietcong supported by the North Vietnamese, and the South Vietnamese supported by the Americans, becomes fiercer.

Mr Wilson and Labour Party win a substantial victory in the General Election.

England wins World Cup in football.

1967 Israel routs the armed forces of Egypt, Jordan and Syria in six days but, despite a hurriedly arranged cease-fire, there is no relaxation of tension in the Middle East.

Civil war rages in Nigeria between the Federal Nigerian Government and the breakaway state of Biafra.

1968 In Czechoslovakia **President Novotny**, a 'Stalinist hard-liner', is ousted by **Alexander Dubcek** and other Communist 'liberals' who introduce political, social and economic reforms. The Russians invade and occupy Czechoslovakia and arrest Dubcek and many of his followers, but when they fail to find any Czechoslovak Communist willing to run the country for them they are forced to reinstate Dubcek. But Dubcek's powers of government are drastically reduced.

Britain announces her intention to withdraw from all her bases East of Suez (with the exception of Hong Kong).

France is brought virtually to a standstill by violent student riots and strikes by more than 8 million workers, and it is several weeks before General de Gaulle restores his authority.

Dr Martin Luther King, the American Negro leader, and **Senator Robert Kennedy**, the late President Kennedy's brother, are assassinated.

Three American astronauts, **Frank Borman**, **Bill Anders** and **Jim Lovell**, become the first men to circle round the moon.

1969 Richard M. Nixon, a Republican and President Eisenhower's Vice-President, is installed as US President. He begins withdrawal of American troops from Vietnam.

Alexander Dubcek is ousted as First Secretary of Czechoslovak Communist Party and replaced by **Dr Husak**. 'Hardline' Communists tighten their control in Czechoslovakia.

American astronauts **Neil Armstrong** and **Edwin Aldrin** become the first men to walk on the moon.

General de Gaulle, defeated in a referendum on local regional reform, retires from public life.

After general elections in West Germany, the Social Democrats become the dominant partners in a coalition government, with **Willy Brandt** as Chancellor.

1970 The Nigerian civil war ends with the capitulation of Biafra.

A treaty, limiting spread of nuclear armaments, comes into force after ratification by 43 states, including Britain, the USA and the Soviet Union, but excluding France and China.

In Britain the Conservatives, led by **Edward Heath**, defeat Labour.

1971 In East Pakistan, the Awami League, victorious in the previous year's elections, demands autonomy for the eastern province and then independence as the Republic of Bangladesh. **President Yahya Khan** treats this demand as sedition. The Awami League's leader, **Sheik Mujibur Rahman**, is arrested and flown to West Pakistan. West Pakistani troops are flown to East Pakistan to suppress all support for independence. Millions of refugees flood across the border into India. India intervenes with its armed forces. In East Pakistan the West Pakistani forces surrender, and Bangladesh is proclaimed. In the West of the

Indian sub-continent, a cease-fire is arranged between India and Pakistan. Yahya Khan resigns and hands over the presidency to **Zulfikar Ali Bhutto**.

Communist China replaces Chiang-Kai-Shek's government as the official representative of China in the UN.

Kurt Waldheim, an Austrian diplomat, is elected fourth Secretary-General of the UN in succession to U Thant.

1972 Pakistan leaves the Commonwealth when some Commonwealth countries recognise Bangladesh as an independent state.

Britain signs a Treaty of Accession to the Common Market. Eire, Denmark and Norway sign similar treaties.

President Nixon visits Peking at the invitation of the Chinese Communist Government, and later Moscow at the invitation of the Soviet Government.

Edward Heath's Conservative Government takes over direct rule of Northern Ireland, suspending the powers of the Northern Irish Government and Parliament.

The British Parliament ratifies the Treaty of Accession to the European Economic Community. Eire and Denmark vote in favour of joining but Norway votes against.

President Amin of Uganda expels tens of thousands of Asians from his country in pursuit of his policy of 'Africanisation'. Britain receives nearly 30,000 Ugandan Asians.

1973 Britain, Eire and Denmark become full members of the enlarged European Economic Community.

President Nixon is sworn in for a second term of office.

Cease-fire agreement in Vietnamese war is signed between US, North Vietnam, South Vietnam and Vietcong.

Elections for a new local assembly are held in Northern Ireland; a 12-man executive is created, and the setting-up of a Council of Ireland is agreed.

In Argentina, **Juan Peron** returns to power.

In Chile, **President Allende's** Marxist government is overthrown by a military junta. Allende is killed.

In Greece, **President Papadopoulos**, having deposed **King Constantine** and the monarchy and declared his country a republic, is overthrown by a rival military junta.

Egypt and Syria attack Israel on Yom Kippur, the Jewish Day of Atonement, and, after initial successes, are fought to a standstill. The United States and the USSR agree to bring the fighting to an end to prevent a world-wide conflagration. The Soviet–US agreement is approved by the UN Security Council; but before the fighting is stopped, a second cease-fire agreement has to be negotiated.

The oil-producing states of Kuwait, Saudi Arabia, Algeria, Abu Dhabi and Libya cut back oil deliveries to countries declared to be pro-Israel. The use of the 'oil weapon' causes an acute energy crisis.

1974 The British Government announces that the working week for most of British industry has to be cut to three days. The miners vote in favour of a national coal strike. Edward Heath calls an election on the issue 'Who governs Britain?' Harold Wilson takes power at the head of a minority Labour Government. The miners accept a settlement of over £100,000,000. In the autumn Wilson calls a second election and wins a narrow majority over all other parties. The British government presses ahead with re-negotiating the terms of British membership of the European Economic Community.

High oil prices cause the economies of many industrial countries, including Britain, to slow down.

President Nixon is forced to resign because of his involvement in the Watergate break-in and the manoeuvres to cover it up— the first President in US history to resign his office.

President Makarios is forced to leave Cyprus after a coup organised by Greek Cypriots who support union with Greece (*Enosis*), encouraged in their action by the military junta in Athens. The Turks invade Cyprus and occupy the northern part of the island. The Turkish invasion leads to the collapse of the military junta in Athens. The Greeks vote in favour of remaining a republic. President Makarios returns but the Turks continue to occupy the north.

In Portugal, 50 years of dictatorship are ended when **Dr Caetano** is ousted. The new government moves rapidly to give Portugal's African colonies—Guinea-Bissau, Mozambique and Angola—their independence.

Emperor Haile Selassie of Ethiopia is deposed by radical elements in his army.

Willy Brandt, West Germany's first Social Democratic Chancellor, resigns when it is revealed that an alleged East German spy has been working in his office.

The IRA extends its terrorist activities to Britain.

1975 In a referendum to decide whether Britain is to stay in the European Economic Community, more than 17 million vote for staying in and more than 8 million against.

Mrs Margaret Thatcher is elected leader of the Conservative Party, replacing Edward Heath.

In Lebanon the Muslims become the largest community in the country, a position previously held by Christians. Fighting breaks out between extremist factions in the two communities. The situation is made worse by the presence in Lebanon of Palestinian refugees, many of them members of the Palestinian Liberation Army. The country slides into civil war.

President Anwar Sadat re-opens Suez Canal and, with the agreement of Israel, the first ships pass through the Canal since its closure after the 1967 war.

In Helsinki, the leaders of 35 countries sign a document intended to reduce tension between East and West.

In Nigeria General Gowon is removed as Head of State by a military coup.

In Indo-China the longest war in the 20th century, lasting 30 years, comes to an end. In South Vietnam, Communist forces capture Saigon, the capital, and rename it Ho Chi Minh City. In Cambodia the Communist Khmer Rouge occupy the capital, Phnom Penh, and **Prince Sihanouk**, ousted in 1970, returns from exile as Head of State. Laos falls to the pro-Communist Pathet Lao after an almost bloodless coup.

In Portugal, more moderate political elements begin to assert themselves. In Mozambique, Portugal hands over power peacefully and smoothly; but in Angola three rival liberation movements are left fighting for control.

President Sheik Mujibur Rahman of Bangladesh and his family are assassinated in a military coup.

In Northern Ireland the number of civilians killed since 1969 passes the 1,000 mark. In Britain the IRA terror campaign is stepped up.

In Spain, General Franco dies at the age of 82, and **Prince Juan Carlos** is sworn in as King and Head of State.

British oil starts flowing ashore from the North Sea. Britain is expected to be self-sufficient in oil by 1980.

1976 Chou-En-Lai, Chinese Prime Minister, **Mao-Tse-Tung**'s

right hand man and the architect of China's policy of rapproche-
ment towards the United States and the West, dies.

The world's first commercial passenger supersonic aircraft,
the Anglo-French Concorde, goes into regular service.

Unemployment in Britain passes the $1\frac{1}{2}$ million mark, and
the pound falls below $2 for the first time in history.

Harold Wilson resigns as Prime Minister and **James Callaghan**
takes his place.

The Americans carry out man's deepest probe into space by
launching two unmanned spacecraft, Viking I and Viking II,
and landing them safely on Mars.

Ian Smith agrees, under pressure from South Africa, to proposals for majority rule within 2 years in Rhodesia.

In South Africa, the independence of Transkei, the first of the
Bantustans, separate homelands for black South Africans, is
proclaimed. The UN General Assembly refuses recognition.

Chairman Mao Tse-Tung dies and is succeeded by the moderate **Hua Kuo-feng**. After a brief power struggle, Mao's widow
and her supporters (the 'Gang of Four') are arrested.

In Lebanon the Syrian army, with the approval of Egypt and
Saudi Arabia, imposes a truce on the warring factions of
Maronite Christians and Muslims after 19 months of civil war
in which more than 50,000 people have been killed and Beirut,
once the business and financial centre of the Middle East,
reduced to rubble.

1977 Jimmy Carter, Democrat, is installed as 39th President of
the USA.

The new Race Relations Bill in Britain strengthens the law
on racial discrimination.

The Labour Government in Britain is kept in power by the
making of a formal pact between itself and the Liberals.

In Israel, Labour, the dominant party since 1948, is defeated,
and **Menahem Begin** forms a coalition cabinet.

Steve Biko, founder and first president of the South African
Students Association, dies while under arrest, and the post
mortem finds 'extensive brain damage'. At the inquiry which
follows world-wide expressions of horror, the police are ex-
onerated from blame for Biko's death.

President Sadat, in an attempt to resolve the conflict in the
Middle East, is the first Egyptian leader to visit Israel.

1978 In Britain, for the first time in six years, there is a balance
of payments surplus, and the inflation rate falls to under 8%.
The radio broadcasting of Parliamentary business begins.

The first baby ever conceived outside its mother is born in
Manchester.

Pope Paul VI dies and is succeeded by **John Paul I**, who dies
of a heart attack 33 days after his election. **Cardinal Karol
Wojtala**, Archbishop of Cracow, becomes the 265th Pope and
the first non-Italian to be elected for four and a half centuries.
He takes the title of **John Paul II**.

A summit meeting between President Sadat and Prime
Minister Begin, arranged by President Carter at Camp David,
ends hopefully, but afterwards many differences prevent the
signing of a peace treaty.

Vietnam and Cambodia fight, and boatloads of Vietnamese
refugees of Chinese extraction seek asylum.

The USA announces that diplomatic relations with Communist China will begin, and those with Nationalist China
(Taiwan) will cease.

1979 In Britain, there are stoppages and strikes in revolt against
the Government's policy of a 5% pay rise and no more. The
BBC is affected; and ITV is off the air for nearly three months.
The Times remains unpublished for nearly a year.

The Iranian people bring about the fall of the Shah. His
enemy, the **Ayatollah Khomeini**, returns from exile and sets up
an Islamic Republic.

President Sadat and Prime Minister Begin sign a peace treaty
and the 30-year war between Egypt and Israel is ended. The
first Israeli ship for 25 years enters the Suez Canal.

Airey Neave, MP, and **Lord Mountbatten** are among victims
of the IRA.

Tanzania invades Uganda and Idi Amin flees.

Margaret Thatcher becomes Britain's first woman Prime
Minister when the Conservatives win the General Election.

The Salt II strategic arms limitation treaty is signed by the
US and the USSR.

The European Parliament has its first session in Strasbourg.

The American Embassy in Teheran is seized by students and
52 hostages are held; the students demand the return to Iran
for trial of the Shah, receiving medical treatment in the US.

In Rhodesia there is an overwhelming vote for the establishment of majority rule. **Bishop Muzorewa** becomes the first black Prime Minister. The state of UDI ends and Lord Soames arrives as British Governor.

Russian troops invade Afghanistan in support of the Communist Government.

1980 In India, three years after defeat, Mrs Gandhi wins an overwhelming victory in a general election.

After elections, **Robert Mugabe** becomes Prime Minister and Southern Rhodesia achieves independence as Zimbabwe.

26 people are taken hostage at the Iranian Embassy in London, but a successful rescue bid is made by the Special Air Service Regiment.

President Tito of Yugoslavia dies, aged 87.

Jerusalem, by Israeli law, becomes the capital city.

In Poland, the Gdansk strikers win the right to form trade unions and to strike and the promise of greater freedom of speech. The Silesian mine and steel workers demand similar concessions, granted when they return to work. Polish radio begins to transmit Sunday Mass for the first time in forty years. Further strikes break out when the Polish Government fails to honour its promises. Fears of Russian intervention mount.

Iraq and Iran drift into an indecisive war over border and territorial rights.

Ronald Reagan, Republican, former Governor of California and film star, is elected President of the USA.

Michael Foot is elected Leader of the Labour Party.

Jiang Qing, Mao's widow, is tried for alleged persecution of the people and responsibility for the death of 30,000 workers.

Iranian students surrender responsibility for the 52 hostages to the Iranian government, which makes demands on America before agreeing to release them. Efforts to free the hostages, including an attack by US commandos, prove fruitless.

John Lennon, erstwhile Beatle, is shot dead in New York.

1981 Immediately after President Reagan is inaugurated as the 40th President of the United States, the American hostages in Iran are released.

Throughout the spring and summer in Britain, there is rioting in major cities.

Twenty-three years of right-wing rule in France end when

François Mitterrand, the socialist candidate, is elected President.

Pope John Paul II and two women are shot and seriously wounded in St Peter's Square by a Turkish gunman.

The Humber Bridge, nearly a mile and a half long and the world's longest single-span bridge, is formally opened.

The Prince of Wales marries **Lady Diana Spencer** in St Paul's Cathedral.

Unemployment in the UK continues to rise to nearly 3 million, only just below the highest ever recorded in 1933.

President Sadat of Egypt is assassinated.

There is increasing dissension in the Labour Party. Polls and by-elections point to strong support for the newly-formed Social Democratic Party, to which a number of Labour MPs defect, and which forms an alliance with the Liberal Party.

The Polish Government announces martial law to break strikes throughout the country organised by Solidarity. Solidarity's leader, **Lech Walesa**, is placed under house arrest.

1982 Unemployment in Britain rises to over three million.

Though some of the last settlers have to be removed by force, Israel evacuates the Sinai and hands it back to Egypt.

The Falkland Islands, territories dependent upon Britain, are annexed, together with South Georgia, by Argentinian forces. The British Foreign Secretary, **Lord Carrington**, resigns and is succeeded by **Francis Pym**. After a turbulent special session of Parliament, a naval task force is assembled and sets sail for the South Atlantic. Attempts at mediation by the American Secretary of State fail, and America calls on Argentina to respond to a United Nations resolution requiring her to withdraw her forces from the Falklands. Britain declares a 200-mile exclusion zone round the islands. South Georgia is reoccupied by a force of British marines. The EEC, the United States and others announce economic sanctions against Argentina. The Argentine cruiser, *General Belgrano*, is torpedoed by a submarine and sinks with the loss of 368 lives. The British destroyer *HMS Sheffield* is lost as the result of an air-launched missile attack, and 30 of her crew are killed. After seven sets of peace proposals are considered Mrs Thatcher tells Parliament that she has grave doubts of the seriousness of the Argentine response to these plans. An attempt to recapture the islands begins with the establishment of a British bridgehead at

Port San Carlos in East Falklands with serious loss on both sides, among British ships and Argentine aircraft. Six of Britain's partners in the EEC agree to trade sanctions against Argentina for an indefinite period.

After six days, the British task force fans out from San Carlos towards Port Darwin and Goose Green, both of which are quickly taken. Twenty-four days after the first landing, British troops enter Stanley, the capital of the islands. The Argentinian forces surrender. British casualties are assessed at nearly 300; Argentinian casualties at 700.

President Galtieri of Argentina is deposed and the newly-formed government announces it will not formally declare an end to hostilities.

In Poland, **General Jaruzelski** lifts some restrictions imposed under martial law, but Lech Walesa is not released. The cost of living rises by 125%, and on the second anniversary of the founding of Solidarity, thousands of protesters clash with the authorities. Walesa is released, but is temporarily held again. Most internees are freed and martial law ends.

The IRA claim the killing of 11 people and the injury of over 50 when bombs explode in London's Hyde Park and Regents Park. Seventeen are killed and over 60 injured when the Irish National Liberation Army explode a bomb in a public house in Co. Londonderry.

The 'Mary Rose', Henry VIII's flagship, is successfully raised from the seabed and taken into Portsmouth Harbour.

The Thames anti-flooding barrier becomes operational after nine years' work and an expenditure of £435 million.

President Brezhnev of the Soviet Union dies and is succeeded by **Yuri Andropov**, a former head of the KGB.

1983 The death sentence on Chairman Mao's widow, Jiang Qing, is rescinded, and she receives a life sentence instead.

The Campaign for Nuclear Disarmament has an estimated 100,000 demonstrators lining the 15 miles between Greenham Common missile site and the Burghfield Ordnance Factory. Similar protests take place all over Europe.

A massive charge of explosive blasts the American Embassy in Beirut, killing over 50 and injuring over 100 others.

In June, the Conservatives win the General Election and Mrs Thatcher is Prime Minister for a second term of office.

Michael Foot resigns as leader of the Labour Party and **Neil Kinnock** is elected in his place.

After the Pope visits Poland, the Polish government declares an amnesty for political prisoners, but Solidarity remains outlawed. Lech Walesa is awarded the Nobel Peace Prize.

In riots in Sri Lanka between Sinhalese and the Tamil minority, 350 die. Many Tamils flee the country before order is restored.

Menachem Begin resigns as Prime Minister of Israel and is succeeded by **Yitzhak Shamir** as a serious financial crisis overtakes the country.

Two hundred and sixty-nine civilians on board a Jumbo jet die when their plane is shot down by Soviet fighters over the island of Sakhalin. An inquiry finds that human error caused the aircraft to stray over Russian territory.

In Grenada, the army scts up a 'revolutionary and military council' after seizing control. Against the advice of the British Government, American troops invade the island. President Reagan claims that a take-over by Cuba has been forestalled. Within a week, hostilities have ceased and US troops begin to withdraw. The nine members of the Organisation of Eastern Caribbean States form an interim government and take over control.

British assets, frozen in Argentina since the Falklands War, are released. Argentina elects a civilian government and, following the discovery of hundreds of bodies buried near the capital, former military leaders are arrested and charged.

1984 The right to trade union membership is withdrawn from employees at Government Communication Headquarters in Cheltenham, on the grounds that it could lead to breaches of security and disruption of nationally vital work. The High Court rules that the ban is unlawful; but a Court of Appeal rules against this.

Captain Bruce McCandless becomes the first man to walk in space without a safety line; and **Svetlana Savitskaya** is the first woman to space-walk.

President Yuri Andropov of the USSR dies, and is succeeded by **Konstantin Chernenko**.

Yorkshire miners are called out on strike in protest at the closing of two pits at Barnsley and Rotherham. The chairman of the National Coal Board, **Ian MacGregor**, confirms the intention to close some 20 more 'uneconomic' pits in the following year. This marks the beginning of a long, bitter and sometimes violent dispute between the NCB and the National Union of Mineworkers, led by their President, **Arthur Scargill**. A majority of miners come out on strike, though the Nottinghamshire men, their demand for a national pithead ballot refused, remain largely at work.

WPC Yvonne Fletcher is killed when shots are fired from the Libyan People's Bureau in London into a crowd of demonstrators. The Bureau is put under siege and diplomats inside the building are given seven days to leave the country.

In India, Sikhs in Amritsar, demanding recognition as a nation, are besieged in the Golden Temple by national troops.

The 6,000,000 population of Ethiopia is pronounced to be on the verge of famine due to drought. Massive international rescue operations are launched.

An IRA bomb explodes at the Grand Hotel in Brighton, where the Prime Minister and members of the Cabinet are staying during the annual Conservative Party Conference. Five people are killed; and over 30 are injured.

In New Delhi, Indira Gandhi, Prime Minister of India, is assassinated by Sikh members of her bodyguard. **Rajiv Gandhi**, her son, is sworn in to replace her and is later elected Prime Minister in her place. Many Sikhs are murdered and have their homes and businesses wrecked.

Ronald Reagan is re-elected as President of the United States.

A natural gas plant explodes in a suburb of Mexico City, killing 600 people and injuring 3,000. At least 2,500 people are killed and many more injured when toxic gas seeps from an underground storage tank at a pesticide plant near Bhopal in India.

Margaret Thatcher and **Deng Xiaoping** sign a joint pact in Peking on the future of Hong Kong, which will pass into Chinese sovereignty in 1997.

1985 The day before the first anniversary of the strike, the longest in British history, the National Union of Mineworkers votes for a return to work.

Konstantin Chernenko, President of the USSR for only fifteen months, dies. **Mikhail Gorbachev** becomes the new leader.

A stand at Bradford City's football ground catches fire: 55 people burn to death, and 200 are injured.

Liverpool football fans fight supporters of the Italian team Juventus in Brussels before the European Cup Final. Thirty-eight people are killed and over 430 injured. FIFA imposes a world-wide ban on English football clubs.

Just before setting out to lead a protest fleet to Mururoa Atoll, the French nuclear testing site in the Pacific, the Greenpeace ship *Rainbow Warrior* is wrecked by explosives and sinks in Auckland Harbour, New Zealand. A member of the crew is killed. Those responsible are quickly proved to be French secret service agents: and Paris admits as much. Two agents are sentenced to ten years' imprisonment for their part in the affair.

The pop singer, **Bob Geldof**, organises a rock concert that raises over £50 million for famine relief.

Over 500 passengers and crew die when a Japanese Boeing 747 crashes into mountains near Tokyo—the worst accident ever involving a single plane. This is also the worst year ever for air disasters: over 2,000 deaths occur. The destruction of an Air India 747 off the coast of Ireland on its way from Canada is judged to be the result of a bomb exploding in the luggage compartment.

When a black woman is accidentally shot by a policeman, riots break out in Brixton, London. Shops are looted and burned and a police station attacked. Riots occur also in Peckham, London, and Toxteth, Liverpool; and when a woman collapses and dies as her home in North London is being searched by police, there is serious rioting in the course of which a policeman is killed.

The struggle against apartheid in South Africa grows more fierce. Soweto and other townships are closed to Press and TV. Cries increase for the release of **Nelson Mandela**, the black African leader imprisoned for nearly a quarter of a century.

The first summit conference for six years takes place between President Reagan and Mikhail Gorbachev. It concludes with a joint statement declaring a new start between the two countries. Later the two leaders promise, in simultaneous broadcasts, to work for peace, trust and the reduction of nuclear armaments.

An agreement is signed between the British and Irish governments, allowing for participation by the Republic in the affairs of Northern Ireland.

1986 Rupert Murdoch, owner of Times Newspapers, transfers much of the operation from Fleet Street to new buildings in Wapping, heavily defended with barbed wire and in other ways.

Most of the journalists concerned agree to make the move, but 5,000 printers and other members of the print unions go on strike, and are sacked. It turns out that a much smaller staff of electricians are ready to operate the new printing technology: this leads to conflict between the electricians' union and the TUC.

Michael Heseltine, Defence Secretary, resigns from the Government in the middle of a Cabinet meeting, and claims that there has been improper prevention of discussion in Cabinet of the affairs of the ailing helicopter company, Westland. As a result of the claims and counter-claims that follow, and of the leak of a letter from the Attorney-General, **Mr Leon Brittan**, Trade and Industry Secretary, also resigns.

The space shuttle Challenger, seconds after its launch from Cape Canaveral, explodes in a ball of fire. Among the crew was a teacher, **Mrs Christa McAuliffe**, chosen from thousands of applicants to be the first civilian to go into space.

Mrs Thatcher and President Mitterrand agree at a meeting at Lille that a rail-only Channel Tunnel should be built.

The National Resistance Army of Uganda enters Kampala, the capital, and its leader, **Yoweri Museveni**, is sworn in as the country's new president.

After claiming to have defeated **Corazon Aquino** in a presidential election, amid allegations of electoral fraud, **President Ferdinand Marcos** is airlifted out of the presidential palace in Manila, capital of the Philippines, and goes into exile. Mrs Aquino is formally declared to have won the election.

Following American deaths in terrorist acts in Europe, American aircraft bomb targets in Tripoli, the Libyan capital, causing a number of civilian deaths and casualties. The United States claims that it has evidence that Libya is behind the acts of terrorism. Outside America, the action is widely condemned, and the claim that the raid was covered by an article of the UN Charter is rejected. In Britain, opinion polls show that a majority disapprove of the decision to allow American aircraft taking part in the raid to fly from bases in Britain. The Western allies agree to sanctions against Libya.

A major accident to a nuclear reactor in a power station at Chernobyl, in the Ukraine, is made known to the outside world two days later, when Sweden detects high levels of radiation in the atmosphere. Meltdown is prevented and the release of radiation limited by dropping sand and other materials on the reactor from helicopters. A radioactive cloud is blown by winds back and forth over Europe and beyond: there is alarm about the effect on rainwater, milk and dairy products.

When President Botha refuses to change the direction of his policy on apartheid after **Sir Geoffrey Howe's** mission to Africa on behalf of the European Economic Community, modest sanctions banning the import of coal, iron, steel and gold coins are brought in by the British Government. The United States introduces more stringent sanctions. Violent unrest continues throughout South Africa and the state of emergency is reimposed. Barclay's Bank and some other multi-national companies decide to dispose of their South African interests.

Britain breaks off diplomatic relations with Syria after the trial and conviction of **Nezar Hindawi** for his attempt to destroy an El Al flight from Heathrow airport. Evidence disclosed at the trial convinces the Government that Hindawi had been aided in terrorist activities by the Syrian authorities.

A meeting takes place at Reykjavik between President Reagan and Mikhail Gorbachev, at which the possibility of banning nuclear weapons is discussed. President Reagan is unable to agree to any constraints on his star wars programme.

Widespread changes in the operation of the London Stock Exchange are introduced, and are popularly referred to as the 'Big Bang'. Visual Display Units in city offices largely take over from the practice of face-to-face trading on the floor of the Stock Exchange. Brokers and jobbers, who traditionally had separate and defined roles, are allowed to embrace both activities.

The release of American hostages held by Muslim extremists in Lebanon, followed by the admission that consignments of United States arms had been shipped to Iran, leads to the suspicion that the two events are connected, despite denials by President Reagan. The disclosure that payment received for the arms has been made available to the Contras fighting the Government forces in Nicaragua provokes a crisis in the US government, and leads to calls for a thorough investigation.

Andrei Sakharov, Soviet dissident, physicist and father of the Soviet hydrogen bomb, is released from internal exile.

1987 In a speech to the Central Council of the Communist Party, Mikhail Gorbachev extends his policy of *glasnost* (openness) by calling for new electoral procedures in the USSR, with the possibility of secret ballots for Communist Party posts: new laws allowing people to pursue complaints against Party officials through the courts: and the encouragement of non-Party members to take a more active part in public life.

The Tower Commission, set up by the US President after the widespread concern over the hostages-for-arms deals, reports that President Reagan, driven by compassion for the hostages, failed to exercise proper control of the Iran deals, and did not seem to be aware of the full consequences of US participation in them.

A cross-channel ferry, the *Herald of Free Enterprise*, capsizes and sinks off Zeebrugge with the loss of nearly 200 lives. It is established that the ferry sailed with its bow doors open.

At the request of the Lebanese Prime Minister, Syrian troops enter West Beirut in an effort to halt the militia wars. The troops bring relief to the Palestinians trapped for months in the Shatila refugee camp.

The United States imposes tariff sanctions against some Japanese imports, allegedly in response to Japanese dumping of semi-conductors in various world markets.

Tamil rebels, fighting for the establishment of a separate Tamil state in Sri Lanka, are blamed for the increasing number of terrorist attacks. An Indo/Sri Lankan agreement allows an Indian peace-keeping force to restrain the Tamils and persuade them to give up their arms in return for autonomy in the north.

The New South Wales Supreme Court dismisses the British Government's attempt to stop publication of **Peter Wright's** memoirs in Australia. As a former member of the Security Service he had undertaken not to reveal details of his work.

The Lebanese Prime Minister is killed when a bomb explodes in a helicopter taking him to Beirut.

At the General Election in June, Margaret Thatcher leads the Conservatives to victory: the first time this century that a Prime Minister has won three consecutive terms of office.

Rudolph Hess, Hitler's former deputy, commits suicide in Spandau prison in Berlin, where he had been incarcerated for 40 years.

In Bangladesh it is reported that one-fifth of the population is affected by floods, and one million are homeless.

In October in southern England there is the worst storm for

nearly 300 years. Nineteen people are killed and huge numbers of trees are lost.

The Chinese 13th Party Congress in Beijing proposes domestic reforms and the continued opening-up of China to the outside world.

Eleven people attending a Remembrance Day service at Enniskillen, Northern Ireland, are killed when an IRA bomb explodes 20 yards from the war memorial.

At a summit conference in Washington, Ronald Reagan and Mikhail Gorbachev sign a treaty to eliminate from Europe every land-based intermediate nuclear missile.

Thirty-one die and more than 50 are injured in a blaze at Kings Cross Underground station in London.

Violence erupts in the Gaza strip as Palestinians protest about the Israeli occupation. Israeli troops and border police are accused of brutality in putting down disturbances.

Five Central American countries support a plan to end the fighting between the Nicaraguan Government and the Contras, the rebel groups supported by the United States.

As attacks on Gulf shipping increase as a consequence of the war between Iran and Iraq, navies of the United States, Britain, France and Italy become involved in defence of their interests.

Mr Robert Mugabe drops the title of Prime Minister of Zimbabwe and is inaugurated as Executive President. This opens the way for Zimbabwe to become a one-party state.

1988 The Prince and Princess of Wales visit Australia for the bicentenary celebrations.

A commission set up by the Austrian Government to examine the wartime record of their President, Dr Kurt Waldheim, reports that he did not initiate illegal acts against prisoners of the German Army but did nothing to resist wrongdoing.

The Liberals and the Social Democrats decide to merge in a new party, the Social and Liberal Democratic Party. **Dr David Owen** announces he will keep alive an independent SDP.

Panama's military strong man, **General Noriega**, ousts the President. Panama is of concern to Washington because of the 10,000 US troops in the Canal zone. General Noriega is linked with cocaine cartels and the US Government introduces sanctions aimed at bringing about his downfall.

Three known IRA terrorists are shot dead in Gibraltar as they act on a plan to bring a car with bombs across the border from Spain. Sectarian killings follow in Northern Ireland, and two British soldiers in a car in West Belfast are beaten and shot.

In the Soviet Union the worst intercommunal violence for many years breaks out in the adjacent republics of Armenia and Azerbaijan.

After 8½ years of occupation the USSR agrees to withdraw its troops from Afghanistan in stages.

François Mitterrand wins a further term of seven years as French President.

A fourth summit meeting between President Reagan and Mr Gorbachev in Moscow results in agreements on arms control, space and cultural exchanges.

Mr Gorbachev announces that the Supreme Soviet will be replaced by a smaller body with legislative powers. In future elections it will be possible to nominate a proportion of candidates who are not members of the Communist Party. A reshuffle in the upper ranks of the Party leads to the election of Mr Gorbachev as President.

After pressure from Washington, Japan agrees to increase its share of the cost of United States forces stationed there.

In error, a US Navy vessel shoots down an Iranian airbus as it takes off and all 290 passengers and crew are killed.

In the world's worst oil field disaster, 167 die in two massive explosions at the Piper Alpha rig in the North Sea.

The strongest hurricane ever recorded in the western hemisphere brings havoc to Jamaica, the Cayman Islands and Mexico.

Opposition to one-party rule in Burma brings civil unrest, and the government concedes that all-party elections should be held. Demonstrations lead to rule by a military junta.

Moscow announces that individuals will have the right to lease land from the state.

A plane carrying **President Zia** of Pakistan explodes in the air and all aboard are killed. A general election held later in the year is won by the Pakistan People's Party. **Miss Benazir Bhutto** becomes the first woman leader of a Muslim country.

There is unrest in the USSR's Baltic States, taken over by the Soviet Union as part of the Nazi–Soviet pact of 1939. Giving recognition to nationalist movements in Estonia, Latvia and Lithuania does little to quieten demands for independence.

In Chile a referendum goes against a further eight-year term for **President Pinochet**, and presidential elections are proposed.

The British Government bans broadcasting authorities in the UK from transmitting direct statements by representatives of Sinn Fein, Republican Sinn Fein and the Ulster Association.

The Education Reform Act introduces a national curriculum for all State primary and secondary schools.

Violence in Sri Lanka leads travel firms to advise tourists to leave the island. The troubles are largely a reaction to the government's Indian-sponsored settlement with the Tamil minority.

Yasser Arafat, chairman of the Palestine Liberation Organisation, announces acceptance of the UN resolution calling for the acknowledgement of the sovereignty of all states in the Middle East. Previously the PLO had been unwilling to recognise Israel. After this announcement the United States indicates it is willing to talk to the PLO about the Middle East.

George Bush, the Republican candidate, is elected 41st President of the United States.

A settlement between South Africa, Cuba and Angola is to lead to the independence of Namibia.

Addressing the United Nations, President Gorbachev announces plans to reduce Soviet armed forces and the number of conventional weapons.

An earthquake strikes Armenia. Rescue teams from many countries go to the Soviet Union. Up to 70,000 die.

British Steel is privatised.

At Clapham Junction in South London, 34 people are killed and 110 injured when three trains crash. Britain's worst air disaster occurs when a Boeing 745 flying from London to New York explodes in the air and crashes into houses in Lockerbie on the Scottish border. The 258 people on board are killed, together with 18 townspeople. Investigations establish that a bomb exploded on board.

1989 Representatives of 149 countries sign a declaration outlawing poison gas and bacteriological weapons.

After a heart attack, **President Botha** of South Africa is replaced as party leader by **Mr F. W. de Klerk**. After a general election, for whites only, Mr de Klerk becomes president. He arranges a meeting with Mr Nelson Mandela, the imprisoned African National Congress leader.

The last Soviet troops leave Afghanistan. In the Soviet Union the first elections offering a choice of candidates result in many official Communist Party candidates being defeated.

In Tibet, Chinese shops are looted and burned as Tibetans chant slogans calling for independence.

Ayatollah Khomeini condemns **Salman Rushdie**'s novel, *The Satanic Verses*, and urges Muslims to kill the author and his publishers. Salman Rushdie goes into hiding. Britain breaks off diplomatic relations with Iran.

An oil tanker runs aground off Alaska and oil spillage causes immense environmental damage.

The Polish Government and Lech Walesa sign an agreement ensuring the legality of the free trade union, Solidarity, and the country is set on a path of democratic reform. Later Solidarity defeats the Communist Party in the elections, and the process is begun of steering Poland towards a market economy.

In Namibia, at the start of the transition period before independence, guerillas from Angola cross the border: over 200 people are killed, and 20 or more of the South African forces. Over-complex administrative arrangements and a too-small UN supervisory force are blamed for the situation.

On a visit to London, President Gorbachev expresses his belief in the possibility of a safe and nuclear-free world. He advocates the steady destruction of stockpiles and elimination of nuclear weapons as the ultimate aim.

Ninety-five spectators are crushed to death at Hillsborough Football ground, Sheffield, when late arrivals at a Cup semi-final cause fatal overcrowding at one end of the ground.

Ayatollah Khomeini dies. **Hashemi Rafsanjani** is elected as Iran's new president.

Mass student protests demanding greater democracy take place in Beijing and other Chinese cities, and coincide with a visit by President Gorbachev aimed at restoring good relations between the two countries. Encouraged by the lack of response from the security forces, the students enlist the support of the workers. A camp is set up in Tiananmen Square, Beijing. Many students go on hunger strike. But the government orders military action, and tanks move into the square and crush all resistance. The bloodshed and the hunting down and arrest of dissidents cause shock throughout the world.

The Marine Band headquarters at Deal, in Kent, is wrecked by an IRA bomb: 10 soldiers are killed, 22 injured.

President Mouawad of Lebanon is assassinated in Beirut. During the year there are outbreaks of fierce fighting between the Syrian-backed Amal and the Iraqi-backed Hezbollah.

A 15-second earthquake inflicts extensive damage around San Francisco Bay, with nearly 100 deaths.

Vietnamese troops withdraw from Cambodia after 11 years, so ending their involvement with the civil war.

The political changes in Eastern Europe, begun in Poland, continue when East German refugees cross the now open border into Hungary, en route for West Germany. Protests and demonstrations, particularly in Leipzig and East Berlin, force the resignation of the President, Eric Honecker. Having introduced reforms, the ruling communist party begins to dismantle the Berlin Wall, and after 28 years of separation, Berliners can pass freely in both directions. Opposition parties are admitted to the government.

In Hungary, reforms are already under way, and a rewritten constitution pledges multi-party democracy. As it becomes clear that the Soviet Union has abandoned its interventionist policy in Eastern Europe, the emergence of protest movements spreads to Bulgaria and Czechoslovakia: leading in Bulgaria to reforms by the communist government, and in Czechoslovakia to a loss of overall power by the communists, the establishment of an interim government with the promise of free elections, and the election of the playwright **Vaclav Havel** as President.

Despite brutal attempts at repression, the pattern is repeated in Romania: the army supports the protest groups. **President Ceausescu** and his wife are summarily tried and executed.

Chancellor Kohl of West Germany speaks of the re-unification of Germany in stages, and western political leaders attempt to adjust their thinking to the defence implications of these extraordinary and unforeseen events.

President Gorbachev visits the Pope, ending 70 years of hostility between the Vatican and the Soviet Union. At a summit meeting in the Mediterranean, President Bush and President Gorbachev promise economic co-operation. This is crucial for the USSR, where the President comes under increasing pressure because of the spread of multi-party democracy in its Eastern European partners, the disappointing results of Soviet efforts to improve farming and industrial productivity, and the continuing poor choice of goods in the shops. Meanwhile, in the Baltic states and Azerbaijan, demonstrations continue for greater independence.

The proceedings of the House of Commons are televised for the first time.

The Congress Party loses its overall majority at the Indian general election. Rajiv Gandhi resigns as premier and is succeeded by V. P. Singh, of the Janata Dal party.

There are widespread accusations of ballot-rigging in the general election in Panama. General Noriega claims victory, but foreign observers give it to the opposition. More United States troops are sent to the canal zone, and US sanctions are tightened. In December their troops invade Panama on the grounds that US citizens are at risk. This action brings sharp criticism from the United Nations. Noriega surrenders and is taken to face trial in the United States.

Britain begins the forced repatriation of the 'boat people' by sending a small party back to Vietnam. There is widespread criticism of the British policy.

The Ethiopian government steps up its 14-year-old war against the northern rebels as an estimated 4 million people face starvation in the disrupted territories.

1990 Gales strike England and Wales, causing widespread damage. There are 47 deaths, and many need hospital treatment.

The Yugoslav government announces plans to go ahead with changes in the constitution and to introduce a multi-party state. The Supreme Soviet of the USSR decides on a new-style executive presidency, and President Gorbachev is appointed for a four-year term. Gradual progress towards a multi-party system is accepted.

Moscow sends in the army, navy and KGB in an effort to halt violence between the predominantly Muslim Azerbaijanis and the Christian Armenians in the trans-Caucasus.

President Gorbachev calls for the withdrawal of a declaration of independence by Lithuania, saying legislation being prepared will give republics an ordered procedure for leaving the Soviet Union if a given majority votes for it. Soviet pressure grows as sanctions against Lithuania are introduced.

At the East German elections, the Social Democrats (the conservative party favoured by Chancellor Kohl of West Germany) wins the largest share of the vote. German reunification is to be discussed by the East and West German governments and by the four powers occupying Germany at the end of the Second World War—the UK, France, the USA and the USSR.

In South Africa, Nelson Mandela is freed. The 30-year-old ban on the ANC is lifted, prisoners are to be freed, and restrictions on the media removed. Britain ends the limited sanctions imposed on South Africa, but other countries say they will not follow this example while apartheid remains in place.

There is a surprise defeat for the Sandanistas in the Nicaraguan elections, won by **Violeta Chamorro**'s coalition.

There is conflict in the Kashmir valley between Hindu and Muslim fundamentalists. Tens of thousands of Hindus flee from the Muslim uprising aimed at secession from India. The heavy Indian military presence leads to tension with Pakistan.

The community charge, or poll tax, is introduced in England and Wales a year later than in Scotland. There are widespread protests at what many see as an unfair tax.

A riot at Strangeways jail, Manchester, turns into the longest siege in British penal history, lasting 25 days.

In the wake of military repression of the pro-democracy demonstrations in China in June, 1989, and to restore confidence among business managers and administrators, 50,000 heads of households in Hong Kong are offered UK passports.

The Social Democratic Party is wound up.

Free elections take place in Bulgaria, Czechoslovakia and Romania. But it becomes clear that the main reason for the collapse of communist rule in these countries was the rapidly-failing economic system, which could not meet even basic consumer needs. It is estimated that years of hard work will be needed before market economies bring greater prosperity.

The President of Pakistan dismisses Benazir Bhutto as Prime Minister, accusing her of corruption and nepotism. In a general election her Pakistan People's Party is unsuccessful, and **Mian Nawz Sharif** becomes Prime Minister.

Iraq invades Kuwait. When their forces reach the Saudi Arabian frontier, the United States gives the Saudis immediate armed assistance to prevent further aggression. The United

Nations condemns the invasion and demands withdrawal. An embargo is placed on trade with Iraq and a naval and air blockade are authorised. Twenty-eight nations are involved in the coalition. Britain decides to send forces. Iraq announces it has annexed Kuwait as a new province. In many quarters it is felt that sanctions alone will not make Iraq withdraw within a reasonable period; and at the end of November the Security Council approves the use of all necessary force to drive Iraq out if it has not left Kuwait by January 15. **President Saddam Hussein** allows hostages held in Baghdad to return to their own countries by Christmas.

The civil war in Lebanon, which has lasted since 1975, ends with the surrender of **General Michael Aoun's** army to the Syrian forces supporting the Lebanese government.

The UK joins the European Exchange Rate mechanism.

Changes in the law in South Africa begin to make it easier for blacks and whites to work and play alongside each other. But discussions between the South African government and the African National Congress on plans for a multi-national democracy slow down because of clashes between rival black groups—the ANC and the mainly Zulu supporters of Inkatha.

President Gorbachev wins the Nobel Peace Prize. There are reports of serious food shortages in Leningrad. Food shortages in the cities constitute one reason for the EC report on the state of the Soviet economy, which emphasises the urgent need for changes in agriculture, distribution, energy and manufacture. The EC promises help with food and technical assistance. President Bush plans to allow the Soviet Union to buy grain and other commodities at favourable prices, and offers help with medical supplies and technical advice. Aiming to save the unity of the Soviet Union, President Gorbachev takes additional powers to ensure that central policies are carried out in the 15 republics. **Edward Shevardnadze**, the Foreign Minister, resigns, telling the Soviet Parliament that he fears the new powers voted for the President could lead to renewed dictatorship.

In the worst rioting in Jerusalem since 1967, eighteen Arabs are killed when police open fire.

The two halves of the Channel Tunnel meet in mid-channel, and British and French engineers shake hands. (See J38).

At the conference on Security and Co-operation in Europe

attended by 34 nations (European and North American), four decades of military confrontation between East and West are formally ended.

In July East Germany celebrates as the Deutschmark becomes legal tender. After the re-unification of the two Germanies in October, Helmut Kohl's coalition win a general election.

V. P. Singh resigns as India's Prime Minister after a crushing defeat in Parliament. He is replaced by **Chandra Shekhar**, leader of the Janata Dal group, which is supported by the Congress Party.

At the Rome summit of the European Council all members, except the UK, state that their aim is to move towards the next stage of economic and monetary union by January 1994. Mrs Thatcher accuses her EC partners of conducting business incompetently and living in cloud-cuckoo-land. Sir Geoffrey Howe resigns his cabinet post, and in his resignation speech warns that the Prime Minister is risking Britain's future by her attitude towards its European partners. Mrs Thatcher is challenged for the leadership, and when a second round of voting becomes necessary, resigns. **John Major** is elected leader and becomes Prime Minister.

The presidential election in Poland is won by Lech Walesa.

In spite of reforms introduced in Albania, unrest grows. Some Albanians illegally cross into Greece and Yugoslavia, and others seek refuge in foreign embassies. In some cases the authorities allow refugees to leave the country.

In the UK, December brings the fifth highest monthly rise in unemployment on record, 80,400, taking the total to 1.84 million.

1991 The Soviet Government employs troops to halt moves towards independence in the Baltic republics. In Vilnius, Lithuania, tanks are used to occupy the Defence Department and the press and TV centres. Some civilian protesters are crushed whilst trying to defend key buildings: 15 people die. In Riga, Latvia, similar actions by troops from the Soviet Interior Ministry lead to four deaths. Fighting industrial unrest and falling production, the government tries to stem the growing desire of many of the republics to become independent, and to overcome their reluctance to contribute to the central budget. In support of these efforts to keep the country as a single state a referendum is held, and the Soviet leadership claims victory when 110 million people vote for the continuance of the Soviet Union as a 'renewed federation of equal sovereign republics . . .' Cooked meats, fruit and sweets without ration coupons are offered at polling stations as inducements to vote. Six of the 15 republics refuse to take part in the referendum.

Price rises are introduced, subsidies for food are cut by about two-thirds to ease the country's worsening debt. In June **Boris Yeltsin** becomes the Republic of Russia's first President directly elected by popular vote. This strengthens his position in relation to Mikhail Gorbachev, who is not a directly-elected leader.

South African repeals the Population Registration Act 1950, regarded as the cornerstone of apartheid. In theory blacks, Indians, and mixed races can now live where they please, but few have the means to do this and the vast majority will continue to live in a tribal homeland or one of the townships. In an effort to end the clashes between the feuding black political parties, the African National Congress and the Inkatha Freedom Party, a peace agreement is reached following a meeting of their leaders; but violence continues.

As the Prime Minister is about to start a cabinet meeting, the IRA fires mortar bombs at 10 Downing Street from a van parked off Whitehall. A bomb explodes in the garden outside the cabinet room, breaking windows; two others land without exploding behind the Foreign Office building.

The civilian government in Thailand is overthrown by a military coup, the army claiming government corruption as the reason for its action.

After 16 years imprisonment, the six men jailed for the death of 21 people in two pub bombings in Birmingham are released by the Court of Appeal. Forensic and police evidence are found to have been unsafe. As this follows the decision in 1989 that the four imprisoned for bombings in Guildford were wrongly convicted, the Home Secretary appoints a Royal Commission to examine the system of criminal justice.

Last-minute attempts to avert war in the Gulf fail, and the air attack begins on January 16. The Iraqi air force proves ineffective and soon ceases to fly. The allied forces, led by the Americans, bomb troops, supply lines, airfields and strategic installations over a period of five weeks. Iraq fires Scud missiles at Israel and Saudi Arabia: but Iraqi hopes of involving Israel in the war and causing a split in Arab opinion do not succeed. The Iraqis set fire to over 650 Kuwaiti oilfields. Kuwait City is captured within three days of the start of the ground war, with the Iraqi army cut off from its supply lines. A ceasefire is declared, and there are uprisings against Saddam Hussein by Kurdish separatists and Shia rebels. All are put down by the Iraqi army with great severity. Huge numbers of Kurdish refugees flee to the mountains on the Turkish border where they face freezing conditions without tents, blankets or fresh water. Many nations join the relief effort but poor access roads slow the operation. Iraq agrees to United Nations representatives entering the country to carry out relief work. Even larger numbers of Kurdish refugees cross the Iranian border, but Iran's relief efforts cannot match their needs. The allied nations impose a 'safe havens' plan for the Kurds, and set out to persuade the refugees to return to Iraq.

Results from Albania's first multi-party elections since 1944 give the communists a clear majority. But widespread strikes soon bring about the resignation of the government. A coalition is formed; wages are increased and prices controlled.

In the House of Commons it is announced that the unpopular poll tax is to go, to be replaced by a local tax largely based on property, as in the past.

Rajiv Gandhi, former prime minister of India, is killed in a bomb explosion during the election campaign. The election results in the Congress Party forming a minority government with **P. V. Narasimha Rao** as prime minister.

On the morning of 19 August tanks are sent into the streets of Moscow and other cities, and it is announced that President Gorbachev has been deposed. He and his family are held under house arrest in the Crimea. Boris Yeltsin leads the opposition to the coup, and his power and influence are greatly enhanced when the coup fails. The leaders of the revolt, politicians and army chiefs opposed to any loosening of central control in the Soviet Union, do not gain sufficient support from the army or the KGB, and their action collapses in three days. When President Gorbachev returns to Moscow he has to give ground to his rival Boris Yeltsin who takes over the government communications centre, and soon has joint control of government appointments. Russia takes over the financial institutions of the Soviet

Union. Attempts by President Gorbachev to keep the Soviet Union as a single unit fail, and, led by Boris Yeltsin and Russia, the republics form a Commonwealth of Independent States. Russia assumes control of the USSR's nuclear weapons. Gorbachev resigns and the world's second superpower ceases to exist. The communist experiment started by Lenin's Bolshevik Revolution had lasted a little over 74 years.

In Kenya **President Moi** orders raids on the houses of his political opponents, followed by police arrests. This is after demonstrations by crowds demanding an end to one-party dominance by the Kenya African National Union.

At the end of 27 years of one-party rule in Zambia, **Kenneth Kaunda** and his party are defeated in the elections and **Frederick Chiluba**, leader of the Movement for Multi-Party Democracy, is elected president.

Jean-Bertrand Aristide, Haiti's first democratically elected president, is deposed in a violent military coup.

In Madrid, delegates from Israel and Palestine are brought together for a peace conference after extensive negotiations by the United States.

Prince Norodom Sikanouk returns to Cambodia and to its 8.5 million people, exhausted by civil war. He aims to work for a multi-party democracy.

Mr Kitchi Miyazawa becomes Japan's prime minister after taking over the leadership of the Liberal Democratic Party. But his draft legislation to allow Japan to send peacekeeping forces overseas becomes limited by many conditions imposed by the Diet.

After a new agreement with the United Kingdom on repatriation, 59 people are deported back to Vietnam from Hong Kong against their wishes. This is the first forced repatriation for nearly two years.

A number of Western hostages held in Beirut are released including **Terry Waite**, captured nearly five years earlier when trying to negotiate the release of earlier hostages.

The declining influence of the central government, and increasing ethnic minority troubles and border incidents between the republics in Yugoslavia, decide Croatia and Slovenia to declare their republics independent. Serbia, the largest republic, wants to retain a federal united Yugoslavia. The Yugoslav army, largely controlled by Serbs, takes action to try and prevent the independence moves, and there are the beginnings of a civil war. The European Community makes numerous efforts to introduce a ceasefire. Serbian forces shell the ancient walled town of Dubrovnik. Serbia makes it plain that, because of its ethnic minorities living in Croatia and Slovenia, there would be territorial claims on those republics before any settlement based on independent countries.

Heads of government of the 12 member countries of the European Community meeting at Maastricht decide to prepare for a single currency for the Community by 1999.

In Algeria's multi-party elections the Islamic Salvation Front wins sufficient support to suggest it would become the principal party after the second round. A military-backed five-man council assumes power, cancels the country's first free elections, and bans the Islamic fundamentalist party.

1992 In a referendum of white South African voters an overwhelming majority vote in favour of the process aimed at leading to a power-sharing deal with the black majority.

In the General Election in April, the Conservatives under John Major win a majority of 21 seats. Neil Kinnock resigns as leader of the Labour Party and **John Smith** is elected in his place.

The UN conference on the Environment and Development, known as the Earth Summit, is held in Rio de Janeiro. Broad principles of environmentally sound development are laid down, but many regard the compromise decisions as unsatisfactory.

Chris Patten, the Governor of Hong Kong, receives a hostile reception in China for his proposals to introduce greater democracy into elections to the Hong Kong Legislative Council.

The Japanese parliament approves a bill that allows its forces to serve overseas on UN peacekeeping duties.

Accusing the South African government of complicity in violence against its supporters, the African National Congress withdraws from the Convention for a Democratic South Africa. Before the end of the year, efforts are made to re-start the talks.

Los Angeles has the worst rioting in recent US history; nearly 60 are killed and 4,000 injured, with a thousand million dollarsworth of damage to property. This follows from the decision of an all-white jury to acquit four police officers on charges of

savagely beating a black motorist stopped for a traffic violation—
an event captured on video by an amateur cameraman.

To stop attacks by Saddam Hussein's forces against Shia
Muslim communities in southern Iraq, the UN establishes an air-
exclusion zone south of the 32nd parallel. US fighter aircraft
patrol to ensure there are no Iraqi flights over the area.

In September there is a European currency crisis. Sterling,
the lira and the peseta are forced below their Exchange Rate
Mechanism floor by currency speculators. The British government withdraws sterling from the ERM and allows the pound
to float against other currencies. As a result it falls about 10%
against the German mark.

Elections in Israel result in a victory for the Labour Party,
ending 15 years of rule by the Likud Party. There is worldwide
condemnation of Israel when 415 Palestinians are deported to
the no-man's land between Israel's border and Lebanon. This
follows the abduction and killing of an Israeli guard.

The General Synod of the Church of England decides that
women may be ordained as priests. Opponents of the reform
talk of leaving the Church.

Bill Clinton wins the US presidential election, the first Democratic victory for 12 years.

To tackle the famine in Somalia, which causes at least 350,000
deaths during the year, US Navy commandos land near the
capital, Mogadishu, at the start of a massive relief mission. The
aim is to secure safe routes for food convoys to regional centres
in southern Somalia. For over a year, looting and protection
rackets have disrupted relief efforts by voluntary organisations.

The civil war in Yugoslavia worsens: the further invasion of
Bosnia by Serbian forces leads to the Muslim section of the
population being driven into detention camps. This is described
as 'ethnic cleansing'—a policy denounced by the West and the
Muslim countries. UN forces, including a British contingent,
are sent to provide humanitarian aid by opening routes for
supplies of food and medicine for Bosnians and other groups
cut off from distribution centres. All sides in the conflict make
accusations of atrocities. At a UN conference in London, the
Serbs agree to close the detention camps; but months later
there is evidence that many still exist. UN economic and diplomatic sanctions aimed at putting pressure on Serbia seem to

have little effect. Attempts are made to construct a peace plan based on the division of Bosnia into self-governing provinces.

In a referendum in Denmark there is a narrow 'No' vote on the issues of whether the Maastricht treaty should be ratified. This causes widespread concern in the other EC countries: it may be possible to save the treaty only if all twelve countries sign. But at an EC summit in Edinburgh, Denmark is exempted from key areas of Maastricht such as political and monetary union and the single currency. These changes allow the Danish government to plan for a second referendum.

In Russia Mr Yeltsin introduces western-style reforms such as the privatisation of industry and allowing wages and prices to find their own level in a free market. These moves are attacked by the conservatives, largely former Communist Party members, who claim that change is being introduced too rapidly. At a meeting of the Congress of the People's Deputies, Mr Yeltsin is obliged to accept a slowing down of the rate of reform. His prime minister is forced to resign and is replaced by a conservative. Mr Yeltsin insists that this change will not affect the aim of his programme.

After the destruction by Hindu extremists of an ancient Muslim mosque at Ayodya, riots develop across India and many are killed and injured, with thousands becoming homeless.

The High Court decides that the British Government's plan to close half the nation's coal pits was unlawful, and that both government and Coal Board had ignored the right of mine workers and unions to be consulted. This follows widespread public demonstrations of support for the miners.

Fire wrecks part of the state apartments in Windsor Castle, including St George's Hall which dates from the time of Edward III.

It is announced that the Prince and Princess of Wales are to separate.

1993 After 74 years of union as an independent country, elections in Czechoslovakia result in its division into the Czech Republic and Slovakia.

An IRA bomb explodes in the centre of Warrington, Cheshire, and two children are killed. Anger at this outrage is much more widespread than for many terrorist acts, and there is considerable impact on public opinion in the United States, where the IRA has sometimes found sympathy.

After the overwhelming victory of the parties of the right in a general election, **Eduard Balladur** of the Gaullist Party takes over as Prime Minister in France.

Chris Hani, general secretary of the South African Communist Party, is assassinated and tens of thousands of the black population take to the streets in protest.

In Texas 86 men, women and children die in a devestating fire that destroys the compound of the fanatical Branch Davidian religious sect. This is after the FBI had injected tear gas into the buildings to bring a 51–day siege to an end.

In a referendum in Italy on electoral reform, a very large majority vote to end proportional representation in favour of a mainly first-past-the-post system of electing members of parliament. The hope is that the change will bring to an end the years of corrupt party politics.

At a meeting in Vancouver between Presidents Clinton and Yeltsin, the United States agrees a 1.6 dollar aid programme for Russia.

In a referendum in Russia, President Yeltsin receives overwhelming support.

HISTORIC ACTS OF PARLIAMENT

Act	Date	What it did
Catholic Emancipation Act	1829	Gave full civic rights to Catholics.
Combination Acts	1799 & 1800	Made trade unions and meetings of men to discuss wages and hours illegal. Repealed, 1824. Trade Unions made legal, 1871.
Conventicle Act	1664	Made it illegal for more than five people to meet for religious worship. An anti-Catholic measure.
Corn Laws	1815	Prohibited import of foreign corn till wheat reached famine prices. Repealed, 1846.
Corporation Act	1661	Required that anyone taking up a municipal office should receive communion according to the rites of the Anglican Church and should declare it unlawful on

Act	Date	What it did
		any grounds to take up arms against the king. An anti-Presbyterian measure.
Education Act	1870	Introduced elementary education for all.
Education Act	1944	Introduced secondary education for all.
Education Reform Act	1988	Introduced a national curriculum for all State primary and secondary schools.
Factory Acts	Throughout 19th century	Regulated conditions of work. The Act of 1833 provided for the appointment of factory inspectors; the Act of 1847 limited the working day to 10 hours.
Government, Act	1657	Made Cromwell's rule legal, and enabled him to name his successor.
Habeas Corpus	1679	Made it illegal to hold a man in prison without trial.
Heresy, Statute of	1401	Provided that all heretics (people whose beliefs were not those of the Church) were to be imprisoned and, if they refused to give up their heresy, to be burned alive. Repealed, 1548.
Indemnity, Bill of	1660	First measure passed after restoration of Charles II; pardoned all offences committed during the Cromwellian period.
Kilkenny, Statute of	1366	Forbade the mixing of the English in Ireland with the Irish people.
Labourers, Statute of	1349	Passed during the labour shortage that followed the Black Death; bound a labourer to serve under anyone requiring him to do so for wages current two years before the plague began.
Libel Act	1791	Made the decision as to what was libellous a matter for the jury and not the judge.
Mines Act	1842	Prohibited the employment in mines of women, girls and boys under 10.

Act	Date	What it did
National Insurance Act	1916	First introduced compulsory national health contributions and a scheme of insurance against unemployment.
Navigation Act	1652	Prohibited the importation in foreign ships of any but products of the countries to which the ships belonged. Aimed at the Dutch.
Old Age Pensions Act	1908	Introduced old age pensions for the first time.
Parliament Acts	1911 & 1949	Limited the powers of the House of Lords.
Poor Laws	1562–1601	Placed on local authorities the responsibility for settling and supporting the poor.
Poyning's Act	1494	Forbade the Parliament of the Pale in Ireland to deal with matters not first approved of by the English king and his Council. Repealed, 1779.
Public Health Act	1848	Set up the first Central Board of Health.
Reform Bill	1832	Took away the right to elect MPs from 56 'rotten boroughs', gave the seats to counties or large towns hitherto unrepresented in Parliament, and gave the vote to £10 householders. Followed by the Act of 1867, which extended the vote to working people in towns; the Act of 1884, which gave the vote to country labourers; and the Acts of 1918 and 1928, which gave the vote to women.
Rights, Bill of	1689	Established the right of the people, through their representatives in Parliament, to depose the king and set on the throne whomever they chose.
Security, Act of	1706	Required the sovereign to swear to support the Presbyterian Church.

Act	Date	What it did
Settlement, Act of	1701	Confined the succession to the throne to Protestants and settled it on the House of Hanover.
Six Articles, Act of the	1539	An anti-Protestant measure, establishing the celibacy of the clergy, monastic vows and private masses. Repealed, 1548.
Stamp Act	1765	Imposed a tax on all legal documents issued within the colonies. Repealed, 1766.
Succession, Act of	1534	Required an oath to be taken by all acknowledging that Henry VIII's marriage with Catherine of Aragon was invalid.
Supremacy, Act of	1534	Ordered that the king 'shall be taken, accepted and reputed the only supreme head on earth of the Church of England'.
Test Act	1563	First anti-Catholic Act, exacting from all office-holders an oath of allegiance to Queen Elizabeth and a declaration that the Pope had no authority. A similar act was passed in 1673, and set aside in 1686.
Toleration Act	1689	Established freedom of worship.
Treaty of Accession to European Communities, Act	1972	It made Britain a full member as from 1 Jan 1973, of the three European Communities, i.e. the Economic Community, the Coal and Steel Community and of Euratom.
Triennial Bill	1641	Enforced the assembly of the House of Commons every three years.
Uniformity, Act of	1559	Restored the English Prayer Book and enforced its use on the clergy.
Union, Act of	1707	United England and Scotland.
Union with Ireland, Act of	1800	United England and Ireland.
Winchester, Statute of	1285	Bound every man to serve the king in case of invasion or revolt and to pursue felons when the hue and cry was raised against them.

EXPLORATIONS AND DISCOVERIES

Date	Explorer	Nationality	Exploration or Discovery
982	Eric the Red	Viking	Discovered Greenland
c. 1000	Leif Ericsson	Viking	Reached N. America
1255	Nicolo and Maffeo Polo	Venetian	Travelled to Peking
1271–94	Marco Polo	Venetian	Journeyed through China, India and other parts of Asia
14th century	João Zarco, Tristão Vas and others	Portuguese	Discovered Madeira and the Azores
1487–88	Bartholomew Diaz	Portuguese	Rounded Cape of Good Hope
1492	Christopher Columbus	Italian in Spanish service	Discovered San Salvador (now Watling Island), the Bahamas, Cuba and Haiti
1493–96	Christopher Columbus	Italian in Spanish service	Discovered Guadeloupe, Montserrat, Antigua, Puerto Rico and Jamaica
1497	John Cabot	Genoese in English service	Discovered Cape Breton Island, Newfoundland and Nova Scotia
1497–1503	Amerigo Vespucci	Florentine	Explored Mexico, part of E. coast of America and S. American coast
1498	Vasco da Gama	Portuguese	Discovered sea-route from Europe to India
1498	Christopher Columbus	Italian in Spanish service	Landed on mainland of S. America
1501–16	Various	Portuguese	Discovered Ceylon, Goa, Malacca, Canton, Japan and E. Indies
1502–4	Christopher Columbus	Italian in Spanish service	Discovered Trinidad

Date	Explorer	Nationality	Exploration or Discovery
1509	Sebastian Cabot	Genoese in English service	Explored American coast as far as Florida, Brazilian coast and mouth of R. Plate
1519–22	Ferdinand Magellan	Portuguese in Spanish service	First to sail round the world; discovered the Magellan Strait, reached the Philippines and named the Pacific
1534–36	Jacques Cartier	French	Discovered Canada, explored the St Lawrence and named Mount Royal (Montreal)
1539	De Soto	Spanish	Discovered Florida, Georgia and the R. Mississippi
1554	Sir Hugh Willoughby and Richard Chancellor	English	Discovered the White Sea and the ocean route to Russia
1576	Martin Frobisher	English	Began search for N.W. Passage
	John Davis	English	Discovered Davis Strait between Atlantic and Arctic Oceans
1577–80	Sir Francis Drake	English	Sailed round the world in the *Golden Hind*
1606	William Janszoon	Dutch	Discovered Australia
1606	Capt. John Smith and a party of colonists	English	Explored Chesapeake Bay, discovered Potomac and Susquehannah
1611	Henry Hudson	English	Sought N.E. and N.W. Passages; discovered Hudson River, Strait and Bay
1642	Abel Tasman	Dutch	Discovered Tasmania, New Zealand, the Tonga and Fiji islands

Date	Explorer	Nationality	Exploration or Discovery
1700	William Dampier	English	Explored W. Coast of Australia
1728	Vitus Bering	Danish in Russian service	Discovered Bering Strait between Asia and America
1740–44	George, Lord Anson	English	Sailed round the world in the *Centurion*
1767	Capt. Wallis	English	Discovered Tahiti
1768–71	Capt. James Cook	English	Sailed round the world in the *Endeavour*; charted New Zealand coasts and surveyed E. Coast of Australia, naming New South Wales and Botany Bay
1772	Capt. James Cook	English	Discovered Easter Island, New Caledonia and Norfolk Island
1776	Capt. James Cook	English	Discovered several of the Cook (or Hervey) islands. Rediscovered Sandwich (now Hawaiian) islands
1776	Mungo Park	Scottish	Explored the course of R. Niger
1831	Sir James Clark Ross and Rear-Admiral Sir John Ross	English	Located the magnetic pole
1839–43	Sir James Clark Ross	English	Discovered Victoria Land, Mounts Erebus and Terror, the Ross ice barrier
1847	Rear-Admiral Sir John Franklin	English	Lost in Arctic Ocean while seeking N.W. Passage
1852–73	David Livingstone	Scottish	Discovered the course of the Zambesi, the Victoria Falls and Lake Nyasa

Date	Explorer	Nationality	Exploration or Discovery
1856	Capt. John Speke	English	Discovered Lake Tanganyika
1858	Capt. John Speke	English	Discovered Lake Victoria Nyanza
1862	Capt. John Speke and Lt.-Col. J. A. Grant	English	Discovered source of White Nile
1901	Capt. R. F. Scott	English	Discovered King Edward VII Land
1903–6	Capt. Roald Amundsen	Norwegian	First navigation of the N.W. Passage
1908–9	Sir Ernest Shackleton	English	Reached within 100 miles of South Pole
1909	Rear-Admiral Robert Peary	American	Reached North Pole
1911	Capt. Roald Amundsen	Norwegian	First reached South Pole (December 14)
1912	Capt. R. F. Scott	English	Reached South Pole (January 18)
1929	Admiral R. Byrd	American	First flight over South Pole
1957–58	Sir Vivian Fuchs and Sir Edmund Hillary	English and New Zealander	First crossing of the Antarctic Continent
1961–62	Major Yuri Gagarin, Major Gherman Titov, Commander Alan Shepard, Capt. Virgil Grissom and Col. John Glenn	Russian and American	First journeys into space
1963	Valentina Tereshkova	Russian	First woman in space
1965	Col. Leonov, Major White	Russian and American	First men to 'walk' in space

Date	Explorer	Nationality	Exploration or Discovery
1968	Frank Borman, Bill Anders, and Jim Lovell	American	First men to circle moon
1969	Neil Armstrong and Edwin Aldrin	American	First men to step on the moon
	Charles Conrad and Alan Bean	American	Second pair to step on the moon

BRITISH PRIME MINISTERS

REIGN OF GEORGE I

Sir Robert Walpole (*Whig*)	1721–27

REIGN OF GEORGE II

Sir Robert Walpole (*Whig*)	1727–42
Earl of Wilmington (*Whig*)	1742–43
Henry Pelham (*Whig*)	1743–46
Henry Pelham (*Whig*)	1746–54
Duke of Newcastle (*Whig*)	1754–56
Duke of Devonshire (*Whig*)	1756–57
Duke of Newcastle (*Whig*)	1757–60

REIGN OF GEORGE III

Duke of Newcastle (*Whig*)	1760–62
Earl of Bute (*Tory*)	1762–63
George Grenville (*Whig*)	1763–65
Marquess of Rockingham (*Whig*)	1765–66
Earl of Chatham (*Whig*)	1766–67
Duke of Grafton (*Whig*)	1767–70
Lord North (*Tory*)	1770–82
Marquess of Rockingham (*Whig*)	1782

Earl of Shelburne (*Whig*)   1782–83
Duke of Portland (*Coalition*)   1783
William Pitt (*Tory*)   1783–1801
Henry Addington (*Tory*)   1801–4
William Pitt (*Tory*)   1804–6
Lord Grenville (*Whig*)   1806–7
Duke of Portland (*Tory*)   1807–9
Spencer Perceval (*Tory*)   1809–12
Earl of Liverpool (*Tory*)   1812–20

REIGN OF GEORGE IV

Earl of Liverpool (*Tory*)   1820–27
George Canning (*Tory*)   1827
Viscount Goderich (*Tory*)   1827–28
Duke of Wellington (*Tory*)   1828–30

REIGN OF WILLIAM IV

Earl Grey (*Whig*)   1830–34
Viscount Melbourne (*Whig*)   1834
Sir Robert Peel (*Tory*)   1834–35
Viscount Melbourne (*Whig*)   1835–37

REIGN OF VICTORIA

Viscount Melbourne (*Whig*)   1837–41
Sir Robert Peel (*Tory*)   1841–46
Lord John Russell (*Whig*)   1846–52
Earl of Derby (*Tory*)   1852
Earl of Aberdeen (*Peelite*)   1852–55
Viscount Palmerston (*Liberal*)   1855–58
Earl of Derby (*Conservative*)   1858
Viscount Palmerston (*Liberal*)   1858–65
Earl Russell (*Liberal*)   1865–66
Earl of Derby (*Conservative*)   1866–68
Benjamin Disraeli (*Conservative*)   1868
W. E. Gladstone (*Liberal*)   1868–74
Benjamin Disraeli (*Conservative*)   1874–80
W. E. Gladstone (*Liberal*)   1880–85
Marquess of Salisbury (*Conservative*)   1885–86
W. E. Gladstone (*Liberal*)   1886
Marquess of Salisbury (*Conservative*)   1886–92
W. E. Gladstone (*Liberal*)   1892–94
Earl of Rosebery (*Liberal*)   1894–95
Marquess of Salisbury (*Conservative*)   1895–1901

REIGN OF EDWARD VII

Marquess of Salisbury (*Conservative*)	1901–2
A. J. Balfour (*Conservative*)	1902–5
Sir Henry Campbell-Bannerman (*Liberal*)	1905–8
Herbert H. Asquith (*Liberal*)	1908–10

REIGN OF GEORGE V

H. H. Asquith (*Liberal*)	1910–15
H. H. Asquith (*Coalition*)	1915–16
D. Lloyd George (*Coalition*)	1916–22
A. Bonar Law (*Conservative*)	1922–23
Stanley Baldwin (*Conservative*)	1923–24
J. Ramsay MacDonald (*Labour*)	1924
Stanley Baldwin (*Conservative*)	1924–29
J. Ramsay MacDonald (*Labour*)	1929–31
J. Ramsay MacDonald (*National Government*)	1931–35
Stanley Baldwin (*National Government*)	1935–36

REIGN OF EDWARD VIII

Stanley Baldwin (*National Government*)	1936

REIGN OF GEORGE VI

Stanley Baldwin (*National Government*)	1936–37
Neville Chamberlain (*National Government*)	1937–40
Winston S. Churchill (*Coalition*)	1940–45
Clement R. Attlee (*Labour*)	1945–51
Winston S. Churchill (*Conservative*)	1951–52

REIGN OF ELIZABETH II

Sir Winston S. Churchill (*Conservative*)	1952–55
Sir Anthony Eden (*Conservative*)	1955–57
Harold Macmillan (*Conservative*)	1957 63
Sir Alec Douglas-Home (*Conservative*)	1963–64
Harold Wilson (*Labour*)	1964–70
Edward Heath (*Conservative*)	1970–74
Harold Wilson (*Labour*)	1974–76
James Callaghan (*Labour*)	1976–79
Margaret Thatcher (*Conservative*)	1979–90
John Major (*Conservative*)	1990–

THE ENGLISH LINE OF SUCCESSION

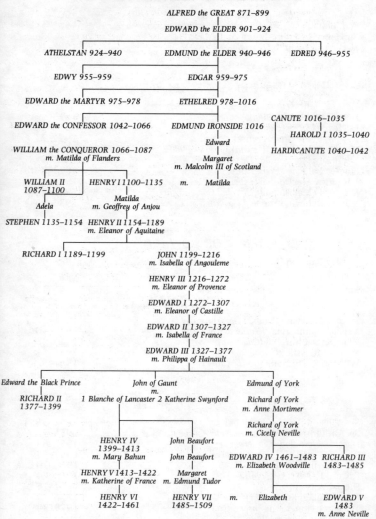

ALFRED the GREAT 871–899

EDWARD the ELDER 901–924

ATHELSTAN 924–940   *EDMUND the ELDER 940–946*   *EDRED 946–955*

EDWY 955–959   *EDGAR 959–975*

EDWARD the MARTYR 975–978   *ETHELRED 978–1016*

EDWARD the CONFESSOR 1042–1066   *EDMUND IRONSIDE 1016*   *CANUTE 1016–1035*

HAROLD I 1035–1040

Edward

WILLIAM the CONQUEROR 1066–1087   *Margaret*   *HARDICANUTE 1040–1042*
m. Matilda of Flanders   *m. Malcolm III of Scotland*

WILLIAM II   *HENRY I 1100–1135*   *m.   Matilda*
1087–1100

Adela   *Matilda*
m. Geoffrey of Anjou

STEPHEN 1135–1154   *HENRY II 1154–1189*
m. Eleanor of Aquitaine

RICHARD I 1189–1199   *JOHN 1199–1216*
m. Isabella of Angouleme

HENRY III 1216–1272
m. Eleanor of Provence

EDWARD I 1272–1307
m. Eleanor of Castille

EDWARD II 1307–1327
m. Isabella of France

EDWARD III 1327–1377
m. Philippa of Hainault

Edward the Black Prince   *John of Gaunt*   *Edmund of York*
m.

RICHARD II   *1 Blanche of Lancaster 2 Katherine Swynford*   *Richard of York*
1377–1399   *m. Anne Mortimer*

Richard of York
m. Cicely Neville

HENRY IV   *John Beaufort*
1399–1413
m. Mary Bahun   *John Beaufort*   *EDWARD IV 1461–1483*   *RICHARD III*
m. Elizabeth Woodville   *1483–1485*

HENRY V 1413–1422   *Margaret*
m. Katherine of France   *m. Edmund Tudor*

HENRY VI   *HENRY VII*   *m.*   *Elizabeth*   *EDWARD V*
1422–1461   *1485–1509*   *1483*
m. Anne Neville

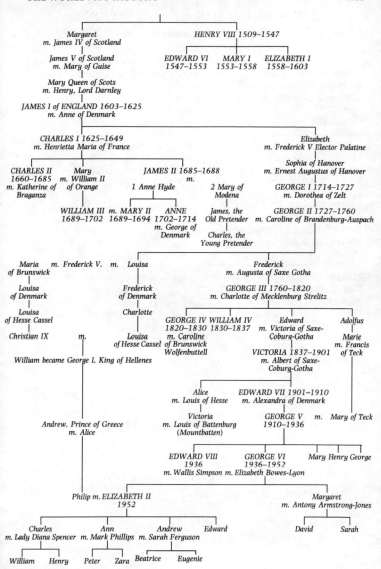

LIST OF KINGS AND QUEENS OF SCOTLAND

ALPINES

Kenneth I, 843–60
Donald I, 860–63
Constantine I, 863–77
Aedh, 877–78
Eocha, 878–89
Donald II, 889–900
Constantine II, 900–43
Malcolm I, 943–54
Indulf, 954–62
Duff, 962–67
Colin, 967–71
Kenneth II, 971–95
Constantine III, 995–97
Kenneth III, 997–1005
Malcolm II, 1005–34
Duncan I, 1034–40
Macbeth, 1040–57
Malcolm III, 1057–93
Donald Bane, 6 months in 1093
Duncan II, 6 months in 1094
Donald Bane again, 1094–97
Edgar, 1097–1107
Alexander I, 1107–24
David I, 1124–53
Malcolm IV (The Maiden),
   1153–65

William I (The Lion), 1165–1214
Alexander II, 1214–49
Alexander III, 1249–86
Margaret, 1286–90
No king, 1290–92
John Baliol, 1292–96
No king, 1296–1306

BRUCES

Robert I, 1306–29
David II, 1329–71

STUARTS

Robert II, 1371–90
Robert III, 1390–1406
Regent Albany, 1406–19
Regent Murdoch, 1419–24
James I, 1424–37
James II, 1437–60
James III, 1460–88
James IV, 1488–1513
James V, 1513–42
Mary, 1542–67
James VI, 1567–1625

Until 1603 James VI reigned over Scotland only; in 1603 he became King of England and Ireland. From 1603 onwards the kings of Scotland are the same as the kings of England.

PRESIDENTS OF THE UNITED STATES

George Washington (*Federalist*)	1789–97
John Adams (*Federalist*)	1797–1801
Thomas Jefferson (*Republican*)	1801–9
James Madison (*Republican*)	1809–17
James Monroe (*Republican*)	1817–25
John Quincy Adams (*Republican*)	1825–29
Andrew Jackson (*Democrat*)	1829–37
Martin Van Buren (*Democrat*)	1837–41
William Henry Harrison (*Whig*)	1841
John Tyler (*Whig*)	1841–45
James Knox Polk (*Democrat*)	1845–49
Zachary Taylor (*Whig*)	1849–50
Millard Fillmore (*Whig*)	1850–53
Franklin Pierce (*Democrat*)	1853–57
James Buchanan (*Democrat*)	1857–61
Abraham Lincoln (*Republican*)	1861–65
Andrew Johnson (*Republican*)	1865–69
Ulysses Simpson Grant (*Republican*)	1869–77
Rutherford Birchard Hayes (*Republican*)	1877–81
James Abram Garfield (*Republican*)	1881
Chester Alan Arthur (*Republican*)	1881–85
Grover Cleveland (*Democrat*)	1885–89
Benjamin Harrison (*Republican*)	1889–93
Grover Cleveland (*Democrat*)	1893–97
William McKinley (*Republican*)	1897–1901
Theodore Roosevelt (*Republican*)	1901–9
William Howard Taft (*Republican*)	1909–13
Woodrow Wilson (*Democrat*)	1913–21
Warren Gamaliel Harding (*Republican*)	1921–23
Calvin Coolidge (*Republican*)	1923–29
Herbert C. Hoover (*Republican*)	1929–33
Franklin Delano Roosevelt (*Democrat*)	1933–45
Harry S. Truman (*Democrat*)	1945–53
Dwight D. Eisenhower (*Republican*)	1953–61
John F. Kennedy (*Democrat*)	1961–63
Lyndon B. Johnson (*Democrat*)	1963–69
Richard M. Nixon (*Republican*)	1969–74
Gerald Ford (*Republican*)	1974–77
Jimmy Carter (*Democrat*)	1977–81
Ronald Reagan (*Republican*)	1981–89
George Bush (*Republican*)	1989–93
Bill Clinton (*Democrat*)	1993–

GOVERNMENT IN BRITAIN

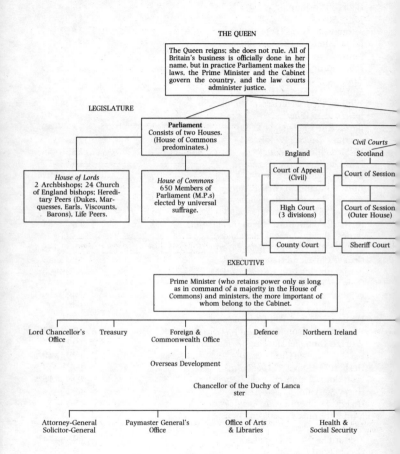

THE QUEEN

The Queen reigns; she does not rule. All of Britain's business is officially done in her name, but in practice Parliament makes the laws, the Prime Minister and the Cabinet govern the country, and the law courts administer justice.

LEGISLATURE

Parliament
Consists of two Houses.
(House of Commons predominates.)

Civil Courts

England

Scotland

House of Lords
2 Archbishops; 24 Church of England bishops; Hereditary Peers (Dukes, Marquesses, Earls, Viscounts, Barons), Life Peers.

House of Commons
650 Members of Parliament (M.P.s) elected by universal suffrage.

Court of Appeal (Civil)

Court of Session

High Court (3 divisions)

Court of Session (Outer House)

County Court

Sheriff Court

EXECUTIVE

Prime Minister (who retains power only as long as in command of a majority in the House of Commons) and ministers, the more important of whom belong to the Cabinet.

Lord Chancellor's Office   Treasury   Foreign & Commonwealth Office   Defence   Northern Ireland

Overseas Development

Chancellor of the Duchy of Lancaster

Attorney-General
Solicitor-General

Paymaster General's Office

Office of Arts & Libraries

Health & Social Security

Note that there is *no* upward line of appeal from the Scottish High Court of Justiciary to the House of Lords.

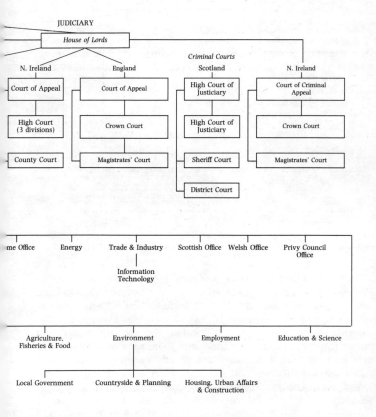

JUDICIARY

House of Lords

N. Ireland	England	Criminal Courts Scotland	N. Ireland
Court of Appeal	Court of Appeal	High Court of Justiciary	Court of Criminal Appeal
High Court (3 divisions)	Crown Court	High Court of Justiciary	Crown Court
County Court	Magistrates' Court	Sheriff Court	Magistrates' Court
		District Court	

me Office   Energy   Trade & Industry   Scottish Office   Welsh Office   Privy Council Office

Information Technology

Agriculture, Fisheries & Food   Environment   Employment   Education & Science

Local Government   Countryside & Planning   Housing, Urban Affairs & Construction

GOVERNMENT IN BRITAIN: LOCAL AFFAIRS

The management of local affairs is left to local authorities subject to supervision—largely exercised through financial control—by the central Government in London.

In a drastic reorganisation in 1974, the 1,400 local authorities formerly existing in England and Wales (County Councils, County Borough Councils, Municipal Boroughs, Rural Districts, Urban Districts, Parish Councils and Meetings) were replaced by:

6 Metropolitan counties —large conurbations— West Midlands, Mersey-side, West Yorkshire, South Yorkshire, Tyne and Wear, Greater Manchester—responsible for education and personal social services.	52 new counties responsible for planning, transport, education and personal social services.	some 375 new district authorities responsible for housing, refuse collection, play- and sports-grounds etc.

The 430 local authorities formerly existing in Scotland (counties, counties of cities, town councils and district councils) were in 1975 replaced by:

8 regional authorities responsible for major planning, transport, education and personal social services.	47 district authorities responsible for housing, refuse collection, parks and sports grounds.

Under the Local Government Act of 1985 the Greater London Council was abolished together with the six Metropolitan county councils, and most of their functions became the responsibility of the existing borough and district councils. The running of the fire service in London and the fire, police and public transport services in the Metropolitan counties was taken over by new joint authorities, composed of borough and district councillors. Education in Inner London was made the responsibility of a new Inner London Education Authority, directly elected. Under the Education Reform Act 1988 the Inner London Education Authority was abolished in March 1990, and the responsibility for education passed to the inner London boroughs.

THE COMMONWEALTH

The Commonwealth grew out of the British Empire. All the states, nations and territories which belong to it today were once governed by men sent out from England who received their orders from London.

The transformation from dependence to independent nationhood usually followed this broad pattern:

Once British power was firmly established, the British Government would try to draw local notabilities into the business of running the country, consulting them on important matters, and even appointing them to be his official advisers; in due course he would set up a legislative Council or Parliament, but he would make certain of being able to get his way in the last resort by allowing only a minority of its members to be elected by the local population and by appointing the majority himself; later on he would gradually increase the number of locally elected members until in the end there would be no officially appointed members left; at that stage London would usually surrender its powers to run the affairs of the country concerned, the leader of the majority in the Legislative Council or Parliament would become Prime Minister, the Governor would cease to play an active part in politics and, like the Queen in Britain, would be able to act only as advised by the Prime Minister.

The first countries to reach the top of the ladder of self-government were those settled by people of British or European stock. They were known as 'Dominions', and in defining their relationship to one another and to Britain, the Imperial Conference of 1926 described them as 'autonomous communities within the British Empire, equal in status, in no way subordinate one to another in any aspect of their domestic or foreign affairs, though united by a common allegiance to the Crown, and freely associated as members of the British Commonwealth of Nations.'

They were—apart from Britain—five in number:

Australia   Canada   New Zealand
Newfoundland (after a referendum joined Canada as a

Province in 1949 and ceased being an independent
Dominion)
South Africa (left the Commonwealth in 1961).

After the Second World War the number of countries which
attained independent nationhood increased rapidly and, since
many of them had populations which were not predominantly of
British or European descent, it became customary to refer to the
Commonwealth and not the British Commonwealth.

In January 1993 the following were fully independent members
of the Commonwealth, in addition to those listed above:

Antigua and	Kiribati[3]	Seychelles
Barbuda	Lesotho[4]	Sierra Leone
Bahamas	Malawi[5]	Singapore
Bangladesh	Malaysia	Solomon Islands
Barbados	Malta	Sri Lanka
Belize	Maldives (The)	Swaziland
Botswana[1]	Mauritius	Tanzania[6]
Brunei	Namibia	Tonga
Cyprus	Nauru	Trinidad and
Dominica	Nigeria	Tobago
Gambia (The)	Pakistan	Tuvalu
Ghana	Papua New Guinea	Uganda
Grenada	Saint Kitts-Nevis	Vanuatu[7]
Guyana[2]	Saint Lucia	Western Samoa
India	St Vincent and	Zambia[8]
Jamaica	the Grenadines	Zimbabwe[9]
Kenya		

(Burma became independent in 1948 but decided to leave the
Commonwealth. Pakistan left the Commonwealth in 1972 and
rejoined in 1989. Fiji ceased to be a member in 1987 when a
military coup arbitrarily removed the Queen's Governor General.)

There are altogether 50 independent countries within the
Commonwealth (including Britain). They form an association of
countries. They are not a state or even a federation. There is no
single parliament or government, no central defence force or
executive power. They are no longer 'united by a common allegiance to the Crown'. For example, twenty-five member countries
are republics although all recognise the Queen as Head of the
Commonwealth. And there is no common foreign policy. Britain,

Former names: [1]Bechuanaland. [2]Brit. Guiana. [3]Gilbert Islands. [4]Basutoland.
[5]Nyasaland. [6]Tanganyika and Zanzibar. [7]New Hebrides. [8]N. Rhodesia. [9]S. Rhodesia.

Canada, Australia and New Zealand belong to military alliances designed to stop the spread of Communism; India, Sri Lanka, Ghana and Tanzania are 'uncommitted'. Four countries, The Maldives, Nauru, St Vincent and Tuvalu, are special members, with the right of participation in all functional Commonwealth meetings and activities, but not of attendance at meetings of Commonwealth Heads of Government.

The essence of the Commonwealth relationship is consultation, and the most important forms of consultation are the Commonwealth Prime Ministers' Conferences which, whenever possible, are held in London at least once every two years and now have a permanent home in Marlborough House.

Other Commonwealth bonds:

> Constant consultation between the Commonwealth delegations at the United Nations in New York.
>
> Commercial ties and Imperial preferences.
>
> Language (Many Commonwealth leaders with multilingual populations find that English is the only language in which they can talk to all their people.)
>
> Common political traditions and habits of thought.
>
> Education (Many Commonwealth universities are linked to British universities in order to ensure high academic standards. Moreover, many Commonwealth countries continue to have their doctors, scientists, engineers, administrators and soldiers trained in Britain.)
>
> Sport (Cricket and cricketing language are familiar in countries like Britain, Australia, New Zealand and the West Indies, but hardly outside the Commonwealth.)

Despite the rapid increase since the end of the Second World War in the number of independent countries within the Commonwealth, there still remain territories which continue to be dependent on Britain. Some are well advanced in self-government; others are little more than small island communities, fortresses, anchorages or former coaling stations which may have difficulty in surviving as independent states. The still dependent territories are:

> In the Atlantic: Bermuda, Falkland Islands, St Helena
>
> In the Caribbean: Leeward Islands, Windward Islands
>
>> Four of the larger islands units in these two groups—
>> Antigua, Grenada, Dominica, St Lucia and the island group

of St Kitts—Nevis and Anguilla—were in 1967 granted the new status of 'Associated States', i.e. complete self-government except in foreign and defence policy. St Vincent joined the group in 1969. Grenada, Dominica, St Lucia, St Vincent, St Kitts-Nevis and Antigua ceased to be associated states when they became independent.

In the Mediterranean: Gibraltar
In and around the Indian Ocean: Aldabra Is.
In the Far East: Hong Kong
In the Pacific: Ellice Islands, Pitcairn Islands

Total population of the Commonwealth: about 1,385 million, or a quarter of the world's total.

THE UNITED NATIONS

The United Nations came into existence on October 24, 1945, and every year October 24 is celebrated as United Nations' Day throughout the world.

The aims of the United Nations are set out in its Charter in these words: 'to save succeeding generations from the scourge of war ... to reaffirm faith in fundamental human rights, in the dignity and worth of the human person, in the equal rights of men and women and of nations large and small, and to establish conditions under which justice and respect for the obligations arising from treaties and other sources of international law can be maintained, and to employ international machinery for the promotion of the economic and social advancement of all peoples'.

Members of the UN in 1945: 51 countries.
Members of the UN in 1993: 180 countries.

The principal organ of the UN is the General Assembly. Around it are grouped the other five main organs of the UN:

General Assembly All other UN bodies report to it. It controls the UN budget and assesses each country's contribution. It elects new members on the recommendation of the Security Council. On 'important' questions, i.e., questions affecting the world's peace and security or the election of new members or the budget, a two-thirds majority of those present and voting is

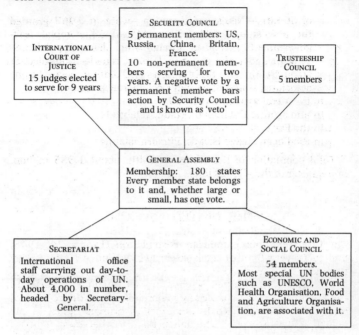

SECURITY COUNCIL
5 permanent members: US, Russia, China, Britain, France.
10 non-permanent members serving for two years. A negative vote by a permanent member bars action by Security Council and is known as 'veto'

INTERNATIONAL COURT OF JUSTICE
15 judges elected to serve for 9 years

TRUSTEESHIP COUNCIL
5 members

GENERAL ASSEMBLY
Membership: 180 states Every member state belongs to it and, whether large or small, has one vote.

SECRETARIAT
International office staff carrying out day-to-day operations of UN. About 4,000 in number, headed by Secretary-General.

ECONOMIC AND SOCIAL COUNCIL
54 members.
Most special UN bodies such as UNESCO, World Health Organisation, Food and Agriculture Organisation, are associated with it.

essential before any action can be taken. It meets every year in regular session beginning on the third Tuesday in September.

Security Council It is primarily responsible for keeping international peace and security. Any nation—whether a member of the UN or not—may bring a dispute or threat to peace to its attention and ask it to take action. Any of the five permanent members can block action by voting 'No'. This is known as the veto. Its ten non-permanent members are elected by the General Assembly.

International Court of Justice Its 15 judges are elected by the General Assembly on the recommendation of the Security Council. They consider legal disputes brought before them by nations which cannot agree between themselves. They also give advice on international law when asked to by the General Assembly, the Security Council or other UN bodies.

Trusteeship Council It looks after the interests of non-self-governing territories in different parts of the world which have been placed under the trusteeship of the UN. Its aim is to help these territories towards full self-government as quickly as possible.

Secretariat It consists of international civil servants who, while they belong to it, must forget their national loyalties and work only for the best interests of the UN. The head of the Secretariat is the Secretary-General, who is appointed by the General Assembly on the recommendation of the Security Council, usually for a five-year term.

The UN has had four Secretaries-General:

1. Trygve Lie, of Norway (1945–1953).
2. Dag Hammarskjoeld, of Sweden (1953–1961. Killed in an air crash in Africa).
3. U Thant, of Burma (1961–1971).
4. Kurt Waldheim, of Austria (1972–1982).
5. Javier Perez de Cuellar of Peru (1982–91).
6. Boutros Boutros Ghali of Egypt (1992–).

Economic and Social Council (ECOSOC) Its aim is to establish lasting world peace by helping the poor, the sick, the hungry, the illiterate in all parts of the globe. It is responsible for assisting under-developed countries and promotes health and education schemes. In a broad sense it supervises the work of many special UN bodies like the UN Educational, Scientific and Cultural Organisation (UNESCO), the International Bank for Reconstruction and Development, the International Labour Organisation (ILO), the Food and Agriculture Organisation (FAO), the UN International Children's Emergency Fund (UNICEF) and the International Atomic Energy Agency which seeks to help countries by encouraging and supporting the use of atomic energy for peaceful development purposes.

Location of UN Headquarters: New York.

Official languages in which the UN conducts its business:
Chinese, English, French, Russian, Spanish.

THE EUROPEAN COMMUNITY

The European Economic Community (EEC), also known as the Common Market, was set up by the Treaty of Rome in 1958.

There were then six full members—Belgium, France, Holland, Italy, Luxembourg and West Germany. Britain had taken part in the negotiations, but took another point of view on several issues: it was, for example, opposed to free trade in agricultural products. As a result, Britain joined with six other countries—Austria, Denmark, Norway, Portugal, Sweden and Switzerland—in forming the European Free Trade Area (EFTA). Britain acceded as a full member in 1973, with two of her partners in EFTA—Ireland and Denmark. Greece signed the Treaty of Accession in 1979 to become the tenth member. Portugal and Spain became the eleventh and twelfth members in 1986.

The EEC forms a common market: there are no tariffs or trade controls within it, and there is a Common External Tariff. There is also a Common Agricultural Policy (CAP): free movement within the Community of capital: and a citizen of any of the Common Market countries is free to seek employment within the 12 member States.

The Single European Act 1986 sought to free further the movement of goods and services within the Community, creating the single market. The Act introduced majority voting for matters relating to the single market (no one country being able to veto proposals). The aim is, by the end of 1992, virtually to abolish frontier controls for Community goods: to harmonise technical standards so that goods produced in one country can be accepted for sale in the other eleven: and to liberalise financial services.

Further measures were adopted by the Council of Ministers at Maastricht in 1991, including: proposals for the Community to switch to a single currency by 1999 – Britain retaining the right to opt-out: the development of a common foreign policy: and an increase in the powers of the European Parliament.

There are five arms through which the Community functions. The **Commission** is able to set Community action going, mediates between member governments and is the guardian of the various treaties involved. The **Council of Ministers** considers proposals submitted to it by the Commission, and makes decisions on them. The **European Parliament** consists of 518 members who are directly elected into office from constituencies covering the whole area of the community countries. The Parliament has to be consulted in all major matters: it has the right to dismiss the Commission through a vote of censure. With the Council it decides the annual budget of the Community. The **European Court of Justice** safeguards the law when it comes to interpreting and applying the Community treaties: decides on whether or not decisions of the Council of Ministers or the Commission are legal: and judges cases where a violation of the Treaties is alleged. Cases may be brought to it by the member States, any of the institutions of the community, firms or individuals. Its decisions are binding. The **European Investment Bank** (EIB) makes long-term loans to public authorities, financial institutions and enterprises of various kinds, for the financing of schemes and projects designed to aid the development of less advanced regions or the renewal of ageing industries.

A GLOSSARY OF POLITICAL TERMS

Absolutism or Absolute Monarchy A system of government where the hereditary ruler, usually a king, has complete power to decide a country's internal and external policy without having to consult anyone. The French Revolution heralded the end of absolutism, and in the nineteenth century absolute monarchies everywhere gave place to constitutional monarchies or republics.

Amnesty An act granting forgiveness (literally, forgetfulness) to political and other offenders.

Anarchism Anarchists (from the Greek word *anarchia*, non-rule) believe that every form of government is evil. Towards the end of the last century anarchists assassinated Czar Alexander of Russia and other political leaders in order to draw attention to their theories. There was a strong anarchist movement in Spain during the 1930s.

Aristocracy From the Greek, meaning government by the best. It has come to mean the best by birth. The government of Britain can be said to have been aristocratic up to the Great Reform Bill of 1832 in the sense that both Houses of Parliament were virtually controlled by members of the great landed aristocratic families.

Autocracy Absolute rule by one man.

Authoritarian A term denoting a dictatorial system of government.

Autonomy A word of Greek origin meaning 'self-government'.

Balance of Payments The balance between the cost of a country's imports and the receipts for its exports. Britain is said to pass through a balance-of-payments crisis whenever the value of her imports exceeds the value of her exports.

Balance of Power The theory that the strength of one group of powers on the European continent should be equal to the strength of the other group, thus preventing any one group from becoming dominant.

Bi-partisan Foreign Policy A foreign policy on which both the government and opposition parties are agreed.

Bourgeoisie French for 'citizen class'. A term used by Marxist socialists to denote manufacturers, merchants and people with a business of their own, as opposed to the 'proletariat', who earn a living only by selling their labour.

Buffer State A small state established or preserved between two greater states to prevent direct clashes between them.

Communism The theory, as expounded by Marx and Engels, which aims at the creation of a society in which the private ownership of land, factories, banks, trading houses, etc., is abolished, and everyone receives what he needs and works according to his capacity. Communists believe that revolution and the use of force are justified to bring about the creation of such a society.

Constitution Document or set of documents which set out how a country is to be governed. Britain is said to have an 'unwritten constitution' because, although there are many documents, such as the Great Reform Bill of 1832 or the Parliament Act of 1911, which deal with constitutional matters, there is no single document which sets out the constitutional machinery of Britain, and such written documents as the Great Reform Bill make sense only against the background of the unwritten customs and traditions which have grown up in Britain over the centuries. By contrast, countries such as the USA, France and Germany are all said to have 'written constitutions' because there is a single document or set of documents to which one can refer.

Constitutional Monarchy A system of government where the king's political power is limited by the constitution: real power usually resting with an elected parliament.

Coup d'état A seizure of power and the machinery of government by force.

Democracy From Greek words meaning 'government by the people'. Democracy may be either direct, as practised in some city-states in Ancient Greece where all the adult citizens met in the market-place to discuss and decide on all questions of policy, or indirect, as practised in modern times when the people elect representatives to some kind of parliament. A democracy can be either a monarchy if its head of State is a king or queen as in Britain, or a republic if its head of State is a president as in the USA and France.

démarche a move or some procedure (especially diplomatic) to achieve some end.

détente This is a French word, meaning an easing of tensions between people or, in the political sense, between nations.

Dictatorship Rule by one man who, in deciding what to do about the internal or external affairs of the country he controls, does not have to consider or consult anyone but himself.

Fascism An authoritarian extreme right-wing nationalist movement which denies the individual all rights in his relations with the state. In Italy Fascism was led by Mussolini, who held power from 1922 to 1943, and there were strong Fascist movements in many other countries between the two world wars. The German version was Hitler's National Socialism. Fascism derives from the Latin word *fasces*, the name for the axe encased in a bundle of rods which was carried in procession before the chief magistrates in Ancient Rome as a symbol of their power over the life and liberty of ordinary citizens.

Federation A union of states or provinces under a common central government to which they surrender some but not all their powers of government. A federal form of government is usually found in countries which cover a vast area such as the USA, Canada and Australia, but in Europe Switzerland is a federation, and its component states, called cantons, enjoy a large measure of autonomy.

Free Trade A policy of allowing goods to move freely between countries without imposing tariffs or customs duties. Adam Smith in 1776 set out the classic case for Free Trade in his *Wealth of Nations*. Britain's superiority as a manufacturing country in the Victorian era made her favour Free Trade, but as other countries became industralised towards the end of the nineteenth century and her superiority vanished, the demand for 'Protection', i.e. tariffs and customs duties to 'protect' goods manufactured in Britain from foreign competition, grew. All countries today are partially 'protected', but many countries, such as Britain and the USA, are working towards making industrial trade as free as possible.

Imperialism In its original sense, the system of government by an emperor. It has come to be used of any policy of political, military or economic expansion carried out at the expense of weaker people. British imperialism saw its heyday in the latter part of the nineteenth century, its leading exponents being Disraeli, Lord Rosebery and Joseph Chamberlain; but since then the tendency within the Commonwealth has been to give colonial people self-government and independence as soon as and wherever possible.

Industrial Revolution Term applied to the economic developments which between the 1750s and the 1830s transformed Britain from a primarily agricultural to a primarily industrial country.

Isolation A refusal to enter into firm commitments and alliances with other powers.

Laisser-Faire The theory that the state should refrain from all interference in economic affairs. From a phrase coined by eighteenth-century French economists, 'laisser-faire et laisser-passer', 'to let go and pass', i.e. to leave the individual alone and let commodities circulate freely. A reaction against laisser-faire set in during the nineteenth century, inspired by a revulsion against the social conditions created by the Industrial Revolution, and found expression, for example, in the Factory Acts regulating working conditions. The twentieth century has seen an ever-increasing degree of state intervention for social and economic reasons.

Liberalism The body of political and social ideas associated with the former Liberal Party in Britain and similar parties elsewhere. The British Liberal Party, which developed out of the Whig Party in the nineteenth century, stood for parliamentary reform, individual liberty, freedom of speech, of the press and of worship, for laisser-faire, i.e. a minimum of state interference in economic affairs, and for international free trade. Towards the end of the century, the Liberal Party modified its views on laisser-faire to ensure minimum living standards for the working class, and, inspired by Lloyd George, the Liberal governments of 1906–14 laid the foundation of what we call today the Welfare State. Since the First World War the influence of the Liberals has declined everywhere, their place as the party of social reform being taken by the Socialists.

Nationalism Term for movements which aim at the strengthening of national feeling and at the unification of a nation or its liberation from foreign rule. Modern nationalism was born in the French Revolution, and under the impact of that event nationalism became a potent factor in European politics in the nineteenth century and helped to bring about the unification of Germany and Italy. With the break-up of the communist states, there has been a revival of nationalism in parts of Europe and the former Soviet Union.

National Socialism A German authoritarian extreme right-wing nationalist movement which denied the individual all rights in his relations with the state, personified by Hitler as the Fuehrer ('Leader').

Neutral Term used to describe the condition of a country which in war refrains from hostilities and maintains a strictly impartial attitude towards the belligerents, and in peace stands aloof from the quarrels of other countries and refuses to enter into military alliances. Example: Switzerland and Sweden.

Neutralist Term which came into use after the Second World War to describe countries which were unwilling to become involved in the Cold War disputes between the Communist and Western power blocs. Example: India.

Plebiscite A direct vote by the voters of a country or district on a specific question. In the usual election the people vote for or against the government on all the policies for which it stands; in a plebiscite or referendum they vote only on one particular question, as in Britain in 1975 when they were asked to vote on whether they wanted Britain to stay in the Common Market or not.

Radical A person seeking political, social or economic reform 'from the root'. Term used to describe the wing of the Liberal party which was most forward in its demands for reform. Radicalism lost much of its popular support with the rise of Socialism in this century.

Reactionary In politics, a person who wants to prevent or undo reforms.

Republic A country where the head of state is a president and not a king.

Responsible Government A country is said to have responsible government where the government is responsible to Parliament for everything it does, and where it must resign if it loses the 'confidence' of Parliament. In this sense Britain has responsible government, but the USA has not, because there the President, elected by the whole country for a term of four years, continues in office whether he has the approval of Congress (Parliament) or not. Both countries are, of course, democracies, despite this difference in their constitutions.

Socialism The political, social and economic theories which aim at the establishment of a classless society, through the substitution of common for private ownership of the means of production (land, factories), distribution (shops, transport), and exchange (banks). Communists believe that all means, including revolution and oppression, are justified in the pursuit of their aims. The Socialists in Britain, Western Europe and most of the African and Asian countries of the Commonwealth are Social Democrats, i.e. they want to bring about a Socialist society by means such as elections and through democratic institutions such as Parliament. Some Social Democrats want a *'mixed economy'*, i.e. one in which not all the means of production, distribution and exchange pass into public ownership, but a large proportion remains in private hands.

Tory Name given to the forerunner of the present Conservative party. Traditionally the Tories were the party of the squire and the parson, as opposed to the *Whigs*, the forerunners of the Liberals who, though led by a group of great land-owning families, drew their support mainly from the business classes and Nonconformists.

White House The official residence of the President of the USA in Washington. It was partially burnt when the British occupied Washington briefly during the 1812–14 war with the USA, and afterwards painted white to hide the scars left by the fire. Hence the name. The term 'The White House' is often used to mean 'the American government', e.g. 'The White House reviews its Far Eastern policy.'

THE WORLD

2: ITS GEOGRAPHY

THE WORLD

The word Geography comes from the two Greek words *geo* and *graphos* and literally means 'writing about the earth'. It is the science that describes and explains the features and patterns of the earth's surface, both those of the physical and natural world and those of the world made by human societies. In particular, Geography studies the links between the physical and human worlds, that is, the relationships between people and land. In its study of the physical world, Geography looks at landforms such as mountains, rivers, seas and plains, and also at climate, vegetation and soils. This brings it close to the borders of other subjects such as Geology, Meteorology (a branch of Physics), Biology and Pedology (the study of soils). In dealing with the human world, Geography looks at population, settlements, agriculture and industry, countries, trade and communications. This brings it close to subjects

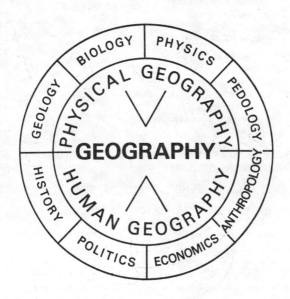

like History, Economics, Politics and Anthropology. But though the subject is divided into physical and human parts, the real role of Geography is to study the influence of nature on people and people on nature.

The Earth: *Some facts and figures*

The earth is one of the nine planets in the solar system which moves around the sun. The others are Mercury, Venus, Mars, Jupiter, Saturn, Uranus, Neptune and Pluto. The earth is the fifth largest of these planets and the third in distance from the sun— about 149,700,000 kilometres. The earth is a sphere, like a ball, but it is slightly flattened at the North and South Poles and bulges a little at the Equator. The earth's path around the sun is known as its orbit; and it takes a year for the orbit, whose path is an ellipse, to be completed.

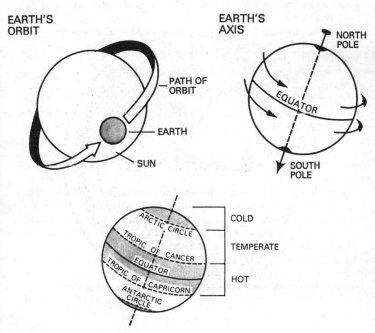

As well as revolving around the sun, the earth also spins on its axis, which is like an imaginary rod passing through the earth's centre from pole to pole. The angle of the axis always stays the same and one complete spin takes about twenty four hours. This spinning, with reference to the light from the sun, produces night and day. The earth's orbit around the sun, together with the angle at which the earth is tilted, is responsible for the seasons. This relationship to the sun causes the earth's major climate and vegetation zones.

The earth can be divided into three main types of climatic regions. The cold regions lie around the North and South Poles, within the Arctic and Antarctic Circles. The tropics are the hot regions north and south of the Equator; their outer boundaries being marked by the Tropic of Cancer in the north and the Tropic of Capricorn in the south. Between these hot and cold regions lie the temperate regions, where climates vary greatly.

Polar diameter (i.e. from pole to pole through the earth's centre), 12,700 km.

Equatorial diameter (between points on the Equator exactly opposite one another), 12,765 km.

Equatorial circumference, 40,076 km.

Total surface area, 510,098,530 sq km.

Area of land, 148,429,000 sq km.

Area of sea, 361,661,020 sq km.

Total mass (weight), about 6,694,000,000,000,000,000,000 (i.e. 6,694 million million million) tonnes.

The Earth's Structure

The earth is made up of a number of concentric layers of material, like the bulb of an onion. The main layers are the core, the mantle and the crust, and each has its own chemical composition and physical properties. Some 4,500 million years ago the earth's surface was molten rock, but as it cooled and hardened the heavier materials sank towards the earth's centre, whilst the lighter (less dense) materials stayed near the surface. During this process, cooling steam was released which condensed to form the oceans and seas. Gases were also given off, and these formed a kind of atmosphere.

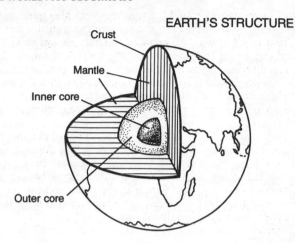

EARTH'S STRUCTURE

The solid crust of the earth, which supports the oceans, the continents and all forms of life, is about as thick in relation to the earth as the shell is to an egg or the skin to an apple. Below the crust, like the flesh of an apple, is the mantle, a section of great thickness and composed of many different layers of material. The mantle is partly fluid. At the earth's centre is the core, and scientists believe that its inner section is solid.

Oceans and Seas

About seven-tenths of the earth's crust is covered with water, forming the main oceans and seas. The other three-tenths is land, and occupies the continents and innumerable islands. If, from outer space, the world was viewed from its Pacific side, hardly any land would be visible at all. All the oceans form one vast and continuous mass of water which, for convenience, is divided into the Pacific, the Atlantic, the Indian and the Arctic Oceans. Some atlases also refer to the Antarctic Ocean, but this is really made up of the southern portions of the Pacific, Atlantic and Indian Oceans.

The seas are smaller, more self-contained water bodies: such as the Mediterranean Sea, the Baltic Sea and the Caribbean Sea. Some of the world's large water bodies are entirely surrounded by land, and are known either as inland seas, such as the Caspian and Aral seas in central Asia (both decreasing in size), or as lakes: e.g. the Great Lakes on the borders of Canada and the United States, and Lake Victoria in East Africa.

Like the world's land masses, the floors of the oceans have many ridges and depressions. They are made up of shelves, slopes and deeps. The continental shelf is the relatively shallow part of the oceans and seas adjoining the continents. The ocean floor gradually slopes away from the continental shelf to the ocean deeps, where submarine plains and trenches are found. The deeps off the coast of the Philippines reach down to 11,033 metres. This is about a mile more than the greatest land height (Mount Everest, 8,863 metres). Within the oceans there are also

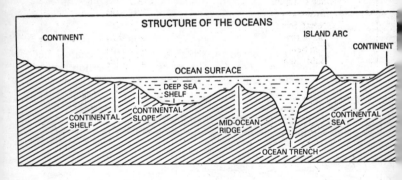

STRUCTURE OF THE OCEANS

huge mountain ranges, such as the Mid-Atlantic Ridge. These mountains were formed in the same way as mountains on land. The average depth of the oceans (3,795 metres) is much greater than the average height of land above sea level. The Mid-Atlantic Ridge marks the boundary of four important *plates* (see B7) in the earth's surface.

Some seas are divided into many names. For example, the South China Sea consists of the following seas: Sulu, Celebes, Molucca, Halmahera, Ceram, Banda, Arafura, Timor, Flores, Bali,

Oceans and Main Seas: *Their Areas*

Ocean or sea	Area (sq km.)
Pacific	165,384,000
Atlantic	82,217,000
Indian	73,481,000
Arctic	14,056,000
Seas	
South China Sea	2,974,600
Mediterranean Sea	2,505,000
Bering Sea	2,268,200
Caribbean Sea	1,943,000
Gulf of Mexico	1,544,000
Sea of Okhotsk	1,527,600
East China Sea	1,249,200
Hudson Bay	1,232,200
Sea of Japan	1,007,500
Andaman Sea	797,600
North Sea	575,300
Black Sea	462,000
Red Sea	437,700
Baltic Sea	422,160

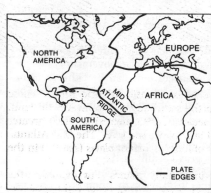

The Mid-Atlantic Ridge

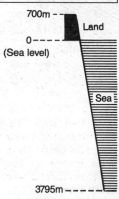

The Average Height of Land Compared with the Average Depth of Ocean

Oceans and Main Seas: *Their Depths*

Ocean or sea	Average depth in metres	Greatest depth in metres
Pacific	4,280	11,033
Atlantic	3,926	9,219
Indian	3,963	8,047
Arctic	1,205	5,441
Seas		
South China Sea	1,212	6,505
Caribbean Sea	2,491	7,680
Mediterranean Sea	1,487	4,846
Bering Sea	2,351	5,121
Gulf of Mexico	1,512	4,377
Sea of Okhotsk	838	3,475
East China Sea	188	3,200
Hudson Bay	128	457
Sea of Japan	1,350	4,000
Andaman Sea	870	3,777
North Sea	94	661
Black Sea	963	2,243
Red Sea	491	2,246
Baltic Sea	58	439

Java and Savu; the following gulfs: Thailand, Tomini and Boni; and the following straits: Malacca, Singapore and Macassar.

Because of waves, currents and tides, the water of oceans and seas is constantly moving. Waves are surface movements of water and are caused by winds. Ocean currents can be either cold or warm and have important effects on the earth's climate. For example, the North Atlantic Drift, of which the Gulf Stream is a part, is a warm current that keeps the harbours of north-west Europe ice-free in winter.

Tides are regular rises and falls of the seas and oceans and are related to the attraction (or gravity pull) of the moon and, to a lesser extent, the sun. Tides ebb and flow twice in every 24 hours 50 minutes, which is the time it takes for the moon to orbit the earth. The highest tides, the Spring Tides, occur when the gravitational pull of the moon and sun act together. The lowest or Neap Tides occur when the gravitational pull of the moon and sun are out of phase with each other.

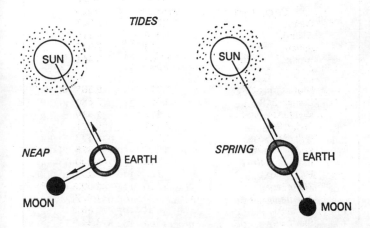

TIDES

The Continents

The land surface of the earth is made up of immense land masses which are divided into continental areas and a great number of islands. A huge land mass, largely in the eastern hemisphere, consists of the continents of Asia, Europe and Africa. The Americas in the western hemisphere are divided between the continents of North America and South America. The two island continents in the southern hemisphere are Australia and Antarctica. Generally, islands are regarded as belonging to the nearest continents. The far-flung islands of the Pacific, however, are usually grouped with Australia, New Zealand and New Guinea under the name of Oceania.

Although the ice that forms over it in winter makes it a solid mass, the Arctic is a sea, not a continent. Antarctica, however, is a land mass covered by ice and snow (see B41–42).

The largest of the world's seven continents is Asia. It covers an area of about 43,000,000 sq km. The next largest is Africa with

The Largest Islands

Island	Ocean	Continent	Area (sq km)	Population
Greenland	Atlantic-Arctic	N. America	2,175,600	55,170
New Guinea	Pacific	Oceania	821,030	6,595,000
Borneo	Pacific	Asia	744,366	9,000,000
Madagascar	Indian	Africa	587,041	12,000,000
Baffin Is.	Arctic	N. America	476,068	2,000
Sumatra	Indian	Asia	473,607	31,000,000
Honshu	Pacific	Asia	230,448	96,700,000
Great Britain	Atlantic	Europe	218,041	55,000,000
Ellesmere Is.	Arctic	N. America	212,688	600
Victoria Is.	Arctic	N. America	212,198	100
Sulawesi	Pacific	Asia	189,036	12,000,000
South Is. N.Z.	Pacific	Oceania	150,460	870,000
Java	Indian	Asia	126,296	94,500,000
Luzon	Pacific	Asia	120,787	30,000,000
North Is. N.Z.	Pacific	Oceania	114,687	2,443,000
Newfoundland	Atlantic	N. America	110,681	571,000
Cuba	Atlantic	N. America	107,832	10,495,000
Iceland	Atlantic	Europe	102,813	256,000
Mindanao	Pacific	Asia	101,505	12,000,000
Novaya Zemlya	Arctic	Asia	82,880	400
Ireland	Atlantic	Europe	82,463	3,540,000
Hokkaido	Pacific	Asia	77,900	5,700,000
Sakhalin	Pacific	Asia	76,400	665,000
Hispaniola	Atlantic	N. America	76,192	13,230,000
Tasmania	Pacific	Oceania	67,800	450,300

about 30,000,000 sq km. North America has an area of 24,000,000 sq km, while South America covers 17,800,000 sq km.

The continent of Europe has a long land boundary with Asia which partly follows the Ural Mountains. Europe's area, including one-quarter of the C.I.S., covers 10,400,000 sq km. Antarctica is bigger, with an area of 14,200,000 sq km. The smallest continent is Australia which combines with the islands mentioned on B9 to form Oceania, covering an area of 8,937,000 sq km.

Origin and Structure of the Continents

Scientists believe there was originally only one large land mass, which they call Pangaea. This split into a northern mass, Laurasia, and a southern one, Gondwanaland. Out of these land masses the continents gradually drifted to where they are today, and movement is still going on. One of the main arguments offered as proof of *continental drift* is that the shores of the continents, particularly South America and Africa, fit together fairly well, like pieces of a jig-saw. Many islands also fit along the edges of larger land masses.

The crust of the earth is made up of several rigid, but slowly moving, *plates* on which the continents sit. They might be said to 'float' like rafts on the denser material of the earth's mantle. (See B5.) The continents split up and drifted apart because, at the edges of the plates, new material came up from the earth's mantle and forced the plates apart. Such movement causes great

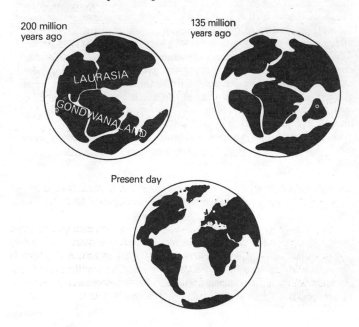

structural cracks called *faults* (see B54) and, as land masses push against each other, rock layers are forced up and folded. An upfold of rock *strata* (layers) is called an *anticline* and a downfold a *syncline*.

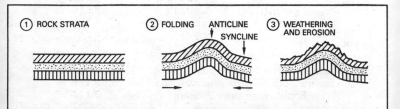

In the process of time the *weathering* and *erosion* of the surface folds produces the rugged scenery of the earth's great mountain ranges: for example, the Rockies, the Andes, the Himalayas and the Alps. Some of the world's mountains are considerably older than others, but most of the highest mountains occur in 'younger' folded ranges.

Weathering and erosion by agents such as temperature changes, running water, moving ice, wind and sea action begin as soon as land forms. Rivers are important etchers of land, as are glaciers (see B54). Large parts of the earth have been shaped by past ice action, and similar processes continue today in high mountain regions and in polar areas.

Wind action also shapes the land, especially in desert areas where material is transported and deposited as high dune ridges.

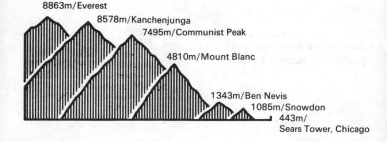

The World's Highest Mountains (See B12)

Peak	Location	Height (metres)
Everest	Nepal-China	8,863
Godwin Austen (K-2)	Pakistan	8,610
Kanchenjunga	Nepal-Sikkim	8,598
Lhotse	Nepal	8,511
Makalu I	Nepal-China	8,481
Dhaulagiri I	Nepal	8,167
Manashlu I	Nepal	8,156
Cho Oyu	Nepal-China	8,153
Nanga Parbat	Pakistan	8,124
Annapurna	Nepal	8,091

Highest Points in each Continent

Continent	Highest point	Height (metres)
Europe	Mt. Elbrus (CIS)	5,642
Asia	Mt. Everest (Nepal-China)	8,863
Africa	Mt. Kilimanjaro (Tanzania)	5,895
N. America	Mt. McKinley (Alaska, U.S.A.)	6,194
S. America	Mt. Aconcagua (Argentina-Chile)	6,960
Oceania	Mt. Yayakusmu (New Guinea)	5,030
Antarctica	Vinson Range	5,140

The sea, too, wears land away and builds it up. Bays, cliffs and caves result from marine erosion. Beaches, sandbars and spits are products of marine deposition (See Dictionary section).

Earthquakes and Volcanoes

Earthquakes and volcanic eruptions occur at the edges of the *plates* in the earth's crust. When plates are forced to move and

Lowest Points in each Continent

Continent	Lowest point	Depth (metres)
Europe	Polders, Netherlands	3·7–4·7
Asia	Dead Sea, Jordan-Israel	403
Africa	Qattara Depression, Egypt	133
N. America	Death Valley, U.S.A.	86
S. America	Rio Negro, Argentina	30
Oceania	Lake Eyre, South Australia	16
Antarctica	Interior	2,499 (ice-filled)

grind against each other, a series of violent jerks and shudders occur. Like the waves which spread from the centre when a stone is thrown into a pond, the vibrations of an earthquake travel out from a centre called a *focus*. The surface of the earth above the focus is called the *epicentre*. Earthquakes cause great damage and can start landslides and floods. The *Richter Scale* is used to measure the strength of the shock waves.

Volcanoes are the earth's most spectacular displays of energy. Volcanic eruptions of molten rock (*lava*), ashes, dust and gases can, like earthquakes, lead to major loss of life. Sometimes the lava reaches the surface through great cracks and flows over large areas to form volcanic plateaus. Other eruptions produce characteristic volcanic cones with vents that link the earth's surface with reservoirs of molten rock below (see B53). Volcanoes that have not erupted for long periods are called *quiescent* or *dormant*. Many other volcanoes are now *extinct*.

Earthquakes and volcanic eruptions occur in well-defined areas which lie at the edges of the earth's plates. For example, the largest belt is called the 'Fiery Girdle' and extends around the shores of the Pacific Ocean. A second belt runs through the Mediterranean to the Himalayas and south-east Asia. A third belt follows the

Mid-Atlantic Ridge (see B7) from Iceland in the north to Tristan da Cunha in the south. There are about 430 volcanoes in all with recorded eruptions—275 in the northern hemisphere and 155 in the southern. Some of the world's countries that have experienced disastrous earthquakes in recent times include Turkey, Iran, Greece, Italy, Morocco, Mexico, Armenia (CIS) and the Philippines.

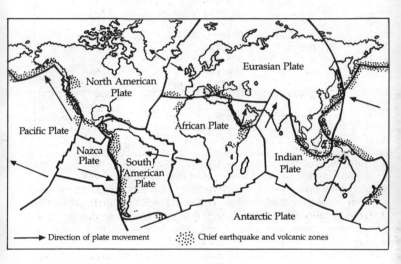

→ Direction of plate movement   ⠐⠐⠐⠐ Chief earthquake and volcanic zones

The World's Population

Of all the inhabitants of the earth's surface, humans have been the most inventive and successful, but also the most destructive. In 1993 the world's population was estimated as being 5,545 million. Every five days this figure is said to increase by more than 1 million. One of the major problems facing the world is that of providing food and resources for this huge population explosion. Many parts of the world are at starvation level, and food production in many countries has been greatly affected by disastrous droughts. Ethiopia and Sudan, for example, are countries experiencing acute hunger, and millions of people have died from the lack of food. Similar conditions occur throughout the (cont. B21)

The Principal Volcanoes of the World

I. Active

Volcano	Height (metres)	Volcano	Height (metres)
Ojos del Salado (Argentina)	6,895	Fuego (Guatemala)	3,835
Cotopaxi (Ecuador)	5,911	Kerintji (Indonesia)	3,805
Cayambe (Ecuador)	5,796	Erebus (Antarctica)	3,794
Popocatapetl (Mexico)	5,452	Santa Maria (Guatemala)	3,768
Sangay (Ecuador)	5,230	Rindjani (Indonesia)	3,726
Cotacachi (Ecuador)	4,966	Teide (Tenerife, Spain)	3,718
Purace (Columbia)	4,756	Semeru (Indonesia)	3,676
Klyuchevskaya (Russia)	4,750	Ichinskaya (Russia)	3,607
Wrangell (Alaska, USA)	4,270	Atitlan (Guatemala)	3,535
Tajmulco (Guatemala)	4,211	Nyiregongo (Zaire)	3,470
Mauna Loa (Hawaii, USA)	4,170	Irazu (Costa Rica)	3,435
Cameroon (Nigeria)	4,070	Slamat (Indonesia)	3,428
Tacana (Guatemala)	4,064	Spurr (Alaska, USA)	3,374
Acatenango (Guatemala)	3,960	Raung (Indonesia)	3,332
Colima (Mexico)	3,850	Etna (Italy)	3,287

II. Quiescent

Volcano	Height (metres)	Volcano	Height (metres)
Kilimanjaro (Tanzania)	5,985	Welirang (Indonesia)	3,156
Misti (Peru)	5,800	Sundoro (Indonesia)	3,138
Pichincha (Ecuador)	4,783	Apo (Phillippines)	2,954
Kronotskaya (Russia)	3,528	Marapi (Indonesia)	2,891
Lassen (USA)	3,200	Tambora (Indonesia)	2,860

III. Believed Extinct

Volcano	Height (metres)
Demavend (Iran)	5,601
Karisimbi (Zaire)	4,507
Mikeno (Zaire)	4,505
Fujiyama (Japan)	3,776

Volcano	Height (metres)
Aconcagua (Argentine–Chile)	6,960
Chimborazo (Ecuador)	6,267
Orizaba (Mexico)	5,653
Elbrus (Russia)	5,633

Principal Lakes, Rivers and Waterfalls of the World

Lakes of the World [2]

Lake	Location	Area (sq km)	Depth (m)	Salt or fresh
Caspian Sea [1]	CIS (Russia, Kazakhstan, Turkmenistan, Azerbaijan)–Iran, Asia–Europe	393,898	980	Salt
Superior	USA–Canada	82,103	393	Fresh
Victoria	Uganda–Kenya–Tanzania	69,485	470	Fresh
Huron	USA–Canada	59,570	212	Fresh
Michigan	USA	57,760	281	Fresh
Aral Sea [1]	CIS (Kazakhstan, Uzbekistan)	35,000	53	Salt
Tanganjika	(Zaire, Zambia, Tanzania, Burundi)	32,893	500	Fresh
Great Bear	Canada	31,800	200	Fresh
Baikal	CIS (Russia)	31,492	1,620	Fresh
Malawi	Malawi–Tanzania–Mozambique	29,600	472	Fresh
Great Slave	Canada	28,570	158	Fresh
Erie	USA–Canada	25,676	198	Fresh
Winnipeg	Canada	24,500	217	Fresh
Ontario	USA–Canada	19,530	237	Fresh

[1] Some of these lakes are subject to seasonal variations in size. [2] Classified as lakes, despite their names, as they are completely landlocked (See B6).

Principal Rivers of the World

River	Continent	Approx length (km)	Flow (cu m/sec) where known	Outflow into:
Nile	Africa	6,695	3,120	Mediterranean Sea
Amazon	S. America	6,440	180,000	Atlantic Ocean
Mississippi-Missouri	N. America	6,210	18,400	Gulf of Mexico
Ob-Irtysh	Asia	5,570	15,600	Arctic Ocean
Yangtze-Kiang	Asia	5,520	21,800	Pacific Ocean
Hwang Ho (Yellow River)	Asia	4,670	—	Pacific Ocean
Zaïre	Africa	4,670	41,000	Atlantic Ocean
Amur	Asia	4,510	12,400	Sea of Okhotsk (Pacific)
Lena	Asia	4,270	16,300	Arctic Ocean
MacKenzie-Peace	N. America	4,240	11,300	Arctic Ocean
Mekong	Asia	4,180	11,000	South China Sea
Niger	Africa	4,170	11,750	Atlantic Ocean
Yenisey	Asia	4,130	—	Arctic Ocean
Paraña	S. America	3,940	60,000	Atlantic Ocean
Murray-Darling	Australia	3,720	400	Pacific Ocean
Volga	Europe	3,690	9,900	Caspian Sea
Madeira	S. America	3,315	—	Amazon
Purus	S. America	3,220	—	Amazon

N.B. Many tributaries of the world's largest rivers (for example, the Amazon) also rank as major natural waterways.

The World's Great Waterfalls

In Order of Height (Single Leaps Only)

Waterfall	Country	River	Height (metres)
Angel Falls	Venezuela	Tributary of Caroni River	979
Ribbon Falls	California, USA	Tributary of Yosemite River	491
King George VI	Guyana	Utshi River	488
Upper Yosemite	California, USA	Yosemite Creek	436
Gavarnie	Pyrenees, France	Gave de Pau	422
Tugela (*highest fall*)	Natal, Republic of S. Africa	Tugela River	412
Wollomombi	New South Wales, Australia	Wollomombi River	335
Takakkaw	British Columbia, Canada	Tributary of Yoho River	305
Staubbach	Switzerland	Pletschen River	299
Mardola	Norway	Elkesdals Lake	297
Chirombo	Zambia	Ieisa River	268
Vettisfoss	Norway	Utla River	261
King Edward VIII	Guyana	Semang River	256
Gersoppa	India	Sharavati River	253
Sutherland	New Zealand	Arthur River	248

In Order of Volume

Waterfall	Country	River	Height (metres)	Average annual flow (cu m/sec)
Guaira or Sete Quedas	Brazil–Paraguay	Alto Parana River	40	13,310
Khon	Laos–Khmer	Mekong River	21	11,610
Niagara	USA–Canada	Niagara River	51	6,000
Paolo Afonse	Brazil	Sao Francisco River	59	2,830
Urubupunga	Brazil	Alto Parana River	12	2,750
Iguazu	Argentina–Brazil	Iguazu River	72	1,750
Patos-Maribondo	Brazil	Rio Grande	35	1,500
Victoria	Zambia and Zimbabwe	Zambesi River	108	1,100
Grand	Labrador	Hamilton River	75	990
Kaieteur	Guyana	Potaro River	226	660

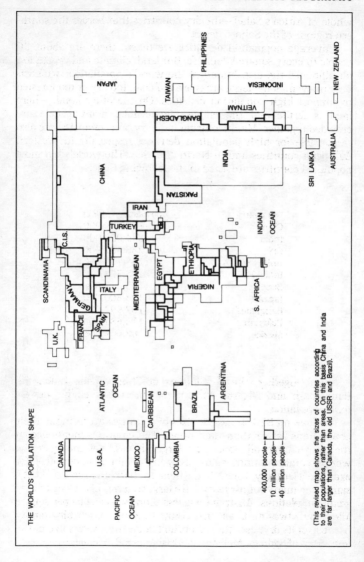

THE WORLD'S POPULATION SHAPE

(This revised map shows the sizes of countries according to their populations, rather than areas. On this basis China and India are far larger than Canada, the old USSR and Brazil.)

400,000 people ▪
10 million people ▫
40 million people ◻

whole of Africa's Sahel—the dry countries that border the south-ern regions of the Sahara desert.

If average population densities are taken, there are about 30 people to every square kilometre. But land, climate and vegetation all influence the distribution of the world's population, which is very uneven. Some large areas are too cold, too dry or too forested to support high population densities. On the other hand, where land is fertile and the climate favourable, many people are crowded together. Manufacturing industry and commerce are also responsible for high population densities, especially in Western European countries and in North America. The world's ten most populated countries are listed in the following table:

Country	Population (1991)
China	1,158,200,000
India	844,000,000
CIS	268,337,000
United States	248,710,000
Indonesia	178,574,000
Brazil	153,322,000
Japan	123,600,000
Bangladesh	107,993,000
Pakistan	113,687,000
Mexico	88,600,000

Added together, the populations of China, India, Indonesia, Bangladesh and Nigeria account for three-fifths of the world's total population.

The map on B20 shows the sizes of countries according to their populations rather than their areas. The countries mentioned in the above table all appear as large shapes. Yet many of the world's smaller countries have very high population densities: for example, Germany, the United Kingdom, Italy and France. At the same time many countries that are large in terms of area have very small populations. Australia has less than two persons per square kilometre: two-thirds of the country being practically empty because of its dryness. More than half of all Australians live in the four cities of Sydney, Melbourne, Brisbane and Adelaide.

The World's Great Cities

In spite of the importance of farming in feeding the world's ever-increasing population, more and more people are leaving the countryside for the towns and cities.

In the richer countries, where agriculture has become mechanised, fewer people are needed to work the land. The towns and cities offer alternative employment, often better-paid jobs and many social amenities: sporting, entertainment and shopping facilities.

In the world's poorer or developing countries, cities are also growing at an extremely rapid rate. Thousands of people flock to them every year, attempting to escape from the poverty of the countryside. Yet poverty, slums and unemployment are found in Western cities, too, and crime rates are high. Whether in rich or poor countries, dwellers in larger cities face similar problems such as air

World's Largest Cities and Urban areas
(*in thousands*)

Mexico City (Mexico)	> 20,207	Bangkok (Thailand)	> 8,200
Sao Paulo (Brazil)	> 18,052	Chicago (USA)	8,150
New York (USA)	17,900	Istanbul (Turkey)	> 8,000
Los Angeles (USA)	14,600	Tehran (Iran)	> 8,000
Osaka-Kobe (Japan)	13,826	Karachi (Pakistan)	> 7,711
Cairo (Egypt)	> 13,700	Ruhrgebiet (Germany)	7,474
Shanghai (China)	12,620	Kinshasa (Zaire)	7,000
Mumbai (India)	> 12,572	Lima (Peru)	> 6,578
Seoul (S. Korea)	12,000	San Francisco (USA)	6,103
Tokyo (Japan)	> 11,900	Lagos (Nigeria)	> 6,000
Calcutta (India)	> 11,663	Philadelphia (USA)	5,899
Buenos Aires (Argentina)	11,500	Bogota (Colombia)	> 5,800
Rio de Janeiro (Brazil)	> 11,428	Hong Kong (Hong Kong)	5,800
London (Greater, UK)	10,500	Madras (India)	> 5,743
Moscow (Russia, CIS)	10,367	Tianjin (China)	> 5,700
Paris (France)	10,000	Guangzhou (China)	> 5,100
Manila (Philippines)	> 9,880	St. Petersburg (Russia, CIS)	5,020
Beijing (China)	9,700	Alexandria (Egypt)	> 5,000
Jakarta (Indonesia)	> 9,588	Pusan (S. Korea)	4,838
Delhi (India)	> 8,375	Milan (Italy)	4,738

Note: > in excess of

pollution, traffic congestion, lack of land for building, and noise. Many countries encourage people to return to the countryside or to new towns, built to attract people away from the overcrowded cities.

The table on B22 lists the world's forty largest urban areas. Many are made up of one or more major city, together with smaller centres and numerous residential and manufacturing suburbs. Such complexes are called *conurbations* or *metropolitan areas*. Tokyo, for example, is the centre of the Kei Hin conurbation, which in 1991 had a population of 28 million. London is the centre of a huge urban region of at least 11 million. In Germany, the urban and industrial area of the Ruhr includes the cities of Essen, Duisburg, Dortmund and Bochum. Another term for the world's largest urban areas is *megalopolitan*.

Race, Language and Religion

As well as varying in density from one part of the world to another, the world's population is divided by factors such as race, language and religion. Scientists describe human beings as *Homo sapiens*, but divide them into three sub-groups or races: **Caucasoids**, **Mongoloids** and **Negroids**.

Most Europeans, and many Asian and North African peoples, belong to the **Caucasoid** race, the largest of the sub-groups. As a result of exploration and migration, European Caucasoids have settled in many parts of the world, particularly in the Americas, Australasia and Africa.

Mongoloid peoples form the second largest racial group. The Chinese, Japanese, Koreans, Malays, Mongols and, as a result of early migrations, the American Indians and Eskimos, all belong to the Mongoloid race.

The **Negroid** races belong mainly to central and north Africa, but slavery transferred many Negroids to North and South America. Some of the world's tallest people (the Nilotes of the White Nile region) and also the shortest (the Negrillos or pygmies of central Africa) belong to the Negroid race.

There are probably over 3,500 languages spoken in the world today. Nobody knows the exact number, since many are spoken only by small groups and tribes and have never been recorded on paper. About two-thirds of the world's population speak twelve principal languages, and another ten important languages account for about half of the remaining population. Differences in language can lead to suspicion, rivalry and conflict between peoples. This is also true of religion. The principal languages and religions of the world are given in the following tables:

Language

Language	Speakers (millions)	Language	Speakers (millions)
Chinese	1,100	French	120
English	490	Bantu (Middle and	
Hindi	410	South Africa)	103
Arabic	360	Urdu	93
Spanish	340	Punjabi (India and	
Bengali (India and		Pakistan)	85
Bangladesh)	260	Korean	71
Portuguese	175	Telugu (India)	68
Russian	170	Tamil (India and	
Malay–Indonesian	142	Sri Lanka)	67
Japanese	124	Italian	66
German	122	Swaheli (East and	
		Central Africa)	65

Religion

	Nominal followers in thousands	
Christianity		
Catholicism	985,000 ⎫	
Protestantism	720,000 ⎬ 1,937,000	
Orthodoxy	200,000 ⎪	
Others	32,000 ⎭	
Islam		
Sunnis	681,000 ⎫	
Shi'ites	190,000 ⎬ 999,000	
Others	128,000 ⎭	
Judaism	19,000	
Asiatic religions		
Confucianism	315,000	
Hinduism	720,000	
Buddhism	420,000	
Shintoism	65,000	
Taoism	32,000	
Sikhs	19,000	
Zoroastrianism	200	
New religions	6,000	

Countries of the World

The world is further divided into political areas called *countries, nations* or *states.* These are by far the most important divisions. The world is made up of over 200 countries and political areas: some very small like Monaco (2 sq km) and the Vatican (0·4 sq km), and others exceptionally large. The world's largest countries in terms of area (but not necessarily in terms of population—see page B20) are:

Country	Area in sq km
CIS	22,031,200
Canada	9,976,139
China	9,560,980
United States	9,363,123
Brazil	8,511,965
Australia	7,682,300
India	3,287,590
Argentina	2,776,889
Sudan	2,505,813
Algeria	2,381,741
Zaire	2,345,409
Greenland (Danish Autonomous Dependency)	2,175,600
Saudi Arabia	2,149,690
Mexico	1,958,201
Indonesia	1,904,569
Libya	1,759,540
Iran	1,648,000
Mongolia	1,566,500
Peru	1,285,216
Chad	1,284,000

Political ideas play an important part in dividing mankind. The world's nations are also grouped into rich and poor countries. These are also known as the *developed countries* (the 'haves') and the *developing countries* (the 'have-nots'). Developing countries are often referred to as *Third World* countries, to distinguish them from communist countries, the largest left in the world being China, and First World developed and non-communist countries.

Countries often combine with one another to form larger units. This might be for economic or military reasons or because they share some common history or identity. The *Commonwealth of Nations* is a very large grouping of countries (see A89). In 1992 its combined area was 28,443,279 square kilometres and its population was 1,450,000,000.

Another important group of countries to which Britain belongs are those which make up the *European Community* (see A94).

Some of the world's most powerful states have formed unions in which they dominate the affairs of other countries. The Soviet Union once did this through the Warsaw Pact (now disbanded) and the United States through the Organisation of American States. There is also the Organisation of African Unity; and in the Middle East, the Arab countries have founded the Arab League.

Groups of countries combine with each other for purely military reasons, as in NATO (North Atlantic Treaty Organisation).

By far the largest of the world organisations is the United Nations (see A85).

The following tables give the areas and populations of all the world's countries and the names and populations of their capital cities. The number of people in any country is constantly changing so only approximate figures, based on the latest counts (or censuses), can be given.

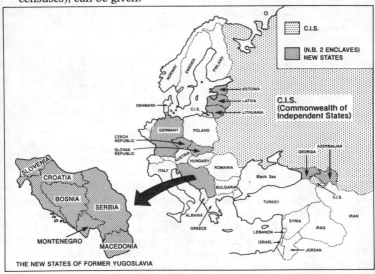

How the map has changed following the end of the Cold War.

EUROPE

Country	Area (sq km)	Population	Capital	Population of Capital
Albania	28 748	3,255,000	Tiranë	230,000
Andorra	453	51,000	Andorra La Vella	19,566
Austria	83,856	7,860,800	Vienna	1,552,200
Azerbaijan	86,600	7,145,600	Baku	1,757,000
Belgium	30,519	9,979,000	Brussels	960,324
Bosnia-Herzegovina	51,129	4,479,000	Sarajevo	450,000
Bulgaria	110,993	8,991,000	Sofia	1,141,140
Croatia	56,538	4,683,000	Zagreb	1,172,000
Cyprus	9,251	701,000	Nicosia	200,000
Czech Republic	78,864	10,364,600	Prague	1,215,100
Denmark	43,092	5,147,000	Copenhagen	1,336,860
Danish Autonomous Dependencies:				
Faeroe Islands	1,399	49,000	Thorshavn	16,000
Greenland	2,175,600	55,558	Godtháb (Nuuk)	12,217
Estonia	45,100	1,583,000	Tallinn	484,400
Finland	338,145	4,999,000	Helsinki	990,000
France	551,500	57,206,000	Paris	10,000,000
Georgia	69,700	5,456,000	Tbilissi	1,264,000
Germany	356,945	80,000,000	Berlin	4,000,000
Gibraltar	6,5	31,000	Gibraltar	31,000

Country	Area (sq km)	Population	Capital	Population of Capital
Greece	131,957	10,270,000	Athens	3,610,000
Autonomous Monk's Republic Athos	336	1,471	Kariaí	235
Hungary	93,033	10,500,000	Budapest	2,018,000
Iceland	103,000	256,000	Reykjavik	142,000
Ireland	70,284	3,524,000	Dublin	900,000
Italy	301,268	56,500,000	Rome	3,767,000
Latvia	64,600	2,687,000	Riga	916,500
Liechtenstein	160	29,386	Vaduz	4,874
Lithuania	65,200	3,730,000	Vilnius	592,500
Luxembourg	2,586	384,000	Luxembourg	95,000
Macedonia-Skopje	25,713	2,111,000	Skopje	520,000
Malta	316	358,000	Valletta	9,196
Monaco	1,95	29,876	Monaco-Ville	1,234
Netherlands	41,473	15,000,000	Amsterdam	1,038,000
Norway	323,878	4,242,000	Oslo	600,000
External inhabited Territories:				
Svalbard	62,700	3,500	Longyearbyen	1,000
Poland	312,683	38,423,000	Warsaw	1,655,690
Portugal	92,389	10,500,000	Lisbon	2,150,000
Romania	237,500	22,761,000	Bucharest	2,014,000
San Marino	60,57	23,243	San Marino	4,185

Country	Area (sq km)	Population	Capital	Population of Capital
Serbia	102,173	10,411,000	Belgrade	1,470,000
Slovak Republic	49,035	5,311,000	Bratislava	445,000
Slovenia	20,251	2,000,221	Ljubljana	330,000
Spain	504,750	39,434,000	Madrid	4,451,000
Sweden	449,964	8,552,000	Stockholm	1,641,700
Switzerland	41,293	6,873,000	Berne	299,000
Turkey	779,452	58,000,000	Ankara	3,900,000
United Kingdom of Great Britain and Northern Ireland	244,100	57,483,000	London	10,800,000
Vatican City	0·44	1,000	Vatican City	1,000
CIS (Commonwealth of Independent States)	21,944,600	268,337,000		
Armenia	29,800	3,580,000	Yerevan	1,300,000
Belorus	207,600	10,259,000	Minsk	1,612,000
Kazakhstan	2,717,100	16,691,000	Alma-Ata	1,152,000
Kirghizia	198,500	4,372,000	Biskek	627,000
Moldova	33,700	4,362,000	Chisinau	720,000
Russia	17,075,400	148,041,000	Moscow	10,367,000
Tadzhikistan	143,100	5,248,000	Dushanbe	604,000
Turkmenia	488,100	3,622,000	Akshkabad	402,000
Ukraine	603,700	51,840,000	Ki'yev	2,602,000
Uzbekistan	447,400	20,322,000	Tashkent	2,100,000

ASIA

Country	Area (sq km)	Population	Capital	Population of Capital
Afghanistan	652,090	16,121,000	Kabul	1,500,000
Bahrain	678	504,000	Manama	150,000
Bangladesh	143,998	107,992,000	Dhaka	4,700,000
Bhutan	46,500	1,400,000	Thimpu	15,000
Brunei Darussalam	5,765	260,000	Bandar Seri-Begawan	70,000
Cambodia (Kampuchea)	181,035	8,500,000	Phnom Penh	900,000
China (People's Republic)	9,560,980	1,158,200,000	Beijing	9,700,000
Taiwan	36,179	20,455,000	Taipei	4,300,000
Hong Kong	1,071	5,800,000	Victoria	1,150,000
Macao	16,92	460,000	Macao	435,000
India	3,287,263	844,000,000	Delhi	8,375,000
Indonesia	1,904,569	178,575,000	Jakarta	9,588,000
Iran	1,648,000	57,000,000	Tehran	8,000,000
Iraq	438,317	18,914,000	Baghdad	4,170,000
Israel	20,770	4,821,000	Jerusalem	545,000
Japan	377,815	123,150,000	Tokyo	11,900,000
Jordan	97,740	3,154,000	Amman	1,300,000
Korea: North	120,538	21,576,000	Pyongyang	2,100,000
South	99,263	43,207,000	Seoul	12,000,000
Kuwait	17,818	1,900,000	Kuwait City	600,000
Laos	263,800	4,186,000	Vientiane	380,000
Lebanon	10,400	2,897,000	Beirut	1,200,000
Malaysia	329,758	17,752,000	Kuala Lumpur	1,250,000

Country	Area (sq km)	Population	Capital	Population of Capital
Maldive Islands	298	214,139	Malé	56,060
Mongolia	1,565,500	2,124,000	Ulan Bator	548,400
Myanmar	676,552	41,609,000	Yangon	4,200,000
Nepal	140,797	19,096,000	Katmandu	845,000
Oman	212,457	1,554,000	Muscat	100,000
Pakistan (incl. Kashmir)	879,902	116,700,000	Islamabad	500,000
Philippines	300,000	62,000,000	Manila	9,880,000
Qatar	11,437	439,000	Doha	225,000
Saudi Arabia	2,149,690	14,902,000	Riyadh	1,500,000
Singapore	626	2,722,000	Singapore	2,722,000
Sri Lanka	65,610	17,002,000	Colombo	1,000,000
Syria	185,180	12,533,000	Damascus	1,700,000
Thailand	513,115	55,801,000	Bangkok	8,200,000
United Arab Emirates	83,600	1,592,000	Abu Dhabi	300,000
Vietnam	331,689	66,473,000	Hanoi	3,000,000
Yemen	527,968	11,612,000	Sana'a	510,000

AFRICA

Country	Area (sq km)	Population	Capital	Population of Capital
Algeria	2,381,741	25,056,000	El Djaza'ir	3,000,000
Angola	1,246,700	10,011,000	Luanda	1,400,000
Benin	112,622	4,741,000	Porto Novo	200,000
Botswana	581,730	1,254,000	Gaborone	138,500
Burkina-Faso	274,200	9,016,000	Ouagadougou	445,000
Burundi	27,834	5,470,000	Bujumbura	300,000
Cameroon	475,442	11,941,000	Yaoundé	860,000
Cape Verde	4,033	371,000	Praia	61,000
Central African Rep.	622,984	3,036,000	Bangui	500,000
Chad	1,284,000	5,679,000	N'Djaména	594,000
Comoros	1,862	475,000	Moroni	25,000
Congo	342,000	2,277,000	Brazzaville	800,000
Côte D'Ivoire	322,463	12,233,000	Yamoussoukro	150,000
Djibouti	23,200	427,000	Djibouti	225,000
Egypt	1,001,449	53,080,000	Cairo	13,700,000
Equatorial Guinea	28,051	417,000	Malabo	33,000
Ethiopia	1,221,900	51,183,000	Addis Ababa	1,600,000
Gabon	267,667	1,135,000	Libreville	360,000
Gambia	11,295	875,000	Banjul	120,000
Ghana	238,537	14,870,000	Accra	1,200,000
Guinea	245,857	6,518,000	Conakry	810,000
Guinea Bissau	36,125	981,000	Bissau	125,000
Kenya	582,646	24,368,000	Nairobi	1,800,000
Lesotho	30,355	1,771,000	Maseru	110,000
Liberia	111,369	2,560,000	Monrovia	400,000
Libya	1,759,540	4,546,000	Tripolis	1,200,000

Country	Area (sq km)	Population	Capital	Population of Capital
Madagascar	587,041	11,620,000	Antananarivo	1,200,000
Malawi	118,484	8,504,000	Lilongwe	255,000
Mali	1,240,192	8,465,000	Bamako	750,000
Mauritania	1,025,520	1,969,000	Nouakchott	500,000
Mauritius	2,040	1,074,000	Port Louis	150,000
Mayotte (Collectivités territoriales)	375	73,900	Dzaoudzi	5,900
Morocco	446,550	25,091,000	Er-Ribât-Salé	1,300,000
Mozambique	801,590	15,784,000	Maputo	1,000,000
Namibia	823,144	1,549,000	Windhoek	114,500
Niger	1,267,000	7,666,000	Niamey	800,000
Nigeria	923,768	88,500,000	Abuja	300,000
Réunion (French Dependencies)	2,512	597,823	Saint Denis	122,000
Rwanda	26,338	7,300,000	Kigali	265,000
St Helena & Dependencies	122	6,000	Jamestown	1,330
Ascension Island	88	1,012	Georgetown	600
Tristan da Cunha	104	300	Edinburgh	180
São Tomé & Príncipe	964	123,000	São Tomé	30,000
Sénégal	196,722	7,428,000	Dakar	1,500,000
Seychelles	280	68,000	Victoria	25,000
Sierra Leone	71,740	4,137,000	Freetown	550,000
Somalia	637,657	6,285,000	Mogadishu	800,000
South Africa	1,221,037	35,914,000	Pretoria	1,000,000
(including 'Homelands')			Cape Town	2,100,000
Spanish Presidios:				
Ceuta	19,5	67,000	Ceuta	67,000
Melilla	12,5	62,000	Melilla	62,000
Sudan	2,515,813	25,191,000	Khartoum	1,700,000

Country	Area (sq km)	Population	Capital	Population of Capital
Swaziland	17,364	789,000	Mbabane	38,000
Tanzania	945,087	24,518,000	Dar es Salaam	1,300,000
Togo	56,785	3,638,000	Lomé	600,000
Tunisia	163,610	8,175,000	Tunis	1,250,000
Uganda	235,880	17,358,000	Kampala	700,000
Western Sahara	266,000	186,000	El Aioun	100,000
Zaïre	2,345,409	35,564,000	Kinshasa	7,000,000
Zambia	752,618	8,122,000	Lusaka	900,000
Zimbabwe	390,759	9,809,000	Harare	1,000,000

NORTH AND CENTRAL AMERICA AND THE WEST INDIES

Country	Area (sq km)	Population	Capital	Population of Capital
Aruba	193	61,000	Oranjested	17,000
Anguilla	96	7,000	The Valley	2,000
Antigua and Barbuda	440	79,000	St John's	36,000
Bahamas	13,878	255,000	Nassau	191,543
Barbados	430	257,082	Bridgetown	102,000
Belize	22,965	191,800	Belmopan	4,000
Bermuda	53,5	58,000	Hamilton	6,000
Canada	9,976,139	26,992,000	Ottawa	820,000
Cayman Islands	259	27,000	Road Town	8,900
Costa Rica	51,100	2,994,000	San José	400,000
Cuba	110,860	10,626,000	Havana	2,200,000

Country	Area (sq km)	Population	Capital	Population of Capital
Dominica	751	82,000	Roseau	17,000
Dominican Republic	48,734	7,170,000	Santo Domingo	1,625,000
El Salvador	21,041	5,253,000	San Salvador	1,040,000
Grenada	344	94,000	St George's	30,000
Guadeloupe	1,780	386,988	Basse-Terre	37,000
Guatemala	108,889	9,454,000	Guatemala City	1,710,000
Haiti	27,750	6,488,000	Port-au-Prince	900,000
Honduras	112,088	5,119,000	Tegucigalpa	645,000
Jamaica	10,990	2,415,000	Kingston	770,000
Martinique	1,102	359,572	Fort-de-France	120,000
Mexico	1,958,201	88,600,000	Mexico City	20,207,000
Montserrat	102	12,000	Plymouth	3,000
Netherlands Antilles	800	191,000	Willemstad	150,000
Nicaragua	130,682	3,853,000	Managua	1,000,000
Panama	75,620	2,418,000	Panama City	620,000
Panama Canal Zone	1,432	31,600	Balboa Heights	120
Puerto Rico	8,897	3,599,000	San Juan	1,100,000
St Kitts-Nevis	262	40,000	Basseterre	14,161
St Lucia	622	150,000	Castries	3,000
St Pierre and Miquelon	242	6,392	St Pierre	5,683
St Vincent & The Grenadines	389	114,000	Kingstown	30,000
Trinidad and Tobago	5,128	1,283,000	Port-of-Spain	250,000
Turks and Caicos Islands	430	13,000	Cockburn Town	2,500
United States of America	9,363,123	248,710,000	Washington, D.C.	3,925,000

Country	Area (sq km)	Population	Capital	Population of Capital
Virgin Islands:				
British	153	13,000	Road Town	4,000
USA	344	110,000	Charlotte Amalie	15,000

SOUTH AMERICA

Country	Area (sq km)	Population	Capital	Population of Capital
Argentina	2,766,889	32,325,000	Buenos Aires	11,500,000
Bolivia	1,098,581	7,314,000	La Paz	2,150,000
Brazil	8,511,965	153,322,000	Brasilia	1,870,000
Chile	756,945	13,386,000	Santiago	4,385,500
Colombia	1,138,914	32,843,000	Bogotá	5,800,000
Ecuador	283,561	9,622,608	Quito	1,300,000
Falkland Islands and South Georgia and South Sandwich Islands	16,263	1,940	Port Stanley	1,200
French Guiana	91,000	114,678	Cayenne	53,000
Guyana	215,083	800,000	Georgetown	170,000
Paraguay	406,752	4,277,000	Asunción	740,000
Peru	1,285,214	21,800,000	Lima	6,578,000
Surinam	163,820	447,000	Paramaribo	246,000
Uruguay	177,414	3,094,000	Montevideo	1,350,000
Venezuela	912,050	19,735,000	Caracas	4,300,000

OCEANIA

Country	Area (sq km)	Population	Capital	Population of Capital
Australia	7,686,848	17,335,900	Canberra	310,500
New South Wales	801,600	5,901,100	Sydney	3,656,500
Queensland	1,727,200	2,972,000	Brisbane	1,301,700
South Australia	984,000	1,456,700	Adelaide	1,049,900
Tasmania	67,800	460,500	Hobart	183,500
Victoria	227,600	4,427,400	Melbourne	3,080,900
Western Australia	2,525,500	1,665,900	Perth	1,193,100
Northern Territory	1,346,200	158,800	Darwin	73,300
Australian Capital Territory	2,400	293,500	Canberra	293,500
Australian Inhabited External Territories				
Christmas Island	135	1,230	Flying Fish Cove	500
Cocos (Keeling) Islands	14	665	Bantam	100
Norfolk Island	35	2,367	Kingston	900
Fiji	18,274	736,000	Suva	120,000
French Polynesia	4,200	197,000	Papeete	25,000
Guam	549	137,000	Agaña	5,500
Kiribati	861	70,000	Bairiki	2,100

Country	Area (sq km)	Population	Capital	Population of Capital
Mariana Islands (Nothern)	475	21,800	Susupe	19,200
Marshall Islands	181	43,400	Uliga	7,600
Micronesia	721	103,000	Pohnpei	5,550
Nauru	21	9,350	Yaren	4,000
New Caledonia	19,058	170,000	Noumea	65,000
New Zealand	270,986	3,427.796	Wellington	325,700
Dependent Inhabited Territories				
Cook Islands	241	19,000	Avarua	5,000
Niue	259	2,267	Alofi	1,000
Tokelau	10	1,690	Fakaofo	500
Palau	458	15,105	Koror	7,685
Papua New Guinea	462,840	3,915,000	Port Moresby	152,900
Samoa (Eastern)	197	39,000	Pago Pago	3,300
Solomon Islands	28,896	324,000	Honiara	35,288
Tonga	748	100,000	Nuku'alofa	22,000
Tuvalu	26	8,300	Vaiaku	2,800
Vanuatu	12,189	157,000	Port Vila	19,311
Wallis & Futuna (French)	274	15,600	Mata Uta	815
Western Samoa	2,831	165,000	Apia	35,000

ANTARCTICA

Antarctica is the world's seventh continent surrounding the South Pole. It was the last to be discovered (after 1819) and explored. Even today it has no permanent settlements, although many nations have claim to the strategic value of the continent and the marketable resources it might contain—oil, perhaps, and other minerals. Rich fishing grounds also surround its coasts. By the Treaty of Antarctica, signed in December 1959, the following countries agreed to freeze all their claims to Antarctic territory for thirty years, without giving them up: Australia, Argentina,

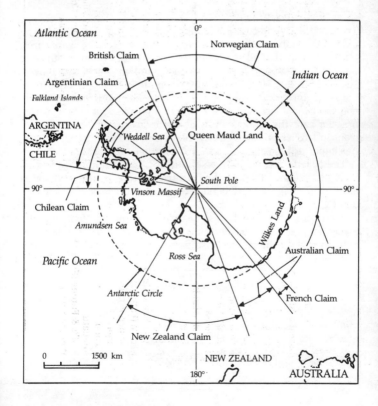

Belgium, Chile, France, Britain, Japan, New Zealand, Norway, the
Republic of South Africa, the USA and the CIS. The aim of the
treaty was to allow the research and peaceful co-operation that
had started during the International Geophysical Year to continue
in this scientifically important area. The main claims and dependencies are shown on the map. Britain has been involved in
Antarctic territory since the days of Captain Cook, but now both
Argentina and Chile lay claim to much of British territory. What
the future holds for Antarctica when the treaty comes to an end
remains, as yet, undecided.

Transport and Communications

Transportation and communications are vital to the functioning of
individual countries and to the world as a whole. There are three
types of transport: land, water and air transport. Developed countries
have good transport systems, and goods and passengers are moved
swiftly from one place to another. In many developing countries,
animal transport is still important: but the main forms of land
transport today are railways, roads and pipelines, the latter being
used for carrying oil, gas and water across country. Inland water
transport relies on lakes, navigable rivers and canals. The world
has important sea canals, as well as inland canals that link rivers.

The oceans and seas are essential to transportation, trade and
communications. In 1991 the countries with the largest shipping
fleets in tonnage were Liberia, Panama, Greece, Japan, Norway
and Cyprus.

Air transport is the fastest form of movement from place to
place today, and the time it takes to travel tends to have become
more important than actual distances.

Railways		
Countries with Longest Networks		
	length in km		length in km

	length in km		length in km
United States	250,863	Brazil	38,000
CIS	144,100	France	35,000
Canada	63,890	Japan	21,091
Germany	45,130	UK	17,435
China	44,000		

Countries with Densest Passenger Traffic		Countries with Densest Cargo Traffic	
	Passenger-km (millions)		Tonne-km (millions)
CIS	417,444	CIS	3,717,012
Japan	383,700	United States	1,513,776
India	277,272	China	1,060,116
China	261,012	Canada	263,436
Germany	66,900	India	233,292
France	63,588	Germany	120,708
Poland	50,376	South Africa	92,184
Italy	40,500	Poland	83,532
UK	34,068	Romania	57,252
South Korea	30,588		

World's Busiest Seaports (1989)

Seaport	Country	Goods (in million tonnes)
Rotterdam*	Netherlands	287,692
Singapore	Singapore	187,789
Kobe	Japan	171,465
Chiba*	Japan	164,182
Shanghai	China	133,000
Nagoya*	Japan	128,934
Yokohama*	Japan	123,873
Antwerpen*	Belgium	102,009
Osaka	Japan	97,378
Kitakyushu*	Japan	95,190
Kawasaki*	Japan	90,442
Marseille*	France	90,323
Hong Kong	Hong Kong	89,005
Tokyo	Japan	79,335
Kaohsiung*	Taiwan	77,987
Long Beach*	USA	74,762
Philadelphia*	USA	68,570
Los Angeles*	USA	67,895
Vancouver*	Canada	66,448
Corpus Christi*	USA	64,789

* denotes oil port

Great Ship Canals of the World

Canal	Year opened	Length (km)	Depth (metres)	Width (metres)
Amsterdam (Netherlands)	1876	26·6	7	26·8
Corinth (Greece)	1893	6·4	8	22
Elbe and Trave (Germany)	1900	66	3	22
Gota (Sweden)	1832	185·1	3	14·3
Kiel (Germany)	1895	98·2	13·7	45·7
Manchester (England)	1894	57·1	8·5–9·1	36·6
Panama (U.S.A.)	1914	81·3	13·7	91·4
Princess Juliana (Netherlands)	1935	32·2	4·9	15·8
Saulte Ste. Marie (U.S.A.)	1855	2·6	6·7	30·5
Saulte Ste. Marie (Canada)	1895	1·8	6·8–7·6	43·3
Suez (Egypt)	1869	161	10·4	60
Welland (Canada)	1887	43·1	7·6	61

World's Busiest Airports (1990)

Airport	Country	Passengers (in thousands)
Chicago (O'Hare International)	USA	59,936
Dallas–Fort Worth	USA	48,515
Atlanta (Hartsfield)	USA	48,515
Los Angeles (International)	USA	45,180
London (Heathrow)*	UK	42,647
Tokyo (Haneda)	Japan	40,188
San Francisco (International)	USA	30,388
New York (J. F. Kennedy)	USA	29,787
Frankfurt (Rhein-Main)	Germany	28,705
Denver (Stapleton International)	USA	27,433
Miami (International)	USA	25,837
Paris (Orly)	France	24,206
Osaka (International)	Japan	23,458
Honolulu (International)	USA	23,132
New York (La Guardia)	USA	22,754

* N.B. Heathrow is the busiest international airport

UNITED KINGDOM OF GREAT BRITAIN AND NORTHERN IRELAND

The UK comprises the island of Great Britain (which includes England, Wales and Scotland) and Northern Ireland (the north-east part of the island of Ireland, also known as Ulster). The UK's total land area is 244,104 square kilometres, of which England covers 130,441 sq km, Scotland 78,775 sq km, Wales 20,768 sq km, and Northern Ireland 14,120 sq km.

There are other countries which, though independent, are attached to the British Crown. The Isle of Man has been a separate state for a thousand years, but the UK is responsible for its defence and external relations. The same applies to the two autonomous Channel Islands of Jersey and Guernsey. Guernsey, also, has its dependencies in the islands of Alderney, Sark, Herm, and Jethou.

The UK's population is estimated (since the 1991 census) as 57,483,000, of which England has 47,886,000, Scotland 5,114,200, Wales 2,885,700 and Northern Ireland 1,597,100. The population of the Isle of Man is 67,000; and of the Channel Islands, 144,000.

After April 1974, when the provisions of the Local Government Act, 1972, came into force, some old county divisions were brought to an end, or their areas and boundaries rearranged. England was given 39 non-metropolitan counties and six metropolitan counties (in addition to Greater London), though the latter were disbanded in Spring 1986. Wales had eight counties, Scotland had twelve regions and Northern Ireland had twenty-six districts. For this edition of the book the former populations and areas of England's six metropolitan counties are given, though in effect (administratively, if not functionally) they have reverted to the pre-1974 arrangement. The following table lists the counties and regions with their areas and populations. The former metropolitan regions are in italic.

UNITED KINGDOM OF GREAT BRITAIN AND NORTHERN IRELAND

Total land area:		244,104 *sq km*
	England	130,441 sq km
	Scotland	78,775 sq km
	Wales	20,768 sq km
	Northern Ireland	14,120 sq km
Population:		57,483,000 *Inhabitants*
	England	47,886,000
	Scotland	5,114,200
	Wales	2,885,700
	Northern Ireland	1,597,100

ENGLAND
National Capital: London   6,754,400 inhabitants
Greater London 10,500,000 inhabitants

Counties	Administrative Headquarters	Area (sq km)	Population
Avon	Bristol	1,338	952,800
Bedfordshire	Bedford	1,235	513,100
Berkshire	Reading	1,256	748,400
Buckinghamshire	Aylesbury	1,883	634,400
Cambridgeshire	Cambridge	3,409	665,000
Cheshire	Chester	2,322	958,600
Cleveland	Middlesbrough	583	552,900
Cornwall & Isles of Scilly	Truro	3,546	464,100
Cumbria	Carlisle	6,809	491,600
Derbyshire	Matlock	2,631	929,400
Devon	Exeter	6,715	1,029,900
Dorset	Dorchester	2,654	656,800

Counties	Administrative Headquarters	Area (sq km)	Population
Durham	Durham	2,436	596,500
Essex	Chelmsford	3,674	1,532,000
Gloucester	Gloucester	2,638	529,500
Hampshire	Winchester	3,772	1,546,000
Hereford & Worcester	Worcester	3,927	675,300
Hertford	Hertford	1,634	987,400
Humberside	Kingston-upon-Hull	3,512	856,300
Isle of Wight	Newport	381	130,500
Kent	Maidstone	3,732	1,523,600
Lancashire	Preston	3,043	1,390,800
Leicestershire	Leicester	2,553	891,900
Lincolnshire	Lincoln	5,885	586,900
Norfolk	Norwich	5,355	748,500
Northamptonshire	Northampton	2,367	576,100
Northumberland	Newcastle-upon-Tyne	5,033	303,600
Nottinghamshire	Nottingham	2,164	1,014,800
Oxfordshire	Oxford	2,611	577,600
Shropshire	Shrewsbury	3,490	403,200
Somerset	Taunton	3,458	460,900
Staffordshire	Stafford	2,716	1,039,900
Suffolk	Ipswich	3,807	641,100
Surrey	Kingston-upon-Thames	1,655	1,000,000
Sussex, East	Lewes	1,795	711,800
Sussex West	Chichester	2,016	704,900
Warwickshire	Warwick	1,981	483,100
Wiltshire	Trowbridge	3,481	558,400

WALES
National Capital: Cardiff (285,000 inhabitants)

Counties	Administrative Headquarters	Area (sq km)	Population
Clwyd	Mold	2,425	411,100
Dyfed	Carmarthen	5,765	352,600
Gwent	Cwmbran	1,376	446,900
Gwynedd	Caernarvon	3,868	240,800
Mid Glamorgan	Cardiff	1,019	538,100
Powys	Llandrindod Wells	5,077	116,800
South Glamorgan	Cardiff	416	404,100
West Glamorgan	Swansea	815	362,800

SCOTLAND
National Capital: Edinburgh (433,200 inhabitants)

Regions	Administrative Headquarters	Area (sq km)	Population
Borders	Newton St Boswells	4,662	102,700
Central	Stirling	2,590	271,400
Dumfries and Galloway	Dumfries	6,475	147,600
Fife	Cupar	1,308	344,800
Grampian	Aberdeen	8,550	503,500
Highlands	Inverness	26,136	201,900

Regions	Administrative Headquarters	Area (sq km)	Population
Lothian	Edinburgh	1,756	742,900
Strathclyde	Glasgow	13,856	2,311,200
Tayside	Dundee	7,668	392,500
Island Authority Areas:			
Orkney Islands	Kirkwall	974	19,400
Shetland Islands	Lerwick	1,427	22,200
Western Isles	Stornoway	2,901	30,610

Administrative
Districts of
Northern
(The six historic
provinces are Antrim,
Down, Derry, Tyrone,
Armagh and
Fermanagh)

NORTHERN IRELAND
National Capital: Belfast (301,500)

District	Area (sq km)	Population	Map ref.
Antrim	562	45,500	1
Ards	361	59,700	2
Armagh	674	49,900	3
Ballymena	634	55,400	4
Ballymoney	417	24,400	5
Banbridge	445	30,600	6
Belfast	115	301,600	7
Carrickfergus	77	28,400	8
Castlereagh	84	59,800	9
Coleraine	484	47,400	10
Cookstown	610	29,300	11
Craigavon	388	73,400	12

District	Area (sq km)	Population	Map ref.
Down	645	54,000	13
Dungannon	779	45,700	14
Fermanagh	1,875	51,600	15
Larne	338	29,300	16
Limavady	589	28,000	17
Lisburn	446	87,900	18
Londonderry	386	96,100	19
Magerafelt	562	34,200	20
Moyle	494	14,500	21
Newry-Mourne	909	83,400	22
Newtonabbey	139	71,900	23
North Down	73	66,800	24
Omagh	1,124	46,900	25
Strabane	861	37,000	26

Other British Isles

Island	Capital or chief town	Area (sq km)	Population
Isle of Man	Douglas	588	67,000
Channel Islands			
Jersey	St. Helier	116	82,809
Guernsey	St. Peter Port	64	55,482
Alderney	St. Anne's	8	2,086
Sark, Brechou & Jethou	Sark	6	610
Isles of Scilly	St. Mary's	16	1,850

Britain's Largest Cities

City	Population	City	Population
London	6,756,400	Bristol	377,700
Birmingham	993,700	Coventry	306,200
Glasgow	715,600	Belfast	301,600
Leeds	709,600	Cardiff	285,000
Sheffield	528,300	Newcastle	279,600
Liverpool	469,600	Leicester	278,500
Bradford	464,100	Nottingham	273,500
Manchester	445,900	Stoke-on-Trent	246,800
Edinburgh	433,200	Kingston upon Hull	246,000

The UK's Main Conurbations
(large urban areas)

Conurbation	Population	Conurbation	Population
London	6,756,400	West Yorkshire	2,040,000
Greater London	10,500,000	Merseyside	1,430,000
West Midlands	2,600,000	South Yorkshire	1,255,000
Greater Manchester	2,500,000	Tyne & Wear	1,120,000
Greater Glasgow	2,100,000		

Britain's Highest Mountains and Largest Lakes

Peak	Height (m)	Lake	Area (sq km)
		England	
Scafell Pike (Cumbria)	978·4	Windermere (Cumbria Lancs)	26
		Wales	
Snowdon (Gwynedd)	1,085	Bala (Gwynedd)	10·4
		Scotland	
Ben Nevis (Inverness)	1,343	Loch Lomond (Central Strathclyde)	70
		Northern Ireland	
Slieve Donard (Down)	852·2	Lough Neagh (Antrim–Londonderry–Tyrone–Armagh)	388·5

Important Rivers of Britain

River	Length (km)	Rises in:	Flows to:
Severn	354	Plynlimmon, Dyfed	Bristol Channel
Thames	336	Cotswold Hills, nr Cirencester	North Sea
Trent	274	N. Staffordshire	Joins Ouse to form R. Humber
Great Ouse	251	Northants.	The Wash
Wye	209	Plynlimmon	Severn, nr Chepstow
Tay	188	Grampian Mts, N. Argyll	Firth of Tay

River	Length (km)	Rises in:	Flows to:
Spey	177	Grampians Mts, Inverness	Moray Firth
Clyde	171	S. Lanark (union of Daer and Potrail Water)	Firth of Clyde
Tweed	156	Tweedsmuir Hills, S. Peebles	North Sea, at Scot-Eng border
Dee	140	Cairngorm Mts, W. Aberdeenshire	North Sea (at Aberdeen)
Ribble	121	Pennine Chain, W. Yorkshire	Irish Sea (nr Southport)
Dee	113	Gwynedd, N. Wales	Irish Sea
Mersey	113	Pennine Chain (union of Goyt and Tame at Stockport)	Irish Sea (at Liverpool)
Tees	113	Cross Fell, Cumbria	North Sea
Forth	106	S. Perth	Firth of Forth
Towy	106	Hills between Cardigan and Radnor	Carmarthen Bay
Eden	105	Pennine Chain (Cumbria-Yorks.)	Solway Firth (Irish Sea)
Wear	105	Pennine Chain (W. Durham)	North Sea
Derwent	97	N. of the Peak (Derby)	Trent
Ouse	97	Yorks (union of Swale and Ure)	Joins Trent to form R. Humber
Tamar	97	Devonian Hills	English Channel (at Plymouth)
Derwent	92	Yorkshire moors	Ouse (between Selby and Goole)
Exe	87	Exmoor (N. Devon)	English Channel (Exeter)
Teifi	85	Llyn Teifi, N.E. Dyfyd	Cardigan Bay (at Cardigan)
Tyne	72	Northumberland (union of N. and S. Tyne)	North Sea (at Tynemouth)

A DICTIONARY OF GEOGRAPHICAL TERMS

Alluvium The fine sand, silt and mud material deposited by rivers to form plains and *deltas*.

Archipelago A sea containing many islands: e.g. Aegean Archipelago between mainland Greece and Turkey. The term is also used to mean any group of islands.

Atoll A low-lying coral island, shaped like a ring or horseshoe around a lagoon. Atolls are typical of the Pacific Ocean.

Avalanche A large mass of snow and ice at high altitudes which crashes down a mountainside under its own weight. Spring, when snow starts to melt, is a common time for avalanches.

Bar A collection of gravel, sand and mud deposited along some coasts, particularly across the mouth of a river or bay.

Basin An area of land drained by a river and its tributaries. The boundary between one river basin and another is known as a *watershed.*

Bay A wide indentation along a coast formed by the sea. Large lakes can also have bays.

Beach An area of sand, pebbles or mud where the land borders the sea. A raised beach is the former sea shore now at a higher level because of a fall in sea level or a rise in the land.

Blow-hole A hole in the roof of a coastal *cave* through which sea spray is blown at high tide.

Bore A tidal wave arising in the estuaries of certain rivers: e.g. the Severn. It is usually associated with spring tides and is also called an eagre.

Butte An isolated, flat-topped and steep-sided hill. It is similar to the larger *mesa* and is part of the remains of old *plateaux* surfaces.

Caldera A large, steep-sided *crater* at the top of a volcano which often contains a lake. Crater Lake, Oregon, is an example.

Canyon A deep, narrow, steep-sided gorge, cut by a river, usually in arid regions: e.g. Grand Canyon of the Colorado River, USA.

Cape This is another name for headland, an area of (usually) resistant land that projects into the sea. It is also known as a promontory.

Cataract A waterfall or series of waterfalls along a river. The term is sometimes used for rapids: e.g. the cataracts along the river Nile.

Cave A hollow beneath the surface of the land produced by river or sea erosion, or volcanic activity. Some of the largest caves and *caverns* are found in limestone regions. These caves often have *stalactites* (giant icicle-like columns of calcium carbonate hanging from their roofs) and *stalagmites* (similar columns, but rising from the floor). See *pothole*.

Col A depression or *pass* in a range of hills or mountains.

Coral Reef A low ridge in the sea formed from the skeletons of vast numbers of dead coral polyps. Fringing and barrier are names given to such reefs. See *atolls*.

Crater A funnel-shaped hollow at the top of a volcanic cone from which gases and lava are ejected. A cone and crater often rise from the centre of a *caldera*. Another type of crater is formed when meteorites strike the earth's surface.

Crevasse A deep crack in the surface of a *glacier*, especially where the ice broadens out or flows over a steep slope.

Delta A low-lying area of deposits (see *alluvium*) found where a river reaches the sea or a lake. Some deltas are fan-shaped (e.g. the Nile Delta), others are called bird's-foot (e.g. the Mississippi) deltas.

Desert Barren areas of the earth's surface where few plants grow on account of aridity (e.g. the tropical and sub-tropical desert) or intense cold (e.g. the Arctic and Antarctic, which can be regarded as cold deserts).

Drumlins A series of low egg-shaped hills formed by the deposition and moulding of material by an ice-sheet or *glacier*.

Dry Valley A valley which once contained a river or stream, but is now dry. Such a valley is a common feature of the chalklands of southern England.

Earthquake A movement or tremor in the earth's crust caused either by volcanic activity or by the existence of a *fault*.

Erosion The wearing away of the land by natural forces such as *weathering*, rivers, winds, seas, glaciers and ice-sheets.

Estuary The part of a river's mouth that is affected by tides, so that river and sea-water mix. Many estuaries are the lower reaches of river valleys that have been flooded by the sea. See *ria*.

Fault A break or fracture in rocks in the earth's crust along which movement has taken place, so that the layers of rock no longer match.

Fjord A deep, steep-sided and long inlet of the sea. Fjords are flooded valleys that were eroded by glaciers.

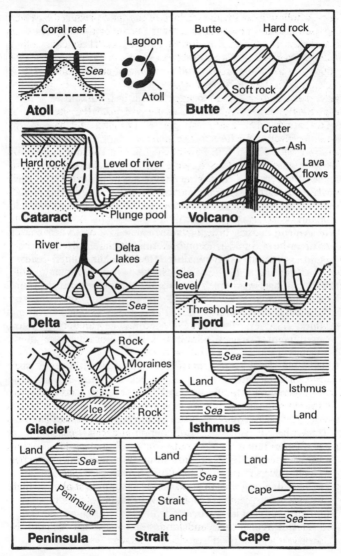

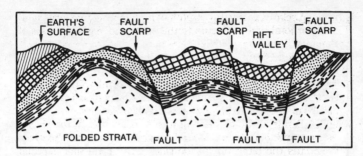

Flood plains These occur when rivers are in their 'old age' stage. They consist of sediment spread over the land during periodic flooding. *Meanders, ox-bow lakes* and *levees* are features of flood plains.

Fold A bend in rock layers (strata) caused by earth movements. The arch of a fold is known as an anticline. The trough of a fold is known as a syncline. Heavy folding often leads to fractures and *faults.*

Geysers Hot springs which shoot jets of hot water and steam into the air at various intervals. Some of the best-known geysers are those of Iceland, New Zealand and Yellowstone National Park, USA. The famous 'Old Faithful' geyser of Yellowstone used to erupt every 66·5 minutes, but is not now so regular in its activity.

Glacier Masses of ice that move very slowly down a valley under the force of gravity. They carry rock material and are major agents of erosion. Glaciers start in a snowfield and end where the rate of melting equals the supply of up-slope ice.

Gorge A deep narrow valley often having almost vertical sides. The Cheddar Gorge in the Mendip Hills is formed in carboniferous limestone.

Hanging valleys These are found in glaciated regions. When glaciers deepen a main valley into a V-shape, tributary valleys are left hanging above the U-shape trough. Water from hanging valleys descends as rapids or waterfalls.

Island Any area of land surrounded by water. Geographers, however, distinguish between islands and continents. See page B10 for the world's largest islands.

Isthmus A relatively narrow stretch of land joining two large land areas or joining a peninsula to the mainland: e.g. isthmuses of Panama, Suez.

Lake An inland body of water. Some of the world's largest lakes are called seas: e.g. Caspian Sea, Dead Sea.

Levee An embankment along a river which forms when the river overflows and deposits material along its banks. Levees can also be man-made to prevent flooding. See *meander*.

Meander Bends in the channel of a river occurring in the river's mature and old stages. Meanders grow in size as the river undercuts the bank on the outside of the bend and deposits *alluvium* on the inside of the bend. See *ox-bow lakes*.

Mesa (the Spanish word for a table) is a flat-topped upland. The hard rocks which cap mesas are parts of the original land surface that has been eroded. Smaller features are *buttes*. See *plateau*.

Mirage An optical illusion, caused when light rays are refracted (bent) as they pass through layers of air with differing densities. In hot deserts, light rays often give the impression that they are coming off a sheet of water. In polar areas the images of ships or icebergs can appear upside down.

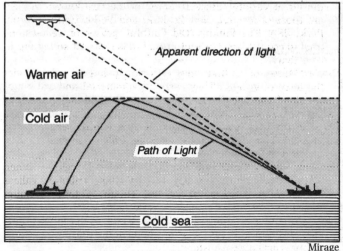

Mirage

Moraine Fragments of eroded rock carried and finally dumped
   by glaciers and ice-sheets. At the snout of a glacier (that is,
   where the glacier melts) this material is dumped in ridges
   called terminal moraine.

Ox-bow lakes These form when the river cuts through a narrow
   bend of a meander. The old meander is then abandoned as a lake.

Peninsula An area of land almost surrounded by water.

Plateau A large, level or mainly level area of highland. In areas
   of horizontal rocks, plateaus are often cut by *canyons*. This river
   erosion can lead to the formation of *buttes* or *mesas*.

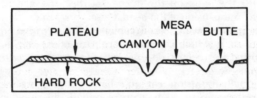

Polder Land claimed from the sea or lake. In the Low Countries,
   polders are protected by artificial dykes or sea walls. They are
   also artificially drained by canals. The greater part of the
   former Zuider Zee has been transformed into polders.

Pothole A hole worn in solid rock, usually at the foot of a
   waterfall, by the constant grinding of stones kept in motion by
   the force of the water. The term is also another name for a
   swallow hole, commonly found in limestone districts. Swallow
   holes can lead to underground *caves* and caverns.

Ria A narrow inlet of the sea that is in fact a drowned river
   estuary. Rias may be caused by the downward sinking of the
   coast or by a rise in sea level. Carrick Roads and the Fal estuary
   in Cornwall form an example of a ria coastline, as does the
   coast of South-west Ireland.

Rift valley This forms when a block of land sinks down between
   long *faults* in the earth's crust: e.g. Great African Rift Valley.

River Terraces Platforms of land lying above the level of the valley
   floor. They are the remains of earlier valley floors and have
   been formed by a river's renewed vertical *erosion*.

Scree This is another name for 'talus'—a pile of loose rocks that
   collect at the foot of mountains or cliffs. Screes are the result of
   rock weathering and form very unstable slopes.

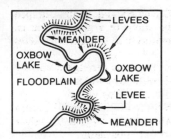 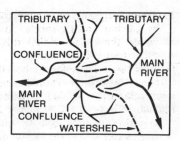

Spit A low ridge of sand and gravel which projects from the land into the sea. It is built up by waves and currents from material transported from another part of the coast. See *bar*.

Strait A narrow stretch of water connecting two large water areas: e.g. the Straits of Gibraltar, connecting the Atlantic and Mediterranean.

Tor An isolated rocky hill often weathered into strange shapes; e.g. the granite tors of Dartmoor.

Tributary A stream or smaller river which joins the main river. The point at which one stream or river joins another is called the confluence.

U-shaped valley A steep-sided trough eroded from an old river valley by a glacier. The *tributaries* often meet the main valleys as *waterfalls* to form *hanging valleys*. See *V-shaped valley*.

Volcano A vent in the earth's surface through which lava, steam and gas are ejected from below the surface. Many volcanoes give rise to conical peaks. See *caldera* and *crater*.

V-shaped valley A valley eroded downwards by a river, but whose slopes have been broadened into a V-shape by weathering. Compare *U-shaped valley* and *canyon*.

Waterfall A vertical fall of river water which often occurs where resistant rocks overlie softer rocks. See *cataract, hanging valley*.

Watershed Also known as a divide, a watershed is the boundary between the drainage area of one river (and *tributaries*) and another. See *basin*.

Weathering The decay and break-up of surface rocks. It can be caused by physical (mechanical) action such as temperature changes, or by chemical action.

THE ATMOSPHERE, CLIMATE AND WEATHER

The earth is surrounded by a layer of air which is known as the *atmosphere*. It provides the gases needed for human, animal and plant life, and also acts as a shield which protects us from the sun's harmful ultraviolet rays. The three main gases of the atmosphere (making up 99·97 per cent of the total) are nitrogen (78·09 per cent), oxygen (20·95 per cent) and argon (0·93 per cent). The remaining 0·03 per cent is made up of minute amounts of other gases including carbon dioxide which is used by plants for photosynthesis. The atmosphere also contains water vapour and specks of dust and salt, the latter coming from sea spray.

Layers of the atmosphere

The atmosphere is divided into four main layers. The lowest zone is known as the *troposphere* which extends to about 18 kilometres over the equator, 10–11 kilometres over the middle latitudes and 8 kilometres over the poles. Most of the air and water vapour in the atmosphere are in the troposphere, which ends in what is known as the *tropopause*.

The *stratosphere* extends from the tropopause to about 80 kilometres above the earth's surface. It contains an important layer of ozone which absorbs harmful radiation from the sun. Strong air currents, moving at more than 60 kilometres an hour, are found in the upper troposphere and lower stratosphere. These so-called *jet-streams* are important to pilots of jet aircraft that fly in these zones.

The *ionosphere* extends for some 80–500 kilometres above the earth. Here the air is extremely rarefied and beyond it is the *exosphere*, where the earth's atmosphere gradually merges into space. Many satellites orbit the earth in the iconosphere.

Other interesting phenomena found in the upper layers of the atmosphere are *meteors* and *aurorae*. Also called shooting stars, meteors consist of large lumps of rocks or metal that sometimes enter the earth's atmosphere, becoming white-hot and glowing. Some leave a trail which is visible for several minutes. The largest known meteorite, estimated to weigh 59 tons, was found in 1920 at Hoba West in Namibia.

Aurorae are lights and colours that occur in the iconosphere and are the result of electrical discharges. They can be seen at night at high latitudes and are particularly common in polar regions. The *aurora borealis* (Northern Lights) occurs in the northern hemisphere and the *aurora australis* in the southern hemisphere.

The circulation of the atmosphere

Weather is the day-to-day conditions of the atmosphere, although most of the features that govern the earth's weather occur in the troposphere. Here the atmosphere is constantly on the move, the chief reason being the heat from the sun. The amount of heat absorbed by the earth's surface varies from place to place. In high latitudes the sun's rays have to pass through a greater thickness of atmosphere and they are also spread out over a larger area (see diagram). It is at the equator that the sun's rays are most concentrated. Here the heated air expands and rises, creating a low-pressure area into which *trade winds* blow from north and south. The *doldrums* is the name given to the area of low pressure around the equator. It is marked by calms: sailing ships tried to avoid the doldrums because they might be stationary for days at a time.

As it rises and spreads north and south, the warm air from the equator cools. Around latitudes 30 degrees north and 30 degrees

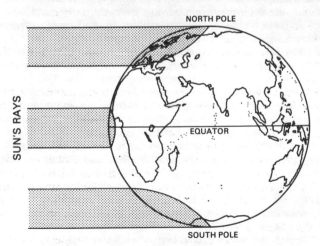

The amount of heat absorbed at the earth's surface

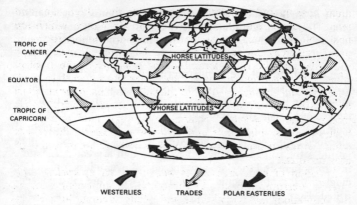

TROPIC OF CANCER

EQUATOR

TROPIC OF CAPRICORN

HORSE LATITUDES

HORSE LATITUDES

WESTERLIES   TRADES   POLAR EASTERLIES

World's major wind belts

south (the *Horse Latitudes*), it finally sinks back to form an area of high pressure. From the Horse Latitudes some of the air flows back to the equator, and some flows towards the poles as winds known as the *westerlies*. These relatively warm westerlies finally meet cold, dense air flowing from the north and south poles. In these ways the winds redistribute heat around the earth's surface.

As the map of the world's major wind belts shows, the air currents do not flow in a north-to-south direction. Instead, they are deflected by the *Coriolis Force*, caused by the earth's rotation on its axis from west to east. This has the effect that winds (and ocean currents) in the northern hemisphere are deflected to the right of the direction in which they are moving. The opposite occurs in the southern hemisphere. The Coriolis Force, therefore, is responsible for the *north-east* and *south-east trade winds*, the *north-westerlies* and *south-westerlies* and the *polar easterlies*.

Air masses

This general pattern of wind systems is greatly complicated by a number of factors, not least the presence of high mountain ranges that deflect the general direction of global winds. Equally important is the distribution of large land and water bodies, for land areas heat up and cool down more quickly than the oceans and seas. These, and other factors, give rise to air masses, which are bodies of air whose physical characteristics are roughly the same over large areas. Air masses over land differ from air masses over the oceans in the same latitudes. For example, in the tropical zone, *tropical maritime* air masses are cooler and wetter than *tropical continental* air masses. Also, in the polar regions, *polar maritime* air masses differ from the colder and drier *polar maritime* air masses. The temperature differences between land and water bodies are very important and give rise to pressure differences where winds are drawn to relatively low pressure areas from high pressure areas.

A region of high pressure is known as an *anticyclone*, the highest pressure occurring in the centre. In anticyclones, weather conditions are fairly stable and winds circulate in a clockwise direction in the northern hemisphere and in an anti-clockwise direction in the southern hemisphere. A *depression* is an area of low air pressure, associated with unsettled, often stormy weather. Where air masses of differing characteristics meet, a *front* is formed which marks the boundary between the two air masses.

In depressions, the *warm front* is the advancing edge of the warm, lighter air at ground level. The *cold front* behind it is the advancing edge of the colder, denser air. Where the cold front

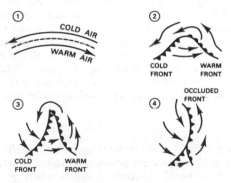

Stages in the development of a depression

overtakes the warm front, the warm air is pushed above ground level, forming an *occluded front* or *occlusion*. Cloudy, rainy weather is associated with the passage of cold and warm fronts and cloud and rain persist for a time along occlusions.

Clouds

The passage of a depression or, indeed, most aspects of a daily weather sequence can be interpreted from cloud types and formations. A cloud is a mass of small water drops or ice crystals, formed by the condensation of water vapour in the atmosphere. This condensation usually occurs at great heights above the earth's surface. The water vapour is the result of evaporation of surface water—oceans, lakes and rivers etc.

Although clouds have a large number of shapes, the three principal formations can be recognised from the translations of their Latin names: *stratus*, a flat layer; *cumulus*, a heap, pile or pack; and *cirrus*, meaning a curl or lock of hair. These frequently combine in other formations. It is helpful to remember that *alto* means high and *nimbo* or *nimbus* means rain.

The internationally agreed classification of clouds is more detailed and describes ten main forms. According to their approximate height above the earth's surface these 10 forms are subdivided as low clouds (up to 2000 metres), medium clouds (2000–6000 metres) and high clouds (6000–12,000 metres). (See following table.)

	Types of Cloud	
Type	*Usual range of height of base in m/ft*	*Description*
Cumulus	300–450 (1,000–1,500)	Flat base, high rounded tops. Small, white, scattered puffs mean fair weather, but heavy, deep clouds often become cumulonimbus.

Type	Usual range of height of base in m/ft	Description
Stratus	Up to 150–600 (500–2,000)	Unbroken grey layer; looks like fog that has lifted from the ground.
Stratocumulus	300–1,400 (1,000–4,500)	Broad layer arranged in round masses or rolls, often so close together that their edges join.
Nimbostratus	Near surface to 6,000 (20,000)	Dark grey with a base that is the same throughout. Often gives continuous rain or snow; if these do not reach the ground the cloud appears to trail.
Cumulonimbus	Up to 600–1,500 (2,000–5,000)	Heavy, dark, very tall—as high as 3 miles. Tops often spread out in anvil-shape. Thunderstorm cloud; gives showers of rain, snow, hail, etc.
Altocumulus	2,000–6,096 (6,500–20,000)	Small, thin rounded patches, resembling cumulus, sometimes so close together their edges meet.
Altostratus	2,005–6,096 (6,580–20,000)	Sheet or veil, sometimes thin, but sometimes so thick it blocks out the moon or even the sun, when it normally indicates continuous rain.
Cirrus	6,096–12,192 (20,000–40,000)	Detached pieces, delicate and feathery ('mares' tails').
Cirrocumulus	6,096–12,192 (20,000–40,000)	Small flakes or rolls in groups or lines ('mackerel sky'). Made up of ice crystals.
Cirrostratus	6,096–12,192 (20,000–40,000)	Thin, milky veil producing a ring of light round the moon.

The Elements of Weather

When applied to weather, precipitation is the deposit of water (in either liquid or solid form) on the earth's surface from the atmosphere. It includes not only rain, but also sleet, snow and hail, which fall from clouds, and dew and hoar frost.

Rain is the main form of precipitation. It falls when water vapour in clouds condenses, the water droplets fusing together to become raindrops. Rain differs from *drizzle* by the size of its water droplets. Raindrops have a diameter greater than 0.5 mm; the diameter of drizzle droplets is $0\cdot2-0\cdot5$ mm.

To understand how and why rain falls, it is necessary to understand *dew point*, which is the temperature at which the air is completely saturated by water vapour. When the temperature falls below dew point, *condensation* occurs and water vapour is changed into water droplets. The temperature of dew point varies because warm air can hold more water vapour than cold air.

The three types of rain are known as *orographic*, *convectional* and *cyclonic*. *Orographic* rain is caused by mountains standing in the path of moisture-laden air. The mountains force the air to rise and when it cools to less than dew point, rain is deposited. *Convectional* rain is caused when the surface layers of the atmosphere are heated, and moisture-laden air rises in a convection current. The air is cooled to below dew point and heavy rain is often deposited. *Cyclonic* rain is associated with the passage of depressions (see page B63). Warm moist air moves upwards over colder, denser air, and when the warm air is cooled to below dew point, rainfall occurs.

Snow falls when the temperature of the atmosphere at cloud level is below freezing; it falls either as individual ice-crystals (always six-sided) or as snow-flakes composed of several ice crystals joined together. Only one-third of the earth's surface experiences snowfalls. Except on high mountain areas, the temperature of the tropics is too warm for snow. On average, 10 centimetres of snow is the equivalent of one centimetre of rain.

Sleet is a mixture of snow and rain. It occurs when the snow has partly melted during its fall to the earth's surface.

Hail consists of ice pellets which fall from clouds, often during thunderstorms. They are caused by the rapid ascent of moist air; the water drops freeze, and the size of the pellets increases as more water vapour freezes onto their surfaces. When they are heavy enough to resist the upward-moving air currents, they fall to the earth's surface.

Dew is moisture deposited by condensation on such things as blades of grass and stones, the moisture coming from water vapour in the air. It occurs at night when the ground surface releases the heat it has stored up during the day, and the air on or immediately above it becomes cooler.

Hoar Frost consists of tiny ice crystals, a kind of frozen dew.

Fog is a mass of small water droplets in the lower air, resulting from air cooling below dew point and water vapour condensing. Fog is, therefore, similar to cloud, except that it occurs near the ground. In some large cities and industrial areas, fog mixes with soot, smoke and gases to produce *smog*, which is harmful to plants, animals and people. Fog is defined as a visibility of less than one kilometre.

Mist is a thinner version of fog where visibility is more than one kilometre, but less than 2 kilometres.

Thunder and lightning These elements are associated with violent storms. Strong upward currents of air form cumulonimbus clouds, and these give rise to heavy rain and sometimes hail. Flashes of lightning are the result of the build-up of static electricity in the clouds, and thunder is produced by the expansion of air, due to the tremendous heat of lightning flashes. Thunderstorms are most numerous in equatorial regions which experience convectional rainfall (page B66).

Wind is an air current, moving with speed in any direction. As well as currents of air that flow across the earth's surface (page B62), there are also upward and downward currents of air. A variety of conditions give rise to local winds, particularly land and sea breezes, which affect coastal and lakeside areas. These breezes are the result of the different rates at which land and water bodies heat up and cool down. This produces local pressure changes, and these determine the direction of the winds.

Wind has an important effect on air temperatures. This is known as the *chill factor*, for wind makes the air feel colder than the thermometer would indicate. As a general rule, subtract 1° C from the temperature for every 3 km per hour wind speed (1° F for every 1 mph). So a strong breeze of 48 km/h (30 mph) in an air temperature of about 15° C (60° F) will feel as cold as if there were no wind and the temperature was about − 1° C (30° F).

Some Violent Kinds of Weather

Typhoons and **hurricanes** are caused by tropical cyclones. These cyclones occur where the pressure of the atmosphere has sunk very much lower than that of the surrounding air. Around its calm centre—known as the 'eye' of the storm—winds of hurricane force (that is, of speeds greater than 121 km (75 mph)) blow continuously. Cyclones cause immense damage in the tropics. They occur most often in the seas of China (typhoons), but nearly as often in the West Indies (hurricanes).

Whirlwinds are like cyclones, having an area of low pressure at their centres, but they are very much smaller, consisting of columns of air whirling very rapidly round an axis that is vertical or nearly so. In the desert they can cause **sandstorms**.

A **tornado** is an extremely violent whirlwind.

A **waterspout** is a tornado occurring at sea; a portion of cloud looking like an upside-down cone reaches down from the base of a thunder-cloud to where it meets a cone of spray raised from the sea to form a continuous column or spout between

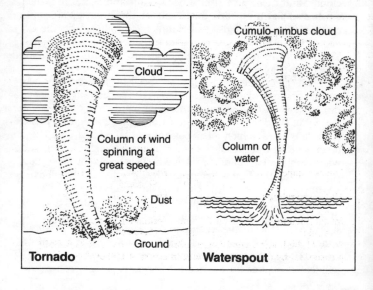

sea and cloud. In the days of sailing-ships waterspouts were
known to tear ships to pieces.
Floods and **droughts** are other examples of the devastating effects
of weather and climate.

World Weather Records

Record	Degree or amount	Where recorded	When recorded
Highest shade temperature	57·8° C (136° F)	San Louis, Mexico	1933
Lowest temperature	−89·2° C (−128° F)	Vostok, Antarctica	21.7.83
Maximum rainfall (24 hours)	1,870 mm (73·62 in)	Cilaos, Ile de Réunion	1952
Maximum rainfall (one month)	9,299 mm (366·14 in)	Cherrapunji, India	1861
Greatest annual total rainfall	26,461 mm (1,042 in)	also at Cherrapunji	1861
Heaviest recorded snowfall in one year	31,102 mm (1,224·5 in)	Mount Ranier Washington State US	1971–2
Largest recorded hailstone	750 grams (11·67 lbs)	Kansas US	1970

British Weather Records

Highest temperature	37°1 C (98° F)	Cheltenham	1990
	37° C (98° F)	Raunds, Northants; Epsom, Surrey and Canterbury, Kent	1911
Lowest temperature	−27·2° C (−17° F)	Braemar, Scotland	1895 and 1982
Maximum rainfall (24 hours)	279 mm (11 in)	Martinstown, nr Dorchester	1955
Maximum annual rainfall	6,527 mm (257 in)	Sprinkling Tarn, Cumberland	1954

Some of the highest wind gusts in Britain were recently (16.1.90)
recorded in the Hebrides. They were in excess of 100 mph.

Further Reading

A Dictionary of Geography, by W. G. Moore (Penguin)

Standard Encyclopaedia of the World's Oceans and Islands, ed. Anthony Huxley (Weidenfeld & Nicolson)

The Observer's Book of The Weather (Warne)

Our Planet Earth (Ward Lock)

Encyclopaedia of the World (Hamlyn)

The Children's World Atlas (Longmans)

The Physical Earth (Mitchell Beazley)

The Modern World (Mitchell Beazley)

THE WORLD

3: ITS FAMOUS PEOPLE
(*Actual and Mythical*)

In *A Dictionary of Famous People* are to be found short biographies of great men and women who lived in both the distant and the recent past. Those in *A Dictionary of Mythology* were, of course, never alive at all, in any ordinary sense—they are the gods and goddesses found in the myths and legends of ancient peoples.

A DICTIONARY OF FAMOUS PEOPLE

When the story of a human life, a biography, is told very briefly it is called a potted biography. The biographies in this section have been potted and then potted again. They are meant to answer the following questions: 'Who were they?' 'When did they live?' 'Where did they come from?' 'What did they do?' For fuller details you should, of course, consult either a separate biography of your man or woman or one of the big encyclopaedias that are devoted entirely to telling the stories of famous lives. (For famous Britons the best source of all is the *Dictionary of National Biography*.)

Left out of this section are most of those people whose achievements are mentioned elsewhere; for example,

> Kings and Queens of England and Scotland (HISTORY);
> British writers (THE ENGLISH LANGUAGE);
> Explorers and discoverers (HISTORY);
> Painters, sculptors and architects (THE ARTS).

In the case of other historical figures, dates of birth and death are given and you are advised to 'see HISTORY'—which usually means the DIARY OF WORLD EVENTS. In some instances people who appear elsewhere in the book are treated fully here (e.g. Captain Scott); this is because there is something important to add that has not been said in the other section where the mention occurs.

The letter *c*. before a date (e.g. *c*. 450 B.C.) is short for the Latin *circa*, 'about', and means that the date is not certainly known.

Aeschylus (*c*. 525–456 B.C.), Greek tragic dramatist.

Akbar, Jalal-ud-din Mohammed (1542–1605), greatest of the Mogul emperors.

Alaric 1st (376–410), King of the Visigoths, who sacked Rome.

Alban, St, lived in the last part of the 3rd century; served as soldier in Rome, was converted to Christianity and, returning to Britain to preach, was martyrised.

Alcibiades (*c*. 450–404 B.C.), Athenian statesman and general, pupil of Socrates.

Alcott, Louisa May (1832–88), American writer, author of *Little Women*.

Alexander II (1818–81), Czar of Russia who emancipated the serfs; assassinated by Nihilists.

Alexander the Great (356–323 B.C.), see HISTORY.

Alfred the Great (849–99), see HISTORY.

Ampère, André Marie (1775–1836), French mathematician, the first to propound the electro-dynamic theory.

Andersen, Hans Christian (1805–75), Danish storyteller and poet; author of famous fairy tales.

Anderson, Elizabeth Garrett (1836–1917), the first woman to practice medicine in England.

Andrew, St, one of Jesus' disciples, and patron saint of Scotland; commemorated on 30 November.

Anselm, St (1033–1109), Archbishop of Canterbury; quarrelled with William Rufus about the authority of the Pope, but regained his position under Henry I.

Antonius Marcus (Mark Antony) (*c*. 83–30 B.C.), see HISTORY.

Aquinas, Thomas, St (*c*. 1225–74), Italian religious teacher and philosopher.

Archimedes (*c*. 287–212 B.C.), Greek mathematician, physicist and inventor; made many discoveries in mechanics (notably the lever) and invented the Archimedean screw. Killed during siege of Syracuse by Romans.

Aristophanes (*c.* 450–*c.* 385 B.C.), Greek comic dramatist.

Aristotle (384–322 B.C.), Greek philosopher and pupil of Plato; took the whole field of knowledge as his subject.

Arkwright, Sir Richard (1732–92), pioneer of British cotton industry.

Arne, Thomas (1710–78), English composer.

Arnold, Thomas (1795–1842), headmaster of Rugby; regarded as the creator of the modern Public School system. The original of the headmaster in *Tom Brown's Schooldays*.

Arthur (*c.* 600), Celtic warrior about whom a great deal of legend has collected.

Atatürk, Kemal (1881–1938), creator of modern Turkey.

Attila (*c.* 406–53), king of the Huns, see HISTORY.

Attlee, 1st Earl (1883–1967), Deputy Prime Minister, 1942–5; Prime Minister, 1945–51.

Augustine, St (354–430), religious philosopher and teacher.

Augustine, St, missionary monk sent to Britain in 597; first Archbishop of Canterbury. Died in 604.

Augustus Caesar (63 B.C.–A.D. 14), first Emperor of Rome; see HISTORY.

Bach, Johann Sebastian (1685–1750), great German composer.

Bacon, Francis, Lord Verulam (1561–1626), English philosopher and statesman; Attorney-General under Elizabeth, Lord Chancellor under James I; author of *Novum Organum* and *Essays*.

Bacon, Roger (*c.* 1214–94), Franciscan friar, the first man in modern times to insist on the importance of experiment in science.

Baden–Powell, Lord (1857–1941), famous for his defence of Mafeking during Boer War; founded Boy Scouts (1908) and Girl Guides (1910).

Baird, John Logie (1888–1946), pioneer of television.

Bakewell, Robert (1725–95), pioneer of modern agriculture.

Ball, John (d. 1381), English priest who was a leader of the Peasants' Revolt.

Balzac, Honoré de (1799–1850), great French novelist; author of 80 novels with the general title of *La Comédie Humaine*.

Banks, Sir Joseph (1744–1820), English botanist and 'father of Australia'.

Barnado, Dr Thomas (1845–1905), devoted his life to the welfare of homeless children; founder of the homes named after him.

Baudelaire, Charles (1821–67), French poet, whose work has had an immense influence on modern poetry.

Becket, St Thomas à (1118–70), see HISTORY.

Bede, 'The Venerable' (c. 673–735), monk and historian, 'the father of English history'.

Beethoven, Ludwig van (1770–1827), great German composer.

Bell, Alexander Graham (1847–1922), inventor of the telephone.

Benedict, St (c. 480–544), founded the Order of Benedictine monks.

Bentham, Jeremy (1748–1832), radical writer and thinker; helped develop the Utilitarian philosophy that the aim of politics should be 'the greatest happiness of the greatest number'.

Berlioz, Hector (1803–69), French composer.

Bernard, St (923–1008), Cistercian monk, patron saint of mountaineers.

Bernhardt, Sarah (1845–1923), famous French tragic actress.

Bismarck, Prince Otto (1815–98), see HISTORY.

Blake, Robert (1599–1657), Parliamentary general in the Civil War; admiral in the wars against Holland and Spain.

Blériot, Louis (1872–1936), French inventor and aviator; first to fly the English Channel, 1909.

Blondin, Charles (1824–97), French tight-rope walker famous for his crossing of the Niagara Falls.

Boadicea (d. A.D. 62), see HISTORY.

Boccaccio, Giovanni (1313–75), Italian novelist and poet.

Bolivar, Simon (1783–1830), 'the Liberator'; revolutionary who broke Spanish power in South America; first president of Venezuela and Dictator of Peru.

Boone, Daniel (1734–1820), American explorer and settler.

Booth, William (1829–1912), founder and first general of the Salvation Army.

Borgia, Cesar (1476–1507), son of Pope Alexander VI, made himself ruler of Romagna by murdering those who stood in his way. Banished by Pope Julius II and died in the invasion of Castile.

Botha, General Louis (1862–1919), Boer general who became first Premier of South Africa.

Boyle, Robert (1627–91), English scientist; the first man to distinguish between a mixture and a compound. Author of Boyle's Law (see DICTIONARY OF SCIENCE AND MATHEMATICS).

Bragg, Sir William (1862–1942), English scientist who received the 1915 Nobel Prize with his son, **Sir Lawrence Bragg** (b. 1890), for their work on X-rays and crystal structures.

Brahms, Johannes (1833–97), German composer.

Brecht, Bertolt (1898–1959), German dramatist and poet.

Bright, John (1811–89), famous Radical statesman, one of those responsible for the introduction of Free Trade.

Britten, Benjamin (1913–1976), English composer.

Brown, Sir Arthur Whitten (1886–1948), made the first transatlantic flight in 1919 with Sir John Alcock.

Brown, John (1800–1859), fanatical opponent of slavery in America. He was hanged for having incited slaves to rebel, and his death was a signal for the outbreak of the Civil War.

Bruce, Robert (1274–1329), see HISTORY.

Brummell, George (1778–1840), 'Beau Brummell', leader of fashion in English society when George IV was Prince Regent.

Brunel, Isambard Kingdom (1806–59), engineer and steamship-designer: constructed Clifton Suspension Bridge and much of the G.W. Railway.

Brunel, Sir Mark Isambard (1769–1849), father of Isambard, and constructor of the Thames tunnel.

Brutus, Marcus (85–42 B.C.), see HISTORY.

Buddha (Sidharta Gautama), the founder of Buddhism in the 6th century B.C.

Burghley, William Cecil, Lord (1520–1598), principal adviser to Queen Elizabeth for 40 years.

Burke, Edmund (1729–97), political philosopher, statesman and orator: most famous for his attacks on the French Revolution.

Butler, Josephine (1828–1906), social reformer.

Byrd, William (1543–1623), English composer.

Cabot, John (c. 1455–c. 1498), see EXPLORATIONS AND DISCOVERIES.

Cabot, Sebastian (c. 1493–1557), see EXPLORATIONS AND DISCOVERIES.

Caesar, Caius Julius (c. 101–44 B.C.), see HISTORY.

Calvin, John (1509–64), French religious reformer who preached his severe doctrine (Calvinism), in Geneva, where he created a Protestant republic.

Campbell, Sir Malcolm (1885–1948), racing driver who held land and water speed records.

Canute the Great (995–1035), see HISTORY.

Carnegie, Andrew (1835–1919), son of poor Scottish weaver who became American multi-millionaire; gave away most of his money to benefit the public, especially the founding of libraries.

Cartier, Jaques (1491–1557), see EXPLORATIONS AND DISCOVERIES.

Casabianca, Louis de (c. 1754–98), captain of a French warship at the Battle of the Nile; he and his 10-year-old son refused to leave the burning ship and died together.

Cassius, Caius (d. 42 B.C.), see HISTORY.

Catherine the Great (1729–96), Empress of Russia; came to the throne by deposing and murdering her husband, the weak Peter; carried Russia's frontiers by conquest to the Black Sea and the borders of Germany.

Cato, Marcus Porcius (234–149 B.C.), Roman statesman, soldier and writer; opposed the luxurious living of his times.

Cavell, Edith (1865–1915), British nurse shot by the Germans for helping wounded British soldiers to escape from Belgium.

Cavour, Count Camillo de (1810–61), one of the founders of modern Italy.

Caxton, William (c. 1422–91), founder of the first English printing press.

Cecilia, Saint, the patron saint of music: martyrised c. A.D. 176.

Cervantes, Saavedra, Miguel de (1547–1616), Spanish novelist, author of *Don Quixote*.

Chaplin, Sir Charles Spencer (1889–1977), the most famous of all film comedians.

Charlemagne (742–814), see HISTORY.

Charles V (1510–58), Holy Roman Emperor who ruled Austria, the Netherlands and Spain.

Chatham, William Pitt, Earl of (1708–78), statesman and Parliamentarian, in control of English policy during Seven Years War.

Chekhov, Anton (1860–1904), great Russian dramatist and short-story writer; author of *The Cherry Orchard*, etc.

Chippendale, Thomas (c. 1717–79), famous furniture designer.

Chopin, Frédéric (1810–49), Polish composer and pianist.

Churchill, Sir Winston (1874–1965), British statesman and author: Prime Minister 1940–45 and 1951–55.

Cicero, Marcus Tullius (106–43 B.C.), most eloquent of the Roman orators.

Cierva, Juan de la (1895–1936), Spanish engineer who invented the autogiro.

Claudius I (10 B.C.–A.D. 54), Roman Emperor; erected many great buildings; visited Britain; murdered by his wife Agrippina.

Clemens, Samuel Langhorne ('Mark Twain') (1835–1910), American writer and humorist, author of *Tom Sawyer* and *Huckleberry Finn*.

Cleopatra (69–30 B.C.), see HISTORY.

Clive, Robert, Lord (1725–74), English general, victor of Plassey, who laid the foundations of the British empire in India.

Cobbett, William (1762–1835), politician, social reformer and writer, author of *Rural Rides*.

Cobden, Richard (1804–1865), statesman, economist and advocate of Free Trade.

Cody, Samuel (1861–1913), the first man to fly in Britain, 1908.

Cody, William (1846–1917), American plainsman and showman known as 'Buffalo Bill'.

Coke, Sir Edward (1552–1634), great English jurist.

Coke, Thomas William (1752–1842), pioneer of scientific farming.

Columbus, Christopher (1451–1506), see EXPLORATIONS AND DISCOVERIES.

Confucius (*c.* 551–479 B.C.), the most celebrated of the Chinese philosophers.

Cook, Capt. James (1728–79), see EXPLORATIONS AND DISCOVERIES.

Copernicus, Nicholas (1743–1543), Polish founder of modern astronomy; author of the Copernican theory that the planets revolve round the sun.

Corneille, Pierre (1606–84), French tragic dramatist.

Cortes, Hernando (1485–1547), Spanish conqueror of Mexico.

Cranmer, Thomas (1489–1556), first Protestant Archbishop of Canterbury; see HISTORY.

Crispin, St (3rd century), patron of shoemakers: commemorated on 25 October.

Croesus (d. *c.* 546 B.C.), last king of Lydia (part of modern Turkey), celebrated for his fabulous wealth.

Crockett, Davy (1786–1836), American frontiersman; fought in Congress for a fair deal for the Red Indians; killed at the Battle of Alamo.

Cromwell, Oliver (1599–1658), see HISTORY.

Cruikshank, George (1792–1878), famous book illustrator and caricaturist.

Cunard, Sir Samuel (1787–1861), founder of the shipping company which became the Cunard Line.

Curie, Pierre (1859–1906) and **Marie** (1867–1934), pioneers of the science of radioactivity, and first to isolate radium.

Daguerre, Louis (1789–1851), French inventor of the earliest photographic process (the daguerrotype).

Daimler, Gottlieb (1834–90), German inventor with N. A. Otto of the Otto gas engine, and also of the motor-car named after him (see CARS).

Dalton, John (1766–1844), English scientist who discovered atomic theory.

Damien, Father Joseph (1840–89), Belgian missionary who volunteered to look after lepers in Honolulu, and himself died of the disease.

Dante, Alighieri (1265–1321), greatest of the Italian poets, author of the *Divine Comedy*.

Danton, Georges (1759–94), President of the Committee of Public Safety during the first French Revolution; supplanted by Robespierre and guillotined.

Darius I (548–485 B.C.), see HISTORY.

Darling, Grace (1815–42), English lighthouse-keeper's daughter famous for saving a shipwrecked crew by putting out with her father in a small boat.

Darnley, Earl of (1545–67), Mary Queen of Scots' second husband, murdered after Mary had entered into an intrigue with Bothwell.

Darwin, Charles (1809–82), English naturalist whose *Origin of the Species* first set out the theory of evolution by means of natural selection.

David (1038–970 B.C.), king who united Israelites in Canaan.

David, St (6th century), patron saint of Wales.

Davis, Jefferson (1808–89), President of the Confederate States during the American Civil War.

Davy, Sir Humphrey (1778–1829), scientist who invented miners' lamp.

Debussy, Claude (1862–1918), French composer.

De Gaulle, General Charles (1890–1970), led Free French in Second World War; President of France, 1958–69.

De Havilland, Sir Geoffrey (1882–1965), a pioneer of civil and military aviation.

Democritus (*c.* 460–357 B.C.), Greek philosopher to whom the conception of the atomic theory is attributed.

Demosthenes (385–322 B.C.), most famous of the Athenian orators; he roused the Athenians to resist Philip of Macedon.

Descartes, René (1596–1650), French philosopher and mathematician.

Diaghilev, Sergei (1872–1929), Russian ballet impresario and founder of the Ballets Russes.

Diocletian (245–313), Roman Emperor under whom the Christians were ruthlessly persecuted; see HISTORY.

Diogenes (412–322 B.C.), Greek philosopher who scorned wealth and social conventions and is said to have lived in a tub.

Disraeli, Benjamin (Earl of Beaconsfield) (1804–81), see HISTORY.

Dominic, St (1170–1221), founder of the Order of Dominicans, or Black Friars.

Dostoevsky, Feodor (1821–81), one of the greatest Russian novelists, author of *Crime and Punishment.*

Drake, Sir Francis (*c.* 1540–96), see HISTORY.

Dumas, Alexandre (1802–70), prolific French novelist and dramatist, author of *The Count of Monte Cristo* and *The Three Musketeers.*

Dunstan, St (909–88), famous Abbot of Glastonbury and Archbishop of Canterbury, who lived through seven reigns.

Duval, Claude (1643–70), notorious French-born highwayman, hanged at Tyburn.

Dvorak, Antonin (1841–1904), Czech composer.

Edison, Thomas Alva (1847–1931), inventor of electric lighting and the gramophone.

Eiffel, Alexandre (1832–1923), French engineer who built the Eiffel Tower and the locks on the Panama Canal.

Einstein, Albert (1879–1955), German mathematical physicist and one of the greatest of all men of science; author of the theory of relativity.

Elgar, Sir Edward (1857–1934), English composer.

Emmet, Robert (1778–1803), Irish patriot; he led a rebellion in 1803, and was executed for high treason.

Empedocles (*c.* 500–*c.* 430 B.C.), Greek philosopher, founder of a school of medicine which regarded the heart as the seat of life.

Epicurus (342–270 B.C.), Greek philosopher who taught that pleasure was the chief good of man and was to be attained through the practice of virtue.

Erasmus, Desiderius (1466–1536), Dutch scholar and philosopher, one of the great figures of the Renaissance.

Essex, Robert Devereux, Earl of (1567–1601), Queen Elizabeth's favourite; he conspired against her and was executed.

Euclid (*c.* 330–*c.* 260 B.C.), Greek mathematician who laid the foundations of modern geometry.

Euripides (480–406 B.C.), great Athenian tragic dramatist.

Evelyn, John (1620–1706), famous for his diaries, and one of the founders of the Royal Society.

Fabius Maximus ('Cunctator') (d. 203 B.C.), the Roman dictator who saved Rome from Hannibal by deliberately avoiding battle. From this policy comes the term 'Fabian tactics'.

Fabre, Jean (1823–1915), French naturalist, life-long observer of the habits of insects.

Fahrenheit, Gabriel (1686–1736), German physicist, inventor of the method of grading a thermometer which bears his name.

Faraday, Michael (1791–1867), English physicist and chemist, founder of the science of electro-magnetism.

Fawcett, Millicent Garrett (1847–1929), educational reformer and leader of the movement for women's suffrage.

Fawkes, Guy (1570–1606), a Yorkshire Catholic, one of the conspirators in the Gunpowder Plot; he was captured in the cellar of Parliament House, tried and executed.

Ferdinand of Spain (1452–1516) and **Isabella** (1451–1504), see HISTORY.

Flaubert, Gustave (1821–80), one of the greatest French novelists.

Fleming, Sir Alexander (1881–1955), discoverer of penicillin.

Fokker, Anthony (1860–1939), famous Dutch airman and aeronautical engineer.

Fonteyn, Margot (1919–1991), the most famous of all British ballerinas.

Ford, Henry (1863–1947), founder of the Ford Motor Co. and pioneer of the cheap motor-car.

Forester, Cecil Scott (1899–1966), author, creator of Hornblower.

Fox, Charles James (1749–1806), Whig statesman who favoured American independence and opposed the war with France.

Fox, George (1624–91), founder of the Society of Friends (the Quakers).

Francis of Assisi, St (1182–1226), founder of the Franciscan Order of monks; lover of flowers, animals and birds.

Franco, General Don Francisco (1892–1975), Head of Spanish State, 1936–75.

Franklin, Benjamin (1706–90), American statesman, philosopher and scientist; played an important part in framing the constitution of the U.S.A.; invented the lightning conductor.

Franklin, Rosalind (1920–58), British scientist who played an important part in the discovery of the structure of DNA.

Frederick I (*c.* 1123–90), Holy Roman Emperor and German national hero; drowned on his way to the Third Crusade.

Frederick II (the Great) (1712–86), King of Prussia; see HISTORY.

Freud, Sigmund (1856–1939), Austrian psychiatrist and founder of psycho-analysis.

Frost, Robert (1874–1963), distinguished American poet.

Fry, Elizabeth (1780–1845), Quaker prison reformer.

Galen, Claudius (131–201), Greek physician, who made important discoveries in anatomy.

Galileo (1564–1642), great Italian mathematician, physicist and astronomer.

Galton, Sir Francis (1822–1911), founder of eugenics and inventor of the device of finger-print identification.

Galvani, Luigi (1737–98), Italian physicist and doctor, who demonstrated the principle of animal electricity.

Gandhi, Indira (1917–84), Indian Prime Minister from 1969 to 1977, and from 1980 until her assassination.

Gandhi, Mohandas Karamchand (1869–1948), great Indian patriot, social reformer and teacher, driving spirit of the movement for national independence.

Garibaldi, Giuseppe (1807–82), Italian patriot who fought for the unification of Italy.

Garrick, David (1717–79), the leading tragic actor of his day.

George, St, patron saint of England; believed to have been a champion of Christianity during the days of Diocletian, and to have been martyrised in A.D. 303.

Gershwin, George (1898–1937), American jazz pianist and composer; wrote *Rhapsody in Blue* and the Negro opera, *Porgy and Bess*.

Gibbons, Grinling (1648–1720), celebrated wood-carver and sculptor.

Gilbert, Sir William Schwenck (1836–1911), English humorist and playwright, best remembered for the famous Savoy operas, in which he collaborated with Sir Arthur Sullivan.

Gladstone, William Ewart (1809–98), see HISTORY.

Glendower, Owen (1359–1415), Welsh chieftain who opposed Henry IV.

Gluck, Christoph von (1714–87), composer, born in Bohemia.

Goethe, Johann Wolfgang von (1749–1832), the most celebrated German writer; novelist, poet, philosopher and scientist.

Gordon, Charles, General (1833–85), see HISTORY.

Gordon, Lord George (1751–93), instigator of the Anti-Popery riots of 1780.

Gorki, Maxim (1868–1936), Russian novelist.

Grace, Dr William (1845–1915), famous cricketer who dominated the game for over 40 years. Altogether he scored 54,896 runs, including 126 centuries, and took 2,876 wickets.

Grahame-White, Claude (1879–1959), the first Englishman to be granted a British certificate of proficiency in aviation, 1909.

Grant, Ulysses Simpson (1822–85), the most famous American general of the Civil War; twice President of the U.S.A.

Gregory, St (257–336), founder of the Armenian Church; his festival is 9 March.

Gregory the Great, St (c. 540–604), one of the most important of the Popes, 590–604.

Gregory XIII (1502–85), Pope who introduced the Gregorian calendar.

Grenville, Sir Richard (1541–91), Elizabethan sea-captain who, with his one ship, the *Revenge*, fought a fleet of Spanish warships in 1591 and died on the deck of the *San Pablo*.

Grieg, Edvard (c. 1843–1907), Norwegian composer.

Grey, Lady Jane (1537–54), see HISTORY.

Grimaldi, Joseph (1779–1837), great English clown.

Grimm, the brothers **Jakob** (1785–1863) and **Wilhelm** (1786–1859), German philologists and folk-lorists who collected the famous fairy-tales.

Gustavus Adolphus (1594–1632), King of Sweden; see HISTORY.

Gwynn, Nell (1650–87), the dancer and actress who became mistress to Charles II.

Hadrian (76–138), see HISTORY.

Hakluyt, Richard (*c.* 1552–1616), geographer; first of the English naval historians.

Halley, Edmund (1656–1742), Astronomer Royal; made first magnetic survey of the oceans, and discovered the comet named after him.

Hampden, John (1594–1643), one of the leaders in Parliament's quarrel with Charles I.

Handel, George Frederick (1685–1759), composer.

Hannibal (247–183 B.C.), see HISTORY.

Hardicanute (1019–42), son of Canute the Great, and the last Danish king of England; imposed the tax known as Danegeld.

Hardie, James Keir (1856–1915), first Socialist M.P. (1892).

Hargreaves, James (d. 1778), inventor and pioneer of modern wool industry.

Haroun-al-Rashid (763–809), the most famous Caliph of Baghdad; hero of the *Arabian Nights*.

Harris, Joel Chandler (1848–1908), American author of the Uncle Remus stories.

Harte, Francis Bret (1839–1902), American poet and author, famous for his stories of Californian mining life.

Harvey, William (1578–1657), English doctor who discovered circulation of the blood.

Hastings, Warren (1732–1818), first Governor-General of India; impeached on charges of cruelty and corruption and acquitted after a trial stretching over 7 years.

Havelock, Sir Henry (1795–1857), hero of the relief of Cawnpore and Lucknow in the Indian Mutiny.

Hawke, Edward, Lord (1705–81), victorious admiral in the battle of Quiberon, fought against the French in a storm, 1759.

Hawkins, Sir John (1532–95), Elizabethan naval officer, vice-admiral in the battle with the Spanish Armada.

Hawthorne, Nathaniel (1804–64), American novelist, author of *The Scarlet Letter*.

Haydn, Franz Joseph (1732–1809), Austrian composer.

Heine, Heinrich (1797–1856), German lyric poet.

Hemingway, Ernest (1898–1961), American novelist, author of *A Farewell to Arms* and *For Whom the Bell Tolls*.

Henry the Navigator (1394–1460), Portuguese prince who inspired many voyages of exploration down the Atlantic coast of Africa.

C14 THE WORLD: ITS FAMOUS PEOPLE

Hepplewhite, George (d. 1786), one of the four great 18th-century cabinet-makers (the others were Chippendale, Robert Adam and Sheraton).

Hereward the Wake, the last of the Saxon chiefs to hold out against the Normans.

Herod the Great (c. 73–4 B.C.), King of Judea under the Romans; to him is attributed the massacre of the innocents.

Herodotus (c. 485–425 B.C.), Greek historian, called 'the father of history'.

Herschel, Sir John (1792–1871), celebrated astronomer.

Herschel, Sir William (1738–1822), father of the last-named; discoverer of the planet Uranus and the satellites of Saturn.

Hill, Sir Rowland (1795–1879), originator of the penny post.

Hippocrates (c. 460–c. 370 B.C.), Greek physician: the 'father of medicine'. Rules of conduct for doctors are still based on his Hippocratic Oath.

Hitler, Adolf (1889–1945), see HISTORY.

Hobbes, Thomas (1588–1679), English philosopher, advocate of strong government, author of *Leviathan*.

Homer (c. 700 B.C.), most famous of all epic poets, and regarded as the author of the *Iliad* and the *Odyssey*; seven Greek towns vie for the honour of having been his birthplace.

Hood, Samuel, Lord (1724–1816), British admiral who captured Toulon and Corsica, 1793.

Hopkins, Sir Frederick Gowland (1861–1947), English biochemist noted for his work on proteins and vitamins.

Horace (65–8 B.C.), great Roman satirist and poet.

Houdini, Harry (1873–1926), American locksmith who went on the stage as an expert in escaping from handcuffs, locked rooms, etc.

Howard, John (1726–90), prison reformer.

Howe, Richard, Earl (1726–99), British admiral who won a famous victory ('the Glorious First of June') over the French in 1794 off Brest.

Hugo, Victor (1802–85), great French poet, dramatist and novelist, author of *Les Misérables* and *The Hunchback of Notre Dame*.

Hume, David (1711–76), Scottish historian and philosopher.

Hunter, the brothers **William** (1718–83) and **John** (1728–93), both famous Scottish physicians, who made many discoveries in anatomy. John is regarded as the founder of modern surgery.

Huss, John (1369–1415), Bohemian religious reformer, whose death by burning alive led to a half century of civil war.

Huxley, Thomas Henry (1825–95), English naturalist and ardent supporter of the theory of evolution of Charles Darwin (*q.v.*).

Ibsen, Henrik (1828–1906), Norwegian writer, one of the world's greatest dramatists.

Innocent III (1160–1216), powerful Pope who initiated the 4th Crusade.

Irving, Sir Henry (1838–1905), great English actor, and the first to be knighted.

Ivan the Terrible (1530–84), first Czar of Russia, who earned his name by his cruel treatment of his subjects.

Jackson, Andrew (1767–1845), American general, twice President of the U.S.A.

Jackson, Thomas (1824–63), most successful general on the Southern side in the American Civil War; known as 'Stonewall' Jackson for the dogged fight he put up at the First Battle of Bull Run.

James, Henry (1843–1916), great Anglo-American novelist.

Jefferson, Thomas (1743–1826), drew up the American Declaration of Independence; twice U.S. President.

Jeffreys, George, Lord (1648–89), judge notorious for his harsh judgements, especially during the so-called 'Bloody Assize', held to try the followers of the Duke of Monmouth who had rebelled against James II.

Jenghiz Khan (1162–1227), Mogul ruler who twice conquered China and drove the Turks back into Europe.

Jenner, Edward (1749–1823), English country doctor who discovered vaccination as a means of preventing smallpox.

Jerome, Jerome K. (1859–1927), humorous writer, author of *Three Men in a Boat*.

Jesus Christ (*c.* 4 B.C.–A.D. 30 or 33), the founder of Christianity; born at Bethlehem, the first-born of His mother Mary. According to Matthew, His birth was miraculous and Joseph was His foster-father. He learned His father's trade of carpentry at Nazareth, and began His mission when He was about thirty. A summary of His teaching is found in the Sermon on the Mount.

Joan of Arc, St (1412–31), see HISTORY.

John, St, the Baptist (executed A.D. 28), the forerunner of Jesus Christ.

Johnson, Amy (1904–41), first woman aviator to fly solo from England to Australia.

Jones, John Paul (1747–92), Scottish mariner who commanded the American fleet during the War of Independence.

Josephine, Empress (1763–1814), wife of Napoleon I until he divorced her and married Marie-Louise.

Julian the Apostate (331–63), Roman Emperor who professed Christianity until the last two years of his life, when he tried to re-establish paganism.

Jung, Carl (1875–1961), Swiss psychiatrist.

Justinian I (*c*. 483–565), see HISTORY.

Kant, Immanuel (1724–1804), German scientist and philosopher.

Kean, Edmund (1787–1833), one of the greatest English tragic actors.

Kelvin, William Thomson, Lord (1824–1907), scientist and inventor; made important discoveries in the field of thermodynamics (the branch of physics dealing with heat).

Kemble, Frances ('Fanny') (1809–93), noted actress, and member of a famous theatrical family, which included her father, **Charles Kemble** (1775–1854), her uncle **John Philip Kemble**, a famous tragic actor, and her aunt Mrs Siddons (*q.v.*).

Kennedy, John Fitzgerald (1917–63), President of the United States from 1961 until his assassination at Dallas, Texas, in November 1963.

Kepler, Johann (1571–1630), German astronomer who worked out the laws of planetary motion.

Khayyam, Omar (11th century), Persian poet and mathematician, whose *Rubaiyat* was translated by the English poet, Edward Fitzgerald.

Kidd, Captain William (*c*. 1645–1701), famous pirate whose crimes were committed under cover of the British flag. Hanged at Execution Dock in London.

King, Martin Luther (1929–68), leader of the black American campaign for civil rights: assassinated.

Kitchener, Horatio, Lord (1850–1916), reconquered the Sudan (1897); Commander-in-Chief in the Boer War; Secretary of State for War, 1914–16. Drowned when the troopship *Hampshire* was sunk by a mine.

Knox, John (1505–72), see HISTORY.

Kruger, Paul (1825–1904), President of the Transvaal who was leader of the Boers in the bitter quarrel with the British that led to the Boer War.

Kruschev, Nikita Sergeyevich (1894–1971), Russian Prime Minister, 1958–64. See HISTORY.

Kublai Khan (1216–94), Mogul Emperor, grandson of Jenghiz Khan; he greatly extended the empire and lived in extraordinary splendour.

Lafayette, Marie-Joseph, Marquis de (1757–1834), French statesman and general, who took an active part in the American War of Independence.

La Fontaine, Jean de (1621–95), French poet and fablewriter.

Lamarck, Jean Baptiste, Chevalier de (1744–1829), French naturalist, author of a theory of the evolution of animals, known as Lamarckism.

Landseer, Sir Edwin (1802–73), most famous English animal painter of his day; designed the lions which are part of the Nelson Monument in Trafalgar Square.

Lanfranc (*c.* 1005–89), Archbishop of Canterbury in the time of William the Conqueror.

Langton, Stephen (1151–1228), Archbishop of Canterbury; one of the leaders of the group that compelled King John to sign the Magna Carta.

Lasker, Emmanuel (1868–1941), world chess champion, 1894–1921.

Latimer, Hugh (*c.* 1485–1555), Bishop of Worcester, one of the founders of English Protestantism; burned at the stake in Oxford.

Laud, William (1573–1645), Archbishop of Canterbury; favourite and chief minister of Charles I; tried for treason and executed under the Long Parliament.

Lavoisier, Antoine (1743–94), French chemist who gave oxygen its name and was the first to establish that combustion is a form of chemical action; guillotined during the French Revolution.

Lawrence, John, Lord (1811–79), marched to the relief of Delhi in the Indian Mutiny.

Lawrence, Thomas Edward ('Lawrence of Arabia') (1888–1935), British soldier and archaeologist; led the Arabs against the Turks in the First World War; described his campaign in *Seven Pillars of Wisdom*.

Leacock, Stephen (1869–1944), Canadian economist and humorous writer.

Lee, Robert Edward (1807–70), Commander-in-Chief of the Southern forces in the American Civil War.

Leibnitz, Gottfried (1646–1716), discovered, independently of Newton, the differential calculus.

Leicester, Robert Dudley, Earl of (1531–88), favourite of Queen Elizabeth and leader of the English forces in the Low Countries, 1585–7.

Lenin, Vladimir Ilyich (1870–1924), see HISTORY.

Leonidas, King of Sparta when Greece was invaded by Xerxes, 480 B.C.; killed leading the defence of the Pass of Thermopylae.

Lesseps, Ferdinand, Vicomte de (1805–94), French engineer responsible for building the Suez Canal.

Lilburne, John (1614–57), English politician and pamphleteer, leader of the Levellers during the English Revolution.

Lincoln, Abraham (1809–65), President of the United States whose pronouncement against slavery led to the outbreak of the Civil War. Soon after the victory of the North, he was assassinated while at the theatre by a fanatical anti-abolitionist, John Wilkes Booth.

Linnaeus, Carl (1707–78), Swedish naturalist, founder of modern botany; he devised a system for naming and classifying plants and animals (see NATURAL HISTORY).

Lister, Joseph, Lord (1827–1912), English surgeon who first established the need for antiseptics in surgical operations.

Liszt, Franz (1811–86), Hungarian composer and pianist.

Livy (59 B.C.–A.D. 17), great Roman historian.

Lloyd George, David, Earl of Dwyfor (1865–1945), see HISTORY.

Locke, John (1632–1704), English philosopher and founder of empiricism, which is the doctrine that all knowledge is derived from experience.

London, John ('Jack') (1876–1916), American novelist, author of *White Fang, Call of the Wild*.

Longfellow, Henry Wadsworth (1807–82), American poet, author of *Hiawatha*.

Lonsdale, Earl of (1857–1944), distinguished sportsman who presented the Lonsdale belts for boxing.

Lope de Vega, Felix (1562–1615), Spanish dramatist and author of more than 2,000 plays.

Louis XIV (1638–1715), King of France for 72 years; called *le grande monarque* (the great king), he gave expression to the idea of absolute monarchy, in which the king claims complete power over his subjects. See HISTORY.

Louis XVI (1754–93), see HISTORY.

Loyola, St Ignatius (1491–1556), founder of the Order of Jesuits.

Luther, Martin (1483–1546), see HISTORY.

Macadam, John (1756–1836), inventor of the Macadam process of road-making.

Macaulay, Thomas Babington, Lord (1800–59), celebrated historian and poet, author of *History of England* and the *Lays of Ancient Rome*.

Macbeth, King of Scotland immortalised by Shakespeare; he reigned from 1040 to 1057.

Macdonald, Flora (1722–90), Scottish Jacobite who sheltered Prince Charles Edward after his defeat at Culloden Moor, 1746.

Machiavelli, Niccolo (1469–1527), Florentine statesman and historian; author of *The Prince*, which describes how a ruler may build up his power.

Macready, William Charles (1793–1873), the greatest tragic actor of his day.

Magellan, Ferdinand (*c.* 1480–1521), Portuguese navigator; see EXPLORATIONS AND DISCOVERIES.

Malory, Sir Thomas (*c.* 1430–70), compiled the *Morte D'Arthur*, which tells the story of King Arthur and his Knights of the Round Table.

Malthus, Thomas Robert (1766–1834), English economist, who regarded the growth of the population as a danger, and proposed that marriage should be discouraged.

Mao Tse-Tung (1893–1976), Chairman of the Chinese Communist Party from 1936 until his death.

Marat, Jean-Paul (1743–93), one of the leading figures in the Reign of Terror during the French Revolution; assassinated by Charlotte Corday.

Marconi, Guglielmo, Marchese (1874–1937), inventor of the first practical method of wireless telegraphy.

Marco Polo (see Polo, Marco).

Marcus Aurelius (121–180), Roman Emperor who drove off the barbarians, and was famous for his wisdom and his taste for philosophy and literature.

Maria Theresa (1717–80), Empress of Austria, Queen of Bohemia and Hungary; see HISTORY.

Marie Antoinette (1755–93), daughter of Maria Theresa, and wife of Louis XVI of France; see HISTORY.

Mark Antony (see **Antonius, Marcus**).

Marlborough, John Churchill, Duke of (1650–1722), perhaps the greatest of all British soldiers; see HISTORY.

Marx, Karl (1818–83), German philosopher and economist, on whose teaching and writings Communism is based.

Masaryk, Thomas (1850–1937), founder and first President of Czechoslovakia.

Maupassant, Guy de (1850–93), famous French novelist and short-story writer.

Maxim, Sir Hiram (1840–1916), inventor of the automatic quick-firing gun named after him.

Maxwell, James Clerk (1831–79), Scottish physicist who formulated the electro-magnetic theory of light; his work made wireless possible.

Mazzini, Giuseppe (1805–72), Italian patriot who worked for the independence and unification of his country.

Mendel, Gregor (1822–84), Austrian botanist and monk whose study of the common garden pea resulted in the law of heredity known as the Mendelian law.

Mendelssohn, Jakob Ludwig Felix (1809–47), German composer.

Mercator, Gerhardus (1512–94), Flemish geographer who simplified navigation by inventing a system of projection in which the longitudes are represented by equidistant parallel lines and the degrees of latitude by perpendicular lines parallel to the meridian.

Mesmer, Friedrich (1733–1815), German doctor who developed the system of animal magnetism known as 'mesmerism'.

Metternich, Prince (1773–1859), Austrian statesman who led the conservative resistance to the ideas of progress spread by the French Revolution.

Mill, John Stuart (1806–73), writer on politics, economics and philosophy, and one of the founders of modern liberalism.

Millikan, Robert Andrew (1868–1953), American physicist who discovered cosmic rays.

Miltiades (d. 489 B.C.), one of the leaders of the Athenians against the Persians at Marathon.

Mithridates (c. 132–63 B.C.), King of Pontius from 120 to 63 B.C., implacable enemy of the Romans; he spoke 22 languages and,

THE WORLD: ITS FAMOUS PEOPLE

surrounded by enemies, was said to have made himself immune from all poisons.

Mohammed (*c.* 570–632), the founder of the Moslem religion; see HISTORY.

Molière (Jean Baptiste Poquelin) (1622–73), the greatest of the French comic dramatists.

Monk, George, Duke of Albemarle (1608–69), general and admiral who fought in the Anglo-Dutch wars; having fought on Cromwell's side against the Royalists, he later helped to restore Charles II to the throne.

Montaigne, Michel de (1533–92), great French essayist.

Montcalm, General Louis, Marquis de (1712–59), French commander in Canada, defeated by Wolfe.

Monteverdi, Claudio (1568–1643), Italian composer.

Montezuma II (1466–1520), last Aztec ruler of Mexico, Emperor when Cortes invaded the country.

Montfort, Simon de, Earl of Leicester (1208–65), powerful baron who forced Henry III to grant the first English Parliament; see HISTORY.

Montgolfier, Joseph (1640–1810) and **Jacques** (1745–99), French brothers who made many ascents in balloons inflated by heated air.

Montrose, James Graham, Marquess of (1612–50), general who raised the Highlands in support of Charles I and II.

Moore, Sir John (1761 1809), British general killed during retreat to Corunna in the Peninsular War.

More, Sir Thomas (1478–1535), Lord Chancellor under Henry VIII who was executed for refusing to take the Oath of Supremacy; wrote *Utopia*.

Morgan, Sir Henry (*c.* 1635–88), Welsh buccaneer who preyed on the Spaniards in the Caribbean; captured Panama in 1671.

Mountevans, Admiral Lord (1881–1957), British sailor and explorer known as 'Evans of the Broke'; wrote *South with Scott*.

Mozart, Wolfgang Amadeus (1756–91), great Austrian composer.

Mussolini, Benito (1883–1945), Fascist dictator of Italy, 1922–43; see HISTORY.

Nansen, Fridtjof (1862–1930), Norwegian explorer and organiser of relief for victims of the First World War.

Napoleon I (Bonaparte) (1769–1821), see HISTORY.

Nasser, Gamel Abdel (1819–70), President of the United Arab Republic, 1958–70.

Napoleon III (1808–73), see HISTORY.

Nelson, Horatio, Viscount (1758–1805), England's greatest naval commander; see HISTORY.

Nero, Claudius Caesar (37–68), Roman Emperor whose reign is notorious for his cruelty and wild living.

Newton, Sir Isaac (1642–1727), probably the greatest of all scientists; famous for his work on the nature of white light the calculus and gravitation; wrote the *Principia*.

Ney, Marshal (1769–1815), one of Napoleon's generals.

Nicholas II, Czar of Russia (1868–1918); shot with his family by the revolutionaries, 16 July 1918.

Nicholas, St (4th century), patron saint of Russia; associated (as Santa Claus) with Christmas.

Nietzsche, Friedrich (1844–1900), German philosopher, who believed that the mass of people must be led by the few Supermen.

Nightingale, Florence (1820–1910), creator of modern nursing and hospital reformer; the 'lady with the lamp' of the Crimean War.

Nijinsky, Vaslav (1890–1950), great Russian ballet dancer, Polish-born.

Nobel, Dr Alfred (1833–96), Swedish inventor of dynamite; in his will he left money for the annual prizes named after him (for work done for the benefit of mankind in physics, chemistry, physiology and medicine, literature and peace).

Northcliffe, Lord (1865–1922), pioneer of modern journalism.

Nostradamus (Michel de Notre Dame) (1503–66), French astrologer.

Nuffield, Lord, William Richard Morris (1877–1963), pioneer motor-car manufacturer and philanthropist.

Nureyev, Rudolf (1938–93), Russian ballet dancer and choreographer.

Oates, Captain L. E. G. (1880–1912), British explorer who was in the sledge party that accompanied Captain Scott in his dash for the South Pole. On the return journey the party became stormbound, and Oates, badly frostbitten, walked out to his death in a blizzard rather than be a burden to his comrades.

Oates, Titus (1649–1705), informer against Roman Catholics in Charles II's reign.

O'Casey, Sean (1883–1964), Irish dramatist, author of *Juno and the Paycock*.

Offa, King of Mercia, reigned from *c.* 757 to 796; built an embankment from the Dee to the Wye, called Offa's Dyke.

Ohm, Georg (1787–1854), discoverer of a law of electric current known as Ohm's Law; see SCIENCE.

Olivier, Laurence (Lord Olivier) (1907–89), great English actor, the first to be made a peer.

Otto, Nikolaus (1832–91), German engineer, inventor of the four-stroke cycle named after him; see CARS.

Ovid (43 B.C.–A.D. 18), Roman poet.

Owen, Robert (1771–1858), social reformer and factory owner; inspired the earliest Factory Acts, trade unionism and co-operative trading.

Paganini, Niccolo (1782–1840), Italian violinist whose virtuosity has become a legend.

Paine, Thomas (1737–1809), English revolutionary writer; after the publication of his *Rights of Man* he was forced to flee to France.

Palestrina, Giovanni de (1525–94), Italian composer.

Palmerston, Viscount (1784–1865), Whig Foreign Secretary, 1830–46; supported liberal uprisings throughout Europe; twice Prime Minister.

Pancras, St (3rd century), patron saint of children; martyred at the age of fourteen.

Pankhurst, Emmeline (1858–1928), leader of movement for votes for women with her daughters **Dame Christabel** and **Sylvia**.

Paracelsus, Philippus (1493–1541), Swiss mystic and alchemist.

Parnell, Charles Stewart (1846–91), leader of the Irish National Party.

Pascal, Blaise (1623–62), French philosopher and mathematician; constructed the first calculating machine.

Pasteur, Louis (1822–95), French chemist and founder of the sciences of bacteriology and immunology; first to show that infectious diseases are caused by germs; devised the process of pasteurisation by which milk can be prevented from going bad.

Patrick, St (*c.* 389–*c.* 461), patron saint of Ireland.

Pavlov, Ivan (1849–1936), Russian physiologist; made many discoveries concerning the digestive system and the brain and nervous system.

Pavlova, Anna (1885–1931), great Russian ballet dancer.

Peel, Sir Robert (1788–1850), British statesman, founder of the modern police service; see HISTORY.

Penn, William (1644–1718), Quaker who founded Pennsylvania.

Pepys, Samuel (1633–1703), naval administrator and famous diarist.

Pericles (*c.* 490–429 B.C.), greatest of the Athenian statesmen; see HISTORY.

Pétain, Marshal Henri Philippe (1856–1951), hero of the defence of Verdun by the French in 1916; in 1940 signed armistice with the Germans, and in 1945 was condemned to death for treason; the sentence was commuted to life imprisonment.

Peter (the Great) (1672–1725), Czar of Russia who did much to modernise his kingdom; founded St Petersburg (now Leningrad).

Peter the Hermit (d. 1115), French monk who raised the army for the disastrous First Crusade.

Petrarch, Francesco (1304–74), Italian poet and scholar, creator of the sonnet.

Petrie, Sir Flinders (1853–1942), British Egyptologist.

Philip II of Macedonia (382–336 B.C.), conqueror of Greece and father of Alexander the Great; see HISTORY.

Philip II of Spain (1527–98), see HISTORY.

Piccard, Auguste (1884–1962), Swiss physicist; ascended into stratosphere in a balloon, 1931 and 1932, and later explored the ocean in his bathysphere.

Pindar (522–443 B.C.), Greek lyric poet.

Pitman, Sir Isaac (1813–97), founder of the Pitman system of shorthand.

Pitt, William (1759–1806), British Prime Minister (at twenty-four, the youngest) throughout the period of the French Revolution and much of the war with France; see HISTORY.

Pizarro, Francisco (*c.* 1471–1541), Spaniard who conquered Peru with great cruelty; killed by his own soldiers.

Planck, Professor Max (1858–1947), German physicist whose law of radiation laid the foundation of the quantum theory.

Plato (427–347 B.C.), great Athenian philosopher, pupil of Socrates, teacher of Aristotle.

Plimsoll, Samuel (1824–96), M.P. who secured the passing of an Act of Parliament which defined a line (the Plimsoll Mark) above which the water must not rise when a ship is loaded. (See SHIPS.)

Plutarch (*c.* 46–210), Greek historian, author of *The Lives of Great Men of Greece and Rome.*

Poe, Edgar Allan (1809–49), American poet and short-story writer; wrote *Tales of Mystery and Imagination*, one of which, *The Murders in the Rue Morgue*, is among the earliest detective stories.

Polo, Marco (1254–1324), Venetian explorer; see EXPLORATIONS AND DISCOVERIES.

Pompey the Great (106–48 B.C.), Roman general; see HISTORY.

Priestley, Joseph (1733–1804), discovered and identified many of the common gases; discovered oxygen.

Proust, Marcel (1871–1922), French novelist; author of 15 novels with the general title, *A la Recherche du Temps Perdu* (*In Search of Lost Time*).

Ptolemy, Claudius (*c.* 90–168), Greek astronomer and geographer, born in Alexandria; according to the Ptolemaic system, the earth was the centre of the universe and the heavenly bodies revolved around it. (See COPERNICUS).

Purcell, Henry (*c.* 1659–95), English composer.

Pushkin, Alexander (1799–1837), great Russian poet, author of *Eugene Onegin.*

Pym, John (1584–1643), Puritan statesman who led the campaign in the House of Commons against Charles I.

Pythagoras (*c.* 582–*c.* 507 B.C.), Greek scientist and mathematician; to him is attributed the discovery of the multiplication table, the decimal system and the square on the hypotenuse.

Rabelais, François (*c.* 1494–1553), French monk and satirical writer, author of *Gargantua* and *Pantagruel.*

Rachmaninov, Serge (1873–1943), Russian composer.

Racine, Jean (1639–99), French tragic dramatist.

Raffles, Sir Thomas Stamford (1781–1826), founder of Singapore, 1819; also of the Zoological Society of London.

Raleigh, Sir Walter (1552–1618), English statesman, poet, sailor and explorer; favourite of Queen Elizabeth; founded the colony of Virginia; was imprisoned in the Tower for 12 years, and there wrote a *History of the World.* Set free in 1615 to lead an expedition to Guiana in search of gold, he was unsuccessful; and on his return was executed.

Rasputin, Grigori (1871–1916), Russian monk who became all-powerful at the court of the last Russian Czar, Nicholas II.

Réamur, René (1683–1757), French chemist; inventor of the thermometer that bears his name.

Rhodes, Cecil (1853–1902), see HISTORY.

Richelieu, Cardinal Duc de (1585–1642), one of the greatest of French statesmen; Prime Minister to Louis XIII.

Ridley, Nicholas (1500–55), Bishop of London, burned at the stake with Latimer.

Rienzi, Cola di (1313–54), Roman patriot who led a popular rebellion in 1347.

Rilke, Rainer Marie (1872–1926), German lyric poet.

Rimbaud, Jean (1854–91), important modern French poet; all his poems were written between his 16th and 19th years.

Rizzio, David (c. 1540–66), Italian musician, favourite of Mary Queen of Scots; stabbed to death in her presence by the jealous Darnley.

Roberts, Field-Marshal Earl (1832–1914), English general who distinguished himself in the Afghanistan campaign; led the campaign against the Boers.

Robespierre, Maximilien (1758–94), French lawyer who was president of the Committee of Public Safety during the Reign of Terror; sent many people to the guillotine, but was himself overthrown and guillotined.

Rob Roy (Robert McGregor) (1671–1734), Scottish highlander noted for his brigandage.

Rockefeller, John Davison (1839–1937), oil magnate who was said to have been the richest man in the world.

Rodney, Lord (1719–92), English admiral, victor in two great battles in the wars with France and Spain, 1780 and 1782.

Roland, Madame (1754–93), one of the leading figures of the French Revolution; she was guillotined, and died pronouncing the famous words, 'Oh liberty, what crimes are committed in thy name!'

Rommel, Field-Marshal (1891–1944), German general; see HISTORY.

Roosevelt, Franklin Delano (1882–1945), four times U.S. President; see HISTORY.

Ross, Sir Ronald (1857–1932), discoverer of the parasite that causes malaria.

Rouget de Lisle, Claude Joseph (1760–1836), French poet who wrote the words and music of the *Marseillaise*.

Rousseau, Jean-Jacques (1712–78), French writer who urged a return to nature and argued that man was naturally good; his ideas had a great influence on the events of his time.

Rupert, Prince (1619–82), Royalist admiral and general; fought for his uncle, Charles I, against Cromwell's troops, and at sea for Charles II against the Dutch.

Russell, Bertrand (Earl Russell) (1872–1970), English philosopher and mathematician.

Rutherford, Lord (1871–1937), New Zealand-born scientist, author of the nuclear theory of the atom and the first man to split the atom.

Saladin (1137–93), Sultan of Egypt and Syria and Moslem hero of the Third Crusade; see HISTORY.

Santos-Dumont, Alberto (1873–1932), famous Brazilian airman, one of the pioneers of modern aviation.

Sappho (*c.* 611–*c.* 592 B.C.), the most famous poetess of the ancient world; a native of the Greek island of Lesbos.

Savonarola, Girolamo (1452–98), Florentine friar who denounced the corruption of his day and was burned at the stake.

Schiller, Johann Friedrich von (1759–1805), one of the greatest German dramatists and poets.

Schliemann, Heinrich (1822–90), German archaeologist who discovered the ruins of ancient Troy.

Schubert, Franz (1797–1828), Austrian composer.

Schumann, Robert (1810–56), German composer.

Schweitzer, Albert (1875–1965), famous musician and organist who became a doctor of medicine in order to devote his life to the work of a medical missionary in Equatorial Africa.

Scipio, Publius (Scipio Africanus the Elder) (*c.* 232–183 B.C.), Roman general who distinguished himself in the Second Punic War.

Scott, Captain Robert Falcon (1868–1912), polar explorer who commanded the Antarctic expeditions of 1901–4 and 1910. With a small party he reached the South Pole on 18 January 1912, only to find that Amundsen had reached it before him. On the return journey the party were storm-bound, and all perished only 11 miles from their next depot.

Scott-Paine, Hubert (1891–1954), pioneer in the construction of flying-boats and high-speed motor-boats.

Selfridge, Harry Gordon (1858–1947), American whose famous shop in Oxford Street (opened in 1909) was the model for the modern British department store.

Shaftesbury, Anthony Ashley Cooper, Earl of (1801–85), the greatest social reformer of the 19th century; inspired changes in the treatment of lunatics, took part in the campaign against slavery and was largely responsible for the Factory Acts that forbade women and children to work underground in the mines and limited working hours.

Sheraton, Thomas (1751–1806), great English cabinet maker.

Sherman, General William (1820–91), great American soldier and leader of the famous 300-mile march across Georgia during the Civil War.

Shostakovich, Dmitri (1906–1975), Russian composer.

Sibelius, Jean (1865–1957), Finnish composer.

Siddons, Sarah (1755–1831), the greatest English tragic actress of her day.

Sidney, Sir Philip (1554–86), poet and soldier, one of Queen Elizabeth's favourites; killed fighting against the Spaniards at Zutphen.

Simpson, Sir James (1811–70), Scottish surgeon; first to use chloroform as an anaesthetic.

Smeaton, John (1724–92), rebuilder of the Eddystone lighthouse after its destruction by fire.

Smith, Adam (1723–90), political economist and first important advocate of free trade; author of *Wealth of Nations*.

Smuts, Field-Marshal Jan (1870–1950), South African soldier, who fought against the British in the Boer War, but afterwards worked for friendship with Britain. Prime Minister of South Africa, 1912–24 and 1939–48.

Sobieski, John (1629–96), King of Poland who freed Vienna from the Turks, 1683; see HISTORY.

Socrates (470–399 B.C.), Greek philosopher, whose teachings are known from the writings of his pupils, Xenophon and Plato. He taught people to think carefully and logically. Charged with corrupting the morals of the young, he was condemned to die by drinking hemlock.

Solomon (10th c. B.C.), son of David, ruler of Israel and Judah.

Solon (638–558 B.C.), great Athenian law-giver.

Somerset, Duke of (1506–52), Protector of England in early days of Edward VI's reign; later deposed and executed.

Sophocles (495–406 B.C.), popular Athenian dramatist; author of *Antigone, Electra, Oedipus*.

Soult, Marshal Nicholas (1769–1851), one of the most successful of Napoleon's marshals, and Wellington's opponent in the Peninsular War.

Spinoza, Benedict (1632–77), Dutch philosopher.

Stalin, Joseph (1879–1953), Soviet dictator from 1923 until his death; see HISTORY.

Stanley, Sir Henry Morton (1841–1904), explorer of Central Africa; in 1867, as a newspaper correspondent, he sought and found the missing David Livingstone.

Stendhal (Marie Henry Beyle) (1783–1842), French novelist.

Stephenson, George (1781–1848), English engineer, inventor of the first successful railway locomotive (see RAILWAYS).

Stephenson, Robert (1772–1850), lighthouse builder who invented the 'flashing' system of throwing light at sea.

Stowe, Harriet Beecher (1811–96), American author of *Uncle Tom's Cabin*, which helped to create strong feeling against slavery.

Stradivari, Antonio (1644–1730), Italian who was the greatest of all violin-makers.

Strafford, Thomas, Earl of (1593–1641), supporter of the authority of Charles I; abandoned by the King, he was impeached and executed.

Strauss, Johann (1825–99), Austrian composer.

Strauss, Richard (1864–1949), German composer.

Stravinsky, Igor (1882–1971), Russian-born American composer.

Strindberg, August (1849–1912), Swedish dramatist and novelist.

Sullivan, Sir Arthur (1842–1900), English composer; collaborator with W. S. Gilbert (*q.v.*) in the Savoy operas.

Sun Yat Sen, Dr (1867–1925), one of the leaders of the Chinese Revolution of 1911; President of the Chinese Republic, 1921–25.

Suvarov, Alexander (1730–1800), great Russian General.

Swedenborg, Emanuel (1688–1772), Swedish philosopher.

Tacitus, Caius (55–*c.* 120), Roman historian.

Tagore, Sir Rabindranath (1861–1941), Indian poet and philosopher.

Talleyrand-Périgord, Charles-Maurice de (1754–1838), Napoleon's Foreign Minister, 1797–1807.

Tamerlane (Timur the Lame) (1335–1405), founder of the Mogul dynasty in India; brutal conqueror of Turkestan, Persia and Syria.

Tarquin Superbus, the last king of Rome; banished 510 B.C.

Tasso, Torquato (1544–95), great Italian poet.

Tchaikovsky, Peter Ilyitch (1840–93), Russian composer.

Telford, Thomas (1757–1834), Scottish road-maker and builder of canals and bridges, including the Menai Suspension Bridge.

Tell, William (14th century), legendary hero of the Swiss struggle for freedom against the Austrians.

Teresa, St (1515–82), Spanish nun famous for her austere life and her vision.

Terry, Dame Ellen (1848–1928), great English actress, long associated with Sir Henry Irving (*q.v.*).

Thales of Miletus (*c.* 624–565 B.C.), Greek philosopher who believed that water was the principal element.

Themistocles (*c.* 514–449 B.C.), Athenian soldier and statesman who defeated the Persian fleet at Salamis, 480 B.C.

Thomson, Sir Joseph (1856–1940), physicist and mathematician, discoverer of the electron.

Thoreau, Henry David (1817–62), nature-worshipping American philosopher; author of *Walden*.

Thucydides (*c.* 460–399 B.C.), greatest of the Greek historians.

Tito, (Josip Broz) (1892–1980), leader of the Yugoslav partisans in the Second World War and President of Yugoslavia until 1980.

Titus (40–81), Roman emperor, son of Vespasian; did much for the welfare of the Roman people, completed the Colosseum; see HISTORY.

Tolstoy, Count Leo (1828–1910), great Russian novelist; author of *War and Peace*, generally regarded as the greatest novel ever written.

Torquemada, Tomas de (1420–98), Inquisitor-General during Spanish Inquisition.

Toussaint L'Ouverture (1743–1803), Negro ex-slave who freed Santo Domingo (the Dominican Republic) from the French.

Trajan (*c.* 52–117), Roman emperor; did much to consolidate the Empire—work that was continued by his successor, Hadrian; see HISTORY.

Trotsky, Leon (1879–1940), one of the leaders of the Russian Revolution; in 1925 was driven into exile in Mexico, where he was later assassinated.

Tubman, Harriet (c. 1821–1913), fugitive slave, abolitionist, and a leading figure in the establishment of an escape route for slaves.

Turgenev, Ivan (1818–83), Russian novelist.

Tussaud, Madame Marie (1760–1850), Swiss who escaped from Paris at the time of the French Revolution and set up her exhibition of wax figures in London.

Tut-ankh-amen (*c.* 1350 B.C.), Egyptian Pharaoh whose tomb was discovered in 1922, with the mummy and the gold sarcophagus intact.

Twain, Mark (see **Clemens, Samuel**).

Tyler, Wat (d. 1381), leader of the Peasants' Revolt; see HISTORY.

Tyndale, William (*c.* 1492–1536), translator of the Bible; put to death for heresy.

Valentine, St, martyred *c.* 273. The habit of sending Valentines is of pre-Christian origin, and is not connected with the saint.

Vaughan Williams, Ralph (1872–1958), English composer.

Verdi, Giuseppe (1813–1901), Italian composer.

Verlaine, Paul (1844–1896), French poet.

Verne, Jules (1828–1905), French writer of early science fiction, author of *Twenty Thousand Leagues under the Sea, Round the World in Eighty Days*.

Vernier, Pierre (1580–1637), inventor of the sliding scale.

Vespasian (A.D. 9–79), Roman emperor; at one time commander of the Roman Army in Britain.

Vespucci, Amerigo (1451–1512), Italian navigator; the first mapmakers gave his name to America.

Villeneuve, Pierre (1763–1806), commanded the French fleet against Nelson at Trafalgar.

Villon, François (1431–*c.* 1489), French poet.

Virgil (**Publius Vergilius Maro**) (70–19 B.C.), great Roman epic poet, author of the *Aeneid*.

Vitus, St (4th century), Roman Catholic saint and martyr; the custom of dancing before his shrine on his commemoration day, 15 June, gave rise to the name, St Vitus Dance, given to a nervous ailment.

Voltaire, François-Marie Arouet de (1694–1778), great and influential French philosopher and writer, author of *Candide*.

Wagner, Richard (1813–83), German opera composer.

Wallace, Alfred Russel (1823–1913), English traveller and naturalist; one of the founders of zoological geography; author of *Travels on the Amazon*.

Wallace, Sir William (*c.* 1270–1305), Scottish patriot; see HISTORY.

Warbeck, Perkin (1474–99), Pretender to the English Crown; claimed to be one of the princes murdered in the Tower; provided with an army by the French and the Scots, he invaded England in 1497, but was defeated and hanged.

Warwick, Richard Neville, Earl of (c. 1428–71), 'The Kingmaker'; see HISTORY.

Washington, Booker T. (1856–1915), black American educationalist.

Washington, George (1732–99), first President of the American Republic, 1789; see HISTORY.

Watt, James (1736–1819), great British engineer, designer of first efficient steam-engine.

Wedgwood, Josiah (1730–95), most famous of the English potters.

Wellington, Arthur Wellesley, Duke of (1769–1852), 'the Iron Duke'; see HISTORY.

Wesley, Charles (1708–88), hymn-writer, brother of John.

Wesley, John (1703–91), founder of Methodism.

Whitman, Walt (1819–92), American poet, author of *Leaves of Grass*.

Whittington, Richard (c. 1358–c. 1423), London apprentice who became four times Lord Mayor of London.

Whymper, Edward (1840–1911), first mountaineer to reach the summit of the Matterhorn.

Wilberforce, William (1759–1833), leading spirit of the successful campaign against the Slave Trade.

Wilkes, John (1727–97), popular Whig politician; expelled from the House of Commons, he was three times elected M.P. for Middlesex, being again expelled each time. In the end his opponents gave way and he was able to take his seat.

William I of Prussia (1797–1888), first German Emperor; see HISTORY.

William II (1859–1941), Emperor of Germany; see HISTORY.

William the Silent (1533–80), Prince of Orange who attempted to free Holland from the grip of Spain; assassinated; see HISTORY.

Wingate, Major-General Orde (1903–44), leader of the Chindit forces that operated behind Japanese lines in Burma during the Second World War. Killed in air crash.

Wolfe, General James (1727–59), British commander at the siege of Quebec, in which he was killed.

Wollstonecraft, Mary (1759–97), Anglo-Irish feminist, author of

Vindication of the Rights of Women: mother of **Mary**, who married the poet Shelley and wrote *Frankenstein*.

Wolsey, Cardinal Thomas (1471–1530), Archbishop of York and Chancellor to Henry VIII; see HISTORY.

Wright, Sir Almroth (1861–1947), discovered the system of inoculation against typhoid.

Wycliff, John (*c.* 1324–84), religious reformer; translator of the Bible.

Xenophon (430–355 B.C.), Greek historian and general, pupil of Socrates.

Xerxes (*c.* 519–465 B.C.), King of Persia; see HISTORY.

Ximenes, Francisco (1436–1517), succeeded Torquemada (*q.v.*) as Inquisitor-General in the Spanish Inquisition.

Young, Brigham (1801–77), Mormon leader and head of the Latter Day Saints of Salt Lake City.

Zeppelin, Ferdinand, Graf von (1838–1917), German inventor of the airship bearing his name.

Zola, Emile (1840–1902), great French novelist.

A DICTIONARY OF MYTHOLOGY

The majority of the gods, goddesses and other mythological characters who appear in this list are Greek or Roman. Some, however, are Egyptian or Norse; and it is important to remember that, though the Greek and Roman myths are the most familiar to us, the Babylonians, the Hebrews, the Chinese, Japanese, Indians and many other peoples built mythical stories, and invented mythical characters, on the basis of their religious beliefs.

The fact that the Romans borrowed many of their myths from the Greeks, giving their own names to the gods, leads often to confusion. The following table shows, side by side, the Greek and Roman names of the principal gods and goddesses.

Greek	*Roman*
Aphrodite (goddess of love)	**Venus**
Apollo (god of light and the arts)	**Phoebus Apollo**
Ares (god of war)	**Mars**
Artemis (huntress)	**Diana**
Athene (goddess of wisdom)	**Minerva**
Cronus (father of Zeus)	**Saturn**

Greek	*Roman*
Demeter (goddess of corn)	Ceres
Dionysus (god of wine and revelry)	Bacchus
Eros (god of love)	Cupid
Hera (mother of the gods and goddess of marriage)	Juno
Hermes (messenger of the gods)	Mercury
Hestia (goddess of the hearth)	Vesta
Pan (god of the flocks)	Faunus
Poseidon (god of the sea)	Neptune
Zeus (father of the gods)	Jupiter

The printing of a name in small capital letters (e.g. VENUS) means that the mythical person named is the subject of a separate entry.

Achilles, King of the Myrmidons, most famous of the Greek heroes of the Trojan War.

Adonis, Greek god: a young man of great beauty, wounded by a boar and changed by APHRODITE into an anemone.

Aeneas, Trojan prince, hero of Virgil's *Aeneid*; the mythical ancestor of the Romans.

Aeolus, wind-god, who unchained the tempests.

Aesculapius, god of medicine.

Agamemnon, King of Mycenae, leader of the Greeks against Troy.

Ajax, Greek warrior at the siege of Troy.

Amazons, mythical race of war-like women.

Amphitrite, sea-goddess and wife of POSEIDON.

Ammon, Egyptian god.

Andromeda, daughter of the king of Ethiopia who, by claiming to be as beautiful as the NEREIDS, roused the anger of POSEIDON, and was condemned to be devoured by a sea monster. She was saved by PERSEUS, who married her.

Antigone, daughter of OEDIPUS. When the king of Thebes forbade the burial of her brother, Polynices, she defied his order, and was buried alive in a cave; there she hanged herself.

Aphrodite, Greek goddess of love; she was said to have sprung from the foam of the sea.

Apollo, Greek and Roman god of light, the arts and divination; also called Phoebus.

Aquilo, the north wind.

Ares, the Greek god of war.

Argonauts, the fifty Greek heroes who, with JASON, sought the Golden Fleece in their ship the *Argo*.

Ariadne, daughter of MINOS of Crete; gave THESEUS the thread which enabled him to find his way out of the Labyrinth.

Artemis, Greek goddess and huntress.

Atalanta, Greek princess who declared she would marry only the man who could beat her at running; she was outrun by Milanion, who dropped three golden apples one after another to tempt Atalanta and slow her down.

Athene or **Pallas**, Greek goddess of wisdom.

Atlas, King of Mauretania who, for warring against ZEUS, was condemned to support the sky on his shoulders.

Bacchus, Roman god of wine.

Baldur, most beautiful of the Norse gods.

Bellerophon, Greek hero who caught PEGASUS, the winged horse, and killed the CHIMAERA.

Boreas, the north wind.

Calypso, nymph who delayed ODYSSEUS for seven years on his way home from Troy.

Cassandra, Trojan princess; she had the gift of prophecy, but was fated never to be believed.

Castor and Pollux, sons of ZEUS and Leda; they were transported to the heavens and became the constellation known as the Twins.

Centaurs, creatures, half-horse and half-man, living on Mt Pelion in Thessaly.

Cerberus, three-headed dog who guarded the gates of HADES.

Ceres, Roman corn goddess.

Charon, boatman who ferried the dead across the STYX.

Chimaera, fire-breathing monster, a mixture of lion, dragon and goat; slain by BELLEROPHON.

Circe, enchantress who turned ODYSSEUS' companions into swine.

Cronus, Greek name for SATURN.

Cupid, Roman name for EROS, the god of love.

Cybele, the 'great mother', goddess of nature.

Cyclops, one-eyed giants who forged ZEUS's thunderbolts.

Danae, daughter of the king of Argos, visited by ZEUS in a shower of gold; mother of PERSEUS.

Daphne, nymph who was changed into a laurel-bush to save her from APOLLO.

Demeter, Greek goddess of the corn.

Diana, Roman goddess and huntress.

Dido, mythical queen who founded Carthage.

Dionysus, Greek god of wine and revelry.

Dryads, Greek goddesses of the forest.

Echo, nymph who, having displeased HERA, was changed into a rock and condemned to repeat the last words of those who spoke to her.

Electra, sister of ORESTES.

Elysium, or **the Elysian fields**, the Greek and Roman paradise.

Endymion, beautiful youth who was loved by the moon.

Erebus, the dark subterranean region below which was HADES.

Eros, the god of love.

Euphrosyne, one of the three GRACES.

Eurydice, wife of ORPHEUS.

Eurus, the south-east wind.

Fates, the three goddesses, Clotho, Lachesis and Atropos, who were in charge of human destinies; they wove the web of each man's life, which ended when Atropos cut the thread.

Fauns, Roman gods of the fields.

Flora, goddess of flowers and gardens.

Freya, Norse goddess of love.

Furies or **Eumenides**, goddesses whose mission was to punish human crimes.

Gorgons, three sisters, MEDUSA, Euryale and Stheno, who had the power to change into stone all who looked at them.

Graces, the three goddesses, EUPHROSYNE, Aglaia and Thalia, who were regarded as the bestowers of beauty and charm.

Hades, the Greek god of the infernal regions; also the infernal regions themselves.

Harpies, winged monsters with women's faces and long claws.

Hector, most valiant of the defenders of Troy: killed by ACHILLES.

Hecuba, wife of PRIAM, King of Troy; nineteen of her children were killed during the siege.

Helen, Greek princess of great beauty; her removal to Troy by PARIS was the cause of the Trojan War.

Helicon, Greek mountain consecrated to the MUSES.

Hera, wife of ZEUS and goddess of marriage.

Heracles, Greek demi-god.

Hercules, Roman name for HERACLES.

Hermes, Greek messenger of the gods.

Hesperides, daughters of ATLAS, guardians of the golden apples stolen by HERCULES.

Hestia, Greek goddess of the hearth, known to the Romans as Vesta.

Horus, falcon-headed Egyptian god.

Hygieia, Greek goddess of health.

Hymen, god of marriage.

Icarus, son of Daedalus; his father made for them both wings fastened with wax. Icarus flew too near the sun; the wax fastenings melted, and he fell into the sea and was drowned.

Irene, Greek goddess of peace.

Iris, the rainbow, a messenger of the gods.

Isis, Egyptian goddess of medicine, marriage and agriculture.

Ixion, thrown into Hell by ZEUS and condemned to be bound to a flaming wheel everlastingly revolving.

Janus, Roman god of beginnings (hence *Januarius*, the first month of the year); he was able to see both the future and the past and is represented with two faces.

Jason, Greek hero and leader of the ARGONAUTS, who won the Golden Fleece.

Juno, wife of JUPITER and goddess of marriage.

Jupiter, Roman name for the father of the gods and king of heaven.

Lethe, one of the rivers of Hell; all who drank its waters became forgetful of the past.

Mars, Roman god of war.

Medea, witch who married JASON and, when he left her, took her revenge by devouring their children.

Medusa, one of the three GORGONS. She offended MINERVA, who turned her hair into serpents. PERSEUS cut off her head and carried it with him to turn his enemies into stone.

Menelaus, King of Sparta and husband of HELEN of Troy.

Mercury, messenger of the gods.

Midas, King of Phrygia to whom the favour was granted that everything he touched turned into gold. When this happened even to his food, he prayed for the power to be taken away.

Minerva, Roman goddess of wisdom and the arts.

Minos, King of Crete who demanded an annual tribute of young men and women from Athens; they were sent into the Labyrinth and devoured by the Minotaur.

Mnemosyne, goddess of memory and mother of the MUSES.

Muses, nine goddesses who presided over the arts: Clio (History), Euterpe (music), Thalia (comedy), Melpomene (tragedy), Terpsichore (dancing), Erata (elegaic poetry), Polymnia (lyric poetry), Urania (astronomy), Calliope (eloquence and epic poetry).

Naiads, nymphs presiding over rivers and springs.

Narcissus, beautiful youth who pined away for love of his own reflection and was turned into a flower.

Nemesis, Greek goddess of vengeance and retribution.

Neptune, Roman god of the sea.

Nereids, nymphs of the Mediterranean.

Notus, the south wind.

Oceanides, nymphs of the sea.

Oceanus, Greek god of the sea.

Odin, or **Wotan**, father of the Norse gods.

Odysseus, King of Ithaca, one of the heroes of the siege of Troy, whose many adventures on his return home are described in Homer's *Odyssey*. The Romans called him ULYSSES.

Oedipus, King of Thebes, who, discovering that he had unwittingly killed his father and married his mother, blinded himself.

Orestes, son of AGAMEMNON and Clytemnestra. When Agamemnon was killed by Clytemnestra, Orestes was saved by his sister ELECTRA, who then drove him to kill his mother in revenge.

Orion, giant hunter; killed by ARTEMIS, he became one of the constellations.

Orpheus, great musician of Greek myth; went into Hades in search of his dead wife, EURYDICE, and so charmed the infernal spirits with his music that they returned Eurydice to him on condition that he should not look behind him until he had left the lower world. He broke this condition and was torn to pieces.

Osiris, Egyptian god, protector of the dead.

Pales, Roman goddess of flocks and shepherds.

Pan, goat-footed Greek god who presided over the flocks.

Pandora, the first woman to be created. ATHENE made her wise; ZEUS gave her a box full of evil things. On earth she married Epimetheus, the first man; then opened the box and so released all the ills from which men suffer.

Paris, Trojan prince who took HELEN from her husband and so caused the Trojan War. Appointed to choose the most beautiful of the three goddesses, HERA, ATHENE and APHRODITE, he chose the last, thus bringing down on Troy the hatred of the other two.

Parnassus, Greek mountain sacred to the MUSES.

Pegasus, winged horse that sprang from the blood of MEDUSA.

Penelope, wife of ODYSSEUS. During his long absence she was pressed to choose a new husband, and promised to do so when she had finished weaving a tapestry; but every night she undid the work she had done that day.

Perseus, son of ZEUS and DANAE. He and his mother were cast adrift and came to the country of King Polydectes. The king, hoping to get rid of Perseus, sent him to bring back MEDUSA's head.

Phaethon, son of the Sun-God, whose father allowed him to drive the sun-chariot for one day only; he was unable to manage the horses, and ZEUS, angered, struck him dead.

Pleiades, the seven daughters of ATLAS who killed themselves into despair and were turned into stars.

Pluto, King of HADES and god of the dead.

Polyphemus, the most famous of the CYCLOPS; he imprisoned ODYSSEUS, who escaped by blinding him.

Pomona, goddess of fruits and gardens.

Poseidon, god of the sea.

Priam, the last King of Troy, killed in the sack of the city.

Procrustes, robber who fitted his victims to a bed, stretching them or lopping their limbs to do so. Slain by THESEUS.

Prometheus, the god of fire. Having formed the first man of clay, he stole fire from heaven to bring him to life. ZEUS had him chained to a mountain, where his liver was devoured every day by a vulture, but grew again every night. He was freed by HERACLES.

Proserpina, wife of PLUTO and mother of the FURIES.

Proteus, sea god who could change his shape at will.

Psyche ('the soul'), beautiful maiden loved by CUPID.

Pygmalion, King of Cyprus who fell in love with a statue of a woman he had made himself.

Remus, brother of ROMULUS.

Romulus, thrown with his brother REMUS into the Tiber at birth;

washed ashore and adopted by a she-wolf. Romulus founded Rome (the traditional date is 753 B.C.).

Saturn, husband of CYBELE and father of JUPITER. A promise made to Titan forced him to eat his children when they were born. Cybele saved Jupiter by putting a stone in his place. Jupiter dethroned his father and Saturn took refuge in Latium, where he showed men how to cultivate the land.

Satyrs, the companions of BACCHUS.

Sirens, monsters, half-woman and half-bird, who lived on the rocks between the isle of Capri and the coast of Italy. By the sweetness of their singing they lured sailors to destruction.

Sisyphus, founder of Corinth, who for his greed and dishonesty was condemned after death to roll a stone for ever uphill; as soon as it got to the top it rolled down again.

Styx, the river flowing round HADES, over which CHARON ferried the dead.

Tantalus, King of Lydia condemned for ever to hunger and thirst.

Tartarus, the lowest region of HADES.

Telemachus, son of ODYSSEUS who set out in search of his father.

Theseus, Greek hero who, among his many adventures, killed the Minotaur (see MINOS).

Themis, goddess of justice.

Thor, the Norse god of war.

Titans, sons of the Heaven and the Earth. Rebelling against the gods, they attempted to climb to Heaven by piling mountain upon mountain; but they were destroyed by JUPITER's thunderbolts.

Triton, one of the sea-gods.

Ulysses, Roman name for ODYSSEUS.

Venus, the Roman goddess of beauty and love.

Vulcan, Roman god of fire.

Zephyrus, the west wind.

Zeus, Greek name for the father of the gods.

THE WORLD

4: ITS ECOLOGY

WHAT IS MEANT BY ECOLOGY?

The word ecology is quite a new one. A little over a hundred years ago scientists who studied plant and animal life began to use it to refer to two branches of their enquiries. One was simply how the different species organised their lives as communities. It meant much the same as 'economy' once meant—not the large-scale movements of money and goods we think of now, but how a way of life was organised in a community or even a household. The words are connected, because the 'eco-' part in both comes from the same Greek word meaning something like 'home-place'. The second way the biologists used the word ecology was similar, only it emphasised how their relationship to their surroundings affected the way the various creatures lived.

But it is only in the second half of this century that we have all begun to hear the word and to use it. The reason for this is that as a result of various human activities a lot of things have begun to go wrong with *our* surroundings. So to most people the word ecology probably suggests something about the cutting down of tropical rain forests and its consequences, and different kinds of pollution. They may also think about the extinction, or threat of extinction, to creatures such as whales; but what lies behind that, once again, is almost always the behaviour of human beings.

It is the way that our own species has begun to disturb the balance of nature that has suddenly made ecology such a familiar word, and has focussed people's urgent interest and attention on the subject. It is because of this that not a day now goes by without some mention of it on the radio and TV and in the newspaper, and why the editor of this book felt that an ecology section should now be added to it. Our quality of life in the future, and perhaps our very survival as a species, may well depend on our understanding how the balance of nature works. So the information offered and the questions raised here will be mainly about *human* ecology and what has gone wrong with it. But it is important to bear in mind that ecology properly means the study of any or all kinds of species as they affect and are affected by their surroundings—usually constructively and in balance. Ecology is the study of living organisms—animals or plants—in relation to their environment.

What is meant by the environment?

The scope of this word too has been changing. It can mean just the immediate surroundings. For example, if it was said that a classroom provided a good environment for learning, that might include its having enough light, being neither too hot nor too cold, being quiet, clean, and giving each of the students enough space. It might also include a valuation of such things as furnishings, plants, wall displays, books and other equipment. On the other hand a room where you were baked or dazzled through big plate glass windows, disturbed by noise and cramped, and where the decor and so on were 'grotty', would be a poor environment in which to learn.

The word is also used scientifically to mean everything that a living being encounters in the course of its existence. And recently the word has come to be used for the whole planet—its earth, air and water—in connection particularly with the way human activities affect it. People who are concerned for the environment in this sense are called *environmentalists*. They are not necessarily professional ecologists, but they will draw on the evidence of ecological science and suggest ways in which we can act, both on our own and together in groups, nations, or internationally, to create and restore surroundings that will make for a better life for all of us.

People sometimes talk about environmentalists as though they were a group with a special interest or axe to grind, like newt-fanciers, say, or those who practise a particular sport. If we don't fancy newts, and don't go in for that particular sport, we feel we can ignore what is being said. The environment is not like that. People who study the environment are not infallible—they may not always get it right; but what they are studying is not something we can opt out of. It affects us all. It is worth remembering this when people say they have heard enough about the environment, or try to make out that it is only one 'issue' among many. Our environment is everything outside ourselves. Even if we were not capable of altering it quite so radically, it is worth everyone's while to think about what affects us so profoundly in every aspect of our daily lives, including the food we eat, the work we do (or don't have), and the way we organise our societies. It would seem sensible to give some thought to what makes the best surroundings for our bodies, minds and spirits to develop healthily, even if things were not going as badly wrong as, unfortunately, they are.

Homo sapiens—Us?

Philosophers, artists, and indeed most of us at some time in our lives ask what human beings are, what they are for, and what is involved in being properly human. But whether we have thought about these questions or not, the way we live will be as a result of what we unconsciously believe to be the answers. Ecology is a science; that is, it deals in physical facts. But it invites us more directly than other sciences do to ask questions about values.

We have called our own species *homo sapiens*. The Latin word *sapiens*, meaning wise or clever, was used to distinguish us from the various other human-like creatures that were steps between us and our ape-like ancestors. We have this quality of cleverness, of brain-power, to a far greater degree than any other creature. But it is a two-edged thing. We have used our wits to make use of the earth's resources so that some of us live more comfortably, and longer, than ever before; in other parts of the world people are dying young of starvation and preventable disease. Other animals seem on the whole to do what is sensible for the good of their species; whereas human beings, especially in the so-called 'developed' world, are increasingly out for themselves as individuals. Many of us have so much more than we need that it has become greed, and the results are not only exploitation of our fellow creatures, but exhausting or damaging the earth itself. This is an 'own goal' which suggests *homo sapiens* has been too clever by half.

We all have a tendency to shift the blame for what is wrong and the responsibility for putting things right onto someone else. We feel it is 'they' who have polluted the sea, cut down the trees, exhausted the soil, or whatever, and not us. But one of the things ecology teaches us is that we are all interconnected and inter-dependent. We may not have done those things with our own hands, but we have consumed the goods and used the energy that led to it happening. Like it or not, we are part of a system that has caused and allowed it. On top of this we fondly imagine that 'they'—a different 'they' this time, the government or the scientists—will sort things out. Unfortunately, this is not true either. Broadly speaking, in a democracy like ours (this is not the place to go into the faults of the British electoral system) the government do what the majority of the people want. But we have to know what we want, and press for it to be done. As for the scientists, they are clever enough to have found out, for example, how to split the atom and give us not only weapons that could destroy our world, but nuclear energy to give us power. But they have not yet discovered any safe way of dealing with the horribly dangerous radioactive waste produced by nuclear power stations. And yet we allow these to go on being built.

Fortunately there are things we can all do to improve our ecological situation that do not involve getting into parliament or becoming high-powered scientists—though more ecological thinking in both those professions would not come amiss. We can all give some thought to what is called our life-style.

Ironically, the one section of society who cannot be held responsible for what has gone wrong with the environment is the one that will be reading this—young people who don't yet vote, work, or spend much money. We adults ought to be very much ashamed of handing the world over to you in such poor ecological shape. All we can do is to suggest that ecologically speaking the philosophy of everyone-for-himself-and-consume-all-you-can has been disastrous, and that the eastern bloc countries have not done any better. Some of the major ecological problems like damage to the ozone layer, acid rain and radioactive contamination do not respect national boundaries. A growing awareness of this led to the first *Earth Summit* being held in 1992 in Rio de Janeiro. Over 100 world leaders met, supposedly to commit themselves to actions aimed at moving towards more *sustainable development*. That means trying to continue to improve the quality of life while not using up or damaging the earth's resources. Unfortunately, because of the conflicting short-term political interests of the different governments, very little was agreed on. But one good result was that the media coverage of the event made people everywhere more aware of the problems. They might now be more inclined to press their governments to put ecological considerations first. At the same time a parallel event, the Global Forum, brought tens of thousands of people from non-governmental organisations (NGO's) together to exchange ideas and work out ways to try to influence government policies.

Some terms often used in connection with ecology

Acid Rain

Sulphur and nitrogen oxides are released from tall industrial chimneys, blown on the wind and in contact with moisture become acids which fall as rain. This can kill fish and trees. Getting something done about it—filtering the emissions or altering or stopping the processes which produce it—is made harder by the fact that the rain often falls over other countries than the ones responsible for it.

Biodegradable

Something which is biodegradable will rot down so that the substances it is made of will return harmlessly into the soil. A good rule of thumb is that things made of animal or vegetable substances will rot, whereas man-made substances such as plastics not only provide a problem of disposal but involve some of the world's finite resources being taken out of use altogether.

Green

The colour green in the plant world is in most cases the most obvious sign that the plant is alive and healthy. Where our bad management of the land is decreasing areas of green and making more desert or industrial wasteland it is bad news for us and for other species too. So the word green has come to be used for a way of thinking that makes what is good for the health of the life of the planet an important priority. It is also used for actions or objects which such an attitude approves. For example, a washing-up liquid which was said to be green in this sense would be one that contained no chemicals that cause damage to the environment. There is a political party called the Green Party in Britain and other European countries. Like other political parties it has a manifesto, a statement of their beliefs and the policies they would have if they were to get into power; but like other political parties the members would not necessarily agree over everything. There is also what is called the green movement, which covers a wide range of thought and activities and concerns, including various kinds of alternative medicine and technology, organic farming and gardening, and an assortment of lifestyles aimed at greater harmony with and less damage to the rest of nature.

Greenhouse effect
When we burn *fossil fuels* (coal, gas and oil) we release carbon dioxide into the atmosphere. Industry and cars are chiefly responsible for the huge increase in this in the last hundred years. At the same time, the forests which help to process the carbon dioxide and keep the balance are being cut down: or, worse still, they are burnt. So more of the sun's energy is being absorbed by the earth, and many scientists believe this is what causes

Global warming
The atmosphere has become 0·5 °C hotter in the last 100 years. Continuing increase could lead to pronounced climatic changes, some places becoming much wetter than they are now, and others drier, the sea level rising and some low-lying places becoming submerged altogether. If we wait the 10 or 20 years needed to prove with more certainty the strong suspicion that greenhouse gases are the cause, the effects will be that much more disastrous. But unfortunately people who make money from the activities causing the emissions tend to oppose cutting down on them.

Ozone layer
Ozone is a poisonous gas, but the layer of it that is in the *stratosphere* (see p. B60) usefully absorbs the ultra-violet rays from the sun, which are harmful to human beings, animals and plants. The gases known as CFCs (chlorofluorocarbons), which are used among other things in the manufacture of some aerosol sprays, are causing holes in this protective layer. In some countries there are already reports of blindness in animals and of an increasing incidence of skin and eye disorders among human beings.

Organic
This word in an ecological context is usually applied to foodstuffs and fertilisers. It is used of naturally-occurring substances that are applied to the soil to re-enrich it, such as animal dung and compost made from rotted-down vegetable matter, as opposed to man-made chemical substances made in factories. It is used of food that has been grown without using chemical fertilisers; and when it is used of meat or other animal products it means that the

animals have themselves been fed with organic food and have not been treated with hormones, antibiotics or other drugs.

Pollution
Pollution is the release into the air, earth or water of substances that disturb the balance of the environment: for example, by being poisonous (toxic), radioactive, causing infectious disease or simply by having a suffocating effect. The result of pollution is, in the short or the longer term, the illness or death of some of the species living in the environment where it occurs.

Re-cycling
Left to itself, nature re-cycles everything. When plants and animals die, their bodies rot back into the earth to enrich it for the following generations. Human beings have begun to use up the earth's resources because they make a lot of things that will not rot, that take a lot of costly energy to produce, and which they do not re-use. Re-cycling is putting something in the way of being re-used—either directly, like re-filling a bottle, or indirectly, like paper which is reprocessed to make new paper, rather than cutting down more trees.

Tropical Rain Forests
These forests, which are situated in a belt round the Equator, serve to regulate our climate and our water supply and to fix precious topsoil. They contain vast numbers of species which may be of use to us (as well as to each other). Less than one in six of their 2 million species have even been identified. They are being cut down for very short-term gain and are irreplaceable.

Earth, Air, Water, Fire

The ancients believed that all physical matter was composed of these four elements, and although our modern physics and chemistry have taught us to analyse in a more complex and accurate way, it is still a helpful grouping. If we translate the simple idea of fire into the more complicated one of power, the four still cover everything in our physical environment—the world of nature on which, for all our cleverness, we are still completely dependent.

Earth
The minerals to be found in the earth, and the structure of the soil and the climate, which determine what it will grow and what kind of creatures live there, all vary from place to place. The earth can produce enough to support all of us, but we have not yet learned how to share it out. So while in wealthy parts (mainly in the north) more and more people are dying of diseases caused by over-eating, in the poorer parts (mainly in the south) there are many people dying of starvation. Both greed and need are causing the earth's resources to be used up and spoiled. Things would be easier if there were fewer of us; but the problem is that it is in the countries where there is least to go round that people tend to have larger families.

Agriculture
The use of *man-made chemicals* as fertilisers, pesticides, fungicides and weed-killers has made the earth a more dangerous habitat for most species, even a deadly one. The notorious DDT which enters the food chain (see p. V23) and becomes concentrated was banned for use in the United States in 1972, but it is still made and exported to the Third World. Residues of chemicals remain in the food, in the soil and in the water supply; and more and more are needed as the soil quality declines. In China, which supports one fifth of the world's population, they have enough to go round using the older farming methods of crop-rotation and organic fertilisation. These methods are not only safer but provide more jobs. It seems a pity if it needs a repressive government to make people live ecologically.

Another big problem is *soil erosion*. Because we over-use the soil in all kinds of ways—eliminating tree cover, over-grazing, reducing it to dust—it is gradually washed and blown off our farmlands and into the sea. All over the world, we are losing topsoil far faster than nature can replace it.

Industry
Most of our ecological problems have come about since we became industrialised. Yet under-developed countries see becoming industrialised as the way to become wealthier, and it is not possible to preach to them about the virtues of a traditional rural lifestyle when we are enjoying so much greater material comfort.

So poorer countries are keen to develop industrially, and even to turn their farming into an industry. They also tend to be exploited by the wealthy nations into taking on the dangerous manufacturing processes, leading to disasters like that at Bhopal in India in 1984 (see p. A51), and to having toxic waste dumped.

Air

After a campaign of over twenty years by far-sighted people who were at first often branded as fools or trouble-makers, it has been recognised by everyone that the lead in car-exhaust fumes was damaging to health, and cars are changing over to unleaded petrol. But cars and industry also emit carbon dioxide which causes noxious smogs in some places and is contributing to global warming.

Water

Seven-tenths of our planet's surface is covered by ocean. It is a vast, astonishing and still largely unknown place, beautiful and rich in species. We are treating it as a drain. Land-dumped waste will eventually find its way to the sea, and some waste is dumped directly into the sea. Certain kinds of fishing, such as purse-seining, 'vacuum' the sea and deplete the fish-stocks. Some species, such as the whales, have been hunted almost to extinction.

In developed countries we take our tap water for granted, although every now and then we are advised not to drink it because of some kind of pollution, either by chemicals or bacteria or poisonous algae. Even so, many people who can afford it have taken to using water filters or drinking bottled spring-water. But in some parts of the world a polluted water supply is all they ever have, and it is a major cause of disease.

Fire

Fossil fuels

In order to produce light and heat in our homes, to run cars, trains and planes, and to make the thousands of things that we think we need or want that are now made in factories, something needs to be burnt in order to create energy. It has usually been either coal, oil or gas. These are found in or under the earth and ocean but they are not replaceable. We are fairly rapidly using them up. And there is the other problem that all this burning causes pollution. In some places, where people drive a very great deal and there is a lot of industry, it causes smogs and is contributing to the greenhouse effect and the destruction of the ozone layer.

Nuclear power
When it was discovered how to produce power by means of nuclear reactions, it seemed that this was the answer. However it is not only proving more costly than was expected and more difficult technically, but the number of leaks and serious accidents over the years have begun to make it seem to many people an unacceptable alternative. The most recent of these was the disaster at Chernobyl (see p. A53), as a result of which hundreds of people died, land in many different countries was contaminated, and many thousands of people will develop cancers in the years to come. Besides accidents, there is the problem of the huge stocks of deadly waste material that arc building up, and for which no safe storage place and no way of de-activating it can be found.

Other sources of power
The wind, the waves and the sun are all sources of power which are not *renewable*: that is, they are not used up by making use of them. Nor does the production of power by these means pollute. The problem is to harness these natural forces to give us power in large enough quantities. At the moment what is called the *political will* does not exist to pay enough clever people to work on this, which is surely not beyond human ingenuity given some of the other things we have managed to do, such as putting men on the moon. The political will simply means that enough people should demand of the government that a thing is done.

Using less
There is one more solution to the problems of non-renewability and pollution that generating power produces, and that is that we should use less. This solution is not politically popular because people who have a lot are loath to let go of it, and people who

have little or nothing are eager to have more. We keep wanting solutions that will enable us to keep up or increase our present level of consumption. A simpler way is to use public transport, cycle or walk, to make things last longer and buy secondhand, to add an extra blanket or sweater rather than turning the heating up, and so on.

What can I do to help?

As well as the suggestions in the section above you can

* Ask questions—think and get others thinking
* Persuade your parents to buy organic food or grow their own
* Encourage them to think green when they go shopping
* Start boxes for collecting household paper, glass and cans for re-cycling
* Try to get your school to recycle paper, and to use recycled paper and ecologically safe cleaning fluids
* Collect used cans for recycling—this can also get money for a good cause
* Start or join an environmental group—you can do more and it is more enjoyable to do things with others. Ecology is partly about our need for each other.

Further Reading

The Gaia Atlas of Planet Management ed. Norman Myers, Pan Books 1985
The WWF Environment Handbook: Mark Carwardine, 1990
The Young Green Consumer Guide: John Elkington and Julia Hailes, Gollancz 1990
The Young Person's Guide to Saving the Planet: Debbie Silver and Bernadette Vallely, Virago 1990
Save the Earth: ed. Jonathon Porritt, Dorling Kindersley, 1991
Global Ecology: Colin Tudge, Natural History Museum Publications, 1991/and go to see the Ecology Exhibition at the Natural History Museum in London
The Pocket Green Book: Andrew Rees, Zed Books, 1991

Organisations to join

Friends of the Earth
26–28 Underwood Street
London N1 7JQ

Greenpeace
Canonbury Villas
London N1 2PN

WATCH
The Green
Witham Park
Lincoln LN5 7JR

A national environmental club
for young people

A DICTIONARY OF SCIENCE AND MATHEMATICS

Very large numbers and very small numbers in this dictionary
are given in *standard form* (q.v.)

Aberration Deviation from perfect image formation in an optical
or equivalent system.

Absolute temperature A temperature scale originally suggested
by *Charles's Law* (q.v.) concerning the expansion of gases. This
law suggests that if a gas could be cooled down to $-273 \cdot 15°$ C
it would occupy zero volume. In fact, all gases liquefy before
reaching such a low temperature, but $-273 \cdot 15°$ C is the
minimum possible temperature, called absolute zero, below
which matter cannot be cooled. Even absolute zero is unattain-
able, although temperatures within one millionth of a degree
have been reached. The Absolute (or Kelvin) scale of temperature measures temperatures from absolute zero, with a degree
Kelvin being the same size as a degree *Celsius*. Consequently
water freezes at $273 \cdot 15°$ K (which is $0°$ C) and boils at $373 \cdot 15°$
K (which is $100°$ C). To convert an absolute temperature from
a Celsius temperature add $273 \cdot 15$.

The importance of the absolute scale is that it is always absolute
temperatures which appear in equations of *thermodynamics*
(q.v.) e.g. the *gas laws* (q.v.). See *Thermometer*.

Acceleration The rate at which velocity increases. Acceleration is
positive when speeding up and negative when slowing down.
Acceleration is measured in metres per second per second
(ms^{-2}) etc.

Accumulator A type of electric *cell* (q.v.) or battery that can be
recharged. The commonest sort (as used for car batteries) has
positive plates of lead peroxide and negative plates of spongy
lead with dilute sulphuric acid as the electrolyte.

Acid An acid is a type of chemical compound. Familiar examples
of acids include vinegar (ethanoic acid), lemon juice and the
juices of many fruits. These are all organic acids. Inorganic
acids include sulphuric acid (H_2SO_4) found in car batteries,
hydrochloric acid (HCl) and nitric acid (HNO_3). All acids contain

replaceable (or *acidic*) hydrogen in their molecules (though in organic acids, only the hydrogen in COOH is acidic), and the most characteristic reaction of acids is for this hydrogen to be replaced by a metal to form a *salt* (q.v.). Some metals react directly with acids to give a salt and hydrogen gas while another example of this kind of reaction is the neutralisation of an acid by a *base* (q.v.) to give a salt and water. E.g. Potassium hydroxide (a base) reacts with dilute nitric acid to give potassium nitrate (a salt) and water. Here the potassium replaces the acidic hydrogen which goes into making the water. The reason why acids so readily lose their acidic hydrogen is that in solutions of acids to a great extent the hydrogen is already separate from the rest of the molecule in the form of positive hydrogen ions.

Acids have a sour taste and when concentrated can be very corrosive and dangerous to handle. *Indicators* (q.v.) can be used to test whether a solution is acidic or not: e.g. in the presence of an acid, blue litmus turns red.

Acoustics The study of *sound*. See RADIO and TELEVISION.

Adsorption The taking-up of a gas by a solid in such a way that a layer of gas only one molecule thick is held firmly in the surface of the solid. Adsorption is an essential part of some chemical phenomena, including *catalysis* (q.v.).

Alkali A *base* (q.v.) that is soluble in water, e.g. the hydroxides of sodium and potassium (caustic soda and caustic potash). Alkalis can be identified in solution by means of *indicators* (q.v.).

Alpha radiation (Alpha Rays, α-Rays) This is a stream of particles that are the nuclei of helium atoms. They are emitted from radioactive substances. Some emitters of alpha rays are: uranium, radium, plutonium. Alpha rays have such little penetrating power that a sheet of paper will stop them, but where they do penetrate they have intense effects, because of their ability to ionise substances they bombard. If present in food which is eaten, for example, they could cause cancer by changing the structure of DNA.

Alternating Current See RADIO AND TELEVISION.

Altimeter An instrument used to measure height above sea level. It is based on the principle that pressure decreases with height and is therefore essentially an aneroid *barometer* (q.v.).

Amino-acid Amino-acids are organic compounds which link to-

gether in chains to produce *proteins* (q.v.). They are of the form
H_2N–CHR–COOH, where R represents a univalent side-chain.
Glycine is the simplest amino-acid in which R is a hydrogen
atom. A large number of amino-acids are possible, but there
are 20 or so which are the building blocks for proteins.

In proteins amino-acids link together by forming a peptide
bond between the carboxyl group (–COOH) of one amino-acid
and the amino group (H_2N–) of the next, with the elimination
of a water molecule. This process can be repeated to give
chains of great length.

Ampere (A) The SI unit of electric *current* (q.v.).

Angle Formed when two lines meet at a point. The angle at the
point is a measure of the proportion of the space round the
point which is between the two lines. The commonest unit of
angle is the degree. The space all round a point is defined to be
360 degrees. If two straight lines intersect at a point at right-
angles they divide the space round the point equally into four
and so each angle is 90 degrees. If three lines divide the space
round a point equally into six, each angle is 60 degrees. Angles
are often measured using a protractor.

The radian (q.v.) is an alternative unit for measuring angles.

If something is rotating around a point (or around an axis) an
angle can be used to measure the amount of the rotation.

Angular velocity The rate of motion through an angle about an
axis. Measured in degrees, revolutions or *radians* (q.v.) per unit
time. The angular velocity of a point in radians/unit time can
be calculated by dividing its linear velocity perpendicular to the
line joining it to the axis by the length of the line. In the diagram, the angular velocity of A (which has linear velocity v)
about C is v/r radians/sec. *Angular acceleration* is the rate of
change of angular velocity.

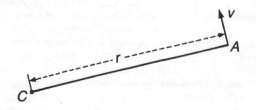

Angstrom (Å) A small unit of length used in atomic physics, to measure the wavelengths of X-rays and the distances between atoms in molecules, and crystals, for example. 1 angstrom = 10^{-10} m. X-rays have wavelengths of between $0 \cdot 1$ Å and 10 Å. The distance between neighbouring copper atoms in copper metal is $3 \cdot 4$ Å.

Anion A negatively charged atom or *radical* (q.v.).

Anode Positive electrode. See *Electrolysis*.

Antibody Antibodies are a very important class of *proteins* (q.v.) found in the blood of higher animals. They play a vital role in the defence against harmful foreign molecules and organisms (e.g. poisons, *viruses* (q.v.) and *bacteria* (q.v.)) which may have entered the body. Each antibody is able to recognise a specific foreign molecule (in the same way as a key is able only to open one lock). When this happens, other parts of the defence system (or *immune system*) are able to break down or inactivate the invading foreign molecule or organism.

    Antibodies against a particular organism are not present in an animal until the animal has been infected at least once with that organism. In other words, the body learns how to make antibodies against an infectious agent only after it has been in contact with that agent. If the animal is infected a second time by the same agent, antibodies against it will already exist and the agent can be destroyed before it can cause noticeable illness. This is why many illnesses are only had once in life (often in childhood); after the first attack, the body becomes *immune* to the illness. *Vaccination* is an artificial way of making someone immune to a disease (e.g. smallpox, cholera or influenza). Attenuated or dead infectious organisms are injected into the body. These do not cause the disease but stimulate the body to make antibodies against the organism. The body is thus prepared in advance and can defend itself in the event of a real infection.

Anti-matter Particles like electrons, protons and neutrons all have corresponding anti-particles: anti-electrons (called *positrons*), anti-protons and anti-neutrons. It has been conjectured that somewhere in the universe there exists anti-matter composed entirely of anti-particles (e.g. an anti-hydrogen atom would have an anti-proton as nucleus and one orbiting positron), but this has never been detected. If anti-matter were to meet ordinary matter both would be annihilated and much energy released.

Archimedes principle This states that when a body is partially or
totally immersed in a fluid (i.e. a liquid or gas) its apparent loss
of weight is equal to the weight of fluid displaced: i.e. the body
experiences an upthrust equal to the weight of fluid displaced.

Area The amount of space taken up by a two-dimensional object.
Common units of area are square metres, square inches, square
kilometres, square millimetres and square centimetres. To say
that an object has an area of 4 square metres means that it
takes up the same amount of space as 4 squares each of which
has sides of length 1 metre.

 The area of a rectangle can be found by dividing it into
squares. The area can be found by multiplying the number of
squares in a row by the number of rows.

Areas of common shapes

Figure	Area
Rectangle, sides a and b	ab
Triangle, sides a, b, c, vertical height h.	$\frac{1}{2}bh$
And if $s = \frac{1}{2}(a + b + c)$	$\sqrt{s(s - a)(s - b)(s - c)}$
Trapezoid, parallel sides a and c	$\frac{1}{2}h(a + c)$
Parallelogram, sides x and y, where θ = angle between sides	$xy \sin \theta$
Circle, radius r	πr^2
Sector of circle, radius r, θ – angle between radii boundaries	$\dfrac{r^2\theta}{2}$ (θ in radians)
Segment of circle	$\dfrac{r^2}{2} (\theta - \sin \theta)$ (θ in radians)
Ellipse, semi-axes a and b	πab
Surface of sphere, radius r	$4\pi r^2$
Surface of cylinder, height h, radius r	(1) $2\pi rh$ (curved surface only) (2) $2\pi r(h + r)$ (total surface)
Surface of cone, slant height l, radius r	(1) πrl (curved surface) (2) $\pi r(l + r)$ (total surface)

The area of a parallelogram can be found by cutting off a triangle and replacing it to produce a rectangle.

The area of a triangle can be found by halving the appropriate parallelogram.

It is sometimes appropriate to use trigonometry to find areas of triangles. Formulae such as *Heron's formula* (q.v.) can also be useful.

The area of a *circle* (q.v.) involves the use of (*pi*) (q.v.).

Atmosphere, Normal or Standard. A unit of air pressure. 1 normal atmosphere is the pressure needed to support a column of mercury 760 mm high at 0° C at sea-level at Lat. 45°. 1 normal atmosphere = $101\,320\,\text{Nm}^{-2}$.

An alternative unit of atmospheric pressure is the bar, defined to be $10^5\,\text{Nm}^{-2}$. Thus a normal atmosphere is 1.0132 bars = 1013.2 millibars. The millibar is the unit used in weather forecasts for shipping, for example.

Atom The smallest particle of an *element* (q.v.) still retaining the chemical properties of that element.

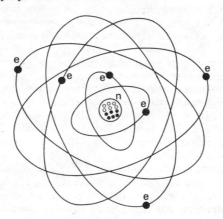

Carbon atom

The carbon atom has 6 electrons, 2 on inner orbits, 4 on outer orbits. These 4 are the valency electrons. The nucleus has 6 protons and 6 neutrons all very close together. Almost all the mass of the atom is in the nucleus.

It consists of a positively charged heavy nucleus surrounded by negatively charged electrons, which can be pictured as moving in orbits similar to the way in which planets move round the sun. The positive charge on the nucleus exactly balances the total negative charge of all the surrounding electrons when the atom is neutral.

The nucleus consists of two types of particle held together by the strong nuclear force (q.v.)—protons and neutrons. A proton carries one unit of positive charge. A neutron has no charge. The mass of a neutron is very slightly more than the mass of a proton.

The chemical properties of the atom are determined by the electrons, which in number, of course, are equivalent to the proton charge in the nucleus. So if a proton is removed from (or added to) the nucleus of an atom it is no longer the same element. The addition or subtraction of neutrons, however, makes no difference to the chemical properties.

The number of protons (and the corresponding number of electrons) determines the element. An atom of carbon, for example, has six electrons, an atom of copper twenty-nine, an atom of uranium ninety-two. The simplest atom is that of hydrogen, whose nucleus is one proton and which has one electron.

Atomic number The number of protons in the nucleus of an atom and therefore also the number of electrons. Elements are often listed in the order of their atomic numbers. See *Elements*.

Atomic pile Original name for a *nuclear reactor* (q.v.).

Atomic weight A number showing how heavy the atom of an element is. The standard for comparison is one of the *isotopes* (q.v.) of carbon, carbon 12, for which the atomic weight is taken to be 12 exactly.

The atomic weight of an element is roughly equal to the total number of protons and neutrons in the nucleus of one of its atoms. There are two reasons why atomic weights are not whole numbers. One is that mass is lost in the form of energy when protons and neutrons fuse together to make a nucleus. The other is that naturally occurring elements frequently consist of a mixture of isotopes.

Avogadro's law Equal volumes of all gases under the same conditions of temperature and pressure contain equal numbers of molecules.

Bacterium (pl.: **bacteria**) Microscopic single-celled living organisms, more complicated than *viruses* (q.v.) but simpler than
animal or plant *cells* (q.v.). Bacteria are found everywhere and
are important in causing the decay of organic matter; in making
atmospheric nitrogen available for use by plants; and in causing
many diseases (such as typhoid, cholera and food poisoning).

Barometer Barometers are instruments used to measure air pressure. A common type of barometer is the aneroid barometer
(aneroid means without the use of liquid). An aneroid barometer consists of a spring attached to an evacuated chamber.
As the air pressure changes the spring is stretched or compressed and this is shown by a pointer attached to the spring.

Base A chemical substance which reacts with an *acid* (q.v.) to
give a *salt* (q.v.) and water only. Bases may be insoluble (e.g.
copper II oxide) or soluble (see *Alkali*).

Battery The name currently given to an electric *cell* (q.v.). Originally a battery meant several cells connected together in series
to give a greater voltage. For example, three cells, each $1 \cdot 5$ V
connected in series give $4 \cdot 5$ V.

Beta radiation (Beta Rays, β-Rays) A stream of very fast electrons emitted by some radioactive substances. These electrons
come from the nucleus by breakdown of neutrons, not from the
planetary electrons. Beta rays are more penetrating than *alpha
rays* (q.v.), the most energetic of them being capable of penetrating 1 mm of lead. Because of their penetrating power they
are used for the measurement of thickness in industry, e.g. the
thickness of the tin layer on iron in tinplate.

Big Bang Theory The currently favoured theory of the origin of
the universe. About ten billion (10^{10}) years ago the universe
was in a state of extreme compression and since then it has
been continuously expanding. The expansion of the universe is
observable today through the rapidity with which galaxies
(distinct groups of many millions of stars) are moving apart
from each other. It is possible that the expansion of the universe
will slow down and change to a contraction in the future. The
universe might then return to its highly compressed state.
However, more recent evidence supports the idea that the
universe will continue to expand for ever.

Billion Now used to mean 10^9. Previously the word billion was
used in USA to mean 10^9 and in the United Kingdom to

mean 10^{12}. Where billion is used in this dictionary it means 10^{9}.

Black hole The term used to describe immensely dense stars with gravitational fields so powerful that nothing, not even radiation, can escape from them.

Bond The method of binding together of atoms to form molecules. Three types of bond account for most compounds. They are:

(*a*) Electrovalent bond (ionic, polar);

(*b*) Covalent bond (non-polar, homopolar);

(*c*) Dative bond (co-ordinate, semipolar).

The *electrovalent bond* exists in simple compounds where one atom needs an electron and the other gives it. Thus a sodium ion is positively charged when giving an electron and a chlorine ion is negatively charged when it accepts an electron. In solution these ions exist separately, but in the solid the positive binds to the negative to form a *crystal* (q.v.).

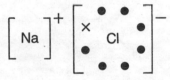

Electrovalent bond

The sodium, less one electron, is positive. The chlorine with an extra electron is negative.

The *covalent bond* works differently. It is created by the giving of an electron from each atom in such a way that each shares the pair of electrons thus formed. This accounts for the binding of atoms that are not ionised in solution and atoms that are the same. For example, it is a covalent bond that makes a molecule of hydrogen from two atoms. It is a covalent bond that holds together the two hydrogen atoms and one oxygen atom in a molecule of water.

The *dative bond* also depends on the sharing of a pair of electrons, but in this case one atom supplies both. This bond is that found in many complex compounds in which some of the atoms remain together as a group even when the compound itself is ionised in solution. For example, potassium ferrocyanide

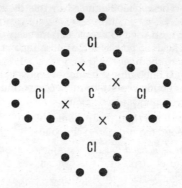

Covalent bond—carbon tetrachloride

The seven electrons of chlorine are shown as dots, the four electrons of carbon as x's.

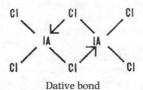

Dative bond

The arrows indicate the giving of electrons by chlorine to aluminium. These arrowed lines show dative bonds, the ordinary lines covalent bonds.

ionises in water to form positive potassium ions and negative 'ferrocyanide' ions.

Boyle's law This states that if a fixed mass of gas is compressed or expanded without change in temperature the product of volume and pressure remains constant. If P is pressure and V is volume the law is usually expressed thus:

$$PV = K \text{ (where } K \text{ is a constant)}$$

Calorie A unit of heat energy. It is the amount of heat required to raise the temperature of 1 gram of water through $1°$ C. The kilocalorie, which is 1000 calories, is used to express the energy content of foods. Confusingly, a kilocalorie is often called simply a calorie. The *joule* (q.v.) is the unit now used to express heat energy in most applications. 1 calorie = 4.187 joules. 1 kilocalorie = $4 \cdot 187$ kilojoules.

Catalysis A process in which a chemical reaction is speeded up, sometimes tremendously, by the presence of an extra substance, called the catalyst, that is the same chemically at the end of the reaction as it is at the beginning. Many industrial processes depend on catalysis. A simple example is the quick combination of hydrogen and oxygen into water where platinum is present. It is believed that the catalysis in this case is due to *adsorption* (q.v.) on the surface of the platinum.

Cation A positively charged atom or *radical* (q.v.).

Cell (a) A source of *electromotive force* (q.v.) caused by chemical action. A primary cell is one that cannot be recharged once its electrolyte or electrodes are used up. A simple primary cell consists of zinc and copper in dilute sulphuric acid. The copper is the positive electrode and the zinc the negative. This is the simple voltaic cell. It is of no use for practical work. A dry cell of the normal type consists of zinc as the negative pole or electrode, in the form of the container, with a jelly of ammonium chloride as the electrolyte and central carbon rod as the positive pole or electrode. This gives $1 \cdot 5$ V. Many other dry cells have been developed for use in rockets and satellites. A fuel cell is one in which primary fuels or derivatives of them are used. A solar cell is not really chemical. It consists of a special substance that generates electricity when light shines on it. A secondary cell can be recharged. See *Accumulator*.

(b) In biology, the cell is the basic structural unit of most living things. Some small organisms such as *bacteria* (q.v.) and the amoeba (a simple animal) consist of only one cell. Higher plants and animals are *multi-cellular*, being composed of many cells fulfilling different functions. A human being consists of approximately 10^{15} cells.

Centripetal force The force acting on a body which constrains it to move in a curved path. For a body of mass m travelling in a circle of radius r at velocity v the force is $m \cdot v^2/r$ and is directed towards the centre of the circle.

Charles's law The law that determines the effect of heat on a gas when the pressure is kept constant. It states that the volume of a gas (*any* gas) increases by a certain fixed amount ($\frac{1}{273}$ of its volume at 0° C) for every degree Centrigrade rise in temperature. Another way of stating this is to say that if the pressure is constant, the volume of a fixed mass of any gas is directly proportional to its *absolute temperature* (q.v.).

Circle A shape in which every point on the *perimeter* (q.v.) is the same distance from a fixed point, called the centre.

The perimeter of a circle is called the circumference.

The radius of a circle means either a straight line segment drawn from the centre of the circle to its circumference, or the length of such a line.

The diameter of a circle means either a straight line segment drawn through the centre of the circle to cut it in half, or the length of such a line.

If R is the radius of a circle, D is its diameter, C is its circumference and A is its area:

$$C = \pi D$$
$$A = \pi R^2$$

See also π (Pi).

Circumference The usual word for the perimeter of a *circle* (q.v.). Also used for the perimeter of other shapes with a curved boundary, such as ellipses.

Coefficient In physics and technology the word coefficient is used to indicate an experimentally determined constant value of importance. Examples are the coefficient of linear expansion of a material, and the coefficient of friction between two materials.

Colloid A material that does not dissolve in a liquid is usually deposited on the bottom if the particles are big enough. If the particles are small enough, however, they remain in suspension though individually invisible, kept up by the random movements of the molecules of solvent. Particles as small as this are said to be colloidal, and the suspension they form is a colloidal solution.

Colour The sensation when the eye receives certain wavelengths of light. Ordinary 'white' light consists of electromagnetic radiation of many different wavelengths from about 4,000 angstroms to about 7,000 angstroms. If these are spread out as in a spectrum so that only a portion enters the eye at a time, then as the eye moves along the spectrum from the short-wavelength end to the long-wavelength end colour is seen, going from violet to red through a series usually given as seven, namely, violet, indigo, blue, green, yellow, orange, red. (Mnemonic: Richard of York Gained Battles in Vain). These are the colours of the rainbow. Actually this is a very rough-and-ready description. If tiny separate parts of the spectrum are exposed one at a time hundreds of different hues can be seen.

The colours of everyday objects are caused by selective absorption of parts of the spectrum of white light.

Complex numbers These are numbers used to extend the set of real numbers.

The letter i (or sometimes j) is used to denote the number which is the square root of -1. Examples of complex numbers are $2 + 3i$, $4 - 7i$, and $-6 - 6i$. In general, a + bi is a complex number (a and b are real numbers).

Complex numbers are often represented geometrically by the points of a coordinate plane (see *coordinates*). The horizontal axis represents the real numbers.

Compound A substance that consists of chemical elements bonded together. Example: the elements sodium and chlorine when combined together chemically make sodium chloride (common salt), a compound.

Conductor An electrical conductor is a material that conducts electricity easily, such as the metals. The best conductor is silver and the next best copper.

Congruent Two shapes are congruent if they have exactly the same shape *and* size (compare with *similar*).

Conversion table

1 cm = 0·3937 in	1 yd = 0·9144018 m
1 m = 39·37 in	1 sq in = 6·451626 sq cm
1 sq cm = 0·1549997 sq in	1 sq yd = 0·8361307 sq m
1 sq m = 1·195985 sq yd	1 acre = 0·404687 hectare
1 hectare = 2·471 acres	1 cu yd = 0·7645594 cu m
1 cu m = 1·3079428 cu yd	1 gal = 4·54596 litres
1 litre = 0·21997 gal	1 lb = 0·4539237 kg
1 kg = 2·204622341 lbs	1 ton (2,240 lbs) = 1·01605 tonnes
1 in = 2·54005 cm	

These figures are very exact. Quick, very rough answers can be obtained by the methods below:

To Turn
Metres into feet multiply by $3\frac{1}{4}$
Feet into metres multiply by 3 and divide by 10
Metres into yards add $\frac{1}{10}$

Yards into metres subtract $\frac{1}{10}$
Kilometres into miles multiply by 5 and divide by 8
Miles into kilometres add $\frac{2}{3}$ of the number of miles
Square metres into square yards add $\frac{1}{5}$
Square yards into square metres subtract $\frac{1}{5}$
Square kilometres into square miles multiply by 2 and divide by 5
Square miles into square kilometres multiply by $2\frac{3}{5}$
Cubic metres into cubic yards add $\frac{1}{3}$
Cubic yards into cubic metres subtract $\frac{1}{4}$
Kilogrammes into pounds add $\frac{1}{10}$ and multiply by 2
Pounds into kilogrammes subtract $\frac{1}{10}$ and divide by 2
Litres into pints add $\frac{3}{4}$
Pints into litres multiply by 3 and divide by 5

Convex A two-dimensional or three-dimensional shape is convex if it does not have any 'dents' in it. A more formal way of saying this is that if a shape is convex, whatever point on the perimeter is chosen, an infinite straight line can be drawn through that point no part of which is inside the shape.

All triangles are convex. Polygons with more than three sides can be convex or non-convex.

Coordinate geometry The study of geometry by using coordinates to represent points. *Pythagoras' theorem* (q.v.) is fundamental to coordinate geometry, because it can be used to find the distance between two points which are given in terms of coordinates.

Coordinates The plane is two-dimensional and so each point in the plane can be represented by two numbers, called coordinates. Two common ways of doing this are called Cartesian and polar coordinates.

To use Cartesian coordinates two perpendicular lines, called axes, are drawn on the plane. The two numbers used to describe a point are the distance of the point from each of the axes.

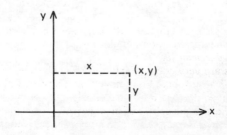

To use polar coordinates a point, called the pole, is defined on the plane and a half-line, called the initial line, is drawn from the pole. The two numbers used to represent any point are its distance from the pole and the angle between the initial line and the direction from the pole to the point.

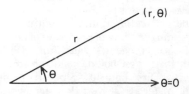

When coordinates are used to represent points in three-dimensional space, each point is represented by three numbers.

Cosine In trigonometry the cosine of an angle is the x-coordinate of the point on the circle, centre origin and radius 1, reached after turning through that angle anticlockwise starting at the x-axis.

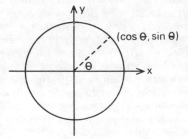

The sine of the angle is the y-coordinate of this point.

The tangent of the angle is the sine of the angle divided by the cosine.

If the angle is less than a right-angle, an equivalent definition of the cosine and sine of an angle can be obtained by drawing a *right-angled triangle* (q.v.).

Cosmic rays are very energetic charged particles which penetrate the Earth's atmosphere from outer space, although their source is still uncertain. They consist chiefly of protons with some electrons, alpha-particles and heavier nuclei. Cosmic rays that collide with gas particles in the atmosphere can produce a variety of *elementary particles* (q.v.) which may be detected using equipment carried by balloons, rockets or satellites. Several elementary particles were first discovered in this way.

Cosmology The study of the origin, evolution and structure of the universe, nowadays carried out using satellite-borne X-ray and ultra-violet telescopes as well as earth-bound optical, infra-red and radio telescopes. See *Big Bang Theory*.

Cryogenics The science of producing and maintaining very low temperatures and the study of properties of matter at those temperatures. Modern cryogenics dates from 1908 when helium, the gas with the lowest boiling point at atmospheric pressure ($-269°$ C), was first liquefied. Since then many remarkable properties of materials at very low temperatures have been discovered: e.g. *superconductivity* (q.v.).

Crystal A solid composed of a group of atoms or molecules which is repeated in space to form a very regular structure, e.g. common salt, sugar, diamond and ice. Each grain of salt is a small crystal of sodium chloride which is composed of positively charged sodium ions (Na^+) and negatively charged chlorine ions (Cl^-) held together by electrostatic *bonds* (q.v.). The crystal consists of millions of tiny cubes stacked together with the Na^+ and Cl^- ions arranged alternately at the corners of each cube. The beautiful hexagonal shapes of snowflakes (which are ice crystals) are due to the very ordered arrangement of the innumerable water molecules (H_2O) in them. However most *metals* (q.v.) are also crystalline even though they do not appear especially regular. Non-crystalline solids (e.g. wood and glass) are called *amorphous* which means without regular structure.

Crystallography The science that investigates the regular structure of *crystals* (q.v.), often by the technique of *X-ray diffraction* (q.v.).

Current Electric current is the rate of flow of electric charge. In a metallic conductor this flow is due to electrons, which drift along between the metal atoms. As electrons are negatively charged, they are going in the opposite direction to the direction of current usually accepted. A current of 1 A is equivalent to the flow of approximately 6×10^{18} electrons per second.

Decagon See *Polygon*.

Decibel See RADIO AND TELEVISION.

Decimal The word means 'based on ten'. Our system of writing

Relative densities (specific gravity) of common substances

Metals			Liquids at 15°C		
Steel	.	. 7·6–7·8	Acetone	.	. 0·79
Brass	.	. 8·4–8·7	Alcohol	.	. 0·79
Aluminium	.	. 2·70	Ether	.	. 0·74
Copper	.	. 8·95	Glycerine	.	. 1·26
Lead	.	. 11·34	Oil (lubricating)		0·9–0·92
Titanium	.	. 4·54	Turpentine	.	. 0·87
Mercury	.	. 13·55	Blood	.	. 1·04–1·067
			Water at 4° C		. 1·00

Miscellaneous Solids			Gases at NTP		
Celluloid	.	. 1·4	Air	. .	. 0·00129
Glass	.	. 2·4–2·8	Argon	.	. 0·0017837
Ice	. .	. 0·92	Carbon dioxide		0·00198
Paraffin Wax	.	0·9	Helium	.	. 0·0001785
Brick	.	. 2·1	Hydrogen	.	. 0·0000899
Coal (soft)	.	. 1·3	Methane	.	. 0·000717
Diamond	.	. 3·52	Oxygen	.	. 0·0014290
Rubber	.	. 0·97–0·99			
Balsa wood	.	0·12–0·2			
Ebony	.	. 1·19			
Lignum vitae	.	. 1·25			
Oak	.	. 0·74			
Boxwood	.	. 0·93			
Cork	.	. 0·24			

numbers is a decimal system because, moving to the left, the digits of a number increase in value by a multiple of ten.

A decimal also means a number which requires a decimal point. 3·4 and 2·75 are decimals.

When the fraction $\frac{1}{3}$ is written in the decimal system a recurring decimal is produced. $\frac{1}{3}$ is 0·3333333. . . . where the 3 is repeated for ever. This is often written as 0·$\dot{3}$. $\frac{1}{7}$ is 0·142857142857142857. . . or 0·$\dot{1}$42857$\dot{7}$.

The fraction $\frac{3}{4}$ is 0·75. A decimal like this which has only a finite number of digits is called a terminating decimal.

Rational numbers (q.v.) can be represented exactly either as terminating or recurring decimals. Irrational numbers cannot.

Density The mass per unit volume of a substance. It can be expressed in kilograms/cubic metre, tons/cubic yard, pounds/cubic foot, etc. The density of a substance varies with temperature. Often the *relative density* or *specific gravity* is used. This is the ratio of the density of a substance to that of water at $4°$ C and is therefore simply a number. The density of water at $4°$ C is 1,000 kg/m^3 or 1 gm/cc. The two densest substances are osmium and iridium.

Deoxyribonucleic acid (DNA) The molecule found in the nucleus of nearly all living cells which carries the genetic code responsible for determining the organism's structure. See *Proteins, DNA.*

Diagonal A diagonal of a polygon is the line segment joining two vertices of the polygon which are NOT next to each other.

Diffraction An important property of light and other *waves* (q.v.). For most everyday purposes light can be assumed to travel in straight lines, although it may undergo *reflection* (q.v.) or *refraction* (q.v.) at the boundary of different media. But because light is a wave motion it can also be spread into secondary waves by objects in its path. This process is known as diffraction and is closely connected with the phenomenon of *interference* (q.v.). Diffraction effects are most marked when the obstacles in the path of the light are roughly of the same size as the wavelength of the light. This is the case in *X-ray diffraction* (q.v.) by *crystals* (q.v.).

Direct current (DC) A current passing in the same direction all the time round a circuit. It can vary in strength, but not in direction.

Dispersion The name given to the splitting-up of light into the spectrum by a prism or lens.

Dissociation The reversible splitting-up of a chemical compound into parts. *Thermal dissociation* may occur when a compound is heated: e.g. ammonium chloride dissociates into the gases ammonia and hydrogen chloride on heating. *Electrolytic dissociation* into charged ions may occur when a compound is dissolved in water: e.g. hydrogen chloride gas dissolves in water to give hydrochloric acid which is dissociated into positive hydrogen ions and negative chloride ions.

DNA (Deoxyribonucleic acid) A very important biological *polymer* (q.v.) which is the genetic material of most living organisms. It contains four different kinds of chemical units called *bases* or *nucleotides.* These can be joined together in any order to form extremely long chains of many thousands of bases. DNA is usually found in a double helical structure, that is with two chains winding around each other. An important feature of this structure, which was first described by Watson and Crick in 1953, is that the two strands of the double-helix are not identical but *complementary*. This means that the sequence of bases in one strand automatically determines the sequence in the other strand and therefore one strand can be used as a template to reconstruct the other.

In plants and animals, the DNA is packed in structures known as *chromosomes* which are found in the nuclei of *cells* (q.v.). The importance of DNA is that it contains the information required by a cell to make the *proteins* (q.v.) necessary for the cell's proper functioning. This *genetic information* is contained in the particular sequence of bases along the DNA chain according to the *genetic code* (q.v.). Before cells divide, the DNA in them is duplicated so that each of the daughter cells has a copy and can therefore produce its own proteins. In this way the characteristics of living things are transmitted from one generation to the next, a process known as *heredity*. The duplication of DNA depends on the fact (mentioned above) that one strand of the double helix can be used to make the other strand.

Electrode The name given to the material through which electricity is led into or away from a gas or liquid. The negative electrode is called the cathode and the positive electrode the anode.

Electrolyte A compound which, when molten or dissolved in solution, *dissociates* (q.v.) into oppositely charged *ions* (q.v.) and can thus carry an electric current.

Compounds formed by electrovalent *bonds* (q.v.), such as *salts* (q.v.), are commonly electrolytes. For example, sodium chloride consists of distinct Na^+ and Cl^- ions, but when solid the ions are held rigidly together in a crystal structure which does not conduct electricity. When molten or dissolved in water, the ions are not held together so strongly and are able to move under the influence of an electric potential. Thus an electrolyte can conduct electricity (see *Electrolysis*).

Electrolysis The movement of ions to form an electric current in an electrolyte, usually as the result of an applied electric potential. Negative ions move towards the anode and positive ions towards the cathode. As a result, gases may be liberated or metal deposited. When metal is deposited on the cathode the process is called electroplating.

Electron *Elementary particle* (q.v.) with small mass and unit negative charge. Electrons can be thought of as orbiting the nucleus of an *atom* (q.v.) rather as the planets orbit the sun.

Electromagnetic radiation This consists of waves of varying electrical and magnetic quantities travelling along at the speed of light. Light, radio waves, X-rays, gamma rays, are all electromagnetic radiation. (See RADIO AND TELEVISION.)

Electromotive force (e.m.f.) The electrical pressure developed by a cell, battery or generator which enables it to produce an electric current in a circuit. Measured in volts.

Elements The chemical units of which compounds are made. There are 92 naturally occurring chemical elements, though some have never been prepared, and a number have been made artificially (transuranic elements) to extend the list to 105 or more.

The elements

Atomic number	Name	Symbol	Atomic weight	Relative densities (gases at NTP)
1	Hydrogen	H	1·008	0·0000899
2	Helium	He	4·003	0·0001785
3	Lithium	Li	6·939	0·534
4	Beryllium	Be	9·012	1·85
5	Boron	B	10·811	2·34
6	Carbon	C	12·011	Diamond 3·52 / Graphite 2·25 / Amorphous 0·5–1·0
7	Nitrogen	N	14·007	0·0012506
8	Oxygen	O	15·999	0·0014290
9	Fluorine	F	18·998	0·0016970
10	Neon	Ne	20·183	0·008999
11	Sodium	Na	22·990	0·97
12	Magnesium	Mg	24·312	1·75
13	Aluminium	Al	26·982	2·70
14	Silicon	Si	28·086	2·33
15	Phosphorus	P	30·974	Yellow 1·82 / Red 2·20
16	Sulphur	S	32·064	Monoclinic 1·96 / Rhombic 2·07
17	Chlorine	Cl	35·453	0·00321
18	Argon	Ar	39·948	0·0017837
19	Potassium	K	39·102	0·862
20	Calcium	Ca	40·08	1·55

Atomic number	Name	Symbol	Atomic weight	Relative densities (gases at NTP)
21	Scandium	Sc	44·956	3·0
22	Titanium	Ti	47·90	4·54
23	Vanadium	V	50·94	6·11
24	Chromium	Cr	52·00	7·18
25	Manganese	Mn	54·94	7·21
26	Iron	Fe	55·85	7·87
27	Cobalt	Co	58·93	8·9
28	Nickel	Ni	58·71	8·9
29	Copper	Cu	63·54	8·95
30	Zinc	Zn	65·37	7·14
31	Gallium	Ga	69·72	5·90
32	Germanium	Ge	72·59	5·32
33	Arsenic	As	74·92	5·73
34	Selenium	Se	78·96	Red 4·45 Grey 4·80
35	Bromine	Br	79·909	3·12
36	Krypton	Kr	83·80	0·003733
37	Rubidium	Rb	85·47	1·53
38	Strontium	Sr	87·62	2·55
39	Yttrium	Y	88·905	4·46
40	Zirconium	Zr	91·22	6·5
41	Niobium	Nb	92·906	8·57
42	Molybdenum	Mo	95·94	10·2
43	Technetium	Tc	99	—
44	Ruthenium	Ru	101·07	12·2
45	Rhodium	Rh	102·91	12·4
46	Palladium	Pd	106·4	12·0
47	Silver	Ag	107·87	10·5
48	Cadmium	Cd	112·40	8·65
49	Indium	In	114·82	7·31
50	Tin	Sn	118·69	7·31
51	Antimony	Sb	121·75	6·69
52	Tellurium	Te	127·60	6·25
53	Iodine	I	126·904	4·94
54	Xenon	Xe	131·30	0·005887
55	Caesium	Cs	132·905	1·90
56	Barium	Ba	137·34	3·5
57	Lanthanum	La	138·91	6·15
58	Cerium	Ce	140·12	6·77
59	Praseodymium	Pr	140·907	6·77
60	Neodymium	Nd	144·24	7·00
61	Prometheum	Pm	147	—

Atomic number	Name	Symbol	Atomic weight	Relative densities (gases at NTP)
62	Samarium	Sm	150·35	7·54
63	Europium	Eu	151·96	5·25
64	Gadolinium	Gd	157·25	7·90
65	Terbium	Tb	158·92	8·23
66	Dysprosium	Dy	162·50	8·54
67	Holmium	Ho	164·93	8·78
68	Erbium	Er	167·26	9·05
69	Thulium	Tm	168·93	9·31
70	Ytterbium	Yb	173·04	6·97
71	Lutecium	Lu	174·97	9·84
72	Hafnium	Hf	178·49	13·3
73	Tantalum	Ta	180·95	16·6
74	Wolfram	W	183·85	19·3
75	Rhenium	Re	186·2	21·0
76	Osmium	Os	190·2	22·5
77	Iridium	Ir	192·2	22·4
78	Platinum	Pt	195·09	21·4
79	Gold	Au	196·97	19·3
80	Mercury	Hg	200·59	13·55
81	Thallium	Tl	204·37	11·85
82	Lead	Pb	207·19	11·34
83	Bismuth	Bi	208·98	9·75
84	Polonium	Po	210	9·32
85	Astatine	At	211	—
86	Radon	Rn	222	0·009725
87	Francium	Fr	223	—
88	Radium	Ra	226·05	5·0
89	Actinium	Ac	227·05	—
90	Thorium	Th	232·12	11·7
91	Protactinium	Pa	231·05	15·37
92	Uranium	U	238·07	18·95
93*	Neptunium	Np	237	20·25
94*	Plutonium	Pu	239	19·84
95*	Americium	Am	241	13·67
96*	Curium	Cm	242	—
97*	Berkelium	Bk	243–250	—
98*	Californium	Cf	251	—
99*	Einsteinium	Es	246, 247, 249, 251–256	—
100*	Fermium	Fm	250, 252–256	—
101*	Mendelevium	Md	256	—

Atomic number	Name	Symbol	Atomic weight	Relative densities (gases at NTP)
102*Nobelium		No	254	—
103*Lawrencium		Lr	257	—
104*Kurchatovium(?)		Ku	—	—
105*Hahnium(?)		—	—	—

* These are called transuranic elements. They have all been artificially created, often in negligibly small amounts, by means of nuclear reactors or machines such as cyclotrons.

Elementary particle Electrons, protons and neutrons are the most common elementary particles that make up *atoms* (q.v.) and nuclei. However, many other particles smaller than atoms are now known to exist, though high energy *particle accelerators* (q.v.) are usually needed to create them. Many of these fundamental or elementary particles are very short-lived and decay into more stable particles or gamma rays in a minute fraction of a second. Examples of these elementary particles are the *neutrino* (a particle with no mass and no charge), the *π-mesons* (which help to explain how the protons and neutrons in a nucleus stay together) and heavier particles like the Σ (*sigma*) and the Ω− (*omega minus*). The list of elementary particles keeps growing as accelerators of higher and higher energy are built. Recent discoveries have been the psi (1974) and upsilon (1977) particles.

All the elementary particles so far discovered seem to fall into two classes called *leptons* (q.v.) and *hadrons* (q.v.). Leptons (e.g. the electron and neutrino) behave as if they are pointlike and indivisible. Hadrons (of which there are well over a hundred e.g. proton, neutron, mesons, Σ, psi) however are thought to be made up of a small number of yet more fundamental particles called *quarks* (q.v.).

Energy The capacity of a body or substance for doing work. It can exist in a number of forms, e.g. mechanical, potential, heat, chemical, electrical, radiant and nuclear energy. The law of conservation of energy states that energy is never lost or gained but only changes from one form to another.

In driving a car to the top of a hill, work is done against the force of gravity and the car gains *potential* energy. This is converted into *kinetic* energy of motion as the car freewheels down the hill. Friction at the moving parts causes wastage of energy as *heat* energy and the car would slow down without the engine which converts *chemical* energy stored in the petrol into kinetic energy.

In Einstein's theory of relativity, mass and energy are equivalent in the sense that all matter is a form of potential energy, and any form of energy (for example, light) has mass proportional to its energy, according to the formula $E = mc^2$ (m = mass, c = speed of light). In nuclear fission and fusion, the energy latent in matter is released in the form of electromagnetic energy. The mass left has been reduced according to the formula $E = mc^2$. This is the origin of the energy released in nuclear bombs and in the Sun. The Sun's energy reaches the Earth in the form of radiant energy (heat and light rays).

All forms of energy are now measured in *joules* (q.v.).

Useful formulae:

Kinetic energy = $mv^2/2$ (m = mass of body, v = velocity of body).

Change in potential energy = mgh (m = mass, g = gravitational acceleration, h = change in vertical height).

Electrical energy = VIt (V = voltage, I = current, t = time).

Change in heat content = $ms (T_2 - T_1)$ (m = mass, s = specific heat, T_2 = final temperature, T_1 = initial temperature).

Enzyme A *catalyst* (q.v.) made by living organisms for the speeding up of biochemical reactions. Enzymes are generally *proteins* (q.v.).

Equiangular A polygon is equiangular if all its angles are equal.

An equiangular quadrilateral is called a rectangle (all its angles are right angles).

An equiangular triangle is also *equilateral* (q.v.). Equilateral polygons with more than three sides are not necessarily equiangular.

Equilateral A polygon is equilateral if the lengths of all of its sides are equal.

An equilateral quadrilateral is called a rhombus.

An equilateral triangle is also equiangular (q.v.). Equilateral polygons with more than three sides are not necessarily equiangular.

Equivalent weight The equivalent weight of an element is the number of units by weight of it that will combine with, or

displace, 1 unit of hydrogen or 8 units of oxygen. It is therefore equal to the atomic weight divided by the valency. The
equivalent weight of an acid is the weight of acid containing
unit weight of replaceable hydrogen (see *Acid*), and that of a
base is the weight of base required to neutralise the equivalent weight of an acid.

Expansion Most substances expand on being heated, and each
has its own capacity for such expansion. The coefficient of linear
expansion is the figure that is used for finding how much a
substance expands in one direction

$$l_2 = l_1 (1 + \alpha t)$$

Where l_1 is the length at the first temperature, t is the rise in
temperature in degrees Centigrade, α is the coefficient of linear
expansion and l_2 is the length at the second temperature.

A similar relationship exists for volume expansion. If V_1 =
volume at first temperature, t = rise in temperature in degrees
Centigrade, β is the coefficient of cubical expansion and V_2 =
the volume at the second temperature

$$V_2 = V_1 (1 + \beta t)$$

For solids $\beta = 3\alpha$ approximately.

Exterior angle To imagine an exterior angle of a polygon one of
the sides of a polygon needs to be extended. The angle between
this side and its neighbouring side *outside* the polygon is an
exterior angle. (See interior angle.)

If an exterior angle is formed at each vertex of a *convex*
polygon, the sum of these exterior angles is always 360 degrees.

Factorial The factorial of a number is the product of all numbers
up to and including that number. Factorial 4, usually written
4!, means $4 \times 3 \times 2 \times 1 = 24$. $7! = 7 \times 6 \times 5 \times 4 \times 3 \times 2 \times 1 = 5040$.

Factorials are important in probability. This is because the
number of different ways in which N objects can be arranged
in a list is N! For example, if you have six cards and shuffle
them thoroughly the number of different orders the cards can
finish up in is $6! = 720$.

Factorising Factorising a whole number means writing the
number as the product of other numbers. For example, $12 = 3 \times 4, 75 = 5 \times 15, 48 = 8 \times 3 \times 2$.

The numbers which are multiplied together are called *factors* of the number.

12 can be written as 12×1 or as 6×2 or as 4×3. So the factors of 12 are 1, 2, 3, 4, 6 and 12.

If a number is written in the form of an algebraic formula this too can sometimes be factorised. Here are some examples.

$3ab + 9b^2 = 3b(a + 3b)$
$a^2 - b^2 = (a - b)(a + b)$
$a^2 + 2ab + b^2 = (a + b)^2$
$a^2 - 2ab + b^2 = (a - b)^2$
$x^2 - 7x + 12 = (x - 3)(x - 4)$
$2x^2 + 5xy - 3y^2 = (2x - y)(x + 3y)$

See also *Prime numbers*.

Factors See *Factorising*.

Fission The splitting of a thing into two more or less equal parts. In nuclear fission, the nucleus of an atom splits into two parts accompanied by the release of nuclear energy and one or more neutrons. Fission may occur spontaneously or by the nucleus being hit by a neutron, but only occurs readily in certain *fissile* materials such as uranium 235 and plutonium 239. It is possible that the neutrons released during fission can hit other nuclei and bring about further fission. This process can be repeated and result in a runaway *chain reaction* with an enormous build-up of energy. However, a chain reaction can only occur if the amount of fissile material is above a *critical size*, so that the number of neutrons continues to rise despite some escaping and some hitting nuclei without causing fission. Atomic bomb explosions are uncontrolled chain reactions of this kind. But nuclear fission can be controlled in *nuclear reactors* (q.v.) and used as a source of energy.

Fluorescence The property of some substances to absorb light of one wavelength and emit light of a longer wavelength: e.g. fluorescein, an organ compound whose solution in alkalis glows bright green due to fluorescence. In fluorescent lighting tubes, the electric current causes mercury vapour to emit ultra-violet light, which then excites fluorescent substances on the sides of the tube to emit visible light. Unlike *phosphorescence* (q.v.), fluorescence stops as soon as the original illumination stops.

Force That which makes a body change its state of rest or uniform motion in a straight line. The SI unit of force is the Newton which is the force needed to change the velocity of a mass of 1 kilogramme by 1 metre per second in a second.

Force F, mass m, and acceleration a are related by the equation $F = ma$.

Friction The force, F, that resists the motion of one surface over another. It results from the fusing together of high points of contact between the surfaces. To overcome the fusion, force must be used. There is another force which bodies in contact exert on one another. This force is called the normal reaction, N. It acts in a direction perpendicular to the surfaces in contact and can be thought of as the force that prevents one body passing straight through another. The coefficient of friction between two bodies is defined as F/N and is roughly constant. It is often written as μ. Frictional forces always act to slow down a moving body by causing kinetic energy to be dissipated as heat. In many machines this is undesirable as it represents a waste of useful energy and also the heat produced may damage the surfaces in contact. To reduce friction between moving parts, lubricants are used as well as ball- and roller-bearings. Friction can however be extremely useful as in belt drives and brakes. The study of surfaces in contact and lubrication is known as *tribology*.

Fusion (i) The melting of a solid substance (used, for instance, in the term 'latent heat of fusion').

(ii) *Nuclear fusion* is the joining together of the nuclei of two atoms to form a single heavier nucleus. Fusion occurs most readily between nuclei of the lighter elements (e.g. the isotopes of hydrogen—deuterium and tritium) but still requires exceedingly high temperatures (hundreds of millions of degrees) before it can proceed. Fusion reactions are accompanied by a vast release of energy and this is thought to be the source of the energy of the Sun and other stars. On Earth, uncontrolled fusion reactions occur in hydrogen bombs, but there is much current interest in the problem of controlling nuclear fusion and using it as a source of energy.

Gamma radiation (Gamma Rays, γ-Rays) Radiation of the same nature as X-rays and light, i.e. electromagnetic radiation, but of much shorter wavelengths. It is emitted by some radioactive substances, e.g. cobalt 60, and is the most penetrating of all radiation.

Gas laws The combination of *Boyle's Law* (q.v.) and *Charles's Law* (q.v.) into one equation:

$$PV = nRT$$

where P = pressure; V = volume; T = absolute temperature; R = gas constant = $8 \cdot 314$ joules per degree per mole; n = no. of *moles* (q.v.).

Gene Originally understood to mean a unit of genetic information that gives to the organism carrying it a certain physical characteristic (e.g. blond hair or blue eyes) which can be transmitted from generation to generation.

　　Today, the gene is understood on the molecular level to be a length of *DNA* (q.v.) coding for one or more *proteins* (q.v.) according to the *genetic code* (q.v.).

Genetic code The code by means of which a particular sequence of bases in a *DNA molecule* (q.v.) is translated into a corresponding sequence of *amino-acids* (q.v.) in a *protein* (q.v.).

　　The code works by assigning to each possible group of three DNA bases (triplet) a particular amino-acid. Thus a protein chain of, say, 100 amino-acids in length is coded for by a DNA chain of 300 bases in length. From the four different kinds of DNA bases (called A, T, C and G for short) it is possible to make 64 different triplets e.g. AAA, AAT, AGC, CGA . . . As there are only 20 different amino-acids found in proteins, some amino-acids are coded for by more than one triplet e.g. the amino-acid glycine is coded for by the four triplets GGG, GGA, GGT and GGC.

　　The genetic code is found to be the same for all living organisms, a strong argument for the common origin of all life forms.

Genetic engineering The artificial manipulation of the genetic material of an organism by deletion, insertion or modification of *genes* (q.v.). A typical application is the insertion of the gene for a particular *protein* (q.v.) from one organism into the *DNA* (q.v.) of another organism, often a *bacterium* (q.v.) or yeast, which then becomes capable of making the protein. Such a process is possible because naturally occurring *restriction enzymes* are available to cut DNA at very specific places, thus enabling individual genes to be isolated. Other *enzymes* (q.v.) are used to join the isolated gene into carrier molecules of DNA (called *vectors*), which can then be incorporated in the organism to be modified. Then by ordinary cell division it is possible to grow colonies of modified organisms each carrying the extra gene, a process known as *cloning*. In this way bacteria have been engineered to produce for example human insulin and human growth hormone.

The techniques of genetic engineering (sometimes called *recombinant DNA*) are extremely powerful tools in fundamental research in *molecular biology* (q.v.) and in understanding the origin of diseases. The enormous potential opened up by genetic engineering is also the basis for the current interest in *biotechnology*. Not only can naturally occurring proteins useful in medicine and industry be produced in large amounts, but in the future it will be possible to design and make new proteins with desired functions. Similarly, organisms can be engineered to have desired properties: e.g. bacteria can be made to break down oil slicks; or the genes present in certain bacteria in the roots of plants such as clover, which enable them to use atmospheric nitrogen, can be transferred to bacteria found associated with the roots of wheat, say, thus eliminating the need for nitrogen fertilisers.

Glass A hard, brittle, usually transparent material. Most everyday glass is made by fusing together sand, limestone and soda ash (sodium carbonate) and has composition 70% silica (SiO_2), 15% sodium oxide (Na_2O), 10% calcium oxide (CaO) and 5% other metal oxides. Pyrex is a particularly heat and shock-resistant glass in which some of the silica has been replaced by boron oxide (B_2O_3). Solid glass is formed by cooling molten glass in such a way that it does not have time to form *crystals* (q.v.). It therefore has an amorphous (disordered) structure.

Glass was in use in Ancient Egypt, but is continually being found in new applications: e.g. fibre optics, very fine glass fibres carrying beams of light used to transmit information such as telephone messages, computer data and television programmes.

Gram–atom The weight in grams equivalent to the *atomic weight* (q.v.). For example, the atomic weight of oxygen is 16, so a gram–atom of oxygen is 16 grams.

Gram-equivalent The weight in grams of a substance equal to the *equivalent weight* (q.v.).

Gram-molecule The weight in grams equal to the molecular weight of an element or compound. For example, the molecular weight of H_2SO_4 is 98, so a gram-molecule of H_2SO_4 is 98 gm.

Gravity Every object attracts every other object with a force directly proportional to the product of the masses of the objects and inversely as the square of the distance between them. If m_1 is the mass of one object, m_2 the mass of the other, d the distance between them, then the gravitational force $F = \dfrac{Gm_1m_2}{d^2}$, where G is a constant. $G = 6\cdot67 \times 10^{-11}\,\text{Nm}^2\text{kg}^{-2}$.

For objects on or near the Earth, the mass of the Earth is very much greater than an object, and so the gravitational force between them makes the object 'fall' towards the Earth. The acceleration as it does this is called the acceleration due to gravity. At the Earth's surface this is $9\cdot8$ m per sec per sec in the SI system and 32 ft per sec per sec in the f.p.s. system.

Hadron Elementary particles which are subject to the *strong nuclear force* (q.v.). Hadrons are much more numerous than *leptons* (q.v.) and include stable particles like the proton and neutron as well as the mesons and the most recently discovered (and extremely unstable) psi and upsilon particles. Hadrons are believed to be composed of more fundamental particles called *quarks* (q.v.).

Half-life The time for half the nuclei in a sample of radioactive material to decay. This ranges from a fraction of a second for some man-made radioisotopes to 4,510 million years for Uranium 238. (See *Isotope*.)

Heat Energy possessed by a substance in the form of random motions of the atoms which make up the substance. In a red-hot piece of iron the atoms are vibrating back and forth very fast, and so the iron contains more heat than when it is cold and the atoms are moving much less fast. However, heat must not be confused with *temperature* (q.v.). The adding of heat to a substance usually causes a rise in temperature but the amount of this rise depends on the mass and *specific heat* (q.v.) of the substance. Adding heat to a substance may cause a *change of* *state* (e.g. a solid melting to a liquid) without a change in temperature (see *Latent heat*). Measured in *joules* (q.v.).

Heavy water Water in which the hydrogen is replaced by the *isotope* (q.v.) deuterium and hence written as D_2O rather than H_2O. The nucleus of ordinary hydrogen is simply one proton, while that of deuterium is one proton and one neutron.

Heptagon See *Polygon*.

Heron's formula This formula is used to find the area of a triangle if the length of its three sides are known.

The area of a triangle is $\sqrt{s(s-a)(s-b)(s-c)}$ where a, b and c are the lengths of the three sides of the triangle and s is its semi-perimeter (i.e. half its perimeter).

Hexagon See *Polygon*.

Hologram A photograph taken with the light from a laser which, when even a small part of it is illumined by laser light, reconstitutes the entire picture. The discovery of Professor Denis Gabor of Imperial College, London, for which he was awarded the 1971 Nobel prize for physics.

Indicator A substance added in small quantities to a chemical reaction which shows when the reaction is complete by a sudden change of colour. The most familiar indicators change colour depending on whether a solution is acidic or alkaline: e.g. litmus is red in acids but blue in alkalis, and phenolphthalein is colourless in acids but purple in alkalis.

Infra-red light *Electromagnetic waves* (q.v.) with wavelengths longer than those of visible light and in the range 7,500–100,000 angstroms, or 0·75–10 micrometres. Infra-red radiation is invisible to the eye but has a heating effect and can be detected at great distances by modern crystal detectors. Every warm body emits infra-red radiation.

Insulator A material, such as glass, rubber, porcelain, plastics, that has no free electrons, and so will not allow electric current to pass when an e.m.f. is applied.

Integer An integer is a whole number. 5, 27 and 4218 are positive integers. -4, -39 and -231 are negative integers. Zero is also an integer.

Interference When *waves* (q.v.) from different sources superimpose they can either reinforce each other (*interfere constructively*) or cancel each other out (*interfere destructively*). In the case of light this can give rise to characteristic dark and light bands called an *interference pattern.*

Interferometer A device in which the phenomenon of *interference* (q.v.) of light or radio waves is used as a tool, e.g. in spectroscopy and astronomy.

Interior angle The interior angle of a polygon is the angle between two adjacent sides of the polygon inside the polygon. (See *Exterior angle.*)

The sum of the interior angles of any two polygons with the same number of sides is the same. To find the sum of the interior angles in degrees, multiply the number of sides by 180 and subtract 360.

Ion An atom or group of atoms that is electrically charged due to an excess or deficiency of electrons. Negatively charged ions are called *anions*; positive ions are called *cations.*

Ionisation The process by which mobile *ions* (q.v.) are produced from atoms and molecules. This can occur when *electrolytes* (q.v.) become molten or dissolve to form solutions, or when gases are subjected to electrical discharges and become *plasmas* (q.v.).

Familiar radioisotopes		
Name	*Type of radiation*	*Half-life*
Carbon 14	beta	5,600 years
Phosphorus 32	beta	14·3 days
Cobalt 60	beta, gamma	5·3 years
Strontium 90	beta	28 years
Iodine 131	beta, gamma	8 days
Caesium 137	beta, gamma	30 years
Radium 226	alpha, gamma	1,620 years
Uranium 235	alpha	710 million years
Uranium 238	alpha	4,510 million years
Plutonium 239	alpha	24,400 years

Irrational See *Rational.*

Irregular See *Regular.*

Isosceles A triangle is isosceles if two of its sides are the same length. A consequence of this is that two of its angles are equal.

Isotope One of two or more forms of the same chemical element, differing from other isotopes only in atomic weight. The difference is due entirely to the addition or subtraction of neutrons

from the nucleus. Examples: The hydrogen atom has one proton
and one electron. Add a neutron to the nucleus and it becomes
twice as heavy. It is heavy hydrogen or deuterium. Add another
neutron and it becomes tritium, three times as heavy as the
normal hydrogen. All three isotopes are hydrogen so far as the
chemistry is concerned. Many elements have several stable
isotopes (tin has ten). It is customary to give the mass number
of an isotope after the name in order to indicate which isotope
is present, e.g. uranium 238, uranium 235, plutonium 239,
etc.

Every element can be made to have radioactive isotopes,
called *radioisotopes*. Many of these are used in science and industry because they emit radiation (alpha, beta or gamma). A few
elements have naturally occurring radioisotopes. Tritium is a
radioisotope of hydrogen. See *Half-life*.

Iteration A method of solving equations in which the starting
point is to guess an approximate solution. Better and better
approximations to the solution are obtained using an iteration
formula.

For example, to find the solution of the equation

$$x^3 - 3x + 8 = 0$$

you can rearrange the equation like this:
$x^3 = 3x - 8$ or $x = \sqrt[3]{(3x - 8)}$. The formula on the right is
then used repeatedly to get better and better guesses. If the
guess at an approximate solution is -1, the formula then gives
$-2\cdot224$, $-2\cdot448$, $-2\cdot484$, $-2\cdot491$, $-2\cdot492$, and this last
number is the solution correct to three decimal places. Both
solutions of a quadratic equation can always be found by
iteration. This example illustrates the general method.

$$2x^2 - x - 6 = 0$$
$$2x^2 - x = 6$$
$$x(2x - 1) = 6$$

$$x = \frac{6}{2x - 1} \qquad x = \frac{1}{2}\left(\frac{6}{x} + 1\right)$$

Iteration has become a powerful method of solving equations
since electronic calculators have become readily available.

Joule The SI unit of energy or work. It is the work done when 1 newton acts through 1 metre. Replaces the calorie as the unit of heat energy. 1 joule = 0·239 calories.

Laser A device for producing an intense, narrow beam of light, in which all the waves are in step. The atoms of some gases, if electrically excited, can be persuaded by a 'trigger' pulse of light of a certain wavelength to emit more light of the same wavelength. If such a gas is put into a tube with accurately parallel mirrors at each end, and triggered, the light waves will run up and down, getting stronger as they pass over and re-trigger the atoms of the gas. If some of the light is allowed to escape at one end it emerges in such a narrow beam that a laser can shine a spot only a mile or so across on the moon, and so intense it can burn through steel. An even more interesting possibility is the use of the laser in communications. Since a beam of light has an enormously higher frequency than the shortest radio wave, and since the amount of information a beam can carry is proportional to its frequency, a light beam, if it can be *modulated* (See RADIO AND TELEVISION: modulation), should be able to carry as many as a thousand television channels. (See AIRCRAFT, ROCKETS AND MISSILES: Satellites, Communications.)

Latent heat The latent heat of fusion (vaporisation) is the amount of heat required to turn unit mass of a solid (liquid) into liquid (gas) at the same temperature. The latent heat of fusion of ice is 335 joules per gram; the latent heat of vaporisation of water is 2,257 joules per gram.

Lens A piece of transparent material, usually glass, shaped and

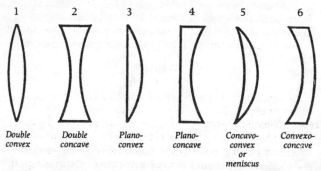

| 1 | 2 | 3 | 4 | 5 | 6 |

| Double convex | Double concave | Plano-convex | Plano-concave | Concavo-convex or meniscus | Convexo-concave |

1, 3 and 5 are convergent; 2, 4 and 6 are divergent

polished to have curved surfaces. The commonest are a double-convex lens and a double-concave lens. Every combination of two of the following surfaces is possible: convex, concave, plane.

A single lens like this is known as a thin lens, and simplified approximate formulae can be used. The principal focus is then the point where parallel rays parallel to the axis come to a point. The distance from the centre of the lens to the point image is called the focal length.

Lenses are of two sorts whatever their surfaces. One sort makes rays of light *converge* when they pass through the lens; the other sort makes rays of light *diverge*.

The focal length of a convergent lens can be found very simply by getting an image of a distant object and the distance from lens to image is then the focal length.

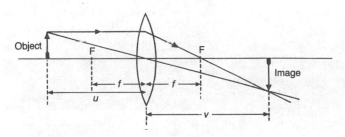

The equation of a simple lens, where u = distance of object from centre of lens, v = distance of image from centre, f = focal length, and distances are considered positive when measured *against* the direction the light is travelling, is:

$$\frac{1}{v} - \frac{1}{u} = \frac{1}{f}$$

All measurements are positive when taken from lens to a *real* image or object.

Lepton/*Elementary particle* (q.v.), distinguished from the generally heavier *hadrons* (q.v.) in not being subject to the *strong nuclear force* (q.v.). Only six leptons (and their corresponding anti-particles—see *anti-matter*) have been discovered: the electron, the muon and the tau (in 1975) and their respective *neutrinos* (q.v.).

Light Radiation that affects our eyes and we 'see'. It is electromagnetic, and the wavelengths of visible light extend from
about 4,000 angstroms (blue) to about 7,000 angstroms (red).
It is customary to speak of all electromagnetic radiation of near
wavelengths to these as 'light', even though it causes no
sensation on the eye.

Magnifying power A measure of how much an optical instrument
magnifies an object. The magnifying power of a single convex
lens used with the eye as a magnifying glass equals 1 plus $\frac{25}{f}$,
where f equals focal length in centimetres.

The magnifying power of an astronomical telescope or a
Galileo-type telescope is the focal length of the objective lens
divided by the focal length of the eyepiece.

Mass The mass of a body is proportional to the amount of matter
in it. It is *not* the same as *weight* (q.v.), because the weight of a
body is the force exerted on it by gravity. An 80 kg person
would be weightless in deep space.

Metals As commonly understood, metals are the substances that
are good conductors of heat and electricity, are lustrous when
polished and so on. In chemistry, however, a metal is characterised as having a tendency towards losing electrons and thus
becoming positively charged. This definition means that only a
very few of the elements are not metals. See Periodic Table on
pages D38–D39.

Microscope A device for getting a magnified image of very small

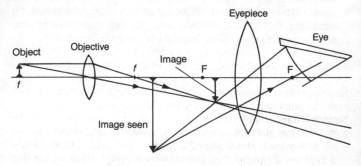

Geometrical Diagram of Microscope

objects. A single magnifying glass is therefore a simple microscope.

A compound microscope consists of two lenses, one of short focal length, the objective, one of long focal length, the eyepiece. The object is placed in the plane of the principal focus.

The magnifying power is found by multiplying the power of the objective by that of the eyepiece. The power of the objective is the *optical tube length* divided by the focal length of the objective. The optical tube length is taken for modern microscopes as being 18 cm. So if, for example, the focal length of an objective is 0·5 cm, then the magnifying power is 36. An eyepiece with a magnification of 3 will then give a total magnification of 108.

The eyepiece and objective are complex lenses, not simple ones, in order to correct for the various errors that a simple lens inflicts on the image, errors that become more and more important as the magnification is increased.

Microscope, Electron A microscope which substitutes beams of electrons for beams of light to form a very greatly magnified image of an object. With the electron microscope, objects as small as individual molecules can be distinguished.

Mole The amount of substance that contains as many elementary units as there are in 0·012 kg of carbon 12. The number of such units is *Avogadro's number* = $6·023 \times 10^{23}$.

Molecular biology The study of how living things work at the level of their component molecules: e.g. *proteins* (q.v.) and *nucleic acids* (q.v.).

Molecule The smallest unit of a chemical compound to retain its identity. If split up, the results are the atoms of elements of which it is compounded. A single element can exist in molecular form. For example, hydrogen can be atomic or molecular. In the latter case two atoms of hydrogen are combined into a molecule.

Momentum The product of a body's mass and velocity.

Neutrino An extremely light, electrically neutral particle. There are various types, all of which are difficult to detect.

Neutron Star See *Pulsar*.

Neutron One of the fundamental particles of nature. Its mass is slightly greater than that of a proton, but the neutron carries no electrical charge. Because of this it is not acted on by the electrical forces in an atom, and so can penetrate more easily.

A neutron is therefore a good nuclear projectile. It is the causing agent in nuclear *fission* (q.v.). Neutrons are produced in immense numbers in a *nuclear reactor* (q.v.).

Newton (N) The SI unit of force. It is the force that would give a mass of 1 kg an acceleration of 1 metre per second per second. The force of gravity on a mass of 1 kg is $9 \cdot 8$ N.

Nonagon See *Polygon*.

Normal Solution A solution of which 1 litre (1,000 cc) contains one *gram-equivalent* (q.v.) of a substance. Indicated by N, e.g. N-hydrochloric acid means normal hydrochloric acid solution in water. Used for quantitative analysis. A more dilute solution is one-tenth normal, shown by $N/10$.

Normal temperature and pressure (NTP) Normal temperature is taken as $0°$ C, normal pressure as 76 cm of mercury. These together give a standard set of conditions for comparing the behaviour of gases.

Nuclear Reactor An apparatus in which a nuclear fuel undergoes *fission* (q.v.) under controlled conditions. The essential parts of a nuclear reactor are: (a) the fuel, which is usually in the form of rods and may be plutonium, natural uranium or enriched uranium (uranium in which the proportion of fissile U-235 to non-fissile U-238 has been made higher than in natural uranium), (b) the *moderator*, which is placed between the fuel rods with the purpose of slowing down the fast neutrons produced during fission so that they produce further fission more readily (moderators commonly used are graphite or *heavy water* (q.v.)), (c) *control rods* (often of cadmium) which absorb neutrons and slow down the rate of fission thus preventing a runaway chain reaction, (d) the *coolant*, which is a fluid (such as carbon dioxide gas or liquid sodium) that is pumped in pipes through the reactor core to remove the vast quantities of heat generated during fission (this heat may be used to generate electricity), (e) a very thick shield of concrete, steel and water to prevent dangerous radiation from escaping from the core. The *fast breeder reactor* is a reactor which 'breeds' more nuclear fuel at the same time as producing energy by fission. This is possible because a fast neutron produced by fission can be absorbed by a non-fissile U-238 nucleus giving a U-239 nucleus which then decays radioactively into fissile plutonium. The reactor at Dounreay, Scotland is of this type. Nuclear reactors are a very important source of electricity but an outstanding problem is what to do with the dangerous radioactive waste products. Public opposition to nuclear power grows as disasters occur such as that at Chernobyl.

Nucleus Means the centre part of anything. Used chiefly to mean the heavy centre part of an atom. Every atomic nucleus consists of protons and neutrons, with the exception of ordinary hydrogen, the nucleus of which is one proton. Examples: oxygen, 8 protons 8 neutrons; iron, 26 protons 30 neutrons; radium, 88 protons 138 neutrons.

Nucleic acid Very important biological *polymers* (q.v.) found in all living organisms. There are two major types of nucleic acid: *DNA* (*deoxyribonucleic acid*) and *RNA* (*ribonucleic acid*) (q.v.).

Octagon See *Polygon*.

Ohm (Ω) The SI unit of electrical resistance. It is defined by means of *Ohm's Law* (q.v.) i.e. if a conductor carries a current of I amps when the potential difference across it is V volts, then the resistance R of the conductor is V/I ohms.

Ohm's law This states that the current I through a conductor is directly proportional to the potential difference V across the conductor and inversely proportional to its resistance R. Discovered by the German physicist, Georg Ohm, in 1827. See DICTIONARY OF RADIO AND TELEVISION.

Ozone (O_3) is a form of oxygen whose molecules consist of three atoms of oxygen instead of the usual two. It can be obtained by passing an electrical discharge through ordinary oxygen. Ozone occurs in large quantities in the ozone layer of the upper atmosphere, between heights of about 15 and 40 kilometres above the Earth. Here it plays a vital role in absorbing a large proportion of the sun's *ultra-violet radiation* (q.v.) which would otherwise be damaging to life on the Earth's surface. There is current concern that the ozone layer is being made thinner at the North and South Poles owing to the effect notably of the use of aerosol cans.

Parallelogram A parallelogram is a quadrilateral whose opposite sides are parallel. A consequence is that the opposite sides are also equal in length.

Particle accelerator A machine which accelerates *elementary particles* (q.v.) near to the speed of light by means of electric and magnetic fields. The resulting beams of high energy particles are allowed to hit stationary atomic targets or to meet other beams of particles head on. By observing the products of such collisions, much is learnt about elementary particles and the atomic nucleus.

Pentagon See *Polygon*.

Perimeter This has two meanings. It means the boundary of a plane shape (consisting of straight line segments or curves or a mixture of straight lines and curves). It also means the total length of the boundary of a plane shape.

Periodic table A table grouping the elements so that certain chemical and physical properties are repeated at regular intervals. It is arranged in horizontal *periods* and vertical *groups*. Elements in one group have similar physical and chemical properties, e.g. fluorine, chlorine, bromine, iodine, all in sub-group *b* of group VII and called the *halogens*. See pages E42 to E43.

Perpendicular Two lines are perpendicular if the angle between them is a right angle.

Phosphorescence Light emitted by some substances without heating, some as the result of irradiation with ultra-violet light or other light, some as the result of chemical action, e.g. phosphorescent organisms in sea-water and creatures like fireflies and glow-worms. See *Fluorescence*.

Pi The number, usually written π, is $3 \cdot 141592 \ldots$ It is important in connection with the *circle* (q.v.). It is defined to be the ratio of the circumference of a circle to its diameter.

The number π has interested people for thousands of years, which is why a Greek letter is used to name it. 22/7 is an approximation to π which dates from ancient times, which is sometimes mistakenly taken to be an exact value for π. In fact, π is an *irrational* number (q.v.).

Plasma A highly-ionised gas i.e. a gas consisting of charged particles, usually electrons and positive ions. It is the state of matter in which most of the universe exists. In extremely high temperature plasmas (as in the interiors of stars) nuclear *fusion* (q.v.) can occur. Plasma physics is therefore of great importance in the attempt to use controlled nuclear fusion as a source of energy.

Polygon A plane shape the perimeter (q.v.) of which consists of straight sides. Polygons have at least three sides. In some cases a special name is used to describe a polygon with a particular number of sides. These are the names for polygons with up to 10 sides.

3 sides	triangle
4 sides	quadrilateral
5 sides	pentagon
6 sides	hexagon
7 sides	septagon or heptagon
8 sides	octagon
9 sides	nonagon
10 sides	decagon

See also *Regular, Irregular, Equilateral, Isosceles.*

Polyhedron Three-dimensional shape whose boundary consists of several plane faces.

Example are a cube (six square faces), a tetrahedron (four triangular faces), a triangular prism (two triangular and three rectangular faces), and a square-based pyramid (one square and four triangular faces).

Polymer A compound consisting of a chain of repeated molecular units. It is formed from the individual *monomer* units by the process of polymerisation. Natural polymers include rubber and *proteins* (q.v.), while synthetic polymers include many plastics (e.g. polythene) and artificial fibres (e.g. nylon).

Power The rate of doing work or using energy. The SI unit is the *watt*, equal to 1 joule per second. In electrical circuits the power in watts is found by multiplying the volts by the amperes. Horse-power was formerly used in mechanics. 1 horse-power = 746 watts.

Pressure The force or weight per unit area acting on a surface. Measured in newtons per square metre (SI units), kilograms per

Conversion table of pressures				
Cm of Hg	*In of Hg*	*Millibars*	*Kg/sq m*	*Lb/sq in*
71·2	28	942	9,650	13·74
73·7	29	976	9,970	14·2
75·5	29·7	1,000	10,220	14·55
76·2	30	1,019	10,400	14·8
78·7	31	1,052	10,750	15·3

THE PERIODIC TABLE

Group →	IA	IIA	IIIB	IVB	VB	VIB	VIIB	←
Period ↓	Alkali metals	Alkaline earth metals	←————— Transition metals —————→					
1	1 ● H* 1.008							
2	3 Li 6.939	4 Be 9.012						
3	11 Na 22.990	12 Mg 24.312						
4	19 K 39.102	20 Ca 40.08	21 Sc 44.956	22 Ti 47.90	23 V 50.94	24 Cr 52.00	25 Mn 54.94	26 Fe 55.8
5	37 Rb 85.47	38 Sr 87.62	39 Y 88.905	40 Zr 91.22	41 Nb 92.906	42 Mo 95.94	43 Tc 99	44 Ru 101.
6	55 Cs 132.905	56 Ba 137.34	57 La** 138.91	72 Hf 178.49	73 Ta 180.95	74 W 183.85	75 Re 186.2	76 Os 190
7	87 Fr 223	88 Ra 226.05	89 Ac† 227.05					

	Metals
●●	Semiconductors
●	Non-metals

** Lanthanides (rare earth met

58	59	60	61
Ce	Pr	Nd	Pr
140.12	140.907	144.24	14

† Actinides

90	91	92	93
Th	Pa	U	N
232.12	231.05	238.07	23

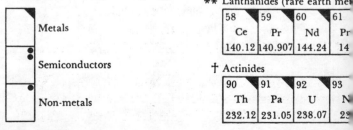

(showing atomic weights)

←VIII→		IB	IIB	IIIA	IVA	VA	VIA	VIIA	O
		Noble metals						Halo-gens	Inert gases
									2 He 4.003
				5 B 10.811	6 C 12.011	7 N 14.007	8 O 15.999	9 F 18.998	10 Ne 20.183
				13 Al 26.982	14 Si 28.086	15 P 30.974	16 S 32.064	17 Cl 35.453	18 Ar 39.948
Co 8.93	28 Ni 58.71	29 Cu 63.54	30 Zn 65.37	31 Ga 69.72	32 Ge 72.59	33 As 74.92	34 Se 78.96	35 Br 79.909	36 Kr 83.80
h 2.91	46 Pd 106.4	47 Ag 107.87	48 Cd 112.40	49 In 114.82	50 Sn 118.69	51 Sb 121.75	52 Te 127.60	53 I 126.904	54 Xe 131.30
r 2.2	78 Pt 195.09	79 Au 196.97	80 Hg 200.59	81 Tl 204.37	82 Pb 207.19	83 Bi 208.98	84 Po 210	85 At 211	86 Rn 222

*Hydrogen is sometimes placed above fluorine at the head of group VIIA. It is not included in the alkali metals.

m .35	63 Eu 151.96	64 Gd 157.25	65 Tb 158.92	66 Dy 162.50	67 Ho 164.93	68 Er 167.26	69 Tm 168.93	70 Yb 173.04	71 Lu 174.97
u 9	95 Am 241	96 Cm 242	97 Bk 247	98 Cf 251	99 Es 254	100 Fm 253	101 Md 256	102 No 254	103 Lr 257

sq m or pounds per sq in etc. Atmospheric pressure, that is the weight of air in a column of unit cross-sectional area up to the top of the Earth's atmosphere, is roughly 15 lb per sq in. Pressure in gases is also expressed as the height of mercury (or other liquid) that the gas will support. A pressure of 0·76 m (760 mm or 29·921 in) of mercury is equivalent to 33·9 ft of water. This is equivalent to 14·696 lb per sq in or 10,332·3 kg per sq m. To turn kilograms weight to newtons multiply by 9·8, the gravitational acceleration in metres per sec. per sec. A *bar* is equivalent to 100,000 newtons per sq m. High pressures, especially in gases, are measured in kilobars. A *torr* is equivalent to 1 mm of mercury and is used to measure low pressures in gases.

Prime numbers A prime number is a positive whole number which has exactly two factors (one of which is the number 1). See *Factorising*.

Here are the prime numbers less than 400.

2, 3, 5, 7, 11, 13, 17, 19, 23, 29, 31, 37, 41, 43, 47, 53, 59, 61, 67, 71, 73, 79, 83, 89, 97, 101, 103, 107, 109, 113, 127, 131, 137, 139, 149, 151, 157, 163, 167, 173, 179, 181, 191, 193, 197, 199, 211, 223, 227, 229, 233, 239, 241, 251, 257, 263, 269, 271, 277, 281, 283, 293, 307, 311, 313, 317, 331, 337, 347, 349, 353, 359, 367, 373, 379, 383, 389, 397.

There is no biggest prime number. The largest prime number so far discovered was found in 1985 (using a computer) and is $2216091 - 1$, a number with 65 050 digits.

Prime factorisation of a number means writing the number as the product of factors all of which are prime numbers (i.e. prime factors). These are examples of prime factorisation.

$12 = 2 \times 2 \times 3$
$75 = 3 \times 5 \times 5$
$48 = 2 \times 2 \times 2 \times 2 \times 3$

Proteins An extremely important class of biological *polymer* (q.v.) which form a vital part of all living organisms.

Proteins consist of long chains formed by the polymerisation (i.e. linking together) of up to several hundred simpler compounds called *amino-acids* (q.v.). About 20 different amino-acids are found in proteins, different proteins varying in the number of each amino-acid they contain and the order in which they are arranged along the chain. Thus an extremely wide variety of protein structures is possible, each fulfilling a specific function; and, in fact, different organisms produce their own set of proteins. Proteins also vary widely in shape; in some the chain is extended, and in others it is folded into a complicated globular structure.

Many proteins are *enzymes*, that is biological *catalysts* (q.v.), which control the multitude of chemical reactions occurring in living organisms. Most enzymes remain inside the cells producing them, while others pass outside: e.g. the digestive enzymes of animals which are secreted into the alimentary canal to catalyse the breakdown of food into simpler compounds.

Other proteins fulfil the function of transporting substances within an organism: e.g. the protein haemoglobin (which contains iron) is found in red blood cells and transports oxygen from the lungs to all cells of the body. Still other proteins compose the muscles and are responsible for the ability of muscles to contract and produce movement. In bones, skin and tendons, protein fibres (rather like lengths of string) play an essential role as building materials.

Proteins are synthesised (e.g. manufactured), when needed, from their component amino-acids inside all animal, plant and bacterial cells. Viruses, the simplest organisms, have to 'hijack' the protein-making machinery of more complicated cells in order to produce the proteins they need; this is what is happening when viruses *infect* animals and plants. The instructions for the production of each different protein are carried by means of the *genetic code* (q.v.) in the genetic material inside the nucleus of the cell (see *Deoxyribonucleic acid* (DNA)). It is copies of these instructions which are passed on when new cells are formed by cell division, thus enabling the new cells to produce the proteins they require.

Proton The positive heavy particle of the nucleus of an atom; also the nucleus of a normal hydrogen atom.

Pulsar A type of radio star discovered in 1968 which gives out pulses of radio waves at very regular intervals. Believed to be composed of very densely packed neutrons (q.v.). A start composed of neutrons is called a neutron star.

Pythagoras' theorem This theorem states that for a right-angled triangle the area of the square drawn on the hypotenuse (the longest side) is the sum of the areas of the squares drawn on the other two sides.

If the lengths of two sides of a right-angled triangle are known Pythagoras' theorem can be used to calculate the length of the third side. For this reason Pythagoras' theorem is a fundamental result in coordinate geometry (q.v.).

See also *Right-angled triangle*.

Quadratic equations These are equations such as

$$x^2 = 16$$
$$x^2 + x = 4$$
$$2x^2 - 3x + 7 = 0$$

There are various ways of solving quadratic equations. One is to use iteration (q.v.). Another way is to use the formula. Any quadratic equation is of the form

$$ax^2 + bx + c = 0$$

The formula for the solutions of this equation are

$$x = \frac{-b \pm \sqrt{b^2 - 4ac}}{2a}$$

Quadrilateral See *Polygon*.

Quark For a long time it has been thought that the nuclei of atoms are composed of protons and neutrons. Now it is thought that these nuclear building blocks (and in fact all other *hadrons* (q.v.)) are themselves made up of more fundamental particles called quarks.

Quarks were first proposed in 1963 and until 1974 only three quarks (and their corresponding anti-quarks) were needed to account for all the observed hadrons. These were the 'up' (u), (down) (d) and 'strange' (s) quarks. The proton consists of two up and one down quark (i.e. uud) while the neutron has composition ddu. To get the electric charge of the proton as $+1$ and that of the neutron as 0, it follows that the u quark must have charge $+\frac{2}{3}$ and the d quark charge $-\frac{1}{3}$. The discovery of the psi particle in 1974 and the upsilon in 1977 necessitated the introduction of two more quarks, the 'charmed' quark (c) and the 'bottom' quark (b). It is not known how many quarks there might be. Free quarks have never been observed. Other particles called *gluons* are supposed to keep them bound tightly together in twos or threes.

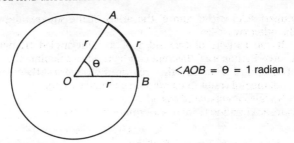

$<AOB = \theta = 1$ radian

Quasar (or quasi-stellar source) Much the brightest and most distant type of giant star so far discovered.

Radian A unit used for measuring angles. To find the radian measure of the angle between two straight lines a circle with its centre where the two lines meet and with a radius of 1 unit is drawn. The length of the arc of this circle which is between the two lines is the radian measure of the angle.

Because the length of the whole circumference of this circle is 2π (see *Circle*) the radian measure of the whole angle round a point is 2π. The radian measure of a *right-angle* (q.v.) is $\pi/2$.

Radical A group of atoms that form part of a compound, and that tend to stay together when the compound dissociates: e.g. SO_4, NO_3, etc.

Radioactivity The spontaneous emission of alpha (q.v.), beta (q.v.) and gamma (q.v.) radiation from a material, resulting from the break-up of the nuclei of atoms. Materials that are abundantly radioactive are radium and uranium and some artificially made radioisotopes (see *isotope*). Large amounts of radiation are extremely dangerous to health. Many materials, however, are known to have a tiny proportion of a radioactive isotope present, and these materials are everywhere—in food, plants, rocks, etc.

Rational A rational is a number which can be written as the ratio of two whole numbers. 3/4, 8/3 and −16/5 are all rationals. All integers are also rationals. For example, 16 is a rational because it can be written as 16/1.

Any rational number can be written as either a terminating or a recurring *decimal* (q.v.).

If a number is not rational it is called an irrational. Examples of irrationals are

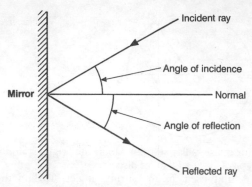

Specular or Mirror Reflection from a Plane Mirror

$$\sqrt{2} \qquad\qquad \sqrt[3]{5} \qquad\qquad \sin 20° \qquad\qquad \pi$$

Reaction The definition for what happens when chemicals combine or split up.

Reagent Chemicals commonly used in chemical laboratories for experiments and analysis, such as dilute hydrochloric acid, ammonium hydroxide, dilute nitric acid, etc.

Reciprocal The reciprocal of a number y is one divided by y and is written $1/y$. E.g. the reciprocal of 4 is $1/4 = 0.25$.

Rectangle A rectangle is a quadrilateral, all four angles of which are right-angles.

The two diagonals of a rectangle are equal in length.

Recurring decimal See *Decimal*.

Reflection The 'bouncing back' of light rays, heat rays, etc. The simple law of reflection is that the angle between the incoming ray and the perpendicular to the surface is equal to the angle between the reflected ray and the same perpendicular. This is expressed as: The angle of incidence = Angle of reflection. With flat or 'plane' mirrors the perpendicular is easy to draw in diagrams, but with curved reflecting surfaces the perpendiculars have to be arrived at by knowledge of the geometry of circles, parabolas, etc.

Such regular reflection is called mirror or specular reflection. At a roughened surface light is reflected in *all* directions and does not obey the above rules. This is called diffused or scattered reflection.

In mathematics a reflection is a transformation of a two-dimensional (2D) or three-dimensional (3D) shape. A 2D shape

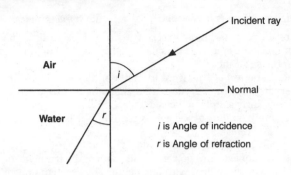

Refraction between Air and Water

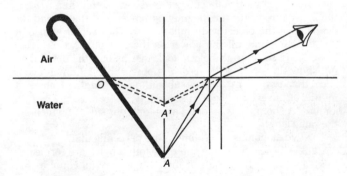

Apparent Bending of Walking-stick in Water Due to Refraction

The point A seems to be at A^1. Similarly with all points on OA so that the part immersed seems to be along OA^1.

is reflected in a line, whereas a 3D shape is reflected in a plane. The reflected image means the same as the mirror image.

Refraction The sudden change of direction of light when passing from one transparent substance into another. A ray of light passing from air into water is bent towards the perpendicular, or normal.

If the angle of incidence (i) is taken as that between the incident ray and the normal and the angle of refraction (r) as that between the refracted ray and the normal, then if the less-dense medium is a vacuum $\dfrac{\sin i}{\sin r} = \mu$, the *refractive index* of the substance. In ordinary experiments, as air is so little different from a vacuum for the passage of light, i is measured in air and r in the substance.

Regular The use of this word in mathematics is different from its everyday use. In everyday use a shape or a design is regular if it looks fairly simple, balanced or repetitive.

In mathematics a polygon is regular if it is both *equiangular* (q.v.) and *equilateral* (q.v.).

A polygon which is not regular is called irregular.

Resolving power The power of an optical instrument or any optical system to deal with fine detail. The resolving power of a telescope is directly proportional to the diameter of the objective lens. Hence prismatic binoculars 8 × 40 are better than 8 × 25, the first figure being the magnifying power and the second the diameter of the objective in millimetres. The second binocular has the same magnifying power as the first but less resolving power, and so, though objects look just as big, the detail does not show up so well. The resolving power of the human eye is such that two point objects subtending an angle of about 1 minute at the eye can be seen separately, i.e. resolved.

Rhombus A rhombus is a quadrilateral all four sides of which are the same length.

The two diagonals of a rhombus are perpendicular.

Right angle When two lines intersect four angles are formed at the point where they meet. If these angles are all equal in size they are right angles.

A right angle is a quarter turn. It is 90 degrees, or $\pi/2$ radians.

Right-angled triangle A triangle one of whose angles is a right angle (q.v.).

The longest side of a right-angled triangle (which is always opposite the right angle) is called the hypotenuse.

Pythagoras' theorem (q.v.) and *cosine* (q.v.) and sine give these relationships between the lengths of the sides of a right-angled triangle.

$a^2 + b^2 = c^2$
$b = c \cos A$
$a = c \sin A$
$a = b \tan A$

RNA (Ribonucleic acid) A *nucleic acid* (q.v.) similar to *DNA* (q.v.) but differing in the chemical nature of the four bases of which it is composed. RNA plays a vital role in living cells, acting as an intermediary in the production of *proteins* (q.v.) from information coded on DNA by means of the *genetic code* (q.v.).

Root One of several equal factors of a number. Thus the square root $\sqrt{}$ or $^2\sqrt{}$ is one of two equal factors: e.g. $3 = \sqrt{9}$ (also written $9^{\frac{1}{2}}$) and $3 \times 3 = 9$. The cube root is one of three equal factors: e.g. $4 = \sqrt[3]{64}$ (also written $64^{\frac{1}{3}}$) and $4 \times 4 \times 4 = 64$. See also *Solution*.

Salt A salt is the compound formed when the hydrogen in an *acid* (q.v.) is replaced by a metal. Examples of a salt are potassium nitrate and calcium sulphate. Sodium chloride (NaCl) is a salt in the chemical sense but is also called common salt in everyday use.

Septagon See *Polygon*.

Similar The use of this word in mathematics is different from its everyday use. In everyday use two things are similar if they are roughly the same. In mathematics, two shapes are similar if they are exactly the same apart from their size.

For example, two squares of different sizes are similar; two circles of different sizes are similar. Two rectangles might not be similar.

Sine See *Cosine*.

SI units The internationally recommended system of *units* (q.v.) in which the base units are:

Quantity	Name of unit	Symbol
length	metre	m
mass	kilogram	kg
time	second	s
electric current	ampere	A
temperature	kelvin	K
amount of substance	mole	mol
luminous intensity	candela	cd

Other quantities are derived by combining these units e.g. the SI unit of volume is the cubic metre (m^3), that of velocity the metre per second ($m\ s^{-1}$), that of energy the joule ($m^2\ kg\ s^{-2}$) and that of electric charge the coulomb (A. s).

Solution Finding the solution to an equation means replacing the variable(s) in an equation by number(s) so that the equation is true.

Examples:

$x = 3$ is a solution of the equation $2x + 5 = 11$.

$x = 2$ and $x = 4$ are both solutions of the equation $x^2 - 6x + 8 = 0$.

$p = 3, q = 4$ is a solution of the equation $p + q = 7$.

$n = 4$ is a solution of the equation $2^n = n^2$.

A solution to an equation is sometimes called a root.

Specific gravity See *Density.*

Specific heat The amount of heat in joules that must be added to 1 kg of a substance to raise its temperature by 1° C. The table gives values for a gram of substance.

Specific heats of common substances			
Aluminium . .	0·846	Alcohol . . .	2·428
Brass . . .	0·384	Chloroform . .	0·980
Copper . . .	0·389	Air	1·009 [1]
Iron	0·474	Carbon dioxide . .	0·846 [1]
Rubber . . .	1·675	Oxygen . . .	0·911 [1]
Wood . . .	1·675	Water . . .	4·187
[1] At constant pressure.			

Square This has two meanings in mathematics. A square is a four-sided polygon (a quadrilateral) which has all its sides the same length and all its angles right-angles.

A square is also a whole number which can be factorised into two equal numbers.

16 is an example of a square because $16 = 4 \times 4$. 289 is a square because $289 = 17 \times 17$. A number like 16 is called a square because 16 objects can be arranged into the shape of a square.

Standard form Very large and very small numbers are often written in standard form. Here are some examples of standard form:

3×10^6 means 3,000,000

$4·1 \times 10^5$ means 410,000

$8·72 \times 10^9$ means 8,720,000,000

$4·3 \times 10^{-5}$ means 0·000043

$7·85 \times 10^{-8}$ means 0·0000000785

A number in standard form is always written as a number between 1 and 10 multiplied by a power of 10.

Strong nuclear force One of the four fundamental forces of nature. The other three are called electromagnetic, gravitational and weak. Strong nuclear force causes the attraction of *hadrons* (q.v.) to each other: for example, protons and neutrons in the nucleus.

Superconductivity This is the remarkable property of many metals and alloys to lose all electrical resistance below a certain critical temperature (usually within 20° of absolute zero). This means that an electric current can flow in a loop of the metal indefinitely without generating heat or decreasing in strength. Because of the low temperatures required (the metal is usually bathed in liquid helium) superconductivity is expensive to use on a large scale. But superconducting magnets which can produce very intense magnetic fields without vast consumption of electrical energy are now quite widely used.

Surface tension A force acting in the surface of a fluid, whether the surface separates one liquid from another or a liquid from a gas such as air. The effect of the force is to make the liquid surface behave rather like a stretched elastic skin with a tendency to reduce its area. It is surface tension which causes water to climb up a narrow capillary tube and causes water surfaces to be meniscus-shaped. Surface tension also governs the formation and shape of liquid drops and bubbles.

Surface tension is measured in newtons per metre. It varies with the temperature. The surface tension of pure water at 20° C is 0·07275 newtons per metre.

Tangent This has two meanings. A tangent to a curve is a line which touches the curve. This means that it is in the same direction as the curve at a point where it meets the curve.

The tangent to a circle meets the circle at just one point. This is not necessarily true of all tangents to all curves.

The tangent to a circle is perpendicular to the radius which it meets.

For the other meaning of tangent, see *Cosine*.

Telescope An optical device for getting an image of a distant object much bigger than the object appears seen with the naked eye. (The image obtained is really much smaller than the actual object.) There are two simple types: the astronomical telescope and the Galilean telescope. The astronomical telescope has a very long focus convergent lens as objective and a very short focus convergent lens (or system of lenses) as eyepiece. The

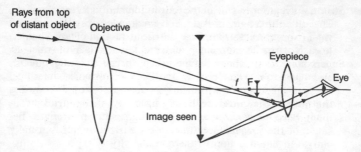

Geometrical Diagram of Astronomical Telescope
F is focus of objective *f* is focus of eyepiece

magnifying power is the focal length of objective divided by the focal length of eyepiece. The bigger the objective in diameter, the greater the resolving power. The image seen is inverted. Prisms can be inserted between the lenses to invert the image and at the same time make the light reflect along paths across and back and across and forward so that the length of the telescope can be short and the optical path long. The result is a prismatic monocular giving the image upright in relation to the object. Two of them make a pair of prismatic binoculars.

The Galilean telescope uses a long-focus convergent lens as objective and a short-focus divergent lens as eyepeice. The image is seen upright. The magnification is again the focal length of objective divided by the focal length of eyepiece, and

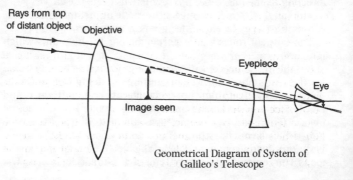

Geometrical Diagram of System of
Galileo's Telescope

as the eyepiece has to be placed within the focal length of the objective the length of the telescope is much less than that of the astronomical telescope for the same magnification. There is, however, one disadvantage, which is that the field of view gets very small as the magnifying power is increased, much more so than the comparable change with an astronomical telescope. Galilean telescopes are therefore for use in everyday life, when the field of view needs to be of reasonable size, restricted to a magnifying power of 2 or 3. Two Galilean telescopes side-by-side make a pair of ordinary non-prismatic field or opera glasses.

All the above are refracting telescopes. Sir Isaac Newton designed a reflecting telescope to get over the difficulty of aberrations in the lenses needed for big magnification. All the very big observatory telescopes of today are reflecting ones.

Temperature The state of hotness or coldness of a body or substance. The heat energy of a body depends on both its temperature and its mass. For example, more heat is required to raise the temperature of a very large mass by 1 degree than to raise the temperature of a small mass by 20 degrees.

Terminating decimal See *Decimal*.

Thermocouple A kind of *thermometer* (q.v.) made by joining one wire at its two ends to another wire of a different material. If one junction is kept cool and the other heated, an electric current flows and can be used as a measure of the temperature of the hot junction.

Thermodynamics The branch of physics dealing with the interconversion of heat with other forms of *energy* (q.v.).

Thermometer An instrument for measuring temperature. The commonest type of thermometer is a glass tube of extremely fine bore and thick walls with a bulb joined at the bottom containing mercury or some other liquid, which also reaches a certain distance up the tube. Warming makes the liquid expand up the tube; cooling makes it contract. A scale of numbers is arrived at by fixing two reference points, usually the melting point of ice and the boiling point of water.

Two temperature scales are in common use. One, called the Fahrenheit scale, has the melting point of ice at 32° and the boiling point of water at 212°. This is in general use in the USA. The second scale is called Celsius and has the lower point at 0° and the upper at 100°. It is in use generally in many countries, and is international for scientific measurement.

To convert Fahrenheit to Celsius, first subtract 32 and then multiply the result by $\frac{5}{9}$.

To convert Celsius to Fahrenheit multiply by $\frac{9}{5}$ and then add 32.

Examples:
(1) 59° F, convert to ° C
    $59 - 32 = 27; 27 \times \frac{5}{9} = 15°$ C
(2) 20° C, convert to ° F
    $20 \times \frac{9}{5} = 36; 36 + 32 = 68°$ F

To convert °C to the *absolute temperature* scale (q.v.) add 273·15.

Liquid-in-glass thermometers are of limited use. Mercury freezes at $-39°$ C; ethyl alcohol boils at 78·3° C. So other devices must be used for very low and very high temperatures. For extreme temperatures a *thermocouple* (q.v.) is frequently used, depending on the electricity generated when two dissimilar metals are joined and the junction heated or cooled. A platinum resistance-thermometer depends on the change of electrical resistance in platinum wire when it is heated. Modern materials called thermistors are also used. The resistance of such materials gets less as it is heated. So an electrical current increases.

Special thermometers of the liquid-in-glass sort are devised to read the minimum or the maximum temperature reached in a certain period of time. A clinical thermometer is a type of maximum thermometer in which the thread of mercury stays put at its highest because of a very narrow constriction at the base of the tube where it joins the mercury-supply bulb.

Ultra-violet light A type of electromagnetic radiation (q.v.) that is invisible to human beings and of shorter wavelength than visible light. Sometimes called 'dark light'. It is very active in affecting chemicals and causing *fluorescence* (q.v.). It is present in the light from the sun, but much of it is filtered out by the earth's atmosphere. It is dangerous for the eyes. Range of wavelengths 1,800–4,200 Å. It is also present in mercury-vapour discharge light.

Units All physical quantities can be expressed in terms of five base units: mass (M), length (L), time (T), electric current and temperature. Thus volume $= L^3$, force $= MLT^{-2}$. The magnitude of the base units is set by convention. In the f.p.s. system they are the foot (L), the pound (M) and the second (S). The currently accepted system is the Système International d'Unités (see *SI units*).

Vacuum Space which contains no matter. In practice unobtainable since, whatever the walls of the container were made of, the container would evaporate slowly and so destroy the vacuum. Usually very low pressures of air or other gases are called vacuums.

Valency The valency of an element is a number that tells in what proportions the element combines with other elements, and so can be used to work out molecular formulae of compounds. Elements of valency 1 (monovalent elements) include hydrogen, chlorine, silver and sodium; of valency 2 (divalent elements) include oxygen, magnesium and calcium; of valency 3 (trivalent elements) include aluminium and nitrogen; and of valency 4 (tetravalent elements) include carbon.

Oxygen being divalent means that one atom of it will combine with two atoms of monovalent hydrogen (giving water H_2O), or with one atom of divalent magnesium (giving MgO, magnesium oxide), or with 'half' an atom of tetravalent carbon (giving carbon dioxide, CO_2). Three atoms of oxygen combine with two of aluminium to give aluminium oxide Al_2O_3.

Valency is closely related to the theory of the chemical *bond* (q.v.) and is not always as simple as above. Many elements can combine with each other in a number of different ways: e.g. nitrogen and oxygen can give the oxides N_2O, NO, N_2O_3, NO_2, and N_2O_5 and two oxides of copper exist, CuO and Cu_2O.

Vapour pressure A liquid loses atoms or molecules into its gaseous surround, usually air. When the pressure of these evaporated atoms or molecules is such that as many are returning to the material as are leaving it the vapour is saturated and its

Vapour pressures of some liquids at 20° C in mm of mercury			
Water	17·5	Benzene	74·6
Mercury	0·0013	Chloroform	161
Acetone	185	Ether	440
Alcohol	44·5	Carbon Tetrachloride	91

pressure is called the vapour pressure of the liquid. It increases
with a rise in temperature and depends only on that temperature and the nature of the liquid. A volatile liquid has a high
vapour pressure at ordinary temperatures. A liquid that has a
low vapour pressure does not evaporate easily. On heating a
liquid there comes a temperature at which the vapour pressure
equals atmospheric pressure. It then boils.

Velocity A positive or negative quantity representing speed. It is
positive or negative to show the direction of motion.

Virus The simplest form of living organism, so small as to be only
visible with the aid of the electron *microscope* (q.v.). Viruses are
inactive when isolated and can only reproduce by invading a *cell*
(q.v.) of a *bacterium* (q.v.), animal or plant and using the more
complicated chemical machinery of the host cell. Viruses come
in various shapes and sizes (up to a few thousand angstroms in
length), but usually a particular kind of virus can only infect
one kind of host. Many infectious diseases (such as influenza
and AIDS in humans) are caused by viruses invading and
disrupting their victim's cells (see *proteins*).

Viscosity The internal friction of fluids, i.e. resistance to flow of
one part over another. Examples: treacle, a very viscous fluid;
ether, a liquid of low viscosity. Viscosity usually decreases with
rise in temperature.

Volt The SI unit of *electromotive force* (*e.m.f.*) (q.v.), potential difference or electrical pressure.

Volume The amount of space taken up by a three-dimensional
object. Common units of volume are cubic metres, cubic
millimetres, cubic centimetres and litres. A litre is 1000 cubic
centimetres.

The following formulae can be used to find volumes of some
objects.

Volumes of common shapes

Cube: l^3, where l = length of one side.
Prism: cross-sectional area × length.
Sphere: $\frac{4}{3}\pi r^3$, where r = radius.
Cylinder: $\pi r^2 l$, where r = radius of base, l = length of cylinder.
Cone: $\frac{1}{3}\pi r^2 h$, where r = radius of base, h = vertical height.
Pyramid: $\frac{1}{3}$ area of base × h, where h = vertical height.

a   b

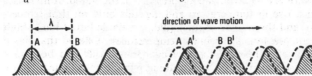

Waves Many kinds of disturbance travel from one point to another as waves, for example, ripples on a water surface, pressure
variations in air (sound) and electrical and magnetic disturbances (light). The important thing is that the disturbance varies
periodically in both space and time. This can be understood by
considering a water wave. If a water wave is photographed at
one time it will look as in diagram (a) where the shape of the
wave is repeated regularly and the distance, λ, between successive crests is called the *wavelength*. If the wave is travelling
from left to right with velocity v, at a slightly later time the
picture will look as in (b) which has the earlier wave shape
dotted in (the crest at A having moved to A'). Moreover if we
remain fixed at B, we have to wait a time T equal to λ/v before
the crest originally at A reaches B. The time T between successive crests arriving at a given point is called the *period*. The
reciprocal $1/T$ is the number of crests passing a point per second
and is called the *frequency, f.* We have shown the important
relationship.

$$T = \lambda/v \text{ or } v = f\lambda$$

which is true for all wave motions. It is important to note that
it is the shape of the wave and the energy carried by it that
moves from A to A' and not the water itself. The water
molecules are actually moving backwards and forwards in the
direction at right angles to the direction the wave is travelling. For this reason, water waves are examples of *transverse*
waves. *Longitudinal* waves, by comparison, are waves in which
the particles are moving back and forth in the same direction
as that in which the wave is moving e.g. sound waves.

All kinds of waves show the characteristic properties of *reflection* (q.v.), *refraction* (q.v.) and *diffraction* (*q.v.*).

Weight The force of attraction exerted on a body by gravity. See
Mass.

The metric system

Linear Measure

10 millimetres (*mm*)	= 1 centimetre (*cm*)
10 centimetres	= 1 decimetre (*dm*)
10 decimetres	= 1 metre (*m*)
10 metres	= 1 decametre (*Dm*)
10 decametres	= 1 hectometre (*hm*)
10 hectometres	= 1 kilometre (*km*)

Measures of Weight

1000 milligrammes (*mg*)	= 1 gramme (*g*)
1000 grammes	= 1 kilogramme (*kg*)
1000 kilogrammes	= 1 tonne (0·984206 tons)

Measures of Capacity

10 millilitres (*ml*)	= 1 centilitre (*cl*)
100 centilitres	= 1 litre (*l*)
1000 litres	= 1 kilolitre (*kl*)

Land Measure
1 hectare (*ha*) = 10,000 sq metres

Imperial Measure

Avoirdupois Weight

16 drams	= 1 ounce (*oz*)
16 ounces	= 1 pound (*lb*)
14 pounds	= 1 stone
28 pounds	= 1 quarter
4 quarters	= 1 hundredweight (*cwt*)
20 hundredweights	= 1 ton (2,240 pounds)
100 pounds	= 1 central, or short hundredweight
2,000 pounds	= 1 short ton (U.S. ton)
7,000 grains	= 1 pound

Linear Measure

12 inches	= 1 foot
3 feet	= 1 yard
5½ yards	= 1 rod, pole or perch
40 poles	= 1 furlong
8 furlongs	= 1 mile
3 miles	= 1 league

Land Measure

7·92 inches	= 1 link
25 links	= 1 rod
4 rods or 100 links	= 1 chain
80 chains	= 1 mile

Square Measure
144 square inches = 1 square foot
9 square feet = 1 square yard
30¼ square yards = 1 square rod, pole or perch
40 square poles = 1 rood
4 roods = 1 acre
640 acres = 1 square mile

Land Square Measure
625 square links = 1 square rod
16 square rods = 1 square chain
10 square chains = 1 acre

Liquid Measure
4 gills = 1 pint
2 pints = 1 quart
4 quarts = 1 gallon

Circular Measure (see also under *radian*)
60 seconds (") = 1 minute (')
60 minutes = 1 degree (°)
90 degrees = 1 quadrant (*quad*)
4 quadrants or 360 degrees = 1 circle (o)

Weights and measures A table of weights and measures is given on pages E60 and E61. In Great Britain the traditional Imperial weights and measures (e.g. inches, pounds and pints) are gradually being replaced by the simpler Metric system (e.g. centimetres, kilograms and litres) which is based on units of ten. To get from one system to the other see under *Conversion table*. See also *SI Units*.

X-ray diffraction A very important technique of *crystallography* (q.v.). The wavelengths of *X-rays* (q.v.) and the size of the repeating units in *crystals* (q.v.) are both of the same magnitude—a few *angstroms* (q.v.). As a result a beam of X-rays incident on a crystal is split up by the process of *diffraction* (q.v.) into a number of secondary beams which leave the crystal in different directions. The intensity and direction of these diffracted beams depend upon the structure of the crystal and can be used by crystallographers to find this structure.

X-rays Electromagnetic radiation of very short wavelength, ranging from a tenth of an angstrom to 20 angstroms. X-rays affect a photographic plate and cause fluorescence in some chemicals. They penetrate matter according to its density. They are used in medical practice for showing up growths, bone fractures, foreign bodies, etc., in the human body.

A DICTIONARY OF RADIO, TELEVISION AND VIDEO

Some of the terms used in discussing radio and television are general scientific terms (e.g. *ampere, ohm*) and if not found in this section should be looked for in the DICTIONARY OF SCIENCE AND MATHEMATICS. At the same time, a number of terms associated with the high fidelity reproduction of records (discs), tape cassettes (e.g. *stylus, Dolby system*) and compact discs are included under the term 'radio', with which this form of hi-fi is so closely integrated.

With the 21st century less than a decade away, a great deal of advance in technology is expected among the European community, resulting in improved radio and television facilities. To take advantage of this, the structure of broadcasting in the United Kingdom is likely to be considerably amended following the Government's Broadcasting Act, based on an earlier White Paper. The provisions of the Act became effective on 1st January, 1993, although the new regulatory bodies took over duties at the beginning of 1991.

Abbreviations

A—ampere	kHz—kilohertz
mA—milliampere (milliamp)	MHz—megahertz
μA—microampere	W—Watt
V—volt	kW—kilowatt
mV—millivolt	mW—milliwatt
μV—microvolt	H—henry
Ω—omega (capital) = ohm	mH—millihenry
MΩ—megohm	μH—microhenry
μΩ—micro-ohm	AC—alternating current
F—farad	DC—direct current
μF—microfarad	emf—electromotive force
Hz—hertz	RMS—root-mean-square

Note: The above abbreviations are in accordance with the ruling of the British Standards Institution.

LF—low frequency	AF—audio frequency
HF—high frequency	DCC—double cotton covered
VHF—very high frequency	SCC—single cotton covered
RF—radio frequency	N. pole—north pole
SWG—standard wire gauge	S. pole—south pole
DSC—double silk covered ⎱ synonymous terms	
DWS—double wound silk ⎰	

Aerial (Antenna) A conductor that can either send out or pick up radio waves and therefore can be the last stage of a transmitter or the first stage of a receiver. In its simplest form it is a metallic rod or wire but efficient, directional aerials can be of complicated design.

A transmitter operating on long or medium waves has an aerial that is a high wire leading through the transmitter to the ground. For waves as short as, or shorter than, those used for television the antenna is free of any earth connection and the length of rod forming the antenna is related to the wavelength. The commonest relationship is that the antenna is a half the wavelength. The usual design is of two rods in line, each rod just under a quarter wavelength long, the two ends at the middle being where the line joining the antenna to the transmitter or receiver is placed. This is the *half-wave dipole* or Hertzian antenna.

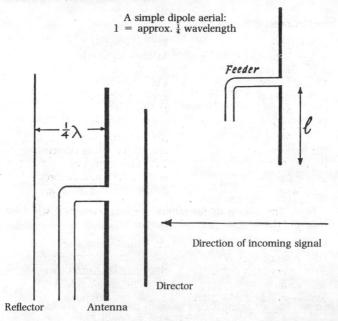

A simple dipole aerial:
1 = approx. ¼ wavelength

A dipole with one reflector and one director

Television video signals are transmitted on various channels of which 57 are available in Britain. Channels 1 to 13 were VHF and were formerly used for the monochrome (black and white) TV service but this has now been discontinued. The channels for colour TV are 21 to 68 on UHF but not all these are used at present. Band VI is on SHF and consists of 20 DBS channels for use in direct broadcasting by satellite. The United Kingdom has been allocated five of these (4, 8, 12, 16, 20).

The audio signals for television are on slightly different frequencies from that of the video signal, so an aerial correctly designed for one will not be accurate for the other. In practice, a compromise is made.

If the electrical component of the electromagnetic wave being transmitted or received is vertical, then the half-wave antenna is vertical. If the electrical component is horizontal

the antenna is horizontal. The higher-powered TV stations and
some of the relays transmit horizontally polarised signals. Most
VHF FM signals are also horizontally polarised although the
majority have been, or will be, converted to 'mixed' polar-
isation for better reception in cars and portables.

Single-dipole antennae transmit and receive in all directions.
Another half-wave rod placed exactly a quarter of a wave-length
behind but unconnected to the transmitter or receiver, enhances
the efficiency in the forward direction, and the extra rod is called
a reflector. Rods placed in *front* of the operative dipole, and at
the correct distance (*not* a quarter wavelength but less), also
enhance the directional efficiency and are called directors.

Satellite broadcasts require a special aerial with a disc reflector to collect the signals.

In modern radios the aerial for medium waves usually consists of an internal ferrite rod, whilst a telescopic aerial provides
reception of FM signals on VHF.

Alternating Current (AC) Electric current which regularly reverses its direction around a circuit. A particular alternating
current is usually described by its *frequency* (q.v.) and its *root-
mean-square* value (q.v.).

Amateur Radio Certain frequencies in the short-wave bands are
allocated internationally for use by amateur radio enthusiasts.
Licences are granted by the Home Office subject to the passing
of a technical examination and a morse code test. No morse
test is required for the Sound Licence 'B' which is limited to
telephony only above 144 MHz or for the amateur TV licence.

Amplification This is the electronics and radio term for magnification, and the circuitry that does the amplifying is an amplifier, of which there are several sorts. The radio-frequency or
RF amplifier amplifies only signals of high frequencies, whereas
the audio-frequency or AF amplifier amplifies signals of frequencies ranging between about 30 and 30,000 Hz in high-
fidelity work and to about 8,000 Hz in a good radio receiver.
These are very low frequencies compared with radio frequencies, which even on the medium waves are of the order of
a million Hz. This enormous difference between the frequencies
handled by an AF amplifier and an RF amplifier means a
considerable difference in the circuits used.

In radio and electronics and television, amplification involves the use of thermionic valves or transistors. Any one such valve or transistor with its associated circuit of resistors, capacitors and perhaps inductance, is called a *stage*. Each stage except the last in a radio receiver is designed as a voltage amplifier, but the final stage has to deliver power to a loudspeaker or the coils of a cathode-ray tube in a television receiver. This final stage is therefore a power amplifier.

The general principle of amplication is that an input alternating voltage, still at radio frequency if it is RF amplication but at audio frequency if it is AF amplification, is applied between the grid and cathode of a thermionic valve. The output is then taken from the anode circuit. If a transistor is used the input is in most cases (i.e. using common emitter connections) applied between base and emitter and the output taken between collector and emitter. In each case what is taken out is bigger than what is put in. The ratio of output to input is called the *stage gain*.

The stage gain depends on various factors which differ according to whether a valve or transistor amplifier is considered.

Amplitude Modulation The addition of an audio-frequency signal to a carrier in such a way that the carrier amplitude varies in response to the signal. See *modulation*.

Anode The positive electrode of an electrolytic cell or thermionic valve or discharge tube.

Astra A medium-power satellite system operated by the Société Européene des Satellites in Luxembourg and backed by several British television companies together with various financial institutions. This satellite is used by BSKYB (q.v.). and by some other stations, including Radio Luxembourg.

Audio Frequency (AF) This means a *frequency* (q.v.) within the range of sound wave frequencies audible to human ears. It can be taken as between 20 hertz and 20,000 hertz, though many people have a much smaller range than this. High-fidelity amplifiers are capable of reproducing from about 30 hertz to 30,000 hertz.

Automatic Gain Control A circuit device which automatically maintains the output of a stage almost constant, even though the input may be varying. It operates by the principle of *feedback* (q.v.), and is used in radio receivers to reduce the effect of *fading* (q.v.).

Bias A voltage applied to transistors and valves to allow them to operate in the most satisfactory manner to avoid distortion. In the case of transistors it may be applied by a battery; but generally it is by an arrangement of resistors.

British Broadcasting Corporation The oldest broadcasting organisation in the world, developing out of a company first formed in 1922.

The BBC broadcasts in sound to countries all over the world in 39 languages beside English. It is organised into two parts, one for the home programmes, with headquarters in Broadcasting House in London, W1, and one for the programmes going overseas—the World Service—with headquarters in Bush House, London WC2. Television Centre at White City controls TV services.

The BBC broadcasts at present in two television services, known as BBC-1 and BBC-2, and in five radio services known as Radio 1, 2, 3, 4 and 5, as well as local radio stations. Radio services are broadcast on medium or low frequencies (MF or LF) and on Very High Frequency (VHF). Details of the frequencies used are printed in *Radio Times* and fuller information is available from the Engineering Information Department.

The new Broadcasting Act provides for the BBC to remain as a 'public service operation', and some revision will be made of radio programmes and frequencies in use. Greater attention is being paid to transmission by FM on VHF. Since its inception the BBC has always been financed by a licence fee decided by the Government, but revision of this method is now being considered.

The World Service is mainly broadcast on the higher frequencies in the bands from 25 to 5 MHz, but some of the services to Europe are broadcast on MF and some of the high frequency programmes are relayed on MF from transmitters in Cyprus and other parts of the world. The World Service can be received in Britain and Eastern Europe on medium wave 648 KHz (463 m).

BBC Television is transmitted on the 625 line standard in the UHF band (band 5). Except for old films, programmes are in colour.

The BBC has set up World Services Television, a twenty-four-hour international news and information channel distributed by satellite; it will be available in every continent by the end of 1993.

BSB British Satellite Broadcasting was a TV system that began in 1989 and merged with SKY television in 1990 to become BSKYB (q.v.).

BSKYB British Sky Broadcasting. On 2nd November 1990 the TV satellite groups known as SKY TV and BSB TV merged their activities into a single operation, the new joint venture being controlled fifty-fifty by News International and BSB. It is anticipated that seven channels will be in operation by the end of 1993. Movies and sport are on a subscription service. BSKYB operates and trades as SKY Television.

Broadcasting Standards Council This is a statutory body under the Broadcasting Act 1990. It monitors the portrayal of violence and sex and matters of taste and decency (such as bad language or the treatment of disasters) in television or radio programmes or broadcast advertisements. The Council deals with complaints about these matters and may make complaints of its own.

Camcorder A name coined by the trade from the words 'camera' and 'recorder' to indicate a video recording camera that produces a tape recording like a 'home movie'.

Capacitance This is the property of a *capacitor* (q.v.) to store electric charge when a voltage is applied across the capacitor plates. The unit of capacitance is the *farad* (F), and a capacitor has a capacitance of one farad if it stores a charge of one coulomb when there is a voltage of one volt across it. The farad is too large for most practical purposes and it is normal to use the microfarad, μF (one millionth of a farad), and the picofarad, pF (one million millionth of a farad).

In understanding how a capacitor behaves in a circuit it is important to remember that electric current is the flow of electric charge. So whenever charge is moving into or out of a capacitor (i.e. the capacitor is *charging* or *discharging*) a current must flow. Also, the charge stored in a capacitor is always equal to the voltage across it times its capacitance.

Suppose a capacitor is connected in a circuit with a battery, a *resistor* (q.v.) and a switch. When the switch is open there is no voltage across the capacitor and therefore no charge stored in it. On closing the switch, current flows for a short time, charging up the capacitor until the voltage across it is equal to that of the battery. The insulating layer in the capacitor then prevents any further current flow. If the battery is now removed from the circuit, the capacitor discharges through the resistor and a current again flows for a short time (but in the opposite direction) until there is no voltage across the capacitor. If the battery is now reconnected, but with positive and negative reversed, the capacitor will again charge up (in the opposite direction to before) and current will again flow. Thus we can see that if we connect a capacitor to an AC generator whose voltage is regularly changing from positive to zero, zero to negative, and negative through zero to positive again, the capacitor will regularly charge up, discharge and recharge in the opposite direction. An alternating current will therefore flow even though there is an insulating layer in the capacitor. The AC is exactly of the same *frequency* (q.v.) as the voltage but the current maxima coincide with the voltage zeros: i.e. the voltage and current are 90° out of *phase* (q.v.). The magnitude of the current is given by V/X_C, where V is the voltage and X_C is called the *capacitive reactance*. For a capacitor of capacitance C farads and AC of frequency f, $X_C = 1/2\pi Cf$ ohms.

Capacitor A circuit component which has the property of *capacitance* (q.v.). The simplest form of capacitor is the parallel plate capacitor which consists of two plates of metal separated by an insulating material called a *dielectric*. The capacitance C is given by the formula

$$C = \frac{\varepsilon A}{d} \times \frac{10^{-9}}{36\pi} \text{ farads}$$

where A is the area of the overlapping plates, d is the distance between the plates and ε is a constant which depends on the dielectric used and is called the *dielectric constant*. For low values of capacitance the dielectric may be air ($\varepsilon = 1$). This is often the case for variable capacitors used in tuning radios. When the dial is turned, one set of plates interleaves with another set separated by air gaps and A in the above formula is increased or decreased. Fixed capacitors of higher values are made with ceramic, mica, paper, polyester or polystyrene dielectrics. Very high values are provided by electrolytic capacitors. Here the dielectric is formed by a thin layer of oxide,

itself formed by the action of an electric current: to retain it, the
capacitor is polarised (i.e. + and − poles).

Carrier Wave Electromagnetic waves of the frequencies of speech
and music cannot be transmitted efficiently over long distances.
So in telecommunications a wave of much higher frequency,
the carrier wave, is used to 'carry' the desired signal by the
technique of *modulation* (q.v.).

Cartridge The operative part of a record player which is actuated
by the *stylus* (q.v.) and carried by the *pick-up* (q.v.).

Cassette A compact form of reels of magnetic tape upon which home
recording may be carried out. They are available for both audio
and television use. To record or play back video cassette tapes a
video recorder is required. At one time there were two methods,
BETA and VHS, but only the latter is now in use.

Cathode The negative electrode of an electrolytic cell or a thermionic valve or discharge tube.

Cathode-ray Tube This device is a glass envelope roughly conical

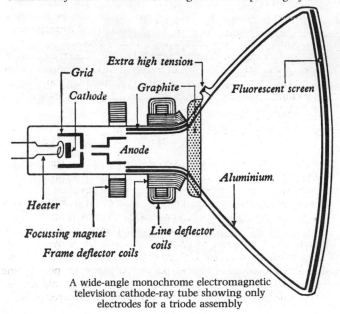

A wide-angle monochrome electromagnetic
television cathode-ray tube showing only
electrodes for a triode assembly

in shape with a long neck in which a cathode emits electrons which travel towards a fluorescent screen on the large end of the envelope. A metal electrode in the neck is the anode to attract the electrons and speed them on their way to the screen. The cathode and focusing electrodes and anodes constitute the *electron gun*. When correctly designed a narrow intense beam of electrons travels to the screen and produces a tiny spot of light.

There are several uses for a cathode-ray tube. The most well-known are in television receivers and computer terminals. With extra apparatus they make an oscilloscope, an apparatus that allows waves and oscillations to be seen as visible traces and measured. The electron beam is forced to traverse the screen in lines, each successive line being below the one before it, so that the whole of the working area of the screen is *scanned*. In order to make the beam do this its movements are controlled by electromagnetic coils on the neck. The colour picture tube has three electron guns to provide red, green and blue signals. These combine to form the colour picture.

Channel 3 This is the title the Broadcasting Act gives to the former ITV television band; but the ITC (q.v.) has decided to continue to call it ITV. From January 1, 1993, licences for ten years have been granted to fifteen regional contractors and one national breakfast-time contractor. Of the original ITV contractors, three regional and one breakfast-time licensees have been replaced by new ones. From the same date Channel 4 (currently a subsidiary of ITC) will become a licensee as a non-profit-making corporation.

Contractors will be financed by the selling of air-time to advertisers.

CB Radio CB Radio or Citizens Band Radio has now been legal for some years. A form of radio-telephone, it enables truck drivers and other road users to keep in touch with one another and exchange details of road hazards, etc. In 1981 the Government legalised CB Radio with the proviso that FM only could be used and the frequencies allocated are 27 and 934 MHz. A licence fee of £10 is payable annually. Use of AM apparatus remains illegal.

Chip The popular name for an *integrated circuit* (q.v.) derived from silicon chip or micro-chip. It is encapsulated in a small plastic box with connecting lugs on each side.

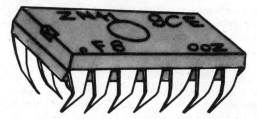

A silicon chip

Circuit The name given to the arrangement of conductors, capacitors, inductances, valves, etc., that make up the theoretical picture of an electronics device. All these components are shown in diagrams by conventional graphical symbols and the connecting wires by straight lines. The circuit diagram must be distinguished from the wiring diagram, which shows the natural disposition, soldering points, etc., of the real components. The circuit diagram merely tells the theory on which the behaviour of the apparatus is based and can be calculated.

Classic FM The first national commercial radio station established under the new Broadcasting Act; it plays classical music.

Coil Conducting wire wound on a former and used in AC circuits as a source of *inductance* (q.v.). There may be many or few turns and the core may or may not be of a magnetic material, depending on the application. Coils are widely used in *tuning* (q.v.) circuits and as *chokes* when a high impedance to AC is required.

Colour Code A form of marking by coloured bands or spots to indicate the values of components, different colours being given to the figures 1–10. Usually used for resistors but sometimes applied to capacitors.

Colour Television The first British colour television broadcast was made on 2 July 1967, and the BBC's full colour service on BBC 2 opened on 2 December. Programmes from all stations are now generally in colour.

Compact Disc As its name implies, a small gramophone record capable of carrying as much information as the conventional record. It is not played by the usual stylus and pick-up but special apparatus enables it to be traversed by a laser beam by which the disc's contents are conveyed to the amplifier. Very fine quality of reproduction is secured by the system.

Condenser See *capacitor*.

Crystal Detector An early form of rectifier consisting of a thin pointed wire (the 'cat's whisker') in contact with a *semiconductor* (q.v.) crystal. Used as a detector for radio waves prior to the invention of diode valves and *p–n junction* (q.v.) diodes.

Decibel (dB) A unit which compares two levels of *power* (q.v.). To say that two power levels, P_2 and P_1, differ by n dB means that $n = 10 \times \log_{10} P_2/P_1$. Depending upon whether P_2 is greater or less than P_1, n may be positive or negative. If, for example, $P_2 = 2P_1$, then P_2 is $10\log_{10}2$ (about 3) dB up on P_1. In electronics, decibels are often used to compare the output power of a circuit with the input power, i.e. to give a measure of the circuit gain or loss. A bel is ten decibels.

Decibel Table			
(Based on 1 milliwatt reference)			
Milliwatts	*Decibels*	*Milliwatts*	*Decibels*
1	0	3·981	6
1·259	1	5·012	7
1·585	2	6·310	8
1·995	3	7·943	9
2·512	4	10·000	10
3·162	5	1 watt	30

If it is required to give actual power levels instead of just relative power levels, the *decibel referred to one milliwatt* (dBm) is often used. In this case P_1 is fixed at a reference level of one milliwatt. The table gives the correspondence between power levels measured in milliwatts and dBm.

Decoder Circuitry required to enable stereo radio broadcasts on VHF to operate a stereo amplifier. It is inserted between the tuner and the stereo amplifier. The term is also used to describe the apparatus needed to allow reception of satellite TV on the normal TV receiver.

Detection (Demodulation) The reverse process to *modulation* (q.v.): i.e. the separation of the original signal from the modulated *carrier wave* (q.v.). This is usually done in radio and television receivers (after changing from a frequency-modulated signal to an amplitude-modulated signal if necessary) by rectifying the high frequency signal to give a direct current varying at audio frequencies. See *rectification.*

Diagrams There are certain standard *graphical symbols* (q.v.) used in electrical, electronic, radio and television circuit diagrams. Straight lines indicate conducting connections (lengths of copper wire when an amateur is wiring up a piece of apparatus). Today this is more likely to be a printed circuit board or 'vero-board'.

Digital Electronics It would seem inevitable that two branches of the science known as electronics should ultimately become associated, and digital electronics, which are related to computers and data processing, are becoming increasingly important in the radio field. Details and graphical symbols are outside the scope of this section, but see **Nicam**.

Digital Stereo Sound A development by which television broadcasts may be made in stereo and which is generally known as nicam (*q.v.*) digital stereo sound.

DIN In general use in Europe as a standard specification. There is an accepted DIN standard for high-fidelity amplifiers and there are DIN plugs and sockets standardised for general use. It derives from Deutscher Industrie Normenausschuss, the German Industrial Standards Board.

Diode This means 'two electrodes' and refers to a component that will allow the passage of an electric current in one direction only and hence can be used for *rectification* (q.v.). The diode may be a thermionic valve with only a cathode and an anode or a semiconductor *p-n junction* (q.v.).

Distortion There are a number of forms of distortion which can affect the reproduction of a radio or other signal by an amplifier. These include noise and hum, but the most prevalent is *harmonic distortion* (q.v.).

Dolby System A system named after the inventor which reduces the hiss which is an undesirable feature of tape recording (particularly cassettes). Also known as DNL (dynamic noise limiter), it enables cassettes to compete with discs as a source of hi-fi recording.

Doping The adding of small quantities of impurities to a *semiconductor* (q.v.). Adding of antimony or arsenic to germanium gives *n-type* germanium. This has a higher conductivity (see *resistivity*) than undoped germanium because the impurity atoms bring extra electrons which are readily available for carrying electricity. Adding aluminium or indium to germanium gives *p-type* germanium. This also has an increased conductivity but due to the presence of positively charged *holes* which, like electrons, can carry electricity. See *p–n junction* and *transistor.*

Early Bird The world's first commercial communications satellite, launched by the United States in the spring of 1965.

Earth A term much used in radio and electronics. For ordinary circuits, including telephone and distribution lines, the earth, being a conductor of electricity, though a poor one, can be used as the return wire to complete the circuit. For circuits involving electromagnetic oscillations and waves the earth is the conductor to which the transmitter or receiver is connected, the antenna being the other. Thus when medium or low frequencies are used the antenna system is a long, high wire or system of wires and the earth connection is a system of wires buried in the ground. For an ordinary receiver the water pipe is a good enough earth. The word 'earth' is also used, however, to mean the common metallic connection to all the circuits, frequently the metal chassis on which everything is mounted. The advantage of an earth connection is that stray currents use the earth as a 'sink' and in receiving weak signals on medium and long waves the signal is increased. Modern receivers frequently need no earth connection at all. Transmission and reception of television signals and any others using dipole antennae make no use of an earth connection.

Electric Field An electric field is a region of space in which an electric charge experiences a force.

Electromagnetic Waves (EM waves) Waves (see DICTIONARY OF SCIENCE) consisting of both electric and magnetic quantities varying regularly in space and time and travelling together at the speed of light.

Diagram (a) gives an instantaneous picture of an EM wave. The *electric field* (q.v.) is in the x-direction and oscillates between $+$ ve and $-$ ve values as in diagram (b). The *magnetic field* (q.v.) is in the y-direction and varies in a similar way. The whole wave travels in the z-direction at the speed of light so that at a later time the electric field will vary as shown dotted in (b). The wavelength, λ, is the distance between one crest and the next. The frequency,

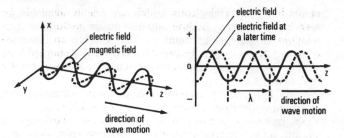

(a) Simplified diagram of an   (b) Diagram showing how
    electromagnetic wave   the electric field varies

Wavelengths and Frequencies			
λ	n	λ	n
2,000 m	150 kHz	50 m	6 MHz
1,000 m	300 kHz	10 m	30 MHz
500 m	600 kHz	3 m	100 MHz
300 m	1,000 kHz	1 m	300 MHz
	(1 MHz)	10 cm	3,000 MHz
200 m	1,500 kHz	3 cm	10,000 MHz
100 m	3,000 kHz	1 cm	30,000 MHz
	(3 MHz)	5 mm	60,000 MHz

The Electromagnetic Spectrum		
Wavelength	Frequency	Name
0·01 Å	3×10^{14} MHz	}
0·1 Å	3×10^{13} MHz	} Gamma rays and X-rays
10 Å	3×10^{11} MHz	}
100 Å	3×10^{10} MHz	} Ultra-violet light
4,000 Å	$7·5 \times 10^{8}$ MHz	} Visible light { violet / red
7,500 Å	4×10^{8} MHz	} Infra-red light
1,000,000 Å	3×10^{6} MHz	
(0·01 cm)		
0·1 cm	300,000 MHz	} Radio waves from millimetre
1,000,000 cm	30 kHz	} waves to long waves

f, is the number of oscillations per second at a given point. These are related to the speed of light, c, by the equation.

$$c = f.\lambda$$

The value of c for EM waves in free space, c_0, is 3×10^8 m per sec or 186,000 miles per sec. Note that EM waves do not need a medium through which to travel, unlike sound waves. EM waves do of course travel through other materials but at a velocity c_0/μ where μ is the refractive index of the material.

EM waves have very different properties depending on the wavelength. Different names are given to different ranges of wavelength, and these make up the *Electromagnetic Spectrum.* (See DICTIONARY OF SCIENCE for *Gamma rays, Ultra-violet light,* etc).

Fading The variation in strength of a received radio signal. Medium waves suffer from this at night when the ground ray and the sky ray are received together and the sky ray is varying. Short waves suffer from it because of variations in the conditions of the reflecting ionosphere. It can be reduced in a receiver by *automatic gain control* (q.v.).

Farad The SI unit of *capacitance* (q.v.).

Feedback This is the feeding back from a later part of a circuit to an earlier part. The feedback may be negative, in which case it stabilises, reduces amplification and, if it varies according to the input, provides automatic gain control. Negative feedback is usually introduced into audio amplifiers as it reduces most forms of distortion. Positive feedback can cause instability but, if controlled (reaction), will increase amplification.

Ferrite A material made like a ceramic, i.e. by baking at a high temperature. It is made of a number of oxides, including iron oxide, and can be designed so that it has any magnetic properties desired. Moreover, it can be moulded into any shape. The magnetic coils used on the cathode-ray tubes of some television receivers are wound on ferrite cores. A long rod of ferrite inside a coil constitutes a ferrite 'aerial' for a radio receiver.

Filter A circuit device for passing oscillations of only certain desired frequencies, e.g. low-pass filter, high-pass filter, band-pass filter (for passing only a band of frequencies and cutting off everything of higher and lower frequencies).

Quartz crystal or ceramic filters are also used in IF stages: tuned to the IF they increase selectivity.

Frequency An alternating quantity (such as an alternating current or a radio wave) consists of repeated *cycles*, one cycle

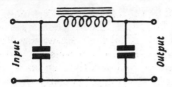

Low-pass filter: the higher the frequency of the input signal the more easily it is short-circuited. The lower the frequency the more easily it is passed on.

High-pass filter: the higher the frequency of the input signal the more easily it is passed on. The lower the frequency the more easily it is short-circuited.

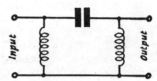

being the sequence of variation of the quantity from zero to maximum positive, from maximum positive through zero to maximum negative and then back to zero. The number of such cycles per second is called the frequency and is measured in *hertz* (one hertz is the same as one cycle per second).

Frequency Modulation (FM) A special way of making a *carrier wave* (q.v.) take an audio-frequency variation. Instead of the amplitude of the carrier being made to vary, the frequency is made to vary instead. It is done on VHF transmissions by the BBC to give a high-quality signal fairly free of interference by locally-made electrical noise. An FM receiver must have extra circuitry to transform the signal into an amplitude-modulated one for audio-frequency amplification in the usual way. The two stages needed are called the *limiter* and *discriminator*, usually combined into one stage called the *ratio detector*.

Galvanometer An instrument which measures small electric currents.

Ganging The mechanical coupling of variable capacitors or resistors in order to control two or more circuits with one knob.

Graphical Symbols There is a convention for representing in circuit diagrams the many sorts of components involved in electronics, radio and television. Most of these are now standardised, but some still have a few variations.

Ground Ray Radio waves on the long and medium wave lengths are sent out by an earthed antenna and travel along attached

Graphical Symbols

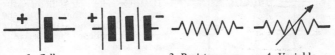

1. Cell   2. Battery   3. Resistance or   4. Variable
                                   fixed resistor   resistor

5. Capacitance   6. Variable   7. Electrolytic   8. Inductance or
   or fixed   capacitor   capacitor   fixed inductor
   capacitor   (air core)

9. Fixed inductor   10. Inductor   11. Mains
   (iron core)   variable by   Transformer
                      moving iron-
                      duct or ferrite
                      core

12. Simple   13. Antenna   14. Earth
   switch

15. Rectifier   16. Loudspeaker   17. Mains Triode
                                        Valve

18. P–N–P Transistor   19. N–P–N Transistor   20. Field Effect
                                                Transistor

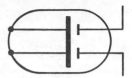

21. Mosfet

22. Integrated Circuit (Micro-chip)

to the ground. This is the ground ray. It provides the commonest and most widespread system of broadcasting. The range varies according to the power of the transmitter and the nature of the ground over which it travels. For the sort of power in use today, the reliable range of a ground ray can be up to two or three hundred miles.

Half-wave Aerial See *aerial.*

Harmonic Distortion Each fundamental note also has harmonics which arise at multiples of the original. If an amplifier over-emphasises the harmonics in relation to the fundamental it suffers from harmonic distortion. The 'goodness' of an amplifier is often judged by, among other things, the minimal percentage of harmonic distortion.

Henry (*H*) The SI unit of *inductance* (q.v.).

Hi-fi An Americanism which is short for, and has been adopted as meaning, high-fidelity: that is, reproduction of an original performance exactly as performed without any coloration or distortion. It is not yet entirely attained, but modern results are superb (at a price). There is a generally accepted *DIN* (q.v.) specification for Hi-fi which is rather lower than the standard at which many modern amplifiers can now operate.

Hum Continuous, low frequency *noise* (q.v.) in audio equipment usually originating from the mains supply and caused, for example, by inadequate earthing or an unsmoothed power supply.

IBA The Independent Broadcasting Authority (formerly the Independent Television Authority) was set up by the Television Act 1954 to provide a service, additional to that of the BBC, for broadcasting entertainment, disseminating information, religious and educational programmes. (See ITC).

The Authority was abolished as at 1st January, 1991 by the Broadcasting Act, and replaced by the Independent Television Commission (I.T.C.) (q.v.) and by the Radio Authority.

ILR Independent Local Radio was part of the IBA, but has been replaced by the new Radio Authority.

Impedance (Z) The word used to represent for AC circuits the equivalent of *resistance* (q.v.) in a DC circuit. The impedance depends on the actual resistance and the *reactance* (q.v.) due to capacitance and inductance. Impedance has the same relationship to emf (E) and current (I) as resistance. So

$$I = \frac{E}{Z}$$

Independent Music Radio (IMR): the second national commercial radio station, devoted to rock and pop music.

Inductance Whenever a coil has a varying magnetic field through it, an emf is set up in the coil causing a current to flow if the circuit is complete. This is known as *induction* and was discovered by Faraday. Whenever an electric current flows in a coil, a magnetic field is created through the coil. Therefore a varying current in a coil will produce a varying magnetic field through the coil and, by induction, will give rise to an induced current in the coil. However, the induced current is always in a direction which opposes the effect of the original current. This opposition to the passage of a varying current is called *inductive reactance* and depends on (a) the rate of change of current in the coil and (b) the *self inductance* (L) of the coil, which is a quantity that takes into account the diameter of the coil, the number of turns and the nature of the core. L is measured in *henries* and a coil has an inductance of one henry if a current varying at the rate of one ampere per second induces in the coil an emf of one volt. If AC of frequency f flows through a coil of inductance L, the inductive reactance (X_L) is $2\pi fL$ ohms, so that with an applied emf of V volts, the current will be $V/2\pi fL$ amps. By induction it is possible for a varying current in one coil to cause an induced current to flow in another coil. This is known as *mutual inductance* and is the basis of *transformers* (q.v.).

Inductance–Capacitance Circuit (*L–C Circuit*) In an AC circuit the voltage across an inductor leads the current through it by 90° (see *phase*), while that across a capacitor lags the current by

90°. This behaviour leads to interesting effects in both the series L–C circuit, in which an inductor is connected in series with a capacitor, and the parallel L–C circuit, in which an inductor is connected in parallel with a capacitor. In the series circuit, because the current through each component is the same, the voltage across the capacitor is 180° out of phase with that across the inductor. This means that the two voltages will cancel out if they are of the same magnitude. In the parallel circuit, because the voltage across each component is the same, the current through the capacitor is 180° out of phase with that through the inductor and the currents will tend to cancel each other out. The condition for complete cancellation is the same in each case, namely that the inductive reactance (X_L) equals the capacitive reactance (X_C), where both quantities depend on the frequency f of the electricity.

Now, $X_L = 2\pi f L$ and $X_C = 1/2\pi f C$
so if $X_L = X_C$
then, $2\pi f L = 1/2\pi f C$
$$f^2 = 1/4\pi^2 LC$$
$$f = 1/2\pi\sqrt{LC}$$

This special frequency is called the *resonant frequency*. At the resonant frequency in the series circuit, the combination of inductor and capacitor present no opposition to the current, though resistance in the wires does limit the current. The series L–C circuit is known as an acceptor circuit as, at the resonant frequency, the opposition to current is at a minimum. At the resonant frequency in the parallel circuit, the total current is zero. In practice, however, resistance in the wires means that the cancellation is not exact, but the circuit still has a maximum opposition to current at this frequency. It is therefore called a rejector circuit.

Because of this peculiar behaviour of series and parallel L–C circuits, they are used in *tuning* (q.v.) and other applications where it is necessary to pick out a particular frequency.

Integrated Circuit (IC) ICs are complete circuit elements (e.g. an amplifier), the individual components (transistors, capacitors and resistors) of which are all together on a single 'chip' of silicon. As individual containers for each component are not required and very little power is needed to make the circuit work, the chip can be made very small (up to 100 components per sq mm).

Intermediate Frequency (IF) This is the fixed frequency that results when an incoming signal is mixed with a locally generated oscillation. The IF in Britain for the *superhet* (q.v.) reception of long waves and medium waves is 470 kHz. The IF for BBC VHF frequency modulation programmes is 10·7 MHz.

Ionosphere High above the earth's surface, starting at 70 miles or so, there are deep layers of gas electrified by the sun's rays. These electrified atoms and molecules affect radio waves and are known under the general term 'ionosphere'. The ionosphere varies daily and seasonally and according to the behaviour of the sun.

Medium waves are reflected from its lowest layers during the day and from higher layers at night (when the lowest layers have disappeared, this giving good intensity of reception some distance away). Short waves are reflected from the ionosphere and enable long-distance communication to take place. Very short waves penetrate the ionosphere and are lost.

ITC The Independent Television Commission is the new body created by the Broadcasting Act to take over the duties of the TV element of the old IBA. The franchises of the ITV companies expired in December 1992 and ITC was empowered, by way of competitive tender, to renew them or allot new ones. (See *Channel 3*) The commission's powers cover also BSKYB and cable TV.

ITV (Independent Television) See *Channel 3*.

Load The purpose of a circuit is to generate a signal or to modify an incoming signal and then to deliver the new signal into another apparatus known as the load. The load takes energy from the circuit that 'drives' it and the nature of the load (e.g. its impedance) alters the behaviour of the circuit. The load for an audio amplifier is usually a loudspeaker, and that for a radio transmitter is an *aerial* (q.v.).

Loudspeaker A device for turning electrical variations into variations of air pressure that reach the ears. There is commercially only one widely-used type—the moving-coil loudspeaker. In this a magnet, usually a permanent magnet, has an annular gap. In this gap floats a tiny light coil of fine wire held in position by a 'spider'. Attached to the coil is a diaphragm, the whole moving in sympathy with current floating through the coil.

For an ordinary commercial loudspeaker the ability of the loudspeaker is usually restricted to about a range of 100–5,000 Hz. By special construction a loudspeaker can be made to cover a wider range than this, and a combination of loudspeakers can be made to cover from 30 to 20,000 Hz.

The loudspeaker is, of course, the final stage of a sound-radio receiver or the audio part of a television receiver.

Magnetic Field A region of space in which a magnet experiences a turning force (couple). Magnetic fields are produced by permanent magnets and electric currents.

Magnetometer An instrument for measuring the intensity of a magnetic field.

Marco Polo 1 The British satellite owned and operated by BSB. Its use, under licence granted by ITC, ended on December 30, 1992.

Maser A device for the amplification of electromagnetic waves. Used in radioastronomy for amplifying the very small signals received from distant radio galaxies, and for picking up the signals received from communications satellites.

Measuring Instruments To measure current an ammeter (milli-ammeter, microammeter) is used. For voltage (emf, potential difference) a voltmeter is used. For resistance it is an ohmmeter that is required.

Microelectronics Microelectronics is concerned with the minia-turisation of electronic circuits. This is achieved by use of *integrated circuits* (q.v.) and *printed circuits* (q.v.), which enable complicated circuits (as in computers) to be kept to a very small size.

Microphone An apparatus for changing pressure waves in air (sound) into electrical variations. There are several sorts, such as the crystal microphone, the ribbon microphone, the moving-coil microphone, etc.

Microwaves An electromagnetic wave with a wavelength be-tween fifty and one-fiftieth of a centimetre.

Modulation This is the term for changing a carrier wave in such a way that it has with it the audio-frequency variations corres-ponding to speech or music. *Amplitude modulation* (q.v.) occurs when a carrier increases and decreases in amplitude. *Frequency modulation* (q.v.) occurs when a carrier varies in *frequency* according to the amplitude of the current from the microphone.

For reception of radio-telephony the modulation must be separated from the carrier. This is usually called *detection* (q.v.), but is sometimes called demodulation.

Molniyas The name given to the first series of Russian communications satellites.

National Transcommunications Ltd. The provider of transmission facilities for ITV and Channel 4. It is, in effect, the former IBA engineering department, but is now independent of ITC.

Nicam Near-instantaneously Companded Audio Multiplex: the system by which digital stereo sound (*q.v.*) is included in TV broadcasts. (Companding is a system of transmitting or re-producing sound by compressing and then re-expanding the volume range so as to produce a clearer signal by reducing the contrast). It has been jointly developed by the BBC, IBA and BREMA (representing manufacturers). Nicam digital stereo sound came into operation experimentally in London and some other regions late in 1989. During 1993, between 80% and 90% of the country will be covered by BBC, ITV and Channel 4 stereo broadcasts.

Noise In electronic equipment, noise is unwanted hissing, humming and crackling heard as a background to the wanted signal. Noise may be generated by the equipment itself (for instance due to the random thermal motions of electrons), and this is particularly troublesome in high frequency circuits carrying small signals. An important factor in such circuits is therefore the *signal-to-noise ratio* which needs to be large if the noise is not going to swamp the signal. Noise may also be picked up from outside sources, e.g. mains *hum* (q.v.) and 'atmospherics' in radio receivers. In TV reception, 'noise' can appear as 'snow' on the picture.

Ohm's Law The most important law of simple electrical circuits. It states that the current through a conductor is directly proportional to the potential difference across the conductor and inversely proportional to its resistance. Ohm's Law is directly applicable to most simple DC circuits. By introducing the idea of *impedance* (q.v.), it can be generalised to AC circuits that include capacitors and inductors.

Oscillation An oscillation is one complete cycle of a regularly varying quantity. See *frequency*.

Oscillator An electronic circuit designed to generate continuous *oscillations* (q.v.). This is usually achieved by connecting an *inductance-capacitance circuit* (q.v.) to a valve or transistor amplifier and arranging positive *feedback* (q.v.) to keep the oscillations going. The *frequency* (q.v.) of the oscillations depends on the values of capacitance and inductance in the *L–C* circuit. Oscillators have numerous uses, e.g. to generate the *carrier wave* (q.v.) needed to transmit radio signals.

PAL Phase Alternative Line, the system of transmission used in Britain for colour TV.

Parallel A method of connecting circuit components. If components have ends ab, a_1b_1, a_2b_2, etc, then they are connected in parallel if all the a's are joined together and all the b's joined together. If electric cells of the same emf are joined in parallel, the total emf is that of any one of them but greater power is available from cells connected in this way. The diagram shows how to calculate the resultant resistance (or

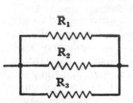

Resistors in parallel.

Total given by $\dfrac{1}{R} = \dfrac{1}{R_1} + \dfrac{1}{R_2} + \dfrac{1}{R_3}$

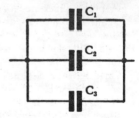

Capacitors in parallel.

Total $C = C_1 + C_2 + C_3$

capacitance) when resistors (or capacitors) are connected in parallel.

Phase This is a term which describes the time relationship of two oscillatory currents or waves of the same *frequency* (q.v.) If both are zero together, increase to their maximum positive together and subsequently remain in step, the two oscillations

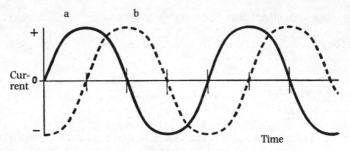

Two oscillations out of phase by 90° or one quarter of a cycle;
(b) 'lags' on (a)

are said to be *in phase*. If, when oscillation (a) is at its maximum positive, oscillation (b) is zero, then (b) is said to be 90° *out of phase* with (a). The diagram shows the case of (b) *lagging* (a) by 90° (or equivalently (a) *leading* (b) by 90°) because when (a) is at its maximum positive, (b) is zero but increasing towards its maximum positive. If when (a) is at its maximum positive, (b) is at its maximum negative, then (a) and (b) are said to be *180° out of phase* and if combined would cancel each other out completely provided they were of the same magnitude. A phase difference of 360° means that the oscillations are again in phase as an oscillation merely repeats itself every 360°.

Pick-up The device which carries the cartridge and stylus and enables the latter to follow the grooves of a disc recording. The cartridge it carries may be either magnetic or crystal.

Piezoelectricity Electric current produced by mechanical stimulation of crystals.

p–n junction The boundary between a piece of *n*-type and a piece of *p*-type *semiconductor* (q.v.). (See *doping*). The *p–n* junction has the property of *rectification* (q.v.), and is therefore widely used in *diodes* (q.v.).

Power Power is the rate of doing work or using energy and is measured in *watts*. The rate of work done by an electrical apparatus in watts is equal to the voltage across it (in volts) multiplied by the current through it (in amps).

Pre-amplifier Amplifies the signal input sufficiently to load the main amplifier. Usually contains tone controls.

Prefixes Standard prefixes are:

    p = 1 million millionth = pico, e.g. 2 picofarads, 2 pF
    n = 1 thousand millionth = nano, e.g. 4 nanoseconds, 4 ns
    μ = 1 millionth = micro, e.g. 3 microamperes, 3 μA
    m = 1 thousandth = milli, e.g. 6 milliamperes, 6 mA
    k = 1 thousand = kilo, e.g. 10 kilovolts, 10 kV
    M = 1 million = mega, e.g. 10 megahertz, 10 MHz
    G = 10^9 = giga, e.g. 11·7 gigahertz, 11·7 GHz

Printed Circuit This is an insulating board with a layer of copper on one side. The copper is dissolved away except along protected paths which then act as connections between components mounted on the board. Photographic methods are often used to scale down the size of printed circuits.

Quadraphony Quadraphonic stereo or 'quad sound' is a system which allows stereo reproduction to be fed into four loudspeakers via four amplifiers, sound coming from each corner of the room.

Radio Authority This is a new body to encourage and develop radio broadcasting, and it absorbs those functions of the former Independent Local Radio. It is to develop, in particular, greater opportunity for commercial, ethnic and 'special interest' radio broadcasting.

Radio Data Systems The following extract from their Engineering Information Handbook is printed by kind permission of the BBC: *FM Radio Data System [RDS]*. This is a radio tuning-aid system which the BBC has played a major role in developing. It enables suitably designed radios to identify FM stations and programme services by detecting inaudible digital signals which are inserted into a normal FM broadcast. A Radio Data receiver could then display the name of the service, for example "BBC R4", and automatically search for a particular station. In a car, the radio would automatically retune as the car travels from the service area of one transmitter to that of another. Using a radio with RDS facilities frees a listener from the need to know a station's frequency or wavelength or its whereabouts on the radio dial.

RDS has been specified by the European Broadcasting Union and CCIR, and BBC FM transmitters are being equipped to include Radio Data signals in their transmissions. A full RDS service is provided by all BBC Local Radio and National Radio transmitters in England and installation at BBC transmitters in Wales, Scotland and Northern Ireland was completed by 1989.

Radio Receiver When broadcasting began, seventy years ago, the most popular form of receiver was a crystal set consisting of a tuning circuit, a crystal detector (q.v.) and telephones. Design then progressed to one- or two-valve receivers and ultimately to the superhet (q.v.), which even today is the basis of most commercial radio receivers. After valves, circuits were based on transistors: from which were developed integrated circuits (ICs). These last, with their associated components, mounted on printed circuit boards, are used by modern receivers.

The germanium diode (see *diode*) could be used in a simple home-built receiver for headphone reception in a similar circuit to that in the crystal set. But it needed a longish aerial, and the trend of modern broadcasting is away from AM (amplitude modulation—q.v.) to FM (frequency modulation—q.v.): so that such a receiver, suitable only for AM reception, is no longer viable. Ferranti, manufacturers of electronic apparatus, have produced an IC that, though designed for the reception of AM signals only, requires merely a small ferrite-rod aerial. This is the ZN414. The circuit of a suitable receiver is shown at Fig. 1.

The coil is wound on a ferrite rod 100 to 140 mm long which serves as the aerial and consists of 55 turns of 28 dcc (double cotton-covered) wire wound side by side on a tube formed of cartridge or drawing paper placed tightly round the

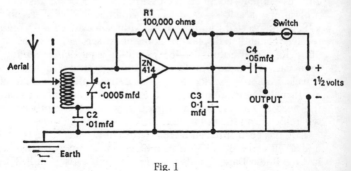

Fig. 1

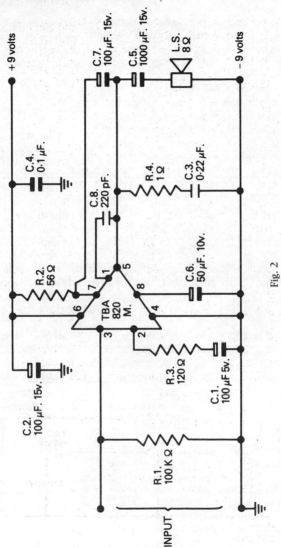

Fig. 2

rod (and held in place with a scrap of sticky tape). A tap is
made at the twentieth turn by twisting the wire and cleaning
off its insulation. Other components required are shown in the
diagram; the whole receiver can be built on a piece of Vero-
board.

Reception of FM signals needs a more complicated receiver:
but again, advanced technology has designed an IC which
provides most of the circuitry needed. This is the TDA 700
manufactured by Phillips Semiconductors. (They have permitted the reproduction of the circuit diagram in Fig. 3). Everything within the box is part of the IC, the size of which is 20
mm × 5 mm. Capacitors and a few external components are
required as shown, and an FM receiver could be constructed
by experienced students, components being available from
Maplin or other mail-order suppliers. The output is fed into
ear-phones or into an amplifier such as that shown in Fig. 2.
This will operate a small loudspeaker and is also built around
a silicon chip IC, which with its associated components can
be mounted on a piece of Veroboard. The amplifier may also
be used with the receiver shown in Fig. 1.

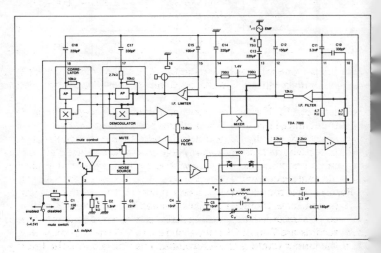

Fig. 3

RSGB Radio Society of Great Britain, the national body for British amateur radio enthusiasts, particularly transmitting amateurs, **Radio Waves in Use**

	Wave-	Names commonly used	
Frequency	lengths	Wavelength range	Frequency range
Low frequency	Long waves	Above 600 m	Below 500 kHz
Medium frequency	Medium waves	200–600 m	500–1,500 kHz
High frequency	Short waves	10–80 m	3,750 kc/s to 30 MHz
VHF Very-high frequency	Ultra-short waves	Band I 4·41–7·32 m Band II 3–3·43 m Band III 1·39–1·72 m	41–68 MHz 87·5–100 MHz 174–216 MHz
UHF Ultra-high frequency		Band IV 51–63 cm Band V 31–49 cm	475–585 MHz 610–960 MHz
	Micro-waves	7·5 mm–15 cm Divided into several bands—S Band, X Band, J Band, etc.	2,000–40,000 MHz

but anyone interested in radio may join. The address of RSGB is Lambda House, Cranborne Road, Potters Bar, Herts EN6 3JN.

Reactance (X) This is the term for the effect of capacitance or inductance in cutting down alternating current. It is given the symbol X, usually with suffixes L and C to denote whether it is inductive reactance or capacitive reactance, thus X_L, X_C. It is measured in ohms. It varies with the frequency of the applied alternating current. See *impedance*.

Records Flat round discs, formerly made of a wax/shellac compound, now moulded in plastic material upon which music, etc., is recorded by pressing from a master record. Modern records are 7 in (175 mm) and 12 in (305 mm) in diameter, the former rotating at 45 revolutions per minute and the latter (long playing) at 33⅓ rpm. These plastic (vinyl) records are now being phased out in favour of CDs and cassettes. *Compact discs* (q.v.) were introduced in 1983.

Rectification Alternating current reverses its direction every half cycle. Rectification is the process by which AC is converted to a direct current which always flows in the same direction. This is achieved by the use of rectifiers or *diodes* (q.v.) which allow current to pass through them in one direction only. In the *half wave* rectifier the $-ve$ half of the cycle is simply suppressed, while in the *full wave* rectifier, the $-ve$ half of the cycle is inverted so as to flow in the desired direction.

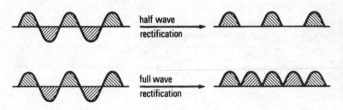

Rectification is very important because the mains supply is AC while most electronic circuits need a DC supply. However to be suitable, the rectified supply has to be *smoothed* so that the voltage is nearly constant.

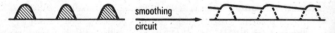

Resistance This is the tendency for all materials to oppose the flow of an electric current and to convert electrical energy into heat. It is measured in ohms and the resistance of a conductor depends, in simple cases, on the *resistivity* (q.v.) of the material and the dimensions of the conductor. A resistance of R ohms carrying a current of I amps converts electrical energy into heat at the rate of I^2R watts.

Resistivity This is the resistance (measured in microhms) of a cubic centimetre of material, and is a measure of how badly the material conducts electricity. The reciprocal of resistivity is *conductivity*, a measure of how well a material conducts electricity. Copper and other metals are good conductors, with a low resistivity which increases with temperature. Glass and plastic are insulators with a very high resistivity. Between these limits lie *semiconductors* (q.v.).

Resistivities			
Resistivity in microhm centimetres at room temperature			
Aluminium .	.	2·82	Amber .	.	.	5×10^{16}
Brass	.	About 8	Celluloid	.	.	2×10^{10}
Copper .	.	1·72	Germanium .	.	46×10^{6}
Iron	.	9·8	Graphite	.	1,375
Magnesium .	.	4·46	Mica (clear) .	.	4×10^{16}
Nichrome	.	About 100	Paraffin wax .	.	3×10^{18}
Nickel .	.	7·24	Plate glass	.	2×10^{11}
Steel, hardened	.	About 45	Silicon .	.	10
Tin	.	11·4	Sulphur	.	.	2×10^{23}

Resistor An electronic component used in a circuit to provide a known *resistance* (q.v.). Both fixed and variable resistors are very widely used.

Resonance When an *inductance–capacitance circuit* (q.v.) responds at a maximum to one frequency only, it is said to be in resonance with a signal of that frequency. *Tuning* (q.v.) consists of selecting the point of resonance.

Root-mean-square (RMS) The average value of a quantity that takes positive and negative values equally (e.g. an alternating current) is zero. If the values are squared, the mean found and then the square root taken, the non-zero result is called the RMS value. Because the heating effect of an electric current depends on the square of the current, the RMS of an AC is equal to the constant DC needed to produce the same heating effect as the AC. The peak value (or amplitude) of an AC is $\sqrt{2} = 1·414$ times the RMS value.

Satellite TV Systems which enable viewers to view programmes received directly from a satellite. Signals are beamed towards the satellite and bounced off it back to earth, where they are received on a special aerial system. (See the note on F3 regarding DBS channels).

This form of broadcasting seems certain to change the scene in the UK, as elsewhere in the world, radically.

Scanning The traversing of a scene or screen by a spot of light in an orderly fashion. It is scanning in successive lines in a very short time that allows a scene to be turned into electrical variations by a television camera and then into a pattern of light on a television-receiver screen.

Selectivity The ability of a radio receiver to tune to one radio station without interference from stations with nearby frequencies.

Semiconductor A material whose *resistivity* (q.v.) is much higher than that of metals but much less than that of insulators. E.g. the elements germanium, silicon and selenium and the compounds copper oxide and indium antiminide. Semiconductors have three special electrical properties which make them very useful. (a) Unlike metals, the conductivity of semiconductors can be increased by the addition of small quantities of impurities. This is called *doping* (q.v.), and is the basis behind all modern semiconductor devices such as the *transistor* (q.v.). (b) Some semiconductors (notably selenium) increase their conductivity if light is shined on them. This is useful in photocells and in copying by the process of *xerography*. (c) Over some temperature ranges, semiconductors increase their conductivity very fast with increasing temperature, and can therefore be used where sensitivity to temperature is needed.

Series A method of connecting circuit components such that they are joined end to end. The current through each component is therefore the same, though the voltage across each will differ. The diagram below shows how to work out the total resistance (capacitance) when resistors (capacitors) are connected in series. See *parallel*.

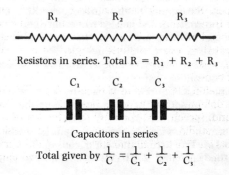

$$R_1 \qquad\qquad R_2 \qquad\qquad R_3$$

Resistors in series. Total $R = R_1 + R_2 + R_3$

$$C_1 \qquad C_2 \qquad C_3$$

Capacitors in series

Total given by $\dfrac{1}{C} = \dfrac{1}{C_1} + \dfrac{1}{C_2} + \dfrac{1}{C_3}$

Sky Sky Television service is the satellite TV service operated by Rupert Murdoch's company. It began early in 1989 and uses the ASTRA satellite based in Luxembourg. (But see *BSKYB*). Sky Television is now the name under which BSkyB operates and trades.

Sky Ray Radio waves going out into space and not following the ground.

Sound Sound is the sensation felt when our ears pick up pressure waves (i.e. sound waves) transmitted through a gas or other fluid from a vibrating source (e.g. a violin string). Sound waves through a gas consist of alternate compressions and rarefactions of the gas travelling along at the speed of sound. This is 332 metres per second or 760 miles an hour in air. The *pitch* of sound heard depends directly on the *frequency* (q.v.) of vibration of the source. Thus the note middle C corresponds to a frequency of vibration 256 cycles per second. The octave higher is always double the frequency.

　　Music and speech are built up from a large number of simple waves of different frequencies all mixed together. Even a single note played on a violin, say, consists of a lowest frequency which is called the *fundamental* (and corresponds to the pitch of the note), as well as a number of higher frequencies present in lesser strength. These are called *harmonics* and they determine the tone or quality of the note heard. This is why audio equipment sensitive to frequencies up to 30,000 cycles per second is needed for the faithful reproduction of sound.

SSB A modulated carrier wave has two sets of sidebands, lower and upper. Single sideband working is very popular with amateur transmitters and is a system whereby the carrier and one sideband are eliminated and all the transmitter power is concentrated in the remaining (single) sideband. One of its advantages is an improvement in selectivity in the crowded amateur bands.

SSTV Slow scan television, as used by amateur transmitters.

Stereo Stereophonic reproduction is designed to allow each ear to hear sound, speech, etc., correctly from the left or right of the orchestra, studio or other source of transmission. Radio broadcasts on VHF are often in stereo, as are most gramophone discs or tape cassettes. For receiving stereo, two amplifiers (or a twin amplifier) and two loudspeakers are required. The latter should be placed about 6 ft apart.

Stylus The correct name for the 'needle' which is placed in the groove of a disc recording and which transmits its vibrations to the cartridge for amplification and reproduction. The stylus may be made of diamond (the best and longest lasting) or of sapphire or ruby. Standard tip radii are: mono LP or 45's = 0·029 mm and stereo or 'compatible' (i.e. either mono or stereo) = 0·0175 mm by 0·0075 mm, these being the latest elliptical tips.

Superhet The superheterodyne receiver. This is the common commercial type for sound and television. It enables high *selectivity* (q.v.) suitable for today's overcrowded air to be obtained without too much loss of quality.

The principle is to mix two oscillations together in a frequency-changer in such a way that no matter what the frequency of the incoming signal is, the outgoing frequency from the frequency-changer is always the same, the *intermediate*

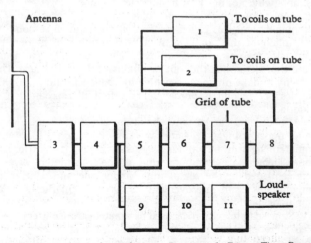

Block Diagram of Superhet Television Receiver: 1. Frame Time Base. 2. Line Time Base. 3. RF Amplifier. 4. Frequency Changer. 5. IF Amplifier. 6. Video Detector. 7. Video Amplifier. 8. Sync. Separator. 9. IF Amplifier. 10. Audio Detector. 11. Audio Amplifier

frequency (q.v.). At this fixed frequency it is comparatively easy to make satisfactory band-pass filters and transformers.

Symbols For the mathematical treatment of current, emf, etc., symbols in the form of letters are used:

λ = lambda = wavelength μ = mu = amplification factor
n or f = frequency   of valve, some-
v = velocity   times written m
R = resistance g = mutual conduct-
I = current   ance of valve
E = emf L = inductance
R_a = AC resistance of valve C = capacitance

Synthesiser An electronic musical instrument which is played by means of a keyboard like a piano. The sounds are produced by oscillations which can be varied to give musical sounds based on orchestral instruments or a variety of noises.

Tape Plastic tape coated with ferromagnetic particles (iron oxide), which can be magnetised by a magnet in a tape head. Varying the force of the magnetisation by feeding audio currents into the tape head enables the tape to record the matter carried by them. Tapes comes in varying widths and narrow ones are fitted into cassettes. Tapes may be wiped clean and used again. For better frequency response and wider range, tape using chromium dioxide particles is coming into more general use. Similar tapes are available for recording television programmes.

Teletext A form of TV newspaper requiring a special receiver on which can be obtained news, weather, train times, etc. The BBC system is called Ceefax and the ITV Teletext.

Telstar The first television satellite, orbited by the United States.

Terrestrial television Television emanating from ground stations as opposed to TV from satellites.

Transceiver By special circuit arrangements a set can be switched for use either as a transmitter or a receiver. Generally hand-held, has recently come into prominence in *CB Radio* (q.v.). Often called a 'rig' or a 'walkie-talkie'.

Transformer A device for increasing or decreasing the magnitude of an alternating voltage. A step-up transformer consists of a primary coil of few turns and a secondary coil of a larger number of turns both wound on the same iron core but forming separate circuits. In a step-down transformer the primary has more turns than the secondary. The ratio of the voltage in the secondary to that in the primary is nearly equal to the ratio of the number of turns in the secondary to that in the primary. If the voltage is higher in the secondary than in the primary then the current in the secondary is proportionately lower than that in the primary, so that the power in each coil is the same. Transformers work by means of electromagnetic induction (see *inductance*). The AC in the primary produces a varying magnetic field through the secondary and so induces an emf in the secondary.

Transistor An electronic device consisting of three layers of *semiconductor* (q.v.). The *n–p–n* transistor has two layers of *n*-type semiconductor sandwiching a layer of *p*-type, and the *p–n–p* transistor has two layers of *p*-type sandwiching one of *n*-type (see *doping*). In either case, the middle layer is called the *base* and the outer layers are called the *collector* and *emitter*. The transistor is principally used as an amplifier, since a small current flowing in the base–emitter circuit can be used to control a much larger current in the emitter–collector circuit.

    The transistor was invented in 1948 and since then has rapidly been replacing the *valve* (q.v.) in electronic circuits. The advantage of using transistors is that they can be made very small and reliable since they do not require the vacuum tube, the heater or the high voltage power supply necessary for valves. Most circuits, however, now use ICs (see *Radio Receiver*) rather than individual transistors.

Triode A thermionic valve with three electrodes—cathode, grid, anode.

Tuner The 'front end' of hi-fi equipment whereby broadcast programmes are received. Usually VHF only, but can include medium and long waves. Some tuners incorporate a *decoder* (q.v.) for stereo.

Tuning In a radio receiver the frequency of the radio station heard is determined by the resonant frequency of an *inductance-capacitance circuit* (q.v.). By varying the capacitance in the circuit, the resonant frequency is changed and so different stations can be selected. See *resonance*.

UK Gold A joint venture by Thames TV and the BBC to broadcast, via satellite, old classic TV programmes and films.

Valve (Thermionic Valve) Known as 'tube' in USA, this is an evacuated glass bulb containing a cathode, an anode and one or more electrodes called grids. The cathode is heated and emits electrons. Valves are now only used for transmitting and industrial purposes.

Video The word indicating the vision side of a television signal. It has come by popular usage to mean a video recorder. Recorders are available for the purpose of 'taping' programmes for later viewing or for playing through the TV set commercially produced cassettes of films, etc.

Video has produced a new branch of the electronics industry and its own vocabulary. For digital stereo sound, see *Nicam* and *Camcorder*. Video recorders in use at the moment will be neither compatible nor adaptable for Nicam stereo.

Video Tape A means of recording TV programmes on tape which is simpler and cheaper than recording on film. Most TV programmes are no longer 'live' but 'video-taped'.

Watt (W) The SI unit of electrical *power* (q.v.).

Wavelength From the earliest days of radio, stations have been known by their wavelengths which have been measured in metres. Today the use of frequency, measured in kiloHertz, is preferred but many older sets in the UK are marked in wave-lengths. The following formula shows how to calculate a wave-length from a frequency:

$$\frac{300,000}{\text{frequency (in kHz)}} = \text{wavelength (in metres)}$$

Conversely, dividing three hundred thousand by the wave-length will give the frequency.

Zener diode A special form of junction diode usually used for voltage regulation or stabilisation.

Further Reading

Practical Electronics Handbook (revised edition) by Ian Sinclair (Heinemann/Newnes)

Projects in Amateur Radio and Short-wave Listening by F. G. Rayer (Newnes Technical books) (for those interested in home-construction)

Beginner's Guide to Digital Electronics by Ian Sinclair

There are a number of leaflets about TV and radio to be had from BBC Engineering Information (Broadcasting House, London, W1A 1AA); they will be glad to help with any reception difficulties.

A DICTIONARY OF AIRCRAFT, ROCKETS AND MISSILES

(With a section on Astronomy)

Abbreviations

AAM	Air-to-air missile
ADF	Automatic direction-finding
AEW	Airborne early warning
AFCS	Automatic flight control system
APU	Auxiliary power unit
ASI	Airspeed indicator
ASM	Air-to-surface missile
ASTOVL	Advanced short take-off and vertical landing
ASW	Anti-submarine warfare
ATC	Air traffic control
AUW	All-up weight
AWACS	Airborne warning and control system
BCAR	British Civil Airworthiness Requirements
CAA	Civil Aviation Authority (UK)
CAB	Civil Aeronautics Board (USA)
DF	Direction-finding
DME	Distance-measuring equipment
EAS	Equivalent airspeed
ECCM	Electronic counter-countermeasures
ECM	Electronic countermeasures
EHP	Equivalent horsepower (turboprop)
ELINT	Electronic intelligence
EPNdB	Effective perceived noise decibel
ESA	European Space Agency
EVA	Extravehicular activity
FAA	Federal Aviation Administration (USA)
FAI	Fédération Aéronautique Internationale
FAR	Federal Aviation Regulations
FBW	Fly-by-wire
FLIR	Forward-looking infra-red
GCI	Ground-controlled interception
GPU	Ground power unit
GPWS	Ground-proximity warning system
HF	High-frequency
HUD	Head-up display
IAS	Indicated airspeed
IATA	International Air Transport Association
ICAO	International Civil Aviation Organisation

IFF	Identification friend or foe
IFR	Instrument flight rules
ILS	Instrument landing system
INAS	Integrated nav/attack system
INS	Inertial navigation system
ISA	International Standard Atmosphere
LGB	Laser-guided bomb
LLTV	Low-light TV
M	Mach number
MAD	Magnetic anomaly detector
MLS	Microwave landing system
MTBF	Mean time between failures
MTOGW	Maximum take-off gross weight
NASA	National Aeronautics and Space Administration (USA)
NASP	National Aerospace Plane
Notam	Notice to Airmen
NTP	Normal temperature and pressure
RAE	Royal Aerospace Establishment
RPV	Remotely piloted vehicle
RVR	Runway visual range
SAC	Strategic Air Command, US Air Force
SAR	Search and rescue
SHP	Shaft horsepower
SL	Sea level
SLAR	Sideways-looking airborne radar
SSR	Secondary surveillance radar
SST	Supersonic transport
STOL	Short take-off and landing
STOVL	Short take-off and vertical landing
TAS	True airspeed
TBO	Time between overhauls
TCAS	Traffic Alert and Collision Avoidance System
UHF	Ultra-high-frequency
VFR	Visual flight rules
VHF	Very-high-frequency
VLF	Very-low-frequency
VOR	VHF omni-directional range beacon
VTOL	Vertical take-off and landing
ZFW	Zero-fuel weight

Aerofoil Section through a wing, rotor blade or tailplane so shaped that it can generate *lift* (q.v.).

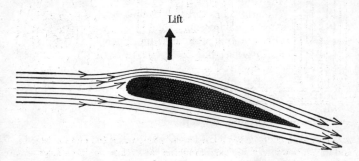

Airflow over an aerofoil surface, caused by forward motion of the aerofoil, results in a reduction of pressure above the upper surface and a smaller increase of pressure beneath. The result is an upward force, known as lift, at right-angles to the direction of the airflow.

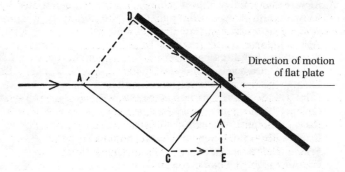

Action of air on a flat plate drawn forward If the pressure due to the air is *AB*, this can be resolved into *CB*, at right-angles to the plate, and *DB* along the plate. *CB* can be resolved into *EB* at right-angles to the air direction and *CE* in the same direction as the air. *EB* represents the lift, and *CE* a retarding force known as drag.

In the same way, an aerofoil inclined at an *angle of attack* (q.v.) to airflow in the direction *AB* will produce lift *EB* in addition to the lift already produced by its cambered upper surface.

(a)   (b)   (c)

Air action on a flat plate and a streamlined object In (a) the plate is edge-on and the air flows smoothly past. In (b) the plate is face-on and a large area of low pressure and turbulence is produced, slowing down the air. In (c) the air is flowing more smoothly past a streamlined object.

Aerospace companies Aerospace manufacturing is dominated by companies in Europe, Russia and the United States. Here are some of the most important aircraft builders:

Airbus Industrie (International): Jet airliners
Antonov (Russia): Jet and turboprop transport aircraft
Bell (USA): Civil and military helicopters
Boeing (USA): Airliners, military aircraft and helicopters
British Aerospace (UK): Combat aircraft, airliners, business jets
Cessna (USA): Utility aircraft, business jets
Dassault-Breguet (France): Combat aircraft, business jets
Embraer (Brazil): Military trainers, commuterliners
Fokker (Netherlands): Short/medium-range airliners
Grumman (USA): Combat aircraft
Lockheed (USA): Combat aircraft, military transports
McDonnell Douglas (USA): Military aircraft, airliners
Mikoyan-Gurevich (Russia): Combat aircraft
Mil (Russia): Military and civil helicopters
Panavia (International): Tornado combat aircraft
Rockwell International (USA): Combat aircraft, Shuttle Orbiter
Saab-Scania (Sweden): Combat aircraft, regional airliners
Sikorsky (USA): Civil and military helicopters

Afterburning Burning fuel in the jetpipe of a turbojet or turbofan engine to increase its thrust. Also called *reheat*.

Aircraft markings All civil aircraft must be registered and carry their registration markings in prominent external positions. The markings consist of letters/numbers indicating country of origin followed by individual aircraft letters/numbers. Principal national markings are given below:

CIVIL AIRCRAFT MARKINGS			
AP	Pakistan	LN	Norway
A6	United Arab Emirates	LQ/LV	Argentina
		LX	Luxembourg
B	China	LY	Lithuania
C/CF	Canada	N	United States
CC	Chile	OB	Peru
CN	Morocco	OD	Lebanon
CP	Bolivia	OE	Austria
CR/CS	Portugal	OH	Finland
CU	Cuba	OO	Belgium
CX	Uruguay	OY	Denmark
C5	Gambia	P	Korea, Democratic Republic of
C6	Bahamas		
C9	Mozambique	PH	Netherlands
D	Germany	PK	Indonesia
EC	Spain	PP/PT	Brazil
EI/EJ	Ireland	RA	Russian Federation
EP	Iran	RH	Armenia
ES	Estonia	RP	Philippines
ET	Ethiopia	SE	Sweden
EW	Belarus	LZ	Bulgaria
F	France	SL	Slovenia
G	United Kingdom	SP	Poland
HA	Hungary	ST	Sudan
HB	Switzerland	SU	Egypt
HC	Ecuador	SX	Greece
HK	Colombia	TC	Turkey
HL	Korea, Republic of	TF	Iceland
HS	Thailand	TG	Guatemala
HZ	Saudi Arabia	TL	Central African Republic
I	Italy		
JA	Japan	TS	Tunisia
JY	Jordan	UA	Azerbaijan

UR	Ukraine	4R	Sri Lanka
VH	Australia	4X	Israel
VP/VQ/	UK colonies and	5A	Libya
VR	protectorates	5B	Cyprus
VT	India	5H	Tanzania
XA/XB/	Mexico	5N	Nigeria
XC		5X	Uganda
XV	Vietnam	5Y	Kenya
XY/XZ	Myanmar	6Y	Jamaica
	(Burma)	7T	Algeria
YA	Afghanistan	9A	Croatia
YI	Iraq	9G	Ghana
YK	Syria	9H	Malta
YL	Latvia	9J	Zambia
YR	Romania	9K	Kuwait
YV	Venezuela	9M	Malaysia
ZA	Albania	9Q	Zaire
ZK/ZL/ZM	New Zealand	9V	Singapore
ZS/ZT/ZU	South Africa	9Y	Trinidad and Tobago

Air data computer Digital computer fitted to an aircraft to serve as a central source of information on the surrounding atmosphere and the flight of the aircraft through it. A typical air data computer senses, measures and helps to display pressure altitude, outside air temperature, Mach number, equivalent airspeed, angle of attack, angle of yaw and dynamic pressure.

Airframe Assembled structure of an aircraft, together with those system components which are integral with the structure and influence its strength or shape. Such components include transparencies, flush aerials, radomes, fairings, doors, internal ducts, and pylons for externally carried stores. Usually includes landing gear but not systems (eg electrical, hydraulics and electronics), equipment, armament, furnishings and other readily removable items.

Airspeed indicator Speed through the air increases the pressure due to ram effect. A small tube directed into the air, called a *pitot tube*, can be used to direct the airstream to a pressure-measuring device. At the same time a closed tube with holes in its sides can be used to measure the static atmospheric pressure. The difference between the two is a measure of airspeed.

Airway An air route supervised by ground-based controllers. Most airline flights follow airways, which are typically 18 km (10 nm) wide and have a centreline defined by radio navaids located at regular intervals on the ground.

Altimeter The normal height-measuring instrument is essentially an aneroid barometer. Atmospheric pressure decreases with height above the Earth's surface, at a rate of approximately 40 mm (1.57 in) on the barometer for every 500 m (1,640 ft) up to about 2,000 m (6,560 ft). The barometer can be linked to a clock-like height display to produce a *pressure altimeter*. Such an altimeter measures only height above sea level, and the zero may be adjusted to reflect variations in atmospheric pressure or the terrain over which the aircraft is flying.

A *radio altimeter* relies on the reflection of radio signals to give the true height above the ground over which the aircraft is flying.

Anhedral Angle at which a wing is inclined downwards from root to tip (see also *Dihedral*).

Apogee The point in an Earth orbit which is furthest from the Earth.

Artificial horizon An instrument designed to show a pilot flying blind whether his aircraft is straight and level. The gyroscopically driven display consists of a line, representing the horizon, and an aircraft symbol. The line moves in relation to the symbol as the aircraft climbs, dives and turns.

Atmosphere The layer of gas round the Earth. It consists chiefly of oxygen and nitrogen, with small quantities of other gases such as carbon dioxide, argon and helium.

The pressure of the atmosphere is greatest at sea level. It gets less and less the farther one goes away from the Earth, though not in direct proportion to the height. The temperature also gets less with height up to about 11,000 m (36,089 ft), where it reaches a constant $-56 \cdot 5°$ C. This level is called the *tropopause*. Below it is the *troposphere*. Above it is the *stratosphere*.

Because the atmosphere is not a single gas with constant characteristics, a *standard atmosphere* has been internationally agreed. Figures for aircraft performance records must be related to the standard conditions. Standard pressure at sea level and $0°$ C is $1 \cdot 03$ kg/sq cm ($14 \cdot 7$ lb/sq in) or 760 mm ($29 \cdot 92$ in) of mercury. Standard temperature is taken as $15°$ C or $59°$ F.

THE STANDARD ATMOSPHERE

Altitude		Pressure		Temperature
m	(ft)	mmHg	(lb/in²)	°C
				Ambient temperature
				remains constant
				above 11,000 m
				(36,089 ft)
30,000	(98,425)	8·790	(0·170)	
25,000	(82,021)	18·834	(0·364)	
20,000	(65,617)	41·065	(0·794)	
15,000	(49,213)	90·342	(1·747)	−56·5
10,000	(32,808)	198·288	(3·834)	−50·0
8,000	(26,247)	267·020	(5·163)	−37·0
5,000	(16,404)	405·182	(7·835)	−17·5
4,000	(13,123)	462·339	(8·940)	−11·0
3,000	(9,843)	525·857	(10·168)	−4·5
2,000	(6,562)	596·263	(11·529)	2·0
1,000	(3,280)	674·114	(13·035)	8·5
Sea level		760·000	(14·696)	15·0

(mmHg = millimetres of mercury, lb/in² = pounds per square inch)

Attack, angle of Angle between the mean *chord* (q.v.) and the free-stream direction at which the airflow meets an *aerofoil* (q.v.).

Autogyro Type of rotary-wing aircraft invented by Juan de la Cierva of Spain. Thrust is provided by a conventional propeller, lift by an unpowered rotor (see also *Helicopter*).

Autopilot A device which allows an aircraft to fly automatically on an even keel and a selected course without the attention of the pilot. Any roll, yaw or pitch or change in direction causes signals to be sent to servo mechanisms, which make the necessary correcting adjustments to the control surfaces.

More elaborate autopilots can also maintain a rate of climb or descent or a constant height.

Avionics Aviation electronics, including radio, radar, navigation systems and computers.

Ballistic missile See *Missiles*.

Boundary layer The thin layer of air close to the surface of a moving aerofoil. The airflow at the leading edge is usually laminar, i.e. parallel to the surface, but further back it is broken up, with the resulting turbulence producing drag. Several attempts have been made to avoid this. An important one— laminar flow control—is an arrangement for sucking in air through surface holes in the aerofoil.

Bypass ratio The ratio between the airflow through the fan and the airflow through the core in a turbofan engine.

Chord The distance from the leading edge to the trailing edge of an aerofoil measured parallel to the longitudinal axis of the aircraft.

Clean Configuration of aircraft with undercarriage, flaps and slats retracted and without external stores.

Control surface Hinged flap at trailing edge of aerofoil providing control of aircraft movement about its longitudinal, lateral and vertical axes; called *aileron, elevator* and *rudder* respectively. An *elevon* combines the functions of elevator and aileron.

Decca Navigator A navigation system developed in the 1950s for use by both aircraft and ships.

A Decca *chain* consists of a master transmitter whose low-frequency signals (70–130 kHz) are closely related to those of three associated slave transmitters. The latter transmit so that their signals are in exact phase with that of the master. By the time they are received by a ship or aircraft they are out of phase to some degree, and it is from these differences that position is calculated. This can be presented in a number of ways: either numerically, by a coded light system or, in the more advanced receivers, directly on a map. Each transmitter can be received over a distance of about 1,500 km (950 miles), and a number of chains cover most of Europe, the eastern seaboard of the United States and some other parts of the world, particularly in areas of heavy ship traffic. It is a very accurate aid—fixes of better than one mile accuracy are usual—and is standard on a number of aircraft, including the larger helicopters used in North Sea oil exploration. Although it has not gained universal acceptance, it is still being developed and new chains are occasionally opened.

Delta wing A wing with a triangular platform. It has many of the aerodynamic advantages of a swept-back wing and is structurally more efficient.

Dihedral Angle at which a wing is inclined upwards from root to tip. Most aircraft have some dihedral angle, which tends to add to stability in the rolling plane.

θ = dihedral angle

Drag The force resisting the motion of an aircraft through the air. It can be broken down into two parts: *induced drag* caused by the lift-generating pressure differences over the wing; and *profile drag* caused by *turbulence* (q.v.) due to roughness of the skin, interference of airflow round different parts of the aircraft, and projections such as aerials, radomes and cockpit canopies.

Drone A pilotless aircraft, usually used for reconnaissance or as a target.

Escape velocity The velocity that a body must have to get away from the gravitational pull of Earth. It is given by the equation

$$V = \sqrt{2gR}$$

where R = distance from centre of Earth, g = acceleration due to gravity at distance R.

For ordinary purposes the escape velocity from the Earth is taken as about 11 km per second or 6·8 miles per second. At this velocity a projectile will follow a parabolic course and never return to Earth.

Fail-safe Describes aircraft structure or system whose failure will not endanger the aircraft.

Feathering Aligning the blades of an unpowered propeller so that it does not 'windmill' in the airflow and create drag (see also *Propeller*).

First flights Some significant first flights by new aircraft in the period February 1992 to January 1993:

February 1992	3	Airbus A340-300 long-range airliner, second example
	13	BAe Hawk 200 combat aircraft, first radar-equipped example
March 1992	24	LTV/Aerospatiale AS.565 Panther 800 military utility helicopter

	26	Saab 2000 high-speed turboprop regional airliner
	27	BAe Jetstream 41 29-seat regional airliner, third prototype
April 1992	1	Airbus A340-200 long-range airliner, first example
	1	Dassault Falcon 20 radar testbed for Rafale combat aircraft
	11	Cabri G.2 light helicopter
	15	McDonnell Douglas AH-64D Longbow Apache combat helicopter
	18	Boeing 727 powered by Roll-Royce Tay engines
May 1992	18	McDonnell Douglas C-17 military transport, first production example
June 1992	4	CH-53/2000, Israel Aircraft Industries upgrade of Sikorsky CH-53 Stallion heavy helicopter
	15	Learjet Model 60 business jet, first production example
	23	McDonnell Douglas C-17 military transport, second production example
July 1992	3	Saab 2000 high-speed turboprop regional airliner, second prototype
	8	BAe Jetstream 41 29-seat regional airliner, fourth prototype
August 1992	14	Tupolev Tu-204 short/medium-range twinjet airliner re-engined with Rolls-Royce RB.211-535D4 turbofans
	21	Bell UH-1 utility helicopter re-engined with GE T700 turboshaft
	30	Indian Advanced Light Helicopter
September 1992	10	Saab JAS39 Gripen combat aircraft, first production example
	13	AASI Jetcruzer pusher-powered six-seat executive transport
	22	McDonnell Douglas/BAe AV-8B Harrier II Plus radar-equipped short take-off/vertical landing combat aircraft
October 1992	20	Dornier Do 328 33-seat turboprop-powered regional airliner, third prototype
November 1992	2	Airbus A330 twinjet airliner
	8	Yakovlev Yak-112 single-engined light utility aircraft
December 1992	3	Airbus A330 twinjet airliner, second example
	17	Molniya Design Bureau Molniya 1 pusher-powered six-seat light aircraft

	18	McDonnell Douglas MD Explorer light twin helicopter, first prototype
January 1993	15	Deutsche Aerospace/Rockwell International FanRanger military jet trainer
	27	Fokker Maritime Enforcer II twin-turboprop maritime patrol aircraft
	31	Sikorsky UH-60Q medical evacuation helicopter

Flap Control surface used to provide temporary increase in lift of a wing for take-off or landing.

Fly-by-wire Flight control system in which the pilot's demands are transmitted to the control surfaces by electrical signals rather than mechanical linkages. Fly-by-light uses fibre-optics instead of electrics.

Free fall The state of non-resistance to a gravitational field, experienced by a body falling towards the Earth before it enters the atmosphere and by orbiting satellites. A passenger inside a vehicle in free fall has the sensation of being weightless. It is possible to experience this state for a few seconds in an aircraft making an outside loop in which the centrifugal force balances the Earth's gravitational force. Astronauts and cosmonauts are regularly weightless for long periods in manned space vehicles.

Fuels Petrol is used in piston engines, gas turbines (turbojets, turboprops, turbofans) burn kerosene or paraffin-based fuel. For rockets see *Propellant*.

Fuselage Central body of an aeroplane or helicopter. Carries crew, passengers and cargo, and provides mounting point for wings, engines and control surfaces.

g The acceleration due to gravity, which on the surface of the Earth is taken as roughly 9.81 m per second per second or 32 ft per second per second. Also used as a unit of acceleration for analysis of forces acting on aircraft and spacecraft and their occupants. An airman flying at 800 km/hr (500 mph) along a curved path of about 1·5 km (1 mile) radius would experience a centrifugal force equivalent to an acceleration of 5 g.

Gas turbine See *Jet propulsion*.

Geostationary Orbit in which a satellite has no motion in relation to the surface of the Earth, so that it appears to hover over a selected point. To achieve this the satellite must be orbiting at a height of 35,800 km (22,245 miles) and in the same plane as the Earth's equator.

Gravity The law of gravitation states that any two bodies in the universe attract each other with a force that is directly proportional to the product of their masses and inversely proportional to the square of the distance between them:

$$\text{Force} = \frac{km_1m_2}{d^2}$$

where k is a gravitational constant $= 6 \cdot 67 \times 10^{-8}$ in metric units, m_1 and m_2 the two masses, and d the distance.

The acceleration due to gravity (g) at the Earth's surface is about $9 \cdot 81$ m (32 ft) per second per second. This varies with geographical position, however, and gets very much less with height above the Earth's surface.

Guided missile See *Missiles.*

Gunship Helicopter designed for battlefield attack.

Gyroscope Used in many navigational instruments in aircraft and ships. Consisting essentially of a heavy wheel spun at high speed by an electric motor or a turbine, it has two properties: (i) if it is supported in frictionless gimbals so that it can rotate freely in all three dimensions, it will remain parallel to its original position, i.e. it has 'rigidity in space'; (ii) if it is not supported in gimbals but is made to turn it will *precess*, shifting its axis of rotation through 90° to its original direction and exerting a force proportional to the rate of turn. This is used, for example, to correct gunsights for the movement of the aircraft.

These properties can be combined: if a gyro is held in one direction in its gimbals so that it has to turn with the Earth it will precess until it points north and the axis of the Earth's rotation is parallel to its own. It will then continue to point north and can be used as a true compass (i.e. indicating geographical rather than magnetic north).

Heat barrier At very high speeds the kinetic energy of the air flowing past an aircraft is turned into significant amounts of heat energy: at Mach 3 skin temperature can reach the melting point of steel. Aircraft designed to travel at these speeds must therefore be made of heat-resisting materials, and the crew, passengers and avionics must be protected by cooling systems. Spacecraft leave the atmosphere too quickly for kinetic heating to be a problem, but it becomes a major factor during re-entry.

Helicopter An aircraft that can rise vertically by the use of rotating wings. These wings, known as *blades*, are attached to a hub and together constitute the *rotor*. The lift provided by the passage of the blades through the air propels the aircraft vertically. There has to be enough engine power to produce lift exceeding the total weight of the aircraft.

For forward movement the plane of the rotor is, in effect, tilted forwards. This is achieved by altering the pitch of the rotor blades so that as each passes through the rear part of the rotation its pitch is increased and as it passes through the front part of the rotation its pitch is decreased. The resulting difference in lift between the front and the rear of the rotor disc produces a forward propulsive force.

If the helicopter fuselage were free to rotate it would go round in the opposite direction to that of the rotor. It is prevented from doing so by a small rotor mounted on the side of the tail boom. The pitch of this rotor can be varied to give control for changing the helicopter's direction of flight. Another way of overcoming the turning tendency of the fuselage, or *torque*, is to have a main rotor at the rear rotating in the opposite direction to that of the front rotor, or to have counter-rotating main rotors on concentric shafts. A third method is *Notar* (no tail rotor), in which high-pressure air from the powerplant is ducted along the tailboom and ejected through controllable louvres on either side of the tailboom tip.

One very important new development related to the helicopter is the Bell-Boeing V-22 Osprey military aircraft, in which twin rotors tilt forward to become propellers for forward flight.

Incidence Angle at which the wing mean *chord* (q.v.) is set in relation to the aircraft's longitudinal axis. This is different from *angle of attack* (q.v.).

Inertial navigation The only type of modern airborne navigation system to be independent of outside information sources. Accelerometers are mounted on a platform which is kept level by a set of gyroscopes. The accelerometers measure velocity changes in the fore-and-aft, lateral and vertical planes, and from this information an onboard computer calculates speed, heading and distance travelled. The crew tell the computer their latitude and longitude at the start of the flight, and thereafter the system automatically calculates and displays the aircraft's current position. The system can be linked to the autopilot, allowing the cruise phase of the flight to be conducted automatically.

Mechanical drift in the gyros causes inertial to lose accuracy with time, though recent advances in gyroscope technology mean that after a transatlantic flight the error will usually not exceed 10 km (5·4 nm). Developments now being investigated will result in further improvements in accuracy.

A new form of inertial navigation, known as *laser inertial*, has recently been developed. Based on ring-laser instead of mechanical gyros, such systems are fitted to the latest generation of airliners and will be standard on the attack aircraft of the 1990s.

A laser gyro is a small, usually triangular structure enclosing a very fine channel running parallel to all three of its sides. The total length of the channel, known as the *path length*, varies according to the application, but is typically 43 cm for transport aircraft systems, 20 cm or less for missiles. The greater the path length, the more accurate the navigation.

A beam of laser light is passed around the channel, starting from one corner, being reflected by mirrors at the other two and then received back at the start point. Any motion of the system about an axis perpendicular to the plane of the light path will be seen as a change in the phase of the light detected at the exit receiver. This phase change is then computed to give acceleration about that axis. Three mutually perpendicular laser gyros give accelerations about all three axes. Thereafter the calculation of velocity and distance is just as for a conventional mechanical gyro system.

Because they are less complex, laser gyros are far more reliable than mechanical systems. They are also more accurate. Mechanical gyros are cheaper to buy, but their lower reliability makes them more costly in the long run. Laser gyros are therefore likely to become the standard in most airborne applications over the next few years.

Instrument landing system (ILS) Landing aid comprising two radio beams: the *localiser* for horizontal guidance, *glideslope* for vertical. Scheduled to be replaced by *microwave landing system* (MLS) or satellite-based systems.

Jet propulsion The pushing forward of a vehicle by the rapid rearwards efflux of a mass of gas. Although both *rockets* (q.v.) and air-breathing powerplants produce such jets, the expression is usually restricted to the gas-turbine engine. The world's first jet-powered flight was carried out by the German Heinkel He178 on August 27, 1939.

The gas turbine works by taking air in at the front, compressing it, mixing vaporised fuel—usually kerosene—with it, igniting the mixture, making the burning gases flow through a turbine to drive the compressor (which is mounted on the same shaft), and letting them escape in a jet to drive the aircraft. In most gas turbines the compressor and turbine are *axial*, consisting of many small blades set on a central drum and moving between stationary blades mounted on a closely fitted casing. Some small gas turbines have a *centrifugal* compressor, in which the blades are mounted on a rotating plate and shaped

IMPORTANT MODERN JET ENGINES

Manufacturer	Designation	Maximum thrust (kN)	Typical aircraft application
Rolls-Royce	RB.211-524D4	236	Boeing 747
	RB.211-535C	166·4	Boeing 757
	Tay 620-15	61·61	Fokker 100
	RB.168 Spey (military) Mk 250	53·3	Nimrod MR.2
	Olympus 593	167·7 (dry)	Concorde
	Pegasus 11-F402-RR-404	94·21	AV-8B Harrier II
CFM International	CFM56-5	111·25	Airbus A320
Turbo-Union	RB.199 Mk 103	42·95 (dry)	Tornado
Garrett	TFE731-5R-1H	16·46	BAe 125-800
General	F404-GE-400	71·2	F/A-18A Hornet
Electric	CF6-80E1A2	300	Airbus A330-300
	F101-GE-102	133	Rockwell B-1B
Pratt &	JT8D-17R	77·4	Boeing 727-200
Whitney	JT9D-59A1	234	Airbus A300B4-200
	F100-PW-100	65·2 (dry)	F-15 Eagle
	PW4000	267	Boeing 747-400
Kuznetsov	NK-86	127·5	Il-86
Soloviev	D-90A	157·1	Il-96-300
Tumansky	R-29B	78·45 (dry)	MiG-23/27
	R-31	91·18 (dry)	MiG-25

N.B. To obtain thrust in kg weight multiply kilonewtons (kN) thrust by 1,000 and divide by g (9·81 m per sec per sec). Thrust (dry) in table refers to unreheated thrust, which can be much increased by afterburning.

to compress the air by forcing it outwards. In a *ramjet* the forward motion of the engine is used to compress the incoming air sufficiently for combustion to take place. This can happen only at very high speeds, from about Mach 3 upwards.

Lasers Over the past ten years lasers have become a primary aid to attack-aircraft pilots in delivering their weapons accurately. Low-powered laser beams are also used in a new form of *inertial navigation system* (q.v.).

A laser is a coherent (i.e. single, stable frequency) beam of light with a very narrow spread; that is, it remains tightly concentrated even at great distances from its source.

In an airborne laser system the pilot can steer the beam on to the target; he then launches weapons capable of following reflected laser energy to the target. Although the beam is invisible to the human eye, its direction can be seen by the pilot as a symbol on a display in front of him. The beam is positioned on the target by adjusting the location of the symbol, using a simple hand controller connected to the laser transmitter.

In some applications the aircraft system is both laser transmitter and receiver. By measuring the time taken for a pulse of laser light to travel to and from the target, the aircraft's weapon-aiming computer can accurately calculate the distance. Since the direction of the beam is also known, the computer can calculate the exact moment at which to release the weapons so that they hit the target.

The laser transmitter can also be carried by a ground observer, who uses it to identify or *designate* the target. The attacking aircraft detects the laser light reflected from the target, which the pilot need never see, and launches laser-homing bombs or missiles.

Because the laser beam is both invisible and very narrow, the target receives very little warning of impending attack.

Lift Vertical force due to the flow of air round an aerofoil. About three-quarters of the lift of a wing is composed of suction due to low pressure on the upper surface of the aerofoil; the other quarter is due to positive pressure on the underside. The lift increases with the *angle of attack* (q.v.) until the aerofoil *stalls* (q.v.).

Localiser Equipment giving steering guidance in an instrument landing system (ILS).

Loran Navigation system which is broadly similar to *Decca* (q.v.) but based on time rather than phase-linked transmissions by master and slave stations. Each station in the chain emits a short pulse at exactly the same time. The intervals between the arrival at the aircraft of the pulses from the master and each of the slaves give a position fix.

Mach number Ratio of the speed of an aircraft to the local speed of sound. Mach 1, the speed of sound, is taken as 333 m (1,094 ft) per second in air at NTP. Under the same conditions Mach 2 is 667 m (2,188 ft) per second and Mach 3 1,000 m (3,280 ft) per second. Mach 1 is 1,225 km/hr (761 mph) at sea level, falling with atmospheric pressure to a constant 1,062 km/hr (660 mph) at 11,000 m (36,000 ft) and beyond.

Missiles Generally, rocket-powered weapons with remote or onboard guidance. They are classified into strategic or tactical; short, medium, intermediate or intercontinental in range; whether ballistic or not; and by role, whether surface-to-air, air-to-air, etc.

Strategic missiles have nuclear warheads and are deployed to threaten a potential adversary's territory, population, government, industry and long-range weapon systems in order to deter attack. Tactical missiles have both conventional and, less commonly, nuclear warheads and are designed for use in battle against an enemy's forces. Strategic missiles can be either intermediate or intercontinental in range. The former are based on submarines; until the signing of the Intermediate Nuclear Forces Treaty by the Soviet Union (now the Commonwealth of Independent States) and the United States in 1988 they were also to be found on the territory of allies adjoining a potential enemy. The latter are based on the operating nation's own territory and are capable of covering several thousand miles to reach their targets.

Medium-range missiles are directed at targets that are beyond visual range: the second wave of an attacking armoured force, for instance, or a strategic bomber detected by radar. Short-range missiles usually require visual identification of the target by the user. Examples are anti-tank and air-to-air 'dogfight' missiles.

Missiles are usually powered all the way from launch to target. Exceptions include the intercontinental ballistic missile (ICBM) and, at the other end of the scale, the glide bomb. The

ICBM is powered and guided only for the first few minutes of flight, during which it leaves the atmosphere in the same way as a spacecraft entering orbit. The rocket motors and fuel tanks then fall away and the warhead follows a ballistic trajectory—like that of a thrown stone—to the target. The glide bomb is guided throughout—often by *laser* (q.v.)—but has no propulsion. Comprising a conventional bomb fitted with guidance and large lifting and control surfaces, it glides all the way to the target, either homing on reflected laser light or obeying commands from an airborne operator. Laser-guided bombs were used very successfully during the Gulf War of January-February 1991.

Various propulsion methods are used, the choice depending on the task of the missile. Rocket motors—both solid and liquid—are the most common, but turbojets and ramjets are chosen when range is more important than acceleration or maximum speed.

Choice of guidance method also depends on mission. Ballistic missiles have *inertial navigation* (q.v.), while cruise missiles (see below) compare the terrain over which they are flying with a pre-loaded computer image of the required track; this technique is known as *terrain comparison*, or Tercom. Anti-ship missiles combine inertial with active radar homing, in which the missile illuminates the target with its own radar and then follows the reflections. Anti-tank missiles are flown by remote control in much the same way as a model aeroplane, while many of the weapons designed for use against aircraft are attracted by exhaust heat.

Missiles have the following roles: strategic, surface-to-surface, air-to-surface, anti-ship, anti-submarine, surface-to-air, air-to-air, and anti-tank.

Strategic Invariably nuclear-armed, strategic missiles can be either ballistic or, in the case of cruise missiles, jet-powered and wingborne. Ballistic missiles are land or submarine-based; cruise missiles can also be launched from ships and aircraft.

The cruise missile—essentially a small pilotless aircraft powered by a single jet engine and fitted with a miniature nuclear warhead—has been added to strategic arsenals in recent years for several reasons. First, its small size and mobility makes it easy to conceal, reducing its vulnerability to a first strike or counter-attack. Second, the wider variety of platforms capable of launching cruise missiles allows the user to present a more complex and therefore more effective threat. Finally, cruise missiles armed with conventional warheads are also useful for tactical purposes.

Examples of strategic missiles are the Russian SS-18 Satan ICBM and the US Boeing AGM-86B Air Launched Cruise Missile.

Surface-to-surface This category comprises land-launched weapons capable of carrying nuclear or conventional warheads over ranges of tens to hundreds of miles. They are most commonly designed for battlefield support, attacking reinforcements and supply formations to prevent them from assisting front-line forces. Examples are the Russian Scud-B and US Lance.

Air-to-surface Launched by aircraft at land targets, these missiles are usually rocket-powered and fitted with conventional warheads, though nuclear-tipped and jet-powered types do exist. Some are designed specifically to attack certain types of target: anti-radiation missiles (ARMs) home on radar signals, while the stand-off submunition dispensers now under development would scatter powerful bomblets on runways and armoured columns. Examples are the US Hughes AGM-65 Maverick, British Aerospace Alarm ARM and Russian AS-7 Kerry.

Anti-ship Launched by ships, submarines, aircraft and, occasionally, shore batteries, anti-ship missiles can be rocket or jet-powered and are most often fitted with conventional warheads. They are usually cylindrical in shape, with fins for lift and control, though some Russian and Chinese designs resemble small

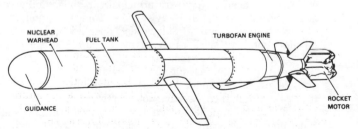

Tomahawk cruise missile

aircraft. Range—65 km (40 miles) is typical—tends to be greater than that of air-to-surface missiles. Anti-ship missiles have proved to be very effective in recent conflicts, notably the Falklands War. Examples are the French Aérospatiale Exocet, British Aerospace Sea Eagle and US McDonnell Douglas RGM-84A Harpoon.

Anti-submarine Launched by ships and submarines, these weapons usually comprise a vehicle—a missile or small aircraft—and an independent payload. Following launch from the deck of a ship or torpedo tube of a submarine, the vehicle flies to the suspected location of the target. The payload—a nuclear depth charge or conventionally armed homing torpedo—is then released into the water. Homing torpedoes—the British Stingray and French Murène are typical—can search for and attack their targets without external assistance. Current anti-submarine missile systems include the Australian/British Ikara, US Asroc and Subroc, and Russian SS-N-14 Silex.

Surface-to-air Designed to destroy aircraft and other missiles, these weapons can be fired from fixed land sites, vehicles, man-portable launchers, and surface vessels. Surface-to-air missiles (SAMs) are rocket or ramjet-powered and almost always have conventional warheads. They vary in size from the few pounds of weapons such as the US Stinger and French Mistral, designed to give infantrymen a last-ditch defence against air attack, to the 2,000 kg (4,400 lb) of the Russian SA-12b Giant, which can counter tactical and, possibly, strategic ballistic missiles.

Air-to-air Launched from aircraft to destroy other aircraft, air-to-air missiles are rocket-powered and armed with high-explosive warheads. They vary principally in range and guidance method. The US Navy's F-14 Tomcat fighter, for example, carries a mix of Sidewinder, Sparrow and Phoenix missiles. Phoenix has a range of more than 200 km (125 miles) and homes on the reflections of a radar beam directed at the target by the launch aircraft. Sparrow is similarly guided but has less range, about 65–100 km. Sidewinder homes on the heat (infra-red) energy given off by the engines of opposing aircraft and is launched when they are well within visual range and manoeuvring to gain the advantage.

Anti-tank Launched from lightweight ground firing posts,

armoured vehicles and helicopters, anti-tank missiles are rocket-powered and usually command-guided; that is, they are remotely steered to the target by a human operator. Designed to penetrate large thicknesses of modern armour, their high-explosive warheads are of the hollow-charge type. On impact a hollow charge forms a very hot, high-velocity jet of material which forces its way through the armour. Current anti-tank missiles include the Euromissile HOT and Milan, US Hughes BGM-71 TOW, and Russian AT-4 Spigot, AT-5 Spandrel, AT-6 Spiral and AT-8 Songster.

Navigation The means by which a vehicle (ship, aircraft, motor car) is steered towards a desired point. In aeronautical applications radio beacons, maps and *inertial* (q.v.) are used for position-fixing, while a magnetic or, more usually, gyroscopic compass indicates heading. Ground radio beacons of the VHF omni-directional range (VOR) and non-directional beacon (NDB) type are arranged so that the navigator can calculate a fix from differing bearings, while *Decca* (q.v.) uses phase difference and *Loran* (q.v.) time difference between received signals. In ertial navigation uses self-contained sensors to determine position without outside reference. The satellite-based Global Positioning System (USA) and Glonass (Russia) could be cleared for routine air transport use by the mid-1990s.

For basic navigation *dead reckoning* and *astro* (star) navigation are used. The first depends on knowing wind speed and direction accurately so as to correct the known heading, while the latter relies on tables of the elevation angles of given stars at given times. Neither is effective in fast-moving aircraft.

Omega Very-low-frequency (10 kHz) navigation aid originally developed by the US Navy for the underwater navigation of its nuclear submarines and since widely adopted for aeronautical use. The eight transmitters give global coverage and accuracies of better than 2 km are generally possible, making Omega currently the most accurate worldwide navigation aid. It is employed particularly as a back-up to other systems such as inertial. Its main shortcoming is the fact that, since it is primarily a military-sponsored tactical navigation aid, it is not guaranteed to be fully operational at all times.

Orbit The closed path of a satellite around the Earth, or of any body round any other. The Earth is in orbit around the Sun, while the Moon and many artificial satellites are in orbit around the Earth. Orbits are usually elliptical in shape, though certain types of artificial satellite follow circular paths.

Payload That part of the disposable load of an aircraft which yields a commercial or, in the case of combat aircraft, military benefit. Commercial payloads comprise passengers and freight. Military payloads are made up of bombs, missiles and other weapon systems.

Perigee The point in an Earth orbit which is nearest to the Earth.

Port The left-hand side of an aircraft as seen by the pilot looking forward. Associated with a red wing-tip light.

Propellant Any substance used to generate propulsive gases in a rocket engine. There are two major classes of propellant: liquid and solid.

Liquid propellants consist mostly of a fuel, which is burned, and an oxidant to provide the necessary oxygen when the rocket is operating in a vacuum. The fuel can be paraffin, petrol, alcohol, hydrazine, aniline or any other liquid that can be oxidised to form large volumes of gas. Oxidants include liquid oxygen, red fuming nitric acid, hydrogen peroxide and fluorine.

There are a few single-liquid propellants, such as monomethyl hydrazine and high-test peroxide, which have no need of an added oxidant.

The simplest solid fuel is gunpowder. Others include: JPN, a mixture of nitrocellulose, nitroglycerine, diethyl phthalate, carbamite, potassium sulphate, carbon and wax; galcit, a mixture of potassium perchlorate and a fuel such as asphalt; NDRC, a mixture of ammonium picrate, sodium nitrate and resin.

The efficiency of a propellant is known as its *specific impulse*, given by the equation

$$\text{Specific impulse} = \frac{\text{Thrust in kilograms}}{\text{Rate of loss of mass in kilograms}}$$

Specific impulse is related to the exhaust velocity of the gas produced by the equation

$$\text{Specific impulse} = \frac{\text{Exhaust velocity}}{g}$$

Propeller Device used to draw an aircraft through the air. Its action is similar to that of a ship's propeller. It consists of two or more blades attached to a hub, which itself is fixed to the drive shaft from the engine. When the propeller is turning, the speed of the tip of a blade is greater than that of its root, or the part nearest the hub. If this were not corrected, the force produced by the blade would vary from a high value at the tip to a low one at the root. The blade is therefore twisted so that the tip is nearer position (c) in the diagram than the root, which may be in position (d). Because the force produced by the blade depends on both its speed and its angle of attack, the fast-moving tip has thus been given a smaller angle than the slower-moving root.

As the forward speed of an aircraft changes, so does the efficiency of the propeller. The higher the forward speed, the coarser should be the propeller pitch. The pitch of some propellers can therefore be varied by the pilot to suit his requirements; these are known as *variable-pitch* propellers.

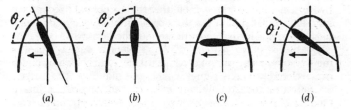

(a)   (b)   (c)   (d)

Section of propeller blade end-on, looking towards the hub The angle between the *chord* (q.v.) of the blade and the transverse axis of the hub is called the *pitch* of the blade (symbol θ). The pitch is greater (coarser) in (a) than in (d). In (b) it is coarsest and the propeller is said to be *feathered*. In (c) pitch is zero and the propeller generates no propulsive force. The arrow in each case indicates the direction of rotation of the blade section. In some cases the blade may be rotated to achieve reverse pitch (i.e. θ is negative), allowing the whole aircraft to be slowed down or reversed.

Pylon Structure for attaching an external load to an aircraft (e.g. engine nacelle, drop-tank or weapon).

Radar Developed during the Second World War, radar is an electronic system for determining the position of air and surface targets. A large ground-based radar aerial emits extremely high-frequency pulsed radio signals in a beam about one degree wide. The aerial rotates at about 5 to 10 r.p.m., covering the whole sky with the beam.

If the beam encounters an aircraft, some of its energy is reflected back to the aerial, where it is collected and the time taken for the two-way passage determined. From this, and the direction in which the beam was transmitted, a computer determines the position of the aircraft, which is then displayed on a cathode-ray tube as a fluorescent dot. Returns from nearby buildings or other stationary objects some distance away are filtered out. Information such as aircraft heading and speed can be calculated from successive returns and displayed alongside the radar return and the identity of the aircraft.

Most air traffic over or close to land is controlled by radar. Aircraft can be brought in to within half a mile of touchdown using either PAR (precision approach radar) or GCA (ground-controlled approach). Aircraft themselves can be equipped with radar for storm avoidance, when it is used for locating clouds (the beam reflects off the rain droplets). Secondary surveillance radar (SSR), a development of ordinary (primary) radar, is a back-up facility for air traffic control. The radar beam has a pulse pattern which triggers a device called a *transponder* in the aircraft. Once triggered, the transponder emits a coded radio signal which is unique to the carrier aircraft. The coded reply can be correlated with the primary radar return from the aircraft to show its position and identity. SSR techniques are also used to distinguish hostile from friendly aircraft in combat; such systems are called *identification friend or foe* (IFF). Aircraft height also can be transponded.

Airliners are now being fitted with Traffic Alert and Collision Avoidance System (TCAS), a radar-based system which alerts crews of the possibility of mid-air collision and issues advice on the necessary evasive action.

For military purposes, low-level navigation at night is made possible by the display to the pilot of a radar picture of the route ahead. This data can also be fed into a terrain-following computer, which then directs the aircraft's autopilot to climb over the hills ahead and keep low down in the valleys to minimise the chances of detection.

Airborne radars which look almost vertically downwards

can be used for mapping, either for simple cartographic purposes or for the precise location of enemy installations.

The development of high-powered airborne radars has led to the development of airborne early warning (AEW) aircraft, which can detect aircraft, road vehicles or ships up to 350 km away from the platform.

Radio beacons The *Decca* and *Loran* (q.v.) beacon systems used for long-range aerial navigation are complemented by various short-range systems, notably VOR, NDB and DME.

A VOR (very-high-frequency omni-directional range) transmits in the 108–118 MHz frequency band. An unmodulated reference tone which has the same phase regardless of direction has superimposed on it a second tone whose phase varies with the direction of transmission. A Morse code beacon identifier is superimposed on the transmission. The airborne receiver picks up the signal, works out the phase of the varying signal and displays the bearing from the aircraft to the beacon.

The older NDB (non-directional beacon) transmits in the medium-wave band. A constant tone, with Morse code identification, is transmitted uniformly in all directions. The airborne receiver determines the direction from which the signal is coming by rotating an aerial until the signal is strongest, and then displays that bearing.

DME (distance-measuring equipment) and its military cousin Tacan (tactical air navigation) determine the time taken for a pulse to travel from the beacon to the aircraft, where this value is then converted into distance. Tacan also gives bearing information.

Range The permissible distance that an aircraft can fly with a specified load, usually with allowances for diversions and other contingencies.

Records Aerospace performance records are recognised officially only if they have been set under conditions defined by the Fédération Aéronautique Internationale (FAI). Unofficially, a number of aircraft have flown faster than the FAI-recognised record.

The official absolute world records correct to May 1990 are:

Speed in a straight line over 15 to 25 km Capt Eldon W. Joersz and Maj George T. Morgan Jr (USAF), at Beale Air Force Base, California, in a Lockheed SR-71A on July 28, 1976, 3,530 km/hr (2,193 mph).

Height Alexander Fedotov, USSR, in an E-266M (MiG-25) on August 31, 1977, 37,650 m (123,523 ft).

Distance in a straight line and distance in a closed circuit Dick Rutan and Jeana Yeager, USA. Circumnavigation of the world in Voyager aircraft, starting and finishing at Edwards Air Force Base, California, December 14-23, 1986, 40,212 km (24,987 miles).

Height in sustained horizontal flight Lt Ed Yielding (USAF) in a Lockheed SR-71A on March 6, 1990, 27,432 m (90,000 ft).

Speed in a closed circuit Maj Adolphus H. Bledsoe Jr and Maj John T. Fuller (USAF), over a 1,000 km circuit at Beale Air Force Base, California, in a Lockheed SR-71A on July 27, 1976, 3,367 km/hr (2,092 mph).

Reciprocating engine Another name for piston engine, in which the in-and-out action of pistons in cylinders is transformed into rotational motion of a shaft. All early aero engines were piston engines.

Re-entry Return of an Earth-originating object from space into the atmosphere of the planet. A vehicle in orbit at speeds of thousands of miles an hour runs the risk of burning up as a result of frictional heating by the air when it re-enters the atmosphere. First-generation spacecraft like the US Apollo and Russian Vostok were protected by *ablative* heatshields, which dispersed heat by gradually charring and falling away. Modern vehicles like the US Space Shuttle Orbiter and the Russian Buran are covered with tiles made of materials which radiate heat extremely rapidly.

Rocket Reaction motor which, unlike a jet engine, does not need an external supply of oxygen with which to burn its fuel. It is therefore able to function in the vacuum of outer space.

Fuels called *propellants* are burned to create immense volumes of gas which stream at high speed out of the motor's single, rearwards-facing opening. The resultant reaction is forward, causing the rocket to move in that direction. The simplest rocket, used in fireworks, has gunpowder or similar fuel lit by a paper fuze.

As the rocket travels upwards it loses the fuel that is being consumed. So the total weight gets less and the rocket accelerates until all the fuel is spent. The ratio of the initial mass of the rocket to the final mass when the fuel is gone is called the *mass ratio*. The velocity at burnout is given by the equation

$$V = 2 \cdot 3 \, c \log_{10} R$$

where R = mass ratio; c = jet velocity.

The bigger the final velocity required, the more fuel there must be and the bigger (and heavier) the fuel tanks or casing and rocket engine. For this reason rocket vehicles used to launch spacecraft are divided into at least two stages. When the first stage has burned out its heavy tanks and engines can be thrown away. The next stage, already moving at high speed, then starts to fire, further accelerating the payload until it reaches orbital speed. By permitting redundant structure to be discarded, staging reduces the total mass of the vehicle.

The world's largest rocket vehicle, the Russian Energia launcher, generates a maximum thrust of 4 million kg and can put 105,000 kg into low Earth orbit. Its core stage has four engines fuelled with oxygen and hydrogen and each producing 150,000 kg of thrust. Attached to the core are four boosters fuelled with oxygen and kerosene and each rated at 590,000 kg thrust.

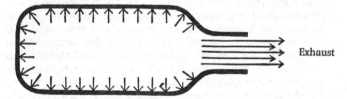

Exhaust

How a rocket works The fuel burns very quickly to form immense volumes of gas which expand and gather speed before escaping through the exhaust. This rearwards action is matched by a powerful forwards reaction which propels the vehicle.

Safe life Period during which an aircraft component can be expected to function safely before replacement is required.
Satellite Any body in orbit round a bigger body is a satellite. The

Moon is a satellite of the Earth, and the Earth can be described as a satellite of the Sun.

Artificial satellites are man-made objects put into orbit, usually round the Earth. To get a satellite into Earth orbit it must be launched parallel to the surface, high above the atmosphere, and at a certain minimum speed. If the speed is too low the intended satellite will fall back to Earth. If the speed is above *escape velocity* (q.v.) the satellite will fly off into space. Launch speed and orbital height and shape are related. For example, any speed between 7·9 and 11·1 km/sec is sufficient to launch an object into an orbit with a lowest point 480 km above the Earth. But a vehicle launched at the lower speed would follow a circular orbit, whereas one launched at exactly the higher speed would depart into deep space on a parabolic path. If launched at a speed between these values the vehicle would follow an ellipse, being farthest away from the Earth at one end and nearest at the opposite end.

Since the successful orbital flight of the Soviet Sputnik 1 in October 1957 many thousands of satellites have been launched. Most of these have since fallen out of orbit; the time a satellite lasts depends on how deeply it dips into the Earth's atmosphere. At 160 km (100 miles) high a satellite will last a week before air resistance slows it down and causes it to fall back and burn up; at 1,300 km (808 miles) it will last indefinitely.

The amount of man-made material in Earth orbit is a matter of increasing concern. In addition to dozens of operational satellites there are thousands of spent upper stages, dead satellites and large fragments of exploded spacecraft, plus countless items of 'space rubbish' which include an astronaut's glove and myriad copper needles. In 1991 Space Shuttle Orbiters twice came close to colliding with space debris.

Satellites serve many purposes:
Science Earth-orbiting satellites have made an enormous contribution to our knowledge of the magnetic fields, radiation and particles in near-Earth and deep space. Planetary probes like the Soviet Veneras and US Mariner and Voyager have told us more about the planets of the Solar System in the last 25 years than had been learned in the previous 3,000 years of human observation.

Earth observation Optical, infra-red and other sensors mounted on satellites like the US Landsats, French SPOT and Russian Resurs are giving scientists, industrialists and politicians a view of the world in its entirety for the first time. The first warnings of damage to the atmosphere from spray-can propellants, carbon dioxide emissions and destruction of forests were given by Earth-resources and weather satellites.

Navigation Satellites like the US GPS Navstar and Russian Glonass emit precisely timed radio signals as a navigational aid for ships, aircraft and land vehicles. Satellites are used also for surveying and mapping and for geological and other environmental research.

Reconnaissance USAF Big Bird and KH-11 and Russian Cosmos satellites carry cameras to monitor military activity in potentially hostile countries.

Communications Satellites are used routinely to relay international (Intelsat), regional (Eutelsat, PanAmSat) and national (Palapa, Insat, Molniya) telecommunications, principally telephone and television. Other communications applications include direct-broadcast television (Astra), links with mobile users (Inmarsat), corporate data-transfer (Satellite Business Systems) and road haulage location and messaging (Qualcomm).

Search and rescue The Cospas-Sarsat international sea, air and land distress alerting and location system relays signals from emergency radio beacons aboard ships, aircraft and land vehicles to rescue co-ordination centres around the world.

Manned spaceflight The first generations of manned spacecraft—Mercury, Gemini, Apollo, Vostok, Soyuz—were little more than simple satellites fitted with life-support systems and, sometimes, docking equipment. The current US Space Shuttle Orbiter and Russian Buran are true aerospacecraft capable of re-entering and gliding back to fully controlled runway landings, and of being re-used repeatedly. The Russians and Americans have also launched space stations, large modular satellites capable of accommodating crews for protracted stays in space. The Russians have built up many man-years of experience with their Salyut and Mir stations, while the USA completed the successful Skylab programme in the 1970s and is now working with Europe, Canada and Japan on the International Space Station for service in the late 1990s.

Shock wave When air encounters an object which is moving
faster than the speed of sound it no longer has time to move
gradually out of the way. Instead it is pushed sharply aside in
a series of jumps; the lines along which these jumps occur are
called *shock waves* and mark the boundary between regions of
different pressure. The boom of an aircraft passing through the
sound barrier is simply a shock wave reaching one's ears: the
sudden change of pressure is heard as an explosion, or frequently as a double bang.

Space probe Unmanned vehicle which is launched to escape from
Earth orbit and to continue on a voyage of exploration within
the Solar System or beyond. About 100 space probes have
been launched since the first, Pioneer 1, was put up by the
United States in 1958. All have been listed in *Junior Pears Encyclopaedia*.

The first probe to hit the Moon was the Soviet Lunik 2 in
September 1959, followed by the American Ranger 4 in April
1962. Lunik 3 achieved lunar orbit and photographed the far
side of the Moon, unseen previously by man, in October 1959.
The Soviets made the first soft landing on the Moon in
January 1966 with their Luna 9 probe and obtained pictures
of the lunar surface. Surveyor 1, an American probe, followed
in May 1966 and transmitted TV pictures from the surface.

Meanwhile, the Americans had launched Mariner 2, which
radioed back much information as it passed close to Venus in
December 1962. Mariner 4 and the Soviet Zond 4 both took
photographs of Mars in 1964–65, and Mariner 5 passed within
3,200 km of Venus in 1967.

Soviet and American lunar programmes continued, with
Surveyor 3 finding 15 cm pebbles on the Moon in 1967. The
Soviets brought back soil samples in Luna 16 in September
1970, and their Luna 17, which landed in the Sea of Rains,
put the first 8-wheel Lunokhod robot vehicle on the lunar
surface.

Pioneer 10 went to Jupiter in 1973, crossed Neptune's orbit
on June 13, 1983, and then passed on into deep space beyond
the solar system. The Soviet Venus 8 probe made a parachute
landing on the planet in July 1972. The USSR put the Mars 6
capsule on the Martian surface in March 1974 but it failed to

Continued on page G47

Spacecraft placed in orbit during 1992

Spacecraft	Launcher	Mass (kg)	Purpose	Country	Date
Cosmos 2175	A2 Soyuz	6,500?	Reconn	Russia	21.1.92
STS 42 Discovery	Space Shuttle	98,543	Reusable launcher (with International Microgravity Laboratory 1)	USA	22.1.92
Cosmos 2176	A2e Molniya	1,900?	Missile	EW Russia	24.1.92
Progress M11	A2 Soyuz	7,250?	Mir resupply	Russia	25.1.92
Cosmos 2177–2179 (Glonass)	D1e Proton	1,400? each	Nav	Russia	29.1.92
Defence Satellite Communications System 3	Atlas II	1,130	Mil comms	USA	10.2.92
JERS-1 Fuyo	H1	1,340	ER	Japan	11.2.92
Cosmos 2180	C1 Cosmos	825?	Mil nav	Russia	18.2.92
Navstar GPS 2-12	Delta 2/7925	845	Nav	USA	23.2.92
Superbird B1	Ariane 44L	2,560	Comms	Japan	26.2.92
Arabsat 1C	Ariane 44L	1,360	Comms	International	26.2.92
Molniya 1-83	A2e Molniya	1,600?	Comms	Russia	4.3.92
Cosmos 2181	C1 Cosmos	?	Nav	Russia	9.3.92
Galaxy 5	Atlas I	1,413	Comms	USA	13.3.92
Soyuz TM-14	A2 Soyuz	7,150	Mir ferry	Russia	17.3.92
STS 45 Atlantis	Space Shuttle	93,008	Reusable launcher (with Atlas 1)	USA	24.3.92
Cosmos 2182	A2 Soyuz	6,500?	Reconn	Russia	1.4.92
Gorizont 25	D1e Proton	2,125	Comms	Russia	2.4.92
Cosmos 2183	A2 Soyuz	7,000?	Reconn	Russia	8.4.92
Navstar GPS 2-13	Delta 2/7925	845	Nav	USA	9.4.92
Cosmos 2184	C1 Cosmos	825?	Nav	Russia	15.4.92
Telecom 2B	Ariane 44L	2,200	Comms	France	15.4.92
Inmarsat 2-F4	Ariane 44L	1,310	Comms	International	15.4.92
Progress M12	A2 Soyuz	7,250?	Mir resupply	Russia	19.4.92
US elint satellite	Titan 2	?	Elint	USA	25.4.92
Resurs-F2 5	A2 Soyuz	6,300?	ER	Russia	29.4.92
Cosmos 2185	A2 Soyuz	6,500?	Reconn	Russia	29.4.92
STS 49 Endeavour	Space Shuttle	91,213	Reusable launcher	USA	7.5.92
Palapa B4	Delta 2/7925	1,260	Comms	Indonesia	13.5.92
SROSS-C (Stretched Rohini Satellite Series)	ASLV-3	106	Science	India	20.5.92
Cosmos 2186	A2 Soyuz	6,500?	Reconn	Russia	29.5.92
Cosmos 2187-2194	C1 Cosmos	45? each	Mil comms	Russia	3.6.92
Extreme Ultra-Violet Explorer (EUVE)	Delta 2	4,000	Science	USA	7.6.92
Intelsat K	Atlas IIA	2,840	Comms	International	9.6.92
Resurs-F1 10	A2 Soyuz	6,300?	ER	Russia	23.6.92

Spacecraft	Launcher	Mass (kg)	Purpose	Country	Date
STS 50 *Columbia*	Space Shuttle	103,813	Reusable launcher (with US Microgravity Laboratory 1)	USA	25.6.92
Progress M13	A2 Soyuz	7,250?	Mir resupply	Russia	30.6.92
Cosmos 2195	C1 Cosmos	825?	Nav	Russia	1.7.92
Defence Satellite Communications System 3	Atlas II	1,130	Mil comms	USA	2.7.92
Solar, Anomalous and Magneto-spheric Particle Explorer (SAMPEX)	Scout	180	Science	USA/Germany	3.7.92
Navstar GPS 2-14	Delta 2/7925	845	Nav	USA	7.7.92
Cosmos 2196	A2e Molniya	1,900?	Missile	EW Russia	8.7.92
Eutelsat 2-4	Ariane 44L	1,877	Comms	International	9.7.92
Insat 2A	Ariane 44L	1,906	Comms/ER	India	9.7.92
Cosmos 2197-2202	F2 Tsyklon	225? each	Comms	Russia	13.7.92
Gorizont 26	D1e Proton	2,125	Comms	Russia	14.7.92
Geotail	Delta 2/6925	1,009	Science	USA/Japan	24.7.92
Cosmos 2203	A2 Soyuz	6,500?	Reconn	Russia	24.7.92
Soyuz TM-15	A2 Soyuz	6,850	Mir ferry	Russia	26.7.92
Cosmos 2204-2206 (Glonass)	D1e Proton	1,400 each	Nav	Russia	30.7.92
Cosmos 2207	A2 Soyuz	6,300?	Reconn	Russia	30.7.92
STS 46 *Atlantis*	Space Shuttle	94,675	Reusable launcher	USA	31.7.92
Eureca 1	Space Shuttle	4,491	Science	International	31.7.92
Molniya 1-84	A2e Molniya	1,700?	Comms	Russia	6.8.92
FSW-2 1	Long March 2D	2,500?	Science/Reconn	China	9.8.92
Topex/Poseidon	Ariane 42P	2,402	ER (ocean topography)	USA	10.8.92
Kitsat-A (Uribyol 1)	Ariane 42P	48	ER/Comms	South Korea	10.8.92
S80/T	Ariane 42P	48	Comms/nav	France	10.8.92
Cosmos 2208	C1 Cosmos	900?	Comms	Russia	12.8.92
Optus B1	Long March 2E	1,580?	Comms	Australia	14.8.92
Progress M14	A2 Soyuz	7,250?	Mir resupply	Russia	15.8.92
Resurs-F1 11	A2 Soyuz	6,300?	ER	Russia	19.8.92
Pion 5 and 6	A2 Soyuz	78 each	Passive satellites	Russia	19.8.92
Satcom C4	Delta 2/7925	1,400	Comms	USA	31.8.92
Navstar GPS 2-15	Delta 2/7925	845	Nav	USA	9.9.92
Cosmos 2209	D1e Proton	2,200?	Comms	Russia	10.9.92
Hispasat 1A	Ariane 44LP	2,194	Comms	Spain	10.9.92
Satcom C3	Ariane 44LP	1,375	Comms	USA	10.9.92
STS 47 *Endeavour*	Space Shuttle	99,450	Reusable launcher (with Spacelab J)	USA	12.9.92
Cosmos 2210	A2 Soyuz	6,700?	Reconn	Russia	22.10.92
Mars Observer	Titan 3 Commercial	2,580	Science	USA	25.9.92

Spacecraft	Launcher	Mass (kg)	Purpose	Country	Date
FSW-1 14	Long March 2C	2,100?	Reconn	China	5.10.92
Freja	Long March 2C	259	Science	Sweden	5.10.92
Photon 5	A2 Soyuz	6,800	Science	Russia	8.10.92
DFS-3 Kopernikus	Delta 2	1,420	Comms	Germany	12.10.92
Molniya 3-42	A2e Molniya	1,750?	Comms	Russia	14.10.92
Cosmos 2211-2216	F2 Tsyklon	225? each	Mil comms	Russia	20.10.92
Cosmos 2217	A2e Molniya	1,900?	EW	Russia	21.10.92
STS 52 *Columbia*	Space Shuttle	97,201	Reusable launcher	USA	22.10.92
Lageos 2	Space Shuttle	405	Science	USA	22.10.92
Canadian Target Assembly (CTA)	Space Shuttle	?	Science	Canada	22.10.92
Progress M15	A2 Soyuz	7,250?	Mir resupply	Russia	27.10.92
Galaxy 7	Ariane 42P	2,968	Comms	USA	27.10.92
Cosmos 2218	C1 Cosmos	825?	Nav	Russia	29.10.92
Ekran 20	D1e Proton	2,000?	Comms	Russia	30.10.92
Resurs 500	A2 Soyuz	6,300?	ER	Russia	15.11.92
Cosmos 2219	J1 Zenit 2	9,000?	Elint	Russia	17.11.92
Cosmos 2220	A2 Soyuz	6,500?	Reconn	Russia	20.11.92
MAK-2	Ejected from Mir	?	Science (aeronomy)	Russia	20.11.92
Miniature Seeker Technology Integration (MSTI-1)	Scout	135	Mil test	USA	21.11.92
Navstar GPS 2-16	Delta 2/7925	845	Nav	USA	22.11.92
Cosmos 2221	F2 Tsyklon	2,000?	Elint	Russia	24.11.92
Cosmos 2222	A2e Molniya	1,900?	Missile	EW Russia	25.11.92
Gorizont 27	D1e Proton	2,125?	Comms	Russia	27.11.92
US reconnaissance satellite	Titan 404	?	Reconn	USA	28.11.92
Superbird A1	Ariane 42P	2,780	Comms	Japan	1.12.92
Molniya 3-43	A2e Molniya	1,750?	Comms	Russia	2.12.92
STS 53 *Discovery*	Space Shuttle	87,565	Reusable launcher	USA	2.12.92
DOD-1	Space Shuttle	10,530	Military	USA	2.12.92
Cosmos 2223	A2 Soyuz	7,000?	Reconn	Russia	9.12.92
Cosmos 2224	D1e Proton	2,200?	Science	Russia	17.12.92
Navstar GPS 2-17	Delta 2/7925	845	Nav	USA	18.12.92
Cosmos 2225	A2 Soyuz	6,500?	Reconn	Russia	22.12.92
Cosmos 2226	F2 Tsyklon	1,000?	Geodesy	Russia	22.12.92
Cosmos 2227	J1 Zenit	9,000?	Elint	Russia	25.12.92
Cosmos 2228	F2 Tsyklon	2,000?	Elint	Russia	25.12.92
Bion 10/Cosmos 2229	A2 Soyuz	6,000?	Biosatellite	Russia	29.12.92

Note: Russian (formerly Soviet) launch vehicles are designated using the system created by the late Dr Charles Sheldon of the US Library of Congress. Up to the present day there have been eight basic types of launcher: A, B, C, D, F, G, J and K. Added upper stages are labelled "1" and "2". An escape stage, used to boost payloads beyond low Earth orbit, is designated "e". Russian names are also given: Vostok (A1), Soyuz (A2), Molniya (A2e), Cosmos (C1), Proton (D1, D1e), Tsyklon (F1m, F2), Zenit (J1), Energia (K1).

Abbreviations: **Comms** Communications **Elint** Electronic intelligence **ER** Earth resources **EW** Early warning **Glonass** Soviet navigation satellite system **Met** Meteorology **Mil** Military **Nav** Navigation **Reconn** Photo-reconnaissance/surveillance **Sigint** Signal intelligence.

Manned space vehicles launched to January 1992

Name	Activities and duration	Country	Crew	Launch date
Vostok 1	1 orbit, 1 hr 48 min	USSR	Gagarin	12.4.61
Freedom 7	Suborbital, 15 min 28 sec	USA	Shepard	5.5.61
Liberty Bell 7	Suborbital, 15 min 37 sec	USA	Grissom	21.7.61
Vostok 2	17 orbits, 1 day 1 hr 18 min	USSR	Titov	6.8.61
Friendship 7	3 orbits, 4 hr 55 min 23 sec	USA	Glenn	20.2.62
Aurora 7	3 orbits, 4 hr 56 min	USA	Carpenter	24.5.62
Vostok 3	64 orbits, 3 days 22 hr 22 min	USSR	Nikolayev	11.8.62
Vostok 4	2 days 22 hr 57 min	USSR	Popovich	12.8.62
Sigma 7	6 orbits, 9 hr 13 min 11 sec	USA	Schirra	3.9.62
Faith 7	22 orbits (manually controlled descent after system failure), 1 day 10 hr 19 min	USA	Cooper	15.5.63
Vostok 5	81 orbits, 4 days 23 hrs 6 min	USSR	Bykovsky	14.6.63
Vostok 6	48 orbits, 2 days 22 hr 50 min	USSR	Valentina Tereshkova*	15.6.63
Voskhod 1	16 orbits, 1 day 0 hr 17 min	USSR	Komarov, Yegorov, Feoktistov	12.10.63
Voskhod 2	18 orbits, 1 day 2 hr 2 min	USSR	Belyaev, Leonov[1]	18.3.65
Gemini 3[2]	3 orbits, 4 hr 52 min 52 sec	USA	Grissom, Young	23.3.65
Gemini 4	62 orbits, 4 days 1hr 50 min	USA	McDivitt, White[3]	3.6.65
Gemini 5	120 orbits, 7 days 22 hrs 56 min	USA	Cooper, Conrad	21.8.65
Gemini 6[5]	16 orbits, 1 day 1 hr 51 min	USA	Schirra, Stafford	15.12.65
Gemini 7[5]	206 orbits, 13 days 18 hr 25 min	USA	Borman, Lovell	4.12.65
Gemini 8	4 orbits, 10 hr 18 min	USA	Armstrong, Scott	16.3.66
Gemini 9	48 orbits, 3 days 0 hr 21 min	USA	Stafford, Cernan	3.6.66
Gemini 10	44 orbits, 2 days 22 hr 48 min	USA	Young, Collins	18.7.66
Gemini 11[6]	48 orbits, 2 days 23 hr 18 min	USA	Conrad, Gordon	12.9.66
Gemini 12[7]	63 orbits, 3 days 12 hr 26 min	USA	Aldrin, Lovell	11.11.66
Soyuz 1	17 orbits, 1 day 0 hr 36 min	USSR	Komarov[8]	23.4.67
Apollo 7	163 orbits, 10 days 20 hr 9 min. Live TV, rendezvous with booster	USA	Schirra, Eisele, Cunningham	11.10.68
Soyuz 3	64 orbits, 3 days 22 hr 50 min. Rendezvous with Soyuz 2, no docking	USSR	Beregovoi	26.10.68
Apollo 8	6 days 3 hr. First manned flight around Moon	USA	Borman, Lovell, Anders	21.12.68
Soyuz 4	48 orbits, 2 days 23 hr 20 min. Docking target for Soyuz 5	USSR	Shatalov	14.1.69
Soyuz 5	49 orbits, 3 days 0 hr 54 min. Docked with Soyuz 4	USSR	Volynov, Khrunov, Yeliseyev	15.1.69
Apollo 9	151 orbits, 10 days 1 hr. LM manned flight 6 hr	USA	McDivitt, Scott, Schweickart	3.3.69
Apollo 10	8 days 0 hr 3 min. LM manned flight 8 hr in 60 nm lunar orbit	USA	Stafford, Young, Cernan	18.5.69

* Valentina Tereshkova was the first woman cosmonaut.
[1] Leonov was the first man to leave a spaceship and float tethered in outer space.
[2] Gemini 3 was a manoeuvrable spacecraft and changed its flight path three times.
[3] White was the second man and the first American to step out into space.
[4] The approximate time that would be required to fly to the Moon, briefly explore and return to Earth.
[5] These spacecraft carried out a successful rendezvous in orbit, approaching to within 2 m of each other and flying in formation for more than 2 circuits of the Earth.
[6] First-orbit docking achieved.   [7] Docking achieved on third orbit.
[8] Komarov was first in-flight space fatality: parachute shroud lines became entangled.

Name	Activities and duration	Country	Crew	Launch date
Apollo 11	8 days. LM 'Eagle' made man's first landing on the Moon, 20 and 21.7.69	USA	Armstrong, Aldrin, Collins	16.7.69
Soyuz 6	5 days. Rendezvous trials of three Soyuz craft in Earth orbit	USSR	Shonin, Kubasov	11.10.69
Soyuz 7	5 days. Rendezvous trials as above	USSR	Filipchenko, Volkov, Gorbatko	12.10.69
Soyuz 8	5 days. Rendezvous trials as above	USSR	Shatalov, Yeliseyev	13.10.69
Apollo 12	10 days. LM 'Intrepid' on Moon 19 and 20.11.69	USA	Conrad, Gordon, Bean	14.11.69
Apollo 13	6 days. LM 'Aquarius' used as lifeboat	USA	Lovell, Haise, Swigert	11.4.70
Soyuz 9	17 days	USSR	Sevastyanov, Nikolayev	1.6.70
Apollo 14	10 days. Landing in Fra Mauro highlands. Use of wheeled cart. Exploration of Cone Crater	USA	Shepard, Mitchell, Roosa	31.1.71
Soyuz 10	2 days. Docked with Salyut but trouble with hatch prevented transfer	USSR	Rukavishnikov, Shatalov, Yeliseyev	22.4.71
Soyuz 11	24 days. Rendezvous with Salyut. Mission ended with death of cosmonauts	USSR	Dobrovolski, Volkov, Patsayev	6.6.71
Apollo 15	12 days. Landing in Apennines. Use of Lunar Roving Vehicle. Exploration of Hadley Rille	USA	Scott, Worden, Irwin	26.7.71
Apollo 16	11 days. Landing in Descartes highlands. 17-mile exploration in LRV2	USA	Young, Duke, Mattingly	16.4.72
Apollo 17	12 days. Landing in Taurus-Littrow area. Exploration in LRV3 found volcanic evidence	USA	Cernan, Evans, Schmitt	7.12.72
Skylab 2	First manned flight to Skylab space station (launched 14.5.73). Deployed sunshade to reduce internal temperature and released solar panel. Manned duration 28 days to 22.6.73	USA	Conrad, Kerwin, Weitz	25.5.73
Skylab 3	Second manned flight to Skylab space station. Manned duration 59 days to 25.9.73	USA	Bean, Lousma, Garriott	28.7.73
Soyuz 12	First Soviet manned flight for two years, tested improved Soyuz. Manned duration 2 days to 29.9.73	USSR	Lazarev, Makarov	27.9.73
Skylab 4	Final flight to Skylab space station. Manned duration 84 days to 8.2.74. Skylab finally re-entered Earth atmosphere 11.7.79	USA	Carr, Pogue, Gibson	16.11.73

Name	Activities and duration	Country	Crew	Launch date
Soyuz 13	Verification of Soyuz modifications. Manned duration 8 days to 26.12.73	USSR	Klimuk, Lebedev	18.12.73
Soyuz 14	Rendezvous and docking with Salyut 3 on 4.7.74. Manned duration 15 days to 19.7.74	USSR	Popovich, Artyukhin	3.7.74
Soyuz 15	Overshot Salyut 3 when booster over-burned. Returned in 2 days	USSR	Sarafanov, Demin	26.8.74
Soyuz 16	Successful rehearsal of ASTP mission. Manned duration 6 days to 8.12.74	USSR	Filipchenko, Rukavishnikov	2.12.74
Soyuz 17	Rendezvous and docking with Salyut 4 on 12.1.75. Manned duration 29 days to 9.2.75	USSR	Gubarev, Grechko	10.1.75
Soyuz 18	Rendezvous and docking with Salyut 4 on 25.5.75. Manned duration 63 days to 26.7.75	USSR	Klimuk, Sevastyanov	24.5.75
Soyuz 19	Apollo/Soyuz Test Project (ASTP). Docked with Apollo 18 17.7.75. Astronauts exchanged visits. Manned duration 6 days to 21.7.75	USSR	Leonov, Kubasov	15.7.75
Apollo 18	Apollo/Soyuz Test Project (ASTP). Docked with Soyuz 19 17.7.75. Astronauts exchanged visits. Manned duration 9 days to 24.7.75	USA	Stafford, Slayton, Brand	15.7.75
Soyuz 21	Rendezvous and docking with Salyut 5 on 7.7.76. Scientific and weather experiments. Manned duration 49 days to 24.8.76	USSR	Volynov, Zholobov	6.7.76
Soyuz 22	Carried multi-spectral camera for East German geology survey. Watched Norway NATO exercise. Manned duration 8 days to 23.9.76	USSR	Bykovsky, Aksyonov	15.9.76
Soyuz 23	Rendezvous with Salyut 5 on 15.10.76, failed to dock. Manned duration 2 days to 16.10.76	USSR	Zudov, Rozhdestvensky	14.10.76
Soyuz 24	Rendezvous and docking with Salyut 5 on 9.2.77. Manned duration 18 days to 25.2.77	USSR	Gorbatko, Glazkov	7.2.77
Soyuz 25	Rendezvous with Salyut 6 on 9.10.77 but docking unsuccessful. Manned duration 2 days to 11.10.77	USSR	Kovalyonok, Ryumin	9.10.77
Soyuz 26	Rendezvous and docking with Salyut 6 on 10.12.27. Spacecraft returned on 16.1.78	USSR	Romanenko, Grechko (This crew returned in Soyuz 27 after 96 days on 16.3.78)	10.12.77

Name	Activities and duration	Country	Crew	Launch date
Soyuz 27	Rendezvous and docking with Salyut 6 on 11.1.78. Spacecraft returned on 16.3.78	USSR	Dzhanibekov, Makarov (This crew returned in Soyuz 26 after 5 days on 16.1.78)	10.1.78
Soyuz 28	Rendezvous and docking with Salyut 6 on 3.3.78. Manned duration 8 days to 10.3.78	USSR	Gubarev, Remek (Czech)	2.3.78
Soyuz 29	Rendezvous and docking with Salyut 6 on 17.6.78. Spacecraft returned on 3.9.78	USSR	Kovalyonok, Ivanchenkov (This crew returned in Soyuz 31 after 140 days on 2.11.78)	15.6.78
Soyuz 30	Rendezvous and docking with Salyut 6 on 27.6.78. Manned duration 6 days to 5.7.78	USSR	Klimuk, Giermaszewski (Polish)	27.6.78
Soyuz 31	Rendezvous and docking with Salyut 6 on 27.8.78. Spacecraft returned on 2.11.78	USSR	Bykovsky, Jähn (E. German) (This crew returned in Soyuz 29 after 7 days on 3.9.78)	26.8.78
Soyuz 32	Rendezvous and docking with Salyut 6 on 25.2.79. Spacecraft returned unmanned 13.6.79	USSR	Lyakhov, Ryumin (This crew returned in Soyuz 34 after 175 days on 19.8.79)	25.2.79
Soyuz 33	Rendezvous with Salyut 6 on 10.4.79, but docking unsuccessful. Manned duration 2 days to 12.4.79	USSR	Rukavishnikov, Ivanov (Bulgarian)	10.4.79
Soyuz 34	(Launched unmanned. Rendezvous and docking with Salyut 6 on 8.6.79. Returned with Lyakhov and Ryumin on 19.8.79)			
Soyuz 35	Rendezvous and docking with Salyut 6 on 10.4.80. Spacecraft returned on 3.6.80	USSR	Popov, Ryumin (This crew returned on Soyuz 37 after 185 days on 11.10.80)	9.4.80
Soyuz 36	Rendezvous and docking with Salyut 6 on 27.5.80. Spacecraft returned on 31.7.80	USSR	Kubasov, Farkash (Hungarian) (This crew returned in Soyuz 35 after 7 days on 3.6.80)	26.5.80
Soyuz T-2	Rendezvous and docking with Salyut 6 on 6.6.80. Manned duration 4 days to 9.6.80	USSR	Malyshev, Aksyonov	5.6.80
Soyuz 37	Rendezvous and docking with Salyut 6 on 24.7.80. Spacecraft returned on 11.10.80	USSR	Gorbatko, Pham Tuan (Vietnamese) (This crew returned in Soyuz 36 after 8 days on 31.7.80)	23.7.80
Soyuz 38	Rendezvous and docking with Salyut 6 on 19.9.80. Manned duration 8 days to 26.9.80	USSR	Romanenko, Mendez (Cuban)	18.9.80
Soyuz T-3	Rendezvous and docking with Salyut 6 on 28.11.80. Manned duration 13 days to 10.12.80	USSR	Kizim, Makarov, Strekalov (First 3-man crew since June 1971)	27.11.80
Soyuz T-4	Rendezvous and docking with Salyut 6 on 13.3.81. Manned duration 75 days to 26.5.81	USSR	Kovalyonok, Savinykh (100th person in space)	12.3.81

Name	Activities and duration	Country	Crew	Launch date
Soyuz 39	Rendezvous and docking with Salyut 6 on 22.3.81. Manned duration 8 days to 30.3.81	USSR	Dzhanibekov, Gurragcha (Mongolian)	22.3.81
Space Shuttle *Columbia* STS 1	2 days 6 hr 21 min. First space vehicle to land back as a winged aircraft and to be reusable	USA	Young, Crippen	12.4.81
Soyuz 40	Rendezvous and docking with Salyut 6 on 15.5.81. Manned duration 8 days to 22.5.81	USSR	Popov, Prunariu (Romanian)	14.5.81
Space Shuttle *Columbia* STS 2	2 days 6 hr 13 min. Carried Osta-1 scientific experiment, which failed to separate. Landed back at Edwards AFB	USA	Engle, Truly	12.11.81
Space Shuttle *Columbia* STS 3	8 days 0 hr 5 min. Carried OSS-1. Extra day in space. Landed back at White Sands, New Mexico	USA	Lousma, Fullerton	22.3.82
Soyuz T-5	Rendezvous and docking with Salyut 7 on 14.5.82. Launched Iskra 2 amateur radio satellite on 17.5.82	USSR	Berezovoi, Lebedev	13.5.82
Soyuz T-6	Rendezvous and docking with Salyut 7 on 25.6.82. Manned duration 8 days to 2.7.82	USSR	Dzhanibekov, Ivanchenkov, Chrétien (French)	24.6.82
Space Shuttle *Columbia* STS 4	7 days 1 hr 9 min. Landed back at Edwards AFB 4.7.82	USA	Mattingly, Hartsfield	27.6.82
Soyuz T-7	Rendezvous and docking with Salyut 7 on 20.8.82. Manned duration 8 days to 27.8.82	USSR	Popov, Serebrov, Savitskaya (2nd Soviet woman cosmonaut) (This crew returned in Soyuz T-5)	19.8.82
Space Shuttle *Columbia* STS 5	Deployed SBS-C and Telesat-E. Landed back at Edwards AFB 16.11.82. 5 days	USA	Brand, Overmyer, Lenoir, Allen	11.11.82
Space Shuttle *Challenger* STS 6	Deployed TDRS-1. Landed back at Edwards AFB 9.4.83. 5 days.	USA	Weitz, Bobko, Musgrave, Peterson	4.4.83
Soyuz T-8	Failed to dock with Salyut 7 on 21.4.83. Landed safely on 22.4.83. Manned duration 2 days	USSR	Titov, Strekalov, Serebrov	20.4.83
Space Shuttle *Challenger* STS 7	Deployed Anik C2 (Canada) and Palapa B1 (Indonesia). Released and retrieved Spas 01. Landed back at Edwards AFB 24.6.83. 6 days	USA	Crippen, Hauck, Fabian, Thagard, Ride (1st US woman astronaut)	18.6.83
Soyuz T-9	Rendezvous and docking with Salyut 7 on 28.6.83. Manned duration 149 days to 23.11.83	USSR	Lyakhov, Alexandrov	27.6.83

Name	Activities and duration	Country	Crew	Launch date
Space Shuttle *Challenger* STS 8	Deployed Insat 1B (India). Landed back at Edwards AFB 5.9.83. 6 days. First night landing	USA	Truly, Brandenstein, D. Gardner, Bluford, W. Thornton	30.8.83
Space Shuttle *Challenger* STS 9	First Spacelab mission. Landed back at Edwards AFB 8.12.82. 10 days	USA	Young, Shaw, Parker, Garriott, Lichtenberg, Merbold (German)	28.11.83
Space Shuttle *Challenger* STS 41B	Deployed Westar 6 and Palapa 4. Landed back at Kennedy Space Centre 11.2.84. 8 days	USA	Brand, Gibson, Stewart, McCandless, McNair	3.2.84
Soyuz T-10	Rendezvous and docking with Salyut 7 on 9.2.84. Manned duration 237 days to 2.10.84	USSR	Kizim, Solovyov, Atkov	8.2.84
Soyuz T-11	Rendezvous and docking with Salyut 7 on 4.4.84. Manned duration 7 days to 11.4.84	USSR	Malyshev, Strekalov, Sharma (Indian)	3.4.84
Space Shuttle *Challenger* STS 41C	Deployed LDEF. Landed back at Edwards AFB on 13.4.84. 7 days	USA	Crippen, Hart, van Hoften, G. Nelson, Scobee	6.4.84
Soyuz T-12	Rendezvous and docking with Salyut 7 on 18.7.84. Manned duration 11 days to 29.7.84	USSR	Dzhanibekov, Savitskaya (1st woman to walk in space), Volk	17.7.84
Space Shuttle *Discovery* STS 41D	Deployed SBS 4, Leasat 2 (Syncom IV-2) and Telstar 3C. Landed back at Edwards AFB 5.9.84. 6 days	USA	Hartsfield, Coats, Resnik, Hawley, Mullane, C. Walker	30.8.84
Space Shuttle *Challenger* STS 41G	Deployed ERBS. Landed back at Cape Canaveral 13.10.84. 8 days	USA	Crippen, Sullivan, Leestma, McBride, Ride, Scully-Power, Garneau (Canadian)	5.10.84
Space Shuttle *Discovery* STS 51A	Deployed Telesat 8 (Anik D2) and Leasat 1 (Syncom IV-1). Landed back at Cape Canaveral 16.11.84. 8 days.	USA	Allen, A. Fisher, D. Gardner, D. Walker, Hauck	8.11.84
Space Shuttle *Discovery* STS 51C	Deployed USA 8 military satellite. Landed back at Cape Canaveral 27.1.85. 3 days	USA	Mattingly, Shriver, Onizuka, Buchli, Payton	24.1.85
Space Shuttle *Discovery* STS 51D	Deployed Anik C1 (Telesat 9) and Syncom IV-3. Landed back at Cape Canaveral 19.4.85. 7 days	USA	Bobko, Williams, Griggs, Seddon, Hoffman, C. Walker, Garn	12.4.85
Space Shuttle *Challenger* STS 51B	Deployed Nusat small satellite. Landed back at Edwards AFB 6.5.85. 7 days	USA	Overmyer, Gregory, Lind, W. Thornton, Wang, Thagard, van den Berg	29.4.85
Soyuz T-13	Rendezvous and docking with Salyut 7 on 8.6.85. Manned duration 112 days to 26.9.85. Dzhanibekov returned 25.9.85 with Grechko in Soyuz T-13	USSR	Dzhanibekov, Savinykh	6.6.85

Name	Activities and duration	Country	Crew	Launch date
Space Shuttle *Discovery* STS 51G	Deployed Morelos 1, Arabsat 1B, Telstar 3D and Spartan 1 satellites. Landed back at Edwards AFB 24.6.85. 7 days	USA	Brandenstein, Creighton, Fabian, Lucid, Nagel, Baudry (French), Al Saud (Saudi Arabian)	17.6.85
Space Shuttle *Challenger* STS 51F	Deployed Plasma Diagnostics Package (PDP). Landed back at Edwards AFB 6.8.85. 8 days	USA	Fullerton, Musgrave, England, Bartoe, Bridges, Henize, Acton	29.7.85
Space Shuttle *Discovery* STS 51I	Deployed Aussat 1, ASC 1 and Syncom IV-4 satellites. Landed back at Edwards AFB 3.9.85. 7 days	USA	Engle, Covey, van Hoften, G. Nelson, W. Fisher, Lounge	27.8.85
Soyuz T-14	Rendezvous and docking with Salyut 7 on 19.9.85. Volkov, Vasyutin and Savinykh returned 23.11.85 in Soyuz T-14	USSR	Vasyutin, Grechko, Volkov	17.9.85
Space Shuttle *Atlantis* STS 51J	Deployed USA 11 and USA 12 military communications satellites. Landed back at Edwards AFB 7.10.85. 4 days	USA	Bobko, Grabe, Hilmers, Stewart, Pailes	3.10.85
Space Shuttle *Challenger* STS 61A	Spacelab mission. Deployed GLOMR satellite. Landed back at Edwards AFB 6.11.85. 7 days	USA	Hartsfield, Nagel, Bluford, Buchli, Dunbar, Furrer (German), Messerschmid (German), Ockels (Dutch)	30.10.85
Space Shuttle *Atlantis* STS 61B	Deployed Morelos 2, Aussat 2, RCA Satcom K2 satellites and OEX target. Landed back at Edwards AFB 3.12.85. 7 days	USA	Shaw, O'Connor, Spring, Cleave, Ross, C. Walker, Neri (Mexican)	27.11.85
Space Shuttle *Columbia* STS 61C	Deployed Satcom K1 commercial communications satellite. Landed back at Edwards AFB 18.1.86. 6 days	USA	Gibson, Bolden, Hawley, G. Nelson, Cenker, Chang-Diaz, W. Nelson	12.1.86
Space Shuttle *Challenger* STS 51L	Destroyed in explosion 73 seconds after launch due to O-ring seal failure	USA	Scobee, Smith, McNair, Onizuka, Jarvis, McAuliffe, Resnik, all perished	28.1.86
Soyuz T-15	Rendezvous and docking with Mir on 15.3.86. Spacecraft returned 16.7.86	USSR	Kizim, Solovyov	13.3.86
Soyuz TM-2	Rendezvous and docking with Mir 49 hr 50 min after entering orbit. Romanenko set duration record of 326 days 11 hr 37 min 59 sec. Laveikin returned early because of heart problem. (TM-1 was unmanned test flight.)	USSR	Romanenko, Laveikin	5.2.87

Name	Activities and duration	Country	Crew	Launch date
Soyuz TM-3	Rendezvous and docking with Mir 28.7.87. Viktorenko and Faris completed flight of 7 days 23 hr 4 min 5 sec, returning in TM-2 with Laveikin.	USSR	Viktorenko, Alexandrov, Faris (Syrian)	22.7.87
Soyuz TM-4	Rendezvous and docking with Mir 22.12.87. Titov and Manarov went on to set new duration record with world's first one-year spaceflight. Levchenko, training as shuttle pilot, returned in TM-3 with Romanenko and Alexandrov (USSR) after 7-day flight.	USSR	Titov, Manarov, Levchenko	21.12.87
Soyuz TM-5	Rendezvous and docking with Mir 9.6.88. Crew returned in TM-4 after 9 days 20 hr 10 min. Alexandrov second Bulgarian in space.	USSR	Solovyov, Savinkyh, Alexandrov (Bulgarian)	7.6.88
Soyuz TM-6	Rendezvous and docking with Mir 31.8.88. Lyakhov and Mohmand returned in TM-5 after 8 days 20 hr 27 min. Polyakov stayed to monitor health of Titov and Manarov.	USSR	Lyakhov, Polyakov, Mohmand (Afghan)	29.8.88
Space Shuttle Discovery STS Mission 26	First post-Challenger Shuttle flight. Deployed TDRS-3 data-relay satellite. Landed at Edwards AFB 3.10.88. 4 days 1 hr.	USA	Hauck, Covey, Lounge, Hilmers, G. Nelson	29.9.88
Soyuz TM-7	Rendezvous and docking with Mir 28.11.88. Chrétien performed first non-Soviet, non-US EVA 9.12.88 and returned in TM-6 with Titov and Manarov 21.12.88. Volkov, Krikalev and Polyakov returned in TM-7 27.4.89	USSR	Volkov, Krikalev, Chrétien (French)	26.11.88
Space Shuttle Atlantis STS Mission 27	Deployed Lacrosse reconnaissance satellite. Landed at Edwards AFB 6.12.88. 4 days 9 hr 6 min.	USA	Gibson, G. Gardner, Ross, Mullane, Shepherd	2.12.88
Space Shuttle Discovery STS Mission 29	Deployed TDRS-4 communications relay satellite, performed Space Station radiator test. Landed at Edwards AFB 18.3.89. 4 days 23 hr 39 min.	USA	Coats, Blaha, Bagian, Buchli, Springer	13.3.89

Name	Activities and duration	Country	Crew	Launch date
Space Shuttle *Atlantis* STS Mission 30	Deployed Magellan Venus radar mapper. Landed at Edwards AFB 8.5.89. 4 days	USA	D. Walker, Grabe, Thagard, Cleave, Lee	4.5.89
Space Shuttle *Columbia* STS Mission 28	Deployed Defence Department KH-12 Ikon reconnaissance satellite. Landed at Edwards AFB 13.8.89. 5 days 2 hr.	USA	Shaw, Richards, Leestma, Adamson, Brown	8.8.89
Soyuz TM-8	Rendezvous and docking with Mir 7.9.89 Installed Kvant 2 module. First Soviet manned manoeuvring unit flight, 1.2.90. Viktorenko and Serebrov returned in TM-8 19.2.90 after 166 days.	USSR	Viktorenko, Serebrov	6.9.89
Space Shuttle *Atlantis* STS Mission 34	Deployed Galileo Jupiter probe. Landed at Edwards AFB 23.10.89. 4 days 23 hr 41 min.	USA	Williams, McCulley, Lucid, Baker, Chang-Diaz	18.10.89
Space Shuttle *Discovery* STS Mission 33	Deployed Magnum Defence Department sigint satellite. Landed at Edwards AFB 27.11.89. 5 days 0 hr 7 min 32 sec.	USA	Gregory, Blaha, Carter, Musgrave, K. Thornton	22.11.89
Space Shuttle *Columbia* STS Mission 32	Deployed Leasat 5 US Navy communications satellite. Retrieved Long Duration Exposure Facility. Landed at Edwards AFB 20.1.90. 10 days 21 hr 0 min 36 sec. Shuttle record.	USA	Brandenstein, Wetherbee, Dunbar, Low, Ivins	9.1.89
Soyuz TM-9	Rendezvous and docking with Mir 13.2.90. Solovyov and Balandin returned in TM-9 9.8.90 after 198-day flight.	USSR	Solovyov, Balandin	11.2.90
Space Shuttle *Atlantis* STS Mission 36	Deployed Defence Department AFP-731 reconn/ sigint satellite. Landed at Edwards AFB 4.3.90. 4 days 10 hr 19 min 43 sec.	USA	Creighton, Casper, Hilmers, Mullane, Thuot	28.2.90
Space Shuttle *Discovery* STS Mission 31	Deployed Hubble Space Telescope. Record Shuttle altitude of 331 nm. Landed at Edwards AFB 29.4.90. 5 days.	USA	Shriver, Bolden, Hawley, McCandless, Sullivan	24.4.90
Soyuz TM-10	Rendezvous and docking with Mir 3.8.90. Landed with Japanese cosmonaut Akiyama 10.12.90 after 130 days 19 hr.	USSR	Manakov, Strekalov	1.8.90
Space Shuttle *Discovery* STS Mission 41	Launched Ulysses solar probe. Landed at Edwards AFB 10.10.90. 4 days 2 hr 10 min 4 sec.	USA	Richards, Cabana, Shepherd, Melnick Akers	6.10.90

Name	Activities and duration	Country	Crew	Launch date
Space Shuttle *Atlantis* STS Mission 38	Defence Department mission, deployed AFP-658 elint(?) satellite. Landed at Cape Canaveral 20.11.90. 4 days 21 hr 55 min 22 sec.	USA	Covey, Culbertson, Springer, Meade, Gemar	15.11.90
Space Shuttle *Columbia* STS Mission 35	Carried Astro 1 payload of ultra-violet telescopes and Broad-Band X-Ray Telescope. Third-longest Shuttle flight. Landed at Edwards AFB 10.12.90. 8 days 23 hr 5 min 8 sec.	USA	Brand, G. Gardner, Lounge, Hoffman, Parker, Parise, Durrance	2.12.90
Soyuz TM-11	Rendezvous and docking with Mir 4.12.90. After 7 days 22 hr journalist Akiyama returned in TM-10 with Manakov and Strekalov 10.12.90. Afanasyev and Manarov returned in TM-11 26.5.91 after 175 days 1 hr 52 min.	USSR	Afanasyev, Manarov, Akiyama (Japanese)	2.12.90
Space Shuttle *Atlantis* STS Mission 37	Deployed Gamma Ray Observatory. Two EVAs by Ross and Apt, first US for 5 years. Landed at Edwards AFB 11.4.91. 5 days 23 hr 32 min	USA	Nagel, Cameron, Ross, Apt, Godwin	5.4.91
Space Shuttle *Discovery* STS Mission 39	US Air Force/Strategic Defence Initiative organisation payload, including Infra-red Background Signature Survey (IBSS), Cryogenic Infra-red Radiance Instrument for Shuttle (CIRRIS). Launched IBSS/SPAS (retrieved), CRO-A, B and C (chemical-release satellites). Landed at Cape Canaveral 6.5.91. 8 days 7 hr 22 min.	USA	Coats, Hammond, Harbaugh, McMonagle, Bluford, Hieb, Veach	28.4.91
Soyuz TM-12/ Juno	First British manned spaceflight, first British woman. Rendezvous and docking with Mir 20.5.91. After 7 days 21 hr 15 min Sharman returned in TM-11 with Afanasyev and Manarov 26.5.91. Artsyebarsky returned in TM-12 10.10.91 after 144 days 15 hr 22 min; he was accompanied by TM-13 crew Aubakirov and Viehbock. Krikalev returned in TM-13 25.3.92 after 310 days 20 hr; he was accompanied by Volkov and Flade (launced in TM-14).	USSR	Artsyebarsky, Krikalev, Sharman (British)	18.5.91

Name	Activities and duration	Country	Crew	Launch date
Space Shuttle *Columbia* STS Mission 40	Spacelab mission Spacelab Life Sciences 1 (SLS-1). Landed at Edwards AFB 14.6.91. 9 days 2 hr 14 min.	USA	O'Connor, Gutierrez, Bagian, Seddon, Gaffney, Jernigan Hughes-Fulford	5.6.91
Space Shuttle *Atlantis* STS Mission 43	Deployed TDRS-5, tested Space Station radiator. Landed at Cape Canaveral 11.8.91. 8 days 21 hr 21 min.	USA	Blaha, M. Baker, Lucid, Low, Adamson	2.8.91
Space Shuttle *Discovery* STS Mission 48	Deployed Upper Atmosphere Research Satellite. Manoeuvred to avoid old rocket debris. Landed at Edwards AFB 18.9.91. 5 days 8 hr 27 min	USA	Creighton, Reightler, Buchli, M. Brown, Gemar	12.9.91
Soyuz TM-13 AustroMir	Rendezvous and docking with Mir 4.10.91. After 7 days 22 hr 13 min Aubakirov and Viehboeck returned in TM-12 with Artsyebarsky 10.10.91. Volkov due to return in TM-13 25.3.92.	USSR	Volkov, Aubakirov, (Kazakh), Viehboeck (Austrian)	2.10.91
Space Shuttle *Atlantis* STS Mission 44	Deployed DSP-16 early-warning satellite, carried out military Earth-observation trials. Landed at Edwards AFB 1.12.91. 6 days 22 hr 50 min.	USA	Gregory, Henricks, Musgrave, Runco, James Voss, Hennan	24.11.91
Space Shuttle *Discovery* STS Mission 42	International Microgravity 1 (IML-1). Landed at Edwards AFB 30.1.92. Duration 8 days 1 hr 14 min	USA	Grabe, Oswald, Hilmers, Thagard, Readdy, Bondar (Canadian) Merbold (German)	22.1.92
Soyuz TM-14/ Mir 92	Rendezvous and docking with Mir 19.3.92. After 7 days Flade returned in TM-13 with Krikalev and Volkov 25.3.92. Viktorenko and Kaleri returned in TM-15 27.7.92 after 146 days.	USSR	Viktorenko, Kaleri, Flade (German)	17.3.92
Space Shuttle *Atlantis* STS Mission 45	Atmospheric Laboratory for Applications and Sciences (Atlas) 1. Landed at Cape Canaveral 2.4.92. Duration 8 days 22 hr 9 min	USA	Bolden, Duffy, Sullivan, Foale, Leestma, Frimout (Belgian), Lichtenberg	24.3.92
Space Shuttle *Endeavour* STS Mission 49	Intelsat VI-F3 rescue. EVA duration record; first simultaneous EVA by three astronauts. Landed at Edwards AFB 16.5.92. Duration 8 days 21 hr 17 min	USA	Brandenstein, Chilton, Thuot, K. Thornton, Hieb, Akers, Melnick	7.5.92

Name	Activities and duration	Country	Crew	Launch date
Space Shuttle Columbia STS Mission 50	US Microgravity Laboratory 1. First flight with Extended Duration Orbiter (EDO) pallet; Shuttle duration record. Landed at Cape Canaveral 9.7.92. Duration 13 days 19 hr 30 min	USA	Richards, Bowersox, Meade, E. Baker, Dunbar, DeLucas, Trinh	25.6.92
Soyuz TM-15 Antares	Rendezvous and docking with Mir 29.7.92. Tognini returned in TM-14 with Viktorenko and Kaleri 10.8.92 after 14 days. Solovyov and Avdeyev returned in TM-15 1.2.93 after 190 days	USSR	Solovyov, Avdeyev, Tognini (French)	27.7.92
Space Shuttle Atlantis STS Mission 46	Deployed TSS-1 Tethered Satellite (reel mechanism jammed), Eureca 1. Landed at Cape Canaveral 8.8.92. Duration 7 days 23 hr 16 min.	USA	Shriver, A. Allen, Chang-Diaz, Nicollier (Swiss), Hoffman, Ivins, Malerba (Italian)	31.7.92
Space Shuttle Endeavour STS Mission 47	Spacelab J. Landed at Cape Canaveral 20.9.92. Duration 7 days 22 hr 31 min	USA	Gibson, C. Brown, Apt, Davis, Jemison, Lee, Mohri (Japanese)	12.9.92
Space Shuttle Columbia STS Mission 52	Deployed Lageos 2. Landed at Cape Canaveral 1.11.92. Duration 9 days 20 hr 56 min	USA	Wetherbee, M. Baker, Shepherd, Jernigan, Veach, MacLean (Canadian)	22.10.92
Space Shuttle Discovery STS Mission 53	Defence Department mission, deployed DOD-1 satellite. Landed at Edwards AFB 9.12.92. Duration 7 days 7 hr 19 min	USA	D. Walker, Cabana, Bluford, James Voss, Clifford	2.12.92
Space Shuttle Endeavour STS Mission 54	Deployed TDRS-6 data relay satellite. Landed at Cape Canaveral 19.1.93. Duration 5 days 0 hr 23 min	USA	Casper, McMonagle, Harbaugh, Runco, Helms	13.1.93
Soyuz TM-16	Rendezvous and docking with Mir 26.1.93. Crew due to occupy Mir for six months; relieved Solvyov and Avdeyev, who returned in TM-15 1.2.93 after 190 days	USSR	Manakov, Polishchuk	24.1.93

Continued from page G32

transmit any data. The Americans put Viking 1's Mars lander on the surface in July 1976.

The spectacular success of NASA's Voyager 1 space probe in November 1980 underlines best what can be achieved by space probes. Voyager 1 flew within 4,500 km of Titan, Saturn's largest moon, and found its atmosphere to be composed of nitrogen rather than methane, as had been supposed. It also flew close to

Saturn's rings and sent back superb photographs which revealed that they are not made up of broad bands but of hundreds of ringlets, some interwoven. Voyager 2's pictures in August 1981 were even more spectacular.

During 1983 the Soviet Union launched its Venus 15 (June 2, 1983) and Venus 16 (June 7, 1983) probes, which went into orbit around the planet in October 1983 to map its surface by radar. The Soviet Vega 1 and Vega 2 probes were launched on December 15 and 27, 1984, respectively. They flew close to Halley's Comet in March 1986. The European Space Agency's Giotto, a Halley's Comet probe, was launched by Ariane 1 on July 2, 1985, and Japan's Suisei (Planet A), also a Halley's Comet probe, was launched by Mu-3S on August 18, 1985. Both completed their missions in 1986. Giotto passed within 540 km of the comet's nucleus on March 14, 1986. It survived the encounter and returned much scientific information. One of the most recent planetary probes is the US Mars Observer, launched in September 1992 and due to reach the planet in August 1993.

Space travel Exploration of other planets by man began in 1969 with the United States' Apollo 11 mission to the Moon. The complete success of Apollo 11 set the stage for more extensive lunar exploration. Between then and 1972 there were a further five successful Apollo landings, bringing to 12 the total of astronauts to have set foot on the lunar surface.

Following the failure of their own unpublicised manned lunar programme the Soviets decided to confine themselves to what proved to be a very successful series of unmanned probes.

The most likely target for the next manned landing on another body in the Solar System is Mars. The very successful series of Soviet long-duration flights in Earth orbit is believed to have been directed in part at demonstrating the ability of cosmonauts to tolerate the long periods of weightlessness and confinement demanded by a journey to Mars.

Specific fuel consumption A measure of engine efficiency based on the rate of fuel consumption divided by the power supplied.

Stall Separation of *boundary layer* (q.v.) from upper surface of *aerofoil* (q.v.), resulting in large loss of *lift* (q.v.). Generally occurs at low airspeed or high *angle of attack* (q.v.).

Starboard The right-hand side of an aircraft as seen by the pilot looking forward. Indicated by a green wingtip light.

Strategic Defence Initiative (SDI) The United States is developing satellite and ground-based systems designed to destroy enemy nuclear missiles soon after launch. Various means of attacking the missiles and their warheads are being investigated, including lasers, particle beams and high-speed projectiles.

Supercritical wing Wing in which lift is generated over whole upper surface instead of close to leading edge.

Supersonic flight Flight at speeds greater than Mach 1. It is characterised by a sharp increase in drag and a rearwards shift of the centre of pressure of the wing, leading to significant changes in longitudinal stability. These effects are contained by the adoption of sweep (forwards or back) and thin-section aerofoils. See also *Shock wave*.

Sweepback Rearwards sweep of aerofoil surface, as seen from above. Measured relative to longitudinal axis, usually at quarter-chord line.

Sweepforward Forwards sweep of aerofoil surface, as seen from above. Measured relative to longitudinal axis, usually at quarter-chord line. Grumman's forward-swept-wing X-29 experimental aircraft, which first flew on December 14, 1984, proved the aerodynamic advantages of this type of configuration. These include a 35% drag reduction at transonic speeds.

Thermal imaging A new technology gaining rapid acceptance for sensors for use in military aircraft. It enables objects to be detected at night or through cloud or mist, with a clarity far better than is achieved by even the most advanced radar. Thermal imaging systems receive heat from an object and do not transmit anything themselves. Unlike radar, therefore, a thermal imager is totally undetectable by opposing forces. Thermal imaging can also be used for mapping, resource surveillance and in numerous land and sea-based applications, both civil and military.

The thermal radiation detected by an imager is seen by the human eye only when a body becomes red-hot. Advanced thermal imagers can detect differences in temperature as small as 0.5°C, allowing a very detailed picture to be built up. Such images can be recorded on film for later analysis—to detect enemy installations or troop movements, for example—by intelligence teams.

Transceiver Radio transmitter/receiver.

Turbofan Development of the jet engine in which a larger amount of air than is needed for combustion is taken in and mixed with the hot exhaust stream. The exhaust stream becomes heavier and slower so that less energy is wasted in *turbulence* (q.v.). The result is lower fuel consumption and reduced noise.

Turbojet Basic jet engine with compressor, combustion chamber, turbine and propulsive nozzle. See *Jet propulsion*.

Turboprop Powerplant in which a propeller is driven by a gas turbine. Turboprops, vibrationless and powerful, have proved successful in airliners such as the Fokker 50 and military transports such as the Lockheed C-130 Hercules. Advanced turboprops are now being developed.

Turboshaft Gas turbine used to drive a shaft (as opposed to the propeller of a turboprop) which powers a helicopter rotor via a reduction gearbox.

Turbulence Air moves in two states: *laminar flow* (composed of orderly streams) or *turbulent flow* (a disorderly mass of small swirls). Whether flow is laminar or turbulent generally depends on the value of the *Reynolds Number*, a dimensionless function of the size of the object, the viscosity of the air and the velocity of flow. Turbulent flow absorbs much more energy than laminar flow, so aircraft designers try to prevent it occurring. It begins in the *boundary layer* (q.v.), a thin skin of relatively stationary air close to the surface of the aeroplane. A promising system for preventing turbulence is to suck this layer away through fine holes in the wing skin.

Types of aircraft, some outstanding modern

FRANCE

Dassault Mirage IIIE Delta-wing fighter-bomber/intruder. One Snecma Atar 9C turbojet rated at 60·8 kN (13,670 lb) thrust with reheat. Maximum speed Mach 2·2.

Dassault Mirage F.1 Swept-wing fighter/attack aircraft. One Snecma Atar 9K-50 turbojet rated at 70·6 kN (15,873 lb) thrust with reheat.

Dassault Mirage 2000 Delta-wing interceptor, air-superiority fighter and attack aircraft. One Snecma M53-5 turbofan rated at 88·3 kN (19,840 lb) thrust with reheat. Maximum speed over Mach 2·3. Mirage 2000N carries ASMP nuclear missile. Latest version is 2000S two-seat conventional strike aircraft, now on offer to export customers.

Dassault Rafale France's next-generation combat aircraft, designed to replace Air Force Jaguars and Mirage IIIs, Vs and F.1s and Navy Crusaders and Etendard IVs. Air Force version is called Rafale C, naval variant is Rafale M. Features fly-by-wire, giving high manoeuvrability, advanced composite structure and twin Snecma M88-2 turbofans. Maximum speed Mach 2.

Dassault Falcon 900 Trijet intercontinental business aircraft seating up to 19 passengers. Latest version is 900B, with more powerful Garrett TFE731-5B turbofans and improved avionics.

INTERNATIONAL

Airbus A300 Wide-bodied medium-range airliner built by consortium comprising Aérospatiale (France), British Aerospace, CASA (Spain) and Deutsche Aerospace (Germany). Two US General Electric CF6-50C turbofans. Seats up to 320 passengers. A310 has shorter cabin for up to 280 passengers. A300–600R is extended-range version.

Airbus A320 Advanced-technology short/medium-range single-aisle airliner. Seats up to 179 passengers, typical range

Airbus A320

3,576 km (2,222 miles). Powered by two CFM56-5 or IAE V2500 turbofans rated at 111·2 kN (25,000 lb) thrust each.

Airbus A330/A340 New family of long-range airliners, with two and four engines respectively. A340 first flew in October 1991, A330 in November 1992.

Concorde Supersonic transport designed and produced by British Aerospace and Aérospatiale of France. Faster than Mach 2. Four Rolls-Royce Olympus 593 engines.

Panavia Tornado Multi-role combat aircraft, powered by two Turbo-Union RB.199-34R-2 turbofans, each of 71 kN (16,000 lb) thrust with reheat. Maximum speed 2,337 km/hr (1,320 mph) at altitude. Produced by consortium of Aeritalia (Italy), MBB (West Germany) and British Aerospace. Around 1,000 ordered for air forces of Britain, Italy, Germany and Saudi Arabia. Interdictor/strike, air defence and electronic warfare variants. Tornados saw action with the British, Italian and Saudi air forces in the 1991 Gulf War, delivering anti-runway munitions, anti-radar missiles and laser-guided and conventional bombs.

NETHERLANDS

Fokker 50 Development of F.27 Friendship twin-turboprop airliner. Can carry up to 58 passengers over typical range of 1,000 km (625 miles). Powered by two P&WC PW125B turboprops, each rated at 1,678 kW (2,250 shp).

Fokker 100 Development of F.28 Fellowship twinjet short/medium-range airliner. Can carry up to 119 passengers over typical range of 2,400 km (1,500 miles). Powered by two Rolls-Royce Tay Mk 650-15 turbofans, each rated at 67 kN (15,000 lb).

RUSSIA

Antonov An-26 Curl Twin-turboprop short-haul passenger transport. Two Ivchenko AI-24VT engines. Wing span 29·20 m (95 ft 9½ in). Carries up to 5,500 kg (12,125 lb) of cargo. An-32 Cline is developed version with almost twice as much power.

Ilyushin Il-62MK Classic Long-range jet transport powered by four Soloviev D-30KU turbofans. Carries up to 174 passengers. Capable of non-stop flight from Moscow to Havana, Cuba.

Il-76T Candid   Strategic transport powered by four Soloviev D-30KP turbofans. Similar to US Lockheed Starlifter. Carries 40,000 kg (39 tons) of payload. Wing span 50·5m (165 ft 8 in).

Il-86 Camber   Wide-body medium-range airliner powered by four NK-86 turbofans. Wing span 48 m (157 ft). Carries up to 350 passengers.

Il-96-300 Long-range derivative of Il-86. Distinguished from earlier design by new wing with winglets, taller fin and Soloviev D-90A high-bypass-ratio turbofans. Carries up to 300 passengers over 7,500 km (4,660 miles). Il-96M is improved, Westernised version.

Mikoyan MiG-29 Fulcrum   Air combat/attack fighter powered by two Tumansky RD-33 turbofan engines. Carries six AA-10 missiles. Wing span 12 m (39 ft $4\frac{1}{2}$ in).

MiG-31 Foxhound   Two-seat interceptor designed to counter low-flying bombers and cruise missiles. Derived from earlier MiG-25 Foxbat. Maximum speed Mach 2·83, maximum endurance with aerial refuelling more than six hours.

Sukhoi Su-25 Frogfoot   Twin-engined ground attack air-

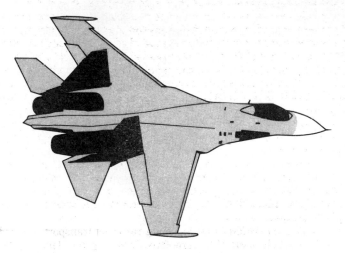

Sukhoi Su-27

craft. Two Tumansky R-13 turbojets. 23 mm gun and 10 weapon pylons.

Su-27 Flanker   Highly manoeuvrable long-range air-superiority fighter, comparable with US F-15 Eagle. Two Tumansky R-32 turbofans, each rated at about 133 kN (30,000 lb) thrust with afterburning. One 30 mm gun and up to 10 AAMs.

Tupolev Tu-154M Careless   Medium/long-range transport powered by three 103 kN (23,150 lb) thrust Soloviev D-30KU turbofans. Carries up to 180 passengers.

Tu-160 Blackjack   Variable-geometry strategic bomber comparable with US B-1B. About 30 are believed to be in service. Maximum speed Mach 2. Armed with 3,000 km-range AS-15 Kent cruise missiles.

UNITED KINGDOM

BAe RJ70, RJ80, RJ85, RJ100, RJ115 Family of four-turbofan regional airliners based on the BAe 146 and seating between 70 and 120 passengers. A twin-engined variant seating up to 139 passengers is being studied under the designation RJX.

BAe Jaguar Tactical support aircraft powered by two Rolls-Royce/Turboméca Adour Mk 102 turbofans, each of 32·5 kN (7,305 lb) thrust with reheat. Maximum speed Mach 1·5 at 11,000 m (36,000 ft). Saw action with British and French air forces in 1991 Gulf War. Hindustan Aeronautics continues to licence-build Jaguars for the Indian Air Force.

BAe Jetstream 31 and 41 Twin-turboprop commuter airliners, seating 19 and 29 respectively. The Jetstream 41 first flew in September 1991 and is now being delivered to airlines in Europe and the USA

BAe Harrier V/STOL close support and armed reconnaissance aircraft. Has two pairs of rotating nozzles which direct thrust downwards for lift or aft for propulsion. Rolls-Royce Pegasus 103 of 95.6 kN (21,500 lb) thrust. Maximum level speed over 1,186 km/hr (737 mph). Harrier GR.5 is the RAF version of US Marine Corps AV-8B Harrier II. A radar-equipped version of the AV-8B, the Harrier II Plus, is being acquired by Italy, Spain and the US Marine Corps. GR.7 is RAF night attack version.

BAe Hawk Two-seat basic and advanced jet trainer with air

defence and ground attack capability. One Rolls-Royce/Turboméca Adour Mk 151 non-afterburning turbofan of 23·13 kN (5,200 lb) thrust. Maximum level speed 1,038 km/hr (645 mph). Ordered by air forces of Britain, Finland, Kenya, Indonesia, Zimbabwe, Dubai, Abu Dhabi, Kuwait, Saudi Arabia, Switzerland, South Korea, Oman, United Arab Emirates and Malaysia, and US Navy (as T-45A Goshawk). Hawk 100 is two-seat ground attack/trainer, Hawk 200 is single-seat attack variant.

BAe Nimrod MR.2 Maritime reconnaissance aircraft developed from Comet first-generation jet airliner. Four Rolls-Royce Spey Mk 250 turbofans of 54 kN (12,140 lb) thrust each.

BAe 125-800 Twin-jet executive transport powered by 19·13 kN (4,300 lb) thrust Garrett-AiResearch TFE731-5R-1H turbofans. Seats crew of two and up to eight passengers. Maximum cruising speed 845 km/hr (525 mph). U-125A is search and rescue version for Japan. Latest 125 version is designated BAe 1000.

Pilatus Britten-Norman Islander Twin-engined light transport carrying up to ten passengers. Two 194 kW (260 bhp) Lycoming O-540 engines. Speed 274 km/hr (170 mph). Trislander is three-engined version. Turbine Islander has Allison 290 turboprops.

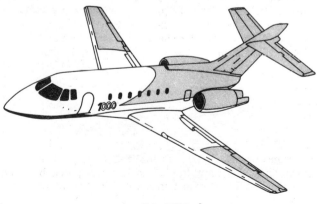

BAe 1000

Shorts 330 Widebody commuter airliner. Two 1,020 shp Pratt & Whitney of Canada PT6A-45A turboprops. Standard seating for 30 passengers. Sherpa freighter version serves with US Air Force in Europe, designated C-23A.

Shorts 360 Commuterliner with airline-standard 36-seat cabin. Two Pratt & Whitney PT6A-65R turboprops.

Shorts Tucano Two-seat basic trainer built under licence from Embraer of Brazil. RAF has ordered 130. Shorts version powered by Garrett TPE331 turboprop.

Slingsby T.67 Firefly Single-engined military primary trainer operated by Hong Kong, the Netherlands, Norway and Turkey and selected by the Canadian Armed Forces as a primary trainer and by the US Air Force for pilot trainee screening. Powered by 149kW (200 bhp) Lycoming AEIO-360.

USA

Boeing 727 Trijet airliner. Powered by three Pratt & Whitney JT8D turbofans. Stretched 727-200 seats up to 189 passengers.

Boeing 737 Twinjet airliner. Powered by JT8D turbofans. Seats up to 168 passengers. West's most numerous jet airliner.

Boeing 747 Four-jet long-range airliner nicknamed the 'Jumbo Jet'. Powered by four Pratt & Whitney JT9D, General Electric CF6 or Rolls-Royce RB.211 turbofans. Basic accommo-

Boeing 747-400

dation for 452 passengers, but capable of carrying up to 511 in extended-upper-deck versions. Latest version, with wingtip winglets and updated systems, is -400.

Boeing 757 Short-to-medium-range narrow-body jet airliner with two Rolls-Royce RB.211-535C or 535E4 or Pratt & Whitney PW2037 turbofans. 178–239 seats.

Boeing 767 Medium-range wide-body airliner. Powered by two JT9D or CF6 turbofans. Competes with Airbus A310. Seats 255 passengers.

Boeing E-3A Sentry Airborne warning and control (AWACS) aircraft based on Boeing 707 transport. Large circular radome above fuselage. Four Pratt & Whitney turbofans.

Boeing/Sikorsky RAH-66 Comanche Winner in April 1991 of the US Army's Light Helicopter competition. First flight of this combat helicopter is scheduled for 1994.

General Dynamics F-16 Lightweight air combat fighter. One Pratt & Whitney F100-PW-200 turbofan. Mach 2 + .

Grumman F-14 Tomcat Two-seat naval all-weather interceptor. Two TF30 or General Electric F110 reheated turbofans. Mach 2 + at altitude. Armed with Phoenix ultra-long-range air-to-air missiles and exceptionally capable fire-control system.

Lockheed/Boeing/General Dynamics F-22 Lightning II Winner in April 1991 of the USAF's Advanced Tactical Fighter competition, the stealthy and highly manoeuvrable F-22 will fly for the first time in 1996. Powered by two Pratt & Whitney F119 turbofans.

Lockheed C-5B Galaxy Heavy military transport. Four General

C-130 Hercules

Electric TF39 turbofans, each 183 kN (41,000 lb) thrust. Span
68 m (223 ft). Carries 101,600 kg (100 tons) of payload. Used
by USAF Military Airlift Command.

Lockheed C-130 Hercules Military transport. Four T56 turboprops. C-130K RAF version carries 128 troops. Other variants
are used for maritime patrol, search and rescue, ground attack,
electronic warfare, tanking, special operations and Antarctic
support.

McDonnell Douglas F-4 Phantom II Multi-role fighter capable
of more than Mach 2. Span 11·75 m (38·55 ft). Basic powerplant is Pratt & Whitney J79 turbojet, but Israel Aircraft
Industries is developing Super Phantom version powered by
91·2 kN (20,600 lb) thrust PW1120s; performance gains
include 15% better turn rate, 33% better climb rate.

McDonnell Douglas F-15 Eagle Air-superiority fighter. Two
Pratt & Whitney F100-PW-100 turbofans. Maximum speed
exceeds Mach 2·5.

McDonnell Douglas F/A-18 Hornet Versatile naval fighter and
attack aircraft developed for US Navy and Marine Corps and
subsequently selected by air forces of Australia, Canada,
Kuwait, Spain and Switzerland. Powered by two GE F404
turbofans rated at 71·2 kN (16,000 lb) each. Maximum level
speed Mach 1·8 + , maximum weapon load 7,710 kg (17,000
lb). Newest versions, now under development, are the F-18E
and two-seat F-18F.

McDonnell Douglas MD-80 Twin-turbofan short/medium-
range airliner. Seats up to 172 passengers. MD-90 derivative
is due to make its first flight in 1993.

McDonnell Douglas MD-11 Derived from DC-10, widebody
airliner powered by three General Electric CF6 or P&W
PW4000 turbofans. Up to 405 passengers.

Rockwell B-1B Supersonic bomber. Carries air-launched
cruise missiles (ALCMs). Four General Electric F101 reheated
turbofans.

Variable-geometry Aircraft able to alter its configuration in flight,
particularly by varying the sweepback of the wings.
Vertical take-off and landing (VTOL) Although the principal quality
of the helicopter is its ability to take off and land vertically, the
term VTOL is applied exclusively to fixed-wing aircraft which

can do likewise. Developed originally to reduce the dependence of military aircraft on conspicuous and vulnerable runways, VTOL can be achieved in various ways. One is to direct jet exhaust down for take-off and horizontally when airborne, as in the British Aerospace Harrier. Another way, used in the Short SC.1 experimental type, was to have separate engines for vertical and horizontal flight. Because vertical take-off greatly increases fuel consumption, the most usual Harrier operating method is to perform a short rolling take-off and a vertical landing (STOVL).

Wind tunnel An experimental device in which air is made to flow past model or full-scale aerofoils and aircraft. Instruments attached to the models measure lift, drag and other parameters at varying airspeeds. Modern high-speed wind tunnels can achieve speeds as high as Mach 18 for fractions of a second by means of the rapid expansion of compressed air.

Wing loading Aircraft weight divided by wing area.

A LOOK AT THE FUTURE

Until the end of the 1960s aviation progress was marked by regular great leaps forward in performance: from 200 mph biplane to 350 mph monoplane, 400 mph piston fighter to 600 mph jet, subsonic airliner to Mach 2 Concorde. But for the last 20 years the emphasis has been on less spectacular improvements which, while making aircraft more efficient, have created fewer strange new shapes in the sky.

Civil aircraft are quieter and use less fuel. Military types are more manoeuvrable, better armed, easier to fly and harder for defences to detect, thanks to 'stealth' techniques such as radar-absorbent materials, careful airframe design and low-smoke engines. Both airliners and fighters have benefited from the use of light but strong new materials, fly-by-wire controls, advanced electronics and engines giving more and more power for less and less weight.

This process continues, so much so that the next generation of long-range airliners—the McDonnell Douglas MD-12, Boeing 777 and Airbus A330 and A340—outwardly appear little different from their predecessors. But closer inspection reveals some subtle improvements intended to increase efficiency and profitability still further. Airbus and McDonnell Douglas are following Boeing's example by fitting wingtip aerofoils called winglets. Clever design means that these fin-like surfaces not only help to control the drag-inducing air vortices spilling off the wingtip, but also actually produce a small amount of thrust to contribute to that of the engines.

Other drag cures to watch for on new airliners over the next few years include 'riblets'—microscopic grooves in a plastic skin applied to the exterior of the aircraft—and laminar flow control. Drag is at its lowest when the air passes in smooth sheets over the skin of the aircraft. Called laminar flow, this condition can be encouraged by careful shaping of the wing and the use of pumps to draw air in through tiny holes in the leading edge.

Look too for plate, 'canoe' or blade-shaped satellite communications antennas on the upper fuselage. At present the shortcomings of high-frequency radio mean that airliners are effectively out of touch with the ground when they are over mid-ocean. Using the Inmarsat satellite system, passengers on a growing number of aircraft can make in-flight telephone calls to friends and business contacts all over the world.

Airliner crews will also be able to send and receive important operational information. Near-instant, reliable contact between pilots and air traffic controllers will make it possible for more aircraft to use the same airspace, so reducing congestion and delays, and for crews to save fuel by changing their routes to take advantage of favourable winds.

Developments like these, contributing to steady improvements in the efficiency and safety of air travel, look set to continue indefinitely. But the aerospace world is also gathering itself for a giant stride that will take effect early in the 21st century. A renewed interest in speed is being signalled by projects such as the proposal by Aérospatiale of France for a second-generation supersonic transport capable of carrying more than twice as many passengers as the Concorde. It would also be faster, have more range and be cheaper to operate. Japan is studying the possibility of even greater speeds, in the form of a 300-seat hypersonic (Mach 5) transport.

Most spectacular of all is America's National Aerospace Plane. Due to fly towards the end of the 1990s, NASP is being built to stimulate development of the technology needed for a true aerospacecraft, equally at home in the atmosphere or in the vacuum of space. Such a machine would be able to take off from a runway and fly straight into orbit without wastefully discarding spent stages. Alternatively, it could fly a partial orbit, allowing it to go from Britain to Australia in an hour and a half, compared with today's 24 hr.

Success will require great advances in every area: propulsion, materials, structures, control systems and avionics. Most crucial of these is the engine. To keep weight to a minimum and avoid the need to throw away a large part of the vehicle on every flight—as all space launchers currently do—the aerospacecraft will need a powerplant capable of changing the way it operates to match the huge range of conditions it will meet. For take-off and flight low in the atmosphere it will have to be a turbojet or turbofan. At higher altitudes and hypersonic speeds it will act as a ramjet, and at the edge of the atmosphere and in space it will turn into a rocket. Such powerplants are known as combined or variable-cycle engines.

An effective aerospacecraft would greatly reduce the cost of launching satellites or carrying astronauts to and from space stations. At present it costs about $50 million to put a communications satellite into orbit. A Shuttle launch, typically carrying half a dozen people, costs $250 million. Easier to launch and completely reusable, an aerospacecraft would be much cheaper. Satellites would cost less to build because they could be more readily recovered for maintenance and repair. This in turn would cut the cost of their services—communications, Earth resources and weather information, scientific data—and make their benefits more widely available to mankind.

ASTRONOMY

Astronomical measures The nearest star to the Earth (Bungula in the constellation Centaurus) is 40,000,000,000,000 km (25,000,000,000,000 miles) away. Measurements as huge as this become meaningless when given in kilometres or miles, so until recently stellar distances (distances between stars) were expressed in *light-years*. A light-year is the distance light travels in one year. The speed of light is 299,300 km or

186,000 miles per second, so a light-year represents some 9,600,000,000,000 km or 6,000,000,000,000 miles.

A newer astronomical measure of distance is the *parsec*, which is the distance at which the mean radius of the Earth's orbit would subtend an angle of 1 second. A parsec is rather more than 30,600,000,000,000 km (19,000,000,000,000 miles) or roughly 3.25 light-years.

Comets Bodies made of ice, condensed gases and solid particles which travel round the Sun in highly eccentric orbits that take them out of sight of Earth for decades at a time. The solar wind causes material to stream away from each comet, forming a characteristic 'tail'. One of the most famous comets, Halley's, was examined closely by spacecraft from Europe, Japan, the USA and USSR in 1986. Europe's Giotto came within 540 km of the comet, producing clear images of its peanut-shaped nucleus. Soviet Vega 1 and Vega 2 probes flew by on March 6 and 9, 1986, respectively.

Constellations On a cloudless night between 2,000 and 3,000 stars are visible to the unaided eye. The observable stars are divided into groups or *constellations* (a word that means 'star-groups') named for their resemblance to animals, objects and mythological figures (see pages G63–67).

Magnitude Stars are classified according to their brightness as seen from the Earth. The unit of brightness is called the *magnitude*. Stars that can be seen without the help of telescopes are of magnitude 0–6. Magnitude 0 is the brightest; each magnitude that follows is about 2·5 times less bright than the one before it.

There are four stars (given in the list on page G67) that, being brighter than magnitude 0, are given minus magnitudes.

The brightness of the Sun in this scale is −26·7, that of the Moon − 11·2.

THE CONSTELLATIONS

Those in capital letters are invisible from Great Britian

Scientific name	*English name*
Andromeda	The Chained Lady
ANTLIA	The Pump
APUS	The Bird of Paradise
Aquarius	The Water-Pourer
Aquila	The Eagle
ARA	The Altar
ARGO	Jason's Ship Argo
Aries	The Ram
Auriga	The Charioteer
Bootes	The Herdsman
Caelum	The Graving Tool
Camelopardalis	The Giraffe
Cancer	The Crab
Canes Venatici	The Hunting Dogs
Canis Major	The Great Dog
Canis Minor	The Little Dog
Capricornus	The Horned Goat
Cassiopeia	The Lady in the Chair
CENTAURUS	The Centaur
Cepheus	Cassiopeia's Consort
Cetus	The Sea Monster
CHAMAELEON	The Chameleon
CIRCINUS	The Pair of Compasses
Columba	The Dove
Coma Berenices	Berenice's Hair
CORONA AUSTRALIS	The Southern Crown
Corona Borealis	The Northern Crown
Corvus	The Crow
Crater	The Cup
CRUX	The Southern Cross
Cygnus	The Swan
Delphinus	The Dolphin
DORADO	The Goldfish
Draco	The Dragon
Equuleus	The Little Horse
ERIDANUS	The River
Fornax	The Furnace
Gemini	The Twins
GRUS	The Crane
Hercules	The Legendary Strong Man
HOROLOGIUM	The Clock

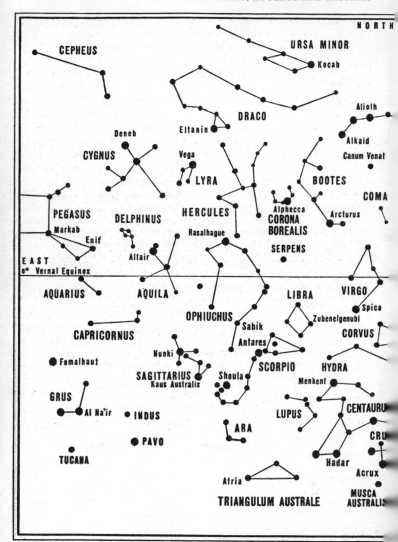

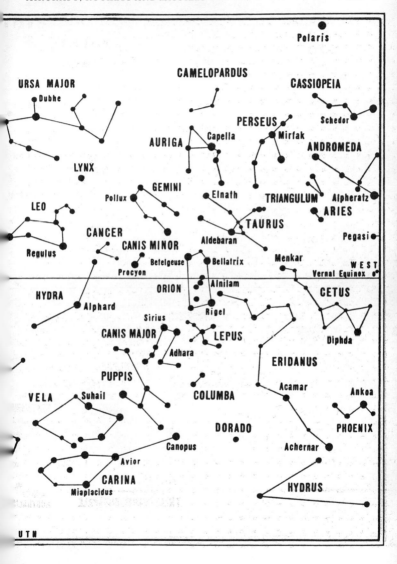

Scientific name	English name
Hydra	The Sea Serpent
HYDRUS	The Water Snake
INDUS	The Indian
Lacerta	The Lizard
Leo	The Lion
Leo Minor	The Little Lion
Lepus	The Hare
Libra	The Balance
LUPUS	The Wolf
Lynx	The Lynx
Lyra	The Lyre
MENSA	The Table Mountain
MICROSCOPIUM	The Microscope
Monoceros	The Unicorn
MUSCA	The Fly
NORMA	The Square
OCTANS	The Octant
Ophiuchus	The Serpent
Orion	The Giant Hunter
PAVO	The Peacock
Pegasus	The Winged Horse
Perseus	The Legendary Hero
PHOENIX	The Phoenix
PICTOR	The Painter's Easel
Pisces	The Fishes
Piscis Austrinus	The Southern Fish
RETICULUM	The Net
Sagitta	The Arrow
Sagittarius	The Archer
Scorpius	The Scorpion
Sculptor	The Sculptor's Workshop
Scutum	The Shield
Serpens	The Serpent
Sextans	The Sextant
Taurus	The Bull
TELESCOPIUM	The Telescope
Triangulum	The Triangle
TRIANGULUM AUSTRALE	The Southern Triangle
TUCANA	The Toucan
Ursa Major	The Great Bear
Ursa Minor	The Little Bear
Virgo	The Maiden
VOLANS	The Flying Fish
Vulpecula	The Fox with the Goose

THE TWENTY BRIGHTEST STARS

Star	Constellation	Magnitude
Sirius	Great Dog	− 1·43
CANOPUS	Jason's Ship Argo	− 0·73
RIGIL KENTAURUS	Centaur	− 0·27
Arcturus	Herdsman	− 0·06
Vega	Lyre	0·04
Capella	Charioteer	0·09
Rigel	The Giant Hunter	0·15
Procyon	Little Dog	0·37
ACHERNAR	The River Eridanus	0·53
AGENA	Centaur	0·66
Altair	Eagle	0·80
Aldebaran	Bull	0·85
ACRUX	Southern Cross	0·87
Betelgeuse	The Giant Hunter	0·90
Antares	Scorpion	0·98
Spica	Maiden	1·00
Fomalhaut	Southern Fish	1·16
Pollux	Twins	1·16
Deneb	Swan	1·26
BETA CRUCIS	Southern Cross	1·31

The Solar System The centre of the Solar System is the Sun, our Earth being one of the planets revolving round it.

THE SUN

Diameter, km/miles	1,390,500/864,000
Mass, reckoning the Earth as 1	330,000
Density, reckoning the Earth as 1	0·25
Volume, reckoning the Earth as 1	1,300,000
Force of gravity on the surface, reckoning the Earth as 1	27·7
Period of rotation on its axis	25·38 days
Speed of rotation at its equator	7,092 km/hr/4,407 mph
Surface area	12,000 times that of Earth
Mass	2,030,073,000,000,000,000,000,000,000 tonnes/ 1,998,000,000,000,000,000,000,000,000 tons
Temperature	c. 5,500°C
Height of biggest flames from the surface	460,276 km/286,000 miles

THE MOON

Diameter	3,481 km/2,163 miles
Surface area	37,970,000 sq km/14,660,000 sq miles
Mass	79,252,000,000,000,000,000 tonnes/ 78,000,000,000,000,000,000 tons
Orbital speed	3,682 km/hr/2,288 mph
Estimated temperature, day	+ 101°C
Estimated temperature, night	− 157° C
Force of gravity at surface, reckoning the Earth as 1	0·16
Time of revolution round the Earth	27 days 7 hr 43 min 11 sec
Number of visible craters	30,000 (many more on the far side of the Moon)

THE PLANETS

	Average distance from the Sun (in millions of miles/km)	Time taken to orbit Sun	Diameter (in miles/km)
Mercury	36/58	88 days	3,100/4,990
Venus	67/108	224·75 days	7,700/12,390
Earth	93/159	365·25 days	7,927/12,575
Mars	141/227	687 days	4,200/6,760
Jupiter	483/771	11·86 years	88,700/142,750
Saturn	886/1,426	29·46 years	75,100/120,860
Uranus	1,783/2,869	84·01 years	29,300/47,150
Neptune	2,793/4,485	164·79 years	27,700/44,580
Pluto	3,666/5,899	248·43 years	3,600/5,790

Relative gravitational pull If the Earth's gravitational pull is reckoned as 100, the relative pull on the surface of the Sun and the other planets is:

Sun	2770	Jupiter	261
Mercury	38	Saturn	119
Venus	86	Uranus	88
Mars	38	Neptune	110

MOTOR CARS
MOTORCYCLES, MOPEDS
AND 3-WHEELERS

MOTOR CARS

MOTORCYCLES, MOPEDS, 3-WHEELERS
AND SCOOTERS

HISTORY AND DEVELOPMENT

1876 is perhaps the birth year of the motor car of today. It was then that the internal-combustion engine was developed to a workable form by Otto.

Cugnot Steam Carriage

But the dream of the self-propelled carriage is a very old one. As far back as the sixteenth century, Johann Hautach made a vehicle propelled by coiled springs—a clockwork car. Steam carriages were also developed. The Frenchman Cugnot constructed a workable steam carriage in 1770—a three wheeler. Murdock, Dallery, Symington, Gurney and others all achieved a varying degree of success with steam-propelled carriages during the next fifty years (see models and drawings at the Science Museum). Gurney's steamer could climb Highgate Hill—a long, steep ascent—and in 1831 a Gurney coach ran regularly between Cheltenham and Gloucester at speeds up to 12 m.p.h. At the same time, Ogle and Summers built a car which achieved no less than 35 m.p.h. on the rough roads of that time—a speed greater than Stephenson's 'Rocket' locomotive of the same period, which had the advantage of running on rails.

But on the whole, these were triumphs that led nowhere. Opposition to any new kind of road vehicle was intense, and these early cars were constantly under attack from the highly organised horse-drawn coaching systems. Even more important, the first cars coincided with the almost fantastically rapid growth of Britain's railway systems: men with money chose to invest in railways, not horseless carriages.

Thus when Otto made a workable internal-combustion engine of the sort used in cars today, his achievement was of very little interest to Britain. Cars continued to be thought of as dangerous and unpleasant toys until the turn of the century. In France, however, Panhard and Levassor built a car round the new engine. There was activity in America, too, with petrol-driven cars such as the Duryea. In Germany, Benz constructed a petrol-engined three-wheeler (1885). Daimler made a two-cylinder V engine in 1889. Incidentally, the names Benz and Daimler are still seen on motors today. Meanwhile in Britain what few cars there were had to proceed at walking pace behind a man carrying a red warning flag!

Prescott Steamer, 1903   Benz, 1885

In 1896 this ridiculous law was repealed (the London-Brighton run for Veteran cars celebrates the event each year) and motoring began to be taken more seriously in Britain.

At the turn of the century motorists had a choice of three sorts of self-propelled vehicle: steam, petrol-driven and electric. Electric cars were silent and very easy to manage, but useful only as town carriages. They could not go far without having their batteries recharged—a problem still to be solved.

Steam cars were very numerous. Serpollet, White, Stanley and other manufacturers produced silent, fast and powerful vehicles with hill-climbing power that the petrol cars of the time could not approach. In addition, they involved none of the noisy and difficult gear-changing inseparable from the early petrol-engined cars. An American Stanley Steamer held the world speed record in 1906 at no less than $127\frac{1}{2}$ m.p.h.—an extraordinary speed, for petrol-driven road cars of the same date were not expected to reach more than 30 or 40 m.p.h.

But steam cars had their disadvantages. They were difficult to run. They used a lot of water. They could be very dirty. And it took up to 20 minutes to get steam up.

While the design of the steam car remained static and unchanging, the petrol car developed very rapidly indeed. Britain had an extremely advanced design in the Lanchester, a car that was many years before its time. A host of famous car makes, many of them still familiar names, came into being—Peugeot, Audi, Sunbeam, Rolls-Royce, Fiat and Rover among them.

Most important of all, petrol cars were developed that rivalled steam cars in speed and silence—and beat them in ease of operation and cost. The first Rolls-Royces (1905–10) in particular set an entirely new standard of refinement, luxury and (from the owner's point of view) simplicity. They were an example to all other makers of petrol cars and a clear indication that the days of the steam car were numbered. Another nail in the steam coffin was the self-starter—an American invention—which gave the petrol car an additional lead over the hard-to-start steamers.

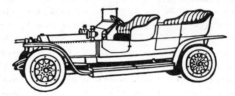

Rolls-Royce Silver Ghost

The Rolls-Royce was a craftsman-built car, individually made. In America Henry Ford started to build cars by mass-production: that is, in batches of thousands of cars, all made from interchangeable parts and assembled by largely unskilled labour. Ford's contribution to motoring development, although very different from that of the Rolls-Royce, was just as important. While Rolls-Royce set a new standard of perfection, Ford made cars available to people the world over. Motoring for the masses began with Ford.

By 1914 the car had settled into a pattern that has not changed very greatly. The engine was a multi-cylinder unit fed with controlled amounts of petrol and air by means of a jet carburettor (the earliest cars had a wick carburettor). The rear wheels drove the car and the front wheels steered it. Steering was effected by a wheel (earlier cars often had tillers) and braking by internal expanding hub brakes—though only on the rear wheels. Electricity was generally responsible for starting and lighting the most modern cars—and almost invariably responsible for engine ignition. The car's body and chassis were separate, although the first all-steel, 'unit construction' chassis bodies so common today had been produced. Early troubles of quick tyre wear and constant puncturing had been largely overcome.

During the First World War car design was neglected. Engine design advanced rapidly, however. In particular, many new and better metals were developed that allowed higher speeds within the engine and greater power development. It became apparent that the huge, thundering racing cars powered by massive engines were not necessarily the fastest; the comparatively tiny feather-weight racing cars of Ettore Bugatti—an immortal name—were beginning to steal the thunder. Smaller, lighter cars of fairly good performance and refinement began to appear. The Peugeot Bébé, designed by Bugatti, was a very early arrival. And in 1923 the first Austin 7 appeared. The Austin 7 and cars like it brought motoring for the masses to Europe just as the Model T Ford brought it to America. Motoring now became world-wide.

By 1925 steam and electric cars had virtually disappeared from the scene. More and more saloon cars were being made. Economy

Model T Ford, 1927

Peugeot Bébé, 1913

Austin 7, 1926

cars of various sorts were successfully produced in huge numbers. Mass-production methods inevitably superseded hand fitting. Motoring was beginning to change people's habits and to expand their horizons.

During the next fifteen years the car finally overthrew the old order. For hundreds of years people had lived their lives within an area of a few square miles. A villager stayed in his village. But now the motor bus took him to other towns, other districts. Charabancs brought visitors to his village. More and more people could afford cars. Road networks covered whole countries and continents. The motor car that had started as a toy had become a near-necessity.

Morris Cowley

Car development was comparatively undramatic during the period 1925–40. Finally cars became much cheaper and shoddier. Sports cars increased their power and speed, but not violently. Racing became a nationally subsidised affair as well as a sport for rich amateurs. Luxury cars were smoother in outline but little else. Towards the end of the period, streamlining made an uneasy appearance as a styling feature, but had little effect on car performance. Citroën, the giant French manufacturer, developed a unit-built car with front-wheel drive that was to remain ahead of its time for twenty years. Other leaders in design were Riley (small,

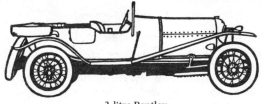

3-litre Bentley

comfortable, fast sports saloons from 1930 on); Lancia of Italy (small saloons of very advanced design, including independent suspension for all four wheels—1937 on); BMW of Germany (tubular backbone chassis frames, unusually powerful engines); Fiat of Italy (the tiny 500-c.c. 'Topolino', 1937, the first miniature car to behave like a full-size model); and MG (the sort of small and inexpensive sports car for which Britain found world markets).

Riley Falcon, 1937   Fiat 500, 1937

Racing cars saw their peak in the big-engined Mercedes-Benz and Auto Union machines of Germany, which developed more than 600 B.H.P.—compared with today's 900 +.

Mercedes-Benz Grand Prix racing car, 1937

American cars developed almost exclusively along the lines of size, comfort and silence. Problems of more power from less fuel— or of getting more passenger space in a compact vehicle—were of little interest to American car-owners, who could get all the petrol (and therefore power) they needed at very low prices.

Which brings the story to World War Two.

Second World War to the Present

After the Second World War, car production was at once resumed on pre-war lines. At first slowly, the designers and makers explored and incorporated new developments. The most important concerned suspension systems (q.v. this section), brakes (particularly discs, q.v.), tyres, luxuries such as radios and heaters, automatic transmissions, better fuels and oils—and new layouts for cars. Another very important development was the rapid rise of the Japanese motor industry, now the world's largest producer of cars.

Today there is no such thing as a typical car. The motorist can choose between rear-engine, rear-wheel-drive cars; front-engine, front-wheel-drive cars; front-engine, rear-wheel-drive cars. It is generally true to say that present-day cars offer more space, convenience and comforts, performance, mechanical reliability and fuel economy than old models, at the expense of greater complication and more difficult, expensive, 'only-the-garage-can-do-it' servicing.

The future? Already, cars have proved to be their own worst enemies. There are simply too many of them. We fight for road space and parking space; indeed, in Tokyo car owners are required

Fiat 127

Volkswagen

Mini

Volkswagen, Mini, Fiat 127—three very different postwar small cars by law to own a parking place. There is also a worldwide uneasiness about motoring's demands on fuels, materials and the environment. To combat this, motor manufacturers are beginning to produce cars that can be recycled. Alternative environmentally-friendly power sources are also being sought. Electric or diesel/electric 'hybrid' vehicles already exist. But even these may not meet future laws. In the USA a zero-emissions target has been set, so future vehicles will not be allowed to pollute at all. Does this spell the end of the private motor car, to be replaced by slow mobile bubbles piloted by computers?

Probably not; cars, unlike buses or airliners, mean much more to us than transport. They are treasured personal possessions and agents of personal freedom.

HOW CARS WORK

Engine

The Otto cycle (see History, above) is the name given to the four-stroke cycle of operation by which most car engines work. A very few cars use two-stroke engines. Diesels are increasingly used.

With a four-stroke engine each cylinder is fired once during each two revolutions of the crankshaft. With a two-stroke engine, a cylinder fires at every revolution. Four-stroke engines use mechanically timed and driven valves to regulate the entrance and exit of gases into the cylinder. The basic two-stroke engine needs no valves; the flow of gases in and out of the cylinder is brought about by pressures within the engine itself.

Four-strokes are generally smoother at low speed, more economical and capable of developing smoother power. And they do their work without the smoky emissions of two-strokes. Two-strokes are, however, becoming more popular in small cars, because of their high ratio of power to size.

Both engines work on a similar principle. One part of petrol is mixed with about 20 parts of air in a carburettor or by measured squirts of fuel (fuel injection). This highly inflammable mixture is compressed by a piston rising within a cylinder. The piston has springy rings to ensure a gastight seal. When the mixture is exploded by the spark plug, the piston is driven down. (Some cars have compression-ignition Diesel engines, which don't need spark

Two Stroke Cycle

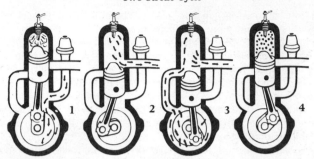

1. Ignition, induction.   2. Exhaust, crankcase charge compressed.   3. Exhaust, fresh charge enters cylinder.   4. Compression, partial vacuum in crankcase.

plugs.) The piston is attached to a connecting-rod, in turn attached to a journal of the crankshaft. Thus the explosion drives the crankshaft round, and this movement is carried to the driving wheels (see Transmission). The action of the engine is like that of a man's arm cranking a car; the straight, up-and-down movement of his arm (his shoulder is the piston, his arm the connecting-rod) becomes a rotary or circular movement when applied to the crank.

Most European cars, both medium-sized and large, have four- or six-cylinder four-stroke engines with cylinders in line. Some

Four Stroke Cycle

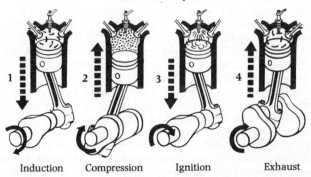

Induction   Compression   Ignition   Exhaust

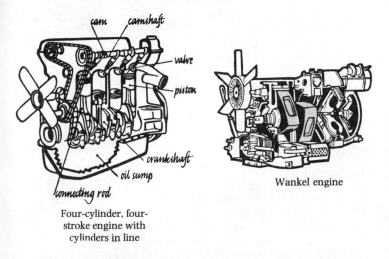

cam   camshaft

valve

piston

crankshaft

oil sump

connecting rod

Four-cylinder, four-
stroke engine with
cylinders in line

Wankel engine

'baby' cars have fewer cylinders—the Fiat 126 has two. Three-
cylinder and five-cylinder engines are now being produced. Big
cars with six, eight or twelve cylinders may have V engines; if
they did not, the engines might be too long or their crankshafts
too flexible. Some engines have opposing cylinders laid flat.

All the engines described so far are Reciprocating engines—
that is, they contain parts that go up and down, driving other
parts that go round and round. Many attempts have been and are
being made to construct engines with parts that all spin (Rover
long ago made a gas-turbine engine, for example). The spinning,
rotary engine should, in theory, be smoother and less wasteful.

In fact, the Wankel engine is the only rotary design in international production. The drawing (page H12) shows the Wankel
operating cycle. The lobes (shown *a*, *b*, *c*) describe patterns within
the casing of the engine that cause pressure/suction areas for the
mixture and exhaust. The advantages of the Wankel engine include compactness and astonishing smoothness, but no manufacturer has achieved fuel economy comparable with the piston
engine's—economy matters more and more. To try to get the best
from both worlds—piston economy and rotary smoothness—
several manufacturers are experimenting with orbital engines.

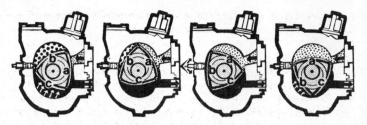

Wankel cycle
Rotary sequence of Induction, Compression, Ignition, Exhaust

Lubrication

Two-stroke engines may be lubricated by a small amount of oil added direct to the petrol. As the mixture must pass through the crankcase as well as to the cylinder, the oil vapour provides enough lubrication for every part. However, modern engines have a positive, pumped oil supply from a separate oil tank.

Four-stroke engines are elaborately lubricated from a reservoir called the sump. Oil is drawn from the sump by a pump which passes it under pressure through channels drilled through such components as the crankshaft, connecting-rods and valve gear.

Cooling

Car engines develop great heat, not only through the explosions within the cylinder but also through friction of the moving parts. This heat must be got rid of, either by cooling with water or air. The VW 'Beetle' was air-cooled.

Most car engines are *water-cooled*. The cylinder-head, where the explosions take place, and also the cylinder block that contains the cylinders, are channelled with water passages. Water is passed through these passages, generally with the aid of a pump driven by the engine itself.

The constantly flowing water in the engine is cooled by the radiator, a grille of small water tubes supported by a lattice of fins. This is joined to the top and bottom of the engine by short lengths of hose so that a loop circuit is formed. The radiator is exposed to the outside air, and may be further cooled by an engine-driven or electric fan. Hot liquids rise above cool: so the hottest part of the radiator is the top, and the coolest the bottom.

The flow of cooling water is thus from bottom to top of the engine and from top to bottom of the radiator.

Air Cooling

The cylinders of an air-cooled car are covered with fins (as on a motorcycle engine) which present a large area of coolable metal to the passing air. The fins are generally supplemented by a powerful engine-driven fan to make sure of a good supply of cooling air even when the car is in heavy traffic.

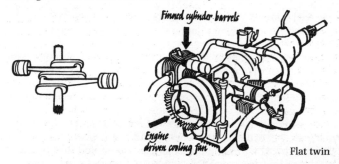

Finned cylinder barrels

Engine driven cooling fan

Flat twin

Air-cooled engines need no cooling water, of course, and this is an advantage, as water may leak or freeze or cause corrosion. Air-cooling disadvantages include extra noise (water is a good sound damper) and the large amount of engine power needed to drive an adequate fan.

Surplus engine heat warms the car interior.

Engine Power and Capacity

The size of a car engine is described in terms of the amount of water that would be needed to fill all cylinders, with pistons down. In Europe we describe this amount in cubic centimetres (c.c.) or litres—thus 'Daimler 4·2', in which the engine is of approximately 4,200 c.c. (4 litres) capacity. A small 4-seater is about 1·0–1·3 litres; a medium-size family car, 1·5 or 2 litres; an 'executive' saloon, around 3 litres.

The power that an engine develops is described in Brake Horse Power or B.H.P. 'Austin A60' was so called because its engine developed approximately 60 B.H.P.

Capacity and power should not be confused. A racing-car engine may develop seven times as much B.H.P. as a family saloon of the same capacity. Both c.c. and B.H.P. must be known to get an idea of an engine's characteristics.

Engine power depends on the rate at which it can digest fuel and get rid of the exhaust. Thus, the faster an engine can be made to turn—the more gulps of fuel it can consume—the more power it will deliver. Modern family-car engines often exceed 6,000 revolutions per minute. Modern racing-car engines may turn at 10,000 r.p.m. or more.

To feed a family car with fuel, one carburettor may be enough. Sports and racing engines demand more fuel and therefore more carburettors to mix and deliver it. In high-performance and Diesel engines, *fuel injectors* replace the carburettors. Yet more fuel may be given to the engine by a *supercharger*—a high-speed fan that forcibly feeds air to the carburettor (or mixture to the engine) under pressure; or by *turbocharger*, a high-speed blower using exhaust gases to 'charge' the engine. Other ways to increase engine power include multi-valve cylinder heads. Instead of one inlet and one exhaust valve per cylinder many cars now have two of each, which can increase engine speed and hence power. Variable valve timing or VTEC has also been used—this varies the engine's timing with the throttle demand—giving more power. Several manufacturers have also tried using two spark plugs per cylinder to boost performance.

Hugely increased road traffic has produced, worldwide, its own special threat—various pollutants from burned fuel. To minimize the damage, *lead-free* petrol is now commonplace; and *catalytic converters*, which 'eat' and nullify dangerous emissions, are increasingly fitted to new-car exhaust systems.

Transmission

The power developed by a car's engine must be transmitted to its driving wheels through the clutch, gearbox, various drive shafts and a differential. All these parts are transmission parts.

The Clutch

The clutch is used to join or separate the engine from the rest of the transmission. In starting a car from rest the clutch is 'let in'

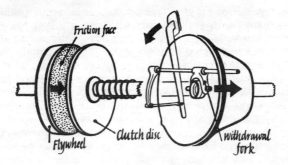

Friction face

Flywheel Clutch disc withdrawal fork

with a pedal so that the engine can *gradually* start the driving wheels turning without damage to other transmission parts.

The clutch is made up of three disc-like plates, two joined to the engine and one to the transmission. When the clutch pedal is pushed the plates are separated. When the pedal is released the friction-lined plates are pushed together by springs so that they become one.

The Gearbox

The gearbox allows the driver to match the speed and power of the engine to the road conditions. Car engines work efficiently only when they are turning fast: thus a car with only top gear (highest) working would be unable to climb a hill, as the engine would steadily lose speed and therefore power. The same is true of a child attempting to climb a steep hill on an adult's bicycle.

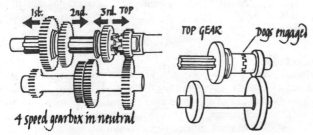

1st.   2nd.   3rd. TOP

TOP GEAR   Dogs engaged

4 speed gearbox in neutral

Most cars have five gears. A number have six. First is the lowest, used for starting the car from rest or for climbing steep hills. Top is used for easy cruising conditions and for maximum speed. Some cars today are fitted with—

Overdrive, in effect a separate gearbox giving a higher gear. This allows high-speed cruising under easy conditions with the engine turning over slower than it would in direct 'top'.

The majority of cars still make use of a gearbox containing trains of gear-wheels that are engaged by a lever: the clutch helps the operation. But there have always been many other kinds of gearboxes, and recently more and more cars have—

Automatic Gears A car with a fully automatic gearbox has no clutch pedal, and the driver need only set a lever to select the *conditions* under which the car is to be operated. If he selects 'normal driving' he need do nothing further except brake or accelerate. The car itself will do whatever gear-changing is necessary. But although automatic gearboxes simplify driving, they themselves are inevitably complicated, as the basic gearbox must be controlled by electric, hydraulic and vacuum systems that relate engine conditions to the car's needs.

Other kinds of gearing include epicyclic 'preselectors', in which the next gear wanted is 'dialled' for in advance; and the *variable-pulley* gearbox, in which belts are driven by two pulleys which change in relative size, and so give the most suitable of an infinite range of gears automatically, like this:

$$\text{Engine} \to \bigcirc \to \bigcirc \; = \text{low gear}, \quad \bigcirc \to \bigcirc \; = \text{medium},$$
$$\bigcirc \to \bigcirc \; = \text{high}.$$

This old idea was revived in sophisticated form by Ford and Fiat.

Computer 'manager'—more and more makers offer cars and motorcycles whose engine/transmission performance is monitored or controlled by sophisticated chips and computers.

Differential

When a car turns a corner the inner of the two driven wheels travels a lesser distance than the outer, and therefore turns slower.

The differential is a mechanism that allows the two wheels to turn at different speeds, yet both remain driven. Some high-powered cars have a limited slip differential, which prevents the driven wheels spinning by limiting the amount of power delivered. Several four-wheel-drive cars have locking differentials which make all driven wheels turn at the same speed—this helps in very slippery off-road conditions.

Drive Shafts and Universal Joints

When the clutch has taken up the engine's power and the gearbox has adjusted it to road conditions there still remains the necessity to take the power to the driving wheels. How this is done depends on the layout of the car. Many cars have the engine at the front and the driving wheels at the back: in this case power is led to the differential, and thence to the driving wheels, through the *propeller shaft*. Generally, this shaft is a simple tube with a universal joint at either end.

Propeller shaft between gearbox and rear axle

Two other shafts, called half-shafts, must then carry power from either side of the differential to each driving wheel. These may be enclosed in a rigid casing. If the car has independent rear suspension (described later) each shaft must have universal joints.

If the car is front-engined and front-wheel driven, or rear-engined and rear-wheel driven, then a propeller shaft is unnecessary. The drive can be taken from the differential straight to the rear wheels by two short shafts, each with universal joints.

Some 'workhorse' and high-performance cars have 4-wheel drive.

Universal Joints allow a stiff shaft to transmit power through an angle, or through constantly changing angles.

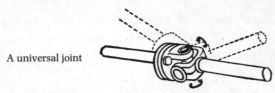

A universal joint

They must be fitted to a propeller shaft because the rear axle moves up and down on its springs while the gearbox remains stationary.

If the driving wheels are driven direct by shafts from the differential, then universal joints must be provided to allow for the wheels' up-and-down movements.

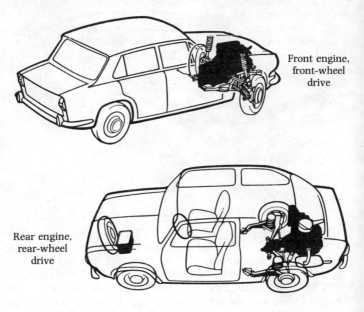

Front engine, front-wheel drive

Rear engine, rear-wheel drive

The most commonly used universal joints are the Hardy-Spicer type, which is comparable to gimbals; and the constant-velocity type, which uses metal balls running within tracks cut into two half-spheres, one cupping another.

Brakes

By the end of the Second World War, the majority of the world's cars were braked on all four wheels by internal-expanding drum brakes operated by hydraulic power (H19). Hydraulic systems are preferred to mechanical systems because there are no mechanical power losses; because hydraulic power is simply transmitted along flexible pipes instead of by rod or cable systems; and because each of the four brakes must automatically receive exactly the same proportion of the power exerted by the driver.

During the Second World War, disc brakes (external-contracting brakes in which brake pads close like pincers on a disc attached to the road wheel) were successfully developed for aircraft and are now commonplace equipment for cars and motorcycles.

Whatever system is used, an additional and separate braking system must also be supplied. This is called the 'parking brake' or 'hand-brake', and is used only to hold the car when at rest or to stop the car in the event of a failure of the main braking system. Hand-brakes are normally mechanically applied to one pair of wheels only.

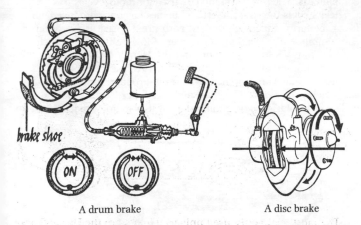

A drum brake   A disc brake

Various systems have been and are being used to prevent braked wheels from 'locking up' (ABS, Anti-lock Braking System). A skidding tyre brakes ineffectively, even dangerously.

Body and Chassis

The chassis of a car is the framework that supports the body, engine and other components. This 'skeleton' is often visible in old sporting cars. However, the majority of present-day mass-produced cars use the body itself as a chassis. The 'Unit Construction' modern car body is an all-metal welded box structure of great rigidity, and no separate chassis is needed. Sometimes additional local strength is given by a small chassis-like structure. Sometimes the engine and perhaps the transmission and driving wheels are mounted on a small separate chassis that may be removed from the body quickly and easily for servicing.

'Unit Construction' is not the only method. Until quite recently, Triumph mass-produced small cars with a separate chassis frame; and luxury-car makers supplied a chassis on which various specialist coach-builders could fit individual bodywork. Sports and racing cars are often built up round a complicated arrangement of tubes called a Space Frame, which gives great rigidity with minimum weight; or with a chassis taking the form of a massive spine with outriggers to hold bodywork, engine, suspension and other components. The same systems are used for motorcycles.

Sheet steel is the raw material of bodies for mass-produced cars. It can be formed in huge presses with great speed and economy. Aluminium is also used for a number of low-volume cars, including the Audi V8 luxury saloon and the Honda NSX supercar. Its main advantages are low weight and rust-resistance.

Plastics bodies are popular with small-production makers of kit cars, racing cars, etc. The time and space needed to produce the bodies forbid large-scale production. But a major producer tried

Du Pont, Model G, 1930; its chassis is clearly visible

Renault Clio 'hot hatch' 1764 c.c. Choice of engines

combining both techniques with a central steel 'cage' to which various plastic front and rear assemblies were attached to provide a range of cars.

Steering

Steering by the front wheels only was the rule. Now, however, a few important manufacturers offer 4-wheel steering. In most cases the rear wheels are steered in the opposite direction to the fronts at low speed to make the car more manoeuvrable and in the same direction at high speed to make turning more stable.

A typical steering linkage consists of a steering wheel, whose

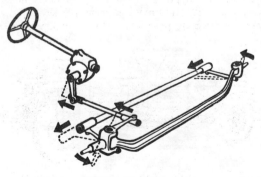

Basic steering linkage

motion is translated through the steering box to push the drop
arm. This is connected by a drag link so that it steers one road
wheel. The other road wheel is connected to the first by the track
rod.

Electrical System

The equipment of a car includes a complete electrical generating
system, a storage battery to hold the electricity and a variety of
systems and mechanisms that use it.

Electricity is supplied by dynamo or the more modern alternator, usually driven by belt from a pulley on the engine's
crankshaft. The output of the dynamo or alternator charges the
battery (usually 12-volt, but sometimes 6). A voltage regulator or
cut-out keeps the output at a suitable level.

The battery stores electric power and passes it on demand. The
greatest demand is that of the self-starter motor, which makes the
battery supply enough power to turn over the engine quicker and
for longer than a man could.

The petrol/air mixture within the cylinders is fired by sparking-
plugs. These are supplied by the ignition coil with current stepped
up in voltage from the battery's 6 or 12 volts to 6,000–12,000
volts. The coil current is directed by a mechanical or electronic
distributor to each sparking-plug in turn. (Diesels don't need spark
plugs: the compressed mixture fires itself).

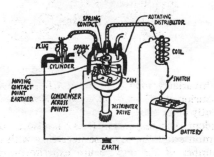

Electricity from the battery powers a host of other components
and accessories. On a modern family car they will certainly include

the lighting system, direction indicators, horn and panel lights; and, even, computers. The windows, hood and even mirrors may be raised and lowered by separate electric motors. The clutch, various panel instruments, gearbox and/or overdrive may also use electricity.

Electricity must complete a circuit to do a job. Thus one wire may be used to take current from the battery to a lamp bulb, and another wire to take current back to the battery. Sometimes, however, the car itself is used as a conductor of current, thus halving the considerable amount of wiring.

Suspension

Suspension is the word used to describe those parts of the car that join the road wheels to the chassis or body.

The traditional method of suspension was by leaf springs supporting an axle, and this method is still quite often used for the rear axle.

Leaf spring

Almost invariably today, the front wheels have independent front suspension (i.f.s.): with i.f.s., each wheel is free to behave independently of the other.

Independent rear suspension (i.r.s.) is also becoming increasingly common and is in any case necessary with a rear-engined car. A number of car makers are experimenting with 'active suspension'. This automatically adjusts the springing to the road conditions, making the most comfortable and stable ride at all times.

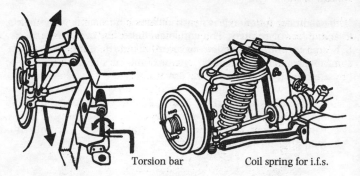

Torsion bar   Coil spring for i.f.s.

Springs

Springs may be in the form of leaves, coils, compressed liquids or torsion bars (bars twisted along their length). Citroën introduced inert gas as a springing medium—rather as if the car were suspended on four interlinked footballs. Others followed.

Ride Controllers and Shock Absorbers

If a car were suspended only on springs it would meet a bump, bounce over it and keep on bouncing. So-called shock absorbers or dampers let the spring do its work but prevent it from bouncing. They control the ride of the car and keep it steady.

With most cars, this control is the result of keeping each wheel steady. But ideally, it would be better to control the ride of the car as a whole: Citroën and others found ways of achieving this by linking each inert-gas suspension unit to the other by means of a hydraulic mechanism so that the behaviour of any one road wheel affects the behaviour of the others. The car is in fact self-levelling. Some British cars have front and rear wheels collectively sprung by liquid-filled tubes ('Hydrolastic').

Anti-Roll Bars

Anti-roll bars are used to link the behaviour of one road wheel to another. Thus on heavy cornering the heavily loaded outside wheels transfer some of their load to the inside wheels and the car remains more nearly level.

Tyres

Tyres, while not part of the suspension, will affect its behaviour.

Over- or under-inflation has drastic effects both on the way a car feels and how it behaves. Attempts have been and are being made to design tyres having renewable treads; and there are tyres that can be run flat for limited distances. Some cars even have tyre-pressure monitors that warn the driver if a tyre is going flat.

Jaguar World Sportscar racer

ELECTRIC CARS

At the dawn of motoring, electric cars battled for supremacy with the noisy, smelly internal-combustion-powered machines on the roads. But the convenience of petrol power won through and resulted in the modern car. Electric car development stagnated, and almost no progress was made. While petrol cars got faster and quieter, electric cars almost stood still.

But now all those years of fossil fuel-burning are catching up with us. The greenhouse effect and lead in fuel have caused untold damage to the environment. And with legislation forcing car makers to produce lower and lower emission levels—culminating in a zero-level for two per cent of cars sold in California in 1998—the electric car has resurfaced.

At the forefront of the race to produce the first practical electric cars are General Motors in America, with their Impact, and BMW in Germany with their E1.

The Impact relies on a large number of conventional lead acid batteries (similar to those found under the bonnet of a normal car). Thanks to its super-sleek shape and lightweight construction, the Impact makes efficient use of simple battery technology. BMW, however, is pushing forward with sophisticated new sodium-sulphur batteries which give better power and range and

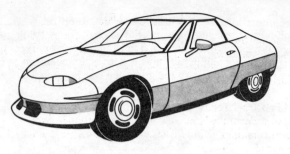

General Motors, Impact

BMW, E1

save weight. The downside is that these batteries run at a temperature of 300 degrees C.

In France the PSA group (Peugeot and Citroen) are experimenting with a network of electric car-refuelling points where cars can plug in to recharge their batteries.

Meanwhile, a number of simpler electric vehicles are making their way to Britain from Europe. From Denmark come a peculiar single-seat three-wheeler called the Citi-el PCV and a two-seater four-wheel car called the Kewet El-Jet; and the French are offering a two-seater called the Agora Electric—all three having a limited range for city use only.

The number of electric cars being developed grows each day as more manufacturers join the race. By 1996 they should be on sale and the electric car will finally have its revenge on the petrol-engined polluters that almost killed it nearly 100 years before.

RACING CARS

Apart from the fun of it, motor racing has always been of enormous value to every motorist. Fuels, metals, oils, tyres, brakes—in fact, nearly every part of the ordinary car—all gain from the high-pressure testing and development that racing gives.

Grand Prix track racing is undertaken only by thoroughbred, out-and-out 'Formula 1' machines. (Other Formulae, read on.) The World Championship is decided by Grand Prix events all over the world.

Track Racing also includes events for production, sports, 'Enduro', historic and Veteran cars, Karts, etc.

Road Racing includes the classic Le Mans 24-hours—open to all kinds of sports/racing cars driven over a closed road circuit.

Rallies are typified by the classic, all-Europe Monte Carlo and by the Lombard/RAC Rally of Great Britain—a five-day 2000 + miles event incorporating speed trials and forest stages. The winners of the various classes are those who lose the fewest number of points.

Time Trials, Sprints, Hill Climbs, Rallycross, etc., are events that pit the driver 'against the clock'. The winners are those who cover a given distance, climb a certain hill or complete a number of circuits in the shortest time.

Trials are winter events held over deserted country roads or in

Ford F Series pickup, American favourite

muddy fields and up hills. Often no one can complete the course, in which case the team that gets farthest wins. Special cars and skills are needed.

Club Racing takes place all over Britain and the world. In Britain such races are the proving grounds for new drivers. Cars range from true racing machines to Vintage Sports Cars.

Drag Racing. An American motor sport that has invaded Europe. Aim: to achieve the highest speed in a straight line over a short distance.

Formula Track Racing Cars True racing cars are defined by Formulae arrived at by international agreement. At present those in force include:

Formula 1—3½-litres unsupercharged engines in single-seater bodies. 12 cyls max.

Formula 3000—Racing cars with single-seater bodies. Engine capacity up to 3,000 c.c. normally aspirated.

Formula 3—2 litre. Limited modifications to engines from cars produced in units of 5,000 or more. There are other such Formulae, mostly aimed at producing cars based on standard components, such as *Formula Ford, Renault, Vauxhall/Lotus.* Also, *World Sports-prototype Championship* (big cars, big engines); and classes for production motor vehicles, such as *Gran Turismo* (fast touring) and *Saloon* cars; also *Sports* cars, *Touring* cars. The popular *Group A* is for standard production saloons.

Vauxhall/Lotus 'Challenge' 2-litre budget racer

LAND SPEED RECORD

Some important figures (wheel-driven cars):

			mph
1925	Campbell	Sunbeam	150·9
1926	Thomas	Higham Special	171·1
1927	Segrave	Sunbeam	203·8
1932	Campbell	Napier–Campbell Bluebird	254
1935	Campbell	Rolls-Royce–Campbell Bluebird	301·1
1938	Eyston	Eyston Thunderbolt	357·5
1947	Cobb	Railton	394·2
1965	Summers (USA)	Goldenrod	409·6

Not wheel-driven:

1970	Gary Gabelich	Blue Flame	622·4
1983	Richard Noble	Thrust II	633·5

IDENTIFYING CARS

Cars are identified and described in various ways. Engine capacity and power have already been discussed (see Engine). Descriptions such as saloon, convertible or station wagon are well known to you. But every car also carries a variety of identity marks:

Registration Letters and Numbers (number plates) are allotted to each new car. The same letters and numbers appear in the car's official registration document. However many owners the car may have, its number plate never changes.

Chassis and Engine Numbers are among other details appearing in the registration document. These are permanently stamped on cars of every nationality. Car makers are now being encouraged to display visible vehicle identification numbers (VIN) on their cars to make them more easy to identify.

Saturn by GM—USA's answer to imported Compacts. 4 cyl. 1901 c.c.

Proton, Japanese/Malaysian-built saloon cars 1·3–1·5 litres

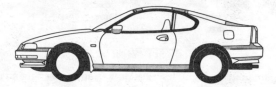

Honda Prelude—4-wheel steering

Lotus Carlton, big 'muscle' car, 377 B.H.P.

Alfa Romeo 164 3-litre V6 LUSSO

Old and new car logos and badges

Alfa Romeo

Honda

SAAB

ASTON MARTIN

AUSTIN ROVER

BUGATTI

Citroën

DKW

Daimler

FIAT

Ford

Ferrari

Audi

Mazda

Toyota

Jensen

LAGONDA

Renault Espace 2000 TSE

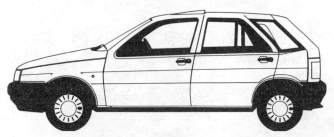

Fiat Tipo

Citroën XM, Computer-controlled springing, 4-cyl or V6 3 or 2 litre

GROUP MANUFACTURERS

Which parent company makes or owns which cars is a question
difficult to answer. Ford, the American giant, now owns the
Aston Martin–Lagonda group and Jaguar. GM (General Motors)

Lancia Delta HF Integrale, turbo rally car

Lamborghini Diablo, V12, 200 mph

Mazda Revue, Tiny saloon 1·3 or 1·5 litres

of America has various makes of cars, including Vauxhall, Opel and Lotus. Chrysler of USA owns Dodge and Jeep.

The Japanese giants include Toyota, Honda which owns 20 per cent of Rover, Nissan, Mitsubishi and Mazda.

Land Rover 'Discovery', 4-wheel drive, petrol or turbo-Diesel engines

In Europe the French PSA Group owns Peugeot and Citroën, the German VAG group of VW and Audi also owns Spain's SEAT and Czechoslovakia's Skoda. The Italian giant Fiat owns the country's three greatest marques, Alfa Romeo, Lancia and Ferrari.

In short, there is little room left for the brilliant independent maker. The capital and technical resources of a giant are, in the end, almost certain to be needed.

Further Reading
Autocar, Car, Motor Sport, Auto Express, etc—the weekly and
    monthly magazines.
The Observer's Book of Automobiles
Picture History of Motoring, L. T. C. Rolt
Which? Magazine's test reports; and other Road Test compila-
    tions.
About a Motor Car, Puffin Book (Penguin)

Places to Visit
Science Museum, Kensington, London
National Motor Museum, Beaulieu, Hants
Stratford Motor Museum, Gloucester

MOTORCYCLES, MOPEDS, 3-WHEELERS AND SCOOTERS

1911 Zenith Gradua, J.A.P.   1922 Matchless twin
engine

HISTORY

The history of the motorcycle begins, like that of the motor car, with the internal combustion engine. Gottlieb Daimler, pioneer of cars, can perhaps be credited with the first motorcycle (1885) although an Englishman, Edward Butler, produced a motor tricycle a year before.

Whatever its origins, the motorcycle took some time to establish itself. The bicycling craze of the 1890s submerged whatever interest there might have been in motorcycles. At the turn of the century, however, social conditions changed radically in every way. Times were ripe for motorisation of any sort—bicycles included.

And indeed the first motorcycles were very similar to the powered bicycles—the mopeds—of today. Like mopeds, they were power-*assisted* vehicles. You pedalled when the motor needed help. Later and more powerful machines remained as simple as mopeds. They had no gears, or only two; there was no kick-starter—you pedalled or ran alongside the machine to get it going. Transmission was by belt (as it still is with some very modern machines). Lighting was by acetylene—a romantic but smelly and time-consuming method.

Suddenly, though, the motorcycle caught on. From 1910 on, design developed fast. During the First World War, the motorcycle came into its own: motorcycle dispatch riders were popular heroes and machines like theirs were greatly coveted when the war ended.

In the 1920s, no fewer than 200 firms produced motorcycles. The pattern of these machines did not change greatly for 20 years.

Spring front-forks, electric lighting, greater power, the kick-starter, three or four gears, a pillion—all these features were adopted as standard.

The motorcycle thus emerged as an international form of transport, appealing particularly to those who enjoyed transport for its own sake (and there is still no more exhilarating way of getting about): and to those who wanted personal transport at rock-bottom prices.

1930 Scott Squirrel, water-cooled 2-stroke   1928 Coventry Victor twin

As we have said, the motorcycle began as a moped. Oddly enough this form of the motorcycle more or less disappeared in the 1930s—and the scooter, although it was invented soon after the First World War, was never commercially developed either. Three-wheelers, blending both motorcycle and car features, did make some progress. But the standard motorcycle, often with sidecar, was the most-used vehicle.

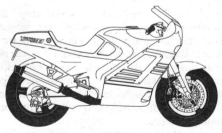

Norton

Second World War to the Present

Wars leave nations poor. After the Second World War, everyone wanted personal transport and few could afford it. Two-wheelers became popular. The moped, the minimal motorcycle, became, and remains, part of the world transport scene.

Italian companies invented the motor scooter, whose advantages included weather protection, a soft ride and simple controls. The scooter flourished for some years—but the Japanese were busily re-thinking all markets for powered two-wheelers. In the 1960s they launched today's stylish, colourful, fully-sprung, highly developed machines. These killed off traditional British designs; and the scooter fashion too.

The bigger machines have also changed. A liquid-cooled, multi-cylinder motorcycle is today a common sight—and a very handsome one. Common too are imaginative finishes, luggage carriers, self-starters, aerodynamic fairings and the sort of engineering that make oil stains old-fashioned.

The new crises in fuel, money, materials, parking space and public transport have led to interest in all kinds of two-wheelers. Commuters may find it necessary to keep a two-wheeler handy. Shoppers may take to smart little plastic-clad mini scooters. Electrically powered bicycles are in production. But 'mainstream' motorcycles may have become too expensive and complex for their own good.

HOW MOTORCYCLES WORK

The Frame
The wheels, engine and other parts of the machine are mounted in or on the frame—typically, a double loop of steel tubing (the 'duplex' frame). But then, a fat banana-like pressing may form the spinal frame; so may complex steel and alloy structures. The engine is sometimes used as part of the frame. All those parts of the motorcycle that help it to roll or steer are called 'cycle' parts.

Engine
Motorcycles and motor cars are very closely related mechanically. To avoid wasting space, we refer you back to the section on **Motor Cars** when talking about common features.

Like cars, motorcycles have either 2-stroke or 4-stroke engines (H9, 10). Some turbocharged engines (H14) are in production,

Harley-Davidson (USA) FXDB Sturgis, V-twin, 1340 c.c.

even for medium-sized engines. The Wankel rotary motor (H12) has been tried and is used now in Norton machines.

The advantage of the 2-stroke used to be its mechanical simplicity—it is possible to make a 2-stroke with only three working parts. But today's 2-strokes have some sort of valve to admit the fuel mixture and a metered supply of lubricating oil from a separ-

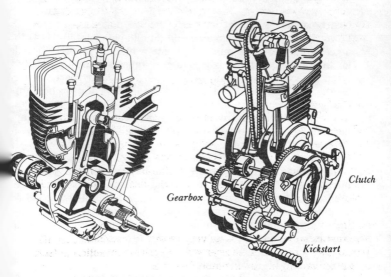

Above left: 2-stroke single-cylinder engine
Above right: Honda overhead-cam 4-stroke engine and gearbox

ate tank instead of the old petrol-and-oil mix in the fuel tank. In vibration and noise they are comparable with 4-strokes but can be more powerful. The important advantages of the 4-stroke are considerably better fuel economy; less annoyance from fouled plugs and exhaust systems; and a smokeless exhaust.

Most motorcycle engines are air-cooled (H12, 13) and have fins outside the cylinders. Many 'superbikes' (and even some small-engined bikes) have liquid cooling—look for the radiator. Engine capacity varies from less than 50 c.c. for moped and beginners' machines to over 1,000 c.c. The vast majority of motorcycles have one or two cylinders, but multi-cylinder machines are on the increase—even 6-cylinders.

Motorcycle engines can be made to develop astonishing power for their size. 100 B.H.P. per litre is not uncommon (H13) which means that some of the 500 c.c. motorcycles you see on the road can develop as much power as a small car. A multi-cylinder 250 c.c. racing motorcycle may give as much as 160 B.H.P. per litre. Some racing engines exceed 12,000 rpm (H14).

Gearboxes

Power from the engine is taken via a multi-plate clutch (H14) to a gearbox working in much the same way as a car's (H15) and for the same reasons (H14). Five gear ratios are usual, and six-speed boxes fairly common. A footchange—a lever rocked down by the toe for downward changes, and up by toe or heel for changes up—is usual. Automatic and infinitely variable gearboxes (H15) have been used with success. Scooters and mopeds may have two-stage or 'stepless' transmissions, self-changing.

Final drive

Almost always, the drive from engine to gearbox—the 'primary' drive—is by chain. So too is the final drive—although belts are used on at least a few motorcycles; and are suitable for light-weights in conjunction with automatic, scooter-type transmissions. A few makers use shaft-drive on expensive and luxurious machines. 2-wheel drive is being tried.

Ignition and Lighting

Larger motorcycles and an increasing number of scooters use car-type electrical equipment (H21).

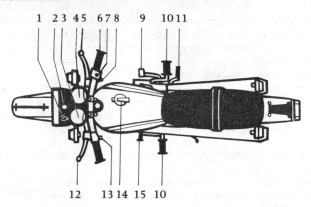

1 Headlight control switch
2 High beam indicator light
3 Speedometer
4 Tachometer (engine rpm)
5 Front brake lever
6 Throttle grip
7 Emergency switch
8 Headlight control switch (above)
   Starter button (below)

9 Rear brake pedal
10 Foot rests
11 Kick starter pedal
12 Clutch lever
13 Turn signal switch
   Horn button (below)
14 Fuel tank cap
15 Gear-change pedal

Smaller, simpler, cheaper machines may get electricity for ignition and lighting from a Magneto—a rotary electric mechanism fitted within the flywheel of the engine.

Controls
Here is a typical enough layout of the controls found on a modern motorcycle. Some machines have rocking, heel-and-toe gear-change levers. Most motorcycles have steering-column locks and quite a number have lockable petrol-tank fillers. Old motorcycles had controls not shown here; decompressors to help starting and so on. Virtually all motorcycles have a petrol tap (not shown) with a position for 'reserve'. Even 50 c.c. machines may have self-starters operated by a tiny button on the handlebars.

Brakes
Drum brakes (H19), mechanically operated by rods or cables,

Bimota Dieci 4-cylinder injection 1000 c.c.

were general, but today hydraulic front and rear discs are
common. An increasing number of motorcycles now have anti-
lock brakes.

Suspension

The majority of motorcycles have telescopically-sprung front forks
with dampers (H23) incorporated. Some have sophisticated anti-
dive systems as well. The rear wheel is mounted in a sprung
pivoted fork with a suspension system like a stubby version of the
telescopic front fork; but again, there are sophisticated variations
designed to enhance the drive-line geometry that have only a
single strut supporting the wheel.

MOTORCYCLE SPORT

Grand Prix Racing Various formulae. FI—750 c.c. 4-stroke, 500
c.c. 2-stroke. International events—the World Championship
Series (controlled by the FIM)—in a dozen countries worldwide.
6 classes from 50 c.c. (including turbos); sidecars. Also road-
circuit events.

Circuit racing Club, national, and international (including 24
hours at Le Mans). Formulae variable—designed to attract
entries.

Motocross (125, 250 and 500 c.c.—also sidecar events) which is
virtually the same thing as a *Scramble*—a race over rough
territory; *Trials* (mixed territory, observed sections, competitors
lose marks for each failure); *Arena* (closed-circuit obstacle race);
or *Grass track* or *sand* racing. All these events (and similar

Ducati 907 ie fuel-
injected V-twin

Kawasaki ZXR400, 400 c.c.

events for sidecar machines) are open to anyone who can get his
entry accepted at Club, Local, National or International level.
Speedway schools are held at venues throughout Great Britain.
Drag racing events are 'against the clock' straight-line speed
competitions. *Enduro* events stretch over days. *Schoolboy Sport*
covers some of these activities up to age 16. *Supercross* is new,
spectacular, circuit racing

SCOOTERS, LIGHTWEIGHTS, RUNABOUTS

The scooter craze of some 30 years ago opened up motorcycling.
Girls flashed by on Vespas and Lambrettas. Young men jazzed
up their mounts. Office workers commuted by scooter. But then
the Japanese lightweights arrived. They handled and braked
safely, gave amazing power from their 100–250 c.c. engines,
had 4 to 6 gears, didn't leak oil—and were colourful, fashion-
able.

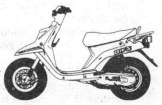

Honda CN250 feet-first scooter.
244 c.c. 4-stroke

Yamaha BW's (50 c.c.)
—the 'Bi-Wiz'

Suzuki DR350S Street-legal trail bike, 349 c.c. 4-stroke

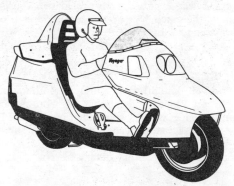

Voyager 850 c.c. Feet-first, enveloping bodywork

The scooter market was swamped not only by the light-weights, but by other Japanese offerings—the sober, quiet, reliable step-throughs; an endless variety of mopeds; and now, bright little mini-scooters with self-starters and shopping bags. These are supplemented by bigger, plastic-shelled machines rather like the original Italian scooters.

So, today, you have the choice of 'masculine' or 'feminine' characteristics—big or small wheels—a near-silent 30 mph or a rorty 70 mph.

SIXTEENERS, LEARNERS

The law has been tightened. L-riders are allowed on the road only after taking on- and off-road training (CBT) which allows the issue of the DL196 form validating licences and permitting unaccompanied riding on public roads. In short—you must be trained and you must pass two sorts of test, on the road and off it. 16-year-old riders are restricted to machines of not more than 50 c.c. giving a maximum speed of 35 mph.

Tula (Russian) Snow bike, 197 c.c. 2-stroke

Honda XR80 junior bike, 80 c.c.

THREE-WHEELERS

The aim of the three-wheeler has always been to give the benefits of a minimal car with advantages in terms of first cost, economy, tax and 'garageability'. Another benefit is that holders of a motor-cycle licence may use it to drive a three-wheeled car.

The three-wheeler was at its most popular in the 1930s when firms like Morgan produced a range of exciting sportsters. These trikes, with two wheels at the front and a single driven rear wheel, were extremely successful.

In recent years, however, the three-wheeler has in many minds become something of a joke. The Reliant Robin with its unstable handling and very low power is the only popular trike on our roads today. A brave attempt to produce an electric three-wheeler, the 'Sinclair C5', never really caught on.

So—does *Junior Pears* need a page on three-wheelers? The question could be argued—until now. Things are changing rapidly. Today's questions may be: 'The two-car family . . . shouldn't the second car be simply a local runabout?' 'Towns and cities . . . could they be decongested by allowing only quiet, small, vehicles?'

Major manufacturers are looking at these very questions, and one even came up with an answer—a three-wheeler that is practical, quiet, yet also harks back to its sporting roots. The VW

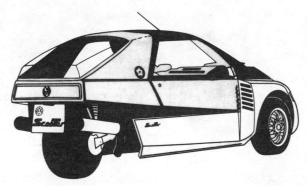

VW Scooter

Scooter had a supercharged engine and offered almost supercar performance in a pocket-sized package. Unfortunately, it never made it into production.

RAILWAYS

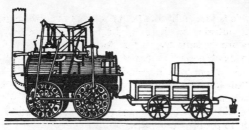

Locomotion No. 1

THE AGE OF THE TRAIN

Today, for many long-distance journeys and for carrying large numbers of people into city centres to work or for shopping, we take trains for granted. Although many people use cars for trips into town for business or to the country or seaside for holidays, using motorways, and even with buses linking country villages with nearby towns, and serving suburban areas in large cities, the railway is still the best form of transport for mass travel. Much of our freight traffic goes in large juggernaut lorries by road, but railways are far better for bulk traffic: that is, large amounts of material from a single loading point to a single unloading point. This includes coal from mines to power stations, iron ore from mines and quarries to steelworks, clay from clay workings to pottery or china factories, or paper mills, petrol and other fuel from oil refineries to storage depots, and containers carrying general goods all over the country and to ports.

On longer journeys of more than about 500 km (or roundly 300 miles) jet airliners are faster than trains. Up to those distances, even though aircraft are faster from airport to airport, the train is often quickest from city centre to city centre because of the added time taken by taxi, bus, or local train to travel between the city centre and the airport at each end.

Thus the modern train in many parts of the world is beating the competition from private cars, buses and long distance coaches, and, in some cases on longer journeys, aircraft as well. Many trains now reach speeds of 200 km/h (125 mph), and in a few cases travel at around 300 km/h (186 mph). They are quiet and comfortable, and many have air conditioning so that the temperature inside is just right for the passengers even though it may be snowing outside, or there might be a heat wave. Above all, railways are far safer than other forms of transport—particularly roads. In six of the last 17 years—1976, 1977, 1980, 1982, 1985 and 1990—not a single passenger was killed in a train accident on British Rail compared with about 5000 people killed in Britain in car accidents every year. Even 1988 would have been free of passenger deaths in train accidents but for the Clapham disaster in which 35 people were killed.

Today in most countries trains are powered by diesel or electric traction; in a few countries, particularly South Africa, Zimbabwe, India and China, a few trains are still hauled by steam locomotives but diesel and electric trains are gradually taking over although steam will last for a short time yet. In Britain and a few other countries there are many tourist railways run with pre-served steam locomotives, sometimes with qualified railway en-thusiasts helping to work the line in their spare time as a hobby. Yet even in 1992 three new steam locomotives were built in Switzerland for mountain lines in that country and Austria.

The steam locomotive was one of man's greatest inventions for, without it, we would not have the industrial world we know today. This is because something more powerful and faster than the horse was needed to speed up journeys and to carry heavier loads. For thousands of years until the early 1800s, movement around Britain and other countries was limited to the speed of the horse: about 30 km/h (roundly 20 mph) for a rider on horseback, and less than half that for the average speed of a horse-drawn coach or wagon. Canals—that is, man-made waterways—had been built in many parts of Britain towards the end of the eighteenth century to allow boats to carry bulk cargoes between inland towns and cities not near the sea or navigable rivers. Although a horse-drawn barge could carry much heavier loads than a horse-drawn wagon on the bad roads of the eight-eenth century, speeds were no more than 5 km/h (3 mph).

How Railways Began

(1800–1850)
The railway which has evolved into the modern systems of today has its origins nearly 190 years ago in the development of

two separate forms of technology. On the one hand was the rail way or guided track, and on the other the steam engine. It was the successful combination of these two that started the great railway expansion from the 1830s.

Nobody knows when the first railway was built. The first mention of one, in which a special track of wooden rails was used, is found in the sixteenth century. Men had discovered that a cart or wagon ran more easily on a track than on the rough roads of the time. The earliest railways were purely local lines, no more than a few hundred metres long; with the coming of iron works and coal mines, they were used to help move wagon-loads of material. The wagons were pulled by men or horses. One of the oldest mineral railways in the world, the Middleton Railway at Leeds, can trace its origin back to 1758; it survives today and is operated by students of Leeds University.

The first railways to carry merchandise from one town to another were built in the 1800s. The Surrey Iron Railway, from Wandsworth to Croydon, was approved by Parliament in 1801 and opened, for goods only, in 1804, while the first passenger-carrying railway in the world, the Oystermouth Railway from Swansea to Oystermouth (closed as recently as 1959), was opened in 1806. Both lines employed horses. The Stockton & Darlington Railway was opened in 1825, followed in 1830 by the Liverpool & Manchester and Canterbury & Whitstable Railways using steam locomotives.

At the time that the first railways were being built engineers were experimenting with steam locomotives—at first with little success. The development of the stationary steam engine working on low pressure steam and atmospheric pressure by Thomas Newcomen in the early eighteenth century and used for pumping water out of mines, was followed by experiments by other pioneers later in the century. James Watt saw that steam of a higher pressure had power. Richard Trevithick's road steam locomotive, one of the first effective models, was patented in 1802. It was followed a year later by his first rail steam locomotive, built at the Coalbrookdale Iron Works tramway in Shropshire. Little is known about this engine. In 1804 came the more famous Trevithick steam locomotive at the Penydarren Iron Works in South Wales. It was now that George Stephenson, one of the greatest railway engineers of them all, came upon the scene. At the time he was employed at Killingworth Colliery, Northumberland, and by 1815 he had built a type known as the 'Killingworth' locomotive, used on a number of colliery lines. A development of this type was built in 1825 for the Stockton & Darlington Railway by the newly founded firm of R. Stephenson & Co. This was the famous *Locomotion No. 1*, still in existence today.

The Stockton & Darlington was the first public railway in the world to use steam locomotives—though they were used only with goods trains. In quest of suitable locomotives the Liverpool & Manchester Railway held trials in 1829 at Rainhill; the most successful entry was the *Rocket*, built by R. Stephenson & Co.

The Rocket

George Stephenson not only built locomotives but also surveyed, planned and engineered many pioneer railway routes. The first trunk line was the London & Birmingham Railway, engineered by Robert Stephenson, George's son and partner, and completed in 1838. At Birmingham it connected with the Grand Junction Railway opened at the same time, which provided a through route to Liverpool and Manchester. In the same year the Great Western Railway completed the first section of its line between London and Bristol. Railway schemes were now introduced by the hundred. All had to be submitted to Parliament for approval. Many were rejected; but many were approved.

The Battle of the Gauges

From the beginning George Stephenson had had the foresight to realise that lines then only connecting neighbouring towns would one day be joined to form great trunk routes. He therefore standardised a gauge (the distance between the inner edges of the running rails) of 1·435 m (4 ft 8½ in) for all the railways with which he was connected—a familiar gauge to Stephenson, since it was used on some colliery lines in the north-east. Other engineers, however, had their own ideas as to what the gauge should be. Isambard Kingdom Brunel, engineer of the Great Western Railway, adopted a gauge of 2·140 m (7 ft 0¼ in) for the line from London to Bristol, and many lines between London and the West of England and West Midlands were built to this 'Broad Gauge'. Very soon the immense disadvantages of using different gauges for neighbouring lines became obvious. At junction stations where standard and broad tracks met, passengers and goods had to be transferred from one train to another. In the end Parliament decreed that the standard gauge should be used for all main-line railways; and in 1868 the Great Western began to convert its tracks. During the period of change mixed-gauge tracks were used—these having three rails, one of which was common and the other two set to standard and broad gauge respectively; but broad-gauge tracks on the main line from London to Penzance remained until 1892, when the last stretch was converted in one weekend to standard gauge.

But the broad gauge is not lost for ever; the Great Western Society depot at Didcot has a short length reconstructed over 80 years after it was abolished, and the Science Museum has had a replica GWR broad gauge 4–2–2 built. In 1985 celebrations were held to mark the 150th anniversary since the Great Western Railway was formed, with exhibitions and special steam trains.

1850–1900
Gradually the pattern of railway routes became the one we know today. Small local companies soon realised the advantages of amalgamating with other lines to form larger companies.

Meanwhile, more and more railways were built, many of them competing with other railways already in existence. Some companies were on friendly terms with their neighbours, but others were keen rivals and built railways simply in a spirit of competition. This explains why, today, some towns have more than one route to London or other big cities.

During the second half of the nineteenth century, locomotives began to look less like the *Rocket*; boilers were made larger, chimneys shorter and cabs began to appear. By 1870 the loco-

motive had taken the shape familiar to us now with preserved
engines, and coaches had lost their resemblance to wagons.

1900–1990s

By 1900 the main-line railway map was almost complete. The
last main line to be built in what might be called the first century
of railways was the Great Central route to London from Nottingham and Leicester, opened in 1899. From then on, at least as far
as main line railways were concerned, the railway system was
generally complete. During the present century, though, new
railways have been built at intervals, mostly underground routes
in London, suburban lines to open up new residential areas and
even a few lengths of main line for long-distance express services
such as the Westbury and Frome by-passes opened in 1933 on
the Paddington–Plymouth route. It was just 50 years later that
another main line by-pass was built when a new line, $14\frac{1}{2}$ miles
long, avoided mining work at Selby and at the same time provided
a high-speed link between Doncaster and York on the East Coast
main line. In 1991 a new branch was opened to Stansted Airport
and later during the 1990's there is likely to be a new branch
from Hayes, on the main line from Paddington, to Heathrow
Airport, and there are plans for a new underground line called
Crossrail for BR trains under London linking Paddington and
Liverpool Street. There is also likely to be a new high-speed
railway from the Channel Tunnel to London: this is now planned
to run near Maidstone to the Thames where it will cross to the
north bank and approach London from the east to Stratford: it
will then continue by tunnel to Kings Cross where it will link
with the lines to the north and north west.

From about 1900 competition from road transport began to
take traffic from the railways; first came the electric trams and,
later, cars, lorries and buses. Railway companies could no longer
afford to compete both against each other and against the new
forms of transport, and in 1923 all 123 of them were amalgamated into four groups known as the London, Midland & Scottish,
the London & North Eastern, the Great Western and the Southern.
The LMS served the country from London to the Midlands, North
West, North Wales and part of Scotland, reaching to the far north
at Wick. The LNER covered the country from London to the
North and East and the remainder of Scotland. The GW's area

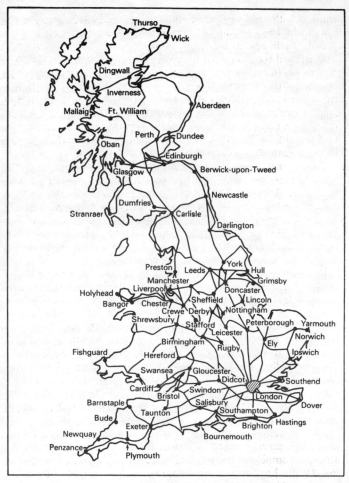

Main BR Lines

stretched from London to the West of England, West Midlands and most of Wales. The SR operated from London to the South Coast from Kent to Devonshire and North Cornwall.

On January 1, 1948, together with canals and some road

transport, the railways were nationalised and taken over by the nation. In 1963 Britain's railways came under the control of the British Railways Board, with independent boards to manage canals, road transport and transport hotels and catering. The first British Railways Board chairman was Dr Richard (later Lord) Beeching: the present chairman is Sir Robert Reid. Although there have been six BR regions in the last few years much of BR's administration is based on what are called business sectors by type—InterCity, Provincial Services, Network SouthEast, Parcels, and Freight, each with its own financial budgets and distinctive colour schemes for rolling stock.

For the last 30 years the railways of Britain have struggled to adapt themselves to the modern world. When he was chairman of British Railways, Dr Beeching found that half the railway system carried about 95 per cent of the traffic while the other half carried the remaining 5 per cent and was losing money. The Beeching Plan called for the closure of a large number of lines. Many branch lines were closed and also some main lines. Yet since 1982 around 60 stations have been opened.

During the ten years from 1960 to 1970 the British railway system changed considerably. As we shall see later, steam loco-motives finally gave way to diesels and electrics in 1968. Train speeds were higher than ever and 160 km/h (100 mph) became common; new types of signalling were brought into use on a large scale, and new operating methods introduced. In 1974 BR completed the electrification at 25,000 volts a.c. of the West Coast main line over the 645 km (401 miles) between Euston and Glasgow. From 1976, new diesel High Speed Trains known as Inter-City 125 started regular 200 km/h (125 mph) services. But again in the 1990s BR is having to fight against rising costs in running trains.

After a period in the 1980s when more people used trains, additional services were introduced, and several electrification schemes completed, the general recession right from the start of the 1990s has seen fewer passengers, less freight, increasing money problems for BR and a tight investment programme by the government. This has delayed new signalling schemes and means that old trains have to remain in service for much longer. The reason is because the government wants to continue its privatisa-tion of nationalised industries. Early in 1993 the government introduced to parliament its plans to privatise many parts of BR. It plans to offer services to private companies to operate under a franchise, and hopes that these companies will pay for new trains. As this edition closed for press many details were not known. Many organisations do not like the proposals and will try to alter them.

Railways in Other Countries

The railway was really Britain's gift to the world. After the success of the Stockton & Darlington and Liverpool & Manchester railways, businessmen and engineers in other countries soon saw the advantages of the railway. British engineers were behind the planning and building of new railways in Europe and North America. Later, as European countries developed colonies in Africa and Asia, and Britain opened up the Indian sub-continent, Australia and New Zealand, railways spread to many countries of the world during the latter part of the nineteenth century. Many countries by this time had their own engineers who were able to design railways and supervise construction. Often their ideas were different from those developed in Britain, particularly in track gauge. Some, like Brunel, preferred a wider gauge than the 1·435 m (4 ft 8½ in) which was standard in much of Europe and North America. In countries with hills and mountains, where it would be difficult to build a straight and easily graded railway, narrower gauges were used because the smaller narrow-gauge engines and trains could go round sharper curves and climb steeper gradients than 1·435 m gauge trains, although at much lower speeds and with lighter loads. This is why today there are so many different track gauges in use. Australia for example has three different gauges—1·067m (3 ft 6 in), 1·435 m (4 ft 8½ in) and 1·600 m (5 ft 3 in), depending on which State you are in. Nobody thought about the complications of through running. It was not until the early 1970s that a 1·435 m gauge route was completed right across Australia from Sydney to Perth by using existing sections of 1·435 m gauge and adding a third rail set at 1·435 m gauge to wider or narrow gauge tracks.

Cecil Rhodes, founder of Rhodesia in the last century (see A30), dreamed of a through rail route from Cape Town to Cairo for the whole way across Africa from South to North. Alas it did not happen, partly because there were large areas, particularly towards the north of Africa, where railways were never built, and partly because in Central and Southern Africa two different gauges were used, 1·067 m (3 ft 6 in)—'Cape gauge'—in the countries today known as South Africa, Zimbabwe, Zambia, Mozambique, Botswana, Malawi, Zaire and Angola, and 1·000 m (3 ft $3\frac{3}{8}$ in) in Kenya, Uganda and Tanzania.

In Europe, where Spain and Portugal use 1·676 m (5 ft 6 in) gauge and the CIS and Finland use 1·524 m (5 ft) gauge, wagons and coaches can run through to the 1·435 m lines used in the rest of Europe by changing wheels or bogies at frontiers. New high speed lines in Spain, the first of which opened between Madrid and Seville in 1992, are being built to the standard 1.435 m gauge with the aim in the longer term of being linked to the rest of Europe without change of gauge. It will be very costly to change existing tracks and may never happen.

In Zambia in 1976 a new railway of 1·067 m gauge was completed to the Tanzanian port of Dar es Salaam on the Indian Ocean and railways in other developing countries are being upgraded or rebuilt where they have fallen into disuse through civil war or previous lack of investment. In other countries like Japan, France, Germany and Italy governments are spending large sums of money in building new high speed railways on straighter routes alongside or parallel to existing lines which may be restricted by curves or traffic congestion. All these new high speed railways are electrified, and many countries have converted to electric operation on their most heavily used routes and diesel operation on the others, and steam locomotives are no longer used in many countries. Just a few countries still have steam locomotives as we have mentioned in the introduction to this section, but in China steam locomotives were still being built until 1988, the workshops at Datong constructing over 200 steam locomotives each year. But even in China diesels are replacing fairly new steam locomotives.

Railways in most countries of the world are usually state-owned, since even if they were built by private companies they have been nationalised. However, some countries are now having second thoughts about the State running the railways as in Britain; in Japan, for example, the railways have been sold to private companies, and in Germany there is talk about the railways being privatised. Railways are very expensive to build and operate and many now lose money, but without them the life of the country would come to a stop. National governments sometimes help to pay for the losses by giving money called subsidies or grants, which means that the people of the country have to pay for the railways through taxes. In some cases governments pay for new trains, track, or resignalling, or the building of major projects like new tunnels. In Switzerland the government is trying to get people to use trains much more to try to reduce air pollution from car and truck exhausts. As part of a package of measures called 'Rail 2000' the Swiss railways are to run more frequent train services in regular interval timetables which already operate all over the country, with new lines and stations, modern trains and cheaper fares, and all with the help of government subsidies. And the most exciting new development in Switzerland will be the building of new rail tunnels under the Alps at a much lower level than existing lines and therefore much longer. The Gotthard base tunnel will be nearly the same length as the Channel Tunnel at 49 km, while the Lötschberg will be shorter at 28 km. They will take the next 12 to 18 years to build.

Locomotives

Steam locomotives reigned supreme on the railways of the world for over a century until, in the face of more modern forms of traction powered by diesel engines or electricity, the last steam locomotive was withdrawn from regular service on Britain's main lines in August 1968.

Steam: Some Classic Locomotives of the Past

Steam locomotives were classified according to the 'Whyte' table of wheel arrangements (see J13). In the days when there were 123 different companies the number of locomotive designs ran into hundreds. Yet the same wheel arrangements were adopted by many companies for locomotives on the same type of work. In late Victorian times 2–4–0 and 4–4–0 locomotives were used for passenger duties and 0–6–0 locomotives for goods trains and for shunting. In the first years of the present century locomotive designers began to think in terms of larger locomotives than had been used until then. Some railways built 4–4–2 (Atlantic) loco-

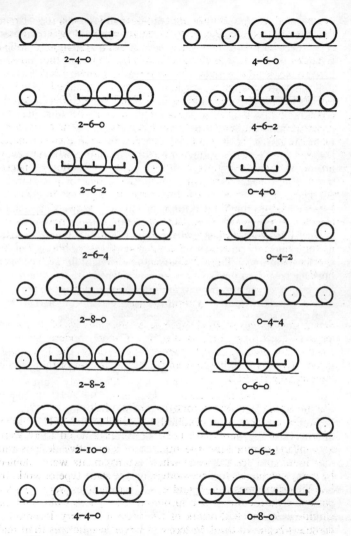

Whyte Classification of Steam Locomotive Wheel Arrangements

motives for express duties and others had 4–6–0s. The Great
Western built a solitary 4–6–2 (Pacific) locomotive, but it was not
very successful and was later rebuilt as a 4–6–0. After the
grouping in 1923 designs were standardised and express passenger trains were built right up to the maximum size and weight
that the British loading gauge permitted. Some of the most famous
express locomotives built during this period were the Great Western 'King' class 4–6–0, most powerful of all 4–6–0 designs; the
LNER streamlined 'A4' 4–6–2; the LMS 'Coronation' class 4–6–2,
which began as a streamlined engine; and the SR 'Merchant
Navy' 4-6-2, which appeared in 1941 originally partly streamlined.

BR Types

After nationalisation British Railways introduced twelve standard
classes of steam locomotives. They were: three types of 4–6–2, for
express passenger duties; two types of 4–6–0 for lighter express
and intermediate passenger or freight working; three types of 2–
6–0 for main-line and branch passenger or freight duties; a 2–6–4
tank for suburban passenger trains; two types of 2–6–2 tank for
branch passenger and freight; and a 2–10–0 for heavy express or
ordinary freight. Many BR and earlier steam locomotives have
been preserved.

The Last of the Line

The very last locomotive built specially for express passenger
work, No. 71000 *Duke of Gloucester*, was completed in 1954; but
even this engine was withdrawn after a life of only eight years.
The last steam locomotive of all, a class '9' 2–10–0 freight
engine, No. 92220, was built at Swindon Works for the Western
Region in 1960. This engine did not carry the last number, since
another batch, Nos. 92221-50, built at Crewe Works, was
actually completed first. No. 92220 was specially named *Evening
Star*, painted in green livery and given a copper-capped chimney.
Both 92220 and 71000 have been preserved, the latter being
restored to working order in 1986 on the Great Central Railway.

Modernisation

During the Second World War and the years immediately following, the railways were not able to replace old and worn-out

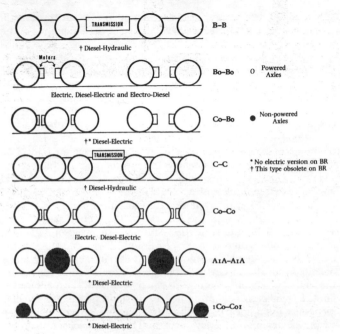

Classification of Diesel and Electric Locomotive
Wheel Arrangements

equipment. Coal of a quality suitable for steam locomotives was
becoming difficult to obtain and very expensive. It was difficult,
too, to find men to train as firemen. So when, in 1955, the British
Transport Commission announced an immense plan to modernise
its locomotives, coaches, signalling and other equipment, part of
the plan was that diesel and electric trains should replace steam
locomotives, which would gradually disappear. Some trunk routes
and suburban lines would be electrified; on others, diesel locomotives would haul express passenger and freight trains. Trains
with diesel engines built on the coaches themselves (known as
multiple-units) would be used for local and semi-fast journeys.

The multiple-unit system is widely used on BR with both diesel
and electric types. Each unit has its own diesel power plant in the

case of diesel trains, and electric traction motors in the case of electric trains. Each unit has driving cabs at the outer ends of the coaches at each end. When two or more units are coupled together, control cables are joined up between them so that all the diesel engines or all the electric motors can be controlled at the same time by the one driver from the leading driving cab. Many locomotives on BR can be coupled in pairs and driven from the leading cab by one man. But locomotives hauling separate coaches are gradually becoming a thing of the past in many areas as multiple-unit trains take over most of the local services run by Regional Railways, and InterCity trains are operated by 125 diesel trains or 225 push-pull electric locomotives. And the cross-Channel Eurostar trains will have a power car at each end operating as a multiple-unit.

It took only 13 years from the announcement of the modernisation plan in 1955 until the last steam locomotive ran in daily service on BR in August 1968. Although steam locomotives no longer run on regular all-year services on BR you can still see and travel behind steam locomotives on the numerous privately-operated railways in Great Britain which are listed at the end of the railway section. Moreover, since 1971 BR has allowed a limited number of steam-hauled excursions to run on selected secondary main lines. BR itself runs some regular summer season steam excursions on a few routes. The steam locomotives are mostly privately-owned by preservation societies, but some belong to the National Railway Museum. They have to be up to the highest standards of maintenance.

Diesel and electric locomotive wheel arrangements are expressed by the Continental system; the Whyte notation for steam locomotives cannot be used, since it does not distinguish clearly between driving wheels and non-driving wheels. In the Continental system the number of axles are counted; driving axles are shown by a letter (A = 1 driving axle, B = 2, C = 3, D = 4) and unpowered axles by a figure. Each bogie or group of wheels is separated from the next by a hyphen. In addition, if in a group of driving axles each has its own driving motor a small suffix 'o' is added after the letter. If several driving axles are driven from one source either by gearing, shaft drive or coupling rods, no suffix is used. For example, if an electric locomotive has two four-wheel bogies with all axles individually powered it would be described as a Bo-Bo. If one motor on each bogie was connected to both driving axles by coupling rods or driving shafts it would become a B-B. Sometimes the suffix 'o' is not included even if separate motors power the axles.

Modern Traction Developments

Since 1968 new diesel and electric types have been introduced and many of the first generation diesel locomotives and multiple-units have reached the end of their lives and been withdrawn, and a few preserved. With experts telling us that the world's oil reserves are limited and with oil still costing more than coal for the same power, BR and the government have been looking at possible longer term electrification, where coal will still play an important but reduced part as a power station fuel for electricity generation, alongside nuclear fuel and gas used at some power stations.

During the last decade BR has embarked on the development of second-generation diesels with new types of locomotives and multiple-units and new electrics, with more-advanced locomotives using electronic and micro-processor technology for controls, and multiple-unit trains to replace not only the Southern dc electric trains of the 1950s but also the original a.c. electric trains now getting on for 30 years old. Diesel locomotive-hauled passenger trains are gradually becoming a thing of the past as more lines are electrified and new types of diesel multiple-unit take over more services. Indeed the diesel locomotives of Classes 56, 58, 59 (the privately-owned Foster Yeoman locomotives for stone trains) and the Class 60 are all intended for freight. Most diesel passenger trains will be formed by the Skipper and Pacer four-wheel railbuses operating as two- or three-car units on the lighter services, or the bogie Sprinter units of Classes 150 to 159, some of which will be fully air conditioned and designed to run at up to 145 km/h (90 mph). Three of the sprinter classes include the longest coaches ever to run in Britain, 23 m (75 ft 5½ in) over the body. Most of these units are operated by BR's Provincial sector but Network SouthEast also has new diesel trains of Classes 165 and 166.

New electric locomotive classes were introduced in the late 1980s. The first was a type with six-wheeled bogies giving a Co-Co arrangement for ac lines principally for hauling freight over the steeply graded West Coast route over Shap and Beattock; but it was not developed after the first prototype of Class 89, and was

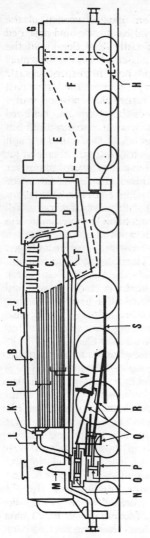

Simplified Diagram of British Railways 4–6–2 Express Steam Locomotive

A Smokebox
B Boiler
C Firebox
D Cab
E Coal space
F Water space
G Water tank filler
H Water pick up scoop for taking water at speed from troughs
I Firebox stays
J Safety valves
K Regulator valve operated by rodding from regulator lever in cab
L Steam pipe taking 'live' steam to cylinders

M Blast pipe for exhausting used steam from the cylinders out of the chimney
N Valve chest
O Piston
P Cylinder
Q Valve gear
R Connecting rod
S Coupling rod
T Brick arch
U Tubes carrying superheater elements. 'Wet' steam on its way from the regulator to cylinders passes through the superheater to dry it and make it more efficient
V Tubes to carry exhaust gases from firebox to smokebox

later withdrawn. The Class 90 is an updated version of the Class 87, although visually with sloped back ends, and designed to run at 177 km/h (110 mph) for both West Coast and the newly electrified East Coast routes on passenger and freight trains, and the Class 91 which is a brand new high-speed electric locomotive for 225 km/h (140 mph) operation on the fastest East Coast route trains. The Class 91s are rather like a power car in a fixed formation train in one sense since they have a streamlined front at one end, normally leading the train in one direction, but the end normally coupled to the coaches is flat-fronted though with a driving cab. Thus they can be driven from either end for slower-speed services when not required on high-speed passenger duties. Occasionally they have been known to run on high-speed trains with the flat end leading. Dual voltage electric locomotives for Channel Tunnel freight and overnight sleeping car trains will be in Class 92. They will work through to France. Some will actually be owned by SNCF (French Railways).

New electric multiple-unit designs have appeared in both a.c. overhead and d.c. third rail variations for local duties in London, Liverpool, and Glasgow, including the Class 319 ThamesLink services between the Bedford line north of the Thames and Southern lines to the south which started in May 1988. Another new type of electric train entered service in 1988, the stylish Class 442 Wessex Express sets for services to Weymouth, working as five-car sets of 23 m long coaches, with the driving cabs having wrap-round windscreens and plug doors.

At the end of 1991 BR took delivery of the first of the new Networker multiple-unit trains in two basic patterns, the diesel Networker Turbo units of Class 165/6 for Chiltern and Thames services out of Marylebone and Paddington, and the third-rail electric units of Class 465 for services from Charing Cross and Cannon Street. Although the 465s take direct current electricity from the third rail, the modern thyristor converter equipment on these trains turns the electricity into three-phase alternating current for the motors which are much more energy-efficient than the old style direct current motors. By the end of 1992 enough diesel Networker Turbo units were delivered for Paddington services to allow the elimination of locomotive-hauled trains into the terminus so that all services are either InterCity 125s or diesel multiple-units.

Locomotive Numbering on BR

BR diesel and electric locomotives are numbered in a series in which the class number forms the first two figures of the complete number. Shunting locomotives are numbered in classes 03 to 09, main-line diesel locomotives in classes 20 to 60 and electric locomotives from 73 to 92 though with gaps as classes have been withdrawn. The first locomotive in each class is numbered 001. Inter-City 125 units are in class 253 and 254 as part of the multiple-unit series 100 to 254. Electric multiple-units are numbered in the 300 series for a.c. units, the 400 series for SR d.c. units and 500 series for other d.c. types. The Cross-Channel Eurostar trains are in Class 373. In 1977 BR resumed locomotive-naming with classes 50 and 87 and later selected locomotives in other classes as well as Inter-City 125 units and the electric Class 442s. Preserved steam locomotives have usually kept their BR numbers or in some cases have reverted to older numbers of the pre-BR companies, but the BR computer records on the TOPS system have special numbers for the steam locomotives as Class 98, with the third figure denoting power class and the last two figures being the final two figures of the actual locomotive number.

How Locomotives Work

Steam

A steam locomotive has five principal parts—firebox, boiler, smokebox, cylinders and wheels. The firebox is at one end of the boiler, which surrounds it. Tubes from the firebox pass to the front of the boiler and into the smokebox, from which smoke and gases escape through the chimney. A steam pipe leads from the top of the boiler through the regulator valve to the cylinder valves, and from the cylinder valves to the smokebox. A piston inside the cylinder is connected to the driving wheels so that when it moves backwards and forwards the connecting-rods to the driving wheels make them turn. Engines have at least two cylinders, sometimes three or even four.

Coal is burnt in the firebox and heats the water in the boiler, turning it to steam. Because the steam cannot escape, pressure builds up. When the driver opens the regulator valve, steam passes through the pipe leading to the cylinders. Depending on the position of the driver's reversing lever, which operates part of the valve gear, the valves admit steam to one side of the pistons. The steam forces the piston to the opposite end of the cylinder, and the connecting-rods to the wheels push or pull the wheels round. When the steam has made its push the valves let it out of the cylinder into another pipe which leads it to the smokebox. Here, with the smoke and gases from the fire, it is exhausted out of the chimney as a 'puff'. Meanwhile, the valves let in more steam to the other side of the piston, and this pushes the piston back again. So a continuous action is built up, steam pushing first on one side of the piston, then on the other, propelling it backwards and forwards and in turn causing the driving wheels to revolve and the locomotive to move.

As the steam is exhausted out of the chimney it creates a vacuum in the smokebox and draws air through the fire. Thus when the engine is working hard the fire automatically burns fiercely, making a lot of steam. When the engine is eased and steam shut off, the fire dies down and the boiler does not make so much steam—an early form of automation developed by Robert Stephenson nearly 150 years ago. The fireman has to keep the firebox well covered with coal, and the boiler properly filled with water through what is called an injector, a steam-operated device which forces water into the boiler at high speed against the pressure of the steam.

Diesel

The diesel locomotive (or multiple-unit) power equipment is in two parts, the engine and the device for connecting the power output from the engine to the wheels, called the transmission.

The principle of the engine is the same for locomotives and multiple-units, but it is in the methods of transmission that variations occur. There are three of these: mechanical, electric and hydraulic.

The cylinders are the most important part of a diesel engine. There may be as few as four or as many as sixteen. Each has a piston sliding up and down inside it, connected to a crankshaft. Sometimes the pistons from two banks of cylinders drive a single crankshaft; in others, a cylinder may be open at both ends and have two pistons opposing each other, driving separate crankshafts connected by gearing. The diesel engine works by compression ignition. As the piston moves into the cylinder it com-

Diesel Locomotive with Mechanical Transmission

Typical diesel-mechanical shunting locomotive; A is the engine and B the gearbox, from which the torque is transmitted by a jackshaft drive to the road wheels

presses the air in the cylinder to a high pressure and to a very high temperature. Just before the piston stroke is completed a minute amount of fuel oil is injected into the cylinder by fuel pump, and the high temperature causes the fuel to ignite and explode, forcing the piston back. Several cylinders and pistons are arranged so that each fires in turn and, as one piston is rising to compress the air, the next will just be firing, the next driven half-way down, another at the end of its power stroke waiting to return to compress the air again. Generally four-stroke engines are used, in which the pistons make two strokes up and down for every one firing movement. The intermediate stroke cleans out the exhaust gas from the previous firing stroke and draws in fresh air for the next one.

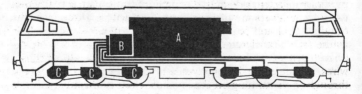

Diesel Locomotive with Electric Transmission

A typical diesel-electric locomotive; A is the diesel engine, which drives the generator, B, that provides current for C, the electric traction motors

The mechanical form of transmission employs a clutch and gearbox to transmit the drive from the output shaft of the engine to the wheels, almost as in a motor-car. Its use in this country is limited to engines of less than about 400 h.p., and on British Rail is confined to some small shunting locomotives and to the first generation diesel multiple-units now being withdrawn rapidly, nearly all of which are equipped with this form of transmission, though with a fluid clutch.

In the second system of transmission the diesel engine drives an electric generator which feeds current to electric motors coupled to the locomotive axles. This is the main system used on British Rail locomotives, and it is also in use on some SR diesel multiple-unit trains. The diesel-electric system is used on BR's Inter-City 125 HST units but with alternating current rectified for the d.c. motors. In addition, of course, the diesel generator supplies electricity at lower voltages for the control units worked from the driver's controller, which regulate engine speed and electric power and thus the train speed.

The third of the transmission systems, hydraulic drive, was used for some main line diesel locomotives in the late 1950s and 1960s but then went out of fashion. However hydraulic drive, with an impeller driven by the engine forcing oil under pressure to turn a mating part in a torque converter linked to the wheels, is making a comeback, for it is the form of transmission used by the new generation of diesel multiple-units of the Sprinter family, and the Networker Turbos.

Electric

Unlike a steam or diesel locomotive, which generates its own power, an electric locomotive or multiple-unit train must obtain its power from some outside source. Electricity is taken from the National Grid and passed to railway sub-stations along the line, where it is transformed (and rectified in many cases) to the correct voltage and fed either to conductor rails or to overhead wires. The electric locomotives and trains collect the current through *shoes* running on the conductor rail or through a device called a *pantograph* which is mounted on the roof and rubs along the underside of the conductor wire. The current then passes through the control system and into the electric traction motors. The return current is generally passed into the running rails.

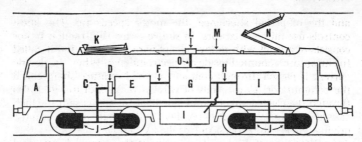

Simplified Diagram of British Rail Main Line Bo-Bo Electric Locomotive
Operating on 25,000 Volts Alternating Current from Overhead Contact
Wire

A *Cab No. 1*
B *Cab No. 2*
C *Relatively low voltage direct cur-*
    rent (about 1,900 volts)
D *Control equipment*
E *Main rectifier*
F *Relatively low voltage alternating*
    current (about 2,000 volts)
G *Main transformer*
H *Low voltage alternating current*
    (1000 volts or less)
I *Other equipment, such as com-*
    pressor and ejector motors for
    train brakes, and air-operated

control apparatus, lighting on
locomotive, train heating and
control equipment
J *Traction motors*
K *Second pantograph not in use (most*
    locomotives have only one pan-
    tograph)
L *Circuit breaker*
M *Supply from pantograph*
N *Pantograph collecting electricity*
    from overhead wire
O *High voltage alternating current*
    (25,000 volts)

British Rail has standardised electrification at 25,000 volts a.c.
with overhead current collection except on the SR and one or two
other local lines where the 660-750 volts d.c. third rail system is
used.

An electric locomotive or train works by passing an electric
current through the traction motors. At one time the main
method of controlling speed was by increasing or reducing the
voltage applied to the motors, either by passing the current
through resistances in the case of direct current, or by different
tappings from the transformer in the case of alternating current.
In recent years other methods have been used, including 'chop-
pers' in which full voltage is applied but in a series of on-off
pulses. With the off-period long and the on-period short the
motors run slowly; but as the on-pulses are increased in length

and the off-period shortened, the motor speeds up. The latest controls use microprocessors. In simple terms the traction motor consists of a shaft with many coils of wire wound round it called the armature, mounted inside an electromagnet. When an electric current is passed through contacts on the armature shaft, called the commutator, to the coils of wire in the armature, and also through the electromagnet, a magnetic attraction is set up which causes the armature shaft to revolve. As this shaft is geared to the driving wheels, the process moves the locomotive.

Another type of modern locomotive is the electro-diesel, used on the Southern Region. This works as an electric locomotive when running on an electrified line but has a diesel engine for running on non-electrified sidings or lines. This type of locomotive, together with some of the SR diesel locomotives, can work certain Southern express trains push–pull fashion, that is with the loco-motive at either end of the train. When the locomotive is pushing, the driver controls it from a driving cab in the leading coach. Push-pull working is also used on many services on the East and West Coast main lines with an electric locomotive at one end of the train and a driving van trailer (DVT) at the other.

Brakes

If you want to stop a train it's not much good turning off the power alone; a train can coast for several miles, particularly if it is running downhill, without appreciably slowing down.

A train's brakes usually consist of blocks which, when applied, press hard on the treads of the wheels. Latest freight wagons and many passenger coaches have disc brakes—special brake pads which press against discs on the axle. The means of applying and releasing them is by variations in air pressure. For many years two forms of power brakes have been in use, the *vacuum* system and the *compressed air* system, originally called the Westinghouse brake after its inventor George Westinghouse. Both were developed by the late 1880s. In the former a vacuum in the brake system holds the brake off and, admitting air at atmospheric pressure, applies them. In the Westinghouse system compressed air through the train equipment keeps the brake off but, letting the air out of the continuous pipe through the train, allows compressed air in reservoirs on each coach to pass through a distributor valve into the brake cylinders to apply the brakes. Because pressures in air brakes can be higher than the vacuum system, owing to atmospheric pressure limits, compressed air brakes can be more powerful and use smaller components, but are more complicated.

Before the grouping of railways into the four 'big' companies in 1923 some railways used the Westinghouse brake and others used the vacuum brake. And to allow through working between lines with different brakes some coaches and locomotives had both systems. In 1923 the vacuum brake was adopted as the future standard, although a few pockets of Westinghouse brakes remained, particularly on the Isle of Wight and on local services from Liverpool Street in London. Compressed-air brakes were also used on electric trains. This situation lasted for over 40 years until BR decided to adopt the compressed-air brake as the new future standard during the late 1960s.

On multiple-units this is applied and released electrically—a much quicker process—although there is still automatic application in case of emergency. The modern compressed-air brake system uses two pipes running throughout the train, one to apply the brakes when the compressed air is let out through the driver's brake valve, the other full of high pressure compressed air to recharge the system to release them. If a passenger operates the alarm signal or a train becomes uncoupled accidentally and breaks the flexible train pipe between the coaches, air enters the brake system and applies the brakes.

Some electric trains or locomotives have electric braking by which the motors become generators in order to slow down. Sometimes the electricity is fed back into the third rail as in the case of the Networker Class 465 units, called regenerative braking, and sometimes into resistors on the train when it is termed rheostatic braking.

Coaches

BR main-line coaches built between 1951 and 1966 weigh about 32–34 tonnes each, are 19·660 m (64 ft 6 in) long over the body ends and 2·743 m (9 ft) wide over the body (2·819 m—9 ft 3 in if you count the door handles). Corridor coaches seat 48 or 64 second-class passengers or 42 first-class passengers. The latest coaches are of 'integral' construction in which the coach body is self-supporting without a heavy underframe. Since 1966 all new second class coaches have been of the open pattern, with pairs of seats on each side of a central passageway. BR's Mark III coaches, in use on HST trains and on other lines, are 22·570 m (74 ft) long. They weigh 32 tonnes and seat 48 first or 72 or 76 second class. In 1989 the first of BR's latest Mark IV coaches entered service as part of electrification between Kings Cross and Leeds. The coaches are 23 m (75 ft 5 in) long and seat 46 first or 74 standard (formerly second) class passengers. Inside they have even better decor and lighting than the Mark IIIs and include space for disabled wheelchairs and disabled toilets. Some trains have restaurant or buffet cars so that passengers can eat or drink.

In 1971 BR made history by introducing trains with fully air-conditioned coaches on ordinary services; until then they had been used for only a few special luxury expresses on which supplementary fares were charged. On air-conditioned coaches the windows do not open and the air is filtered and heated or cooled before being circulated inside the coach.

Freight Services

Until the 1970s goods wagons on British Rail did not change very much in size from the early days of railways, 150 years or so ago. The normal open wagon or covered goods van was still a four-wheeler nearly 5 m (16 ft) long. One reason for the continuity in size was the limitation of some goods stations where short loading platforms were designed for only one wagon at a time, and sidings in some places could only be reached by short turntables or traversers.

But these small wagons were not suited to today's high speeds and the operating methods adopted over the last 20 years by the railways. Until the end of the 1960s the normal British goods train was slow moving, with each wagon or group of wagons starting from different stations and terminating at different stations. There were several thousand goods stations which handled all the different types of freight traffic. Very often a wagon would pass through two, three or even more marshalling yards on its journey. Many small stations and goods yards were then closed and freight trains were reorganised to run between main centres

J28

without remarshalling. Lorries collect and deliver freight from
factories and shops to the main goods stations.

British Rail developed the Freightliner train for carrying goods.
These consist of long flat bogie wagons, able to travel at up to
120 km/h (75 mph) carrying containers. They run as block
trains, that is without intermediate remarshalling. Containers are
loaded in the factory or warehouse, then taken by lorry to the
Freightliner yard where the container is lifted on to one of the
railway wagons. One wagon can often carry up to three containers. When loaded the train sets off on its journey. At the other
end the containers are again taken by road to their destination.
Sometimes containers are sent overseas by ship, thus being carried
by lorry, train, ship, without the goods being handled. A new
similar development uses what are called *swap bodies* between
lorry chassis and rail wagons for the same purpose. Swap bodies
may be shaped or have soft tops and cannot be stacked (in depots
or ships) like containers. Another development new to Britain is
piggy-back in which lorry trailers are carried complete on rail
wagons or special rail bogies.

Coal in special hopper wagons and oil in tank wagons are often
taken in block loads, from a colliery or port to a power station or
oil storage depot. For today's freight services BR has been developing new types of wagon, longer and carrying heavier loads than
the old types. Some are four-wheelers but others, particularly tank
wagons, are large bogie types weighing 100 tonnes fully loaded.
Some coal trains between collieries and power stations are loaded
and unloaded while moving slowly at each end of their journey.
They are called merry-go-round trains.

Computers are used by BR in the TOPS (Total Operations
Processing System) network to record the movement of every
locomotive, coach and wagon. The computer can print out
the whereabouts of wagons, or tell operators when a locomotive
is due for maintenance, and advise crews of train speed
limits applying to wagons in their train.

Track

The rails used on early railways were of cast iron and later the
stronger wrought iron; but for very many years now the rail has
been made of steel. Until the 1950s *bull-head* was used almost

exclusively on British railways and is still in use on many lines. This has a cross-section rather like a figure 8 with a square-ish head. It is laid in cast-iron *chairs* and held by wooden blocks or spring steel *keys* wedged between the rail and the side of the chair. The chairs are bolted to wooden sleepers, and the sleepers themselves are held in position by stone ballast, often limestone but sometimes granite.

Since about 1946 the place of bull-head as a standard rail has been taken by what is called *flat-bottomed rail*. This, as its name suggests, has a flat base and is capable of standing upright without support. It is held in position by *baseplates*, and the rail and baseplates are spiked, clipped or bolted to the sleeper.

Rails are normally 18·288 m (60 ft) long and are supported by 24 sleepers to a length: there are 2,112 sleepers in 1·609 km (1 mile) of track. Each length is joined to the next by *fishplates*— lengths of steel plate about 600 mm (2 ft) long bolted through the rail ends with four bolts. When new track is laid, small gaps are left between rail ends to allow for expansion in hot weather. The holes through which the fishplate bolts pass are oval, to allow the rail to expand.

Welded track is now used extensively in Britain. In this type of track the 60 ft lengths of rail are welded together into one piece, sometimes up to 1½ km (1 mile) or more in length without a break. In the previous paragraph we mentioned that gaps allow for the rails to expand in hot weather. If special measures are not taken, continuously-welded rail would be badly distorted when it expands in very hot weather. To overcome this difficulty, welded rail is nearly always carried on concrete sleepers which are so heavy that the rail is held tightly in position. The sleepers are spaced slightly closer at about 26 for every 60 ft. Moreover, soon after it is laid the rail is heated artificially to average summer-time temperatures, starting at one end and working through to the far end. As the rail is heated it expands, and is fastened down tightly in its expanded form. In subsequent hot weather, therefore, it cannot expand any more; in cold weather it tries to contract but since it is rigidly held it is unable to do so. In some ways it is like a piece of elastic which has been stretched a little and fastened down while stretched. The engineers responsible for heating the rail try to fix it in position at a temperature about halfway between the extremes of cold and hot weather. Deep stone ballast

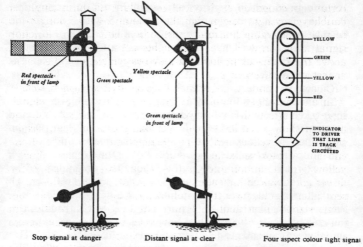

Stop signal at danger   Distant signal at clear   Four aspect colour light signal

British Rail Semaphore and Colour-light Signals

At some signals on high speed routes preceding junctions, the single and double yellow aspects are flashing to show that the train must slow down to turn off the main line at points ahead.

also helps to hold the track rigidly. By 1992 more than 65 per cent of BR track was welded.

A new form of track in which sleepers and ballast are replaced by a solid bed of reinforced concrete paving to which the rails are attached is also used in a few places by British Railways.

Signalling

First the signals themselves. Most main lines have *colour-light signals* in which powerful lamps with coloured glass lenses, which can be seen by day or night, give the signal indications so that the driver knows whether it is safe to proceed at top speed or whether he must slow down or stop. The indications are: red—danger, stop; single yellow—caution, be ready to stop at next signal; double yellow—preliminary caution, be ready to stop at second signal ahead; green—clear, proceed at normal speed. At certain junctions on high speed main lines flashing single or double yellow lights mean that the route ahead is set for a train to take a diverging line and must slow down. At the junction signal itself a row of five white lights pointing to left or right above the main colour indication shows which way the points are set for the divergence.

On some secondary and branch lines old style *semaphore signals*, with an arm about $1\frac{1}{2}$ m (5 ft) long, are still used. *Stop* signals have a red arm with a white vertical stripe near the left end, and at night show a red light for danger and green for clear. *Distant* signals have a yellow arm with a vee notch cut from the left-hand end and a black vee stripe near the end. At night they show a yellow light at caution and green for clear. These signals give the driver an advanced indication of the next stop signals ahead. All semaphore signals have the arm horizontal for danger or caution. Some signals, nearly all on former GWR routes, have the arm lowered at about 60 degrees to show clear, but most semaphore signal arms are inclined 45 degrees above horizontal for clear.

All passenger lines on British Rail are worked on the 'absolute block' system of signalling. In this system each line is divided into sections. With modern colour-light signalling there is usually a signal capable of showing a red aspect at the entrance to each section so that in effect there shall not be more than one train on one line between successive signals. The block system, though, was devised over 100 years ago when all signalling was controlled mechanically. Where mechanical signalling is used there is usually a signalbox where the sections, called 'block sections', meet.

The principle is that there shall not be more than one train in a block section on one line at a time. The signalboxes are equipped with 'block instruments' and bells for each line, so that signalmen in neighbouring boxes can keep each other fully informed about the passage of a train through the sections they control. The block instrument has a dial resembling a clock face but without any figures. The dial is marked with three panels; one says 'line blocked', another 'line clear' and the third 'train on line'. The indications are given by a needle pivoted in the centre which points to the appropriate panel. The needle is deflected by an electro-magnet when the signalman turns a switch on the block instrument to the appropriate position. The indication is

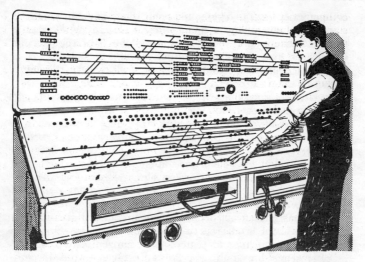

electrically repeated by the block instrument applying to the same section in the signalbox at the entry end of the section.

When a signalman wants to signal a train he must carry out the routine laid down by regulations in which he 'offers' the train by coded bell signals to the next signalbox ahead and if the line is clear the signalman there 'accepts' the train by a repetition of the bell signal. Bell signals are exchanged when the train enters and leaves the section of line between the two boxes and indicators show whether the section is clear or occupied by a train.

At one time the safety of trains depended solely on the correct operation of the block system by the signalmen, but today, lines carrying fast, frequent services are equipped with additional safeguards to prevent a signalman from forgetting a train. Many of these devices are worked by the trains themselves from what are known as *track circuits*. A track circuit is an electrically-insulated section of line which has a weak electric current passed through the running rails and connected to an electro-magnetic relay at one end of the section. As the train passes over the line, its wheels short-circuit the current, which is cut off from the relay. The relay arm therefore falls away from the magnet and makes contact with other electrical circuits, which can be used to operate such equipment as locks on signal and point levers and can prevent a signalman from pulling a signal lever to clear a signal when a train is standing on a track circuit ahead of it. Track circuits can also be used to control signals automatically.

The track circuit is in fact the basis of all modern signalling, because it allows the signalman to 'see' trains many miles away. In mechanical signalling, where the signalman works points and signals from levers which operate rods or wires, Government regulations limit mechanical operation of points to no more than 320 m (350 yds) from the signalbox. At big junctions, several signalboxes were often needed to control the layout. But with electric operation of points and signals there is no limit, and signal cabins often work points and signals 80 km (50 miles) or more away. Track circuits are used to show the signalman the positions of trains by lights on a track diagram in the signal cabin. Track circuits are also used to initiate the operation of barriers at level crossings, the ones in which barriers automatically lower across half the road when a train is coming. Other level crossings with full barriers are often controlled from a signalbox many miles away, the signalman 'seeing' the crossing by closed-circuit television. These types of crossing, which also have flashing lights to stop cars and pedestrians when a train is approaching, are gradually replacing the old type with swing gates. By the way, NEVER try to pass over a crossing when the barriers are down and the red lights flashing. All improvements and developments in railway signalling over the last 150 years have come piece by piece, added on to what was already there so that it could be proved to be absolutely reliable and fail safe. This means that if a piece of equipment breaks down the signals will go to danger and trains will stop.

Modern centralised signal cabins have been introduced on many sections of British Rail over the last 30 years. In some, the signals and points are controlled from the banks of thumb-switches. But in the signalling centres commissioned between the 1960s and 1980s the controlling miniature push-buttons or thumb-switches are placed in their appropriate positions on a diagram which consists of a replica of the track layout. The buttons usually work on the route-setting principle; that is, the operation of two buttons will set up a complete route from signal to signal—the equipment checking first that no other train is on the line concerned, then changing the points needed for the route and finally clearing the signal.

Illustrated is a route setting panel of the 1960s and still in use today. To set up a route the signalman turns the thumb-switch at the entrance to a signal section and presses a button at the end of it. When the route is set, white lights are illuminated on his diagram along the track concerned so that he can see the path the train will take. As the train passes along the route, the lights change from white to red to show the signalman the position of the train. After the train has passed the signalman restores the thumb-switch to its normal position until it is needed again and the white lights are extinguished. Where there is a junction, the button he presses determines the route that is set.

The signalmen in these modern cabins advise each other of approaching trains by the train describer. Usually the describer displays a code of figures and letters indicating the train's classification, its destination area and its number. The code is set up on the describer by the signalman who dials the code on a telephone-type dial or operates push buttons. The code description automatically moves from aperture to aperture along the track diagram in step with the train, so the signalman can see its description at a glance. When the train continues on its way towards the next signal cabin its description is automatically passed to the describer there so that the signalman knows what train is approaching him. He can watch its progress, too, from his track circuit diagram. Usually there are several automatic signal sections controlled solely by track circuits between the areas worked by the push-button panels. Colour-light signals are installed throughout the 645 km (401 miles) between Euston and Glasgow, as part of electrification, mostly controlled from centralised power signalboxes supervising long sections of line. There are only 6 signalboxes between Euston and Nuneaton—a distance of 156 km (97 miles), and over the 354 km (220 miles) from the Warrington area to Glasgow only five signalboxes. Edinburgh signalbox controls more than 320 route kilometres.

Most British Rail main lines, whether equipped with semaphore or colour light signals, are fitted with 'AWS'—the automatic warning system. This device, situated at all semaphore distant signals and nearly all colour-light signals, operates a bell in the driver's cab if the signal is clear; if it is at caution a horn sounds

and the brakes are applied automatically unless the driver acknowledges the warning.

More advanced than AWS is a new sophisticated form of
signalling in which the signals ahead (if indeed lineside signals
are retained) or the condition of the line ahead and the safe
running speed are displayed continuously in the driver's cab. This
form of signalling is used in some countries for running at over
200 km/h (125 mph). On other railways, Holland for example,
cab signalling is used on lower speed lines. It can be achieved by
pairs of wires laid along the centre of the track which transmit
signalling codes to a train passing above by induction—a form of
magnetism. If the wires are crossed at, say, 100 metre intervals
the transmitted code operates a counter on the train which shows
the distance travelled. Another means of transmitting details of
line conditions on to a display in the driver's cab is by transponders. These are packages of electronic equipment which are
placed between the rails and are normally dead. When a train
passes over a transponder an inducted signal from the train is
aimed at the transponder, which is energised by it and replies
with coded details of its location (for example, distance from
London, and such fixed details as permanent speed restrictions or
other operating and signalling information for display to the
driver). It works rather like a bar-code reader at a supermarket
check-out.

During 1991 work started on the development of AWS, known
as automatic train protection (ATP), which will give BR train
drivers more positive cab-indications of safe top speed and automatic brake applications if they do not respond to caution or
danger signals, or speed restrictions. First trials are on lines from
Marylebone and Paddington and then on the Kings Cross—
Edinburgh line, which will then allow the new electric trains to
run up to 225 km/h (140 mph).

The next stage beyond that is the introduction of automatic
speed control. Automatic trains which drive themselves after the
train operator has pressed the start button are at work on
London's Victoria Line underground route. The trains pick up
inducted codes transmitted through the running rails as signalling
and safety codes, without which the trains cannot move on their
own. Other codes are transmitted to the train to reduce speed and
stop within a metre or so of the correct place at stations, all

without any action on the part of the train operator. Trains automatically slow down and stop at signal sections if there is another train close ahead, and automatically restart when the line is again clear. At junctions, points are set automatically by programme machines. These have long paper rolls with holes punched in to represent the day's train service and denoting train number, time and route. Feeler arms 'read' the punched holes for each entry and, by switching electrical circuits on and off, act on the normal signalling equipment to set the route, provided the train describer shows that the right train is approaching. The paper roll steps forward line by line for each train as it passes through the junction.

On the Tyne & Wear Metro in Newcastle, although there is a central control office which includes a push-button signalling panel and a diagram showing every track on the system and all the trains as a row of red lights, the trains normally signal themselves through junctions by a different system from that used by London Transport. The driver sets up the train working number and its destination by dials on his control desk which puts a code into a transponder underneath the train. When the train approaches a junction area a loop of wire on the track detects the code on the train and sends this information as electrical impulses to the relay room so that the equipment can set the points and signals automatically if the line is clear.

The Docklands Light Railway in London is fully automated with trains controlled through a central computer at the main control centre linked to a computer on each train. A train captain rides on each train to operate doors and the train-start button, and check tickets, but does not drive the train except in an emergency.

Computers are used at most modern BR signalboxes to record train movement and operate train describers. In the newest signalling in England and in other countries, computers initiate the route-setting operation automatically when fed from the train describer with the number of a particular train as it approaches within two or three miles of a junction and the computer-based timetable information.

The newest type of signalbox is called an integrated electronic control centre (IECC) and brings BR right into the age of computer technology. The principles of control are similar to the signalling centres described on page J32 but with a visual display unit showing the details of the track diagram and train position, and control through a qwerty keyboard supplemented by a tracker ball which controls a cursor on the screen with a push-button on the ball to start a route-setting sequence. Automatic route-setting is used and at the heart of the system are microprocessors. Details of the scheduled train service, the routes booked and alternatives in the event of disruption are held in the memory, and the actual train-running details fed in from track-circuit occupation. If trains are running to time the routes are set automatically, triggered from the microprocessor through the interlocking equipment. If trains are late and start to delay others, the equipment is able to cope with alternative routes and platform alterations up to a point; but the signalman, normally supervising, can then step in to set routes manually since there is a limit on the variations that can be pre-programmed.

BR is also using computer-controlled radio signalling direct to the driver's cab, particularly on remote cross country lines, as for example in the Scottish Highlands and East Anglia. It is called Radio Electronic Token Block (RETB). The lines concerned have a single track, at passing loops the points are self-resetting, there are no signals in the normal sense although there are indicators to show that the points are properly set, and the driver's authority to move out of a passing loop on to the single line is a message displayed on a receiver on the locomotive control desk, transmitted to the train by radio from the control centre many miles away. There are even trains on some remote routes in certain parts of the world where space technology is used with train positions being detected by satellite through track transponders and radio links to the control centre.

Underground Railways

In many cities of the world underground electric railways for many years have helped to move passengers quickly and to avoid street congestion. London underground railways were among the earliest, in the last century, with most of the system built between 1900 and 1910. Now new lines have been built, not only in London with the Jubilee Line, but also in rapid transit form—a cross between a tram and a train—in Newcastle and in other world cities. In Newcastle, which was the first railway of its type in

Britain, the trains are lightweight, articulated, two-unit electric cars, which can be coupled in three-car formations. They have open saloon interiors, with plenty of room for standing, and sliding doors. They work from overhead catenary at 1,500 volts d.c. New tunnels have been built under Newcastle city centre, and a new bridge across the River Tyne links existing suburban railways to Whitley Bay and South Shields which are served by the new Tyne & Wear Metro. In Liverpool, new underground lines have been built across the city, and the famous Glasgow Subway has also been modernised.

Other new Light Rapid Transit (LRT) systems are being discussed, planned or actually being built. In Manchester the new Metrolink services running over former BR lines to Bury and Altrincham and through the streets through the city centre started running in 1992. The Metrolink light rail trains owe much to modern mainland European tramway practice for they are basically single-deck articulated tramway type cars. This type of vehicle is expected to be used for the various LRT schemes now being planned. A new light rail system has been approved for Sheffield to open in stages between 1993 and 1995, while other plans are being developed for Birmingham, Leeds, Nottingham, and elsewhere. In London the successful London Docklands Light Railway has been extended into the City commercial area around the Bank of England and other extensions are planned into East London. This is a case where the line has carried so many passengers it would almost justify a normal railway rather than a 'light' railway where the trains are related to trams, but the planners at the start did not realise it would be so well used. At Birmingham Airport a new form of transport called Maglev was opened in 1984 in which small cabins without wheels run on a guided way; electro-magnets hold the cars hovering above the track and electric conductors along the track pull the cars by magnetic attraction.

The Channel Tunnel

History was made at 11.13 am on 1 December 1990 when the men boring the first of the three tunnels forming the Channel Tunnel project from the French side and the British side met under the Channel; for the first time in almost 10,000 years man could make a land crossing between England and France. The Channel Tunnel is undoubtedly the greatest civil engineering project of our time, certainly as far as Britain and France are concerned. The project was finally approved by both governments in 1987, the treaty to build the tunnel was confirmed, and the money needed was guaranteed by banks and shareholders, because the scheme is not being paid for by the state but by private investors and the Eurotunnel consortium. The idea of a tunnel under the English Channel dates back to the early 1800s, and a century ago trial boring actually started but was stopped on military objections. The name Channel Tunnel is a misnomer because there are three tunnels side by side, the large outer ones each carrying a single railway track and a smaller middle tunnel linked to the other two at intervals by cross passages for services, cables, and maintenance staff access, also emergencies. The final break-through of the third tunnel—the south-running tunnel— took place on 28 June 1991, completing the boring of this great civil engineering project. The tunnels were bored through the chalk under the English Channel and run for 50.50 km (31 miles) between Folkestone and Sangatte near Calais. As this edition is being prepared work continues on laying rail tracks and fitting signalling, safety and other systems through the tunnels to allow trial running to start during 1993 and public services to start during winter 1993/4.

There will be through trains between London (Waterloo), Paris and Brussels, taking around 3 hours, and through services between other places in Britain and on the European mainland, and the tunnel is expected to increase through rail freight. There will also be ferry trains running between terminals at each end of the tunnel carrying cars, lorries and road coaches, the cars in double deck rail wagons and the bigger road vehicles in single deck rail wagons. The road vehicles will simply drive on to the train at one end and drive off about 35 minutes later at the other end. French and Belgian railways are building connecting high-speed TGV lines to the tunnel as well as providing new links between Paris, Brussels and Amsterdam.

A new high-speed rail link between the Channel Tunnel at Folkestone and London has been planned by Union Railways, a subsidiary of BR, to be built over the next few years. From Folkestone it will run through North Kent, crossing the River

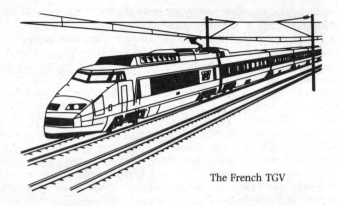

The French TGV

Thames and heading into London near the north bank of the Thames to reach Stratford. From there final plans will be published in autumn 1993 for the route to a new international station probably at St Pancras. Although trains between London, Paris and Brussels will run to and from London's Waterloo station from opening in 1994, when the high speed link is built trains will use St Pancras and connections to main lines north of London will allow passenger and freight trains between the North of England and mainland Europe direct access to the Channel Tunnel high-speed line.

Signalling through the Channel Tunnel is similar to the latest version used on the French high speed TGV lines, called TVM430. The line is divided into 500m block sections and there are virtually no lineside signals other than marker boards. Instead, drivers have a cab display showing the maximum speed at which they can run, the speed figures flash to show a change of speed ahead, and the figures have different colour backgrounds depending on conditions. 160 on green means continue at 160 km, 000 on red means stop before the next marker-board. For a normal service braking to a stop, a train is slowed down over four sections from 160 km/hour. Although the signalling interlocking is relay-based, computers are at the heart of technology which sends the signalling information through the track circuits with induction transmission to decoding equipment on the trains. And for the first time a full speed supervision control has been incorporated on trains running in Britain over the Eurotunnel tracks so

British Rail's High
Speed Train 'Inter-City 125'

that if a driver does not slow down or stop as required the
automated equipment takes over and automatically regulates the
speed within the safety limits.

Trains through the Channel Tunnel are of three basic types:
the Eurotunnel shuttles for road vehicles, which have a Bo-Bo-Bo
locomotive at each end of long formations of car- and lorry- or
coach-carrying wagons; through freight trains which are worked
by Class 92 locomotives suitable for running on British and
French railways, and which will also work the overnight sleeping
car trains; and jointly-owned Eurostar trains for London–Paris–
Brussels services. These will be lengthy eighteen-coach formations
plus a power car at each end capable of running over British and
Continental lines, triple voltage to run on BR Network SouthEast
750V d.c. third rail, Eurotunnel and French TGV lines at 25,000V
a.c. overhead, and Belgian 3,000V d.c. overhead. Broadly similar
trains are also being built for through operation between Manchester and Edinburgh and Paris and Brussels. They will be shorter
formations of two power cars and fourteen intermediate coaches.
Because of delays in finalising the specification, these 'north of
London' trains will not be ready for service until 1995.

The Railway Speed Record Holders

Railway speeds in the last few years have increased, but until

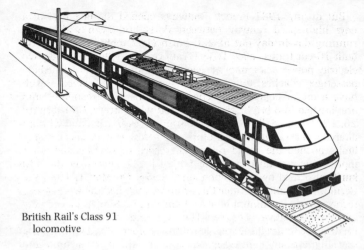

British Rail's Class 91
   locomotive

1976 British trains did not normally exceed 160 km/h (100 mph), with averages of 130–40 km/h (80–90 mph). The first 160 km/h (100 mph) run by rail ever was claimed for the Great Western's 4-4-0 *City of Truro*, which was said to have reached 164·5 km/h (102·3 mph) on May 9, 1904, with a Plymouth to London mail often disputed since. LNER 4472 *Flying Scotsman* made the first authentic 160 km/h (100 mph) run in 1934. The world's speed record for steam locomotives is held by Great Britain's No. 60022 *Mallard*, which, in July 1938, reached 202·5 km/h (126 mph) with a test train between Grantham and Peterborough.

Japan was the first country to go beyond the 160 km/h (100 mph) speeds at one time thought to be the practicable limit for trains in daily service, with regular speeds of up to 209 km/h (130 mph) on the New Tokaido line between Tokyo and Osaka, built specially for high-speed running and opened in 1964. During 1972 the Japanese opened a second high-speed railway, the New San Yo line, and more high speed railways are being built. On some, trains run every 15 min. Then, during the late 1960s and early 1970s Britain, France, Germany and Italy started experiments with trains running at up to 200 km/h (125 mph). In Italy a new line—the Direttissimo—between Rome and Florence is being opened in sections and has a top speed of 250 km/h (155 mph).

But during 1981 French Railways opened the first part of a new high-speed railway between Paris and Lyon with trains running day-in day-out at 260 km/h (162 mph). The specially-built 10-car trains called TGVs (Train Grande Vitesse) include two electric power cars one at each end, and eight intermediate passenger coaches, two of which next to the power cars each have a motor bogie at one end. The trains are streamlined and are finished in a bright orange-red and white livery. On February 26, 1981 a specially formed TGV train of seven cars, and with an altered gear ratio to the motors, on a test run to check safety limits pushed the world rail speed record to 380 km/h (236·1 mph). This was an increase of 50 km/h (31 mph) over the 330 km/h also held by the French since 1955. On May 1, 1988 the German experimental Inter City trainset snatched the world speed record with a maximum of 406·9 km/h (252·8 mph) on the new high speed railway between Hanover and Würzburg. But the French recaptured the record on December 12, 1988 with a specially formed and equipped TGV on the Paris–Lyon route which attained 408·4 km/h (253·5 mph).

Since 1989 another TGV line to the west and south west of France called TGV Atlantique has trains running at 300 km/h (186 mph) in daily service. However the French were not content to hold the absolute speed record by a mere 2 km/h and on a special test run on the new TGV-Atlantique on December 5, 1989 first pushed the world speed record to 482·4 km/h (300 mph) and then in the Spring of 1990 conducted a series of high speed test runs to assess the performance of motors, wheels, track, catenary and pantographs in which speeds exceeded 500 km/h on several occasions, with a new world record set on 18 May 1990 at a top speed of 515·3 km/h (320 mph) near Vendome. Again the runs were made by a specially adapted TGV train of five coaches, the power cars were equipped with slightly larger than normal wheels and the voltage to the catenary was increased. The record has certainly put France way out in front in the world high speed train race. These trials are not just for the honour of having the fastest train; they have a real value for the future of rail travel since they are all part of the proving process for the next stage of development, a European rail system with 1000 km journeys covered in three hours and regular top speeds of 350 km/h (217 mph) with beginnings from the mid-1990s.

The Japanese, particularly, and engineers in other countries (including at one time Britain), have also been running trials with other forms of guided land transport. The coaches run astride a basically concrete beam but do not touch it since they are held just above it either by an air cushion as in a hovercraft or by the repellent force of magnets under the car and in the track. Linear electrical conductors on the track and on the car propel the car along. Speeds of over 600 km/h (around 400 mph) have been reached. So far such systems have not been used for long-distance routes.

In Britain new high-speed railways have not been considered to be worth the large amount of money they would cost. It was found that by making certain curves less sharp and banking other curves with more superelevation, several existing Inter-City main lines could take trains of normal construction at up to 200 km/h (125 mph). This has allowed the development of the High Speed Train (HST), which consists of fixed formation units of seven or eight Mark III passenger coaches with two diesel-electric streamlined power cars, one at each end, so that there is no locomotive shunting at terminals. In 1985 BR raised the world's speed record for diesel traction from the 227 km/h (141 mph) which it set in 1973 to 231 km/h (144 mph) on the inaugural run of the Inter-City Tees-Tyne Pullman as it ran down Stoke bank between Grantham and Peterborough, the same stretch on which *Mallard* gained the world's speed record for steam in 1938. The main feature of the Tees-Tyne Pullman run was the high average speed, for it ran the 432 km (268½ miles) between Newcastle and London in 2 hours 19 min 37 sec, an average speed for the entire journey of 185 km/h (115·4 mph), itself a world record for a diesel train. In 1986, in bogie trials, a special Inter-City 125 reached 144·7 mph. and later runs have squeezed an extra one or two miles an hour faster still. Inter-City 125 trains are normally run from London to Bristol, Penzance and South Wales, and during 1982 were also introduced to the Bristol, Birmingham, Derby line, and to Sheffield–St Pancras services. Inter-City 125 trains have high-power brakes and stop in the same distance as ordinary 160 km/h (100 mph) trains.

The train originally designed in the 1970s for running at 240 km/h (150 mph) on existing track was known as the Advanced Passenger Train (APT). Practically everything about it was new. The coach bodies tilted as trains went round curves, and it had special braking and suspension. The first experimental unit, which was on trial for several years, was powered by gas turbines. This train finished its trials and went into the National Railway Museum. Alas, the prototype electric units were never really successful and reliable and the whole project was abandoned and the trains withdrawn in 1987. Nevertheless on its last trial in Scotland it became the fastest train in Britain, on December 20, 1979 reaching 261 km/h (162·2) descending Beattock bank. On September 17, 1989 almost the same speed was attained on a trial trip of the new East Coast electric trains hauled by locomotive No 91010, which reached 260 km/h on Stoke bank between Grantham and Peterborough. For the East Coast route electrification which started operation over the London–Leeds section in 1989 and London–Newcastle–Edinburgh in 1991 the high-speed trains are worked by Class 91 locomotives with Mk IV coaches, designed to operate at 225 km/h (140 mph), and known as Inter-City 225. Already BR has been thinking about the next generation of Inter-City trains using Mark V coaches and known by its metric speed as Inter-City 250. But development towards production and improvements to upgrade the West Coast Main Line on which the InterCity 250s would run have been postponed until the future services and needs of a franchise operator under privatisation become clearer.

Colour Schemes

In the days of individual railway companies before nationalisation each company had its own colour schemes for trains and stations. The locomotives and coaches were usually the most distinctive. Green was a popular colour for locomotives, although of different shades, while the LMS used crimson lake (related to maroon) for its express passenger locomotives and coaches. In its early years British Railways used dark green for its express locomotives—rather like the former GWR green, with red and cream coaches. Then some of the older colours came back on a regional basis; but from the mid 1960s the blue and light grey which can still be seen on trains all over the country became the new standard colours, although some local and suburban trains and most locomotives were all blue for a few years.

But since the reorganisation into sectors each type of service has had its own colour schemes, and the provincial services in particular have different colours for each of the main areas. Some of the schemes are the brightest ever seen in Britain with Glasgow's mainly orange and black being most noticeable, while Network SouthEast has a multi-colour scheme with grey, white, red and blue. Inter-City colours are pale grey, red, white, and black, with pale grey repeated above the windows except on first class coaches which have a yellow stripe. Even freight trains have bright colours since, although the basic livery is red and grey, many of the wagons, particularly those owned privately, carry the colours of their owning companies. All locomotives and multiple units have yellow ends—a colour which on latest stock is designed to blend in along the sides with the regular colours.

In 1987 the Railfreight sector introduced new coloured symbol panels painted on locomotive sides to show the traffic to which they are allocated, and metal plates with symbols showing the depot to which they are attached.

Preservation

Although British Rail no longer runs daily steam locomotives on main lines, steam locomotives are by no means extinct in Britain. Over the last 25 years as steam engines were withdrawn most went for scrap but some were sold to private owners for preservation. One of the most remarkable scrapyards was at Barry in South Wales where over 200 steam locomotives were sent for breaking up but most were actually saved for preservation. Some are not in working order and can be seen only as static exhibits at museums. Others, including several large express locomotives, are kept in working order ready to run on BR main line specials.

Numerous smaller tank and tender engines can be seen running on standard gauge lines operated by preservation societies or private companies. These branches are all in private ownership and new railway companies have been formed to operate services mainly as tourist attractions. Most employ volunteer railway enthusiasts to help run and maintain the line under the guidance of a few professional engineers and other staff. There are also narrow gauge lines, a few of which are newly built. One of the latest is the 381 mm (15 in) gauge Bure Valley Railway in

Norfolk which opened in 1990 over the nine miles between Wroxham and Aylsham on a former BR trackbed.

In September 1975, the new National Railway Museum was opened at York. It houses the state collection of locomotives, coaches and other relics. There is another branch of the Museum at Swindon, concentrating on former GWR relics.

Principal Lines run by Private Railways with Steam Locomotives

Standard gauge 1·435 m

Name	Location
Bluebell	New Coombe Bridge–Sheffield Park
South Devon	Buckfastleigh–Littlehempston
Paignton & Dartmouth	Paignton–Kingswear
Keighley & Worth Valley	Keighley–Oxenhope
Middleton	Leeds
Severn Valley	Bridgnorth–Kidderminster
Lakeside & Haverthwaite	Windermere Lakeside–Haverthwaite
North Yorkshire Moors	Grosmont–Pickering
Kent & East Sussex	Tenterden–Bodiam
West Somerset	Minehead–Bishops Lydeard
Nene Valley	Wansford–Peterborough
North Norfolk	Sheringham–Weybourne
Gwili	Bronwydd Arms–Penybont
Mid-Hants	Alresford–Alton
Strathspey	Boat of Garten–Aviemore
Great Central	Loughborough–Rothley–Leicester North
Isle of Wight	Smallbrook Jet–Havenstreet–Wootton
Llangollen	Llangollen–Berwyn
Bo'ness & Kinneil	Bo'ness–Kinneil
Midland Trust	Butterley–Ironville
East Lancashire	Bury–Ramsbottom
Bodmin & Wenford	Bodmin Parkway–Bodmin General
Swanage	Swanage
East Somerset	Cranmore
Dean Forest	Norchard
Gloucestershire & Warwickshire	Toddington
Embsay	Embsay
Foxfield	Blythe Bridge

Narrow gauge

gauge (mm)

Festiniog	600	Porthmadog–Blaenau Ffestiniog
Talyllyn	685	Tywyn–Nant Gwernol
Welshpool & Llanfair	762	Llanfair Caereinion–Welshpool
Ravenglass & Eskdale	381	Ravenglass–Eskdale (Dalegarth)
Romney, Hythe & Dymchurch	381	Hythe–Dungeness
Sittingbourne & Kemsley	762	Sittingbourne
Fairbourne	310	Fairbourne
Llanberis Lake	600	Llanberis
Snowdon Mountain	800	Llanberis
Bala Lake	600	Llanuwchllyn–Bala
Vale of Rheidol	600	Aberystwyth–Devils Bridge
Brecon Mountain	600	Pontsticill–Pant
Leighton Buzzard	600	Pages Park–Vandyke Road
Isle of Man	914	Douglas–Port Erin
Wells & Walsingham	261	Wells–Walsingham
Mull & W. Highland	261	Craignure
Launceston	600	Launceston
Bure Valley	381	Wroxham–Aylsham
South Tynedale	600	Alston

NOTE: Some other lines are attempting to complete arrangements to open services as this edition closed for press. There are also numerous other standard gauge depots with short operating lines, narrow gauge and miniature railways.

Some British Railways Facts and Figures

Largest station area: Clapham Junction, 11·23 Ha (27¾ acres)
Largest number of platforms: Waterloo, 21
Busiest station: Clapham Junction, 2,400 trains each 24 hours
Longest platform: Colchester, 603 m (1.980 ft)
Steepest Main-line Gradients:
    Lickey Incline, 1 in 37·7 (nearly 3·2 km/2 miles)
    Exeter (St David's-Central), 1 in 31·3 (150 m/7½ chains)
    Dainton Bank (near summit), 1 in 37 (240m/12 chains)

Highest altitude: Druimuachdar, 448 m (1,484 ft) above sea-level
Longest Bridge: Tay Bridge, 3·551 km (2 miles 364 yd)
Longest Tunnel: Severn Tunnel, 7·011 km (4 miles 628 yd)*

* The BR longest tunnel is exceeded by London Underground Northern Line from East Finchley to Morden 27·842 km (17 miles 528 yd), and Eurotunnel Channel Tunnel (see opposite).

Total number of locomotives in service (April 1992):
Diesel, 1,634†   HST power cars, 197
Electric, 262
† Plus 11 locomotives privately owned.

British Rail route open for traffic at April 1992 (the latest date for which
figures are available): 16,558 km (10,289 miles)
Route electrified: 4,885 km (3,036 miles)
(includes 2,938 km (1,826 miles) electrified on high-voltage a.c. system;
1,944 km (1,208 miles) d.c. third rail system)
Total track length: 37,757 km (23,462 miles) including sidings
(The reduction since April 1991 mainly arises from the transfer of 26 km
(16 miles) of BR route to Manchester Metrolink).

Some World Railways Facts and Figures

The total length of the world's railway routes is over 1,207,000
km (750,000 miles), of which over 320,000 km (200,000 miles)
is in the USA.

The country with the largest single system is the CIS with
over 136,800 km (85,000 miles) of 1·524 m (5 ft) gauge railway.

The journey between Moscow and Vladivostok, on the Trans-
Siberian Railway (nearly 9,298 km/5,778 miles, taking 7 days) is
the longest that can be taken without changing trains.

The longest stretch of perfectly straight line in the world runs
for 526 km (328 miles) across the Nullarbor Plain, Australia.

The highest railway station in Europe is 3,454 m (11,333 ft)
above sea-level, on the Jungfrau Railway in Switzerland.

The highest railway in the world is in Peru at La Cima where it
reaches 4,818 m (15,806 ft) above sea-level.

From 1921 to 1980 the world's longest rail tunnel (other than
underground systems) was the Simplon No. 2, linking Switzerland
and Italy, 19·823 km (12 miles 559 yd) long, but in 1980 it was
exceeded by the 22·2 km (13 miles 1,320 yd) Shimuzu Tunnel
on the new Joetsu line in Japan. In 1988 the Seikan Tunnel,
linking the Japanese islands of Honshu and Hokkaido, was opened.
It is 53·9 km (33 miles 1,232 yd) long of which 23·3 km (14
miles 827 yd) is under the sea. Boring of the three tunnels
forming the Channel Tunnel project was completed in June 1991,
each with a total length of 50·50 km (31½ mile), of which 38 km
(23½ miles) is under the sea.

The fastest trains in the world

Date	Motive power	Location	Maximum speed
3/7/1938	**Steam.** LNER A4 4–6–2 No. 4468 (now 60022) *Mallard*	Grantham–Peterborough	202·5 km/h (126 mph)
9/11/1986*	**Diesel** BR Inter-City 125	Darlington–York	232 km/h (144·7 mph)
18/5/1990	**Electric** SNCF (French) TGV Atlantique	Vendôme	515·3 km/h (320 mph)

*Average speed Newcastle–Kings Cross over 432 km (268½ miles) 185 km/h (115·4 mph). Later trial runs have raised the record to 237 km/h (148 mph)

The fastest train in Britain

20/12/1979	Electric Prototype APT	Beattock	261 km/h (162·2 mph)

SHIPS

SAILING SHIPS

What Is a Ship?

An odd question? Well, strictly speaking the word applies only to vessels with three or more masts, all of them *square-rigged*. And a vessel is square-rigged when its main sails are square and are stretched by yards suspended by the middle at right angles to the mast. The other kind of rigging is *fore-and-aft*—that is, the sails are turned so that they run lengthwise of a ship. Look at the picture of sailing-ships: you'll see that one rigged fore-and-aft on the mizzen mast (the mast at the back) is a *barque*. Rig her fore-and-aft on the main mast, too, with only the foremast square-rigged, and she is a *barquentine*. A two-masted vessel with a square rig on both masts and a boom mainsail (you'll see what that is in the picture) is a *brig*; rig the main mast fore-and-aft, and she's a *brigantine*. A vessel rigged entirely fore-and-aft is a schooner; give her a square top sail and she's a *topsail schooner*.

Note: Despite what we've said about the strict meaning of the word 'ship', we shall use it in this section, as everyone in practice does, to mean any sea-going vessel.

SHIP'S FLAGS AND SIGNALS

The International Code

On the sea, with its traffic of ships from all parts of the world, there must be no barriers of language. The International Code enables ships to communicate with one another no matter what tongue is spoken on board.

A set of signal flags consists of 26 alphabetical flags, 10 numeral pennants (a pennant is a flag that's triangular instead of rectangular), 3 substitutes and the answering, or code, pennant.

Now, every ship at sea has signal letters assigned to it. There are four of these in every case, the first letter or first two letters indicating the nationality of the ship. (For example, British ships' signal letters begin with G or M.)

If you want to signal to a particular ship you first hoist the flags that make that ship's signal letters. If you don't do this, it will be understood that you are addressing all ships within signalling distance.

Fore-and-aft Schooner

Topsail Schooner

Brig

Brigantine

Barque

Barquentine

Cutter

Ships receiving a signal have to hoist their answering pennant *at the dip* (that is, about half-way up) when they see each flag hoisted, and *close up* (that is, as high as it will go) when they have understood it. The ship sending the message hoists its own answering pennant to show that the message is completed.

The substitutes are used to repeat a letter. If, for example, one wanted to use the letter A three times in a single group of flags, one would clearly need three complete sets of flags to do it, were it not possible to use the substitutes.

All the signal flags have special meanings when flown alone. For example:

> A—I have a diver down; keep well clear at low speeds.
> B—'I am taking in, or discharging, explosives.'
> G—'Pilot wanted.'
> H—'Pilot on board.'
> P—Departure flag.
> QQ—'Infectious disease on board.'
> W—'Medical assistance required.'
> Y—'I am dragging my anchor.'
> N and C together—SOS.
> C—'Yes.'
> N—'No.'

Sirens
One short blast on a ship's siren means that she is directing her course to starboard, two short blasts to port, three short blasts for engines full-speed astern. In fog one long blast at intervals not longer than two minutes means a ship is under way, two long blasts that she is under way but not moving through the water.

Distress Signals
(a) A gun or other explosive signal fired at intervals of about a minute.

(b) A continuous sounding of any fog-signal apparatus.

(c) Rockets or shells throwing red stars fired one at a time at short intervals.

(d) A signal by radio or any other method consisting of the letters SOS in Morse Code.

(e) A signal sent by radio consisting of the spoken word 'Mayday' (from the French *m'aidez*, meaning 'help me').

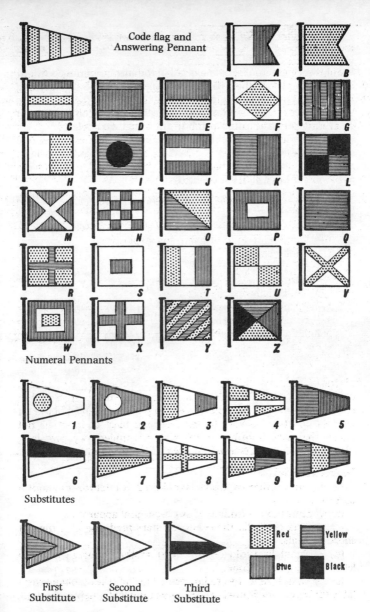

Code flag and Answering Pennant

A B
C D E F G
H I J K L
M N O P Q
R S T U V
W X Y Z

Numeral Pennants

1 2 3 4 5
6 7 8 9 0

Substitutes

First Substitute
Second Substitute
Third Substitute

Red   Yellow
Blue   Black

International Code of Signals

(*f*) Hoisting of the signal flags NC in the International Code.

(*g*) A signal consisting of a square flag having above or below it a ball or anything resembling a ball.

(*h*) Flames on the ship (as from a burning tar barrel).

(*i*) A rocket parachute flare showing a red light.

The ensign hoisted upside down is generally understood as an unofficial distress signal.

MEASURES OF WIND AND WAVE

The **Beaufort Scale** for measuring the force of winds at sea is used internationally.

Scale No.	Wind force	Mph	Kph
0	Calm	1	1·6
1	Light air	1–3	1·6–4·8
2	Light breeze	4–7	6·4–11·2
3	Gentle breeze	8–12	12·8–19·2
4	Moderate breeze	13–18	20·8–28·8
5	Fresh breeze	19–24	30·4–38·4
6	Strong breeze	25–31	40·0–49·6
7	Near gale	32–38	51·2–60·8
8	Gale	39–46	62·4–73·6
9	Strong gale	47–54	75·2–86·4
10	Storm	55–63	88·0–100·8
11	Violent storm	64–72	102·4–115·2
12	Hurricane	73–82	116·8–131·2
13	Hurricane	83–92	132·8–147·2
14	Hurricane	93–103	148·8–164·8
15	Hurricane	104–114	166·4–182·4
16	Hurricane	115–125	184·0–200·0
17	Hurricane	126–136	201·6–217·6

Wave Scale

		Height of waves, crest to trough (*ft and m*)	
0	Calm		
1	Calm	$\frac{1}{4}$	0·077
2	Smooth	$\frac{1}{2}$–1	0·15–0·30
3	Smooth	2–3	0·61–0·91
4	Slight	3–5	0·91–1·50
5	Moderate	6–8	1·87–2·44
6	Rough	9–13	2·74–3·96
7	Very rough	13–19	3·96–5·79

8	High	18–25	5·49–7·62
9	Very High	23–32	7·01–9·75
10	Very High	29–41	8·84–12·50
11	Phenomenal	37–52	11·28–15·85
12	Phenomenal	45 and over	13·7 and over

Note: the highest sea in the Bay of Biscay is 8.23 m (27 ft). In mid-Atlantic the waves will sometimes top 12·19 m (40 ft).

NAVAL VESSELS

In general

Warships are usually painted grey. Unlike a merchant ship, a warship has no raised deck at the stern. Propulsion is usually by gas turbine, although steam turbines and diesels are still used. Nuclear-powered propulsion is now found in many classes of submarine, and also in some surface warships. It is likely that more surface warships will be nuclear-powered in the future, although it remains an expensive option: hence the very limited use, so far, in merchant ships. Armour plating at water-level and below is generally no longer used in modern warship construction, although aircraft carriers normally have armoured flight decks. Aerial and sensor arrays above the upper deck and superstructure are prone to heavy damage from missile attack, but top-weight and stability factors do not allow heavy armour in these areas. A warship's *standard displacement* is a measurement made when it is ready for sea with ammunition and stores, but omitting fuel and reserve feed water. *Load displacement* refers to the ship ready for sea with all stores, fuel and ammunition.

Cruiser. *Blake*, 1961. 172·2 m (565 ft)

ASW Carriers

These have replaced the former general-purpose warships, fast and heavily armed, called cruisers. The Royal Navy no longer has any of these: HMS *Blake* was finally paid off at the end of 1979, and her silhouette is retained as a reminder of a very important type of Royal Navy vessel. The successors to the cruisers, as far as helicopter platforms are concerned, are the Invincible Class Anti-Submarine Warfare (ASW) Carriers. There are three of this new class, *Invincible*, *Illustrious* and *Ark Royal*: they carry Sea Harrier VSTOL fixed-wing multi-purpose aircraft as well as Sea King ASW helicopters. The main armament is the Seadart anti-air/anti-surface missile. These ships form the centre-piece of the Royal Navy's future task groups and have the command facilities to exercise control over wide areas above, below and on the surface of the sea.

The Destroyer

A smaller warship, though now the same tonnage as Second World War light cruisers. Can be used for general purposes, but their primary role is anti-missile defence of major units or formations. Destroyers are organised in flotillas, the leader having a black band round the top of the forward funnel. The Royal Navy has 12 guided missile destroyers (standard displacement, 5,000 tonnes: 158·5 m (520 ft) long: speed, 32 knots: armed with two 4·5-in guns and guided missile launchers, and equipped with a Wessex anti-submarine helicopter). The latest class is the Type 42 of which there are nine. Type 42 armament is the Seadart missile, but it also carries a Lynx helicopter, Seacast close-defence missiles, and 4·5-in automatic gun and anti-submarine torpedoes.

Destroyer. Type 42

The Frigate

Again, a general purpose ship but with a major anti-submarine role. The Broadsword class (Type 22), all-missile ship, carries Exocet and Sea Wolf weapon systems and is capable of carrying two Lynx anti-ship and anti-submarine helicopters. (The helicopter has become a major feature in the weapons systems of most modern warships.) There are fourteen of these. Other modern frigates are from the Type 21 and Leander classes: the latest, *Norfolk*, *Argyll*, *Lancaster*, *Iron Duke*, *Monmouth* and *Marlborough*, are Type 23. The Royal Navy has 34 frigates in the Operational Fleet or engaged in trials and training.

Frigate. Type 21

Escort vessels

Modern destroyers and frigates are often discussed as escort vessels. Although they can and do operate independently on patrol and in a variety of peacetime roles, their organisation is in the form of mixed flotillas: which enables them, with their complexity of weapon systems and sensors, to afford protection to groups of other ships, whether they be amphibious groups, hunter-killer groups or merchant convoys.

The Submarine

There are three main parts to a submarine. The *pressure hull*, inside which the crew lives and works, is circular in section to balance-out the enormous pressures exerted on the submarine

Submarine. *Dreadnought*, nuclear propelled. 266 ft

when dived—four 'atmospheres' (4 × 15 p.s.i.) for every 100 feet of depth. The *casing* is for streamlining and to give the crew something to walk on when the submarine is surfaced. The fin ('sail' in the US Navy) houses the upper sections of five or more retractable masts (e.g. periscopes) and provides a raised platform as a bridge and look-out position.

There are three main types of submarine. The *ballistic-missile* submarine (SSBN) acts as an underwater launching platform extremely difficult to locate and destroy, and is nuclear-reactor-powered; the missiles are usually armed with nuclear warheads. There are two types of *hunter-attack* submarines built to seek out and, if necessary, sink enemy surface ships and other submerged submarines; *Fleet* submarines (SSNs) which are nuclear-reactor-powered, and *Patrol* or *Conventional* submarines (SSKs) which have diesel-clcctric propulsion. The Royal Navy has four SSBNs, the *Resolution*-class (8,500 tons, crew 147) armed with Polaris missiles, 13 SSNs and 11 SSKs. The first Type 2400 submarines are *Upholder*, *Unseen* and *Ursula*. The very first SSN was *H.M.S. Dreadnought*, followed by *Valiant*, *Churchill*, *Swiftsure* and *Trafalgar* classes—all approximately 3,500 tons, crew 100–120. Many other countries have SSKs. The normal submarine weapon is the torpedo. Some modern types (such as the British *Tigerfish*) have advanced guidance systems. An even newer anti-ship missile is coming into common use: the Royal Navy version is called *Sub-Harpoon*. Fired like a torpedo while submerged, the weapon travels up to the surface, where wings unfold and it flies at its target over long ranges at rocket-powered speed. Nuclear-reactor-powered submarines can remain submerged for many weeks without surfacing, travelling at underwater speeds of 25 knots or more if required. Their undetectability is based not only on 'invisibility', but also on operating as silently as possible so that anti-submarine forces fail to locate them with noise-seeking sonar. Nuclear-

Resolution class Polaris submarine (*SSBN*)

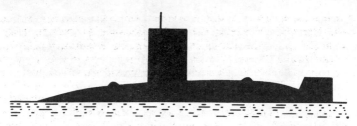

Swiftsure class Fleet submarine (SSN)

Oberon class conventional patrol submarine (SSK)

powered hunter-attack submarines have been recognised for some years as the capital ships of modern sea-power: even a suspicion that an enemy SSN is in his vicinity can cause the commander of a powerful group of surface warships, including aircraft carriers, to go to the defensive and possibly withdraw. The SSN is also the best weapon for detecting and destroying hostile submarines.

Other ships in the Operational Fleet include the Royal Navy's two assault ships, *Fearless* and *Intrepid*, which can carry an Army battalion and a brigade group HQ, landing craft capable of carrying heavy tanks, and RAF as well as RN helicopters. There are also 1 ice patrol ship and 36 ships which constitute the Mine Counter-measure Force, and are divided between minehunters and minesweepers. There are a number of offshore patrol vessels and 24 support and auxiliary vessels supplying fuel and stores to the Fleet at sea. There are also some 35 patrol vessels of various kinds, training ships, numerous vessels for survey purposes, a number of ships in reserve as support ships, and some 700 vessels forming the Royal Maritime Auxiliary Service.

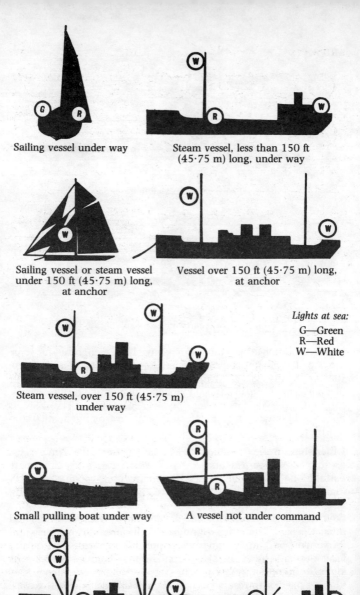

Sailing vessel under way

Steam vessel, less than 150 ft
(45·75 m) long, under way

Sailing vessel or steam vessel
under 150 ft (45·75 m) long,
at anchor

Vessel over 150 ft (45·75 m) long,
at anchor

Lights at sea:
G—Green
R—Red
W—White

Steam vessel, over 150 ft (45·75 m)
under way

Small pulling boat under way

A vessel not under command

Vessel towing another

There are also numerous mooring, salvage and boom vessels, 2 seaward defence boats, 2 fleet maintenance ships, 1 submarine depot ship, 1 royal yacht/hospital ship, 84 fleet and some support and auxiliary vessels, ranging from minesweeper support to fleet replenishment tankers.

NAUTICAL TERMS

abaft, behind; towards the ship's stern.

abeam, opposite the centre of the ship's side.

admiral, from the Arabic *Amir-al-Bahr*, Commander of the Seas.

aft, towards the stern.

alee, away from the wind; to put the helm over to the lee side of the boat.

avast, hold fast, stop; from the Italian *basta*, enough.

aweigh, anchor just raised from the sea bed.

ballast, weight put in a ship or boat to help keep her stable; nowadays, usually sea-water.

batten down, to fix tarpaulins to the hatches with iron battens and wedges.

beam, the width of a ship at her widest part.

belay, to make a rope fast to a cleat or belaying pin.

bells, are struck to give the time every half-hour, starting anew at each change of watch. 12.30 is one bell; 1, two bells; 1.30, three bells; and so on until 4, which is eight bells; then the pattern is repeated from 4.30, one bell, to 8, eight bells; 8.30 being one bell again, and 12 noon and midnight, eight bells.

bilge, the broadest part of a ship's bottom.

binnacle, the case in which the compass is housed.

boom, a spar for stretching the foot of a sail; any long spar or piece of timber.

bow, the front or forepart of a ship.

bowsprit, a spar projecting from the bow.

bulkhead, a partition dividing a cabin or hold.

bulwark, a ledge round the deck to prevent things falling or being washed overboard.

cable, a sea measure of 100 fathoms: 182·88 m or 600 ft.

cleat, a piece of wood or metal fastened on parts of a ship, and having holes or recesses for fastening ropes.

coaming, the rim of a hatchway, raised to prevent water from entering.

companion, a wooden hood over a hatch.

companion-ladder, steps leading down to a cabin.

coxswain, a petty officer in charge of a boat and crew (a 'cock' was a small rowing boat).

davits, iron fittings that project over a ship's side for hoisting a boat.

Davy Jones' locker, the bottom of the sea. There are three possible explanations for this term:

1. Davy Jones was a noted pirate, given to putting his victims over the side.
2. In Negro language 'duffy' or 'davy' is a ghost, and 'Jones' means 'Jonah'.
3. The Hindu goddess of death is called Deva Lokka.

deadlights, a storm-shutter for a cabin window.

displacement, the quantity of water displaced by a boat afloat.

dog watch, a division of the usual four hour's watch, to make a change of watches; from 4 to 6 and 6 to 8 p.m.

draught, the depth to which a ship sinks in the water.

fathom, a nautical measure of $1 \cdot 8288$ m or 6 ft.

fender, a buffer made of bundles of rope, cork or other material, to prevent a ship from scraping against a pier when moored.

fid, a wooden tool used for separating the strands of a hemp or nylon fibre rope in splicing.

first watch, 8 p.m. till midnight.

flukes, the part of an anchor that hooks into the sea bed.

fore-and-aft, lengthwise of a ship.

forecastle (fo'c'sle), the forepart of the ship under the maindeck, the crew's quarters. The term is a survival from the old days when high wooden castles were built on each end of a fighting ship. The *aftercastle* is a term no longer used, but it is interesting to note that the cleaning gear for the after parts of ships in the Royal Navy is still stamped AX, the old sign for 'aftercastle'.

galley, a ship's kitchen.

grapnel, a small anchor with several claws or arms.

halyards, ropes by which sails are hoisted.

hatch, the cover for a hatchway.

hatchway, the opening in a ship's deck into the hold, or from one deck to another.

hawse, the bows or forward end of a ship.

hawser, a small cable; a large rope.

Jacob's ladder, a ladder with rope sides and wooden treads.

knot, one nautical mile per hour.

lanyard, a short rope used for fastening or stretching.

larboard, the port side: the term was officially banned in 1844, and 'port' substituted, to avoid confusion with 'starboard'.

lee, the sheltered side of a ship.

leeway, the distance a ship is driven to leeward of her true course.

marline spike, an iron tool used for separating the strands of a rope in splicing.

middle watch, from midnight till 4 a.m.

nautical, or sea-mile, one-sixtieth of a degree measured at the equator; 1,853·18 m or 6,080 ft.

offing, to seawards; towards the horizon.

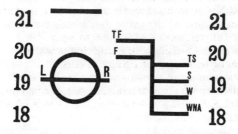

The line and the circle are the original Plimsoll Mark. The top line is the Deck Line. TF = Tropical Fresh Water. F = Fresh Water. TS = Tropical Summer. S = Summer. W = Winter. WNA = Winter North Atlantic. LR = Lloyd's Register. The figures show the amount of water the ship is drawing. They are 15·24 cm (6 in) high and the bottom of the figure represents the foot.

Plimsoll line, a line 45.72 cm (18 in) long running through a ring painted on both sides of a merchant ship. A ship may be safely loaded until this line is awash. It is named after Samuel Plimsoll, who was responsible for bringing it into use.

poop, the raised after-part of a ship.

port, the left side of a ship looking forward.

quarter, a ship's sides near the stern.

quarter-deck, the after end of the upper deck.

ratlines, the rope steps placed across the shrouds to enable sailors to go aloft.

scuppers, holes in a ship's sides for draining water from the decks.

shrouds, very strong wire ropes which support the masts on both sides.

splicing, joining two ropes by weaving together the untwisted strands.

starboard, the right side of a ship looking forward.

stay, a rope supporting the mast or a spar.

stern, the rear end of a ship.

superstructure, the parts of a ship built above the upper deck.

taffrail, the rail on the counter, or projecting stern, of a ship.

tonnage: The gross and net tonnage of a ship are measures of space, not of weight. Gross tonnage is the number of tons enclosed in a ship, 100 cu. ft counting as 1 ton or 1,016 kg. Net tonnage is the amount of space devoted to passengers and cargo. Deadweight tonnage is the number of tons weight that a ship can carry.

1 tonne = 1,000 kg.

topside (or **freeboard**), the part of a ship that is out of the water.

trick, a turn or spell of duty at sea. A trick at the wheel or as look-out lasts for two hours.

truck, the circular cap at the top of a mast.

waist, amidships.

warp, to haul a ship into position with a hawser.

watches, divisions of a ship's crew into two or three sections, one set having charge of the vessel while the others rest. Day and night are divided into watches of four hours each, except the period of 4 p.m. to 8 p.m., which is divided into two dog-watches of two hours each. Men not included in the watches are known as 'Daymen'.

weather side, the side of a ship on which the wind is blowing.

weigh, to heave up the anchor.

yawing, the swinging of a ship's head, first in one direction and then in another, due to bad steering or to a high sea.

NAUTICAL MEASURES

1 nautical mile = 6,080 ft = 1,853.18 m

1 knot = 1 nautical mile per hour = 1·151 mph = 1·853 km/h

THE ENGLISH LANGUAGE

SOME OF THE TECHNICAL TERMS OF LANGUAGE

These are a few of the terms you will meet, and need, when you are thinking or talking about language. It is largely for the sake of those of you who are studying foreign and classical languages that we have included terms like *inflexion*, *gender* and *case*. They are now of little concern to the ordinary user of English; and for this we have to thank William the Conqueror. He brought with him to England not only his capacity for castle-building and strong government but also the French language. This became the official language of England for nearly 300 years. The result was that English for that period escaped from the hands of writers and teachers, who tend to fix a language in all its formality, and passed into the care of the ordinary people, who, by the time it got back into official use, had gaily lopped off nearly all the difficult word-endings, inflexions and marks of gender and case.

affix, a syllable, not a word in itself, which can be added to an existing word in order to change its meaning. See PREFIX and SUFFIX.

alliteration, the use in a phrase or sentence of words that begin with, or contain, the same letter or sound: e.g.

> Lord Lundy from his ear*l*iest years
> Was *f*ar too *f*reely moved to tears.

anagram, a re-arrangement of the letters of a word or phrase which produces another word or phrase: e.g. 'Florence Nightingale' becomes, 'Flit on, cheering angel'.

antecedent, a word which determines the form of another word coming later in the sentence: e.g. in 'Few boys would say that they enjoy washing behind their ears', *boys* is the antecedent of the pronoun *they*, which therefore must be in the plural.

antithesis, words arranged to stress a contrast: e.g. 'To err is human, to forgive divine.'

antonym, a word whose meaning is directly opposite to that of another word: e.g. *light* and *dark*, *large* and *small*, *clean* and *dirty*.

apposition, a second description of a person or thing placed side by side with the first, the second having grammatically the same value as the first: e.g. 'Jones, *captain of Wales*, scored the final try.'

auxiliary verb, a verb that has no meaning itself but helps to make the meaning of another verb: e.g. *will* in 'I will go', *do* in 'I do see what you mean'.

case, the grammatical function of a noun or pronoun: i.e. whether it is subject, object, genitive, etc. Case has almost vanished from the English language, but it is worth remembering that the *subject* is said to be *nominative*; the *object, accusative*; the *indirect object, dative*; and the *apostrophe form* of the word (Jean's, Jim's), *genitive*.

clause, a group of words containing subject and predicate but not expressing a complete idea: e.g. 'A marshal *who can rid the town of rustlers*—that's what we want.'

complement, a noun or adjective forming the predicate of a verb that cannot govern a direct object: e.g. 'He is *silly*', 'He became *captain*.'

conjugation, the inflexion (*q.v.*) of verbs.

declension, the inflexion (*q.v.*) of nouns or adjectives.

diaeresis, the pronouncing of two successive vowels as separate sounds, often marked by the sign (¨) over the second: e.g. Chloë, aërated.

epigram, a short poem, especially one with a witty twist in it; any sharp, memorable saying.

epithet, an adjective.

etymology, the study of the origin of words.

euphemism, disguising a nasty fact with a nice name: e.g. saying 'he is putting on weight' when you mean 'he's getting fat'.

gender, the distinction of nouns according to sex. (As far as their own language is concerned, lucky Englishmen hardly have to bother about this.)

gerund, a noun formed from a verb by adding *-ing*: e.g. '*Walking* is good for you', '*Parking* is forbidden.'

homonym, a word that looks the same as another word but has a different meaning: e.g. *bear*, meaning 'carry' and 'a shaggy animal'; *peer*, meaning 'a lord' and 'peep'.

hyperbole, use of exaggerated terms for emphasis, as in 'a thousand thanks', 'he's got tons of money'.

indirect object, the person or the thing towards whom an action is directed: e.g. 'I gave *him* a penny.'

inflexion, the change made in the form of words to show what grammatical part they play in a sentence: e.g. *him* is formed by inflexion from *he*.

litotes, deliberate understatement for effect: e.g. saying *not a few* when you mean *a great many*.

malapropism, named after Mrs Malaprop in Sheridan's play, *The Rivals*. 'She's as headstrong as an *allegory* on the banks of the Nile,' said Mrs Malaprop, meaning *alligator*. That is a malapropism: an attempt to use a difficult word and getting it wrong.

meiosis, general understatement—the opposite of hyperbole: e.g. 'Golly, this is *some* game' (meaning it's a terrific game), 'I *didn't half* enjoy it' (meaning you enjoyed it immensely).

metaphor, a telescoped simile (*q.v.*)—instead of saying something is like something else, you say it *is* that other thing. E.g. not 'Sir Jasper is like a fox', but 'Sir Jasper is a fox'. Language is full of metaphors: the *spine* of a book, a *blind* alley, saw-*teeth*, etc.

metonymy, naming something not by its own name, but by something closely associated with it: e.g. 'The Crown' for 'the Government'.

mixed metaphor, using together metaphors that don't match, with ridiculous results: e.g. 'Well, he's a dark horse, and he can paddle his own canoe.'

onomatopœia, the forming of a word so that it resembles the sound of the thing of which it is the name: e.g. *click*, *cuckoo*, *babble*.

oratio obliqua, indirect or reported speech: e.g. a friend says 'I am grateful' and you report this as: 'He said he was grateful.'

oxymoron, using together in one expression words that are contradictory: e.g. *bitter-sweet*, or 'he was a *happy pessimist*'.

palindrome, a word or sentence that reads the same backwards or forwards: e.g. 'Madam, I'm Adam.'

periphrasis, presenting an idea in a roundabout, wordy way.

phrase, any group of words, usually without a predicate.

predicate, the part of a sentence that tells you about, or describes, the subject.

prefix, an affix attached to the beginning of words: e.g. *dis-*, *un-*, *in-* in the words 'disappeared', 'uninterested', 'invaluable'.

prosody, the technique of verse—its rhyme, metre, etc.

pun, a play on words, different in meaning but the same in sound, so as to produce an amusing effect: e.g. Tom Hood's

> A cannon-ball took off his legs,
> So he laid down his arms.

(*Note*: A pun can be used seriously; there are several examples in Shakespeare.)

rhetorical question, a question that isn't asked in order to obtain an answer, but as a striking way of suggesting that the answer is obvious: e.g. 'Did you ever see such a rotten bowler as Smith?'

simile, likening one thing to another: e.g. 'The ice was like iron', 'He ran like the wind.'

spoonerism, getting the initial letters of words mixed up: e.g. the statement of the famous Dr Spooner (after whom this error was named) that an undergraduate had 'hissed all his mystery lectures'.

split infinitive, putting a word between the parts of the infinitive: e.g. 'to quickly run', 'to suddenly fall down'. A safe rule is to avoid it if it sounds clumsy, but not if it is the sharpest and neatest way of saying what you want to say.

suffix, an affix attached to the end of a word: e.g. *-ness*, *-ship*, *-able* in the words 'thinness', 'scholarship', 'bearable'.

syllepsis, e.g. 'He was kicking the football with determination and his left foot', 'She lost her spectacles and her temper'.

synecdoche, naming a part when you mean the whole: e.g. 'a fleet of a hundred sail' (meaning ships).

synonyms, words that are much the same in meaning and use: e.g. beautiful, handsome, good-looking; breakable, fragile, frail.

syntax, the part of grammar that deals with the way words are arranged in sentences.

tautology, unnecessary repetition: e.g. 'I have been *all alone by myself* for hours.'

AN EMERGENCY GUIDE TO PUNCTUATION

If you want to feel in a really dangerous, exposed position, sit down to write a simple, brief guide to punctuation—knowing that

H. G. Fowler, in his *Modern English Usage*, devoted 1,000 worried words to the comma alone, and that punctuation is always to some extent an individual matter. However, this section, as warily as possible, sets down such rules as it is safe to pass on. It is meant as a simple, rough-and-ready guide for emergencies.

Remember: punctuation is only a way of helping your reader to understand the sense of what you write. In speech you make your meaning clear by your pauses and by the way your voice rises and falls (e.g. the listener knows when you're asking a question from the way your voice rises at the end of the sentence). Punctuation is simply a collection of devices for getting these pauses and these rises and falls of voice on to paper. (E.g. your rising voice at the end of a question is suggested by the question-mark.)

A. To mark where a sentence ends we use one of three stops:

(i) a **full stop** (.) where the sentence is a statement;
(ii) a **question mark** (?) where the sentence asks a question;
(iii) an **exclamation mark** (!) where the sentence is an exclamation.

B. The **comma** (,) is the stop that stands for the little pauses after single words or groups of words. Read the following sentence aloud (it comes from *Huckleberry Finn*) and note how the commas mark the pauses and the ups and downs of your voice:

We went to a clump of bushes, and Tom made everybody swear to keep the secret, and then showed them a hole in the hill, right in the thickest part of the bushes.

Warning. Alas, it's not always as easy as this. If you've got tangled up in one of the comma's trickier uses, try pp. 96–99 in Eric Partridge's *You Have a Point There*.

C. A more definite pause in the sentence is marked by a **semi-colon** (;). For example, you might write:

There was no football this afternoon; the weather was far too wet.

You could say there are two sentences here; but (as has happened in the sentence you're now reading) the sense of each is so closely connected with the sense of the other that they gain from not being separated completely.

D. The **colon** (:) is generally used before a list of things or a quotation. E.g.

> *He told us what he had brought with him: a penknife, a fishing-rod, his lunch and half a pound of worms.*

or

> *Shakespeare wrote: 'To be or not to be, that is the question.'*

But *be warned*: some writers like to use the colon (as we have done in this sentence) where others would use a semi-colon.

E. **Inverted commas** or **quotation marks** (" ") are used (i) to mark off the actual words of a speaker where it is *those actual words* that you are writing down, e.g.

> *"Oh Lord," groaned the reader, "punctuation does seem difficult."*

or (ii) to mark off a quotation that comes inside a sentence: e.g.

> *When he got to "See how they run" he made little running movements with his fingers.*

Note: punctuation marks that don't belong to the quotation come outside the quotation marks. E.g.

> *Did I hear you recite "There was an old man of Kilkenny"?* (not *"There was an old man of Kilkenny?"*).

Warning: There are two kinds of inverted commas, (" ") and (' '). It doesn't matter which you use; but note the following:

> *Tom said, "Did I hear you recite 'There was an old man of Kilkenny'?"*

Where—as here—there's a quotation inside a quotation, use your chosen mark for the main quotation and the other mark for the quotation inside it.

F. **Dashes** (—) or **brackets** () are used to enclose things that are really said *aside*—in other words, they don't belong to the main structure of the sentence. If I say:

> *He's a good boy and—as I was saying to his mother yesterday—his work has been excellent,*

my main sentence is *He's a good boy and his work has been*

excellent. As I was saying to his mother yesterday is said aside, and goes either between dashes or between brackets.

G. The **apostrophe** (') is not so difficult as some people make it (we knew a desperate little boy who'd grasped only that it often accompanies the letter 's', and so put it in front of every letter 's' he wrote, even in the middle of a word). There are two main uses of the apostrophe:

    (i) to show possession: *George's book, Mr Davis's Jaguar*;
    (ii) to mark a missing letter: e.g. *don't* (*do not*), *it's* (*it is*). (Of course, in *shan't* the apostrophe marks several missing letters. In the eighteenth century it was written *sha'n't*.)

H. An important use of the **hyphen** (-) is to join words where failing to join them would falsify one's meaning. E.g. a *gold nibbed pen* is a pen made of gold with a nib in it; a *gold-nibbed pen* is a pen (of whatever material) that has a gold nib.

Further Reading

Usage and Abusage, by Eric Partridge (Penguin)
Words! Words! Words! by Andrew Scotland (Cassell)
Modern English Usage, by H. G. Fowler (Oxford)
Roget's Thesaurus of English Words and Phrases (Penguin) is a very useful book (as well as an entertaining one) for the situation where you want to find a synonym (see L4). As an example, you want another word for 'beautiful': you look it up in the index, are directed to a numbered section, and there find: 'Beautiful, beauteous, handsome, fine, pretty, lovely, graceful, elegant, delicate, refined, fair, personable, comely, seemly, bonny . . .'

A DICTIONARY OF WRITERS

This is a list of only the most famous of our writers, giving their dates, saying for which kind of writing they are most famous (as poet, novelist, dramatist or whatever it may be) and giving the name of their best-known work. The list was compiled by someone who would greatly have enjoyed saying more. ('Don't miss the *Canterbury Tales*. They're warm, funny, grave, full of unforgettable

people and phrases, and, though it's worth getting used to the
not-too-difficult Middle English of the original, there's a good
modern translation by Nevill Coghill.' That sort of thing.) But this
is a list purely for reference—by, the compiler hopes, readers who
are busy acquiring for themselves the desire to say more about a
writer than that his dates were this or that, and his best-known
work was that or this.

Addison, Joseph (1672–1719), essayist and dramatist.
Arnold, Matthew (1822–88), poet and critic. *The Scholar Gipsy.*
Auden, W. H. (1907–1973), poet.
Austen, Jane (1775–1817), novelist. *Pride and Prejudice.*
Bacon, Francis (1561–1621), essayist.
Barrie, Sir J. M. (1860–1937), novelist, playwright. *Peter Pan.*
Beaumont, Francis (1584–1616), dramatist, collaborated with
    John Fletcher (1579–1625). *Knight of the Burning Pestle.*
Beckett, Samuel (1906–1989), novelist, playwright. *Waiting for*
    Godot.
Beerbohm, Sir Max (1872–1956), essayist and critic.
Belloc, Hilaire (1870–1953), poet, essayist, historian and novelist.
    Cautionary Tales.
Bennett, Arnold (1867–1931), novelist. *Old Wives' Tale.*
Blake, William (1757–1828), poet. *Songs of Innocence* and *Songs*
    of Experience.
Borrow, George (1803–81), chronicler of gipsy life. *Lavengro.*
Boswell, James (1740–95), biographer, diarist. *Life of Dr Johnson.*
Bridges, Robert (1844–1930), poet. *Testament of Beauty.*
Brontë, Charlotte (1816–55), novelist. *Jane Eyre.*
Brontë, Emily (1818–48), novelist. *Wuthering Heights.*
Browne, Sir Thomas (1605–82), essayist. *Religio Medici.*
Browning, Robert (1812–89), poetry. *The Ring and the Book.*
Browning, Elizabeth Barrett (1806–61), poet. *Sonnets from the*
    Portuguese.
Buchan, John (1875–1940), novelist, historian. *Thirty-Nine Steps.*
Bunyan, John (1628–88), author of *Pilgrim's Progress.*
Burns, Robert (1759–96), poet.
Butler, Samuel (1612–80), poet. *Hudibras.*
Butler, Samuel (1835–1902), novelist. *The Way of All Flesh.*
Byron, Lord (1788–1824), poet. *Don Juan.*
Campion, Thomas (1567?–1619), poet.

Carlyle, Thomas (1795–1881), historian and essayist. *The French Revolution.*

Carroll, Lewis (Charles Lutwidge Dodgson) (1832–98), author of *Alice in Wonderland.*

Chaucer, Geoffrey (1340?–1400), poet. *Canterbury Tales.*

Chesterton, G. K. (1874–1936), poet, essayist and novelist. The *Father Brown* stories.

Clare, John (1793–1864), poet.

Cobbett, William (1762–1835), essayist and social critic. *Rural Rides.*

Coleridge, Samuel Taylor (1772–1834), poet and critic. *Rime of the Ancient Mariner.*

Collins, Wilkie (1824–89), novelist. *The Moonstone.*

Collins, William (1721–59), poet.

Congreve, William (1670–1729), dramatist. *Way of the World.*

Conrad, Joseph (1857–1924), novelist. *Lord Jim.*

Cowley, Abraham (1618–67), poet.

Cowper, William (1731–1800), poet. *The Task.*

Crabbe, George (1754–1832), poet. *The Borough.*

Defoe, Daniel (1661?–1731), novelist. *Robinson Crusoe.*

Dekker, Thomas (1570?–1641?), dramatist.

De la Mare, Walter (1873–1956), poet and novelist.

De Quincey, Thomas (1785–1859), essayist and critic. *Confessions of an Opium-Eater.*

Dickens, Charles (1812–70), novelist. *David Copperfield.*

Donne, John (1573–1631), poet.

Doyle, Sir A. Conan (1859–1930), novelist. *Hound of the Baskervilles.*

Drayton, Michael (1563–1631), poet. *The Ballad of Agincourt.*

Dryden, John (1631–1700), poet and dramatist. *Absalom and Achitophel.*

Eliot, George (Mary Ann Evans) (1819–80), novelist. *Mill on the Floss.*

Eliot, T. S. (1888–1965), poet. *The Waste Land.*

Evelyn, John (1620–1706), diarist.

Fielding, Henry (1707–54), dramatist and novelist. *Tom Jones.*

Fitzgerald, Edward (1809–83), poet. *Rubaiyat of Omar Khayyam.*

Forster, E. M. (1879–1970), novelist. *Passage to India.*

Galsworthy, John (1869–1933), novelist. *The Forsyte Saga.*

Gaskell, Elizabeth Cleghorn (1810–65), novelist. *Cranford.*

Gay, John (1685–1732), poet. *The Beggar's Opera.*

Gibbon, Edward (1737–94), historian. *Decline and Fall of the Roman Empire.*

Gilbert, Sir W. S. (1837–1911), playwright and humorous poet. *The Bab Ballads.*

Gissing, George (1857–1903), novelist. *The Private Papers of Henry Ryecroft.*

Golding, Sir William (b. 1911), novelist. *Lord of the Flies.*

Goldsmith, Oliver (1728–74), poet, essayist and playwright. *Vicar of Wakefield.*

Graves, Robert (1895–1985), poet and novelist.

Gray, Thomas (1716–71), poet. *Elegy in a Country Churchyard.*

Greene, Graham (1904–1991), novelist. *The Power and the Glory.*

Hardy, Thomas (1840–1928), poet and novelist. *Tess of the D'Urbervilles.*

Hazlitt, William (1778–1830), critic and essayist.

Herbert, George (1593–1633), poet.

Herrick, Robert (1591–1674), poet.

Hobbes, Thomas (1588–1679), philosopher. *Leviathan.*

Hood, Thomas (1799–1845), poet. *Song of a Shirt.*

Hopkins, Gerard Manley (1844–89), poet.

Housman, A. E. (1859–1936), poet. *A Shropshire Lad.*

Hudson, W. H. (1841–1922), novelist and naturalist. *Green Mansions.*

Hunt, Leigh (1784–1859), poet and essayist.

Jacobs, W. W. (1863–1943), novelist and short-story writer.

James, Henry (1843–1916), novelist. *Daisy Miller.*

Jefferies, Richard (1848–87), essayist and novelist. *Bevis.*

Johnson, Dr Samuel (1709–84), poet, critic and dictionary-maker. *Vanity of Human Wishes.*

Jonson, Ben (1573?–1637), poet and dramatist. *The Alchemist.*

Joyce, James (1882–1941), novelist. *Ulysses.*

Keats, John (1795–1821), poet. *Endymion.*

Kingsley, Charles (1819–75), novelist. *The Water Babies.*

Kipling, Rudyard (1865–1936), poet and novelist. *Jungle Tales.*

Lamb, Charles ('Elia') (1775–1834), essayist.

Landor, Walter Savage (1775–1864), poet.

Langland, William (1330?–1400?), poet. *Piers Plowman.*

Larkin, Philip (1922–85), poet.

Lawrence, D. H. (1885–1930), poet and novelist. *Sons and Lovers.*

Lear, Edward (1812–88), poet. *The Owl and the Pussycat.*

Lovelace, Richard (1618–58), poet.

Lytton, Lord (1831–91), novelist. *Last Days of Pompeii.*

Macaulay, T. B. (1800–59), historian. *History of England.*

Malory, Sir Thomas (*c.* 1470), author of *Morte d'Arthur.*

Marlowe, Christopher (1564–93), poet and dramatist. *Dr Faustus.*

Marryat, Frederick (1792–1848), novelist. *Children of the New Forest.*

Marvell, Andrew (1621–78), poet.

Masefield, John (1876–1967), poet and novelist. *Dauber.*

Massinger, Philip (1583–1640), dramatist. *New Way to Pay Old Debts.*

Meredith, George (1828–1909), novelist. *The Egoist.*

Milton, John (1608–74), poet. *Paradise Lost.*

Moore, George (1857–1933), novelist. *Esther Waters.*

Moore, Thomas (1779–1852), poet.

More, Sir Thomas (1478–1535), author of *Utopia.*

Morris, William (1834–96), poet. *The Earthly Paradise.*

O'Casey, Sean (1883–1964), dramatist. *Juno and the Paycock.*

Orwell, George (1903–50), essayist and novelist. *Animal Farm.*

Owen, Wilfred (1893–1918), poet.

Peacock, Thomas Love (1785–1866), poet and novelist.

Pepys, Samuel (1633–1703), diarist.

Pope, Alexander (1688–1744), poet. *Rape of the Lock.*

Raleigh, Sir Walter (1552–1618), poet.

Reade, Charles (1814–84), novelist. *Cloister on the Hearth.*

Richardson, Samuel (1689–1761), novelist. *Clarissa Harlowe.*

Rossetti, Christina (1830–94), poet. *Goblin Market.*

Rossetti, Dante Gabriel (1828–82), poet.

Ruskin, John (1819–1900), writer on art. *Stones of Venice.*

Scott, Sir Walter (1771–1832), poet and novelist. The *Waverley* novels.

Shakespeare, William (1564–1616), poet and dramatist. *Hamlet.*

Shaw, George Bernard (1856–1950), dramatist and critic. *St Joan.*

Shelley, Mary (1797–1855), novelist. *Frankenstein.*

Shelley, Percy Bysshe (1792–1822), poet. *The Revolt of Islam.*

Sheridan, Richard Brinsley (1751–1816), dramatist. *The Rivals.*

Sidney, Sir Philip (1554–86), poet.

Skelton, John (1460?–1529), poet.

Smollett, Tobias (1721–71), novelist. *Roderick Random.*

Southey, Robert (1774–1843), poet and historian. *Life of Nelson.*
Spenser, Edmund (1552?–1599), poet. *Faerie Queene.*
Steele, Sir Richard (1672–1729), essayist.
Sterne, Laurence (1713–68), novelist. *A Sentimental Journey.*
Stevenson, Robert Louis (1850–94), poet and novelist. *Treasure Island.*
Suckling, Sir John (1609–42), poet.
Swift, Jonathan (1667–1745), author of *Gulliver's Travels.*
Swinburne, Algernon Charles (1837–1909), poet.
Synge, J. M. (1871–1909), dramatist. *Playboy of the Western World.*
Tennyson, Alfred, Lord (1809–92), poet. *Idylls of the King.*
Thackeray, William Makepiece (1811–63), novelist. *Vanity Fair.*
Thomas, Dylan (1914–53), poet. *Under Milk Wood.*
Thomas, Edward (1878–1917), poet.
Thompson, Francis (1859–1907), poet. *The Hound of Heaven.*
Thomson, James (1700–48), poet. *The Seasons.*
Tolkien, J. R. R. (1892–1973), novelist. *The Lord of the Rings.*
Trollope, Anthony (1815–82), novelist. *The Warden.*
Vaughan, Henry (1622–95), poet.
Webster, John (1580?–1625?), dramatist. *Duchess of Malfi.*
Wells, H. G. (1866–1946), novelist. *Kipps.*
White, Gilbert (1720–93), naturalist. *Natural History of Selborne.*
Wilde, Oscar (1856–1900), poet, critic and dramatist. *Importance of Being Earnest.*
Woolf, Virginia (1882–1941), novelist, critic. *To the Lighthouse.*
Wordsworth, William (1770–1850), poet. *Lyrical Ballads.*
Wycherley, William (1640?–1716), dramatist. *The Country Wife.*
Yeats, William Butler (1865–1939), poet.

MUSIC AND THE ARTS

MUSIC

Very probably, music is historically the first of all the arts. After all, one often hears of babies who sing before they say their first word and who beat out rhythms before they sing. So it is easy to imagine a caveman grunting out some sort of music in an age when even speech—let alone writing—was unknown, and before the first cave paintings adorned the walls of his home.

There is another way in which music can claim to be the first of the arts. One writer put it this way: 'all other arts aspire to the condition of music'. By this, the writer meant that music is the freest of the arts. A writer must say what he means in precise words; a painter must make us a picture of something we recognise; a sculptor must present us with a form that has meaning. Or so it was until very recently. The musician, though, has never had to follow these rules because music has no meaning. He plays a fast tune on a trumpet and we all find it 'lively' or 'stirring'. He plays a slow tune on a violin and we all find it 'melancholy' or 'sad'. We even talk of 'pastoral' music—music that suggests green fields and blue skies. Yet music (as the musician would agree) has no meaning other than the meaning we agree to give it. The astonishing thing is that we all agree about its meaning!

Music, then, is free of the rules that bind the other arts. But there are several rules that apply to music. For instance: the basic recipe for all music includes Melody, Harmony and Rhythm.

Rhythm

Rhythm is the cornerstone of music. To prove this, try humming a very well-known tune (*Pop Goes The Weasel* will do) in a way that has all the notes of the melody in the right order, but with the rhythm deliberately distorted. Most people will find it impossible to recognise the tune. It will have lost its identity with its rhythm. Just the same thing happens when you break up the rhythm of a sentence. For example, you can take these words:

> 'To let a firework off, blue paper must be lit'

and by altering the rhythm, change their sense into:

> 'To let: a firework. Off-blue paper. Must be lit.'

Melody is the tune. Some melodies—*Greensleeves*, for instance—

are so powerful that even drastic rhythm changes cannot conceal them.

Harmony is the structure of notes and chords that fill out the melody and add to its meaning. You could call harmonies the adjectives and adverbs of music. So if the melody is the noun 'cat', it is the harmonies that make the cat happy or sad, black or tortoiseshell.

Most tunes can be given a variety of harmonies. Yet musically gifted people generally agree on what is the right set of harmonies for a given tune—and they will certainly agree in disliking any wrong harmony or false chord they hear.

All the music we hear contains some—usually all—of the elements of rhythm, melody and harmony. One way of classifying musical instruments is to arrange them under the headings of Rhythm, Melody, Harmony. For instance, a drum is a Rhythm instrument; a flute is a Melody instrument; a guitar is a Harmony instrument because it plays chords. Put these three instruments together and you would have a band that could play many kinds of music.

If you are thinking of taking up a musical instrument, you will be wise to find out which sort suits your natural talents best— Melody, Harmony or Rhythm.

MUSIC HISTORY

Wherever history is recorded it is usual to find some record of music. A mural in the tomb of Rameses (about 1150 B.C.) shows players with large, elaborate harps. Another mural in Thebes shows a girl lute player. There is an Assyrian relief in the British Museum picturing a mixed orchestra of players. All these random examples take us well back before the birth of Christ.

Going further afield and still further back to 2500 B.C., we know of a Chinese scholar called Ling Lun who codified the five tones of oriental music then in use and named each tone. Some tones, according to Ling Lun, were upper class and even royal; others were mere peasants! Oddly enough, this idea of naming tones by social qualities, degrees of nobility and so on, is found quite frequently in various periods and countries.

Moving nearer to our own age, there are endless references in fact and fiction establishing the unchanging importance of music throughout history. Everyone knows about David playing his harp to Saul—about the Pied Piper of Hamelin—about Red Indian war chants. Not everyone knows that the rich Romans had water organs; when people came to dinner, the water organ (*hydraulus*) played. Some people hated the noise and wrote peevish comments about it. Rather the same thing happens today with record players!

The tragedy is that although we know that there has always been music, we cannot hear the music itself. We know exactly how the Egyptians, say, looked and dressed. We can read their writings, study their religions, see their own models and paintings and tools in the museums. But we cannot know how their music *sounded.* In fact we can make no sense at all even of some of the earliest written music. We can roughly trace a melodic thread, but we do not know the rhythms or tones; or harmonies, if any. Ancient music is a mystery without a key.

Because of the lack of clearly written music, we can go back only comparatively few centuries to recapture the sound of old music. True, some melodies heard today are truly ancient, even ageless—the chants of Jewish temples, certain Indian pieces and the Catholic Church's Georgian chants—but our sort of music is possibly an invention of the middle ages.

Written Music

Our music is in the main based on the Diatonic scale which can be sung as Doh, Re, Mi, Fa, Sol, La, Ti, Doh. The notes are each a tone apart excepting Mi-Fa and Ti-Doh, which are a semitone (half tone) apart. Doh is the Tonic or 'home' note defining the music's key. Countless simple tunes (e.g., *Three Blind Mice*) employ only the 'natural' tones of the major Diatonic scale (there are minor scales too). Semitones enlarge the scale to 12 notes. Music not restricted to a key may be expressed by the Chromatic scale of 12 semitones.

Several ways of naming notes and writing music have been tried, of course. The simplest were based on sketching a tune like this:

Sing this sketch and with luck you will hear *God Save the Queen*.

To reduce the luck element, notes were named from A to G. Four or more 'stave' lines were added to align the written notes (today we use five, as shown below). This system was developed to its present-day form—an unsatisfactory form, incidentally, for our music uses 12 notes and five into twelve won't go.

A glance above will show you the result of this bad division. The middle C is the only note the two clefs have in common. If you look for any other note—A, for instance—it will occupy one position in the treble clef and a different position in the bass clef.

This system also forces us to use a variety of complicated correction signs. As you can see, our alphabet of notes runs only from A to G—which makes seven notes; but as already pointed out, ours is a 12-note music. To insert the other five notes in written music, we have to make use of signs for sharps—♯, flats—♭ and naturals—♮. But even then it does not work out. Our scale includes notes that could be called either sharp or flat! Here is an octave of notes from a piano:

* Is this note both B and C flat? † Is the black note F sharp or G flat? And for that matter, is there any real difference between D

sharp and E flat? There is not on the piano, naturally. But is there on a violin?

Fortunately we can ask the questions without answering them here. It is enough to say that we live with our musical notation because the cure—introducing a new system—would be worse than the disease! Musicians are used to it, just as typists are used to their typewriter keyboard's layout.

Music's Development From now on we almost ignore all forms of music but our own European and American kinds—that is, the 12-note forms played in various arrangements of melody, harmony and rhythm.

As far as we know (we cannot be sure) this music first took a wide hold of Europe from, say, the tenth century A.D. on. Hucbald, a monk who lived until A.D. 930, describes a raw-sounding two-voice harmony running in fifths (such as C and G, D and A, etc). The effect of playing only in fifths is very crude indeed.

John Cotton (A.D. 1130) wrote of music 'by at least two singers in such a manner that, while one sounds the main melody, the other colours it with other tones'. This suggests that polyphonic (many-voiced) music was only just beginning. Otherwise, why did Cotton bother to explain it?

Polyphonic music developed fairly rapidly. By the fifteenth and sixteenth centuries minstrels' chants freed music of strict, almost mathematical forms and modes. New rhythms became acceptable. Harmonies were used for emotional as well as formal effects. Opera was reborn in Italy in about 1600. Instruments developed fast. Music schools were established. *Some important composers of the period: Monteverdi (opera), Byrd, Palestrina.*

In the seventeenth century, music almost began again with Bach, who developed past forms to an excellence that is still unsurpassed and also reached forward into the future both with his music and instruments (he virtually re-designed the organ, for example). Bach's impact on music is comparable with that of photography on graphic art—but Bach was also the age's supreme artist as well! *Important composers: Purcell, Handel, Bach.*

In the late eighteenth century, the modern symphony orchestra and its music came into being. Music began to move from so-called 'Classical' forms (that is, formal variations-on-a-set-theme forms) into more free and spacious 'Romantic' forms. In our century, painting has received a very similar liberation: the

painter of today need no longer draw to an academic formula—
he can make his own rules and effects. *Typical 'classical' composers:
Mozart, Gluck, Haydn.*

The rest of the story is probably best told by the names of nine-
teenth-century composers such as Beethoven, Mendelssohn, Berlioz, Schubert, Tchaikovsky, Brahms and others. All these are
'Romantic' composers in that they exploited and developed all
that had gone before along their own individual lines; and also
constantly strove to enlarge the range of effects and feelings that
music and musical instruments convey. The restrictions put upon
them, if any, were all self-imposed. They did not follow the Rules
of the Game that existed in earlier centuries. They tried rather to
change the game.

In our century, music has yet again started afresh. The very
nature of 12-note music is in question. Why not a limitless scale?
Or a number of different scales? Why follow any recognised form?
Why accept the instruments of the orchestra as the only instruments—could not music be made electronically, without
human instrumentalists—or even human composers?

Like painting, music need no longer be representational; it need
no longer attempt to establish definite mind-pictures, as it generally did 70 years ago. Anything and everything that the listener
agrees to accept as music—including arrangements of electronic
noises—is now within the composer's scope.

Jazz

When Pepys, the diarist, invited friends to his house for a musical
evening 300 years ago, music was still at its formal stage. The
Rules of the Game were known and followed. Thus the evening's
music could be improvised on a formal theme understood by all
the players present.

As music became more complicated, improvisation became less
likely and less satisfactory. The written notes offered a more
assured performance of more exciting and advanced music. Improvisation therefore slowly died.

It was revived by jazz players early in this century. The jazz
player takes as his basis a set of harmonies that he and the others
are familiar with—the chord structure of *Tea for Two*, for
instance—and improvises melodies and counter melodies that fit
those chords. Almost invariably, the improvisation is solidly

supported by a firm and unchanging rhythm that locks the players together as they perform. This basis of firm harmonies and solid rhythm leaves the jazzman an enormous amount of freedom: and he makes the most of it. He plays round the melody. He adopts new instruments or alters old ones to fit his needs. He welcomes new sounds and ideas—indeed he will go out of his way to surprise his listeners.

The effect of jazz on other musical forms is already felt and felt strongly. Many modern 'classical' composers introduce jazz phrases and passages but seldom with success (the attempts of jazz musicians to use 'classical' forms and methods are equally poor). However, the sheer vitality, inventiveness and virtuosity of the best jazz musicians are heavily infectious. It is very probable that the jazz and 'classical' compositions of the future will move along tracks that meet here and there; and already, both schools are making similar experiments for similar purposes.

Popular Music

Dance, 'pop', 'rock' and most other forms of popular music owe a lot to jazz. 'Folk' music, for instance, is often given jazz elements. However, pop is finding its own, unique 'voices' as the range of (particularly electronic) instruments and sound sources increases. Again, pop musicians are discarding the old recipes for making a tune and reaching out for new freedoms. A pop song of the 1930s had 32 bars, the modern pop song has any number.

No one can predict the future of popular music—but then, the whole idea of pop is that it should please now, this moment.

THE INSTRUMENTS

Instruments can be split into families and groups in various ways, most of them a little vague. For instance, the Flute is a Woodwind instrument—but most modern flutes are made of metal. However, here are some customary groupings:

Strings

Bowed The violin family, particularly the violin—viola—cello—string bass. But also the viols, which have frets.

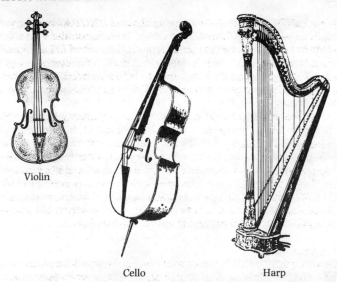

Violin

Cello

Harp

Hand or Plucked The harp. The guitar family—guitar in its 'classical' form with gut or nylon strings plucked with the fingers; or with steel strings plucked with a plectrum. Also banjo, ukelele, lute and many other fretted instruments.

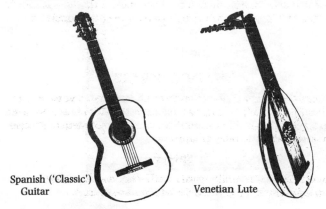

Spanish ('Classic') Guitar

Venetian Lute

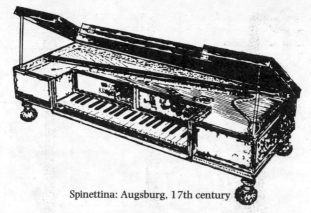

Spinettina: Augsburg, 17th century

Keyboard Piano, harpsichord, klavier, spinet and many others.

Wind

Flute family—flute, piccolo and others, all blown transversely—
  that is, across a hole.
Recorder family The various recorders, small and large; and many
  other instruments that you blow *down*, including the flageolet—a superior penny whistle—and various pipes.

Metal Flute

Piccolo

Flageolet

Tenor Saxophone   Oboe   Recorder

Bagpipes are wind instruments. They consist of a number of pipes blown by the player and also by an air reservoir, the bag. So there is some slight similarity with the—

Organ, which is an arrangement of various kinds of pipes and other sound producers fed air from a chamber that is kept filled by an air pump (but see Electronic instruments, M14).

Reed instruments may have double reeds—oboes and bassoons—or, more commonly, single reeds, as in clarinets, saxophones.

Brass wind instruments

Trumpets, cornets, horns, trombones, bugles. All these can be called **Lip** instruments because the note is formed by the player's lips—not by a reed, or whistle.

All lip instruments are, at heart, a posthorn to which something has been added. A bugle is a simple horn wound into coils. A trumpet is a bugle with valves added to increase the number of notes obtainable. The French horn is a posthorn wound in circles and with valves to increase its range. The

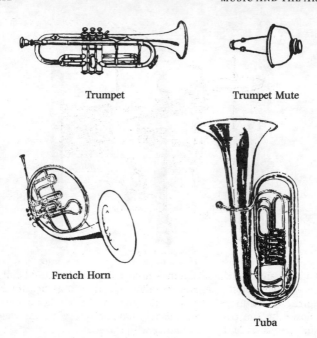

Trumpet   Trumpet Mute

French Horn

Tuba

trombone literally shortens or lengthens itself (thus changing its pitch) when the player operates the slide. Naturally, there are many other differences and the posthorn idea is an over-simplification; but the fact remains that a trumpet with stuck valves or a trombone with a stuck slide reverts to the instrument that founded its family—and that basic instrument is a tapering tube with a mouthpiece, from which about five notes can be produced.

Percussion instruments

This family includes drums, cymbals, bells and other rhythm instruments—including the tunable kettle drums of the symphony orchestra, the jazz drummer's outfit, the huge selection used by a Latin-American band and the electronic drum machine.

Jazz Drum Kit

Once again, the classification is a little vague. One could call a piano a percussion instrument—after all, its strings are hit by hammers.

Tympani

Vibes

From the instruments described so far, one could form anything from a symphony orchestra to a folk group. Throughout history and in every country, instruments have always been basically what they are today. Walt Disney once made a short film about the development of music called TOOT, WHISTLE, PLUNK & BOOM (suggest that they show it at your school) which made this point very well. There is really no *basic* difference between a panpipes and a recorder, or a lyre and ukelele. The differences lie only in additions, subtractions and modifications made over many centuries.

During the last hundred years, though, a completely new class of instruments has appeared. So let us have a new heading:

Electric, Electronic instruments produce their sounds either by amplifying sounds produced by ordinary instruments—the electric guitar is the best example—or by creating original sounds electrically, as in the electric organ and synthesizer. Your local church organ is probably partly electric; its action and air pump may be worked by electricity. But if it is a new instrument, then it is very probably 'electronic'. Its notes and tones have nothing to do with wind and pipes and everything to do with electronic tone-generators, electric amplifiers and so on.

The future of such instruments is limitless. Most of the pop and beat music heard today would be almost inaudible if there

Electric Guitar

Multi-functional keyboard—memory pack, rhythms, various voices, set or
fingered chords, transpose.

were a power failure—most of the sound is made, and all of it
amplified, by electric devices. The modern church organ,
obviously, would be struck dumb if its power supply were cut.
And musicians in nearly all fields are experimenting with
musique concrète—music actually manufactured, stored, edited
and put together from sounds of electronic origin.

SOME MUSICAL TERMS

Many people are not clear about what is meant by the word
'Pitch', what the Conductor actually does and so on. Here are
explanations of a few of these puzzles.

Ballad A song, often sentimental, that tells a story.

Bar Written music is divided into Bars by upright lines. Each bar
contains so many beats. Count the beats and you will know
the rhythm of the music. See MEASURE.

Beat Rhythmic pulse. A waltz has three beats to each bar.

Chamber Music Music for small instrumental groups—music that is best heard in a room, not a hall.

Conductor His function is not simply to make the orchestra play together, but rather to dictate *how* the music should be played. Two separate conductors may produce very different renderings of the same music from an orchestra.

Counterpoint, Contrapuntal Counterpoint is the combining of two or more melodies, played simultaneously. *Contrapuntal* is the adjective.

Fugue A contrapuntal composition for several parts—that is, instruments or voices.

Key Most music is written in the key of the composer's choice. The KEY SIGNATURE indicates to the player which key has been chosen. If the player sees F sharp written at the beginning of the music, he knows that his 'home key' is G—because the major scale of G is distinguished by possessing an F sharp. As the piece may not stick to its 'home key' of G, the composer will have to insert other sharps, flats and naturals as they occur. These are called Accidentals.

Measure A division of music in terms of beats. If there are three beats to the bar, then the writer will draw vertical lines at three-beat intervals and so divide his composition into Measures.

Notation To write a note filling a whole measure, you write a semi-breve, ○. A minim, ℐ. is worth half the time value of the semi-breve and the crotchet, ♩, worth half that. And so on to quaver, semi-quaver and demi-semi-quaver, etc.

Pitch The highness or lowness of a musical sound. Middle A was internationally agreed to have a frequency of 440. A note at the top of the piano, well above middle C, has a higher pitch. People with 'absolute pitch' are able to hear a note and name it correctly.

Synthesizers Electronic musical instruments (including drum machines) that analyse, simulate, modify and create old or new musical sounds.

THE ARTS

Imagine a lucky dip of humanity—a pot filled with cavemen and car-workers, ancient-Egyptian washerwomen and Red Indian warriors. You dip your hand in and take out an SP—a Sample Person. You provide it with the basics of life—the materials for food, shelter and clothing. What will the SP do once settled?

It will first provide itself with the practical things it needs (a bird or beetle would do as much). But later it will do something that hardly any other creatures do. It will add to what it needs something it doesn't need—an individual and personal touch of Art. The latest water-pot will be made in an improved shape and given colour and decoration; fringes will be cut in the edges of sleeves; the home will be decorated.

If your particular SP does none of these things you have chanced on a dull and lifeless specimen. Return it to the lucky dip and try again. You are unlikely to have to make too many tries. Mankind has always produced arts and artists. There were cavemen artists and Victorian ladies who painted flower pictures. There were Eskimos carving walrus tusks and Navajo Indians weaving blankets and rugs. Great artists have sprung from primitive peoples: wicked men have produced work of undying beauty: feeble men have shown huge artistic power.

Ah, but wait. What is all this about 'great' art—'beauty'—'power'? The *Mona Lisa* is only so much rotting pigment. St Paul's Cathedral is simply a large people-container with a useless dome on top. The SP's decorated water-pot holds water no better than the plain one. You can add up the pebbles in a bucketful and get a sure answer—but how do you add up art? Power, beauty, greatness—who says so? How are judgements possible?

One answer is this: you know artistic judgements are possible because you constantly make them yourself. You spend loving hours painting a kit model or getting a garment just right: you become angry with yourself if your achievement falls short of your intention. That is an artistic judgement. You prefer this poster to that—artistic judgement again. Perhaps you are becoming bored with this piece of writing? Then you are making an artistic judgement. There is nothing wrong with the printing or the paper.

How *is* art truly judged? The answer seems to be—time. Quite obviously 'great' art may stem from unusual human powers and mighty themes. But, then, you can see the 'greatness' of an artist in small things. **Leonardo da Vinci**, for example, did working sketches of machines and practice sketches of animals rolling in the grass. There is a quality about the drawings that says, 'The man who made these was a great artist.' There are very small carvings, *netsuke*, made by Japanese craftsmen. Netsuke were merely permanent, solid knots to hold the strings of a purse or pouch together, so no grand intentions or soaring of the spirit were needed in their production: yet in some of these little carvings you may find not only superb craftsmanship but also the work of considerable artists. Time—and the considered opinions of informed and enthusiastic minds—is needed to sort such matters out.

But you have no time. So let us think about—

Your Judgement
'Beauty is in the eye of the beholder.' In other words, you like it, I loathe it, on first sight.

19th-century ivory netsuke

Nevertheless, instant like/loathe decisions are generally worthless. You take the trouble to read the instructions that come with a power tool or dress pattern—to understand how the thing is *meant* to work. The same trouble should be taken with a work of art.

What do you need to know? First, how the thing fits into—or escapes from—its period. What were other artists producing at the time? What were the times like? What rules and conventions governed the artist and his art? Was the artist trying to please himself, or a patron, a customer?

The last question is important. There is a belief that artists are 'free'—they do their own thing, they need satisfy only themselves. This is nonsense, of course. Most artists, including those with the greatest and most revered names, worked to please a patron—the state, the Church, a rich man, a gallery, an agent, a market. Studies, experiments and innovations were private matters. Some artists rebelled against patronage: you may like to look up the fascinating story of James McNeill Whistler. In 1877, he was called a coxcomb who asked 200 guineas 'for flinging a pot of paint in the public's face'. Other artists had to appear in court to speak for or against him. The Court awarded Whistler 'Damages one farthing'. So art *could* be added up then—but the addition did not hold. Today, Whistler is probably considered a 'great' painter. The farthing— or the 200 guineas—must now be multiplied by thousands and hundreds. Yet his work will not surprise *you*, a person living a hundred years later. You will be puzzled by the scandal and outrage caused by an artist determined to please himself.

Once you have understood the motives, methods and 'provenance' (place, time, pedigree) of a work of art, you are in a position to make a judgement. Having made it, look up other judgements, by notable critics. You will probably find that they have seen much more than you have seen.

You will also find that one critic disagrees with another. So your opinion could well be right after all.

A HISTORY

If, as Henry Ford said, 'History is bunk,' then Art History is double bunk, because though most artists are conditioned by the times they live in, many ignore or flout their times yet still emerge as 'significant artists of the period'.

So when you read here that the arts of, say, Ancient Greece were thus-and-thus, take it with a pinch of salt. Imagine, if you like, an Ancient Greek reading the words and saying, 'Well! All I can say is, this writer ought to meet that crazy artist down the road! He doesn't fit this description at all!'

Another point. To avoid getting lost, go back to the first pages of this encyclopaedia—THE WORLD, ITS HISTORY.

Third and most important: there are countless excellently illustrated books about the arts. When something here stirs your curiosity, go to the library and look at the books.

Ancient Times

Farming, home-building, community Man, seems to have started around 7000 B.C. These people left artifacts (things made with tools) and art works all over the world. If you imagine a man of these times to be a shaggy brute with a club for hitting other shaggy brutes, you are probably right: nevertheless, his (or her) cave-drawings are vivid, accomplished and sure. Some we know to be very accurate—for example, we can compare the deer we see today with the deer drawings done all those thousands of years ago and say, 'He got it right.'

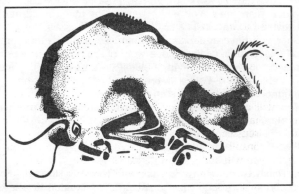

Prehistoric cave painting (from Altamira, Spain)

Benin bronze

For wall and ceiling paintings, all kinds of techniques were used—charcoal sticks, scratchings, shallow relief and so on, often with colour. Frequently the irregularities of the surface were picked up to show the shape of the subject. A protruding lump could be the flank of a beast, for example.

Primitive/Savage/Ethnic Art
It is difficult today to know who are the 'savages'—ourselves, the tool-using technocrats so worried by our knowledge: or them, the primitive peoples, who live close to Nature because they must. The same difficulty strikes us in judging their art. It is only fairly recently that African, Eskimo and such arts from remote, wild places have come to be talked of as 'Art'. Similarly, it is only quite recently that the savageries of some of our present-day artists could be discussed in polite society.

Please consult the books and arrive at your own conclusions. At worst you will find something exciting. At best you may find a half-forgotten something that you will recognise with delight, or fear, or wonder. See books about Lascaux, the Dordogne, Altamira, Bardal, Willendorf, etc.

Neolithic/Megalithic Structures

The ancient men carved and sculpted figures from rock, bone, anything at all. They also made huge structures. Stonehenge (about 2000 B.C.) is one of several European stone circles built at a time when people lived in shallow pits with crude roofs over them. Yet Stonehenge is massive. There are various theories about the purpose of Stonehenge (and obelisks, menhirs, dolmens and other great stone structures). Whatever the truth—probably to do with sun worship—Stonehenge is a staggering example of architecture for a purpose.

China

China has 3,000 years of recorded history. Her influence pervaded the whole Far East—Japan, Korea, Tibet, Mongolia, Annam. A thousand years before Christ was born, the Chinese took for granted sophisticated and beautiful personal possessions—jade, lacquer, bronze, silk, strange stones and crystals marvellously worked, paintings and porcelain (invented 4th–5th centuries A.D.).

All other Chinese crafts and arts were secondary to painting and calligraphy—partly because of the supreme elegance of Chinese writing, but also because the brush strokes could express the matter and spirit of the writer and his message. Thus 'Dear Sir' can be written as an insult or compliment.

Look through books on Chinese art and you will find a strange conflict of simplicity (porcelain, scroll painting, calligraphy, etc.) and outrageous embellishment (certain buildings, fabrics and in-

Chinese calligraphic characters

terior decorations). But invariably you find supreme, sometimes almost unbelievable, skill.

Wood was the material used for Chinese architecture—thus few ancient buildings survive. Intricate systems of interlinking keys supported the curved, tiled roofs.

A word about dynasties: 'Sun', 'Yuan', 'T'ang' are simply the names of ruling families, used to describe the period of a work much as we use 'Georgian' or 'Victorian'.

Japan

From the 7th century A.D. the Japanese adopted China's arts and crafts. From 10th century A.D. on, when China's civilisation was falling apart, the Japanese went their own way, developing un-rivalled skills with lacquer, ivory, pottery, glass and almost any other material—particularly multi-plate colour printing from wood blocks. See books showing *suzuribake* (writing cabinets), *netsuke* (drawstring toggles), *inrō* (little boxes for pills, etc.)—and even bamboo, which was and is the material for anything from plumbing systems to the most delicate craft objects. Sword-making was regarded as a fine art for very good reasons.

Architecture: look up the many Buddhist temples; and Shōsōin (the Imperial Treasure House, 8th century A.D.). The traditional Japanese domestic interior is particularly interesting in its re-finement and simplicity.

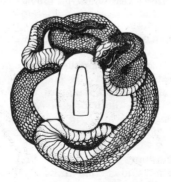

Japanese sword guard: brass, gold,
and silver

India

Great styles of art and architecture had flowered before the birth of Christ. Monasteries, sanctuaries, temples were covered with figures representing innumerable deities. India was, and is, a continent of many faiths and nations—and with an artistic history extending over some 2,000 years. Enough here to say that the golden age of Buddhist art lasted some 300 years, until about A.D. 600 (consult books for examples); that sculpture and architecture are wonderfully mixed—the buildings seem to writhe with figures; and that over the centuries, exquisite works in all materials were produced by artists who found, in their religions, fantastic sources.

Queen Nefertiti (Egypt, 1360 B.C.)

Egypt

The ancient Egyptian civilisations date from about 3000 B.C. The reigning Pharaoh, or king, was regarded as divine. The main function of the artist and the architect was to immortalise him— to record his deeds, to preserve his body and possessions, for all time. Thus architecture and sculpture were monumental (the Pyramids—the Sphinx—the temple of Abu Simbel) and carried out on a staggering scale.

About 2250 B.C., the God/King concept was replaced by that of a heavenly being, Osiris. Now ordinary people could have monumental tombstones and memorials. Because of the Egyptian obsession with death and afterlife, those who could afford it were embalmed, mummified and securely entombed. Today, discoveries are still reported of arts and crafts from the distant past—of works in ivory, wood, glass, gold, precious stones; and, of course, portraiture to commemorate the dead. The painter or stone-carver used his art to report and record as literally as possible—but within certain conventions: an important person was shown large, a less important person small; the side and front of the face could be shown simultaneously; set postures and gestures denoted agreed characteristics and powers (similarly, in Christian art, a halo denoted divine characteristics).

The influence of Egyptian architecture is still to be seen in anything from cinemas to railway bridges and factories. Look up the Egyptian swollen columns and lotus-flower capitals, etc., and see how many echoes you can spot in your district's buildings.

Islam

The Islamic world included Arab, Persian, Syrian and Egyptian peoples who followed the Moslem faith. Islamic art is distinct in that no human and animal figures are represented. The arts were centred on weaving, calligraphy (copying the Koran was a virtuous act), work in precious metals, often inlaid; and in pottery, glass, bronze, enamels. It was largely decorative art: plant forms and geometrical patterns, piercings and curlicues. Thus the term 'arabesque', meaning a curlicue or interlinked decoration.

About a thousand years ago Islam became disunited. Eventually Moslem and Hindu worked together to evolve Mogul art, which could include representations of living animals.

Architecture: Look up in books the Alhambra of Caliph Abd-el-Walid (14th century); mosques, particularly Suleimaniyeh (1550); the Taj Mahal. The pointed arch—from which we derive our Gothic arches and vaulting—was an Islamic innovation.

An Arabesque

The Taj Mahal

Ancient Greece

Rhythm, discipline, order, humanity, harmony, balance—these seem to be the themes of Greek art and architecture. Quite certainly we still follow Greek traditions and find echoes of the Greek in every age that followed. We still describe as 'Classical' (meaning Greek) certain European painters of recent centuries. And we still like to see ideal representations of the human body. We feel at home in public buildings on the Greek scale, with classical Greek decorations. The Greek tradition is probably only a bus ride distant from you as you read.

Greek artists and sculptors tried to express, through the human body, a concept of beauty: see the *Discobolos* (Discus Thrower) by **Myron**, 480–445 B.C. Greek architects sought logical rules and harmonies that could shape a disciplined structure: see for example the Parthenon.

The Greeks were masters of pottery, both in form and decoration; of monumental sculpture in stone and bronze; and of perspective and light-and-shade drawings (q.v.). The Grecian civilisations lasted more than a thousand years and were affected by various religions, scientific advances and philosophies. In the end, it could be said that their greatest achievements were humanistic; for most certainly their art was.

Roman

The Greek civilisation gave way to the all-conquering Romans,

Greek vase

who respected and adopted Greek artistic thinking and methods. But the Romans were not Greeks: thrusting, practical, empire-minded and brilliant engineers, their ideas were less 'human' and

Parthenon front view

their ambitions more grandiose. They enjoyed dreams of glory and their art and architecture showed it. The Pantheon (A.D. 120) and the Colosseum (A.D. 70) are vast structures. A bronze statue of Emperor Nero stood 34 metres high. Their temples, unlike the Greeks', held great congregations. Their villas were centrally heated, lavishly furnished and decorated with wall paintings, mosaic floors and works of art and craft from any corner of their world (which was the whole known world, excluding only China and the Far East). You will find it very easy to discover more in libraries, by visiting the Roman Palace at Fishbourne, Sussex, or simply by reading newspaper stories about Pompeii, the latest 'finds', and so on.

The Pont Du Gard Aqueduct

Etruscan art is often linked with Roman. The Etruscans once dominated Italy and were eventually absorbed by the Romans.

European Art

Western art—the art of Europe, of Europeans in the United States of America and like-minded civilisations—took the forms familiar to us in a comparatively short time: less than a thousand years. When Rome was sacked, Constantinople became the centre of Imperial Roman and Christian culture in northern Europe. A distinct pattern of thought emerged between A.D. 1100 and 1500—the *Gothic* period; you can capture the flavour of this time by visiting Westminster Abbey, the cathedrals of Lincoln and Salisbury and the Keep of the Tower of London. In York Minster you can follow a whole progression of architectural styles and building methods. There are fragments of Roman times, and demonstrations of 'Norman', 'Early English', 'Decorated', 'Perpendicular' developments in the handling of windows, buttresses, vaultings, structures and surfaces. Putting it briefly: what started as massive, thick and round-arched ended as lofty, delicate, airy and filigree. The changes took place over some 300 years.

A section of the Bayeux tapestry

You can also find traces (here we are working backwards) of the arts and sciences of the 'Dark Ages' and Mediaeval times. You can see how the simple pointed arch or the ribbed vault was developed, enlarged and elaborated. You can even see—for instance in the Bayeux tapestry or in stained-glass windows—how people living in the 11th century (the time of William the Conqueror) saw themselves; and judge how important Church and State were in the choice of the subjects the artist might draw from.

Stained-glass window (York Minister)

Section of an illuminated Saxon manuscript

Gothic Art was mainly northern European. In the Byzantine Empire (the Christian, Near East area of Constantinople), great underground burial places, the catacombs, were decorated with paintings on the ceilings and elsewhere. The paintings—like the decorations on lamps and glass objects—were almost always simple representations of Christian doctrines and figures. Great basilicas with lavishly decorated domes were built (Hagia Sophia, Istanbul, A.D. 530). Fine work was done in mosaics, ivories, books, jewellery, enamel and wire-work.

St. Sophia

Renaissance
The word means Rebirth. The new beginning spread through Italy, eventually to affect the whole of Europe, during the 14th-

16th centuries. The works of such artists as **Giotto, Martini** and **Andrea Pisano** hint clearly enough at what was to come.

The Renaissance was one result of a chain-explosion of events, possibilities and attitudes. Links in the chain include the conquest of Constantinople by the Turks (which sent many Greek scholars to Italy); scientific research; voyages of exploration; the spread of printing; the nature of Italy itself—it was then a conglomeration of small city-states ruled by sophisticated families; and perhaps above all, a feeling of personal freedom, very different from that which produced the often strait-jacketed figures seen in, say, old stained-glass windows and sacred statues.

In this climate, the artist could find new aims and bring science to aid his eye and craft. Talent found recognition; and genius, acclaim. Sculptured figures came alive. Painted figures appeared to have roundness and flesh—and to inhabit landscapes painted in depth (see *Perspective, Modelling* below). The very buildings, while keeping the symmetries of ancient Greece, became ornate, colourful, even frivolous—like the new clothes.

The Italian sun slowly thawed even the northern parts of Europe (though here and there, there were dark matters of church and state to keep out the light). By the end of the period, as later artists complained, the Italians seemed to have accomplished everything: colour, perspective, landscape, the use of human figures to express emotion, 'classical' symmetry, 'modern' adventurousness. Looking at the works of **Botticelli, Michelangelo, Giorgione, Titian** and the architect **Palladio**, you say to yourself, 'Only a superb mind could have thought of that. And only a superb hand could have done it!' (e.g., *The Creation of Adam*, a detail from **Michelangelo's** ceiling for the Sistine Chapel. Or **Giorgione's** *Fête Champêtre*. Or **Ghiberti's** bronze doors for the Baptistery, Florence. But really, such lists are pointless because the achievements were endless.)

In countries north of the Alps, the effects of the Renaissance were felt a century later. During the 15th century, a particularly brilliant school of painting arose in the Netherlands (**Hubert** and **Jan van Eyck, van der Weyden, Memling** and others). French architects adopted Italian manners in their architecture and sculpture. England was undergoing the Reformation and the effects of the Renaissance were minor. Germany, too, had other matters to deal with. Yet, throughout Europe, the Renaissance

Madonna and child, Bruges cathedral (Michelangelo)

Supper at Emmaus (Caravaggio)

'took', if only in terms of buildings, clothes, ornaments, furnishings—and a new sense of possibility. **Dürer** of Germany, for example, travelled extensively: he was a supreme master in his own ways—but must have seen and been influenced by the mastery of the very different minds and hands he encountered.

Perspective and Modelling

Western people take it for granted that a two-dimensional work can suggest, 'This thing is near, that thing is distant' (perspective); and 'This thing is rounded, that thing is flat' (modelling).

In Eastern and many other cultures, these effects are not necessarily attempted. No doubt the problems of achieving 'reality' through perspective and modelling have always been recognized by artists of all places and periods: but generally, the problems were sidestepped by the adoption of conventions. For example, a Chinese scroll must be unrolled and viewed bit by bit, from bottom (Near things) to top (Distant things). Again, while the ancient Egyptians gave incised flat surfaces (a rock-face, say) an added drama and interest by using bas-relief—shallow modelling—for

Melencolia I (Dürer)

the figures, they did not bother with perspective. Yet again, you can see 'parallel perspective' in many eastern drawings and paintings. The effect is faintly comical to us, as if the whole scene were slipping off the surface.

In the West, the huge importance of the problem seems always to have been recognised. You see it solved in Ancient Roman

Perspective joke drawing
(after Hogarth)

times and earlier. It was not until some 500 years ago, however, that a general onslaught was made by such masters as **Uccello**, **Masaccio**, **Jan van Eyck**, **Dürer** and **da Vinci**. They found, formalised and set down the answers we have accepted ever since. (The illustration above shows what happens if you don't accept them!) With the mysteries solved, western art could and did stride forward and enter new realms of 'reality'.

Printing, reproduction

To western eyes, there is a respectability and importance in 'oil painting' that may seem to diminish the mere graphic arts of drawing, etching, wood engraving, etc. Yet master drawings (see books with such titles) are masterpieces in their own right—and have always been thought so in China and Japan.

In the east, basically linear works embellished with colour have been hand-printed from blocks for centuries. In the west, printing by mechanical presses began much later and has only recently found techniques that satisfactorily render colour; so superb drawings by great masters could lie neglected because there were no means of reproducing them, or because the drawings were seen as only a step towards the 'serious' work, the oil painting.

Head of Venus (Botticelli)

Yet many great artists and great works were and are linear at heart (see **Botticelli's** *Birth of Venus*) and today it is accepted that a fine artist may be a draughtsman rather than a colourist. See **Brian Steadman's** present-day illustrations for *Alice in Wonderland/Alice Through the Looking Glass*; book illustrations, Victorian and later, by **Rackham, Harry Clarke, Edmund J. Sullivan, Beardsley, Joan Hassall**; 18th century cartoons and illustrations by **Rowlandson, Gillray**; and the numerous works of **Hokusai** (Japan, 19th century). See also the supreme drawings of such masters as **Michelangelo, Titian, Raphael, da Vinci, Dürer**, etc., who will lead you on to, say, **Ingres** (19th century), a 'classical' draughtsman—and so to the experimentalists of later periods and today.

After the Renaissance

Many artists found rich patrons. The royal courts of France and Spain and the Catholic Church, for instance, constantly demanded allegorical, religious and portrait works. The Renaissance skills endured—but not always the conviction, as you may feel when you look at *The Toilet of Venus* (**Guido Reni**). Architects loaded basically classical structures with ornament, statues, pillars, pediments, sweeping stairways. The grandiose styles of, particularly, 17th-century Italy are called *Baroque*. Later, Baroque merged with the still more extravagant *Rococo* manner. The sugar-cake exercises of early 18th-century Rococo are often breath-taking: there may be too much of everything, but how beautifully everything is done! (See paintings by **Bernini**, **Lanfranco**, **Pozzo**, **Fragonard**, **Watteau**. But better—enjoy complete buildings and structures; the Palace of Versailles in France, the Trevi Fountain and much else in Rome. And look at exhibits in the Wallace Collection, London.)

British architects went their own way. They developed a style blended from Classical, Palladian and Renaissance. A very few, like **Inigo Jones**, could be called 'undiluted Classical' (Whitehall, or the Queen's House, Greenwich). **Sir Christopher Wren** and his disciples, however, made endless variations and combinations of classical and baroque themes (e.g., London and City churches, St Paul's Cathedral). Wren's inventiveness and sparkle was, fortunately, echoed by several contemporaries. A great deal of their work stands, though some is hidden or dwarfed by the efforts of present-day architects. St Paul's, for instance, is almost obscured by mean yet massive 20th-century office buildings.

Several 17th-century artists did not follow the trends of the

St Paul's Cathedral

time. **Velasquez** (Spanish) was coolly powerful, darkly dignified. **Rubens** (Flemish) was only incidentally a vivid Baroque painter. The calm, small, glowing interiors of **Jan Vermeer** (Dutch) seem intensely private, where so much painting of the time was public. And of course there was Holland's **Rembrandt**, who would have been considered a giant at any time—among painters.

Eventually the grandeurs and fripperies of Baroque and Rococo were swept away by the French Revolution. Educated tastes now preferred the drier, more severe style of *Neo-Classicism* (at heart, Greek/Roman) typified by the drawings and paintings of, say, **Ingres**—which contrast with the very different approach of the *Romantics*, such as **Delacroix**. In England, **Reynolds** (1723–92) argued a return to the 'Grand Style' of the Renaissance (see his work, and that of his rival, **Gainsborough**). In the Netherlands landscape painting had been highly regarded since the 17th century and in Britain, too, this kind of work found popularity (**Cox**, father and son, watercolourists of 18th-19th centuries; **Constable**, 18th–19th centuries).

Constable represents one of the accepted forms of painting taken to its logical conclusion. There seemed nothing more to say. But then **Turner** (1775–1851) produced—as one of his critics said—'pictures of nothing, and very like'. His stormy handling of paint and extraordinary success in apparently manufacturing light from paint upset the Fine Arts applecart and perhaps led to *Impressionism*. Perhaps not. Certainly his light still shines.

For some time after the French Revolution, artists could depend on the rich, the Church and the State for patronage. From 1800 onwards, most could not. They found themselves in a free market—free to invent, to compete and even to starve. Those painters who did not experiment followed Neo-Classical trends in the main. They produced carefully finished 'painterly' work, obviously worth hard cash. They added a zest and zing by making their work sexier, or more dramatic, or more story-telling, than of old (see the later paintings of **Greuze** [French], a forerunner of the super-sentimentalists of the Victorian age).

In Britain, the architects flourished. During the 18th and early 19th century, they produced some of the most delightful buildings we know. Wren's innovations, it was found, could be adapted to small structures: thus the fine 'Queen Anne' houses, in which various Classical motifs were carried out in brick. The Industrial

Revolution was under way—people were moving into the new, crowded towns—whole strings and squares of housing had to be supplied: even this was done successfully, with a grace that can be admired in cities and towns throughout the country (Edinburgh's New Town; Bath; and in London, see Bedford Square and the other Georgian squares and streets near by). The severely Classical, Inigo Jones manner was carried on by such architects as **Nash**, who not only built, but planned whole areas of cities (go to Regent's Park in London).

Queen Anne, Georgian and Regency styles are at heart ornamented Classical—that is, Ancient Greek/Roman/Palladian/Italian. There were other styles. There was a craze for the 'Gothic Taste', an amazing mixture of castellations, church-y pointed windows, rustic ironwork and twisted chimneys. The craze lasted some seventy years: look for late-Gothic railway stations, lodges, cottages, schools, in your neighbourhood. The date may be shown in bright bricks and will probably be *c.* 1850.

The Prince Regent (later George IV) gave his name to Regency architecture. But his personal interest was in exotic styles—Chinese and Indian and anything else from the East all mixed together. He built Brighton Pavilion. You can go inside this amazing pleasure palace. At the same time (1800 on) the light-hearted, bright, yet formal buildings of Brighton and other seaside resorts and country towns were being built in the Regency style.

Chiswick House—'Classical'

Victorian

In the period 1840–1900 industrialisation, the railways and machines brought changes to all and vast wealth to some; particularly in Britain, the rich and powerful pace-setter. Artists from abroad came to England: native artists prospered. 'Finish'—perfect execution—was one way to the favour of rich patrons. Another was to cram the picture or sculpture with detail and to make it tell a story ('Look, master has died and the dog is sad! See how his eyes glisten!').

Such works were laughed at when the new century arrived—or at any rate, after the First World War. The laughter only recently died down. Victorian craftsmanship was remarkable; and as works of Art—but judge for yourself from, say, *Too early* (**Tissot**); *The Lament for Icarus* (**Draper**); *Derby Day* (**Frith**); *April Love* (**Hughes**). See also the flaming luxury of some of **Lord Leighton's** work; *Pegwell Bay* by **Dyce**; the super-reality of *The Stonebreaker* (**Brett**); and the book illustrations of the period.

There were endless revolts against the fundamentally commercial values of the time. The *pre-Raphaelite Brotherhood* sought to rediscover the purity and truth-to-Nature of an earlier golden age. **Grimshaw** (*Liverpool Quay by Moonlight*) achieved effects that might astonish a present-day colour photographer. There were social realists (*Application for Admission to the Casual Ward*, **Fildes**); and Fairy Painters (**Dadd, Paton** and others). Works from China and Japan influenced **Whistler** the impressionist, and **Aubrey Beardsley** the line artist. **William Morris** founded a sort of Mediaeval arts and crafts workshop whose influence is still seen. The French-inspired *Aesthetic Movement* inspired one, as W. S. Gilbert said mockingly, to 'stroll down Piccadilly/With a poppy or a lily/In my mediaeval hand'. (Get a book about *Art Nouveau* to see what happened later on.)

In France the major revolution brewed. *Modern Art* (q.v.) was starting with the realism of **Courbet**, the rapid emotional effects of the *Impressionists*, the deliberately unclassical nudes of **Manet**, the lushness and freedom of **Renoir**, the posters and paintings of **Toulouse-Lautrec**, the painters of light such as **Monet**. *Post-impressionists* like **Cézanne** and **van Gogh** added strength to the new art.

The Victorians loved to display their wealth. A town house or a sideboard had to be florid, 'important', completely covered with decoration. So much Victorian architecture survives that your own eyes are a sufficient guide. Enough here to say that every conceivable style, ornament and tradition of the past were used, sometimes simultaneously, sometimes disastrously, often delightfully. See St Pancras Station, Big Ben, Balmoral, perhaps your own local railway station or town hall or old public house— anything. Look particularly for uses of cast-iron, a key material of the period.

Modern art

Until the arrival of the French Impressionists of the 19th century, the art of painting had been based on Nature in some form or other. 'Those who take as their standard anything other than Nature,' da Vinci wrote, 'weary themselves in vain.' Whistler, three centuries later, said much the same thing: the job of the painter was 'to pick and choose, as the musician gathers notes and chords,' from Nature.

But then came the Instant Nature-reproducer, the camera— and various machines that appeared more than human in their cleverness and power—and above all a belief that Man could dominate Nature. So the 20th-century architect talked of houses as 'machines for living', the sculptor turned to mechanisms such as mobiles, and the painter to abstract, theoretical, non-representational pictures—and to Isms. Surrealism, vorticism, pointillism, dadaism, expressionism, cubism, futurism . . .

Time has already been unkind to most of the Isms. There is nothing so dated as a 1930s book about Modern Art unless it is a pre-World War One Futurist Manifesto ('HURRAH for motors! HURRAH for speed! HURRAH for draughts!')

Recently, soiled nappies have been displayed in the name of Art—and even naughtier, more shocking articles. 'I admit it's ugly, but is it Art?' is the question we so often have to answer today.

Time will give the answers—and decide which of our present-day artists are truly important, even great. In all periods, innovators have been derided and attacked. Contrariwise, for every old name still remembered, there are a hundred or a thousand forgotten. We wait and see.

Some names: innovators and experimenters who bred modern art include Cézanne, Matisse, Rouault and the Impressionists

Monet, **Renoir**, **Toulouse-Lautrec** and **Degas**. All worked in France, as did **Picasso** (Spanish), the most diverse and prolific of all. Whatever Isms or classifications these artists chose to apply to themselves from time to time, their works are distinct and personal. The same is true of **Paul Klee** (Swiss), **Kandinski** (Russian), **Brancusi** (Rumanian), **Magritte** (Belgian), **Jackson Pollock** (American) and **Henry Moore** or **Graham Sutherland** (English). All are moderns, all produced paintings or sculptures or both that belong to this century and no other. But this is usually their only link.

Younger, present-day artists of note include **Bridget Riley** (fascinating visual conjuring tricks of the Op Art School), **David Hockney** and **Francis Bacon**. A current American school of interest produces super-real paintings—probably a spinoff from *Pop Art*; you may know, from posters, the work of Pop-artist **Roy Lichtenstein** (blow-ups of frames from strip cartoons) and of artists who paint super-real tubes of toothpaste, etc.

Artists who defy classification include **L. S. Lowry** ('naive' industrial landscapes with figures) and an endless list of commercial artists who are coming to be regarded as Fine Artists. But then, the distinction between Fine Arts in a gallery and commercial art on, say, a plastic food pack is becoming blurred.

Sculpture is equally diverse. **Reg Butler's** skeletal structures, **Jacob Epstein's** brutal and massive pieces, the abstract forms of **Barbara Hepworth**, the elongated delicacy of **Giacometti**—all are regarded as important, but so are stacks of bricks and junked cars.

In *architecture*, in this century, new materials—particularly steel-reinforced concrete—have changed the very nature of buildings and, seemingly, have often directed the architect's hand. Concrete and steel lend themselves to modular production of parts that can be endlessly repeated: thus the massive tower blocks and office complexes that dominate our town and city skylines.

Architecture is the functional art. It provides containers for things or people. The functional worth of modern high-rise buildings designed to house humans is under continuous and heavy attack, as is their 'art' element. It seems that the architects and planners of today's familiar, commonplace buildings and centres will be judged harshly tomorrow.

Adventurous and exciting buildings in the modern idioms exist, of course; see the cathedrals of Liverpool and Coventry; various small buildings—aviary, elephant house, giraffe house—in Regent's Park Zoo, London; buildings for the universities of Essex, Southampton, Leicester; the dockland areas of London.

The pioneers of present-day architecture include **Frank Lloyd Wright** of America, **le Corbusier** of France, **Pier Luigi Nervi** of Italy—and **Walter Gropius** of Germany, a founder of the *Bauhaus*, a German institution that influenced the design of houses and household objects after World War I and through the 1930s.

Photography Much of present-day art is wild, provocative and formless. One of many reasons why is—photography, which was already flourishing a hundred years ago.

Picture a successful Victorian artist. He has spent his adult life mastering his craft and art. A photographer sets up his camera beside the artist's easel. The one goes 'click' and the other paints on. Later they compare results. Perspective, modelling, detail, light and shade, 'truth'—the photograph is as perfect as the painting in everything but colour (and that is soon to come!). What should the artist do? Burn his canvases and buy a camera? Or change the very nature of his art?

The problem was and is a real one. The camera cannot eliminate the unwanted or invent the wanted—but the able photographer can find ways to over-ride these difficulties and produce the effect he desires. He can use the camera 'creatively', choose his subjects and settings 'artistically'. There are already Old Masters of photography.

One effect on the non-photographic artist was to make him tackle his art from a different starting point. The camera can show every leaf and twig? Right, then the artist will become an impressionist. Or he will put a frame round a single leaf and call his picture, *Forest.* Or learn computer graphics.

In short—the wilder schools of *modern art* (q.v.) would most probably have emerged anyhow. But photography made quite sure that they did emerge.

Exceptions and rebels

In our history—we warned you at the outset—we may have made it appear that in each period, art and artists followed the general patterns of that period. Probably most artists did just that, just as you talk of television or tennis, not of tatting or tipcat. But there were always exceptions: artists who didn't, wouldn't or couldn't 'belong'. Please look up: the English painters **Turner**, **Samuel**

Palmer, William Blake, Lowry; the works of **Fuseli, Hokusai, Bosch, Henri Rousseau, Pieter Breughel, el Greco**; the architects **Gaudi, Mackintosh**. This short list (you may enjoy extending it) is of artists who have nothing in common but their uncommonness.

Art and Craft
What are they? When does one become the other? A craft can be defined as a high human skill: Art might be defined as a message designed to appeal to the highest human sensibilities. But why cannot a craft object make this appeal? Is a superb pocket watch by **Breguet** craft, or art? Can a pile of tyres (displayed in a recent Art exhibition) truly be art? Is the *Cutty Sark* both a work of art and craft? Can a photograph be art?—and if not, why not?

There are no answers to these old questions. But you must ask them, constantly.

Remarkable books
There are today endless pictorial books about the Arts. Anything you want can be found in libraries and bookshops. Some books, however, are things apart . . .

Homes Sweet Homes; *Pillar to Post*; *Progress at Pelvis Bay*, all by Sir Osbert Lancaster. Architecture, furnishing, period feeling, in words-and-pictures nutshells. Very funny but also piercingly accurate. There are paperback editions, but try to get new or secondhand hardbacks.

First and Last Loves by Sir John Betjeman. Random opinions, enthusiasms, invaluable snippets. Illustrated. Also his *A Pictorial History of English Architecture*.

Architecture by W. R. Dalzell.

One Hundred Details from Pictures in the National Gallery by Sir Kenneth Clark. Also *The Nude* and other works by this author.

Autobiography of Cellini, describing the work of a 16th-century artist/craftsman.

Drawings and Notebooks of Leonardo da Vinci (1452–1519)— thoughts, sketches, theories of a genius.

The Saturday Book was a handsome gift annual for grown-ups. It appeared for more than twenty years. Many beautiful and odd things, expert texts. Look for secondhand copies.

SPORT

At the beginning of this section, sports are arranged alphabetically; under each heading are given details of governing bodies, championships and records. These are followed by a list of those results of the 1992 Olympics and 1992 Winter Olympics not recorded under particular sports.

ARCHERY

Governing body: Grand National Archery Society, National Agricultural Centre, Stoneleigh, Kenilworth, Warks. CV8 2LG.

Olympic Games 1992		
	Men	
Individual	S. Flute (France)	
Team	Spain	
	Women	
Individual	Cho Youn-Jeong (S. Korea)	
Team	S. Korea	
World Championships 1992		
Men (individual)	S. Fairweather (Australia)	
Men (team)	S. Korea	995 pts.
Women (individual)	S. Nyunq-Kim (S. Korea)	
Women (team)	S. Korea	1030 pts.
British Target National Championships 1992		
Men	D. Hughes (Dunlop)	221 pts.
Women	P. Edwards (Atkins)	2290 pts.

ASSOCIATION FOOTBALL

The Football Association was founded in 1863 and the FA Cup competition was first held in 1871/72. Official international matches have been played since 1872.

Governing bodies: Football Association (England), 16 Lancaster Gate, London W2 3LW; Football Association (Scotland), 6 Park Gardens, Glasgow G3 7YE; Football Association (Irish), 20 Windsor Avenue, Belfast BT9 6EG; Football Association (Eire), 80 Merrion Square South, Dublin, 2; Football Association (Wales), 3 Fairy Road, Wrexham, LL13 7PS.

League Champions

Year	Champion	Year	Champion
1889–90	Preston North End	1901	Liverpool
1891	Everton	1902	Sunderland
1892–93	Sunderland	1903–04	Sheffield Wednesday
1894	Aston Villa	1905	Newcastle United
1895	Sunderland	1906	Liverpool
1896–97	Aston Villa	1907	Newcastle United
1898	Sheffield United	1908	Manchester United
1899	Aston Villa	1909	Newcastle United
1900	Aston Villa	1910	Aston Villa

1911	Manchester United	1960	Burnley
1912	Blackburn Rovers	1961	Tottenham Hotspur
1913	Sunderland	1962	Ipswich Town
1914	Blackburn Rovers	1963	Everton
1915	Everton	1964	Liverpool
1920	West Bromwich Albion	1965	Manchester United
		1966	Liverpool
1921	Burnley	1967	Manchester United
1922–23	Liverpool	1968	Manchester City
1924–26	Huddersfield Town	1969	Leeds United
1927	Newcastle United	1970	Everton
1928	Everton	1971	Arsenal
1929–30	Sheffield Wednesday	1972	Derby County
1931	Arsenal	1973	Liverpool
1932	Everton	1974	Leeds United
1933–35	Arsenal	1975	Derby County
1936	Sunderland	1976–77	Liverpool
1937	Manchester City	1978	Nottingham Forest
1938	Arsenal	1979–80	Liverpool
1939	Everton	1981	Aston Villa
1947	Liverpool	1982–84	Liverpool
1948	Arsenal	1985	Everton
1949–50	Portsmouth	1986	Liverpool
1951	Tottenham Hotspur	1987	Everton
1952	Manchester United	1988	Liverpool
1953	Arsenal	1989	Arsenal
1954	Wolverhampton Wanderers	1990	Liverpool
		1991	Arsenal
1955	Chelsea	1992	Leeds
1956–57	Manchester United	1993	Manchester United
1958–59	Wolverhampton Wanderers		

FA Cup

1872–73	Wanderers	1888	West Bromwich Albion
1874	Oxford University		
1875	Royal Engineers	1889	Preston North End
1876–78	Wanderers	1890–91	Blackburn Rovers
1879	Old Etonians	1892	West Bromwich Albion
1880	Clapham Rovers		
1881	Old Carthusians	1893	Wolverhampton Wanderers
1882	Old Etonians		
1883	Blackburn Olympic	1894	Notts County
1884–86	Blackburn Rovers	1895	Aston Villa
1887	Aston Villa	1896	Sheffield Wednesday

1897	Aston Villa	1949	Wolverhampton
1898	Nottingham Forest		Wanderers
1899	Sheffield United	1950	Arsenal
1900	Bury	1951–52	Newcastle United
1901	Tottenham Hotspur	1953	Blackpool
1902	Sheffield United	1954	West Bromwich Albion
1903	Bury	1955	Newcastle United
1904	Manchester City	1956	Manchester City
1905	Aston Villa	1957	Aston Villa
1906	Everton	1958	Bolton Wanderers
1907	Sheffield Wednesday	1959	Nottingham Forest
1908	Wolverhampton	1960	Wolverhampton
	Wanderers		Wanderers
1909	Manchester United	1961–62	Tottenham Hotspur
1910	Newcastle United	1963	Manchester United
1911	Bradford City	1964	West Ham
1912	Barnsley	1965	Liverpool
1913	Aston Villa	1966	Everton
1914	Burnley	1967	Tottenham Hotspur
1915	Sheffield United	1968	West Bromwich Albion
1920	Aston Villa	1969	Manchester City
1921	Tottenham Hotspur	1970	Chelsea
1922	Huddersfield Town	1971	Arsenal
1923	Bolton Wanderers	1972	Leeds United
1924	Newcastle United	1973	Sunderland
1925	Sheffield United	1974	Liverpool
1926	Bolton Wanderers	1975	West Ham
1927	Cardiff City	1976	Southampton
1928	Blackburn Rovers	1977	Manchester United
1929	Bolton Wanderers	1978	Ipswich
1930	Arsenal	1979	Arsenal
1931	West Bromwich	1980	West Ham
	Albion	1981–82	Tottenham Hotspur
1932	Newcastle United	1983	Manchester United
1933	Everton	1984	Everton
1934	Manchester City	1985	Manchester United
1935	Sheffield Wednesday	1986	Liverpool
1936	Arsenal	1987	Coventry City
1937	Sunderland	1988	Wimbledon
1938	Preston North End	1989	Liverpool
1939	Portsmouth	1990	Manchester United
1946	Derby County	1991	Tottenham Hotspur
1947	Charlton Athletic	1992	Liverpool
1948	Manchester United	1993	Arsenal

Rumbelows Cup (formerly Littlewoods Cup)

1961	Aston Villa	1975	Aston Villa
1962	Norwich City	1976	Manchester City
1963	Birmingham City	1977	Aston Villa
1964	Leicester City	1978–79	Nottingham Forest
1965	Chelsea	1980	Wolverhampton
1966	West Bromwich		Wanderers
	Albion	1981–84	Liverpool
1967	Queen's Park Rangers	1985	Norwich City
1968	Leeds United	1986	Oxford United
1969	Swindon Town	1987	Arsenal
1970	Manchester City	1988	Luton
1971	Tottenham Hotspur	1989–90	Nottingham Forest
1972	Stoke City	1991	Sheffield
1973	Tottenham Hotspur		Wednesday
1974	Wolverhampton	1992	Manchester United
	Wanderers	1993	Arsenal

Scottish Cup

1954	Celtic	1973	Rangers
1955	Clyde	1974–75	Celtic
1956	Heart of Midlothian	1976	Rangers
1957	Falkirk	1977	Celtic
1958	Clyde	1978–79	Rangers
1959	St Mirren	1980	Celtic
1960	Rangers	1981	Rangers
1961	Dunfermline	1982–84	Aberdeen
1962–64	Rangers	1985	Celtic
1965	Celtic	1986	Aberdeen
1966	Rangers	1987	St Mirren
1967	Celtic	1988	Celtic
1968	Dunfermline	1989	Celtic
1969	Celtic	1990	Aberdeen
1970	Aberdeen	1991	Motherwell
1971–72	Celtic	1992–93	Rangers

European Cup

1957–60	Real Madrid	1968	Manchester United
1961–62	Benfica	1969	AC Milan
1963	AC Milan	1970	Feyenoord
1964–65	Inter Milan	1971–73	Ajax
1966	Real Madrid	1974–76	Bayern Munich
1967	Celtic	1977–78	Liverpool

1979–80	Nottingham Forest	1987	FC Porto
1981	Liverpool	1988	PSV Eindhoven
1982	Aston Villa	1989–90	AC Milan
1983	SV Hamburg	1991	Red Star, Belgrade
1984	Liverpool	1992	Barcelona
1985	Juventus	1993	Marseilles
1986	Steaua Bucharest		

European Cup Winners' Cup

1961	AC Fiorentina	1978	Anderlecht
1962	Atletico Madrid	1979	Barcelona
1963	Tottenham Hotspur	1980	Valencia
1964	Sporting Club, Lisbon	1981	Dynamo Tbilisi
1965	West Ham United	1982	Barcelona
1966	Borussia Dortmund	1983	Aberdeen
1967	Bayern Munich	1984	Juventus
1968	AC Milan	1985	Everton
1969	Slovan Bratislava	1986	Dinamo Kiev
1970	Manchester City	1987	Ajax
1971	Chelsea	1988	Mechelen
1972	Glasgow Rangers	1989	Barcelona
1973	AC Milan	1990	Sampdoria
1974	FC Magdeburg	1991	Manchester United
1975	Dynamo Kiev	1992	Werder Bremen
1976	Anderlecht	1993	Parma
1977	SV Hamburg		

World Cup

1930	Uruguay	1966	England
1934	Italy	1970	Brazil
1938	Italy	1974	West Germany
1950	Uruguay	1978	Argentina
1954	West Germany	1982	Italy
1958	Brazil	1986	Argentina
1962	Brazil	1990	West Germany

Olympic Games

1908	United Kingdom	1960	Yugoslavia
1912	United Kingdom	1964	Hungary
1920	Belgium	1968	Hungary
1924	Uruguay	1972	Poland
1928	Uruguay	1976	East Germany
1932	No competition	1980	Czechoslovakia
1936	Italy	1984	France
1948	Sweden	1988	USSR
1952	Hungary	1992	Spain
1956	USSR		

Records

Championship wins: Liverpool eighteen times; Arsenal ten times; Everton nine times; Manchester United and Aston Villa seven times; Sunderland six times.

Highest score in FA Cup: Preston North End 26, Hyde 0 (1887)

Highest score in Cup Final: Bury 6, Derby County 0 (1903)

Highest score by one man in League game: 10 goals, J. Payne for Luton Town v Bristol Rovers (1936)

Highest score by one man in Division I: 7 goals, E. Drake for Arsenal v Aston Villa (1935)

Highest score by one man in a full international: 6 goals, G. J. Bambrick for Ireland v Wales (1930)

Most goals during career: 550, by James McGrory (Glasgow Celtic), 1922–38. **English record:** 434, by A. Rowley (West Bromwich Albion, Fulham, Leicester City and Shrewsbury Town)

Most caps won by amateur: 62, by R. Haider (Kingstonian and Hendon), 1966–73

Most caps won by a professional: Peter Shilton (Derby County), 125 for England

Most Welsh caps: I. Allchurch (Newcastle United, Cardiff City and Swansea Town), 1950–66, 68

Most Scottish caps: K. Dalglish (Celtic and Liverpool), 1972–87, 102

Most Irish caps: P. Jennings (Watford, Tottenham Hotspur and Arsenal) 1963–82, 119

ATHLETICS

Governing bodies: British Athletics Federation, Edgbaston House, 3 Duchess Place, Hegley Road, Birmingham.

World and United Kingdom Records

(The records given here are those that have been officially ratified as at December 1992; they are for fully-automatic timing for distances up to and including 400 metres)

	Men	
	World	*United Kingdom*
100 metres	9·86 sec	9·92 sec
	C. Lewis (USA)	L. Christie
200 metres	19·72 sec	20·09 sec
	P. Mennea (Italy)	L. Christie

400 metres	43·29 sec	44.50 sec
	H. Reynolds (USA)	D. Redmond
800 metres	1 min 41·73 sec	1 min 41·73 sec
	S. Coe (GB)	S. Coe
1,000 metres	2 min 12·18 sec	2 min 12·18 sec
	S. Coe (GB)	S. Coe
1,500 metres	3 min 29·46 sec	3 min 29·67 sec
	S. Aouita (Mor)	S. Cram
1 mile	3 min 46·32 sec	3 min 46·32 sec
	S. Cram (GB)	S. Cram
2 kilometres	4 min 50·81 sec	4 min 51·39 sec
	S. Aouita (Mor)	S. Cram
3 kilometres	7 min 29·45 sec	7 min 32·79 sec
	S. Aouita (Mor)	D. Moorcroft
2 miles	8 min 13·45 sec	8 min 13·51 sec
	S Aouita (Mor)	S. Ovett
5 kilometres	12 min 58·39 sec	13 min 0·41 sec
	S. Aouita (Mor)	D. Moorcroft
10 kilometres	27 min 8·23 sec	27 min 23·06 sec
	A. Barrios (Mex)	E. Martin
Marathon	2 hrs 06 min 50 sec	2 hrs 07 min 13 sec
	B. Dinsamo (Eth)	S. Jones
110 metres hurdles	12·92 sec	13·06 sec
	R. Kingdom (USA)	C. Jackson
400 metres hurdles	46·78 sec	47·86 sec
	K. Young (USA)	K. Akabusi
3,000 metres steeplechase	8 min 05·35 sec	8 min 7·96 sec
	P. Koech (Kenya)	M. Rowland
High jump	2·44 metres	2·36 metres
	J. Sotomayor (Cuba)	D. Grant
Pole vault	6·08 metres	5·65 metres
	S. Bubka (Sov)	K. Stock
Long jump	8·95 metres	8·23 metres
	M. Powell (USA)	L. Davies
Triple jump	17·97 metres	17·57 metres
	W. Banks (USA)	K. Connor
Shot-putt	23·12 metres	21·68 metres
	R. Barnes (USA)	G. Capes
Discus-throw	74·08 metres	65·16 metres
	J. Schult (EG)	R. Slaney
Hammer-throw	86·74 metres	77·54 metres
	Y. Sedykh (Sov)	M. Girvan

Javelin-throw	94·74 metres	91·46 metres
	J. Zelezny (Czecho)	S. Backley
Decathlon	8,847 pts	8,847 pts
	D. Thompson (GB)	D. Thompson

Women

100 metres	10·49 sec	11·10 sec
	F. Griffith-Joyner (USA)	K. Cook
200 metres	21·34 sec	22·10 sec
	F. Griffith-Joyner (USA)	K. Cook
400 metres	47·60 sec	49·43 sec
	M. Koch (EG)	K. Cook
800 metres	1 min 53·28 sec	1 min 57·42 sec
	J. Kratochvilova (Czech)	K. Wade
1,500 metres	3 min 52·47 sec	3 min 59·96 sec
	T. Kazankina (Sov)	Z. Budd
1 mile	4 min 15·61 sec	4 min 17·57 sec
	P. Ivan (Rom)	Z. Budd
3 kilometres	8 min 22·62 sec	8 min 28·83 sec
	T. Kazankina (Sov)	Z. Budd
5 kilometres	14 min 37·33 sec	14 min 48·07 sec
	I. Kristiansen (Nor)	Z. Budd
10 kilometres	30 min 13·74 sec	30 min 57·07 sec
	I. Kristiansen (Nor)	E. McColgan
Marathon	2 hrs 21 min 06 sec	2 hrs 25 min 56 sec
	I. Kristiansen (Nor)	V. Marot
100 metres	12·21 sec	12·82 sec
hurdles	Y. Donkova (Bul)	S. Gunnell
400 metres	52·94 sec	53·16 sec
hurdles	M. Stepanova (Sov)	S. Gunnell
High jump	2·09 metres	1·95 metres
	S. Kostadinova (Bul)	D. Davies
Long Jump	7·52 metres	6·90 metres
	G. Chistyakova (Sov)	B. Kinch
Shot-putt	22·63 metres	19·36 metres
	N. Lisovskaya (Sov)	J. Oakes
Discus-throw	76·80 metres	67·48 metres
	G. Reinsch (EG)	M. Ritchie
Javelin-throw	80.00 metres	77·44 metres
	P. Felke (EG)	F. Whitbread
Heptathlon	7,291 pts	6,623 pts
	J. Joyner-Kersee (USA)	J. Simpson

The Mile Record

1884	George (GB)	4 min 12·75 sec
1915	Taber (USA)	4 min 12·6 sec
1923	Nurmi (Finland)	4 min 10·4 sec
1931	Ladoumègue (France)	4 min 9·2 sec
1933	Lovelock (New Zealand)	4 min 7·6 sec
1934	Cunningham (USA)	4 min 6·8 sec
1937	Wooderson (GB)	4 min 6·4 sec
1942	Hägg (Sweden)	4 min 6·2 sec
1942	Andersson (Sweden)	4 min 6·2 sec
1942	Hägg (Sweden)	4 min 4·6 sec
1943	Andersson (Sweden)	4 min 2·6 sec
1944	Andersson (Sweden)	4 min 1·6 sec
1945	Hägg (Sweden)	4 min 1·3 sec
1954	Bannister (GB)	3 min 59·4 sec
1954	Landy (Australia)	3 min 57·9 sec
1957	Ibbotson (GB)	3 min 57·2 sec
1958	Elliott (Australia)	3 min 54·5 sec
1962	Snell (New Zealand)	3 min 54·4 sec
1964	Snell (New Zealand)	3 min 54·1 sec
1965	Jazy (France)	3 min 53·6 sec
1966	Ryun (USA)	3 min 51·3 sec
1967	Ryun (USA)	3 min 51·1 sec
1975	Bayi (Tanzania)	3 min 51·0 sec
1975	Walker (New Zealand)	3 min 49·4 sec
1979	Coe (GB)	3 min 49·0 sec
1980	Ovett (GB)	3 min 48·8 sec
1981	Coe (GB)	3 min 48·53 sec
1981	Ovett (GB)	3 min 48·40 sec
1981	Coe (GB)	3 min 47·43 sec
1985	Cram (GB)	3 min 46·32 sec

Olympic Games (Barcelona 1992)

Men

100 metres	L. Christie (GB)	9·96 sec
200 metres	M. Marsh (USA)	20.01 sec
400 metres	Q. Watts (USA)	43·50 sec
800 metres	W. Tanui (Kenya)	1 min 43·66 sec
1,500 metres	F. Cacho (Spain)	3 min 40·12 sec
5,000 metres	D. Baumann (Germany)	13 min 12·52 sec
10,000 metres	K. Skah (Morocco)	27 min 46·70 sec
Marathon	Hwang Young-cho (S. Korea)	2 hr 13 min 23 sec

110 metres hurdles	M. McKay (Canada)	13·12 sec
400 metres hurdles	K. Young (USA)	46·78 sec (W.R.)
3,000 metres steeplechase	M. Birir (Kenya)	8 min 08·84 sec
20 km walk	D. Plaza (Spain)	1 hr 21 m 45 sec
50 km walk	A. Perlov (Unified Team)	3 hr 50 min 13 sec
4 × 100 metres relay	USA	
4 × 400 metres relay	USA	
High jump	J. Sotormayor (Cuba)	2·34 metres
Long jump	C. Lewis (USA)	8·67 metres
Triple jump	M. Cpo Conley (USA)	18·17 metres
Pole vault	M. Tarosov (Unfied Team)	5·80 metres
Shot putt	M. Stulce (USA)	21·70 metres
Discus	R. Ulbartas (Lithuania)	65·12 metres
Hammer	A. Abduvaliyev (Unified Team)	82·54 metres
Javelin	J. Zelezny (Czecho)	89·66 metres
Decathlon	R. Zmelik (Czecho)	8,611 pts

Women

100 metres	G. Devers (USA)	10·82 sec
200 metres	G. Torrence (USA)	21·81 sec
400 metres	M. Perec (France)	48·83 sec
800 metres	E. Van Langen (Netherlands)	1 min 55·54sec.
1,500 metres	H. Boulmerka (Algeria)	3 min 55·30 sec
3,000 metres	Y. Romanova (Unified Team)	8 min 46·04 sec
10,000 metres	D. Tulu (Ethiopia)	31 min 06·02 sec
Marathon	V. Yegorova (Unified Team)	2 hr 32 min 41 sec
100 metres hurdles	V. Patoulidou (Greece)	12·64 sec
1,600 metres hurdles	S. Gunnell (GB)	52·23 sec
10 km walk	Chen Yueling (China)	44 min 32 sec
4 × 100 metres relay	USA	42·11 sec
High jump	H. Henkel (Germany)	2·02 metres
Long jump	H. Dreschler (Germany)	7·14 metres

Shot putt	S. Krivelyeva (Unified	
	Team)	21·06 metres
Javelin	S. Renk (Germany)	68·34 metres
Discus	M. Marten (Cuba)	70.06 metres
Heptathlon	J. Joyner-Kersee (USA)	7,044 pts

BADMINTON

Governing body: Badminton Association of England Limited, PO Box 553, Loughton, Milton Keynes MK8 9EN.

Thomas Cup
(*Men's International Championship*)

		Venue
1967	Malaysia beat Indonesia	Djakarta
1970	Indonesia beat Malaysia	Kuala Lumpur
1973	Indonesia beat Denmark	Djakarta
1976	Indonesia beat Malaysia	Djakarta
1979	Indonesia beat Denmark	Djakarta
1982	China beat Indonesia	London
1984	Indonesia beat China	Kuala Lumpur
1986	China beat Indonesia	Djakarta
1988	China beat Malaysia	Kuala Lumpur
1990	China beat Malaysia	Tokyo
1992	Malaysia beat Indonesia	Kuala Lumpur

All-England Championships
(*Men's singles*)

1965	Erland Kops	1982	M. Frost
1966	T. Huang	1983	Luan Jin
1967	Erland Kops	1984	M. Frost
1968–74	R. Hartono	1985	Z. Jianhua
1975	S. Pri	1986	M. Frost
1976	R. Hartono	1987	M. Frost
1977	F. Delfs	1988	I. Frederiksen
1978	Lim Swie-king	1989	Y. Yang
1979	Lim Swie-king	1990	Z. Jianhua
1980	P. Prakash	1991	A. Wiranata
1981	Lim Swie-king	1992	Liu Jun

Uber Cup
(*Women's International Championship*)

		Venue
1966	Japan beat USA	Wellington
1969	Japan beat Indonesia	Tokyo
1972	Japan beat Indonesia	Tokyo
1975	Indonesia beat Japan	Djakarta
1978	Japan beat Indonesia	Djakarta
1981	Japan beat Indonesia	Tokyo
1984	China beat England	Kuala Lumpur
1986	China beat Indonesia	Djakarta
1988	China beat S. Korea	Kuala Lumpur
1990	China beat S. Korea	Tokyo
1992	China beat S. Korea	Kuala Lumpur

All-England Championships
(*Women's singles*)

1965	U. Smith	1979	L. Koppen
1966	Mrs. G. C. K. Hashman	1980	C. Köpen
1967	Mrs. G. C. K. Hashman	1981	Sun Ai Hwang
1968	Mrs. E. Twedberg	1982	Z. Ailing
1969	H. Yuki	1983	Z. Ailing
1970	E. Takenaka	1984	Li Lingwei
1971	Mrs. E. Twedberg	1985	P. Hanaiping
1972	Mrs. N. Nakayama	1986	K. Yun-Ja
1973	M. Beck	1987	K. Larsen
1974	H. Yuki	1988	G. Jiewning
1975	H. Yuki	1989	Li Lingwei
1976	G. Gilks	1990	S. Susanti
1977	H. Yuki	1991	S. Susanti
1978	Mrs. G. Gilks	1992	Tang Jiuhong

Inter-County Championship

1962–63	Surrey	1986	Lancashire
1964	Essex	1987	Essex
1965–75	Surrey	1988	Surrey
1976	Lancashire	1989	Surrey
1977–78	Essex	1990	Surrey
1979–81	Lancashire	1991	Yorkshire
1982–85	Surrey	1992	Hertfordshire

Olympic Games 1992
Men

Singles	A. Kusuma (Indonesia)
Doubles	S. Korea

Women

Singles	S. Susanti (Indonesia)
Doubles	S. Korea

BASKETBALL

Governing body: English Basket Ball Association, Calomax House, Lupton Avenue, Leeds LS9 7EE.

Olympic Games 1992

Men	Women
USA	Unified Team

National Championship (Men)

1980	Crystal Palace	1987	BCP London
1981	Sunderland	1988	Livingston
1982	Crystal Palace	1989	Glasgow Rangers
1983	Sunderland	1990	Kingston
1984	Solent Stars	1991	Kingston
1985	Manchester United	1992	Kingston
1986	Kingston		

National Championship (Women)

1981	Southgate	1988	Stockport
1982	Southgate	1989	AC Northampton
1983	Southgate	1990	AC Northampton
1984	AC Northampton	1991	Crystal Palace
1985	AC Northampton	1992	Thames Valley
1986	Crystal Palace	1993	Sheffield Hatters
1987	AC Northampton		

National Cup

1982–84	Solent Stars	1991	Sunderland
1985–88	Kingston	1992	Kingston
1989	Bracknell Tigers	1993	Worthing Bears
1990	Kingston		

National League

1980	Crystal Palace	1987–88	Portsmouth
1981	Team Fiat	1989	Glasgow Rangers
1982–83	Crystal Palace	1990	Oldham
1984	Solent Stars	1991	Kingston
1985	Kingston	1992	Kingston
1986	Manchester United	1993	Worthing Bears

NBA Championship

1980	Los Angeles Lakers	1987	Los Angeles Lakers
1981	Boston Celtics	1988	Los Angeles Lakers
1982	Los Angeles Lakers	1989	Detroit Pistons
1983	Philadelphia 76ers	1990	Detroit Pistons
1984	Los Angeles Lakers	1991	Chicago Bulls
1985–86	Boston Celtics	1992	Chicago Bulls

BOXING

Governing bodies: British Boxing Board of Control, 70 Vauxhall Bridge Road, London SW1V 2RP; Amateur Boxing Association, Francis House, Francis Street, London SW1P 1DE.

Olympic Games 1992

Super Heavy	R. Balado-Mendez (Cuba)
Heavy	F. Savon (Cuba)
Light Heavy	T. May (Germany)
Middle	A. Hermandez (Cuba)
Lightmiddle	J. Garcila (Cuba)
Welter	M. Carruth (Ireland)
Lightwelter	H. Vincent (Cuba)
Light	O. de la Hoya (USA)

Feather	A. Tews (Germany)
Bantam	J. Casamayor (Cuba)
Fly	C. Chol-Su (S. Korea)
Lightfly	R. Garcia (Cuba)

World and European Professional Champions 1992–93

Weight	World (WBC)	World (WBA)	Europe
Heavy	Lennox Lewis (GB)	Riddick Bowe (USA)	Henry Akinwande (GB)
Cruiser	Anaclet Wamba (France)	Bobby Czyz (USA)	Johnny Nelson (GB)
Light Heavy	Jeff Harding (Australia)	Virgin Hill (USA)	*vacant*
Middle	Julian Jackson (Virgin Is)	Mike McCallum (Jamaica)	Sumbu Kalambay (Italy)
Lightmiddle	Terry Norris (USA)	Julio Vasquez (Argentina)	Gary Jacobs (GB)
Welter	Maurice Blocker (USA)	Meldrick Taylor (USA)	Patricio Oliva (Italy)
Lightwelter	Julio Chavez (Mexico)	Edwin Rosario (Puerto Rico)	Valery Kayumba (France)
Light	Pernel Whitaker (USA)	Tony Lopez (USA)	Jean-Baptiste Mandy (France)
Superfeather	Paul Hodkinson (GB)	Joey Gamache (USA)	Daniel Londas (France)
Feather	Goya Vargas (Mexico)	Park Young-Kyun (S. Korea)	Herre Jacob (France)
Superbantam	Daniel Zaragoza (Mexico)	Wilfred da Vasquez (Puerto Rico)	*not recognised*
Bantam	Victor Rabanales (Mexico)	Luisito Espinosa (Philippines)	Vincenzo Belcastro (Italy)
Superfly	Moon Sung Kil (S. Korea)	Khaokor Galaxy (Thailand)	*not recognised*
Fly	Muangchai Kittikasam (Thailand)	Lim Yong-Kang (S. Korea)	Robbie Regan (GB)
Lightfly	Humberto Gonzalez (Mexico)	Yuh Myung-Wood (S. Korea)	*not recognised*

World Heavyweight Champions

1906	Tommy Burns (Canada)	1959	Ingemar Johansson (Sweden)
1908	Jack Johnson (USA)		
1915	Jess Willard (USA)	1960	Floyd Patterson (USA)
1919	Jack Dempsey (USA)	1962	Sonny Liston (USA)
1926	Gene Tunney (USA)	1964	Cassius Clay (USA)
1930	Max Schmeling (Germany)	1970	Joe Frazier (USA)
1932	Jack Sharkey (USA)	1973	George Foreman (USA)
1933	Primo Carnera (Italy)	1974	Muhammad Ali (USA)
1934	Max Baer (USA)	1978	Leon Spinks (USA)
1935	James Braddock (USA)	1979	Larry Holmes (USA)
1937	Joe Louis (USA)	1987	Tony Tucker (USA)
1949	Ezzard Charles (USA)	1988	Mike Tyson (USA)
1951	Jersey Joe Walcott (USA)	1990	James Douglas (USA)
1952	Rocky Marciano (USA)	1991	Evander Holyfield (USA)
1956	Floyd Patterson (USA)	1993	Lennox Lewis (GB)

British Professional Champions
as at March 1993

Heavy	Herbie Hide	Lightwelter	Andy Holligan
Cruiser	Carl Thompson	Light	Billy Schwer
Light Heavy	Crawford Ashley	Superfeather	Sugar Gibiliru
Middle	Frank Grant	Feather	Sean Murphy
Lightmiddle	Andy Till	Bantam	Drew Docherty
Welter	Delroy Bryan	Fly	Francis Ampofo

British Amateur Champions 1993

Super Heavy	M. McKenzie	Lightwelter	P. Richardson
Heavy	P. Lawson	Light	B. Welsh
Light Heavy	K. Oliver	Feather	J. Cook
Lightmiddle	D. Starie	Fly	P. Ingle
Welter	C. Bessie	Lightfly	M. Hughes

Records

Longest reigning world champion: Joe Louis (22nd June 1937–1st March 1949)

Longest reigning British heavyweight champion: Henry Cooper (12th January 1959–13th June 1970)

CRICKET

Governing bodies: The Cricket Council, Lord's Ground, London NW8 8QN; Women's Cricket Association, 16 Upper Woburn Place, London WC1H 0QP.

Test Match Records

England v Australia 1876–1991
The leading records for the series of matches are as follows:

Highest innings totals
  903 for 7 dec.   by England, at The Oval, 1938
  729 for 6 dec.   by Australia, at Lord's, 1930

Lowest innings totals
  36   by Australia, at Birmingham, 1902
  45   by England, at Sydney, 1886–87

Highest individual innings
  364   L. Hutton, for England, at The Oval, 1938
  334   D. G. Bradman, for Australia, at Leeds, 1930
  311   R. B. Simpson, for Australia, at Manchester, 1964
  307   R. M. Cowper, for Australia, at Melbourne, 1965–66
  304   D. G. Bradman, for Australia, at Leeds, 1934

Most runs by a batsman in one series
  England in England: 732 (av 81·33) by D. I. Gower, 1985
  England in Australia: 905 (av 113·12) by W. R. Hammond, 1928–29
  Australia in England: 974 (av 139·14) by D. G. Bradman, 1930
  Australia in Australia: 810 (av 90·00) by D. G. Bradman, 1936–37

Batsmen scoring two centuries in a match
  136 & 130   W. Bardsley, Australia, The Oval, 1909
  176 & 127   H. Sutcliffe, England, Melbourne, 1924–25
  119 n.o. & 177   W. R. Hammond, England, Adelaide, 1928–29
  147 & 103 n.o.   D. C. S. Compton, England, Adelaide, 1946–47
  122 & 124 n.o.   A. R. Morris, Australia, Adelaide, 1946–47

Bowlers taking 9 or 10 wickets in an innings
  10 for 53   J. C. Laker, England, at Manchester (second innings), 1956
  9 for 37   J. C. Laker, England, at Manchester (first innings), 1956
  9 for 121   A. A. Mailey, Australia, at Melbourne, 1920–21

Bowlers taking 15 or more wickets in a match
  19 for 90   J. C. Laker, England, at Manchester, 1956

16 for 137   R. A. L. Massie, Australia, at Lord's, 1972
15 for 104   H. Verity, England, at Lord's, 1934
15 for 124   W. Rhodes, England, at Melbourne, 1903–4

Hat-tricks
For England   W. Bates, at Melbourne, 1882–83
                J. Briggs, at Sydney, 1891–92
                J. T. Hearne, at Leeds, 1899
For Australia   F. R. Spofforth, at Melbourne, 1878–79
                H. Trumble, at Melbourne, 1901–2
                H. Trumble, at Melbourne, 1903–4

Most wickets taken by a bowler in one series
England in England: 46 (av 9·60), J. C. Laker, 1956
England in Australia: 38 (av 23·18), M. W. Tate, 1924–25
Australia in England: 42 (av 21·26), T. M. Alderman, 1981
Australia in Australia: 41 (av 12·85), R. M. Hogg, 1978–79

Record partnerships for each wicket – England
1st   323   J. B. Hobbs & W. Rhodes, at Melbourne, 1911–12
2nd 382   L. Hutton & M. Leyland, at The Oval, 1938
3rd 262   W. R. Hammond & D. R. Jardine, at Adelaide, 1928–29
4th 222   W. R. Hammond & E. Paynter, at Lord's, 1938
5th 206   E. Paynter & D. C. S. Compton, at Nottingham, 1938
6th 215   J. Hardstaff jnr & L. Hutton, at The Oval, 1938
     215   G. Boycott & A. P. E. Knott, at Nottingham, 1977
7th 143   F. E. Woolley & J. Vine, at Sydney, 1911–12
8th 124   E. P. Hendren & H. Larwood, at Brisbane, 1928–29
9th 151   W. H. Scotton & W. W. Read, at The Oval, 1884
10th 130   R. E. Foster & W. Rhodes, at Sydney, 1903–4

Record partnerships for each wicket – Australia
1st   244   R. B. Simpson & W. M. Lawry, at Adelaide, 1965–66
2nd 451   D. G. Bradman & W. H. Ponsford, at The Oval, 1934
3rd 276   D. G. Bradman & A. L. Hassett, at Brisbane, 1946–47
4th 388   D. G. Bradman & W. H. Ponsford, at Leeds, 1934
5th 405   D. G. Bradman & S. G. Barnes, at Sydney, 1946–47
6th 346   D. G. Bradman & J. H. Fingleton, at Melbourne, 1936–37
7th 165   C. Hill & H. Trumble, at Melbourne, 1897–98
8th 243   C. Hill & R. J. Hartigan, at Adelaide, 1907–8
9th 154   S. E. Gregory & J. McC. Blackham, at Sydney, 1894–95
10th 127   J. M. Taylor & A. A. Mailey, at Sydney, 1924–25

Test Cricket 1877–1993
Summarised results of series completed by 1 March 1993

ENGLAND v	W	D	L		AUSTRALIA v	W	D	L
Australia	88	82	104		England	104	82	88
South Africa	46	38	18		South Africa	29	13	11
West Indies	24	37	43		West Indies	30	20	26*
India	31	36	14		New Zealand	10	10	6
Pakistan	14	31	7		India	24	17	8
New Zealand	32	33	4		Pakistan	12	13	9
Sri Lanka	3	1	1		Sri Lanka	3	1	0
SOUTH AFRICA v	W	D	L		SRI LANKA v	W	D	L
England	18	38	46		England	1	1	3
Australia	11	13	29		Australia	0	3	4
New Zealand	9	6	2		New Zealand	1	6	4
India	1	3	0		India	1	4	3
					Pakistan	1	5	6
INDIA v	W	D	L					
England	14	36	31		WEST INDIES v	W	D	L
Australia	8	17	24*		England	43	37	24
West Indies	6	30	26		Australia	26	20	30*
New Zealand	12	13	6		India	26	30	6
Pakistan	4	33	7		New Zealand	8	12	4
Sri Lanka	3	4	1		Pakistan	10	11	7
South Africa	0	3	1					
Zimbabwe	0	1	0		PAKISTAN v	W	D	L
					England	7	31	14
NEW ZEALAND v	W	D	L		Australia	9	13	12
England	4	33	32		West Indies	7	11	10
Australia	6	10	10		New Zealand	13	16	3
South Africa	2	6	9		India	7	33	4
West Indies	4	12	8		Sri Lanka	6	5	1
India	6	12	13					
Pakistan	3	16	14					
Sri Lanka	4	6	1					
Zimbabwe	1	1	0					

* plus one match tied

Leading Run-scorers in Test matches
(series completed by March 1, 1993)

	Innings	Not out	Runs	Highest Score	Average
A. R. Border (Aus)	240	42	10161	205	51.31
S. M. Gavaskar (India)	214	14	10122	236*	51.12
Javed Miandad (Pakistan)	179	21	8569	280*	54.23

	Innings	Not out	Runs	Highest Score	Average
I. V. A. Richards (West Indies)	182	12	8540	291	50.24
D. Gower (England)	204	18	8231	215	44.25
G. Boycott (England)	193	23	8114	246*	47.73
G. S. Sobers (West Indies)	160	21	8032	365*	57.78
M. C. Cowdrey (England)	188	15	7624	182	44.07
G. A. Gooch (England)	183	6	7620	333	43.05
C. G. Greenidge (West Indies)	185	16	7558	226	44.72

* Not out

Greatest number of appearances in Test Cricket (series completed by 1 March 1991)

ENGLAND)

M. C. Cowdrey	114	P. B. H. May	66
D. I. Gower	114	F. E. Woolley	64
G. Boycott	108	E. R. Dexter	62
G. A. Gooch	102	J. E. Emburey	62
I. T. Botham	100	T. E. Bailey	61
A. P. E. Knott	95	R. Illingworth	61
T. G. Evans	91	J. B. Hobbs	61
R. G. D. Willis	90	K. W. R. Fletcher	59
D. L. Underwood	86	A. W. Greig	58
W. R. Hammond	85	W. Rhodes	58
K. F. Barrington	82	R. W. Taylor	57
T. W. Graveney	79	H. Sutcliffe	54
L. Hutton	79	F. J. Titmus	53
D. C. S. Compton	78	P. H. Edmonds	51
J. H. Edrich	77	A. V. Bedser	51
A. J. Lamb	77	E. P. Hendren	51
M. W. Gatting	72	D. L. Amiss	50
J. B. Statham	70	M. J. K. Smith	50
F. S. Trueman	67		

AUSTRALIA

A. R. Border	138	G. S. Chappell	87
R. W. Marsh	96	R. N. Harvey	79

Australia (contd.)

I. M. Chappell	75	G. M. Wood	59
K. D. Walters	74	S. E. Gregory	58
K. J. Hughes	70	K. R. Miller	55
D. K. Lillee	70	W. A. Oldfield	54
W. M. Lawry	67	D. G. Bradman	52
I. M. Redpath	66	D. M. Jones	52
R. Benaud	63	J. R. Thomson	51
D. Boon	63	A. W. Grout	51
R. B. Simpson	62	W. W. Armstrong	50
R. R. Lindwall	61	G. R. Marsh	50
G. D. McKenzie	60	C. Hill	49

South Africa

J. H. B. Waite	50	R. A. McLean	40
A. D. Nourse, sen	45	H. J. Tayfield	37
B. Mitchell	42	D. J. McGlew	34
H. W. Taylor	42	A. D. Nourse, jnr	34
T. L. Goddard	41	E. J. Barlow	30

New Zealand

R. J. Hadlee	86	G. M. Turner	41
J. G. Wright	79	J. J. Crowe	39
M. D. Crowe	63	G. M. Dowling	39
I. D. S. Smith	63	B. A. Edgar	39
B. E. Congdon	61	J. G. Bracewell	38
J. R. Reid	61	J. M. Parker	36
J. V. Coney	52	R. O. Collinge	35
M. G. Burgess	50	K. Rutherford	35
G. P. Howarth	47	K. J. Wadsworth	33
B. L. Cairns	43	R. C. Motz	32
B. Sutcliffe	42	V. Pollard	32
E. J. Chatfield	41		

West Indies

I. V. A. Richards	121	R. B. Kanhai	79
C. H. Lloyd	110	R. Richardson	68
C. G. Greenidge	108	A. I. Kallicharran	66
D. L. Haynes	108	D. L. Murray	62
G. S. Sobers	93	M. A. Holding	60
P. J. L. Dujon	81	H. A. Gomes	60
M. D. Marshall	81	R. C. Fredericks	59
L. R. Gibbs	79	J. Garner	58

WEST INDIES (*contd.*)			
C. A. Walsh	56	E. D. Weekes	48
A. L. Logie	52	A. M. E. Roberts	47
F. M. Worrell	51	B. F. Butcher	44
W. W. Hall	48	C. C. Hunte	44

INDIA			
S. M. Gavaskar	125	C. G. Borde	55
R. N. Kapil Dev	123	V. L. Manjrekar	55
D. B. Vengsarkar	116	M. Azharuddin	54
G. R. Viswanath	91	E. A. S. Prasanna	49
S. M. H. Kirmani	91	Mansur Ali Khan	46
R. J. Shastri	80	F. M. Engineer	46
M. B. Amarnath	69	V. Mankad	44
B. S. Bedi	67	P. Roy	43
P. R. Umrigar	59	K. Srikkanth	43
B. S. Chandrasekhar	58	R. G. Nadkarni	41
S. Venkataraghavan	57		

PAKISTAN			
Javed Miandad	118	Mushtaq Mohammad	57
Imran Khan	88	Wasim Raja	57
Wasim Bari	81	Hanif Mohammad	55
Zaheer Abbas	78	Sarfraz Nawaz	55
Saleem Malik	72	Iqbal Qasim	50
Mudassar Nazar	71	Intikhab Alam	49
Abdul Qadir	67	Mohsin Khan	48
Majid Khan	63	Ramiz Raji	45
Asif Iqbal	58	WalimAkram	45

SRI LANKA			
A. Ranatunga	38	R. J. Ratnayake	23
P. A. de Silva	31	J. R. Ratnayeke	22
L. R. D. Mendis	24	R. S. Madugalle	21
A. P. Gurusinha	23	R. L. Dias	20
S. Wettimuny	23	A. L. F. de Mel	17

County Champions
(*since 1946*)

1946	Yorkshire	1947	Middlesex

1948	Glamorgan	1975	Leicestershire
1949	Middlesex &	1976	Middlesex
	Yorkshire	1977	Middlesex & Kent
1950	Lancashire & Surrey	1978	Kent
1951	Warwickshire	1979	Essex
1952–58	Surrey	1980	Middlesex
1959–60	Yorkshire	1981	Nottinghamshire
1961	Hampshire	1982	Middlesex
1962–63	Yorkshire	1983–84	Essex
1964–65	Worcestershire	1985	Middlesex
1966–68	Yorkshire	1986	Essex
1969	Glamorgan	1987	Nottinghamshire
1970	Kent	1988–89	Worcestershire
1971	Surrey	1990	Middlesex
1972	Warwickshire	1991	Essex
1973	Hampshire	1992	Essex
1974	Worcestershire		

Since 1864 the title has been won outright by:

Yorkshire	31	Worcestershire	5
Surrey	18	Gloucestershire	3
Nottinghamshire	14	Warwickshire	3
Middlesex	10	Glamorgan	2
Lancashire	8	Hampshire	2
Essex	6	Derbyshire	1
Kent	6	Leicestershire	1

Eight times it has been shared by:

Nottinghamshire	5	Gloucestershire	1
Lancashire	4	Surrey	1
Yorkshire	2	Kent	1
Middlesex	2		

Northamptonshire, Somerset and Sussex are the only counties never to have been first in the County Championship.

Gillette/Natwest Bank Trophy

(60-over competition, sponsored initially by Gillette and by NatWest since 1981)

1963–64	Sussex	1967	Kent
1965	Yorkshire	1968	Warwickshire
1966	Warwickshire	1969	Yorkshire

1970–72	Lancashire	1983	Somerset
1973	Gloucestershire	1984	Middlesex
1974	Kent	1985	Essex
1975	Lancashire	1986	Sussex
1976	Northamptonshire	1987	Nottinghamshire
1977	Middlesex	1988	Middlesex
1978	Sussex	1989	Warwickshire
1979	Somerset	1990	Lancashire
1980	Middlesex	1991	Hampshire
1981	Derbyshire	1992	Northamptonshire
1982	Surrey		

Benson & Hedges Cup
(55-over competition)

1972	Leicestershire	1983	Middlesex
1973	Kent	1984	Lancashire
1974	Surrey	1985	Leicestershire
1975	Leicestershire	1986	Middlesex
1976	Kent	1987	Yorkshire
1977	Gloucestershire	1988	Hampshire
1978	Kent	1989	Nottinghamshire
1979	Essex	1990	Lancashire
1980	Northamptonshire	1991	Worcestershire
1981–82	Somerset	1992	Hampshire

Sunday League 40-over Competition
(Sponsored by John Player 1969–86
and by Refuge Assurance 1987–91)

1969–70	Lancashire	1981	Essex
1971	Worcestershire	1982	Sussex
1972–73	Kent	1983	Yorkshire
1974	Leicestershire	1984–85	Essex
1975	Hampshire	1986	Hampshire
1976	Kent	1987–88	Worcestershire
1977	Leicestershire	1989	Lancashire
1978	Hampshire	1990	Derbyshire
1979	Somerset	1991	Nottinghamshire
1980	Warwickshire	1992	Middlesex

World Cup
(60-over competition)

1975 West Indies (runner-up Australia)
1979 West Indies (runner-up England)
1983 India   (runner-up West Indies)
1987 Australia   (runner-up England)
1992 Pakistan   (runner-up England)

Records

Highest score in first-class cricket: 499 Hanif Mohammad, for Karachi v Bahawalpur, 1958–59

Highest score in Test cricket: 365 not out, G. S. Sobers, for West Indies v Pakistan, 1958

Most runs in first-class cricket: 61,237 J. B. Hobbs (Surrey & England), 1905 to 1934

Most runs in a season: 3,816 D. C. S. Compton (Middlesex & England), 1947

Most centuries in a season: 18 D. C. S. Compton, 1947

Fastest recorded century: 100 in 26 minutes T. Moody, Warwickshire v Glamorgan, 1990.* 100 in 35 minutes P. G. H. Fender, Surrey v Northamptonshire, 1920. S. J. O'Shaughnessy, Lancashire v Leicestershire, 1983

Highest team innings: 1,107 Victoria v New South Wales, 1926–27

Most runs in a day: 721 Australians v Essex, Southend, 1948

Highest partnership: 577 V. S. Hazare & Gul Mahomed, for Baroda v Holkar, 4th wicket, 1946–47

Biggest win: Pakistan Western Railways beat Dera Ismail Khan by an innings and 851 runs, Lahore, Pakistan, 1964–65

Most wickets in a season: 304 A. P. 'Tich' Freeman, 1928

Most wickets in a career: 4,187 W. Rhodes (Yorkshire & England), 1898 to 1930.

Most wickets in a match: 19 J. C. Laker, England v Australia, Manchester, 1956

Highest innings by any captain in a Test match: 333 Graham Gooch (England) v India at Lords, 1990. During this match Gooch established a remarkable number of records: his 333 was **the highest ever score at Lords** and **the highest-ever score against India.** In the second innings he scored 123 runs and became **the first batsman to score five Test centuries at Lords,** as well as **the first to score a triple century and a century in the same first class match.**

*Moody was being fed donkey-drops by Glamorgan in the hope of an early declaration.

CROSS-COUNTRY RUNNING

Governing bodies: English Cross-Country Union, 11 Heslop Drive, Darlington, Co Durham; Women's Cross-Country & Race Walking Association, 10 Anderton Close, Bury, Lancs.

English Championship

Men

	Individual	*Team*
1982	D. Clarke (Hercules/Wimbledon)	Tipton Harriers
1983	T. Hutchings (Crawley AC)	Aldershot/Farnham
1984	E. Martin (Basildon)	Aldershot/Farnham
1985	D. Lewis (Rossendale)	Aldershot/Farnham
1986	T. Hutchings (Crawley AC)	Tipton Harriers
1987	D. Clarke (Hercules/Wimbledon)	Gateshead Harriers
1988	D. Clarke (Hercules/Wimbledon)	Birchfield Harriers
1989	D. D. Lewis (Rossendale)	Tipton Harriers
1990	R. Nerurkar (Bingley Harriers)	Valli Harriers
1991	R. Nerurkar (Bingley Harriers)	Bingley Harriers
1992	E. Martin (Basildon)	Tipton Harriers
1993	R. Nerurkar (Bingley Harriers)	

Women

	Individual	*Team*
1982	P. Fudge (Hounslow AC)	Sale Harriers
1983	C. Benning (Southampton/Eastleigh)	Sale Harriers
1984	J. Furniss (Sheffield AC)	Aldershot/Farnham
1985	A. Tooby (Cardiff AAC)	Crawley AC
1986	C. Bradford (Clevedon)	Sale Harriers
1987	J. Shields (Sheffield AC)	Sale Harriers
1988	H. Titterington (Leicester)	Birchfield Harriers
1989	A. Pain (Leeds City)	Parkside
1990	A. Whitcombe (Parkside)	Parkside
1991	A. Whitcombe (Parkside)	Parkside
1992	L. York (Leicester)	Parkside
1993	G. Stacey (Bromley)	Parkside

International Championship

Men

	Individual	*Team*	*Venue*
1979	J. Tracey (Ireland)	England	Limerick
1980	C. Virgin (USA)	England	Paris
1981	C. Virgin (USA)	Ethiopia	Madrid
1982	M. Kedir (Ethiopia)	Ethiopia	Rome

	Individual	*Team*	*Venue*
1983	B. Devele (Ethiopia)	Ethiopia	Gateshead
1984	C. Lopez (Portugal)	Ethiopia	New Jersey
1985	C. Lopez (Portugal)	Ethiopia	Lisbon
1986	J. Ngugi (Kenya)	Kenya	Colombier
1987	J. Ngugi (Kenya)	Kenya	Warsaw
1988	J. Ngugi (Kenya)	Kenya	Auckland
1989	J. Ngugi (Kenya)	Kenya	Stavanger
1990	K. Skah (Morocco)	Kenya	Aix-les-Bains
1991	K. Skah (Morocco)	Kenya	Antwerp
1992	J. Ngugi (Kenya)	Kenya	Boston
1993	W. Sigei (Kenya)	Kenya	Amorebieta

Women

1979	G. Waitz (Norway)	USA	Limerick
1980	G. Waltz (Norway)	USSR	Paris
1981	G. Waltz (Norway)	USSR	Madrid
1982	M. Puica (Romania)	USSR	Rome
1983	G. Waitz (Norway)	USA	Gateshead
1984	M. Puica (Romania)	USA	New Jersey
1985	Z. Budd (England)	USA	Lisbon
1986	Z. Budd (England)	England	Colombier
1987	A. Sergant	France	Warsaw
1988	I. Kristiansen (Norway)	USSR	Auckland
1989	A. Sergent (France)	USSR	Stavanger
1990	L. Jennings (USA)	USSR	Aix-les-Bains
1991	L. Jennings (USA)	Kenya	Antwerp
1992	L. Jennings (USA)	Kenya	Boston
1993	A. Dias (Portugal)	Kenya	Amarebieta

CYCLING

Governing body: British Cycling Federation, 36 Rockingham Road, Kettering, Northants. NN16 8HG.

1992 Olympic Games Winners

Men

1,000 metres time trial	J. Moreno (Spain)
1,000 metres sprint	J. Fiedler (Germany)

4,000 metres pursuit	G. Boardman (GB)
4,000 metres team pursuit	Germany
Individual Points race	G. Lombardi (Italy)
Individual road race	F. Casartelli (Italy)
Road time trial	Germany

Women

Individual Road race	K. Watt (Australia)
1,000 metres sprint	E. Selamae (Estonia)
3,000 metres individual pursuit	P. Rossner (Germany)

1991 World Champions

Men

Professional road race	G. Bugno (Italy)
Amateur road race	V. Rjakskinski (USSR)
Professional sprint	M. Hübner (Germany)
Amateur sprint	J. Fiedler (Germany)
Professional 5,000 m pursuit	M. McCarthy (USA)
Amateur 4,000 m pursuit	J. Lehmann (Germany)
Amateur 4,000 m team pursuit	Germany
Professional 100 km motor-paced	D. Clark (Australia)
Amateur motor-paced hour	R. Konigshoffer (Austria)
Amateur tandem sprint	{ E. Pokorny (Germany) / E. Raasch (Germany)
Amateur 1 km TT	J. Moreno (Spain)
Amateur 100 km team TT	Italy

Women (all amateur)

Road race	L. van Moorsel (Holland)
Sprint	E. Haringa (Holland)
Pursuit	P. Rossner (Germany)

Records

Men's professional motor-paced 1 hour record: 84 km 710 m, A. Romanov USSR, 1987

Men's unpaced standing start 1 hour record: 51·151 km, F. Moser in Mexico, 1984

Men's unpaced flying start 1 kilometre: 58·26 sec, D. Efrain 1986

EQUESTRIANISM

Governing bodies: British Horse Society and British Show Jumping Association, British Equestrian Centre, Stoneleigh, Kenilworth, Warwickshire CV8 2LR.

Olympic Games

(Team winners are shown first followed by individual winners)

Date	Showjumping	Horse trials	Dressage
1952	Great Britain	Sweden	Sweden
	P. J. d'Oriola (Fra)	H. G. von Blixen-Finecke (Swe)	Maj. H. St Cyr (Swe)
1956	West Germany	Great Britain	Sweden
	H. G. Winkler (W. Ger)	P. Kastenman (Swe)	Maj. H. St Cyr (Swe)
1960	West Germany	Australia	No team winner
	R. d'Inzeo (Italy)	L. Morgan (Aust)	S. Filatov (USSR)
1964	West Germany	Italy	West Germany
	P. J. d'Oriola (Fra)	M. Checcoli (Ita)	H. Chammartin (Swi)
1968	Canada	Great Britain	West Germany
	W. Steinkraus (USA)	J. J. Guyon (Fra)	I. Kizimov (USSR)
1972	West Germany	Great Britain	USSR
	G. Mancinelli (Italy)	R. Meade (GB)	L. Linsenhoff (W. Ger)
1976	France	USA	West Germany
	A. Schockemöhle (W. Ger)	E. Coffin (USA)	C. Stückelberger (Swi)
1984	USA	USA	West Germany
	J. Fargis (USA)	M. Todd (NZ)	R. Klimke (W. Ger)
1988	W. Germany	W. Germany	West Germany
	P. Durand (France)	M. Todd (NZ)	N. Uphoff (W. Ger)
1992	Netherlands	Australia	Germany
	L. Beerbaum (Germany)	M. Ryan (Australia)	N. Uphoff (Germany)

World Championships

Date	Horse trials	Dressage
1966	Ireland	West Germany
	Capt C. Moratorio (Arg)	J. Neckermann (W. Ger)
1970	Great Britain	USSR
	M. Gordon-Watson (GB)	E. Petuchkova (USSR)
1974	USA	West Germany
	B. Davidson (USA)	R. Klimke (W. Ger)
1978	Canada	West Germany
	B. Davidson (USA)	C. Stückelberger (Swi)
1982	Great Britain	West Germany
	L. Green (GB)	R. Klimke (W. Ger)
1986	Great Britain	West Germany
	V. Leng (GB)	A-G. Jensen (Den)
1990	New Zealand	West Germany
	B. Tait (NZ)	N. Uphoff (W. Ger)

European Championships

Date	Horse trials	Dressage
1969	Great Britain	West Germany
	M. Gordon-Watson (GB)	L. Linsenhoff (W. Ger)
1971	Great Britain	West Germany
	HRH Princess Anne (GB)	L. Linsenhoff (W. Ger)
1973	West Germany	West Germany
	A. Evdokimov (USSR)	R. Klimke (W. Ger)
1975	USSR	West Germany
	L. Prior-Palmer (GB)	C. Stückelberger (Swi)
1977	Great Britain	West Germany
	L. Prior-Palmer (GB)	C. Stückelberger (Swi)
1979	Ireland	West Germany
	N. Haagensen (Den)	E. Theurer (Aut)
1981	Great Britain	West Germany
	H. Schmutz (Swi)	R. Klimke (W. Ger)
1983	Sweden	West Germany
	R. Bayliss (GB)	A.-G. Jensen (Den)
1985	Great Britain	West Germany
	V. Holgate (GB)	R. Klimke (W. Ger)
1987	Great Britain	West Germany
	V. Leng (GB)	M. Otto Crepin (France)
1989	Great Britain	West Germany
	V. Leng (GB)	N. Uphoff (W. Ger)
1991	Great Britain	Germany
	I. Stark (GB)	I. Werth (Germany)

Nations Cup Trophy
(formerly President's Cup) (Showjumping)

1970	Great Britain	1984	West Germany
1971	West Germany	1985–86	Great Britain
1972–74	Great Britain	1987	France
1975–76	West Germany	1988	France
1977–79	Great Britain	1989	Great Britain
1980	France	1990	France
1981–82	West Germany	1991	Great Britain
1983	Great Britain	1992	Great Britain

King George V Gold Cup

1971	G. Wiltfang (Ger) *Askan*
1972	D. Broome (GB) *Sportsman*
1973	P. McMahon (GB) *Pennwood Forge Mill*
1974	F. Chapot (USA) *Main Spring*
1975	A. Schockemöhle (Ger) *Rex the Robber*
1976	M. Saywell (GB) *Chain Bridge*
1977	D. Broome (GB) *Philco*
1978	J. McVean (Aus) *Claret*
1979	R. Smith (GB) *Video*
1980	D. Bowen (GB) *Scorton*
1981	D. Broome (GB) *Mr Ross*
1982	M. Whitaker (GB) *Disney Way*
1983	P. Schockemöhle (Ger) *Deister*
1984	N. Skelton (GB) *St James*
1985	M. Pyrah (GB) *Towerlands Anglezarke*
1986	J. Whitaker (GB) *Next Ryan's Son*
1987	M. Pyrah (GB) *Towerlands Anglezarke*
1988	R. Smith (GB) *Brook St Boysie*
1989	M. Whitaker (GB) *Next Didi*
1990	J. Whitaker (GB) *Henderson Milton*
1991	D. Broome (GB) *Lannegan*
1992	J. Whitaker (GB) *Henderson Midnight Madness*

British Jumping Derby

1970	H. Smith (GB) *Mattie Brown*
1971	H. Smith (GB) *Mattie Brown*
1972	H. Snoek (Ger) *Shirokko*
1973	M. Dawes (GB) *Mr Banbury*
1974	H. Smith (GB) *Salvador*
1975	P. Darragh (Ire) *Pele*
1976	E. Macken (Ire) *Boomerang*

1977	E. Macken (Ire) *Boomerang*
1978	E. Macken (Ire) *Boomerang*
1979	E. Macken (Ire) *Carroll's Boomerang*
1980	M. Whitaker (GB) *Owen Gregory*
1981	H. Smith (GB) *Sanyo Video*
1982	P. Schockemöhle (Ger) *Deister*
1983	J. Whitaker (GB) *Ryans Son*
1984	Lt. J. Leddingham (Ire) *Gahran*
1985	P. Schockemöhle (Ger) *Lorenzo*
1986	P. Schockemöhle (Ger) *Next Deister*
1987	N. Skelton (GB) *J-Nick*
1988	N. Skelton (GB) *Apollo*
1989	N. Skelton (GB) *Burmah Apollo*
1990	J. Turi (GB) *Vital*
1991	M. Whitaker (GB) *Henderson Monsanta*
1992	M. Whitaker (GB) *Henderson Monsanta*

Badminton Horse Trials

1972	Lt M. Phillips (GB) *Great Ovation*
1973	L. Prior-Palmer (GB) *Be Fair*
1974	Capt M. Phillips (GB) *Columbus*
1975	Cancelled after dressage
1976	L. Prior-Palmer (GB) *Wide Awake*
1977	L. Prior-Palmer (GB) *George*
1978	J. Holderness-Roddam (GB) *Warrior*
1979	L. Prior-Palmer (GB) *Killaire*
1980	M. Todd (NZ) *Southern Comfort*
1981	Capt M. Phillips (GB) *Lincoln*
1982	R. Meade (GB) *Speculator III*
1983	L. Green (GB) *Regal Realm*
1984	L. Green (GB) *Beagle Bay*
1985	V. Holgate (GB) *Priceless*
1986	I. Stark (GB) *Sir Wattie*
1987	Cancelled
1988	I Stark (GB) *Sir Wattie*
1989	V. Leng (GB) *Master Craftsman*
1990	N. McIrvine (GB) *Middle Road*
1991	R. Powell (GB) *The Irishman*
1992	M. Thomson (GB) *King William*
1993	V. Leng (GB) *Welton Houdini*

FENCING

Governing body: Amateur Fencing Association, 1 Barons Gate, 33–35 Rothschild Road, W4 5HT.

1992 Olympic Champions

Men

Foil	P. Omnes (France)
Foil team	Germany
Sabre	B. Szabo (Hungary)
Sabre team	Unified Team
Epee	E. Srecki (France)
Epee team	Germany

Women

Foil	G. Trillini (Italy)
Foil team	Italy

1992 British Championships

Men's foil	W. Gosbee (Salle Boston)
Men's foil team	Salle Boston
Ladies' foil	L. Harris (Salle Paul)
Ladies' foil team	Salle Boston
Men's epee	J. Llewellyn (Reading)
Ladies' epee	G. Usher (Meadow Bank)
Men's sabre	I. Williams (London Thames)
Men's sabre team	London Polytechnic

GOLF

Governing bodies: Royal and Ancient Golf Club, St Andrews, Fife KY16 9JD; Ladies' Golf Union, 12 The Scores, St Andrews, Fife KY16 9AT.

British Open Champions
Since 1946

1946	Sam Snead (USA)	1950	Bobby Locke (South Africa)
1947	Fred Daly (Balmoral)		
1948	Henry Cotton (Royal Mid-Surrey)	1951	Max Faulkner (unattached)
1949	Bobby Locke (South Africa)	1952	Bobby Locke (South Africa)

1953	Ben Hogan (USA)	1973	T. Weiskopf (USA)
1954	P. Thomson (Australia)	1974	G. Player (South Africa)
1955	P. Thomson (Australia)	1975	T. Watson (USA)
1956	P. Thomson (Australia)	1976	J. Miller (USA)
1957	Bobby Locke (South	1977	T. Watson (USA)
	Africa)	1978	J. Nicklaus (USA)
1958	P. Thomson (Australia)	1979	S. Ballesteros (Spain)
1959	G. Player (South Africa)	1980	T. Watson (USA)
1960	Kel Nagle (Australia)	1981	W. Rogers (USA)
1961	A. Palmer (USA)	1982	T. Watson (USA)
1962	A. Palmer (USA)	1983	T. Watson (USA)
1963	Bob Charles (NZ)	1984	S. Ballesteros (Spain)
1964	A. Lema (USA)	1985	S. Lyle (GB)
1965	P. Thomson (Australia)	1986	G. Norman (Australia)
1966	J. Nicklaus (USA)	1987	N. Faldo (GB)
1967	R. de Vicenzo (Argentina)	1988	S. Ballesteros (Spain)
1968	G. Player (South Africa)	1989	M. Calcavecchia (USA)
1969	A. Jacklin (Potters Bar)	1990	N. Faldo (GB)
1970	J. Nicklaus (USA)	1991	I. Baker-Finch (Australia)
1971	L. Trevino (USA)	1992	N. Faldo (GB)

Ryder Cup

1957	Great Britain	1971	USA	1985	GB &
1959	USA	1973	USA		Europe
1961	USA	1975	USA	1987	GB &
1963	USA	1977	USA		Europe
1965	USA	1979	USA	1989	Tie
1967	USA	1981	USA	1991	USA
1969	Tie	1983	USA		

Walker Cup

1957	USA	1971	Great Britain	1985	USA
1959	USA	1973	USA	1987	USA
1961	USA	1975	USA	1989	GB &
1963	USA	1977	USA		Ireland
1965	Tie	1979	USA	1991	USA
1967	USA	1981	USA		
1969	USA	1983	USA		

Curtis Cup

1956	Great Britain	1970	USA	1984	USA
1958	Great Britain	1972	USA	1986	GB & Ireland
1960	USA	1974	USA	1988	GB & Ireland
1962	USA	1976	USA	1990	USA
1964	USA	1978	USA	1992	GB & Ireland
1966	USA	1980	USA		
1968	USA	1982	USA		

World Cup of Golf

1967	USA	1976	Spain	1985	Canada
1968	Canada	1977	Spain	1986	Not held
1969	USA	1978	USA	1987	Wales
1970	Australia	1979	USA	1988	USA
1971	USA	1980	Canada	1989	Australia
1972	Taiwan	1981	Not held	1990	Germany
1973	USA	1982	Spain	1991	Sweden
1974	USA	1983	USA	1992	USA
1975	USA	1984	Spain		

Ladies' British Open Championships 1992

Amateur	*Open*
P. Pedersen (Denmark)	P. Sheehan (USA)

Ladies' Close Amateur Championships 1992

England:	C. Hall
Ireland:	E. Power
Scotland:	J. Moodie
Wales:	J. Foster

HOCKEY

Governing bodies: Hockey Association, Norfolk House, 102 Faxon Gate West, Milton Keynes, MK9 2EP; All England Women's Hockey Association, 51 High Street, Shrewsbury, Shropshire.

Olympic Winners

1920	England	1936	India
1924	No competition	1948	India
1928	India	1952	India
1932	India	1956	India

1960	Pakistan	1984	Pakistan (men),
1964	India		Netherlands (women)
1968	Pakistan	1988	GB (Men)
1972	W. Germany		Australia (Women)
1976	New Zealand	1992	Germany (Men)
1980	India		Spain (Women)

County Championship

	Men		**Women**
1978	Lancashire	1978	Hertfordshire
1979	Kent	1979	Lancashire
1980	Buckinghamshire	1980	Suffolk drew with Leics.
1981	Middlesex	1981	Staffordshire
1982	Buckinghamshire	1982	Suffolk
1983	Lancashire	1983	Leicestershire
1984	Yorkshire	1984	Middlesex
1985	Worcestershire	1985	Lancashire
1986	Surrey	1986	Middlesex
1987	Worcestershire	1987	Staffordshire
1988	Middlesex	1988	Kent
1989	Middlesex	1989	Kent
1990	Middlesex	1990	Middlesex
1991	Middlesex	1991	Lancashire
1992	Yorkshire	1992	Lancashire
1993	Staffordshire	1993	Lancashire

ICE HOCKEY

Governing body: International Ice Hockey Federation, Bellevue-strasse 8, A-1190 Wien, Austria.

World Championships

1976–77	Czechoslovakia	1989	USSR
1978–86	USSR	1990	USSR
1987	Sweden	1991	Sweden
1988	USSR	1992	Unified Team

1992 Olympic Winners (Albertville)
Unified Team

ICE SKATING

Governing body: National Skating Association of Great Britain, 15/27 Gee Street, London EC1V 3RE.

World Records (*as at 1990*)
Men

500 metres	V. J. May (GDR)	36.45 sec	1988
1,000 metres	P. Pegov (USSR)	1 min 12·58 sec	1983
1,500 metres	A. Hoffmann (GDR)	1 min 52·48 sec	1987
3,000 metres	J. O. Koss (Norway)	3 min 57·52 sec	1990
5,000 metres	J. O. Koss (Norway)	6 min 38·77 sec	1992
10,000 metres	T. Gustavson (Sweden)	14 min 03·92 sec	1987

Women

500 metres	B. Blair (USA)	39·10 sec	1988
1,000 metres	C. Rothenberger (GDR)	1 min 17·65 sec	1988
1,500 metres	K. Karnia (GDR)	1 min 59·30 sec	1986
3,000 metres	Y. van Gennip (Holland)	4 min 11·94 sec	1988
5,000 metres	Y. van Gennip (Holland)	7 min 14·13 sec	1988

1992 Olympic Games (Albertville)

Overall winners
Unified Team*

Figure Skating

Men	V. Petrenko (UT)
Women	K. Yamaguchi (USA)
Pairs	N. Mishkutienok and A. Dmitriev (UT)
Ice Dancing	M. Klimova and S. Ponomarenko (UT)

Speed Events

Men's 500 metres	U. J. May (Germany)
Men's 1,000 metres	O. Zinke (Germany)
Men's 1,500 metres	J. O. Koss (Norway)
Men's 5,000 metres	G. Koristad (Norway)
Men's 10,000 metres	B. Veldkamp (Netherlands)
Ladies' 500 metres	B. Blair (USA)
Ladies' 1,000 metres	B. Blair (USA)
Ladies' 1,500 metres	J. Boerner (Germany)
Ladies' 3,000 metres	G. Niemann (Germany)
Ladies' 5,000 metres	G. Niemann (Germany)

Shortrack

Men's 1000 metres	K Ki-Hoon (S. Korea)
Men's 5,000 metres relay	South Korea
Ladies' 500 metres	C. Turner (USA)
Ladies' 3,000 metres relay	Canada

* Former Soviet Union

LAWN TENNIS

Governing body: The Lawn Tennis Association, Palliser Road, London W14 9EG.

Wimbledon Champions
Since 1919

Men's Singles

1919	G. L. Patterson	1956–57	L. A. Hoad
1920–21	W. T. Tilden	1958	A. J. Cooper
1922	G. L. Patterson	1959	A. Olmedo
1923	W. M. Johnston	1960	N. Fraser
1924	J. Borotra	1961–62	R. Laver
1925	R. Lacoste	1963	C. McKinley
1926	J. Borotra	1964–65	R. Emerson
1927	H. Cochet	1966	M. Santana
1928	R. Lacoste	1967	J. Newcombe
1929	H. Cochet	1968–69	R. Laver
1930	W. T. Tilden	1970–71	J. Newcombe
1931	S. B. Wood	1972	S. Smith
1932	H. E. Vines	1973	J. Kodes
1933	J. H. Crawford	1974	J. Connors
1934–36	F. J. Perry	1975	A. Ashe
1937–38	J. D. Budge	1976–80	B. Borg
1939	R. L. Riggs	1981	J. McEnroe
1946	Y. Petra	1982	J. Connors
1947	J. A. Kramer	1983–84	J. McEnroe
1948	R. Falkenburg	1985–86	B. Becker
1949	F. R. Schroeder	1987	P. Cash
1950	J. E. Patty	1988	S. Edberg
1951	R. Savitt	1989	B. Becker
1952	F. A. Sedgman	1990	S. Edberg
1953	E. V. Seixas	1991	M. Stich
1954	J. Drobny	1992	A. Agassi
1955	M. A. Trabert		

Women's singles

1919–23	S. Lenglen	1930	H. Moody
1924	K. McKane	1931	C. Aussem
1925	S. Lenglen	1932–33	H. Moody
1926	K. Godfree	1934	D. Round
1927–29	H. Wills	1935	H. Moody

1936	H. Jacobs	1965	M. Smith
1937	D. Round	1966–68	B. J. King
1938	H. Moody	1969	A. Jones
1939	A. Marble	1970	M. Court
1946	P. Betz	1971	E. Goolagong
1947	M. Osborne	1972–73	B. J. King
1948–50	A. Brough	1974	C. Evert
1951	D. Hart	1975	B. J. King
1952–54	M. Connolly	1976	C. Evert
1955	A. Brough	1977	V. Wade
1956	S. Fry	1978–79	M. Navrātilova
1957–58	A. Gibson	1980	E. Cawley
1959–60	M. Bueno	1981	C. Lloyd
1961	A. Mortimer	1982–87	M. Navrātilova
1962	J. Susman	1988–89	S. Graff
1963	M. Smith	1990	M. Navrātilova
1964	M. Bueno	1991–92	S. Graff

Davis Cup

1951–53	Australia	1977	Australia
1954	USA	1978–79	USA
1955–57	Australia	1980	Czechoslovakia
1958	USA	1981–82	USA
1959–62	Australia	1983	Australia
1963	USA	1984–85	Sweden
1964–67	Australia	1986	Australia
1968–72	USA	1987	Sweden
1973	Australia	1988–89	West Germany
1974	South Africa	1990	USA
1975	Sweden	1991	France
1976	Italy	1992	USA

Wightman Cup

1951–57	USA	1969–74	USA
1958	Great Britain	1974–75	Great Britain
1959	USA	1976–77	USA
1960	Great Britain	1978	Great Britain
1961–67	USA	1979–89	USA
1968	Great Britain	1990	*discontinued*

1992 Olympic Winners		
	Men	*Women*
Singles	M. Rosset (Switzerland)	J. Capriatis (USA)
Doubles	Germany	USA

Records

Longest match (time): 6 hrs. 32 mins. J. McEnroe (USA) beat M. Wilander (Sweden) at St Louis, USA in Davis Cup match, 1982, 9–7, 6–2, 15–17, 3–6, 8–6 (79 games)

Longest match (number of games): 147. R. Leach and R. Dell (USA) beat L. Schloss and T. Mozur (USA) at Newport Casino, Newport, USA, 1967, 3–6, 49–47, 22–20 (6 hrs 10 mins)

Largest number of games in Davis Cup singles: 100 in 1982 H. Fritz (Canada) beat J. Andrew (Venezuela) 16–14, 11–9, 9–11, 4–6, 11–9

Largest number of games in a Wimbledon singles: 112, when R. Gonzales (USA) beat C. Pasarell (USA), 22–24, 1–6, 16–14, 6–3, 11–9 in 1969

Longest Wimbledon match: $5\frac{1}{4}$ hours, when Gonzales beat Pasarell

Greatest number of Wimbledon singles wins: William C. Renshaw (GB) 7 titles (1881–2–3–4–5–6–9); Martina Navrátilova (USA) 9 titles 1978–9, 1982–3–4–5–6–7, 1990

Greatest number of Wimbledon titles: Mrs B. J. King (USA) 20 titles (6 singles, 10 doubles and 4 mixed) (1961–79)

MOTOR CYCLING

Governing body: Auto-Cycle Union, Miller House, Corporation Street, Rugby, Warwickshire CV21 2DN.

World Champions			
	1990	1991	1992
	Road Racing		
80 cc	H. Herreros (Krauser)	H. Herreros (Krauser)	H. Herreros (Krauser)
125 cc	L. Capirossi (Honda)	L. Capirossi (Honda)	G. Gramigni (Aprilie)

250 cc	J. Kocinski (Yamaha)	J. Kocinski (Yamaha)	L. Cadalora (Honda)
500 cc	W. Rainey (Yamaha)	W. Rainey (Yamaha)	W. Rainey (Yamaha)
Sidecar	A. Michel (LCR)	S. Webster (LCR)	R. Briland (LCR)
Moto Cross			
125 cc	D. Schmit	S. Everts	G. Albertyn
Speedway			
	P. Jonsson	J. Pederson	G. Havelock
Trials			
	J. Tarres	J. Tarres	T. Ahrala

Record

Winner of most World Championships: Giacomo Agostini (15, in 1966–75)

MOTOR RACING

Governing body: RAC Motor Sports Association Limited, 31 Belgrave Square, London SW1 8QH.

World Driving Championship 1992: N. Mansell (GB), *Williams*
Shell Oils British Grand Prix 1992: N. Mansell (GB), *Williams*
Le Mans 24-hrs 1992: D. Warwick (GB), Y. Dalmas (France), M. Blundell (GB), *Peugeot*
Lombard RAC Rally 1992: C. Saintz, L. Moya (Spain), *Toyota*
Monte Carlo Rally 1992: D. Auriol (France), *Lancia*

Records

Winner of most World Championships: Juan Manuel Fangio (five, in 1951, 1954, 1955, 1956, 1957)
Winner of most Grand Prix: Alain Prost (44)
Winner of most Grand Prix in one year: Nigel Mansell (nine, in 1992)

NETBALL

Governing body: All England Netball Association Limited, 9 Paynes Park, Hitchin, Herts, SG5 1EH.

World Champions

1963	Australia	1983	Australia
1967	New Zealand	1987	New Zealand
1971	Australia	1991	Australia
1975	Australia		
1979	Australia, Trinidad and		
	New Zealand joint champions		

Inter-County Championship

1979	Essex Met.	1985	Bedfordshire		and E. Essex
1980	Essex Met.	1986	Surrey and		drew
1981	Surrey		Hertford-	1989	Birmingham
1982	Essex Met.		shire drew	1990	Middlesex
1983	Hertfordshire	1987	Kent	1991	Surrey
1984	Hertfordshire	1988	Essex Met.	1992	Surrey

National Clubs Tournament

1979	Old Plastovians	1984	Sudbury	1989	Linden
1980	Linden	1985	Sudbury	1990	New Campbell
1981	New Campbell	1986	Grasshoppers	1991	Harbourne
1982	Wanderers	1987	New Campbell	1992	Toucans
1983	OPA	1988	New Campbell		

ROWING

Governing body: Amateur Rowing Association, 6 Lower Mall, London W6 9DJ.

Grand Challenge Cup

Between 1839 and 1934 the Cup was won 23 times by Leander, 15 times by London BC, 7 times by Oxford University BC, 4 times by Magdalen College, Oxford, 3 times by Thames RC and once each by Sydney RC and Harvard Athletic Association BC. The winners since 1935 have been:

1935	Pembroke College, Cambridge	1939	Harvard University, USA
		1946	Leander Club
1936	FC Zurich RC, Swit-zerland	1947	Jesus College, Cambridge
		1948	Thames RC
1937	R. Wiking, Germany	1949	Leander Club
1938	London RC	1950	Harvard University, USA

1951	Lady Margaret BC, Cambridge
1952	Leander Club
1953	Leander Club
1954	Club Krylia Sovetov, USSR
1955	University of Pennsylvania, USA
1956	Centre Sportif des Forces de l'Armée, France
1957	Cornell University, USA
1958	Trud Club, Leningrad, USSR
1959	Harvard University, USA
1960	Molesey BC
1961	USSR Navy
1962	USSR Navy
1963	London University
1964	USSR
1965	Ratzeburger, WG
1966	TSC Berlin, EG
1967	S. C. Wissenschaft DH f K, Leipzig
1968	London University BC
1969	SC Einheit, Dresden
1970	ASK Vorwärts, Rostock
1971	Tideway Scullers School
1972	WMF Moscow, USSR
1973	Trud Kolomna, USSR
1974	Trud Kolomna, USSR
1975	Leander Club and Thames Tradesmen's RC
1976	Thames Tradesmen's RC
1977	University of Washington RC, USA
1978	Trakia Club, Bulgaria
1979	Thames Tradesmen's RC and London RC
1980	Charles River Rowing Assn, USA
1981	Oxford University BC and Thames Tradesmen's RC
1982	Leander Club and London RC
1983	London RC and University of London BC
1984	Leander Club and London RC
1985	Harvard University, USA
1986	Nautilus RC
1987	Soviet Army, USSR
1988	Leander Club and London University RC
1989	Hansa Dortmund, WG
1990	Hansa Dortmund, WG
1991	Leander and Star
1992	London University RC

Diamond Sculls
First rowed 1844.

1956	T. Kocerka (Poland)
1957	S. A. Mackenzie (Australia)
1958	S. A. Mackenzie (Australia)
1959	S. A. Mackenzie (Australia)
1960	S. A. Mackenzie (Australia)
1961	S. A. Mackenzie (Australia)
1962	S. A. Mackenzie (Australia)
1963	G. Kottman (Switzerland)
1964	S. Cromwell (USA)
1965	D. M. Spero (USA)
1966	A. Hill (Germany)
1967	M. Studach (Switzerland)
1968	H. A. Wardell-Yerburgh (Eton Vikings)

1969	H.-J. Böhmer (DDR)	1981	C. L. Baillieu (Leander)
1970	J. Meissner (W. Germany)	1982	C. L. Baillieu (Leander)
		1983	S. G. Redgrave (Marlow)
1971	A. Demiddi (Argentina)	1984	C. L. Baillieu (Leander)
1972	A. Timoschinin (USSR)	1985	S. G. Redgrave (Marlow)
1973	S. Drea (Eire)	1986	B. Eltang (Denmark)
1974	S. Drea (Eire)	1987	P.-M. Kolbe (FRG)
1975	S. Drea (Eire)	1988	G. H. McGlashan (Australia)
1976	E. O. Hale (Australia)		
1977	T. J. Crooks (Leander)	1989	V. Chalupa (Czech)
1978	T. J. Crooks (Leander)	1990	E. Verdonk (NZ)
1979	H. Matheson (Nottingham)	1991	W. van Belleghem (Belgium)
1980	R. D. Ibarra (Argentina)	1992	R. Henderson (Leander)

University Boat Race

Rowed on the river Thames between Putney and Mortlake (4 miles, 374 yards):

1829	Oxford	1905	Oxford
1836–41	Cambridge	1906–08	Cambridge
1842	Oxford	1909–13	Oxford
1845–48	Cambridge	1914–22	Cambridge
1849–54	Oxford	1923	Oxford
1856	Cambridge	1924–36	Cambridge
1857	Oxford	1937–38	Oxford
1858	Cambridge	1939	Cambridge
1859	Oxford	1946	Oxford
1860	Cambridge	1947–51	Cambridge
1861–69	Oxford	1952	Oxford
1870–74	Cambridge	1953	Cambridge
1875	Oxford	1954	Oxford
1876	Cambridge	1955–58	Cambridge
1877	Dead heat	1959–60	Oxford
1878	Oxford	1961–62	Cambridge
1879	Cambridge	1963	Oxford
1880–83	Oxford	1964	Cambridge
1884	Cambridge	1965–67	Oxford
1885	Oxford	1968–73	Cambridge
1886–89	Cambridge	1974	Oxford
1890–98	Oxford	1975	Cambridge
1899	Cambridge	1976–85	Oxford
1900	Cambridge	1986	Cambridge
1901	Oxford	1987–92	Oxford
1902–04	Cambridge	1993	Cambridge

Cambridge have won 69 times, Oxford 68 times, with one dead heat.

Olympic Games, 1992
Men

Single sculls	T. Lange (Germany)
Double sculls	Australia
Quadruple sculls	Germany
Coxless pairs	Great Britain
Coxless fours	Australia
Coxed pairs	Great Britain
Coxed fours	Romania
Eights	Canada

Women

Single sculls	E. Lipa (Romania)
Coxless pairs	Canada
Double sculls	Germany
Coxed fours	Canada
Quadruple sculls	Germany
Eights	Canada

RUGBY LEAGUE FOOTBALL

Governing body: The Rugby Football League, 180 Chapeltown Road, Leeds LS7 4HT.

Challenge Cup Competition
since 1954:

1954	Warrington	1973	Featherstone Rovers
1955	Barrow	1974	Warrington
1956	St Helens	1975	Widnes
1957	Leeds	1976	St Helens
1958–59	Wigan	1977–78	Leeds
1960	Wakefield Trinity	1979	Widnes
1961	St Helens	1980	Hull Kingston Rovers
1962–63	Wakefield Trinity		
1964	Widnes	1981	Widnes
1965	Wigan	1982	Hull
1966	St Helens	1983	Featherstone Rovers
1967	Featherstone Rovers	1984	Widnes
1968	Leeds	1985	Wigan
1969–70	Castleford	1986	Castleford
1971	Leigh	1987	Halifax
1972	St Helens	1988–93	Wigan

RUGBY UNION FOOTBALL

Governing body: Rugby Football Union, Twickenham, Middlesex, TW2 7RQ.

Five Nations Championship
since 1920

1920	England, Scotland and Wales, tie	1959	France
1921	England	1960	England and France, tie
1922	Wales	1961–62	France
1923–24	England	1963	England
1925	Scotland	1964	Scotland and Wales, tie
1926–27	Ireland and Scotland, tie	1965–66	Wales
1928	England	1967–68	France
1929	Scotland	1969	Wales
1930	England	1970	France and Wales, tie
1931	Wales		
1932	England, Wales and Ireland, tie	1971	Wales
1933	Scotland	1972	series not completed
1934	England	1973	5-way tie
1935	Ireland	1974	Ireland
1936	Wales	1975–76	Wales
1937	England	1977	France
1938	Scotland	1978–79	Wales
1939	England, Wales and Ireland, tie	1980	England
		1981	France
1947	Wales and England, tie	1982	Ireland
1948–49	Ireland	1983	France and Ireland, tie
1950	Wales	1984	Scotland
1951	Ireland	1985	Ireland
1952	Wales	1986	France and Scotland, tie
1953	England		
1954	England, France and Wales, tie	1987	France
		1988	Wales and France, tie
1955	Wales and France, tie	1989	France
		1990	Scotland
1956	Wales	1991–92	England
1957–58	England	1993	France

World Cup

| 1987 | New Zealand | 1991 | Australia |

County Championship
since 1961

1961	Cheshire	1979	Middlesex
1962–65	Warwickshire	1980	Lancashire
1966	Middlesex	1981	Northumberland
1967	Surrey and Durham	1982	Lancashire
1968	Middlesex	1983–84	Gloucestershire
1969	Lancashire	1985	Middlesex
1970	Staffordshire	1986	Warwickshire
1971	Surrey	1987	Yorkshire
1972	Gloucestershire	1988	Lancashire
1973	Lancashire	1989	Durham
1974–76	Gloucestershire	1990	Lancashire
1977	Lancashire	1991	Cornwall
1978	North Midlands	1992–93	Lancashire

Varsity Match
since 1960

1960–63	Cambridge	1979	Oxford
1964	Oxford	1980–85	Cambridge
1965	Drawn	1986	Oxford
1966	Oxford	1987	Cambridge
1967–69	Cambridge	1988	Oxford
1970–71	Oxford	1989	Cambridge
1972–76	Cambridge	1990	Oxford
1977	Oxford	1991	Cambridge
1978	Cambridge	1992	Cambridge

Middlesex Seven-a-Side Tournament
since 1951

1951	Richmond II	1957	St Luke's College, Exeter
1952	Wasps	1958	Blackheath
1953	Richmond I	1959	Loughborough College
1954	Rosslyn Park I	1960	London Scottish
1955	Richmond I	1961	London Scottish I
1956	London Welsh I	1962	London Scottish I

1963	London Scottish I	1977	Richmond I
1964	Loughborough Colleges I	1978	Harlequins I
1965	London Scottish I	1979	Richmond I
1966	Loughborough Colleges I	1980	Richmond I
1967	Harlequins I	1981	Rosslyn Park
1968	London Welsh I	1982	Stewart's Melville FP
1969	St Luke's, Exeter I	1983	Richmond I
1970	Loughborough Colleges I	1984	London Welsh
1971	London Welsh I	1985	Wasps
1972	London Welsh I	1986	Harlequins
1973	London Welsh I	1987–90	Harlequins
1974	Richmond I	1991	London Scottish
1975	Richmond I	1992	Western Samoa
1976	Loughborough Colleges I	1993	Wasps

Records (as at March 1993)

Most Caps: C. M. H. Gibson (Ireland), 69; W. J. McBride (Ireland), 63; J. F. Slattery (Ireland), 61; C. E. Meads (N. Zealand), 55; J. P. R. Williams (Wales), 55.

Highest international score: New Zealand 106 Japan 4 (1987)

Greatest winning margin: New Zealand 106 Japan 4 (1987)

Place kick record: 100 yd., at Richmond Athletic Ground, 1906, by D. F. T. Morkel in an unsuccessful kick for S. Africa v Middlesex. 67 yd., successful by Don Clarke in a club match at Roturua

Longest dropped goal: 90 yd at Twickenham in 1932, by G. Brand for South Africa v England

SHOOTING

Governing bodies: National Rifle Association, Bisley Camp, Brookwood, Woking, Surrey GU24 0PB; National Smallbore Rifle Association (Address as above).

Queen's Prize

1976	Major W. H. Magnay (North London RC)
1977	D. A. Friend (Hurstpierpoint)
1978	R. Graham (Australia)
1979	A. St G. Tucker (Bookham RC)
1980	A. Marion (Canada)
1981	E. M. Ayling (Australia)
1982	L. Peden (Oxford & Cambridge RC)

1983   A. Marion (Canada)
1984   D. F. P. Richards (Manydown RC)
1985   J. T. S. Bloomfield (North London RC)
1986   G. Cox (Royal Air Force Target RC)
1987   A. St G. Tucker (Bookham RC)
1988   J. Pugsley (Pesca RC)
1989   J. Thompson (Central Bankers)
1990   J. T. S. Bloomfield (North London RC)
1991   C. Fitzpatrick (RAF)
1992   A. Bullringer (UBRC)

Olympic Games, 1992
Men

Small-bore rifle (prone)	Lee Fun-chai (S. Korea)
Small-bore rifle (three positions)	G. Petikianc (Unified Team)
Air rifle	Y. Fedkin (Unified Team)
Air pistol	Wang Yifu (China)
Free pistol	K. Loukachik (Unified Team)
Rapid-fire pistol	R. Schumann (Germany)
Running game target	M. Jakosits (Germany)

Women

Sport pistol	M. Loqvinenko (Unified Team)
Standard rifle	L. Melli (USA)
Air rifle	Yeo Kab Soon (S. Korea)
Air pistol	M. Loqvinenko Unified Team)

Open

Trap	P. Hrdlicka (Czech)
Skeet	Zhang Shan (China)

SKI-ING

Governing body: British Ski Federation, Pyrford Road, West Byfleet, Surrey.

1992 Olympic Games (Albertville)
Alpine

Men's downhill	P. Ortlieb (Austria)
Men's slalom	F. Jagge (Norway)
Men's giant slalom	A. Tomba (Italy)
Men's super giant slalom	K. Aamodt (Norway)

Men's freestyle	E. Grospiron (France)
Men's combined	J. Polig (Italy)
Women's downhill	K. Lee-Cortner (Canada)
Women's slalom	P. Kronberger (Austria)
Women's giant slalom	P. Wiberg (Sweden)
Women's super giant slalom	D. Compagnoni (Italy)
Women's freestyle	D. Weinbrecht (USA)
Women's combined	P. Kronberger (Austria)

Ski jumping

Men's 120 metres	T. Nieminen (Finland)
Men's 90 metres team	Japan
Men's 70 metres	E. Vittori (Austria)
Women's 120 metres team	Finland

Biathlon

Men's individual 10 km	M. Kirchner (Germany)
Men's individual 20 km	E. Redkine (UT)*
Men's 4 × 7·5 km relay	Germany
Women's individual 7·5 km	A. Restzova (UT)*
Women's individual 15 km	A. Misersky (Germany)
Women's 3 × 7·5 km relay	France

* Unified Team = former Soviet Union

Nordic

Men's 10 km	V. Ulvang (Norway)
Men's 15 km	J. Daehlic (Norway)
Men's 30 km	V. Ulvang (Norway)
Men's 50 km	B. Duchlic (Norway)
Men's 4 × 10 km relay	Norway
Men's combined	F. Gray (France)
Men's combined team	Japan
Women's 5 km	M. Lukkarinen (Finland)
Women's 10 km	L. Egorova (UT)
Women's 15 km	L. Egorova (UT)
Women's 30 km	S. Belmondo (Italy)
Women's 4 × 5 km relay	UT

British National Alpine Championships

	Men	Women
1975–76	S. Fitzsimmons	V. Iliffe
1977	P. Fuchs	H. Hutcheon
1978	Q. Byrne-Sutton	L. Holmes
1979	S. Fitzsimmons	V. Iliffe

1980	F. Burton	V. Iliffe
1981	M. Bell	M. Langmuir
1982	F. Burton	A. Jochum
1983	R. Duncan	K. Cairns
1984	N. Wilson	L. Beck
1985	F. Burton	L. Beck
1986–87	M. Bell	L. Beck
1988	S. Langmuir	I. Grant
1989	M. Bell	V. MacDonald
1990	Championship cancelled	
1991	R. Duncan	C. de Pourtales
1992	G. Forsyth	L. Beck
1993	G. Bell	E. Carrick-Anderson

SQUASH RACKETS

Governing bodies: Squash Rackets Association, Unit 32, The Salons, Warple Way, London W3; Women's Squash Rackets Association, 345 Upper Richmond Road, Sheen, London SW14 8QN.

British Open Championship

1961	Azam Khan (Pakistan)	1973–74	G. Hunt (Australia)
1962	Mohibullah Khan (Pakistan)	1975	Q. Zaman (Pakistan)
		1976–81	G. Hunt (Australia)
1963–65	Abu Taleb (Egypt)	1982–91	Jahangir Khan (Pakistan)
1966–67	J. Barrington (amateur)		
1968	G. Hunt (Australia)	1992–93	Jansher Khan (Pakistan)
1969–72	J. Barrington (Ireland)		

British Women's Open Championship

1961–64	H. Blundell (Australia)
1965–77	B. McKay (née Blundell) (Australia)
1978	S. Newman (Australia)
1979	B. Wall (Australia)
1980–83	V. Cardwell (née Hoffmann) (Australia)
1984–90	S. Devoy (New Zealand)
1991	L. Opie (GB)
1992	S. Devoy (New Zealand)
1993	M. Martin (Australia)

National Championship

1979	G. P. Briars	1986	B. Beeson
1980	J. P. Barrington	1987	D. Harris
1981	P. S. Kenyon	1988	P. Carter
1982	G. P. Briars	1989	D. Harris
1983	P. S. Kenyon	1990	D. Harris
1984	G. Williams	1991	P. Gregory
1985	P. S. Kenyon	1992	P. Marshall

Women's National Championship

1976	A. Smith	1986–87	L. Opie
1977–80	S. Cogswell	1988	M. Le Moignan
1981	L. Opie	1989	L. Soutter
1982	A. Cumings	1990	L. Soutter
1983	L. Opie	1991	M. Le Moignan
1984	M. Le Moignan	1992	S. Wright
1985	L. Soutter		

SWIMMING AND DIVING

Governing bodies: Amateur Swimming Association, Harold Fern House, Derby Square, Loughborough, Leicestershire LE11 0AL; Channel Swimming Association, 'The Moorings', Alkham Valley Road, Hawkinge, Nr Folkestone, Kent.

Swimming Records

Men

World	European	British
50 m freestyle		
21·81	22·47	22·43
T. Jager (USA)	J. Woithe (GDR)	M. Foster
100 m freestyle		
48·42	49·24	50·24
M. Biondi (USA)	G. Lamberti (Italy)	M. Fibbins
200 m freestyle		
1:46·69	1:46·69	1:50·50
G. Lamberti (Italy)	G. Lamberti (Italy)	Paul Palmer

400 m freestyle

3:45·00	3:45·00	3:50·01
Y. Sadovyi (Unified Team)	Y. Sadovyi (Unified Team)	K. Boyd

800 m freestyle

7:50·64	7:50·64	8:01·87
V. Salnikov (USSR)	V. Salnikov (USSR)	K. Boyd

1500 m freestyle

14:43·48	14:54·76	15:16·05
K. Perkins (Austrialia)	V. Salnikov (USSR)	I. Wilson

50 m breaststroke

	28·12	28·75
	D. Volkov (USSR)	A. Moorhouse

100 m breaststroke

1:01·45	1:01·49	1:01:49
N. Royza (Hungary)	A. Moorhouse (GB)	A. Moorhouse

200 m breaststroke

2:10·16	2:12·08	2:12·90
M. Barrowman (USA)	N. Royza (Hungary)	N. Gillingham

50 m butterfly

	24·61	25·11
	F. Henter (FRG)	A. Jameson

100 m butterfly

52·84	53·08	53·30
P. Morales (USA)	M. Gross (FRG)	A. Jameson

200 m butterfly

1:54·50	1:56·24	2:00·21
D. Loader (NZ)	M. Gross (FRG)	P. Hubble

50 m backstroke

	25·90	25·87
	I. Polianski (USSR)	M. Harris

100 m backstroke

53·93	55·00	56.77
J. Rouse (USA)	I. Polianski (USSR)	M. Harris

200 m backstroke

1:56·57	1:57·30	2:02·58
M. Lopez-Zubero (Spain)	M. Lopez-Zubero (Spain)	M. O'Connor

200 m indiv. medley

1:59·36	1:59·36	2:03·20
T. Darnyi (Hun)	T. Darnyi (Hun)	N. Cochran

400 m indiv. medley
4:07·10	4:14·75	4:24·20
J. Sievinen (Finland)	T. Darnyi (Hun)	J. Davey

4 × 100 m freestyle relay
3:16·53	3:18·33	3:21·71
USA national team	USSR national team	national team

4 × 200 m freestyle relay
7:11·95	7:13·10	7:24·78
Unified Team	FRG national team	national team

4 × 100 m medley relay
3:36·93	3:39·96	3:42·01
USA national team	USSR national team	national team

Women

World	*European*	*British*

50 m freestyle
24·79	25·28	26·01
Yang Wenyi (China)	T. Costache (Rom)	C. Woodcock

100 m freestyle
54·48	54·73	56·11
J. Thompson (USA)	K. Otto (GDR)	K. Pickering

200 m freestyle
1:57·55	1:57·55	1:59·74
H. Friedrich (GDR)	H. Friedrich (GDR)	J. Croft

400 m freestyle
4:03·85	4:05·84	4:07·68
J. Evans (USA)	A. Moehring (GDR)	S. Hardcastle

800 m freestyle
8:16·22	8:19·53	8:24·77
J. Evans (USA)	A. Mohring (GDR)	S. Hardcastle

1500 m freestyle
15:52·10	16:13·55	16:43·95
J. Evans (USA)	A. Strauss (GDR)	S. Hardcastle

100 m breaststroke
1:07·91	1:07·91	1:10·39
S. Hoener (GDR)	S. Hoener (GDR)	S. Brownsdon

200 m breaststroke
2:10·16   2:26·71   2:31·51
M. Barrowman (USA)   S. Hoener (GDR)   J. Hill

50 m butterfly   28·22
                                                               C. Cooper

100 m butterfly
57·93   59·00   1:01·33
M. Meagher (USA)   K. Otto (GDR)   M. Campbell

200 m butterfly
2:05·96   2:07·82   2:11·97
M. Meagher (USA)   C. Polit (GDR)   S. Purvis

50 m backstroke   29·12   29·24
                                K. Otto (GDR)   S. Page

100 m backstroke
1:00·59   1:00·59   1:02·34
I. Kleber (GDR)   I. Kleber (GDR)   S. Page

200 m backstroke
2:08·60   2:09·29   2:14·74
B. Mitchell (USA)   K. Egerszegi (Hun)   J. Deakins

200 m indiv. medley
2:11·65   2:11·73   2:17·21
Li Lin (China)   U. Geweniger (GDR)   J. Hill

400 m indiv. medley
4:36·10   4:36·10   4:46·83
P. Schneider (GDR)   P. Schneider (GDR)   S. Davies

4 × 100 m freestyle relay
3:40·57   3:40·57   3:48·87
GDR national team   GDR national team   national team

4 × 200 m freestyle relay
7:55·47   7:55·47
GDR national team   GDR national team

4 × 100 m medley relay
4:03·69   4:03·69   4:11·88
GDR national team   GDR national team   national team

Olympic Games, 1992

Men

50 m freestyle	A. Popov (Unified Team)	21.91 sec
100 m freestyle	A. Popov (Unified Team)	49.02 sec
200 m freestyle	Y. Sadovyi (Unified Team)	1 min 46·70 sec
400 m freestyle	Y. Sadovyi (Unified Team)	3 min 45·00 sec WR
1500 m freestyle	K. Perkins (Australia)	14 min 43.48 sec WR
4 × 100 m freestyle	USA	3 min 16.74 sec
4 × 200 freestyle	Unified Team	7 min 11.95 sec WR
100 m breaststroke	N. Diebel (USA)	1 min 01·50 sec
200 m breaststroke	M. Barrowman (USA)	2 min 10·16 sec WR
100 m butterfly	P. Morales (USA)	53.32 sec
200 m butterfly	M. Stewart (USA)	1 min 56·26 sec
100 m backstroke	M. Tewksbury (USA)	53.98 sec
200 m backstroke	M. Lopez-Zubero (Spain)	1 min 58·47 sec
200 m indiv. medley	T. Darnyi (Hungary)	4 min 14·23 sec
4 × 200 m indiv. medley	T. Darnyi (Hungary)	4 min 14·23 sec
4 × 100 m relay	USA	3 min 36·93 sec WR
Springboard diving	M. Lenzi (USA)	645·57 pts
Platform diving	Sun Shewei (China)	677·31 pts

Women

50 m freestyle	Yang Wenyi (China)	24·79 sec WR
100 m freestyle	Zhuang Yong (China)	54·64 sec
200 m freestyle	H. Haislett (USA)	1 min 57·90 sec
400 m freestyle	D. Hase (Germany)	4 min 07·18 sec
800 m freestyle	J. Evans (USA)	8 min 39·46 sec
100 m breaststroke	Y. Roudovskaya (Unified Team)	1 min 08·00 sec
200 m breaststroke	K. Iwasaki (Japan)	2 min 26·65 sec

100 m butterfly	Qian Hong (China)	58·62 sec
200 m butterfly	S. Sanders (USA)	2 min 08·67 sec
100 m backstroke	K. Egerszegi (Hungary)	1 min 00·68 sec
200 m backstroke	K. Egerszegi (Hungary)	2 min 07·06 sec
200 m indiv. medley	Li Lin (China)	2 min 11·65 sec WR
400 m indiv. medley	K. Egerszegi (Hungary)	4 min 36·54 sec
4 × 100 m relay	USA	4 min 02·54 sec WR
4 × 100 m medley relay	E. Germany	4 min 03·74 sec
1500 m freestyle	K. Perkins (Australia)	14 min 43.48 sec WR
Synchronised swimming (solo)	K. Babb-Speaque (USA)	
Synchronised swimming (duet)	USA	
Springboard diving	Gao Min (China)	572·40 pts
Platform diving	Minqxia Fu (China)	461·43 pts

TABLE TENNIS

Governing body: English Table Tennis Association, 21 Claremont, Hastings, East Sussex TN34 1HF.

World Championship

Men's singles

1951	J. Leach (England)	1971	S. Bengtsson (Sweden)
1952	H. Satoh (Japan)	1973	J. En-tinh (China)
1953	F. Sido (Hungary)	1975	I. Jonyer (Hungary)
1954	I. Ogimura (Japan)	1977	M. Kohno (Japan)
1955	T. Tanaka (Japan)	1979	Seiji Ono (Japan)
1956	I. Ogimura (Japan)	1981	Guo Yeuhua (China)
1957	T. Tanaka (Japan)	1983	Guo Yuehua (China)
1959	Jung Kuo-Tuan (China)	1985	Jiang Jialiang (China)
1961	Chuang Tse-Tung (China)	1987	Jiang Jialiang (China)
1963	Chuang Tse-Tung (China)	1989	J. Waldner (Sweden)
1965	Chuang Tse-Tung (China)	1991	J. Waldner (Sweden)
1967	N. Hasegawa (Japan)	1993	J. P. Gatien (France)
1969	S. Ito (Japan)		

Women's singles

1951–5	A. Rozeanu (Romania)	1975	Yung Sun Kim (N. Korea)
1956	T. Okawa (Japan)	1977	P. Yung Sun (N. Korea)
1957	F. Eguchi (Japan)	1979	Ge Xinai (China)
1959	K. Matsuzaki (Japan)	1981	Tong Ling (China)
1961	Chiu Chung-Hui (China)	1983	Cao Yanhua (China)
1963	K. Matsuzaki (Japan)	1985	Cao Yanhua (China)
1965	N. Fukazu (Japan)	1987	Zhili He (China)
1967	S. Morisawa (Japan)	1989	Qiao Honq (China)
1969	T. Kowada (Japan)	1991	Deng Yaping (China)
1971	Lin Hui-Ching (China)	1993	Hyun Jung-hwa (S. Korea)
1973	H. Yu-lan (China)		

World Cup

1980	G. Yuehua (China)	1986	Chen Longcan (China)
1981	T. Klampar (Hungary)	1987	Teng Yi (China)
1982	G. Yuehua (China)	1988–89	A. Grubba (Poland)
1983	M. Applegren (Sweden)	1990	J. O. Waldner (Sweden)
1984	J. Jialiang (China)	1991	J. Persson (Sweden)
1985	Chen Xinhua (China)	1992	M. Wange (China)

Swaythling Cup (Men)

1950–51	Czechoslovakia	1973	Sweden
1952	Hungary	1975	China
1953	England	1977	China
1954–59	Japan	1979	Hungary
1961	China	1981	China
1963	China	1983	China
1965	China	1985	China
1967	Japan	1987	China
1969	Japan	1989	Sweden
1971	China	1991	Sweden

Corbillon Cup (Women)

1950–51	Romania	1971	Japan
1952	Japan	1973	S. Korea
1953	Romania	1975	China
1954	Japan	1977	China
1955–56	Romania	1979	Japan
1957	Japan	1981	China
1959	Japan	1983	China
1961	Japan	1985	China
1963	Japan	1987	China
1965	China	1989	China
1967	Japan	1991	S. Korea
1969	USSR		

English Open Championships

Men's singles
1975	A. Strokatov (USSR)
1976	S. Bengtsson (Sweden)
1977	S. Gomozkov (USSR)
1978	Li Chen-shih (China)
1979	K. Yao-hua (China)
1980	D. Douglas (England)
1982	J. Jialiang (China)
1984	D. Douglas (England)
1986	Z. Katinic (Yugoslavia)
1987	J. Persson (Sweden)
1988	A. Cooke (England)
1990	Y. Shentong (China)
1992	J. Gutien (France)

Women's singles
1975	Miss E. Antonian (USSR)
1976	Mrs J. Hammersley (England)
1977	Miss C. Knight (England)
1978	Chu Hsiang-yum (China)
1979	Mrs J. Hammersley (England)
1980	Mrs J. Hammersley (England)
1982	Chen Lili (China)
1984	A. Zacharian (USSR)
1986	E. Kovtun (USSR)
1987	Li Huifen (China)
1988	A. Gordon (England)
1990	M. Hoshine (Japan)
1992	M. Hooman (Netherlands)

Olympic Games 1992

Men
Singles	J. O. Waldner (Sweden)
Doubles	China

Women
Singles	Deng Yaping (China)
Doubles	(China)

VOLLEYBALL

Governing body: English Volleyball Association, 27 South Road, West Bridgford, Nottingham NG2 7AG

Olympic Winners			
Men		**Women**	
1964	USSR	1964	Japan
1968	USSR	1968	USSR
1972	Japan	1972	USSR
1976	Poland	1976	Japan
1980	USSR	1980	USSR
1984	USA	1984	China
1988	USA	1988	USSR
1992	Brazil	1992	Cuba

WATER POLO

Governing body: Amateur Swimming Association, Harold Fern House, Derby Square, Loughborough, Leicestershire LE11 0AL.

Olympic Winners			
1900	Great Britain	1956	Hungary
1904	USA	1960	Italy
1908	Great Britain	1964	Hungary
1912	Great Britain	1968	Yugoslavia
1920	Great Britain	1972	USSR
1924	France	1976	Hungary
1928	Germany	1980	USSR
1932	Hungary	1984	Yugoslavia
1936	Hungary	1992	Yugoslavia
1948	Italy	1988	Italy
1952	Hungary		

YACHTING

Governing body: The Royal Yachting Association, RYA House, Romsey Road, Eastleigh, Hampshire SO5 4YA.

Olympic Games, 1992

Men

Finn	J. Van de Ploeg (Spain)
Star	USA
Flying Dutchman	Spain
Tornado	France
470	Spain
Soling	Denmark
Windsurfing	F. David (France)

Women

470	Spain
Windsurfing	B. Kendah (New Zealand)
Europe	L. Andersen (Norway)

The America's Cup

Shamrock II lost to *Columbia* in 1901
Shamrock III lost to *Reliance* in 1903
Shamrock IV lost to *Resolute* in 1920
Shamrock V lost to *Enterprise* in 1930
Endeavour lost to *Rainbow* in 1934
Endeavour II lost to *Ranger* in 1937
Sceptre lost to *Columbia* in 1958
Gretel lost to *Weatherly* in 1962
Sovereign lost to *Constellation* in 1964
Dame Pattie lost to *Intrepid* in 1967
Gretel II lost to *Intrepid* in 1970
Southern Cross lost to *Courageous* in 1974
Australia lost to *Courageous* in 1977
Australia lost to *Freedom* in 1980
Liberty lost to *Australia II* in 1983
Kookaburra III lost to *Stars and Stripes* in 1987
New Zealand lost to *Stars and Stripes* in 1988

The Admiral's Cup

1969	USA	1981	Great Britain
1971	Great Britain	1983	West Germany
1973	Germany	1985	West Germany
1975	Great Britain	1987	New Zealand
1977	Great Britain	1989	Great Britain
1979	Australia	1991	France

OLYMPIC GAMES 1992 (Barcelona)
(A list of winners not already noted under particular games or sports)

Gymnastics

Governing body: British Amateur Gymnastic Association, 95 High Street, Slough SL1 1DH.

Men

All-round	V. Shcherbo (Unified Team)
Horizontal bars	T. Dimas (USA)
Parallel bars	V. Shcherbo (Unified Team)
Long horse vault	V. Shcherbo (Unified Team)
Pommel horse, equal first	V. Shcherbo (Unified Team)
	Gil-Su Pae (N. Korea)
Rings	V. Shcherbo (Unified Team)
Floor exercises	Li Xiaoshang (China)
Team combined exercises	Unified Team

Women

Team	Unified Team
All-around	T. Goulsou (Unified Team)
Vault	H. Onadi (Hungary)
Asymmetric bars	Lu Li (China)
Beam	T. Lyssenko (Unified Team)
Floor	L. Milosovici (Romania)
Modern Rhythmic	A. Timoshenko (Unified Team)

Modern Pentathlon

Individual	A. Skrzraszek (Poland)
Team	Poland

Weightlifting

Governing body: British Amateur Weight Lifters' Association, 3 Iffley Turn, Oxford.

	52 kg	I. Ivanov (Bulgaria)
	56 kg	C. Byung-Kwan (S. Korea)
	60 kg	N. Suleymanoglu (Turkey)
	67.5 kg	I. Militosian (Unified Team)
	75 kg	F. Kassapu (Unified Team)
	82.5 kg	P. Dimas (Greece)
	90 kg	K. Kakhiashvili (Unified Team)
Under	100 kg	V. Tregubov (Unified Team)
	110 kg	R. Weller (Germany)
Over	110 kg	A. Kurlovich (Unified Team)

Wrestling

Governing body: British Amateur Wrestling Association, 2 Huxley Drive, Bramhall, Stockport, Cheshire.

Freestyle

Light fly	Kim Il (N. Korea)
Fly	Li Hak-Son (N. Korea)
Bantam	A. Diaz (Cuba)
Feather	J. Smith (USA)
Light	A. Fadzaev (Unified Team)
Welter	Park Jang-Soon (S. Korea)
Middle	K. Jackson (USA)
Light heavy	M. Khadartsdev (Unified Team)
Middle heavy	L. Khabelov (Unified Team)
Heavy	B. Baumgartner

Graeco-Roman

48 kg	O. Koutcherenko (Unified Team)
52 kg	J. Ronningen (Norway)
57 kg	A. Han-Bong (S. Korea)
62 kg	A. Pirim (Turkey)
68 kg	A. Rapka (Hungary)
74 kg	N. Iskandarian (Unified Team)
82 kg	P. Farkas (Hungary)
90 kg	M. Bullmann (Germany)
100 kg	H. Perez (Cuba)
130 kg	A. Kareline (Unified Team)

Canoeing

Governing body: The British Canoe Union, Flexel House, 45/47 High Street, Addlestone, Weybridge, Surrey.

Men	
500 m kayak singles	M. Kolehmainen (Finland)
500 m kayak pairs	Germany
1000 m kayak singles	C. Robinson (Australia)
1000 m kayak pairs	Germany
1000 m kayak fours	Germany
500 m Canadian singles	N. Boukhalov (Bulgaria)
500 m Canadian pairs	Unified Team
1000 m Canadian singles	N. Boukhalov (Bulgaria)
1000 m Canadian pairs	Germany
Slalom kayak singles	P. Ferazgi (Italy)
Slalom Canadian singles	L. Pollart (Czech)
Slalom Canadian pairs	USA
Women	
500 m kayak singles	B. Schmidt (Germany)
500 m kayak pairs	Germany
500 m kayak fours	Germany
Slalom kayak singles	E. Micheler (Germany)

Handball

Men	Women
Unified Team	S. Korea

Judo

Governing body: The British Judo Association, 16 Upper Woburn Place, London WC1A 0QP.

Men	
60 kg	N. Goussinev (Unified Team)
65 kg	R. Sampaio (Brazil)
71 kg	T. Koga (Japan)

78 kg		H. Yoshida (Japan)
86 kg		W. Legien (Poland)
95 kg		A. Kovacs (Hungary)
Over	95 kg	D. Khakhaleichvili (Unified Team)

Women

48 kg		C. Nowak (France)
52 kg		M. Martinez (Spain)
56 kg		M. Blasco (Spain)
61 kg		C. Fleury (France)
66 kg		O. Reve (Cuba)
72 kg		Kim Mi Jung (S. Korea)
Over	72 kg	Z. Xiaoyan (China)

WINTER OLYMPICS 1992 (Albertville)

Bobsleigh

Two-man	Switzerland
Four-man	Austria

Luge

Men	G. Hackl (Germany)
Two-man	S. Krausse and J. Behrendt (Germany)
Women	D. Neuner (Austria)

COMPUTERS AND INFORMATION TECHNOLOGY

Abacus A simple counting frame invented by the Babylonians and still used in various parts of the world. It is made of beads which slide along wires. The abacus is similar to a modern computer in that multiplication and division are done by repeatedly adding or subtracting.

Access time is the time taken for a computer to obtain the data, either from the main *memory* or from the *backing store*. This is measured from the time it takes to issue the instruction until the data is stored in the specified location. The times are in millionths of seconds: thus a typical home microcomputer may take 4 millionths of one second to perform a simple memory access. See *direct access*.

Acronym The explosion of computing over the last twenty years has been accompanied by a surge in computing vocabulary. Although acronym itself is not a computing word, it is useful to understand that many computing words are acronyms; they have been derived from a group of letters formed from the initial letters of the words in a name or phrase, e.g. *BASIC* from Beginners All-purpose Symbolic Instruction Code. It often seems that the word is thought of first, and then a cumbersome phrase invented to fit it. Sometimes any letters are chosen, e.g. the word **BIT** comes from BInary digiT.

Address This is a memory location in a computer. Also used as a verb meaning to send to a specified memory location.

ALGOL Acronym for 'ALGOrithmic Language'. A high level computer language, designed for solving scientific and mathematical problems.

Analogue (or **Analog**) Analogue data relates continuously to what is happening. Thus, for example, traditional (analogue) watch hands move constantly round the face, when wound up. The winding of the spring could be said to be the input and the movement of the hands the output. This continuous movement is usually contrasted with the stop/go pattern found in digital systems. A digital watch displays its output in steps of separate units of a second or of fractions of a second. It is either one time or another. Conversion devices are called ADCs (Analogue to Digital Converter) and DACs (Digital to Analogue Converter). See *digit*.

Application This is the task a computer is being used for, e.g. word-processing, games, payroll. Hence an **Application Package** is the set of programs and written instructions which enables the computer to perform a specific task.

Arithmetic and Logic Unit (ALU) That part of a computer's CPU in which calculations and comparisons of values are performed. See *computer*.

ASCII The American Standard Code for Information Interchange. The most common way of representing characters in binary code (see table opposite).

Assembly language See *low level language*.

Assembler The program which translates assembly language into machine code. The machine 'assembles' the translation in the main memory, awaiting execution. Assemblers are 'machine-oriented' rather than 'problem-oriented' since they only work for that type of machine.

Babbage, Charles A mathematician who was concerned with the inaccuracies in astronomical and mathematical tables. In 1822, he thought of producing a machine he called a 'difference engine', a mechanical device for working out the tables he wanted. In the course of his experiments, Babbage conceived the idea of what he called an 'analytical engine', which was to be a general-purpose calculator, as opposed to the one-purpose machine which his difference machine was. In concept, he had created the 'universal computer', since up to then all machines required human intervention at each stage of the problem, wheels had to be set and so on. Babbage proposed that there should be a store for the data, a mill for processing it (i.e. what we now call a central processing unit), and input and output devices; and that is a specification for a computer which any modern computer designer would recognise.

Backing store Although the largest computers have enormous-memories capable of storing several million characters of information, even the largest computers need to store and retrieve data outside the main memory. If one does not have

Some Useful ASCII Character Codes

ASCII Code	Character	ASCII Code	Character	ASCII Code	Character
032	SPACE	064	@	096	space
033	!	065	A	097	a
034	"	066	B	098	b
035	#	067	C	099	c
036	$	068	D	100	d
037	%	069	E	101	e
038	&	070	F	102	f
039	'	071	G	103	g
040	(	072	H	104	h
041	)	073	I	105	i
042	*	074	J	106	j
043	+	075	K	107	k
044	,	076	L	108	l
045	−	077	M	109	m
046	.	078	N	110	n
047	/	079	O	111	o
048	0	080	P	112	p
049	1	081	Q	113	q
050	2	082	R	114	r
051	3	083	S	115	s
052	4	084	T	116	t
053	5	085	U	117	u
054	6	086	V	118	v
055	7	087	W	119	w
056	8	088	X	120	x
057	9	089	Y	121	y
058	:	090	Z	122	z
059	;	091	[	123	;
060	<	092	bkslash	124	<
061	=	093	]	125	=
062	>	094	↑	126	>
063	?	095	back arr	127	DEL

ASCII codes are in decimal

backing storage, then each time the computer is used the program has to be typed in. Backing storage can be held on magnetic tape, discs and drums, and still, in some cases, punched cards and paper tape. An essential feature of backing store is that the information and programs can be both read from, and written onto, the store. See *magnetic disc*.

Bar codes These are a series of alternating lines and spaces printed closely together, often to be found on groceries. The pattern contains information about the product: e.g. its price and product number. A *bar code reader* is an input device used to scan the line patterns. The advantage of bar codes and bar code readers is that as a way of obtaining information and sending it to a computer as data it is much faster than other methods, e.g. keying in on a shop till.

ISBN 0-7207-1666-7

BASIC BASIC stands for Beginners All-purpose Symbolic Instruction Code and is a programming language. Developed in the United States in 1964 as a simple beginner's language, it has, over the years, established itself as the world's most popular learning language. It has always been the most common language available on microcomputers, partly because it has a low memory requirement. Unlike most high level languages it runs in conjunction with an interpreter which executes and runs one BASIC statement at a time. A single statement can make the computer immediately respond; thus BASIC is said to be interactive. Another feature of BASIC compared to other languages is that it uses line numbers. Although easy to use there are a number of drawbacks to BASIC. One arises out of its very ability to respond and be added to; this tends to lead to unstructured ('spaghetti') programming. There have been many attempts to improve BASIC, a notable recent example being that of BBC BASIC.

Baud A baud is a measure of transmission speed, which is particularly important when computers are communicating with one another. Data is transmitted serially: e.g. via the telephone line, *bit* by *bit*. The speed of this transmission is known as the baud rate: a baud is equivalent to one bit per second. The name derives from the engineer, Baudot, who developed the teleprinter in the 1860s.

Binary The binary numbering system is the simplest possible as it uses only two numbers, 0 (zero) and 1 (one). Binary readily represents electrical switching—0 signifies no pulse and 1 a pulse. All data put into a digital computer is transformed into binary signals for storage or processing. In the decimal system each place represents ten times that on its right. In the binary system, each place is worth twice that on its right. The first place on the right is the number of ones, the next the number of twos, the next the number of fours (2 × 2), and so on.

BIT An acronym of **BI**nary Digi**T**. A bit is a binary number only one digit long. A bit must be a 0 or a 1. It is the smallest bit of storage. There are 8 bits in a byte. See *byte* and *binary*.

Boole, George A logician, who in 1854 perfected a way of writing down 'logical operations'. He was concerned with a branch of philosophy called symbolic logic, which tackles problems like, 'If statement A is true and B is true, is statement C also true?' Boole found a shorthand way of writing this which became known as Boolean algebra. This algebra was particularly appropriate to electrical switching, which formed the basis of the binary system and how computers work.

Boot Jargon for starting a computer: from the expression 'to pull yourself up by your own bootstraps'. Hence a **Bootstrap Program** is a program which starts the computer working.

Bug Originally slang, a bug is a mistake or malfunction in a computer program or equipment. Like living bugs they may be easy to detect, but not to remove. The term originates from the moths that damaged the valves on the early ENIAC computer.

Bus The common highway linking components inside the computer along which digital signals travel. Progressively more powerful processors are creating a problem because the highway along which data pours is unable to cope and thus bottlenecks are created. Consequently data may not be accessed or output fast enough. In 1987 IBM introduced Micro Channel Architecture (MCA), a new and faster expansion bus, but totally incompatible with traditional microcomputers. In 1988 a group of manufacturers produced a more powerful alternative standard called EISA (Extended Industry Standard Architecture), which is compatible with existing microcomputers.

Byte A group of 8 bits. Derived from bit 'by eight'. One byte holds one character of information. Take, for example, the letter B. B coded as *ASCII* binary occupies one byte, and is represented as 01000010 requiring 8 binary bits. The decimal equivalent is 66. A byte is the smallest addressable unit of memory.

Cache Memory This is used to hold a copy of data which has recently been accessed by the microprocessor in anticipation of its use again in the near future, when it can be accessed very quickly.

CAD This stands for Computer Aided Design. See *Graphics*.

Ceefax Televised information service put out by the BBC, its name deriving from 'see facts'. See *Teletext*.

Central Processing Unit (CPU) Sometimes called central processor, or the processor. The device at the heart of the computer, it is the part that does the actual computing, controlling the activities of the computer and carrying out arithmetical and other logical operations. For a fuller explanation see *computer*.

Character A letter, digit, punctuation mark or space.

Chip This is the popular name for a wafer-thin slice of silicon onto which integrated electronic circuits have been chemically etched. They are usually, but not always, made from silicon. Most integrated circuits occupy an area less than half that of the nail on a small finger. Memory chips are now being built which house more than a million bits of information. The circuits are said to be 'solid state' because there are no moving parts, so reducing the likelihood of mechanical breakdown.

   The development of integrated circuits gave birth to third-generation computers. Chip-based systems are a thousand times cheaper than the discrete-component ones of fifteen years ago, and tens of thousands of times more compact than systems based on valves or *transistors*. One particular development of chips (not all chips are microprocessors) has meant that all sorts of equipment can be fitted with *microprocessors* ranging from washing machines to toys, and also, the whole range of microcomputers. See *computer generations*.

   Chips are often confused with their casings; the chips are embedded in black plastic rectangles with perhaps 8 or 16 or more metal connectors or 'legs' down the longer sides.

Clipboard The clipboard is a temporary storage area, used in a *windows* environment, to transfer information from one application to another.

COBOL Common Business Orientated Language. A high level computer language that was developed for commercial use. COBOL is very good at handling large files of data, and is by far the most commonly used language in larger computer installations. COBOL is not widely used in microcomputers at present because of the memory requirements.

Compact disc Compact discs are based on laser disc technology, which is also being increasingly used for high quality music recordings. This information is read optically, by laser. A *laser* beam reads these discs without any physical contact and thus minimises wear and tear. The information is carried on the inside of a reflective coating which lines the plastic disc. At present a distinction is being made between CD-ROMs (Compact Disc—Read Only Memories) and CD-I (Compact Disc—Interactive) technology.

A CD-ROM is like a music CD, except that it reproduces words and pictures on a computer screen rather than music through a loudspeaker. CD-ROMS are capable of holding *640* megabytes of information; roughly the equivalent to 100 *million* words of text, or 2,000 novels. As the cost of CD-ROM drives continues to decrease, the number used in business is increasing rapidly. It is estimated that by the end of 1990 more than 200,000 had been installed. The uses vary enormously. One publisher is selling a disc which contains dictionaries in 12 languages which can cross-reference any two languages, thus offering 132 language pairs. Each month a division of FORD publishes a CD-ROM-based inventory list of 300,000 parts for its 2,400 dealers in the UK. Although a CD-ROM can hold significantly more information than a hard disc, the retrieval time can be 10 times slower. One of the problems with CD-ROMS is that they cannot be written to by the user. Hence the emergence of Worm (*Write Once Read Many*) disc technology whereby optical discs with a similar capacity can be written to. **Interactive video discs** also carry vast amounts of data. For example, the Philips LaserVision disc has a density of 16,000 tracks per inch compared with, for instance, 96 per inch for an 80-track floppy disc. Unlike CD-ROMs, this data can be non-digital as well as digital in format, hence the data can be of video and audio recordings. The potential lies in the ability of the user to interact rapidly between digital data and high quality video and/or sound presentation. See *magnetic disc, ROM, RAM.*

Compiler A program which translates from a high level language such as *COBOL* or *FORTRAN* into *machine code.* As instructions in high level languages are complex it is nearly always necessary for each source statement to be broken down into a number of machine code instructions. The original language is known as the source code. Compilers and other items of *system software* provide facilities which help the programmer to debug the code. The set of instructions once compiled is known as the object code. When compilation is complete it is the compiled program which is run. During the process of compilation, errors are identified and listings produced. Contrast with an *interpreter.*

Computer A machine that accepts, processes and stores data ac-

PARTS OF A COMPUTER SYSTEM

INPUT

OUTPUT

BAR CODE READER

KEYBOARD

MOUSE

PROCESSOR

WORKING STORE (SHORT TERM MEMORY)

PRINTER

MONITOR

OPTICAL FIBRE

COMMUNICATION DATA LINK

RADIO

MAGNETIC TAPE

CASSETTE TAPE

FILE STORAGE (LONG TERM MEMORY)

RIGID DISC

FLOPPY DISC

cording to the user's set of instructions. These instructions are known as a program, which has been stored in the computer.

They are calculating machines, but differ from old mechanical (pre-electronic) machines in three ways: their speed of operation; their large memories; and the fact that, by comparing data, they can make decisions which affect the place in the program to which they go next.

Computers are not 'thinking machines'; they are machines which can carry out arithmetic at great speed. (Strictly speaking computers can never make 'value judgements'.)

All program instructions are processed by the *central processing unit* (CPU). The clock, the control unit and arithmetic/logic unit (ALU) together make up the CPU. The CPU co-ordinates the subsystems of the computer. It is the part that does the actual computing, controlling its activities and carrying out arithmetical and other logical operations. The central clock synchronises all the pulses. Once the program is loaded, the CPU will call up the data and process it according to the program instructions.

On mainframe computers the central processor used to occupy the size of a large cabinet. On microcomputers the *microprocessor* may occupy only one chip. See *mainframe, mini and microcomputer systems*.

Computer generations Different generations of computers are often referred to. The first generation machines (1940–52) used vacuum tubes (electronic valves). See *ENIAC*. The second generation machines (1952–64) used transistors and still required air-conditioning and maintenance. The many thousands of separate components still had to be assembled by hand. The third generation used integrated circuits (ICs) as the basic components. At first about ten components could be integrated into an area about 5 mm square. The equipment became more reliable. Much less labour and power was required, and as a result less heat was generated. The process of packing components in a small area continued, and by 1971 Large-Scale-Integration (LSI) chips were being marketed. The microprocessor chip was in production and being used in fourth generation microcomputers. Although not as powerful as the third generation, they were far more compact, robust and versatile. The fourth generation is that which uses LSI circuits, which have now been adopted by the whole range of computers. The next generation, the fifth, is predicted for this decade. Not surprisingly, it is based upon further miniaturisation of circuitry and increasingly sophisticated software. Already there are chips with one million transistors and the Japanese manufacturer NEC is now starting an experimental production line making 16 megabit chips. Each chip will be able to hold roughly 336,000 words. Inspired by Japanese designers, the aim of the fifth generation is to have very large main memories, extremely fast processing times and improved input/output with voice and touch interactions. See *expert systems*, *supercomputer*, *transputer*.

Cursor A movable marker on a screen which shows where the next character will appear.

Daisywheel See *printer*.

Data Data is whatever has been successfully input into the computer. This data can be processed by the program. If resulting output can be understood by users it is said to be information, not data. See *information*.

Database A large collection of data, such as local history records, from which particular information can be retrieved using a computer. In essence it is a comprehensive filing system using a collection of organised data for a particular purpose. See *file*. The use of computers allows a flexible approach to work which would be very cumbersome to do manually. Take, for example, a database of records each containing surnames, first names, telephone numbers, dates of birth and number of children. Searching for a name using only a telephone number becomes easy. It is possible to re-sort the records by first name or by date of birth. Calculations can generate the total and average number of children. Data need only be entered once. A key feature of a database is that it contains as little repeated information as possible. The structure of the data is independent of what is to be done with it. Thus the same database may be used for a wide variety of applications.

Datalogging This is a method of capturing data which can be subsequently processed by a computer. Datalogging is used widely: for example for recording weather variations, counting traffic, and in many types of scientific experiments.

Data Processing (DP) This can be defined as the conversion of raw facts into useful information. A computer is a general purpose data processor; it always processes data. The main use of the phrase 'data processing' arises from use in business organisations; e.g. for payroll, statistical returns, marketing etc. Thus the computer departments within businesses are often called DP departments.

Data Protection Act The Data Protection Act, which was passed in 1984, gives any individual the right to know exactly what is held on computer about them and, if necessary, to request corrections. As a general rule any company or organisation that holds computerised data about individuals has to register with the Data Protection Registrar as a 'data user'. The onus is on the individual to request such data. Organisations that get a request for access must respond within 40 days and give all the information held on computer at the time of request, for which they may charge £10.

Deadly embrace A condition which arises when all the processes going on in a computer system compete for the same resources and the whole system seizes up.

Desk Top Publishing The use of microcomputers to prepare documents on the screen that may contain graphics and text and a variety of print styles. These documents can then be printed on a high-quality printer or stored in a format which can be subsequently fed into a phototypesetter. The quality of the finished product is important; laser printers commonly output a resolution of 300 dots per inch, considerably less than the minimum of 1,000 dots per inch achievable with phototypesetters. Images are often 'captured' and manipulated by means of a scanner. See *printer* and *scanner*.

Digit A single component of a number. Two is a one digit number, 27 is a two digit number, etc.

Digitiser A device that reproduces, in digital format, information originally in non-digital (i.e. analogue): e.g. images and sound. See *datalogging*.

Direct access Direct access is a method of organising data files. If a file is organised in this way, then individual items (records) can be brought from backing store into main memory, updated and written back to their place in the file. Sometimes direct access is called **random access** but, strictly speaking, random

access should refer only to accessing the computer's main
store. Disc backing store can be used for direct access or
sequential access files. Sequential access means that each item
has to be read until the required item is reached. Files held on
magnetic tape have to be sequential and can only be updated
by rewriting the file.

Disc See *magnetic disc*.

Disc drive A machine with a high speed motor which rotates the
disc and a head which reads and writes information to and
from the *magnetic disc or compact disc*.

Dot matrix See *printer*.

Electronic document interchange (EDI) A system of exchanging
commercial documents, such as orders and payment, by electronic means. EDI usually uses electronic mail. It is hoped
that EDI will speed up international transactions, which are
often bogged down by the need to send and complete numerous
paper-based documents.

Electronic mail This is the use of computer systems to transfer
messages between users, using either direct cable links or
indirect links such as telephones and satellites. A variety
of input and output equipment can be used; for example,
telex, word processors, video terminals and facsimile
machines.

ENIAC This is an acronym for Electronic Numeral Integrator And
Calculator. ENIAC was the first modern computer by virtue of
its ability to switch tasks. The breakthrough was made by
storing the program inside the computer, and not building a
machine to do a specific task (e.g. Colossus which was used to
de-cipher German codes in the Second World War). ENIAC
consumed 150 kilowatts of power and contained 18,000 thermionic valves. These are the sort of glass 'bulbs', about 50
mm high, which can be found in old radios.

ENIAC could do additions at amazing speeds, 5,000 per
second, although it rarely worked for more than half an hour
without a valve going. This section of JUNIOR PEARS is being
written with the aid of a micro-computer. In principle it is very
little different from ENIAC. But in practice it takes up 30,000
times less space, is forty times faster, has a larger memory,
consumes the power of an electric light bulb and is about
20,000 times cheaper.

Expert Systems These are computer programs which capture a human expert's knowledge of a particular subject, usually by creating some rules which cover probabilities and approximations. Complex and mammoth amounts of data can be analysed and evaluated until a conclusion is reached.

The first serious expert system—MYCIN—was developed in the mid-1970s to help doctors diagnose meningitis. Until now, the major applications have been where there are a lot of experts—as in medical diagnosis and law. Although there has been much discussion about expert systems, artificial intelligence (see *Turing*), the much-predicted technical breakthroughs are still in the early stages. See *fifth generation computers, transputer*.

Facsimile System (FAX) Transmission of printed words and other images so that the receiver gets an exact copy of the original. A scanner converts the original into electrical signals, which are transmitted by cable or airwaves and printed at the receiving end.

File Any collection of *data* which can be stored or accessed by computer is a file. Each computer file has its own file name consisting of a limited set of characters. Databases use files. In this context, file structure is far more clearly defined. The file becomes a collection of records. Information on each record is divided into separate categories, under the same headings. A **field** is one item of information within a record. Thus the membership secretary of a computer club may have one file containing all the membership details. There will be an individual record for each member. Within each record there will be details about name, address, and so on. Each of these items is an example of a field.

FORTRAN This stands for **FOR**mula **TRAN**slation. A high-level computer language for scientific and technical use.

Games The idea of getting computers to play and even beat humans at games of strategy has been popular for many years. An enormous investment has gone into chess, and the best chess programs are now nearly as good as the best chess players in the world. Games such as noughts and crosses are relatively simple insofar as the number of options are finite and computers are excellent when it comes to *number-crunching*. More difficult techniques involve 'heuristic searches' where programs which can learn from mistakes, and the play of the opponents, develop crude principles. These techniques, related to the development of artificial intelligence, are in their infancy. (See *Turing, Alan*). Chess, draughts and scrabble are examples of **Puzzle Games**, but there are many other types of games that have been spawned by what has become a multi-billion dollar industry.

   Arcade Adventures are mainly concerned with reaction skills and fighting. **Shootem ups** started with *Space Invaders*. Many of the most popular games are **Platform Games**, where the player controls a character who jumps from platform to platform, often through surrealistic landscapes. **Role-playing** games allow one to identify with a character and view the world from that perspective. **Adventure Games** fall within this category. **Simulations**, such as flight and sport, aim at realism. In contrast to the massive amount of simulated violence and destruction there is a generation of adventure games, such as Sim City, where users create cities, civilisations and whole worlds. Many of the best games transcend the above categories. It may be that computer games have done more than any other type of application to bring computers into the home.

Gigabyte Originally the term for 1024 *megabytes* (MB) or 1,048,576 *kilobytes* (K), but increasingly being used to mean 1000 megabytes (1,000,000,000 *bytes*).

GIGO Acronym for 'Garbage In, Garbage Out'—a useful reminder that what comes out is only as good as the programs and data put in.

Graphical User Interface (GUI) A new generation of general purpose user interfaces for computers is emerging. The programs use a combination of a pointing device (such as a mouse), simple pictures (called icons) and pull-down menus instead of traditional but cumbersome keyboard commands. These graphical interfaces are intended to make the casual or novice user more productive. They are not an operating system but an interface which masks the resident operating system. They were first popularised, as part of the firmware, on the Apple Macintosh. As personal computers have become much more powerful, graphical user interfaces have proliferated.

   Microsoft's 'Windows' is perhaps the most well known example of a GUI. More than 9 million copies have been sold world-wide, making the founder of Microsoft, Bill Gates, the richest man in America. More than 5,000 programs which use Windows are now available. They have a common look and feel about them, thereby making them easier to learn and use.

Graphics The creation of non-written text (e.g. pictures, displays and graphs) is an important feature of computers, both on micros (e.g. games, educational programs) and on larger computers (e.g. Computer Aided Design (CAD)). The use of colour has an added impact. In high-resolution graphics, the programmer aims at controlling the individual phospor dots on the display monitor. The only limitation is the memory size of the computer. That unit of the screen addressed by the computer is known as the *Pixel*. In low-resolution graphics, individual shapes, or 'characters', are already constructed and can be built up into an image. These can be conveniently generated by using the keyboard. Each shape is formed by a block, typically eight rows by eight columns.

Hacker Originally a hacker was somebody who spent a lot of time programming computers, perhaps fixing programs, and certainly getting them to do things that others couldn't. The term is now usually used to describe an unauthorised user of a computer system, one who has managed to crack the security systems. Hackers commonly use a computer with a *modem* and gain access to computers thousands of miles away. Hacking tales proliferate, like the one of a shy and brilliant Cornell University student whose coding brought down over 6,000 computers. (See *virus*). Although there may be a tendency to exaggerate their feats, the fact is that, despite security systems, computers remain vulnerable to wily and determined intruders.

Hard copy Data printed onto paper generated by the computer.

Hard disc See *magnetic disc.*

Hardware All the physical equipment in a computer system, e.g. the keyboard, the screen, disc drive, etc. If it can be kicked, it's hardware. Contrast with *software*.

High level languages Programming languages developed to be intelligible and as close as possible to the problem to be solved. These are easier for human beings to use but require a great deal of translation into machine code instructions before they can be executed by the central processing unit of a computer.

There are hundreds of high level languages, which can be divided into four classes: scientific (e.g. ALGOL and FORTRAN), business (e.g. COBOL), specialised (e.g. ADA) and interactive (e.g. BASIC and APL).

A significant development is of application programs which allow the end user to programme the application whilst using it. This allows specific applications to be written much more quickly and be more easily maintained than in a traditional high level language. Programmable applications programs are sometimes called fourth generation languages (*4GLs*), the implication being that they are one step away from the fifth generation of artificial intelligence. See *computer generations*.

Hollerith, Dr Hermann In the late 1880s, the U.S. census bureau had a problem. It was still counting the results from the 1880 census, and had another to deal with in 1890. Hollerith, a census statistician, saw that the only answer was mechanisation. He realised that much of the information being processed could be represented by the presence or absence of holes in paper cards and that the sorting could be done by electrical means, since a contact could be made or broken by the card. This led to the idea of feeding calculating machines with punched cards. The firm Hollerith founded to exploit his invention, the Computing Tabulating Recording Company, later became the International Business Machines Corporation: IBM.

Hypermedia A software environment in which various types and items of information are organised as a stack. Handling a mouse, the user can click onto the stop of the stack, which may be an icon or some text. This then reveals layer upon layer, and the type of information may vary. It may be a pictorial enlargement, possibly accompanied by detailed explanation and sound.

Import This is the process of bringing data such as text, figures and pictures from one application into another. Various applications often handle data in dissimilar ways. Consequently several standard interchange formats have developed. The most famous of these is *ASCII* (American Standard Code for Information Interchange). This and RTF (Rich Text Format) are designed for handling text. TIFF and PCX are standards for importing graphics. It is often the case that some features, e.g. font size, get lost when the data is translated from one format into another.

Informatics This comes from the French word *l'informatique*, and is said to be the science of information handling. The term is useful in so far as it emphasises the importance of information.

Information Information is derived from data. *Data* in itself is meaningless unless it is interpreted. So, information is intelligible data. Take, for example, the number 250646. This could be a date, a telephone number or, for that matter, a reference. The meaning is dependent upon the user. When interpreted it becomes information. Refer to *data*.

Information Technology (IT) This generally refers to the use of microprocessor-based equipment to handle, process and communicate information. There was technology that did this long before the advent of the microprocessor, but the development and powerful coalition of micro-electronics, computers and telecommunications has given rise to the umbrella term 'information technology'. This information is always transmitted in the form of digital data. At its simplest, two computers communicating with each other can be said to be an example of IT. This intercommunication has been crucially enhanced by the development of communication media, e.g. optical fibres and satellites. A particularly important reason for the exploitation of the technology has been the growth of the information sector within modern society. One recent illustration of the scale of this data explosion is the estimation that today's 9,000 daily newspapers contain some 300,000 characters each—2·7 billion characters per day requiring 150,000 human hours for keyboard input.

The deluge of data creates problems for those who design and use information systems. The space agency NASA is said to have analysed only 3 per cent of the data it has collected. The deterioration of the ozone layer could have been detected ten years earlier from data routinely gathered but insufficiently analysed.

I/O Abbreviation for Input/Output.

Input Anything put into the computer system, such as programs and information, which then becomes data. This is done by means of an *input device*: e.g. a keyboard. Other machines for inputting data include magnetic tape and disc drives, card and paper tape readers, bar-code readers and light pens. Whatever the device, it can accept and decode data and transmit it as digital pulses to the computer.

Integer A whole number with no fractions or decimal places.

Integrated circuit see *chip*.

Integrated Services Digital Network (ISDN) This digital communications network permits the communication of voice, computer messages, and other services. The high speeds of data transmission – 64,000 bits per second – allows one to send graphics, faxes and video data while having a phone conversation. See *optical fibre*.

Interactive video see *compact disc*.

Interface This is the circuitry which allows the computer to communicate with one or more *peripheral* devices. Data can be passed from one to the other. The interface translates the differing operating characteristics of the devices.

Interpreter This is a translation program which is called upon whenever a program in a language such as BASIC is executed. It translates one line at a time into machine code. The run will be terminated if the program does not accord with the rules of the programming language—a syntax error occurs—and then the translation process has to start all over again. Contrast with *compiler*.

Kilobytes (K) A measurement of memory or disc capacity and therefore to some extent a measure of computer capabilities. As a kilo refers to a thousand, a Kilobyte generally means a thousand bytes. (It is in fact 2 to the power of 10, which is 1,024 bytes.) A **megabyte** (M) is 1,024 kilobytes (which is approximately one million bytes).

LASER Acronym for 'Light Amplification by Stimulated Emission of Radiation'. A device for producing a concentrated light beam of a single wave length, with many potential applications. See *printer* and *compact disc*.

LOGO A high level programming language designed specifically for learning. LOGO is inter-active (like *BASIC*), and very easy to use. It permits users to build their own vocabulary of instructions. One of LOGO's functions is to control a robotic 'turtle' which can trace its path on the floor with the aid of a pen held between its back legs.

Low level language A programming language in which each instruction corresponds to a single machine-code instruction. Low level languages thus take less time for the computer to interpret than high-level languages. **Assembly** languages are low level. Assembler program instructions use symbols, each of which corresponds (usually) to a single *machine code* instruction: e.g. the instruction LDA (LoaD Accumulator) could have a machine code of 10101001 on the 6502 microprocessor.

Machine code Machine code instructions are the control signals that actually work the machine. They are represented as binary patterns and require no translation. Programs written in other languages must be translated into machine code before the computer can execute them.

Magnetic disc Also spelt disk. A rotatable disc which is used to store and read data. The surface is coated with a magnetisable material. Magnetic discs are the commonest way of storing

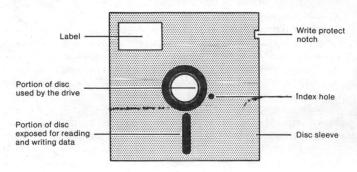

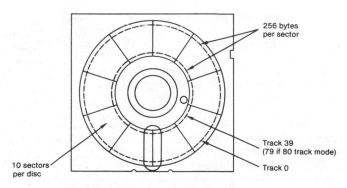

'Tracks' and 'Sectors' on a typical floppy disc

data for direct access. The surface of the disc is divided into tracks: i.e. concentric rings. These tracks are subdivided into sectors. There are a wide variety of discs and disc units used by computers. Floppy discs are commonly used on microcomputer systems, holding from 100K to 1·2 megabytes, although 3·5 discs with a capacity of 4 megabytes are now being manufactured. The common $5\frac{1}{4}$ in discs are being superseded by $3\frac{1}{2}$ in discs. Hard discs sealed inside a drive unit are now relatively cheap and have become a standard feature of business microcomputers. These have greater storage capacity (e.g. 40 megabytes) and faster access time. On larger systems a number of hard discs are often combined to form a disc pack. See *backing store* and *compact disc*.

Magnetic tape An alternative method of storing data is to use magnetic tape wound on spools or cassettes. Tape can only be accessed sequentially but is still widely used in *data processing* installations to store large files: e.g. payroll and employees' records. It is cheaper but slower than disc storage. Tape files are often used as a disc backup and also for long-term storage of files. See also *access* and *backing store*.

Mainframe, Mini & Microcomputer systems The distinction between these types of computer systems is usually based upon the computing power (memory available and the processing capability), the sophistication of the operating system, the number of *peripherals* and the number of users. Thus mainframes work very quickly and can perform many different tasks at once. They can support hundreds of terminals. Mainframe computers require special environments and skilled operators, whereas a microcomputer is usually an isolated unit dependent upon a microprocessor chip. A microcomputer is normally used by a single user, running only one program at a time. In general a mini-computer is smaller than a mainframe but still very fast and capable of performing several tasks at once.

The distinction according to power is not hard and fast, especially because of the advances in technology. Some of today's microcomputers are more powerful than mini configurations of three years ago. Supermicros running powerful operating systems and capable of multiple processing have taken the bottom end of the market from minis. Similar price perform-

ance increases mean that minis now, in turn, threaten mainframes. The combination of fourth generation languages, standard operating systems, networkability and cheap processing
power is now killing off mainframes. The mainframe is not
going to disappear, but the number of new users is tiny.
Intel, the company which produced the world's first microprocessor, have developed a microprocessor which is estimated
to be 135 times more powerful than a PC and more powerful
than most mainframes. These developments should result in
microcomputers becoming more powerful than existing mainframes, at a fraction of the cost. Nearly half of the revenue for
computer manufacturers now comes from microcomputers.
Currently micros with hard discs are available for several
hundred pounds, powerful micros cost several thousands of
pounds and mainframes cost several million pounds. See *computer generations, microprocessor, operating system, supercomputer* and *workstation*.

Megabyte See *Kilobyte*.

Memory The program and the data it needs are stored inside the
main memory of the computer. Sometimes known as immediate access store because data can be instantly retrieved from
any location. See *direct access*. In microcomputers the internal
memory is divided into two parts: **Random Access Memory
(RAM)** and **Read Only Memory (ROM)**. RAM is usually made
up of banks of memory chips that can be used for storing data
and programs for the processor. This memory is known as
volatile: i.e. the contents are lost when the power is switched
off. Therefore programs and data are saved on *backing store*.
ROM is the permanent storage space within the computer,
usually containing important information that the computer
needs all the time: e.g. the operating system. The user can
have access to ROM but cannot change, remove, or add to it
without actually adding on chips. However, the computer
may have sideways RAM which allows programs (in RAM) to
sit alongside the main memory (hence the term 'sideways') and
to be treated as if it were in ROM. See *PROM*.

MHz (Megahertz) Processor speed is described in terms of the
number of electrical pulses that pass through a system a
second. Microprocessors achieve levels of several million times
a second; these are counted in megahertz, abbreviated to MHz.

Microprocessor A *chip* which contains a timing and control unit, and an arithmetic/logic unit. It performs the function of the central processing unit (CPU) found in a traditional computer system. Many people confuse microprocessors with microcomputers. The microprocessor unit (MPU) is not a complete computer because it lacks memory and input/output devices. Processor speed is described in terms of the number of electrical pulses that pass through a system a second. Microprocessors achieve levels of several million times a second; these are counted in megahertz, which is abbreviated to MHz. The microcomputer is just one application of the microprocessor. The importance of the microprocessor is that it permits greater flexibility. Linked with sensors, measuring and switching devices it can be made to run an industrial process; appropriately programmed, it will work a washing machine, sewing machines, calculator, arcade games or many thousands of other devices.

The microprocessor can be said to be the engine of the microcomputer which is often categorised by the type of processor it is using. Microprocessors are distinguished by the number of *bits* they can handle at a time. The Intel 8088 was an eight bit processor used on the original IBM PC which ran at 4.77 *MHz*. The 16 bit 80286 processor is used on PC/AT machines. The 80386 is a 16 bit processor and has reached 33 MHz. This is widely used on what are known as 386 SX and 386 DX machines. The 386 SX uses a 16 bit bus to transmit data and is thus slower than the 386 DX which uses a 32 bit bus. Recently a number of microcomputer manufacturers have preferred to use 32 bit *RISC* processors. Intel are also developing a revolutionary 80586 processor which will have three million transistors. The speed of the computer is based only partly on the processor; the speed of RAM, hard disc and video card all play a major role. The increase of speed in these areas has not been as dramatic as the increase in processor speeds, which leaves the processor waiting for the other parts to catch up. This is known as the I/O bottleneck. See *bus*, *MHz*.

MIDI This stands for Musical Instrument Digital Interface. In the attempt to get over the problems of linking one musical instrument to another, a universal synthesiser interface was built by a US-based music company in 1981, and in the following year

15 other companies adopted the specification and renamed it MIDI. This standard allows different musical instruments to communicate with each other. Many competitive manufacturers were able to come together and share ideas about their systems. MIDI-equipped instruments use the commonly available 5-pin DIN plugs. A relatively simple cable used is capable of carrying 16 different instruments individually, at a speed of over 1000 MIDI instructions per second. These signals are usually communicated to a computer, or an instrument which has computing facilities, which can then manipulate and process the sounds.

MIPS Acronym for Millions of Instructions Per Second. This is the speed of handling by the processor and is a crude indicator of its power.

MODEM This stands for MOdulator-DEModulator. A MODEM allows computers to transmit along communication lines such as the telephone system. The MODEM converts ('modulates') computer data into audio tones and audio tones into data ('demodulates').

Monitor This is the computer display screen which looks like a television set. Developments and demand for improvements in screen resolution and graphics have meant that the standards are ever-changing. For standard applications such as *databases* and *spreadsheets*, the quality of the monitor is largely incidental. But the emergence of applications such as *desk top publishing*, *CAD* and *multimedia* has meant that the quality of the display is crucial. The first widely used colour monitor was the IBM-led CGA (colour graphics adaptor) standard, which was introduced in 1981. This offered just four colours. The next standard, EGA (enhanced graphics adaptor), emerged in 1984. This featured higher resolution and the possibility of 16 co-existing colours from a choice of 64. In 1987 the VGA (Video Graphics Array) standard emerged with a choice of 256 colours from over quarter of a million and a resolution of 640 X 480 dpi (dots per inch). This is now being superseded by SVGA (Super Video Graphics Array).

Mouse Most mice are small boxes, with one or more buttons, which you move around on a flat surface such as a desk top. The movement directs a pointer on a screen, and pressing a button allows you to select or carry out an operation as displayed on the screen.

MS-DOS An acronym of Micro Soft Disc Operating System. See *operating system*.

Multimedia Multimedia permits a computer to handle and combine audio, video and text data which can originate from disparate media. Multimedia has always been a part of microcomputers; even early models offered rudimentary sound and graphics. But, with the dramatic increase of processing power and the development of digital technologies, it is now possible for sound and standard moving video images to be stored on hard disc and *CD-Rom*. While the technology is dramatically evolving, the likelihood of multimedia features being widely exploited depends on the development of common standards.

Multi-plexing The use of a single telecommunications link to transmit a number of different signals virtually simultaneously.

Multi-user A computer system where several users can use the same computer simultaneously.

Network The linking together of computers is called a network. Networks enable individual computers to draw upon the computing power or storage or printing facilities of others. With a network you can distribute computer power. This is a radical departure from the tradition of large computer systems which are 'sun and planets systems' with many satellites revolving around a central pivot. Microcomputers are often networked in order that resources can be shared. LAN stands for Local Area Network. A common LAN configuration is the 'ring' network which consists of one cable linking all the machines. The interconnected points are known as **nodes**. A file server transmits data around the ring before it is claimed by the computer which requested it. The other common LAN set-up is a 'star' network in which data radiates outwards from the central file server(s). Each microcomputer is connected by a separate cable.

Number-crunching This phrase represents the computer's ability to perform—'eat up'—numerical calculations. Thus, for example, the Meteorological Office's massive Control Data Cyber 205 (super) computer, installed in 1982, is capable of 400 million calculations per second. Nearly a trillion calculations are necessary in order to make weather forecasts up to a week in advance. See *supercomputer*.

Numerical Control (NC) In the early fifties the engineering industry started using NC machine tools, which read codes from paper tape, to guide the machines through different stages of cutting. By the 1970s these were being replaced by machines which stored the programs in memory, replacing the paper tape; hence Computer Numerical Control (CNC) machinery.

On-line Directly connected to the computer.

Operating System The operating system acts as an 'interface' between the computer and the user. It determines how the computer responds when turned on and when instructions are keyed in. The first computers did not communicate via an operating system. Indeed a series of switches had to be set by specialists. Now there is great emphasis upon the 'friendliness' of the computer. This is initially determined by the operating system, which is a collection of programs built into the systems software; it contains all the instructions the computer needs. In a microcomputer this is often placed in ROM and is then called firmware. MSDOS (Micro Soft Disc Operating System) was written for 16 bit micros and initially used INTEL 8066 or 8088. This limited users to 640K of memory and 32 megabytes of hard disc, whereas the more powerful 80286, 80836 and 80486 processors can permit much greater access and the use of more powerful operating systems such as UNIX. This is a powerful multi-user, multi-tasking operating system which is also capable of running MSDOS applications. See *graphical user interface* and *microprocessor*.

Optical fibre Optical fibre cables, made of very pure glass, are replacing copper cables as a means of transmission. Light is used as the carrier of the signals. The signals transmitted are superior to traditional methods; data can be transmitted at the rate of about 300 million bits per sec. There is a much higher carrying capacity. Eight optical 'tubes' can do the work of 4,800 traditional phone cables. It is now possible to send sound and vision together along the same line. By the end of the 1980s more than 10,000 km of fibre optic cable had been laid between Japan, the US and the UK.

Output Anything coming out of a computer. This is either to be communicated to the user in a form that can be read (e.g. results printed onto paper or displayed on the VDU) or output in code for other computers and stored on *backing storage* such as disc or tape. See *input*.

Pascal A much admired general purpose high level computer language, designed to encourage structured programming. Named after the French mathematician Blaise Pascal (see C24) who, in 1642, constructed one of the earliest calculating machines.

PC Personal computer. See *mainframe, mini and microcomputer systems*.

Peripherals All the extra machines that can surround, and are controlled by, the computer itself: e.g. a disc drive, printer, keyboard, monitor, plotter, etc. Their purpose is to provide an information link between the outside world and the computer. See *interface* and *backing storage*.

Pixel The tiny dots or PICture ELements that make up a computer graphics picture displayed on monitor or a *VDU*. See *graphics*.

Point of Sale (POS) Terminals Cash registers in supermarkets and shops are being replaced by POS terminals. In addition to providing exact change for the customers, they can keep records of sales and monitor the speed of the operator. There are two main types: free-standing and those directly linked to a central computer. The free-standing terminal is a computer in its own right but is also capable of generating data (e.g. using microcassette tapes) which can be periodically fed into the central computer. The central computer is able to keep records of sales of particular items and make an instant stock check. Potentially, point of sale (POS) devices can be used for checking on the credit-worthiness of shoppers who offer credit cards, direct debiting of the customer's bank account and direct re-stocking to and from the warehouse.

Port A connection on a computer which enables *interfacing* with printers, monitors, etc.

Printer A machine which prints information sent from the computer onto paper. There are many types. Dot matrix, laser and ink-jet printers are commonly used. The dot matrix is the cheapest and most popular computer printer. Dot matrix printers use printed characters formed by ink dots. The printer-hammer pattern is created from a rectangular block of needles, typically 9 by 7.

Only one block of needles is needed to create any of the characters in the given character set which may be as many as 255. As the pins are adaptable they can readily represent drawings and pictures.

The resolution of high-quality printers is commonly measured by the number of dots the printer can print in a line one inch long—dpi for short. The resolution of a standard 9-pin dot matrix printer is roughly 60 dpi, whilst that of a 24-pin device is 360 dpi. Although newer and more expensive *laser printers* are offering 600 dpi, the quality of the standard resolution of 300 dpi for laser printers is considerably better than that of the 24-pin dot matrix printers. This is because the laser printer uses finely powdered ink particles, otherwise known as toner particles, to create the dots. A laser printer does not work by burning an image onto a sheet of paper; a laser beam is burst very rapidly across the paper at each point where part of the image is to appear. The print toner adheres to where the laser has been. An ink jet creates patterns on paper in a way similar to that of the dot matrix, but the dots are squirted by an ink-jet. The tiny ink-jet is activated either by a pump system or, in the case of the bubble jet, by heat. The squirting is repeated many times per second. Ink-jet printers are quieter than dot matrix printers.

Program A set of instructions which tells the computer how to perform any particular task. A computer cannot be useful until it is programmed. These instructions will either be in *machine code* or in a programming language. The program must be capable of being understood and accord to the logic of the language being used by the computer's central processor.

PROM Acronym for Programmable Read Only Memory. A memory into which data is written after manufacture, but which cannot then be altered. See *EPROM*.

RAM Acronym for Random Access Memory. See *memory*.

Real time The ability of the system to respond almost immediately, regardless of the number of terminals, as a result of inputting data. When a person withdraws money from a cash till, or when a travel agency keys in a flight enquiry, the computer system responds almost immediately and is said to be 'real time'. The action must be processed quickly enough so that further action may be taken: for example, when the travel agent books a flight seat, the transaction must be processed before any other agents enquire whether seats are still available. Another application of real time is in controlling industrial processes: e.g. in a chemical plant. 'Real time' services can be very expensive, and may not always be required by the users. Alternative computer configurations may utilise batch processing, or time-sharing.

RISC processor Reduced Instruction Set Chips are based on the discovery that a processor carries out only 20% of its instructions for 80% of the time. Risc processors are therefore designed to carry out these most common instructions as quickly as possible – typically, five or ten times faster than a complex chip. Because RISC chips are smaller and simpler than conventional ones, they can be made to run faster. The latest RISC processor to be unveiled runs at 200 MHz and can process two instructions at once, which gives it a peak speed of 400 *mips*.

Robot Robots are machines designed to replace human labour. ('Robot' comes from the Czech word meaning 'worker'.) For a long time man has dreamed of machines that can both do the work of man and be like man. A robot should to some extent be able to respond 'intelligently' to changes in its environment. A range of sensors should allow the robot to capture data through touch, hearing and vision, crudely like that of a human. Sensors, coupled with microcomputers, give robots so-called 'intelligence'. Many industrial robots do not possess this quality. 'Intelligent' and responsive robots are very expensive and are still under development.

ROM Acronym for Read Only Memory. See *memory*.

Scanner This is an electronic device for capturing predrawn images such as line drawings and photographs and converting them into binary data which can then be manipulated on screen by the computer user. A typical scanner scans 300 dots per inch: which means that high resolution images, such as photographs, suffer badly. In addition, the files produced are very large indeed—2 megabytes is not unusual. See *desk top publishing.*

Semiconductor A material (e.g. silicon, germanium) which can be made to switch from being a good conductor to being a good insulator. This is done by introducing chemical impurities which can very sensitively alter and control its electrical properties.

Software Programs used by the computer. Although software is usually taken to mean the programs loaded by the user, it also includes the systems programs which can come with the machine. See *operating systems* and *systems software.*

Software package Sets of programs to do particular tasks: e.g. stock-control. Like package holidays, they may not be exactly what is required. See *application.*

Speech recognition This is the ability of the computer to 'understand' a series of spoken words. However, speech recognition is still presenting a number of problems because of variations in accent, tone and pitch, and also because of the very flexible and versatile nature of language. In the same way as fingerprints, voice prints can be uniquely identified. Once speech recognition is developed it will be useful in a number of different ways. See *computer generations.*

Speech synthesizers Computer-generated speech is already a feature in some applications. Voice output can either be constructed by adding together previously recorded words and phrases or, much more difficult, by assembling words from a range of sounds (phonemes).

Spreadsheets These are programs which allow the user to set up tables in rows and columns of (usually) financial figures. The data may be entered directly, or it may be derived from calculations performed upon other data. Therefore, a monthly total could be defined as the sum of all the spending, minus the income. A particular advantage of these models is that an imaginary situation can be simulated: for example, the doubling of wage costs, and the consequences tested. Often microcomputers were introduced into businesses because of spreadsheet facilities.

SQL Structured Query Language. This is a language for managing databases and became the first of the expected fourth generation languages suitable for processing huge centralised databases. SQL has been seen as a key to inter-system connectivity, a way of making data accessible to microcomputer users using differing information – retrieval packages. See *high level languages*.

String A distinct group of characters used in programs. These characters may be alphanumeric (a mixture of letters and figures): e.g. 'SRJ855X', or numeric: e.g. '210385'.

Supercomputers Some computers are so much more powerful than other mainframe systems that they are called supercomputers. In May 1985 the world sales of the two main manufacturers of supercomputers (Cray and Control Data) amounted to 130 machines with a projected demand of 50 systems a year. A supercomputer system can cost in the region of £20 million. Supercomputers now available have a performance that is about 3,000 times better than that of the Ferranti Atlas computer of the early 1960s—the supercomputer of its day. One of the latest and fastest is the Cray-2, produced by Seymour Cray. It is only 114 cm (45 in) tall and forms a 300 degrees arc of a circle 134 cm (53 in) in diameter. It has four background processors and a common memory capable of storing 256 million 64 bit words. Its internal state changes every 4.1 billionths of a second. See *number-crunching*.

Systems software These are programs which enable the hardware to be used. They include the *operating system*, editors and translation programs.

Telecommunications Long-distance transmission by cable or radio waves. The developments in this aspect of technology have reflected those in sound and television broadcasting. Now, incorporating elements of light technology (e.g. fibre optics, lasers), it is a vital ingredient of '*information technology*'.

Teletext Both Teletext and Videotext transmit an information service stored in large computer databases. Access depends on microprocessors. There is a crucial difference between Teletext and videotext. Teletext broadcasts information through the air. Teletext uses a part of the same signal which produces the TV picture. The user has a keypad which allows him or her to 'call up' any page of information by number. The microprocessor in the user's television sorts out the correct portion of the signal and displays the information on the screen. The

BBC calls it 'Ceefax'; the Independent Television's service is called 'Teletext'. The service is free, once you have bought or hired the device to decode the pages. See *Videotext*.

Terminal Any device by which data can be sent to or obtained from a computer.

Transistor These came to be used widely in radios, hence the name 'Transistors': also called 'Trannies'. These were the first portable, 'personal' radios. Fundamentally, computers consist of circuits called bistables, which have two stable states. These are known as flipflops and change state according to the electrical pulses they receive. This switching can be done by transistors. Since transistors are simply layers of one substance on another, unlike valves, which are complicated structures of glass envelopes, coils, pins, etc., they can be made very small, and cheaply.

Transputer The transputer, launched in 1985 by a British micro-chip company called INMOS, is a complete computer—processor, memory and communications—on a single chip. Transputers permit parallel processing, which is the carrying out of many operations simultaneously. This capacity may make it suitable for many *fifth generation* computing applications such as artificial intelligence, natural language recognition and vision.

Turing, Alan A British mathematician who proved, in 1937, that any problem with a logical solution, no matter how complex, can be solved by using a small set of simple instructions. Also the 'Turing Test' of computer 'intelligence' is often referred to. According to Turing a machine can be said to be intelligent if its responses to questions are indistinguishable from those of a human being. See *expert systems*.

Unix This is a multi-user, multi-tasking operating system which can be run on a variety of the more powerful processors. See *operating system*.

Validate and **Verify** Accuracy of data is extremely important in *data processing*. Data can be checked by entering it twice; this is known as verification. Computer programs can be used to ensure that the data which is entered is valid: i.e. permissible. For example, a National Insurance number always commences with two letters, followed by 6 numbers and then one letter. It is easy for the program to check that any national insurance number entered follows these criteria. However, it is possible for the wrong number, but valid by independent means, to be entered.

Videotext With videotext information is transmitted by telephone, but unlike *teletext*, it is an inter-active system allowing the user to interrogate the host computer in pursuit of the information needed, following the indexing system adopted by the organisers. The display may be of passages of text. One type of videotext system is viewdata, where the display is of one screen (i.e. page) at a time. British Telecom's version is PRESTEL. See *teletext*.

Virtual Reality Virtual reality allows a person to explore a computer-generated world by pretending to be actually in it. Instead of looking at a screen, the user is totally enclosed in a self-contained environment, including three-dimensional graphics and stereo sounds. This is usually done by means of wearing a helmet, and gloves that capture hand movements. A virtual world must be constantly regenerated in response to the user's actions. The user can seem to walk and move, add objects and take them away; hence the term *virtual reality*.

Virus Computer viruses are rogue pieces of software. The prime feature of a computer virus is that it is designed to replicate itself automatically and to spread from one computer to another, in many ways mimicking the spread of an infectious disease in its behaviour. As they usually originate from a floppy disc, users should check that discs are uncontaminated. Viruses are written by *hackers* who take pleasure in making computers misbehave. The damage varies from flashing messages onto the screen to destroying the entire contents of hard discs, or the computer's own permanent memory. Once in a computer system thay can spread throughout a network. In 1988 the massive US Internet UNIX network suffered a virus attack in which over 6000 computers were infected and reportedly 50,000 man hours of work were required to eradicate it. An infamous virus is called the Friday the 13th virus. This lies dormant in the computer until it is triggered off by the combination by the next Friday which happens to fall on the 13th day of the month. Viruses are now widespread. The National Computing Centre estimates that viral infections could be afflicting, at some time or other, as many as a third of the computers in industry.

Visual Display Unit (VDU). The television-like screen on which a computer displays information. It will often have a keyboard attached to it.

Windows Refer to *graphical user interface*.

Word-processing When using a manual typewriter, it is not possible to make any drastic changes (e.g. move a paragraph or change margins) without re-typing the whole document. Instead of a sheet of paper, the word-processor program uses a VDU screen and computer memory. This allows the user to rearrange layout of text, correction, addition or deletion. When the text has been satisfactorily designed, a printout onto paper may be output. Some word-processing systems don't even print out onto paper; the desired text is directly transmitted to another computer.

With word-processing, standard text (e.g. letters) can be quickly produced with only variations (e.g. names and addresses) having to be typed each time. Word-processor programs usually provide many other features, such as the ability to shift blocks of text around and to search for and change particular words. Word-processors are having a great effect on office work, and are also an invaluable aid for people who are poor typists. Word-processing packages are increasingly popular with home computer users. Nowadays the more sophisticated word-processing packages include a number of *desk top publishing* facilities, such as the use of different print types and sizes and inclusion of drawing facilities.

Workstation These are high-performance networked machines, used typically to run specialised software for scientists, engineers and designers. They use a high-powered 32 bit bus for communicating, allowing them to be networked to a variety of facilities. Traditionally, workstations have been specialised and have not offered the general-purpose software available on stand-alone machines. As workstations are coming down in price and personal computers are increasing in power, the two are beginning to overlap. Hence some personal computers are now being sold as workstations and some workstations are being sold as potential stand-alone machines.

WYSWYG This feature, an acronym for What You See (on the screen) is What You Get (on paper), is useful when using a *word-processing* package.

Further Reading

There are many computer magazines that are essential for the microcomputer enthusiast who wants to keep up-to-date with current developments. Magazines like *Personal Computer World* often have beginner's guides to the jargon. Some national newspapers (e.g. *The Guardian*) run regular computer features. A widely used reference is that written by the British Computer Society: *A Glossary of Computing Terms: An Introduction*. The eighth edition is due to appear in 1993 and will be published by Cambridge University Press. The seventh edition was published in 1992 by Pitman Publishing.

SOMETHING TO JOIN

A section on YOUTH ORGANISATIONS, with notes on the
MORSE CODE, SEMAPHORE, COMPASS and KNOTS.

ORGANISATIONS TO JOIN
(including some courses to apply for)

This is a list of some of the organisations that are either entirely for young people or have sections open to the young. A few of them provide courses only for those who have been specially recommended by their schools or other authorities. Take particular note of the age limits for membership, which are given in most cases. Note also that, in present conditions, subscriptions might well have increased in the months between preparation and publication of this edition.

Air Training Corps A national organisation sponsored by the Ministry of Defence (RAF) with the aim of promoting and encouraging in young men a practical interest in aviation and the RAF, providing training useful both in Service and civilian life, and developing, through the promotion of sports and pastimes in healthy rivalry, the qualities of leadership and good citizenship.

Army Cadet Force The British Army's own voluntary youth organisation. Open to boys, and a percentage of girls, between the ages of 13 and 18. Army Cadet Force Association, Millbank Barracks, John Islip Street, London, SW1P 4RR.

Boys' Brigade Oldest of the national uniformed youth organisations, open to boys from 6 to 18. All BB companies are part of a Christian Church and provide a wide range of activities. For details of the nearest company, write to The Boys' Brigade, Felden Lodge, Felden, Hemel Hempstead, Herts, HP3 0BL: The Boys' Brigade, Carronvale House, Larbert, FK5 3LH, Scotland: or Boys' Brigade, Rathmore House, 126 Glenarm Road, Larne, Co Antrim, BT40 1DZ.

Brathay Exploration Group Each year the Group mounts about 15 expeditions on which groups of young people can discover more about themselves, the world and its inhabitants through challenging and exciting tasks, projects and themes. All the expeditions are led by voluntary leaders who contribute themselves towards their own expedition fee. Recent expeditions have included field work in China, trekking in the Central Alps along the 'Grande Randonnée' route 5, and exploring remote areas of Norway. In the British Isles, expedition teams have studied seals in Orkney, and visited Foula, the most remote inhabited island in Great Britain. The Group also runs basic mountain expeditions for beginners and organises leader training courses from its Lake District base on the northern shores of Windermere. National links with the Young Explorers' Trust and the Expedition Advisory Centre, London, enable the Group to maintain a direct involvement with the world of exploration and travel. Brochure and membership details from: The Administrator, Brathay Exploration Group, Brathay Hall, Ambleside, Cumbria LA22 OHP, England. Tel: 05394 33942 (24 hours).

British Athletic Federation Limited Controls athletics with affiliated clubs throughout the country. Details of clubs, membership open to boys and girls of 11 and over, and of training facilities, instructional booklets and coaching schemes from B.A.F., Edgbaston House, 3 Duchess Place, Hagley Road, Edgbaston, Birmingham, B16 8NM. Tel: 021 456 4050.

British Red Cross Society Membership is open to boys and girls aged from 5–10/11 (Junior members) and from 10/11 up to 18 years (Youth members). Young people aged 15–18 years have the option to join an adult group. Training is offered in first aid, nursing, child care, rescue, survival, accident prevention, tented camping, etc. Young members help at holidays with young people with disabilities and undertake a variety of service activities within their community. They are encouraged to make contact with Youth members abroad and to take part in the organisation's international work. Headquarters: 9 Grosvenor Crescent, London SW1X 7FJ.

British Sub-Aqua Club Devoted to sport diver training, diving safety and underwater exploration, science and sport. Over 1,200 branches. Minimum age: 14, but special Snorkeller Award Scheme for juniors. For information pack, write to: British Sub-Aqua Club, Telford's Quay, Ellesmere Port, South Wirral, Cheshire, L65 4FY.

British Trust for Ornithology A national society for all birdwatchers: invites members to take part in varied field investigations into bird biology and distribution, with emphasis on the interactions between man and birds: the Common Birds Census, Nest Record Scheme, Waterways Bird Survey, Birds of Estuaries Enquiry, bird ringing (by special permit only after considerable training and practice), and other special enquiries including regular censuses of species such as the Heron. Services to members include the newsletter *BTO News*, national conferences—both general and specialist—regional conferences, local meetings in co-operation with local bird clubs, specialist courses in modern techniques, use of the lending and reference libraries at Tring, grants and awards for research, and the option of subscribing at reduced rates to the journals *Bird Study* and *Ringing and Migration*. Annual subscription £17 p.a. Concessionary rates available to members in full-time education on application to: The Membership Secretary, BTO, The National Centre for Ornithology, The Nunnery, Thetford, Norfolk, IP24 2PU.

Camping Club Youth Junior section of the Camping and Caravanning Club. Open to young people aged 12 to 17 inclusive. Annual subscription, £3.50 including entrance fee and VAT. Camping at home and abroad. Instruction given. Greenfields House, Westwood Way, Coventry, CV4 8JH.

Concordia Youth Service Volunteers Runs international workcamps throughout the UK, May–October. The work consists of fruit-, vegetable- and hop-picking. Applicants must be full-time students between 19 and 25. Concordia also place British volunteers in summer international voluntary workcamps throughout western and eastern Europe, Turkey and Tunisia. Age-limit, 17–30. Projects include nature conservation, construction, social work and teaching. Contact: Concordia, 8 Brunswick Place, Hove, East Sussex, BN3 1ET.

Council for British Archaeology Publishes ten issues of *British Archaeological News* which contain advertisements enabling anyone wishing to take part in excavations to get in touch with directors requiring voluntary helpers. For the over-16s mainly. 1993 subscription: £14 (UK). CBA, 112 Kennington Road, London, SE11 6RE. For information about careers and university courses, contact Education Officer, CBA Northern Office, Bowes Morrell House, 111 Walmgate, York, YO1 2UA.

CTC (Cyclists' Touring Club) Britain's largest and oldest national cycling organisation, catering for all ages and abilities of cyclist. They lobby local and central government to protect cyclists' rights and facilities on and off the road. Membership includes free legal aid and third party insurance, free handbook and colour magazines, competitive cycle insurance, free technical and touring advice and information, 200 local cycle groups, national events, world-wide cycling holidays, mail-order shop, sports injury advice service. Junior membership (under 18): £12 per year inc. VAT. CTC, 69 Meadrow, Godalming, Surrey, GU7 3HS. Tel: (0483) 417217.

Field Studies Council The FSC has eleven Centres in England and Wales. Most courses are one week in length (but some are for a shorter period). The courses include fieldwork in archaeology, botany, geography, zoology and art. Junior members (under 16) are welcome on family courses or in groups with their teachers; young people over 16 may join suitable courses individually or in groups. Minimum annual subscription: £8. For further details apply to Central Services, Field Studies Council, Preston Montford, Montford Bridge, Shrewsbury SY4 1HW.

Girls' Brigade An international uniformed movement for girls of all ages from five upwards. It has a varied programme with a wide range of activities. The Brigade is a Church-based movement with the motto: 'Seek, serve and follow Christ'. National Headquarters: Girls' Brigade House, Foxhall Road, Didcot, OX11 7BQ. Tel: (0235) 510425.

The Girl Guides Association Sister organisation of the Scouts; UK membership of about three quarters of a million, world membership of $8\frac{1}{2}$ million in 118 countries. Commonwealth Headquarters: 17–19 Buckingham Palace Road, London, SW1W 0PT.

Junior Astronomical Society Aims to encourage people of all ages interested in astronomy and space. A quarterly, *Popular Astronomy*, includes articles on aspects of astronomy and spaceflight. Regular meetings are held in London. There are special sections to help observers. Subscription: £10 a year. Inquiries and enrolment c/o 36 The Fairway, Keyworth, Nottingham, NG12 5DU.

National Federation of Young Farmers' Clubs YFCs seek to meet the needs of rural young people, aged 16 to 26, through educational, training and social programmes which encourage community involvement and concern for our environment. Members participate in active programmes which include travel, sport, training, vocation and life skills. Headquarters: NFYFC, YFC Centre, National Agricultural Centre, Stoneleigh Park, Kenilworth, Warwickshire, CV8 2LG. Tel: (0203) 696544.

Outward Bound Trust Founded in 1941, the Trust provides

personal and team development programmes divided into four main areas: Meeting the Challenge (for 14-24-year-olds): Meeting Social Needs with Unique Solutions (programmes designed to address issues): Experience of a Lifetime (for over 25-year-olds); and Building Powerful Work Teams (for people at work). A choice of open-enrolment or tailor-made programmes is offered at five centres in the UK. All specialist equipment and clothing is provided. Free brochures are available on request. Contact: Mrs Eva Williams, Marketing Manager, Outward Bound Trust, Chestnut Field, Regent Place, Rugby, Warwickshire, CV21 2RJ. Tel: (0788) 560423 Fax: (0788) 541069.

Quaker International Social Projects (QISP) brings together people of many different nationalities and backgrounds who want to be involved as volunteers in innovative projects aiming to meet community needs. Projects last 1–3 weeks, in the spring and summer months. They involve between 7 and 20 volunteers who live and work as a group. Work may be on play-schemes, environmental projects, manual projects, women-only projects, study projects &c. British volunteers are sent abroad to do similar projects in East and West Europe, Turkey, Morocco and the territory of the former USSR. Open to volunteers of all backgrounds and abilities: applications welcomed from volunteers with special needs. Minimum age 18: no upper age limit. Special youth projects for 16–18 age groups. Friends House, 173–177 Euston Road, London, NW1 2BJ. Tel: 071 387 3601

Ramblers' Association Works with the support of some 700 rambling clubs and over 330 local groups throughout the country; publishes *Rambling Today* four times a year and *The Rambler's Year Book* annually, supplying these free of charge to members. Loans 1/50,000 Ordnance Survey maps for small charge to members. Special rates for unwaged and disabled, as well as juniors and under-18 students. Details: 1/5 Wandsworth Road, London, SW8 2XX. Tel: 071 582 6878.

   Ramblers' Holidays Ltd, organises walking and mountaineering holidays in Britain and on the Continent: details from Box 43, Welwyn Garden City, Herts. 0707 331133.

St John Ambulance Consists of two branches: the Association and the Brigade. The Association organises first-aid training courses in industry, schools and for the general public; the Brigade is a body of volunteer first-aiders providing cover at public events of all kinds, and undertaking nursing and welfare duties in the community. St John Cadets, aged 10–18, can become involved in a wide variety of activities, not only learning first aid but taking part in outdoor pursuits and developing communication and creative skills. Badgers are boys and girls aged 6–10 who belong to the junior section of St John Ambulance. They take part in the 'Badger Course in Absolutely Everything', an extensive training scheme which is fun as well as being directed towards achievement, 1 Grosvenor Crescent, London, SW1X 7EF. 071-235 5231.

The Scout Association Training for Cub Scouts (boys and girls, 8–10½), Scouts (boys and girls, 10½–15½), Venture Scouts (young men and women, 15½–20). Beaver Colonies (boys and girls 6–8) in many places. Outdoor Movement (e.g. camping, hiking, exploring, sailing, climbing, swimming). Community service also important (conservation, help for the needy including Third World projects, etc.). Progress Awards given for achievement. Headquarters: Baden-Powell House, Queen's Gate, London, SW7 5JS.

Sea Cadet Corps A voluntary youth organisation for boys and girls between 12 and 18. Many Units have junior sections for ages 10–12. Naval uniforms are provided. Through discipline, drill and a wide range of boating, offshore and open-air activities, the Cadets develop qualities of self-reliance, self-discipline, leadership and responsible citizenship. Those seeking careers at sea are given every encouragement, but this is not a pre-service organisation, and no cadet is obliged to join the armed forces or Merchant Navy. Headquarters: 202 Lambeth Rd., London, SE1 7JF. 071-928 8978

White Hall Centre Outdoor education courses for schools and individuals. Activities include rock climbing, hillcraft, camping, caving, canoeing, mountain-biking, problem-solving and initiative exercises. Leader-training courses in rock-climbing, mountain-walking, canoeing and caving. Duke of Edinburgh Award Expedition training. Britain's first outdoor education centre open throughout the year. Details from the Principal, White Hall Centre, Long Hill, Buxton, Derbyshire SK17 6SX. Tel: (0298) 23260 Fax: (0298) 25945.

The Woodcraft Folk This is a national voluntary youth organisation for boys and girls, its groups catering for children from six years old. It has a co-operative outlook—encouraging children to learn the value of co-operation, rather than competition, through games, play and adventure activities. Exchange visits are arranged with similar children's organisations from all over Europe and, increasingly, further afield. Activities include games, craftwork, drama, folk singing and dancing, and an educational programme based on badge work. Apply: National Office, 13 Ritherdon Road, London, SW17 8QE. Tel: 081 672 6031.

YMCA A world-wide organisation represented in nearly 100 countries with some 26 million people, mainly young, men and women, participating in a wide variety of programmes guided by trained leaders. There are some 250 centres in England. Headquarters: 640, Forest Road, London, E17 3DZ. 01-520 5599.

Young Explorers' Trust (The Association of British Youth Exploration Societies) Membership is open to groups and societies, however small, setting out to organise expeditions involving a significant element of exploration and discovery. The Trust offers an information and advice service through a national and regional network. A newsletter is published regularly. Overseas expeditions may apply by December or May for the Trust's approval. Grants are made annually to expeditions that reach the appropriate standard of organisation, safety and field tasks. The Jim Bishop Fund gives grant-aid in February to under-19s engaged in adventurous activities. There is a New Opportunities Panel that aims to help disadvantaged young people; it founds mobile units, MOBEX, particularly to help groups in inner city areas, the unemployed and the handicapped. Details from the Young Explorers' Trust at the Royal Geographical Society, 1, Kensington Gore, London, SW7 2AR or direct from the Secretary (0623 861027).

Young Ornithologists' Club Run by the Royal Society for the Protection of Birds for boys and girls interested in birds and wildlife. Runs holidays, local members' groups, activity days, projects and competitions. Publishes its bi-monthly colour magazine *Bird Life* and a newsletter for teenagers. Further details from Youth Unit, The Lodge, Sandy, Beds. SG19 2DL. 0767 680551.

Youth Hostels Associations These organisations have the object of helping young people to explore the countryside. In Britain and Ireland alone they maintain about 400 hostels where members are provided with beds and meals at low rates. A number of

Adventure Holidays are arranged as introductions to new activities such as pony trekking, sailing, skin-diving, etc. Subscription (England and Wales): under 18, £3 a year, 18 and over, £9. Headquarters: *England and Wales*, Trevelyan House, 8 St Stephens Hill, St Albans, Herts, AL1 2DY. *Scotland*, 7 Glebe Crescent, Stirling. *Northern Ireland*, 56 Bradbury Place, Belfast.

Altogether in the 58 countries where the Youth Hostel movement flourishes there are over 5,300 hostels.

A British membership card (with photograph) is accepted in all countries affiliated to the International Youth Hostel Federation. The YHA's Adventure Shop at 14 Southampton Street, London, WC2E 7HY, sells rucksacks, sleeping bags, tents, camping equipment, climbing kit, maps and guides.

YWCA of Great Britain The YWCA is committed to encourage and promote women in decision-making and leadership. It offers women and young people opportunities for challenge and adventure, to learn new skills and, through the development of self-esteem, the self-confidence to help others. It also houses some 10,000 people each year. National headquarters: Clarendon House, 52 Cornmarket Street, Oxford, OX1 3EJ. 0865 726110.

The Morse Code

The Morse code consists of groups of dots and dashes, each group representing a letter or number. You can communicate in Morse by flashing a light, by sound or by using a flag. The dots should

A for	Alfa	·—	N for	November	—·
B	Bravo	—···	O	Oscar	———
C	Charlie	—·—·	P	Papa	·——·
D	Delta	—··	Q	Quebec	——·—
E	Echo	·	R	Romeo	·—·
F	Foxtrot	··—·	S	Sierra	···
G	Golf	——·	T	Tango	—
H	Hotel	····	U	Uniform	··—
I	India	··	V	Victor	···—
J	Juliet	·———	W	Whiskey	·——
K	Kilo	—·—	X	X-Ray	—··—
L	Lima	·—··	Y	Yankee	—·——
M	Mike	——	Z	Zulu	——··

Numerals

1	· — — — —	6	— · · · ·
2	· · — — —	7	— — · · ·
3	· · · — —	8	— — — · ·
4	· · · · —	9	— — — — ·
5	· · · · ·	10	— — — — —

Full stop (AAA) · — · — · —
Apostrophe · — — — — ·
Oblique stroke — · · — ·
Brackets (KK) — · — — · —
Short break · · · ·
Beginning (CT) — · — · —
Hyphen — · · · · —
Inverted commas (RR) · — · · — ·
Underline (UK) · · — — · —
Question (IMI) · · — — · ·
Long break (BT) — · · · —
Ending (AR) · — · — ·
Finish of transmission for indefinite period (VA) · · · — · —

be made as short as possible, and the dashes should be three times as long as the dots. **The Morse alphabet** is used to avoid confusion between letters with similar sounds.

Semaphore

It is immensely important in semaphore signalling that the angles should be clear and the arm and the wrist in a straight line. To ensure this, always press the first finger along the stick of the flag. Choose a position where you can be easily seen and a background that is as far away as possible—the sky being obviously the best.

Rules for Semaphoring

At the end of each word you should drop the arms straight down in front of you—this is known as the 'ready' position—

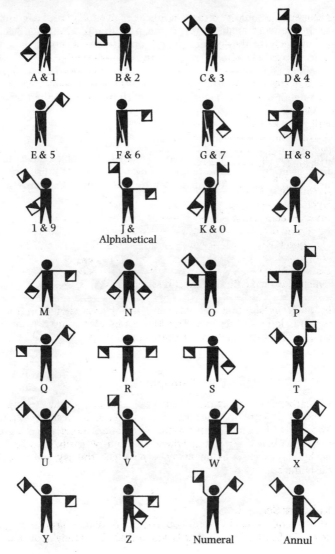

and pause. Should you make a mistake, give the 'annul' sign and begin the word again. ('Annul' means 'rub out', 'cancel'.) Before a number give the 'numeral' sign, and if you are going back to letters give the 'alphabet' sign before you do so.

When you are reading a message, acknowledge each word by making the letter 'A' (the 'general answer' sign). If you are uncertain about a word, make no sign, and the sender will then repeat the word.

The Compass

The magnetic compass is an instrument that enables navigators to steer in any direction required, and also shows the direction of any visible object. It is divided into points, quarter points and degrees.

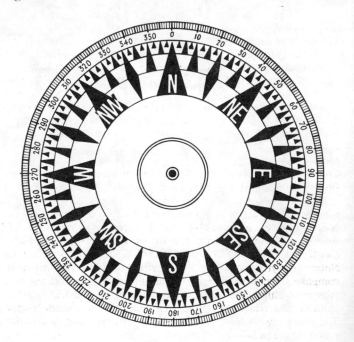

The Points

The compass circle is divided into thirty-two named points. The four main (or cardinal points, N., E., S. and W.), divide the card into four quadrants or quarters. Half-way between the cardinal points are the quadrantal points, N.E., S.E., S.W. and N.W. Half-way again between the cardinal and quadrantal points are the intermediate (three-letter) points, which are named from the cardinal and quadrantal points between which they lie, the cardinal points being named first; N.N.E., E.N.E., E.S.E., S.S.E., S.S.W., W.S.W., W.N.W., N.N.W. Between all these points are sixteen others (called 'by' points) which take their names from the nearest cardinal and quadrantal points.

For example, in the first quadrant (between N. and E.) the points are:

The cardinal	N.
The by-point next to it	N. by E.
The three-letter point half-way between N. and E.	N.N.E.
The by-point next to the half cardinal	N.E. by N.
The half cardinal	N.E.
The by-point	N.E. by E.
The three-letter point between E. and N. E.	E.N.E.
The by-point	E. by N.
The cardinal point	E.

Degrees

The compass circle is also divided into degrees; it is in degrees (by what is called the **Quadrantal Notation**) that a course is usually given and steered. The card is divided into 360°, but is marked 0° at North and South and 90° at East and West. So N.E. would be given as N. 45° E. Gyro compass cards are marked right round from north through 90° (East), 180° (South), 270° (West) and 360° (North). This is called **Circular Notation**. Gyro compasses are carried in addition to magnetic compasses by most warships and many large merchant and passenger ships. The gyro, controlled by the earth's rotation, consists of a wheel turned at great speed by an electric motor. The points, with their equivalents in circular and quadrantal notation, are as follows.

Point	Circular	Quadrantal	Point	Circular	Quadrantal
N.	0	N.	N.E. by E.	56¼	N. 56¼ E.
N. by E.	11¼	N. 11¼ E.	E.N.E.	67½	N. 67½ E.
N.N.E.	22½	N. 22½ E.	E. by N.	78¾	N. 78¾ E.
N.E. by N.	33¾	N. 33¾ E.	E.	90	E.
N.E.	45	N. 45 E.	E. by S.	101¼	S. 78¾ E.
E.S.E.	112½	S. 67½ E.	S.W. by W.	236¼	S. 56¼ W.
S.E. by E.	123¾	S. 56¼ E.	W.S.W.	247½	S. 67½ W.
S.E.	135	S. 45 E.	W. by S.	258¾	S. 78¾ W.
S.E. by S.	146¼	S. 33¾ E.	W.	270	W.
S.S.E.	157½	S. 22½ E.	W. by N.	281¼	N. 78¾ W.
S. by E.	168¾	S. 11¼ E.	W.N.W.	292½	N. 67½ W.
S.	180	S.	N.W. by W.	303¾	N. 56¼ W.
S. by W.	191¼	S. 11¼ W.	N.W.	315	N. 45 W.
S.S.W.	202½	S. 22½ W.	N.W. by N.	326¼	N. 33¾ W.
S.W. by S.	213¾	S. 33¾ W.	N.N.W.	337½	N. 22½ W.
S.W.	225	S. 45 W.	N. by W.	348¾	N. 11¼ W.

Knots

The **Reef Knot** is both the firmest of knots and the quickest to untie. It is used for tying two ropes together.

The **Sheet Bend** is the best knot for tying together ropes of differing thickness. If the end is passed round again the knot becomes a **Double Sheet Bend**, which will neither stick nor jerk undone.

The **Clove Hitch** (an easy knot to make, as the picture shows) is used to make one rope fast to a larger one. When fastened to a pole or another rope it will neither slip up nor down.

The **Bowline** (used at sea for making a loop on a rope's end) makes a fixed loop that will never slip after the first grip. It can be safely used for making a halter for leading an animal.

The **Sheepshank** is used for temporarily shortening a rope.

The **Figure of Eight** is used at sea to prevent a rope unreeving through a block.

The **Half-hitch** is used to tie ropes to poles.

The **Round Turn and Two Half-hitches** is used for securing a rope to a ring or a post.

The **Timber Hitch** is used for dragging timber along the ground.

The **Wall Knot** is a way of whipping, or finishing off, a rope

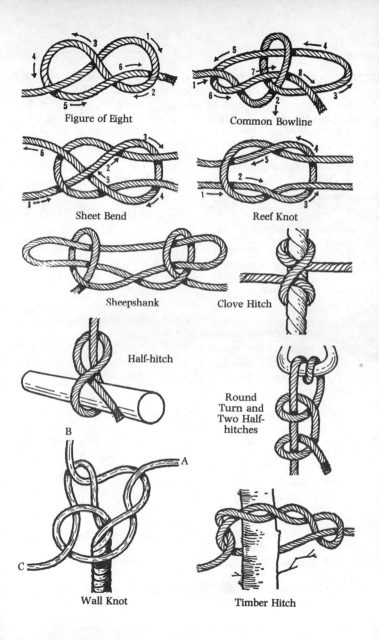

Figure of Eight

Common Bowline

Sheet Bend

Reef Knot

Sheepshank

Clove Hitch

Half-hitch

Round Turn and Two Half-hitches

Wall Knot

Timber Hitch

that is unravelling. Take strand A and loop it back across the front of the rope; then take strand B and loop it over the end of strand A; finally looping strand C over the end of strand B and tucking its end into the loop formed by strand A. Finish by working the knot tight.

THE ARMED SERVICES, THE POLICE AND FIRE BRIGADES

THE ARMED SERVICES

The present integrated Ministry of Defence was created on April 1, 1964. The head of the Ministry is the Secretary of State for Defence, who is also chairman of the Defence Council—the permanent committee of military and civilian chiefs who determine defence policy. He is assisted by a Minister of State and Under Secretary of State for the Armed Forces; and a Minister of State and Under Secretary of State for Defence Procurement.

THE ROYAL NAVY [1]

There is (since 1981) no single Minister responsible for the Royal Navy (senior of the three Armed Services). Before the creation of the unified Ministry of Defence, the title of the department head was First Lord of the Admiralty. The senior naval member of the Navy Board is the Chief of Naval Staff and First Sea Lord.

How the Navy is Organised

Outside the Ministry of Defence, the Navy is under the command of two Commanders-in-Chief: Commander-in-Chief Fleet, who is responsible for all the Navy's ships, and Commander-in-Chief Naval Home Command, who is responsible for all the Navy's shore establishments, units ashore and the training of officers and ratings.

Ships and some submarines are based at three Base Ports, Portsmouth and Plymouth in England and Rosyth in Scotland. The fleet is divided into two flotillas commanded by admirals; submarines are commanded by Flag Officer Submarines: all are responsible to the Commander-in-Chief Fleet. The Dockyard at Chatham has been closed and the appointment FO Medway and Chatham was phased out by the end of 1982.

Under Commander-in-Chief Naval Home Command, establishments in the country are divided into regions which are commanded by admirals located at the three Base Ports and known as Flag Officers Portsmouth, Plymouth, and Scotland and Northern Ireland (Rosyth).

[1] For an account of naval vessels, see the section on *Ships*.

The administration and training of the Fleet Air Arm come under the command of the Flag Officer, Naval Air Command.

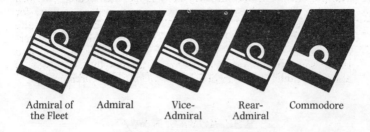

| Admiral of the Fleet | Admiral | Vice-Admiral | Rear-Admiral | Commodore |

| Captain | Commander | Lieut-Commander | Lieutenant | Sub-Lieutenant |

The **Corps of Royal Marines** was founded in 1664 to serve on sea and land. Today they provide three commando units. Apart from serving in ships, the Marines are also drawn upon for the crews of landing craft and for other amphibious operations (that is, those carried out partly on sea and partly on land).

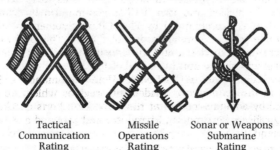

Tactical Communication Rating   Missile Operations Rating   Sonar or Weapons Submarine Rating

Engineering
Mechanic

Air Engineering Mechanic
M (Mechanical), R (Radio/Radar)
or WL (Weapons Electrical)

Petty Officer   Leading Rating

THE ARMY

The man responsible for the detailed running of the Army is the
Minister of State for the Armed Forces, a Member of Parliament. He
is responsible to the Secretary of State for Defence. The Minister of
State controls the Army through the Army Board of the Defence
Council and obtains expert military advice from the Chief of the
General Staff (CGS), the senior military member of the Board.

Principal Branches of the Army

The **Royal Armoured Corps** (RAC), formed in 1939 by amalgamating the Cavalry and the Royal Tank Corps, man tanks and
armoured cars.

The **Royal Artillery** (RA) (the 'Gunners') man both guns and
missiles in Field and Air Defence roles and locating devices.

The **Royal Engineers** (RE) (called the 'Sappers' from the days
when they dug 'saps'—trenches or mines that enabled troops to
advance towards the enemy). In general, their job is to help the

Army to move. They make paths through minefields, provide means of crossing obstacles and carry out any necessary demolition and lay minefields in a withdrawal. They produce maps for the Army and the RAF and operate the Army Postal Service.

The **Royal Corps of Signals** (R. Signals) is responsible for the Army's communications.

The **Infantry** is the fighting core of the Army and includes the Foot Guards, Infantry of the Line, the Brigade of Gurkhas, the Parachute Regiment and the Special Air Service Regiment.

The **Army Air Corps** (AAC) operates the Army's helicopters and aircraft.

The **Royal Corps of Transport** (RCT) replaced the Royal Army Service Corps in 1965.

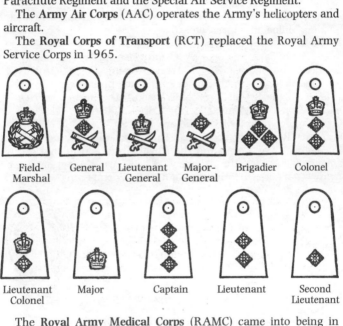

Field-Marshal   General   Lieutenant General   Major-General   Brigadier   Colonel

Lieutenant Colonel   Major   Captain   Lieutenant   Second Lieutenant

The **Royal Army Medical Corps** (RAMC) came into being in 1857, after the Crimean War, as the Army Hospital Corps. Took its present name in 1898.

The **Royal Army Ordnance Corps** (RAOC) is responsible for providing the Army with ammunition, food, equipment and stores. Also provides clerical staff and mobile bath and laundry units on active service.

The **Royal Electrical and Mechanical Engineers** (REME) was

formed in 1942 to meet the needs of mechanised warfare.
Maintains tanks, vehicles, guns, radar, radios, instruments, etc.

The **Intelligence Corps** (Int. Corps) is a small branch consisting
of men trained to collect and evaluate intelligence (that is, largely
information about an enemy or possible enemy).

The **Corps of Royal Military Police** (RMP), the 'Red Caps'.

The **Royal Army Pay Corps** (RAPC).

The **Royal Army Veterinary Corps** (RAVC) looks after the
Army's horses and dogs.

The **Royal Pioneer Corps** (RPC) provides labour for road-
building, unloading stores, etc.

The **Royal Army Educational Corps** (RAEC).

The **Army Catering Corps** (ACC), provides the Army's cooks.

Queen Alexandra's Royal Army Nursing Corps (QARANC)
provides male and female nurses for military hospitals.

In 1993 the Royal Corps of Transport, the Royal Army Ordnance Corps, the Army Catering Corps and the Royal Pioneer
Corps amalgamated with Postal and Courier Services of the RE to
form the Royal Logistic Corps. The Royal Military Police, the
Royal Army Pay Corps and the Royal Army Educational Corps
amalgamated with the Women's Royal Army Corps and the
Army Legal Corps to form the Adjutants' General Corps.

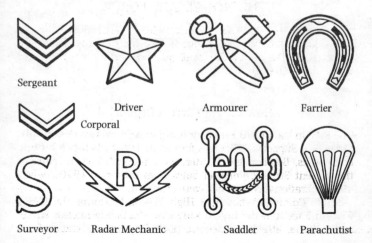

Sergeant

Driver   Armourer   Farrier

Corporal

Surveyor   Radar Mechanic   Saddler   Parachutist

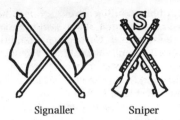

Signaller   Sniper

How the Army is Divided

The standard formation in the modern Army is the division. In wartime the divisions are grouped to form Corps (two divisions or more), armies (two Corps or more) and army groups (two armies or more).

The fighting infantry unit of the Army is the battalion. Nearly 800 strong, it is divided into a Headquarters, Headquarters' Company, Fire Support Company and three Rifle Companies. It is commanded by a Lieutenant-Colonel.

THE ROYAL AIR FORCE

The Secretary of State for Defence, who is Chairman of the Air Force Board of the Defence Council, has ministerial responsibility for the RAF. The most senior RAF member of the Air Force Board is the Chief of the Air Staff.

How the Air Force is Organised

The RAF in the United Kingdom is organised into two Commands: Strike and Support. Strike was formed in 1968 when two historic commands, Bomber and Fighter, were merged. The structure of the present Strike Command dates from the early 1970s, when other operational commands were absorbed.

Strike Command, based at High Wycombe, forms the RAF's front-line teeth in the United Kingdom—including nuclear strike, conventional attack, air defence (including fighters and surface-to-air missiles), airborne early warning, strategic and tactical transport, helicopters, air-to-air refuelling, anti-submarine warfare and air support for the Army in the field. The Command is integrated within NATO, and is responsible for the UK Air Defence Region. Other roles include search and rescue and regular patrolling of the North Sea oil and gas rigs.

Support Command, based at RAF Brampton, in Cambridgeshire has responsibility for engineering and spares support of front-line units. It also has the job of training officers and airmen to front-line standards. The Central Flying School currently at RAF Leeming trains all flying instructors for the RAF, Royal Navy and Army Air Corps, as well as those of other air forces. It also controls the internationally famous RAF aerobatic team—the Red Arrows.

The RAF Staff College and Headquarters Command and Staff Training are located at Bracknell; and at the Second World War fighter base at Biggin Hill, the Officer and Aircrew Selection Centre assesses all candidates for cadetships, scholarships, commissions and aircrew service. In wartime, Support Command would back the operational commands by providing reinforcement of flying and ground personnel.

RAF Germany

Most of RAF Germany's effort goes into providing conventional ground attack, nuclear strike and air defence in support of any NATO land operations.

The RAF Regiment

With RAF Police and Fire Service, the RAF Regiment forms the RAF Security Branch. It protects airfields against ground intruders and low-level air attack, and trains RAF personnel in ground defence. Formed into a number of mobile squadrons, it is armed with Rapier missiles and armoured vehicles of the Scorpion Range.

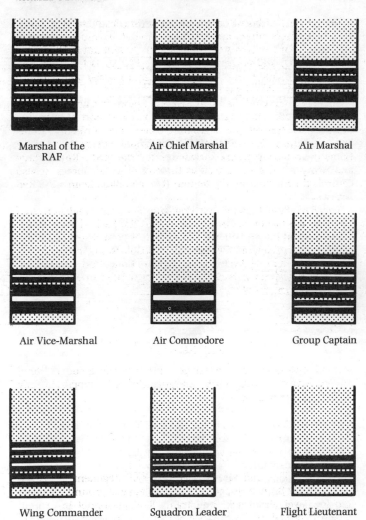

Marshal of the RAF

Air Chief Marshal

Air Marshal

Air Vice-Marshal

Air Commodore

Group Captain

Wing Commander

Squadron Leader

Flight Lieutenant

These are cuff badges worn with No. 1 dress (formal) and mess kit.
Shoulder badges are worn with working dress.

The Women's Royal Air Force

Today some 500 officers and 4,600 airwomen serve in most general branches and trade groups. A few women serve in the air loadmaster category of the General Duties (GD) Flying Branch.

Women enjoy equal rights in pay and employment and compete on equal terms with men for promotion, appointments and training courses.

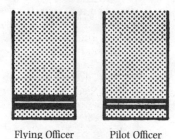

Flying Officer   Pilot Officer

Pilot's Wings

THE POLICE

There are 52 police forces in the UK; 43 of them are in England and Wales and are administered by the Home Office. In Scotland there are eight police forces administered by the Scottish Home and Health Department. In Northern Ireland the Royal Ulster Constabulary is administered by the Northern Ireland Office.

The report of an inquiry to be issued in mid-1993 is likely to suggest the number of police forces in England and Wales should be cut to 20 or 25. In anticipation of the report, the number of police areas in London is likely to be reduced from eight to five: each area being headed by a chief constable.

The main ranks are constable, sergeant, inspector and superin-
tendent. The head of the Metropolitan Police is called the
Commissioner; the head of a provincial force is called the Chief
Constable.

Branches of the Police

The CID All police forces have a Criminal Investigation Department. No officer can be recruited to this section until he has
served as an ordinary uniformed constable. Ranks in the CID
are the same as those in the uniformed police: e.g. detective-
constable, detective-sergeant and so on.

In London, where one in every eight policemen belongs to
this branch, the CID is controlled by an Assistant Commissioner,
with the aid of three Deputy Assistant Commissioners. More
than half of the staff of the CID are attached to police stations.
The headquarters staff includes Central Office (which deals with
national and international crimes), the Criminal Record Office
and Fingerprint Bureau, the Special Branch (which in wartime
works with the forces in counter-espionage, and is also responsible for protecting important public persons), the Flying
Squad and the Fraud Squad (whose job is to detect financial
swindles).

The River Police A few forces (e.g. London, Glasgow) have sections of River Police, whose business is to prevent and detect
stealing from craft on the river and from waterside premises, to
deal with boats found adrift, to help vessels in difficulty, to come
to the aid of drowning persons and to retrieve dead bodies, to
prevent and detect smuggling and to prevent the pollution of
the river.

The Thames Division in London has three river stations—at
Wapping, Waterloo Pier and Shepperton.

The Mounted Police These are used mainly for heading proces-
sions and controlling crowds.

Special Constables These are part-time unpaid men and women
who are employed mainly to help in controlling crowds on
special occasions. They have the same powers as full-time
constables.

FIRE BRIGADES

During the Second World War the 1,059 fire brigades in England and Wales were amalgamated into a single National Fire Service, and after the war an Act of Parliament created 125 brigades, each administered by the local authority. At the same time the 200 Scottish brigades were regrouped into eleven brigades. The Local Government Act of 1972 made the new county councils responsible for the fire services. In Scotland, the Local Government (Scotland) Act, 1973, which came into effect in 1975, gave responsibility to the nine regions. As a result of the Local Government Act of 1985, which came into force in 1986, the fire services in London and the former six Metropolitan counties are run by joint authorities composed of borough and district councillors.

In big cities the brigades are manned by full-time firemen; elsewhere some or all of the crews are part-timers.

The uniform of the British fireman is of dark-blue serge or cloth, with waterproof leggings and rubber or leather boots. The brass helmet of earlier times has given place to helmets made of leather or leather and rubber, which give much better protection against electric shock.

THE LAW

WHAT IS LAW?

The simplest explanation of what law is is to say that it is a body of rules for the regulation of human relationships, in personal and domestic, commercial, industrial and other contexts, which are enforceable by public authority. These rules differ from the rules of manners and morals in that they are made binding and enforceable by the authority of the state, that is, the whole community politically organised. But in subject-matter they frequently coincide with rules of religion or morality, e.g. Thou shalt not steal, or rules of manners or expediency.

The rules take many different forms. Some state what one *may do*, and the consequences of that; thus, if you make a will in proper form, stating what is to happen to your property after your death, the law will ensure that that happens. But you may choose not to make a will; in that case rules of law provide what is to happen to your property. Other rules state what you *must do*, such as pay tax, or debts, and the consequences if you do not. Others again state what you *must not do*, such as commit theft or drive a car recklessly, and what happens to you if you do any of these things.

Law is necessary in any civilised society to avoid or at least minimise conflicts and disputes, to maintain order in society and to ensure that doubtful or disputed claims can be resolved in an orderly way. If there were no system of law, or if it were commonly disregarded, there would be anarchy. Disputes would be settled by force and crime would be unchecked.

Generally speaking, each country in the world, and sometimes distinct parts, states or provinces in a country, have their distinct systems of rules of law. Thus in the United Kingdom there are distinct systems of law in England and Wales, in Scotland and in Northern Ireland. The Isle of Man and the Channel Islands also have distinct systems. The rules of French law, German law and of other countries are different again. Now that the United

Kingdom is a member of the European Communities the system of rules of law of the European Communities is part of the law of the UK and of all of the other (at present twelve) countries which are members. Roughly speaking the laws of England and Wales, Northern Ireland and most English-speaking parts of the Commonwealth and of countries originally settled from Britain, such as the USA, have a distinct family similarity. Again the laws of Scotland, South Africa, Quebec and most European countries have a family similarity, because they originated in the system of law developed in the city of Rome and the Roman Empire. It is noteworthy that the laws of England and of Scotland differ in many respects very substantially. The laws of the CIS and countries of eastern Europe also have a family similarity. While these are the three main families of legal systems, there are a number which do not belong to any of these families. In some countries Islamic law, based on the Koran, is important. The way in which law is made, the actual rules of law, and the way disputes are decided accordingly differs between countries and sometimes within a country, as between England and Scotland or Ontario and Quebec.

The branches of law

The whole body of rules of law of Britain forms a huge mass and for convenience of discovery, study and understanding they are usually grouped under a number of headings, each comprising the rules dealing with particular subjects. The main headings are: *Constitutional law*, dealing with the government of the country, the relations between the government and citizens and the public rights and duties of citizens; *Administrative law*, dealing with the operation of public administration and local government, town planning, new roads, housing and the like; *Social security*, dealing with entitlement to sickness benefit, unemployment benefit and similar payments; *Taxation*, concerned with compulsory payments by persons to the State to defray public expenditure, such as on defence; *Criminal law*, dealing with the kinds of conduct which are treated as punishable, such as murder, theft, reckless driving; *Family law*, concerned with marriage, divorce and children; *Contract*, dealing with agreements and bargains, such as to buy and sell, lease, transport, employ and so on; *Tort* (or, in Scotland, *delict*), concerned with liability for harm done by another, as by injuring in a road accident; *Property*, dealing with rights in land, goods and other things of value; *Trusts*, concerned with persons holding property on behalf of and for others; *Succession*, dealing with wills and the transfer of property when a person dies to those entitled to it. Other branches are sometimes distinguished. These are not distinct branches of law but collections of the rules which are of importance to particular groups of people and are becoming increasingly voluminous and complicated. Thus *Mercantile or commercial law* is not, in Britain, as it is in some countries, a distinct branch of law but a name for various sets of rules which are particularly important for persons and bodies engaged in business and trading, such as those regulating companies, financial institutions, some kinds of contracts, such as transport and insurance, and bankruptcy. *Consumer law* is a name for the increasing sets of rules designed to protect individuals as consumers, buyers or users of goods or services. *Industrial or employment law* is a name for those rules centred on the contract of employment and the powers and functions of trade unions. There are also important bodies of rules about *Civil and Criminal procedure*, or the steps and stages of actions and prosecutions in court, and *evidence*, dealing with how facts in dispute can be proved.

The making of law in Britain

Rules of law are made in several different ways.

(1) There are the rules contained in the Treaties establishing the European Communities, and in regulations, directives and decisions made by the Council and the Commission of the European Communities. These mostly relate to commercial matters and apply in all the countries which are members of the Communities. Some of these affect only the government and require it to act in accordance with the regulations and directives but some have direct effect on individuals in Britain and entitle them to complain to British courts of infringements of rights conferred by EC law.

(2) Rules are also made by the UK Parliament by passing *Acts of Parliament* or *Statutes*. Proposals are put before Parliament by the Cabinet or by individual MPs in the form of Bills. Bills are discussed and debated and, if passed by each House of Parliament, they are given Royal Assent by the Queen and become Acts. This has been happening for hundreds of years. Every year about 100 Acts are passed in this way; some make new law, some change the existing law in some way, some abolish old law.

(3) Parliament frequently authorises Ministers to make rules on matters of detail to give full effect to Acts of Parliament. The rules they make are called *Statutory Instruments*.

(4) In United Kingdom courts it has become accepted that the basic principle underlying a decision of one of the superior courts can lay down a rule regulating future disputes of the same kind. Many such decisions accordingly make new law just as much as Acts of Parliament do. Thus in 1932 the House of Lords decided that if a person was made ill by a poisonous thing in a bottled drink bought for her, the manufacturer of the drink was liable to pay damages (compensation) to her. This had not previously been decided, so that the decision really made new law, and other courts have applied the same rule in similar cases ever since then. Because of this practice the reports of decided cases going back many years have frequently to be examined to see if a court has previously given a ruling which determines a dispute today. Such a previous ruling is called a *precedent*. This kind of law is called *case-law*, and a great deal of law in the UK has been developed by judges in cases.

(5) In early times custom was an important source of law. It is not now very important and if a judge cannot find guidance from any of the foregoing kinds of law he may refer to some very authoritative textbooks, or the rule developed in another country with a similar social and legal system, e.g. USA, or in the last resort do what seems to him right and just.

Deciding legal disputes

Not infrequently people have disputes as to what the law requires them to do in the circumstances. Thus a car knocks down and injures a pedestrian; is the pedestrian entitled to damages for his injuries from the driver? Or was it the pedestrian's own fault? Or again: one man stabs another after an argument. Is that a criminal assault justifying punishment? Or did he act in self-defence? Frequently it is uncertain or disputed what rule of law applies, and what it requires. Frequently the facts are in dispute. How fast was the car going? Were the street lights lit? Did the driver give any warning that he was going to stop? And so on. To decide disputes of various kinds there is a system of courts, staffed by judges. There are separate sets of courts for England and Wales, for Scotland and for Northern Ireland, and different courts for different purposes, dealing with different topics and branches of the law. In particular, there are different courts for civil, criminal and some other kinds of disputes.

The European Court

The *Court of Justice of the European Communities* at Luxembourg consisting of 13 judges drawn from all 12 member-states decides questions of alleged contraventions of the Treaties establishing the European Communities by member-states, companies or individuals. The Treaties and rules made to implement them are applicable in all the member-states. These mostly concern commercial problems. Courts in all the member-states may, and in some cases must, refer to the European Court cases raising a problem of Community law for guidance on the meaning of the Community rules involved and its rulings must be accepted and applied. There is also now a *Court of First Instance* which deals with some cases of lesser importance.

The courts of England and Wales

The highest civil court, which hears appeals from all the parts of the United Kingdom, is the House of Lords which, though in theory it is the same body of peers as comprises one of the Houses of Parliament, is for this purpose composed of a number, usually five, out of eleven Lords of Appeal in Ordinary, very experienced lawyers who have been given peerages to enable them to sit in the House and hear appeals.

Below this is the *Court of Appeal, Civil Division*, which consists of the Master of the Rolls and Lords Justices of Appeal. They sit in groups of two or three and hear appeals from the High Court and County Courts.

The High Court of Justice consists of the Lord Chief Justice of England and a large body of judges, formally called Mr Justice Smith or Mrs Justice Brown. They are grouped in three Divisions, the *Queen's Bench Division*, dealing with contracts, torts and commercial disputes, the *Chancery Division*, dealing with wills and trusts, mortgages, companies and bankruptcy, and the *Family* (formerly Probate, Divorce and Admiralty) *Division*, dealing with family law matters. The judges sit singly, and only very occasionally with a jury. They may sit anywhere in England and Wales, but most of the sittings are at the Royal Courts of Justice in The Strand, London.

The lower English civil court is the County Court. County Courts are held by circuit judges regularly in all the larger towns throughout England and Wales. The procedure is simpler and quicker than in the High Court but in some cases they can deal only with claims not exceeding fixed sums.

In criminal cases the highest court is again the *House of Lords*. Below it is the *Court of Appeal, Criminal Division*, consisting of the Lord Chief Justice, the Lords Justices of Appeal and the Judges of the Queen's Bench Division, which hears appeals only. Serious criminal cases are tried in the *Crown Court*, which may sit anywhere in England and Wales. The Crown Court consists of a judge of the Queen's Bench Division, or a circuit judge, or a Recorder (who is a lawyer sitting sometimes as a judge), in each case with a jury of 12. Cases are allocated according to seriousness. In London the *Central Criminal Court* (the Old Bailey) is staffed by a number of permanent judges. Sittings of Crown Courts are held regularly in the chief towns of England and Wales. These have replaced the centuries-old system of Assizes. The great majority of criminal cases are heard summarily, i.e. without a jury, by *magistrates' courts*, consisting of a stipendiary magistrate i.e. a paid, qualified lawyer, or of three or more justices of the peace who are unpaid, have no training in law, and sit part-time. They are, however, advised by a legally qualified clerk. In serious cases they act as examining justices and decide whether there is a case justifying trial by jury in the Crown Court.

In 1985 a Crown Prosecution Service for England and Wales was established, headed by the Director of Public Prosecutions under the supervision of the Attorney-General, assisted by Chief Crown Prosecutors in areas. The Director and his staff have taken over the conduct of nearly all criminal prosecutions instituted on behalf of a police force by a member of that force or by an ordinary citizen. The staff advise the police and appear for the prosecution in appeals to superior criminal courts.

There are also some *Courts of Special Jurisdiction* which deal only with disputes of particular kinds. Among these are the Employment Appeal Tribunal, consisting of a judge and two laymen, which hears appeals from industrial tribunals, the Lands Tribunal, concerned with compulsory acquisition of land, the Transport Tribunal, the Restrictive Practices Court, and several more. Most of these are composed partly of lawyers, partly of laymen ex-

perienced in the particular subject. Coroner's courts seek to determine the cause of death, where a death has taken place suddenly
or in suspicious circumstances.

Lastly there is a great complex of tribunals, or bodies, usually of
three, of whom frequently only the chairman need have legal
training. Among these are *industrial tribunals* which hear claims
of unfair dismissal from work, and similar claims, *rent tribunals*,
social security tribunals and many more.

The courts of Scotland

The highest civil court is again the House of Lords. Below it is the
Court of Session, Inner House, comprising two Divisions, the First
and the Second Division, presided over respectively by the Lord
President of the Court of Session and the Lord Justice-Clerk of
Scotland, each sitting with two or three other judges. In Scotland
all the judges of the Court of Session have the courtesy title of
Lord. The two Divisions deal mostly with appeals from the Outer
House and the Sheriff Courts. The *Court of Session, Outer House*,
comprises the remaining judges of the Court of Session sitting
singly, occasionally with a jury, trying civil cases at first instance.
The Court of Session sits only in Edinburgh.

The lower Scottish civil court is the *Sheriff Court*. There are 6
sheriffdoms, each having a Sheriff Principal and a number of
Sheriffs, all qualified lawyers. They sit singly in all the major towns
and may hear practically any kind of civil claim. Appeal lies from
a Sheriff to the Sheriff Principal and then to the Court of Session,
Inner House, or direct to the Inner House.

In criminal cases no appeal lies from Scotland to the House of
Lords. The highest criminal court is the *High Court of Justiciary*,
consisting of the same persons as are judges of the Court of Session, but under the titles of Lord Justice-General of Scotland, Lord
Justice-Clerk of Scotland and Lords Commissioners of Justiciary. It
sits, normally in benches of three, to hear appeals, and individual
Lords Commissioners sit with juries of 15 in Edinburgh and other
major towns to try cases of serious crime.

The Sheriff Court also tries criminal cases. A Sheriff-Principal
or Sheriff with a jury tries cases of medium seriousness and a
Sheriff-Principal or Sheriff sitting alone tries summarily lesser
offences, such as traffic offences.

The District Court comprises a stipendiary magistrate or one or more Justices of the Peace and deals with petty offences. In Scotland the JPs are much less important than in England and Wales.

A notable feature of the Scottish system is that all prosecution in criminal cases is in the High Court by the Lord Advocate and his Deputes and in the sheriff court by the Procurator-fiscal of the Sheriffdom and his deputes. There is, that is, a system of public prosecution. The police never prosecute in Scotland.

Scotland has also a variety of courts of special jurisdiction, such as the Scottish Land Court, dealing with agricultural disputes, the Lands Valuation Appeal Court, the Lands Tribunal for Scotland and others. Some courts, such as the Employment Appeal Tribunal, sit also in Scotland. Similarly, it has a range of tribunals generally similar to those in England. There are, however, no Coroner's Courts.

The courts of Northern Ireland
In Northern Ireland the names and powers of the different courts generally follow the English model but there are some variations.

Lawyers
Because law and procedure differ from one country to another, even between the different countries of the UK, lawyers learn and practise the law of a particular country only. In each of the countries of the UK the distinction is drawn between barristers (called advocates in Scotland) and solicitors. Barristers are persons who have been 'called to the Bar' by one of the four Inns of Court in London or by the Inn of Court of Northern Ireland; advocates have been called by the Faculty of Advocates in Scotland. Barristers or advocates are sometimes called 'counsel' and a senior barrister or advocate may be promoted by the Queen to be a Queen's Counsel. The function of counsel is to represent clients in court and argue cases on their behalf. They also do much advisory work. They are the consultants and specialists of the law. Solicitors are persons who have been admitted by the Law Society, the Law Society of Scotland or the Incorporated Law Society of Northern Ireland. They are the general practitioners of the law. They practise from offices, frequently in partnership, and are general legal advisers, drafting wills, dealing with tax problems,

winding up the estates of deceased persons, transferring land and houses, and doing much miscellaneous business. Some represent clients in the lower courts and may in future be allowed to represent them even in the higher courts. Both classes of lawyers have a long and arduous training, normally including study at a University.

The judges of the superior courts are appointed from the senior and experienced barristers or advocates (usually from QCs) and most judges of lower courts are barristers or advocates, though some are solicitors. Many barristers or advocates and solicitors are also employed by Government departments or by local authorities and big companies as legal advisers and to do legal work.

Court procedure

Courts decide cases only when cases are presented to them. In civil cases it is up to the claimant (plaintiff, or in Scotland pursuer) to present his claim against the defendant (or, in Scotland, defender), in the appropriate form. Thereafter a case proceeds through a series of stages, depending largely on its nature and what issues are involved. If there is dispute as to the facts, e.g. whose fault caused the accident, there must be a hearing at which witnesses give evidence of what they heard, saw and so on, and there may be serious dispute as to what conclusions should be reached from the evidence. A layman can present his case himself but in nearly all cases he instructs a solicitor who makes enquiries, collects information and in substantial cases instructs a barrister or advocate to handle the case and appear in court to examine the witnesses and argue the issues of law which arise.

In criminal cases procedure is initiated by the Crown prosecutor or, in Scotland, the Procurator-fiscal, acting in the public interest. The person accused will again normally instruct a solicitor, who may instruct counsel, to defend him.

It is generally unwise for a layman to appear unrepresented. The procedure is frequently complicated and sometimes lengthy. The points of law involved may be complex and difficult and the issues of fact may be tangled. It is very easy for the layman to miss important points of fact or of law.

Non-contentious business

It should not be thought that all legal matters involve disputes. Much legal business does not involve any dispute at all. Thus a man goes to his lawyer to have a will made which will regulate his property after his death, to have a company formed to run a business, to have a charitable trust created, to have a house which he has bought transferred into his name, to arrange for the let of his house and so on. But in all these, and many more, kinds of business, the lawyer has to know what is allowed and what is not, to try to foresee difficulties, to minimise taxation, and to avoid disputes. If disputes arise, the lawyers on each side will try to come to agreement before resorting to a court. Also vast numbers of transactions notably sales of goods and supplies of services, such as servicing a car, are carried through by persons without need to call on lawyers at all.

Legal aid and advice
Since getting legal advice and securing representation in court requires the skill and time of highly-skilled professional men and women, it is expensive. To try to ensure that all people who need it can secure legal advice and, where necessary, representation in court there has developed since 1945 a complex system of Legal Aid and Advice.

Enforcement of the law
The civil law is largely enforced by law-abiding persons who apply it and abide by it in their dealings with one another. Even when a dispute has been taken to court one party, having been found by a court liable to do something or to pay money, will frequently then do or pay voluntarily. If he does not, the party holding the judgment of the court may have to *levy execution* (or in Scotland *do diligence*) against him. Under this, in the last resort, some of the debtor's property may be taken and sold and the proceeds paid to the party holding the judgment. Or the creditor may have the debtor adjudicated bankrupt, in which case all his property is taken and sold and the creditors paid from the proceeds of sale.

The criminal law is largely enforced by the police, who may arrest a criminal or suspected criminal and have him tried in a criminal court. If he is found guilty he may be sent to prison, fined or subjected to another form of punishment.

Law Reform
The rules of law require constantly to be revised, to take account

of new problems, to be suitable for current social conditions, and to take account of gaps and defects which are found in the rules. Consequently the different legal professional bodies all have committees which regularly propose what they consider desirable or necessary reforms to the government. Organisations such as the CBI, TUC, RAC, BMA and many more do the same. Periodically the government appoints a Royal Commission, a group of about 15 people of experience, to make a thorough investigation of the law on a subject, such as trade unions or gambling, and to report and propose changes. If the government agrees to the proposals it will bring forward a Bill to Parliament to enact the necessary changes.

In 1965 there were created the *Law Commission* and the *Scottish Law Commision*, small permanent bodies charged with keeping the whole of English and Scottish law under review, and bringing forward proposals for reform and improvement. Since 1965 many Acts have been passed giving effect to the proposals of the Commissions.

International law
Quite apart from the rules of law applicable in particular countries there is a body of international law regulating relations between states in the world. It grew up initially from rules proposed by legal scholars in books, but in modern times it is largely made by treaties, conventions and agreements between two or more states. Increasingly too there are international organisations, notably the United Nations Organisation, but also many specialised organisations concerned with particular problems, such as the International Labour Organisation and the World Health Organisation. In the past, international disputes have all too frequently been sought to be solved by force, by making war, but the UNO strives hard to prevent resort to force. Disputes may be taken to the *International Court of Justice* but, differing from the courts in states, states which are parties to disputes cannot in general be compelled to go to the International Court and the means of compelling parties to obey judgments of the Court are limited. International law is growing rapidly in importance and bulk, and steadily playing a larger part in the affairs of states.

Human Rights
The United Nations Charter of 1945 expressed member states'

determination to reaffirm faith in fundamental human rights and one of its purposes is to promote and encourage respect for human rights. In 1948 it adopted a Universal Declaration of Human Rights; though not legally binding in any state it sets out standards which civilised countries should observe. These were more precisely defined in an International Covenant on Civil and Political Rights and an International Covenant on Economic, Social and Cultural Rights, both adopted in 1976. There are also numerous international conventions on specific matters such as discrimination in education.

The states which are members of the Council of Europe adopted in 1953 a convention declaring certain Human Rights. Persons who believe that their rights under this convention have been infringed may complain to the European Commission on Human Rights and then to the *European Court of Human Rights*. (This is an entirely different court from the Court of Justice of the European Communities.) But the convention has not been made part of British law and the decisions of this Court are not enforceable in the United Kingdom. They are persuasive on the government only: that is, it is free to decide whether they should be given effect to or not. Individuals cannot appeal to this Court from the British courts. They must initiate a separate complaint.

NATURAL HISTORY

The first thing I do when I get up in the morning is to draw back the curtain and look out through the window at the garden and the new day. If it is a bright summer morning I cannot wait even to get dressed, but go straight downstairs in my dressing-gown. Then I unlock the door and step out into the garden to breathe the fresh morning air 'before many people have used it', as somebody once said. At such times the lawn glitters with beads of dew that glow in different colours, orange, green, turquoise and red, as they reflect separate light waves from the rising sun. A late slug glides towards his shelter, needing to reach it before the sun's heat evaporates the dew and dries the ground. Various flies cluster on sunny patches of the fence to absorb the warming light before they become active, but bumble-bees are already busy at certain flowering shrubs and border flowers, for they are early risers. They set out long before the honey-bees have thought of stirring, and continue to forage later in the evening, sometimes until after sundown. Moreover they fly in light rain or drizzle, which honey-bees never do.

The garden birds, which ceased their singing before sunrise, are now busy collecting food, being hungry after the night. Ladybirds warm their small bodies on sunlit leaves, and a spider circles towards the centre of its orb-web as it spins the last few sticky spirals. Some poppy flowers have split and cast apart their paired sheaths by the delicate pressure of their expanding, crinkly petals—for dawn is their time of opening. I marvel at them, for I can imagine few things so sublimely fresh, or with such a delicately new-born look, as a poppy that has just opened its four satiny, slightly crumpled petals to the rising sun.

So much for a few minutes of sheer enjoyment in my garden at the beginning of the day—but that is what Natural History is about. It is about being aware of the other living things that share this planet with us—the plants that clothe the hills and plains and make them beautiful, and the animals of every shape and size that depend upon the plants for food and shelter. And then, of course, we want to name them, to identify and recognise the many different kinds—but that is not enough. It is not enough to pick a small pink flower by the hedge and say 'This is herb Robert', or to say of a butterfly sunning itself on a bramble in a grassy glade, 'That is a speckled wood', or to point out a jelly-like object on a rock exposed by the ebbing tide and say, 'There is a sea anemone'.

True understanding of Natural History involves enquiry into the whole life of the creatures, their relations with other lives around them, how they feed and reproduce, what are their enemies and by what means they evade them, and how they survive the storms and icy rigours of winter, or the heat and drying winds of summer.

This sort of understanding comes from close contact with living things, and through watching them in the garden, the woods and the open spaces. Books, which contain the accumulated knowledge and observations of devoted men, are of priceless value, of course, and should always be consulted—but nothing can replace the experience of seeing, with your own eyes, the plants and animals in their natural setting. Then there will be other things that you remember, the season and the time of day, the sun that warmed your face, the wind that ruffled your hair, the sudden shower of rain. You will notice how these varying conditions are met, and influence the actions of the creatures that you watch. Thus you will come to know the feel and climate of a creature's life in a direct and personal sense, such as no book alone can ever give you. Then, indeed, you will begin to feel deeply about conserving the wildlife of the earth, and you will want to help in keeping its varied habitats intact and unpolluted for future generations to enjoy.

Now let us return to the subject of gardens, where Nature can be enjoyed simply by stepping out of the back door, or even by gazing through the window. Although gardens are, to a great extent, artificial, man-made habitats, they provide homes and feeding grounds for many wild creatures. In fact, any garden can be enjoyed simply by stepping out of the back door and as country-side gets bulldozed away such private sanctuaries increase enormously in value and importance. Unfortunately, though, there are many kinds of poisons and sprays on the market, and the gardener is urged to use them and to make war on all fronts against aphids, ants, slugs, woodlice, beetles, millipedes, snails and even earthworms, and to scorch and shrivel every kind of weed and wildflower. He is urged to view his garden as a battlefield, where every small creature is a possible threat that must be banished, and where there is little in the way of food for birds.

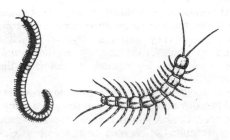

Millipede and Centipede

Such a gardener is apt to wear a worried look and he can never quite relax. Yet, of all places, a garden should be an environment of peace, where one can sit and enjoy the buzz and flutter of wings, the chorus of bird song, the sudden appearance of a shining beetle on the path, as well as the still beauty of the flowers. Surely the peacock butterfly that comes to sip nectar from the herbaceous border is an added bonus, as lovely as any of the flowers on which it sits—but for its caterpillars to feed, there must be nettles.

The Garden as a Wildlife Sanctuary

Now let us consider how to make your garden a welcome sanctuary for wildlife. It should have a fairly well-clipped lawn where thrushes and blackbirds can find worms, where starlings can probe for leather-jackets, wireworms, little slugs and other grass-root creatures, and where pied wagtails can run and flutter in pursuit of surface insects. A lawn that has a natural variety of short-turf plants is much more interesting than one that has only grass. And if it is not mown too hard or frequently, their short-stemmed flowers will bloom. So leave some daisies to spangle the lawn in spring, and patches of white clover that will attract bees in summer. The closely-clustered flowers of round-leaved speedwell make fresh and lovely sky-blue patches on my own lawn in late spring, and the small, clover-like heads of black medick dot the ground with yellow brightness where it spreads, flowering throughout the summer. Above all, though, I love to see that little gem among the short-turf flowers, the dove's-foot cranesbill, and I can seldom resist squatting on the grass to gaze at its small pink stars.

Dove's-foot Cranesbill   Poppy

A slenderish kind of tree, planted on the lawn, relieves its flatness, casts an area of shade and gives a feeling of security to smaller birds. They can fly up into its branches if startled while feeding on scattered crumbs. There should also be a fair-sized tree in the garden, for its topmost branches will provide song posts for a song thrush, or perhaps a mistle thrush. Blackbirds tend to sing from lower branches. In fact, the picture that I carry in my mind is of a blackbird singing amid the yellow tassels of a laburnum tree. Nowadays, however, all these birds may choose a television aerial.

A Place for Wild Flowers
I leave an unmown grassy area at the bottom of my garden, where meadow and hedgerow plants can develop freely. Here grasshoppers can live, and their cheerful stridulations enhance my summer days. Here, too, the umbelliferous plants, such as cow parsley and wild carrot, provide feeding platforms for hover-

A small patch of Wild Flower Garden

flies, greenbottles, solitary wasps and pollen-feeding beetles. Greater stitchwort, herb Robert, bird's-foot trefoil, knapweed, ragwort, meadow vetch, mallow, poppy, white deadnettle, spear thistle, ox-tongue and other hedgerow plants may decorate such an area. The flowers of ragwort and knapweed will attract small tortoiseshell and red admiral butterflies, and meadow browns may come to fly floppily over the grasses. The fruiting heads of spear thistle and ox-tongue are likely to give you the joy of seeing goldfinches feeding from them in early autumn.

In this area, too, the underground larvae of swift moths, summer chafers, skipjack beetles and daddy long-legs will thrive, and the close plant cover will shelter such creatures as slow-worms and the larger ground beetles, even, perhaps, a hedgehog. One summer, when I was clipping back some of the taller grasses in my strip of garden meadow, I found a nest of carder-bees. These smallish, brown bumble-bees had made a soft, snug nest of woven moss and grass, rather like a bird's nest, with a covering of moss to protect the cells. Unlike most bumble-bees, which nest in holes, carder-bees make their nests above ground at the base of tall grasses and other plants.

A stand of nettles in a corner of your wild strip of garden will serve as food for the caterpillars of small tortoiseshell, peacock or red admiral butterflies, and may induce a pair of white-throats to nest among the tangled stems if you live in a rural district.

Homes for Soil Creatures

A few small boulders, wide rather than deep, and flattish below, placed in various parts of the garden but not pressed into the soil, will give daytime shelter to centipedes, slugs, woodlice, beetles and ground-dwelling spiders, or roof the nests of garden ants. When you lift such boulders, however, make sure you replace them with extreme care to avoid harming the sheltering creatures. A well built-up rock garden varies the terrain with its different levels. Snails will find homes in crevices between the rocks, while harvestmen, millipedes, springtails and other creatures lurk beneath the mat-like foliage of aubretia, yellow alyssum, mossy saxifrage and other low-growing rock plants.

Another way of altering the terrain of your garden is to make a sand bank. For this, all you have to do is to collect some buckets of sand from a sandy heath, the beach or a builder's yard, mix it with soil to make it firm and bank it up in a sunny corner. In

Andrena Bee

spring and summer, if you keep it fairly clear of weeds, it will attract mining bees and digger wasps to make their burrows. The first to arrive in spring will probably be the pretty little Andrena bees, easy to recognise by the rich, orange-brown fur on their bodies. These are the female bees, and each will construct a cell at the bottom of her burrow, which she provides with a paste made from pollen and a little honey. Having completed this after several journeys from the flowers, carrying about half her weight of pollen back each time, she lays an egg on the paste and closes the cell. She then makes a few more cells higher up from the tunnel, constructing, provisioning and closing each in turn. Although her offspring emerge from their pupal skins in late summer, they remain resting in their cells until the following spring. This may seem strange, but if they squandered their little store of energy by flying in the autumn sunshine they would be unable to survive the winter months.

Spider-hunting Wasp

One summer I spent a fascinating half hour watching a spider-hunting wasp dragging her paralysed prey to a burrow she had started, under a stone which jutted from the sand bank in my garden. These wasps always seem to be in a desperate hurry. They make short, darting flights, then scurry about on their long legs, poking into crevices as they search for ground-dwelling spiders. This wasp, having already caught her spider, had paralysed it by stinging the nerve centre at the base of its legs.

When I spotted her—only the female wasps hunt spiders—she was running backwards up the slope, dragging the spider along by one leg, gripped in her jaws. Having to move backwards, she could not see very well where she was going, so after dragging the spider a little way, she would drop it and run up the slope to the stone where her burrow was started, to check that she was backing in the right direction. She did not seem able to return in a straight line to the spider, but ran down the slope to the level where she had left it, then ran to and fro until she found it. On most occasions she dropped the spider on a little ledge of the bank and quickly found it—but twice she dropped the spider on smoothly sloping ground, and it rolled down the bank. Then she would rush feverishly up and down the bank for several minutes, until she finally came across it, and her labours would begin again.

Eventually she made her way up to within a few inches from the stone, dropped the spider for the last time and ran up to complete her burrow. Little jets of sand started to shoot out from under the stone as she dug downwards. I had to wait for about ten minutes before she finally came out to pull the spider up under the stone and into her burrow. There, out of sight, she would lay an egg on the paralysed spider, then fill in the burrow and leave.

When a paralysed spider is left while the wasp explores the terrain or digs her burrow it is liable to be attacked by ants, tiger beetles or other predators. This reminds me of another spider-hunting wasp, of a different species, which I happened to notice while on holiday in Majorca. This wasp had a clever idea. I watched her dragging a spider backwards along the ground. After dragging the spider a little way, she dropped it at the base of a plant stem. Then she ran up the stem, explored its small side-shoots, ran down, gripped the spider, dragged it up the stem and placed it firmly in the fork of a branching side-shoot. Here the spider was fairly safe from attack while the wasp flew off to take her bearings or dig her burrow. Unfortunately I was unable to wait for the wasp's return. The action of this wasp was instinctive rather than thought out—none the less, it was still clever.

Bushes for Birds

Your garden should have some evergreen shrubs or trees, such as laurel, privet, *Euonymus japonica*, yew and holly. These will give protection to small roosting birds through the cold winter months. Holly will also produce some winter food, in the form of berries, for thrushes, blackbirds and starlings—but only if it is a female tree, and only if there is a male tree near by so that its flowers can be pollinated.

Ivy is a very useful evergreen climber if it is allowed to cover part of a garden wall. Spiders of several kinds will spin webs between its leaves, or weave silken traps among its clinging stems. The stick-like caterpillars of the swallow-tailed moth eat its leaves, and in late autumn its rounded clusters of yellow-green flowers provide a last bonanza feast of nectar for wasps, bees, bluebottles, hover-flies, butterflies and many moths, before the cold weather ends their activities. Garden snails will hibernate on the wall between its stems in winter, and wrens may roost behind the shelter of its leaves, while sparrows will sometimes bring dry grass and feathers there, and poke them in their roosts for added shelter. Then, in early summer, the purplish-black berries will be gobbled up by blackbirds, thrushes and even woodpigeons.

Rowan and whitebeam are fine berry-bearing trees to grow in the garden, for they will provide a feast for blackbirds, song thrushes and mistle thrushes in the autumn. Elder bushes will grow anywhere in town or country, and their hanging clusters of shining black berries are quickly cleared by birds. Berberis, pyracantha and cotoneaster are useful ornamental shrubs to have. The oval or cylindrical berries of berberis are rich in vitamins, and the fiery-orange, densely clustered berries of pyracantha make a glorious show in October. These, and the small red berries of cotoneaster, offer a late supply of food for birds when most other berries are over. I have watched blackbirds, thrushes and greenfinches feeding on my cotoneaster bush and one day, to my surprise and joy, a couple of waxwings joined them. The inconspicuous, but nectar-rich, flowers of the cotoneaster cause it to hum with the wings of eager honey-bees in summer.

Waxwing

Flowering Bushes for Insects

You will, of course, want to have some bushes in your garden that are especially attractive to butterflies and other insects. For butterflies, buddleia is the bush *par excellence*. In fact, it is also appropriately known as the butterfly bush. Its long, scented, mauve or purple flower-clusters bloom from July until September, when many other shrubs have ceased to blossom. Small tortoise-shells, large whites, red admirals, peacocks, commas and painted ladies may crowd and jostle each other as they probe the small flowers for nectar, while sunning themselves, spread-winged, on the inflorescences.

Red admirals and painted ladies do not survive the winter in Britain, and those we see in spring and early summer are im-migrants from the south—red admirals from southern Europe and painted ladies from North Africa. Both breed in this country. The caterpillars of red admirals feed on nettles, and those of painted ladies feed on thistles, and there is now exciting evidence that some, at least, of the home-bred butterflies migrate south and attempt the return journey in autumn. Whether or not they succeed in doing so has yet to be confirmed, but this is more likely to be the case with the painted lady, which is a rapid and powerful flyer, occasionally reaching as far as Iceland on its northward travels.

Painted Lady

Another good bush for your garden is the flowering currant. Its multitudes of small pink flowers make a beautiful show in spring, and they are favourites of the big queen bumble-bees. Some years ago I had a bedroom on the ground floor where I was working. There was a large flowering currant bush outside my window, and throughout April I woke each morning to the deep hums and buzzings of the bumble-bees which had been busy among its flowers since dawn. In fact, I always think of the flowering currant as the queen bumble-bee bush. I say 'queen bumble-bee' because bumble-bee colonies are annual affairs, and only the young queens, which have already mated, survive the winter.

Queen Bumble-Bee and Flowering Currant

   Thus, after awakening from hibernation, and restoring her
energy with the nectar and pollen of spring flowers, the young
queen must find a suitable hole for her nest, and start the new
colony all on her own. For the first five or six weeks, she must
build the wax cells, lay her eggs, forage for nectar and pollen, feed
her growing batch of grubs, lay in a store of honey for wet days,
make fresh cells and so on, until the first workers hatch and begin
to take over. This is a very different situation from that of the
queen honey-bee, who never leaves the hive after her mating
flight unless accompanied by a swarm of workers, and who is
incapable of building cells, foraging or feeding her young, but
must herself be constantly fed and groomed by attendant
workers.

   Another bush I would recommend is hebe, or veronica, as it is
commonly called. It blooms in late summer and the spikes of
mauve flowers on my own bushes attract hosts of honey-bees,
bumble-bees, hover-flies and silver-Y moths. Most moths fly only
after dark, but silver-Y moths are interesting in that they fly in
bright sunlight, usually in the afternoon, as well as in the evening
and at night. One afternoon, I counted seven of them hovering
round the flower-spikes of my veronicas as they probed the small
corollas with their tongues. When I came out again at dusk, silver-
Y moths were still feeding, impossible to follow as they darted
from one veronica bush to the next, but coming suddenly into
focus as they hovered, like little swaying ghosts, above the dark
foliage. Silver-Y moths do not survive the British winter, but
migrants from the Mediterranean regions arrive in late spring,
often in great numbers. Their caterpillars feed on various wild
and garden plants, and the home-bred moths are believed to make
a return flight south in autumn.

Herbaceous Flowers for Insects

Among the summer-flowering herbaceous plants that I grow in
my garden, red valerian is one of the best for attracting butterflies,
silver-Y moths and others. It is a native of southern Europe, but
garden escapes grow wild on railway banks, old walls and cliffs
by the sea, at least in the south of England where I live. Red
valerian flowers from May throughout the summer, especially if
the flower stems are cut right back when the little feathery fruits
are forming. Its clustered flowers are great favourites of another

immigrant moth from southern Europe and North Africa—the humming-bird hawk-moth. Only recently a friend told me he had seen a humming-bird in his garden, and had called his wife out to have a look. I told him that as all humming-birds are native to America, it must have been the small hawk-moth which flies in bright sunshine and does, indeed, look like a tiny brown and orange bird with a black and white-edged tail tuft. He agreed.

I am always thrilled to see a humming-bird hawk-moth come darting into my garden. I love to watch it flick from flower to

Humming-bird Hawk-moth

flower with marvellously controlled flight, and to see it sway and hover, poised for a magic moment on whirring wings, to probe a nectary with its slender tongue. Indeed, there is no creature that seems to burn with such an intense flame of life as this small hawk-moth, that wings its way over continent and sea, to dart among the flowers of English gardens. Its caterpillars feed on lady's bedstraw, and the generation of moths from these may well make the return flight south.

In late September and October, when the blackbirds feast on blackberries and scatter purple droppings in the nearby scrubby wasteland, the ice plant (*Sedem spectabile*), sometimes called the butterfly plant, attracts small tortoiseshells, peacock butterflies

and occasional commas to my garden. These three butterflies
hibernate as adults in this country, and continue to fly until they
must seek shelter for the winter sleep. They feed and sun themselves on the ice plant's pink, flat heads of glistening flowers, or
join the big, bee-mimicking drone-flies on the Michaelmas daisies.
Both these plants are 'musts' for your garden sanctuary.

Most of the cultivated daisy-type flowers attract butterflies and
other insects, that is to say if they are not the double kind, like
those chrysanthemums, dahlias and asters that have lost the
central disc of yellow florets through artificial selection. The stand
of tall white shasta daisies in my garden attracts a multitude of
summer insects, such as bees, hover-flies, drone-flies, greenbottles,
ichneumon wasps, hunting wasps, soldier beetles, tiny honey-
beetles and delicate green capsid bugs, as well as butterflies.
Another daisy-type flower, the sunflower, should be grown especially for birds. Its enormous disc, when left to seed, will certainly
attract the tits and finches, and if you live in the country near a
wood, then nuthatches may join them.

The Garden Hedge

If you are not lucky enough to have a walled garden there should
be a wooden fence or a hedge to give it shelter and a feeling of
seclusion. These days most farmers use tractor-drawn mechanical clippers to cut and slash the hedges of their fields, leaving
them too low and too narrow to attract nesting birds or shelter
other forms of wild life. Thus it has become particularly important
that gardens should have well-grown border hedges and plenty of
shrubs. Holly, privet, pyracantha, yew and leyland cypress make
good evergreen hedges for birds to nest in during spring and
summer, and to use as roosts in winter. A pair of song thrushes
nested in the privet hedge bordering the front garden of my previous house, and I discovered that the rim of their nest was lined
with toffee papers that children had dropped on the pavement
after visiting the local shop on their way from school. One day,
while lightly clipping the same hedge, I found a young caterpillar
of the privet hawk-moth. I reared the caterpillar in a large jam-jar
and when it was fully grown and ready to pupate, I released it
under the hedge. There it could burrow into the soil, construct an
earthen cell and cast its skin to become a chrysalis.

Dunnocks and wrens like to search the ground below the privet hedge for spiders and tiny insects; and in June, its heavily scented, creamy-white flower-clusters attract the honey-bees by day and moths at night.

The Garden Fence

My present garden is fenced but it contains plenty of shrubs. Flies like to sun themselves on the south-facing side, and in April and early May a queen wasp comes to scrape wood from the upright fence posts. She scrapes the surface with her jaws, backing downwards as she works, until she has a little ball of shredded wood. This she carries to her underground nest, and mixes with saliva to make woodpulp for starting the paper nest that will eventually house her first small batch of grubs. Then, in June, the worker wasps arrive, and on throughout the summer they scrape wood-fibre from the fence. They use this to enlarge the paper nest and add cells to the comb, and later to build fresh combs below it and extend the walls around them as the colony expands.

Zebra Spider

The black-and-white zebra spiders hunt flies and other insects on this south-facing fence, each for ever trailing a hardly-visible line of silk. The little spiders run in short, quick jerks, or twist and swivel to survey the surface round them. When a fly is spotted by a zebra spider she cautiously stalks it until within jumping distance. Then she makes a lightning pounce and, with the fly gripped in her legs and jaws, falls from the fence. However, she falls only an inch or two, because the thread, that she had first fixed to the wall, was spun out as she jumped. If the insect she captures is very small, she grips it with her jaws alone, clutching the fence with her legs to save herself from falling.

Protective Coloration

Garden carpet moths and others choose to rest by day on the
north-facing fence, where their sleep will not be disturbed by the
heat and brightness of the sun. Garden carpets are common even
in town gardens, and may be seen in late spring, and throughout
the summer and autumn. The moth rests with its wings spread
flat against the surface, in the form of a small triangle. Its greyish
white wings are marked with dark patches at the edges. These
serve to break up and obscure its outline, and thus prevent it
from being easily recognised by a bird, as it rests on a fence or
tree. This means of protection, known as 'disruptive coloration', is
widely used by moths and other vulnerable creatures.

Garden Carpet Moth

Another means of protection, known as 'mimicry', is used by
the angle shades moth. This lovely moth is also extremely
common in town and country gardens during early summer and
again in the autumn. I usually see an angle shades moth resting
on the ground at the base of a wall or fence. Its forewings are

Angle Shades Moth

delicately coloured in shades of brown, pink and olive green with angle-shaped markings, and their edges are roughly waved and dented. Thus, as the moth rests by day with wings folded over its back, it strongly resembles a dry and partly withered leaf.

When I am pottering or poking about in the garden I frequently disturb a large yellow underwing. The moth flies rapidly away for a short distance, then drops into a bush or beneath a border plant. It usually rests at the base of plants or low down on the fence where its brown wings, held flat over its back and marked with a few pale lines and darker patches, make it difficult to see. But when the moth flies, its bright yellow hindwings are suddenly displayed, only to vanish as it drops again into the foliage and folds them beneath its forewings. It must be most bewildering to a bird when the yellow-winged moth it was chasing suddenly disappears. The bird may stop to search where the moth plunged, but it continues to look for a yellow moth and misses the concealed brown one. Thus the large yellow underwing is saved from being eaten. This protective device, where vividly marked wings are suddenly displayed in flight, then hidden on alighting, is known as 'flash coloration'.

I have spent several summer holidays abroad in southern Europe. There I like to scramble about among the broom and lavender clumps and pink-flowered cistus bushes on hot, dry, stony hillsides. In such places there are grasshoppers that give very fine displays of flash coloration. The brown, grey or whitish grasshoppers are perfectly camouflaged to match the stony ground where they sit among the sparse dry grasses. As I clamber forwards, they leap up and flutter in front of me, marvellously transformed, and looking like gorgeous butterflies which suddenly vanish as they touch the ground. The broad, gauzy flight-wings of these grasshoppers are brilliant blue or turquoise in some kinds, and vivid red, pink or orange in others, and as the insect alights they suddenly fold like fans beneath its protective forewings. To see them is very well worth toiling up stony tracks, with thorn-scratched arms and legs, in the parching heat of a Mediterranean summer.

Yet another good way to avoid being eaten is to have a nasty taste. However, it is no good being unpalatable if you look much like other creatures that taste nice. You must have distinctive markings that are easily remembered by a predator, and which advertise the fact that you should not be eaten. There are two common garden moths that taste unpleasant, and advertise the fact by means of 'warning coloration'.

One of these is the magpie moth, which I often see resting on bushes in July and August. This attractive moth is very conspicuous. Its body is yellow with black spots, and its broad wings, which are half-spread as it rests, are white with black and yellow spots and marking. When disturbed, it flutters slowly away and settles on the upper surface of a leaf. Not only the moth, but its caterpillar and chrysalis are also distasteful. The caterpillar is marked like the moth, being white with black and yellow spots, and the chrysalis is black with yellow bands. The caterpillars feed on a variety of plants, including the leaves of currant and gooseberry bushes, and I have found them on the euonymus bush in my garden. The chrysalis rests in a very flimsy hammock-like cocoon, which does not hide its yellow-banded form.

The other distasteful moth is the garden tiger. This large and beautiful moth has creamy-white forewings marked with chocolate brown patches, and its hindwings and abdomen are brilliant red with a few black marks. When touched or gently interfered with, the garden tiger does not fly away, but exposes its vivid hindwings and the band of red hairs behind its head. This is its way of saying, 'Leave me alone, I taste nasty.' The furry caterpillar of the garden tiger, commonly known as the 'woolly bear', feeds on dandelions, docks and various other plants.

Garden Tiger Moth

Ladybird Larva

Aphid Predators

Ladybirds are also distasteful, and their bright red, spotted wing-covers advertise the fact to birds. These little beetles and their larvae feed on the aphids that attack the stems and leaves of roses and other cultivated plants; but when the plants are sprayed with poisons the useful ladybirds are killed. Blue tits, willow warblers and other small birds that like to eat aphids, often suffer too, or even die. Nobody can mistake a ladybird, but its larvae are not always recognised. Ladybird larvae look rather like little flattened caterpillars. They are blackish or bluish-grey, with yellow spots and black legs spread out sideways. When the larva is fully grown it turns into a roundish, black-and-yellow pupa, which is fixed by its tail to a plant stem or leaf. So, when you see these little knob-like objects on rose bushes and other plants, remember what they are. One day, when I was at the south coast, I saw hundreds of seven-spot ladybirds on the breakwaters and the promenade, and crawling over the pebbles of the beach. The probable explanation is that they had flown over from the Continent, and were resting before flying inland to settle in gardens and orchards and continue their search for aphids.

In July and August aphids produce winged forms that fly away to start fresh colonies on other plants. As the winged aphids rise into the air, countless numbers are taken by swallows, house martins and swifts. In fact, swifts have been observed to feed their young on round pellets of compressed aphids, taken on the wing and carried home in their throats.

Myriads of winged aphids, too, get trapped in spider webs, sometimes almost covering each sticky spiral with their tiny forms, only to be left untouched by the sickened spiders. However, plenty will survive to start fresh colonies on garden plants; and other enemies, as well as ladybirds, will eat them as they suck the stems and leaves. The loveliest of these is the green lacewing. This insect has a slender, emerald green body, golden eyes and two long pairs of gauzy, iridescent wings, held roof-wise over its back when not engaged in flight. The green lacewing flies chiefly at night, but on a sunny morning, or in the warm light of evening, I often see one fluttering slowly across the garden with a delightful, twinkling motion of its wings.

In late spring and summer you may see tiny, yellowish-green knobs on very slender stalks, that seem to be growing from stems or the underside of leaves. These are the eggs of the green lace-wing. They are laid near aphid colonies, for it is in its larval form that the lacewing feeds on aphids. This little creature, not unlike a ladybird larva in shape, is brownish-yellow, and has a pair of sickle-shaped jaws through which it sucks the captured aphids until only their skins are left. When fully grown and ready to pupate, the larva spins a flattish cocoon of white silk on leaves or the trunks of trees.

In late autumn green lacewings seek shelter, often in houses, where they hibernate in corners near the ceiling. It is at this time that a peculiar thing happens. As the weeks pass, the lacewing loses its lovely green colour and becomes drab yellow or reddish-brown. But months later, when hibernation draws to an end, the yellow or red colour disappears, and the lacewing becomes gradu-ally green, then emerald green once more as it flutters out into the mild spring air.

Green Lacewing

The dainty hover-flies, which are to be seen wherever there is a border of flowers, also lay their eggs near aphid colonies. The yellowish-white or pale green maggot-like larvae which hatch from these are just as avid aphid-eaters as are those of ladybirds or lacewings. The hover-fly larva looks rather like a small, plump caterpillar with suckers instead of legs, but its front part tapers to a very tiny head. When it comes upon an aphid the larva pierces it with its mouth prongs and quickly sucks it dry. The larva then drops the empty skin and pierces another victim. It may consume a dozen or more aphids before taking a short rest to digest its meal. When fully grown the hover-fly larva fixes itself to a leaf or stem and contracts into a little pear-shaped pupa.

If you are an acute observer you may notice a minute insect hovering over a colony of aphids. Keep watching, and you will see it dart down and settle on the colony. This is a braconid wasp, and it is laying an egg in one of the aphids. When the egg hatches, the larva of the braconid wasp will eat its victim from within, until only the empty skin is left. It will then spin a cocoon in the aphid husk and pupate. When ready to emerge, tiny jaws will bite a neat, round hole in the back of the aphid skin, a head will appear, then the little black wasp will struggle out and fly away. However, you need a good pocket lens to watch this happen. I have seen small clusters of aphid skins, still clinging to the stems of plants, each with a round hole in its back where a braconid wasp had left.

Then there is another aphid predator, and a very charming one, that sometimes visits my garden in the autumn. This is the goldcrest, our smallest bird, weighing about six grams or less. I looked out of the front-room window on a dull October morning, and there it was, greenish with a yellow flame along its head, daintily picking aphids from the stems and leaves of my rose bushes. The next day I stood for a quarter of an hour by the sycamore tree in my garden, watching half a dozen goldcrests plucking aphids from the under-surface of the leaves, sometimes hanging on a leaf stalk, or hovering for a few seconds beneath a leaf to do so.

Goldcrest

Well, these are some of the predators of aphids that you may be able to observe in your own garden. One purpose I had in mind in drawing your attention to them, apart from their inherent interest, is to give you some idea of the way a natural balance is maintained by living creatures, preventing any one species from becoming over-numerous. However, where insecticides are used, the predators are killed alongside their prey.

Ants and Aphids

Now let us return once more to the aphid colony. No doubt there is one on a rose bush in your garden, and little black ants are running up and down the stem of the bush between it and their nest. Look closely—you will see ants moving slowly about the colony, tapping or stroking the aphids with their antennae. These ants are inducing the aphids to excrete minute drops of honey-dew, which they greedily lap up. Then with full crops they return to the nest and distribute the liquid, mouth to mouth, among their sister ants. I say 'sister ants' because all worker ants are dwarfed females incapable of mating.

Black garden ants derive much of their food from the honey-dew excreted by aphids. They run up and down the trunk and branches of a sycamore tree in my garden, where their tracks lead to aphid colonies on the leaves. These foraging ants keep closely to invisible tracks, which are really scent trails, laid down and kept fresh by the ants as they travel along. In my previous garden there was a rose bush by the back window. On summer evenings, after sunset, a large toad would come regularly and squat beside the bush. Its tongue would flick out every few seconds and lick up ants from the stem as they ran up and down the track leading to the aphid colonies among the leaves.

Common Toad

Food Chains

A toad and a rose bush—I feel pretty sure that you would never have connected these two things together in your mind. But now you see how a toad may be linked to a rose bush by one item of the food it eats. This sort of who-eats-who linkage is known as a 'food chain'. The rose bush-to-toad food chain may be represented thus: rose bush → aphids → ants → toad. All food chains start with a plant, for only plants can use the sun's energy to trigger the chemical processes that build sugars from the carbon dioxide of air and water from the soil, and only plants can combine the sugars with simple minerals of the same soil water, to make proteins, oils and all the complex matter of their bodies. Thus plants are 'producer organisms', because they produce the food on which all animals depend, whereas animals are 'consumer organisms', for they consume, either directly or indirectly, the various plants. The aphids feed on the rose bush directly, whereas the toad feeds on the rose bush indirectly.

However, rose bushes provide food for mildews, black spot fungi, caterpillars, sawfly larvae, capsid bugs, gall wasps and thrips, as well as aphids, and are themselves nourished by the dead leaves and stems of plants, dead creatures and the droppings of live ones, when these are all consumed and reduced to compost by earthworms, woodlice, millipedes, springtails, mites, soil bacteria and fungi. Aphids may feed on the sap of other bushes, herbs or trees, as well as roses, and are consumed by special predators as you know, besides providing honey-dew for ants. Garden ants feed on seeds, nectar, tiny insects, dead creatures of all kinds and rotting fruit, as well as honey-dew from aphids, and are themselves eaten by various birds. Toads eat earthworms, slugs, newts, young slow-worms, spiders and many other insects besides ants, and may be eaten by grass snakes, tawny owls and herons.

Food Web

I have mentioned all these creatures to show you that food chains are connected up, linking many kinds of plants and animals in an intricate web of inter-dependence. This is called a 'food web'. The plants and animals that compose a food web are in a delicate state of balance, which can easily be upset by breaking the connecting link provided by any one species. For instance, the spraying of bushes with insecticides over a wide area in summer, when the larvae of ladybirds, hover-flies and lacewings are feeding on aphid colonies, may cause a plague of aphids to develop later in the season. The reason for this long-term adverse effect of the spraying is that aphids give birth, without mating or laying eggs, to active female young throughout the summer. Thus those that survive, or are missed by the sprays, are able to reproduce very rapidly and so build up their numbers far in advance of their predators.

I have already mentioned that, especially in late summer, aphids produce winged forms which fly to fresh host-plants and give rise to new colonies of wingless aphids. These winged aphids may be so abundant that you can hardly prevent them from getting into your eyes when you walk outside, and they smear up the wind-screens of cars that travel through the suburbs and along country roads. Now, swifts, being unable to perch or settle on the ground, are entirely dependent on flying insects for their food, and winged aphids form the bulk of their diet. Thus the spraying of trees and bushes with insecticides, when aphid colonies are beginning to produce winged forms, may have a drastic effect on the breeding success of the swifts by forcing them to forage far away from their nesting places.

Mating Swarm of Ants

Winged males and queens of the black garden ant provide swifts with a rich source of food when the ants are swarming. However, the swarms last only for an hour or two on a few days in late summer when the local weather conditions over a stretch of country are just right. The swarms are mating flights, and at three or four o'clock on a warm, sultry afternoon the worker ants construct larger exit holes in their nest and release the males, and the young queens, which are many times their size. The winged ants climb stems and take off, flying slowly up into the sky, where mating occurs between males and queens from nests all over the district.

One afternoon in August I looked out of the window and saw a group of swifts flying to and fro across my garden. I went straight out and down the garden to where winged ants were streaming upwards from a well-stocked nest. Standing beside the nest, I watched the queens ascend like drifting dots diminishing in the sky, and every dot on which I fixed my gaze was engulfed by a swift before it dwindled from sight. It was a fascinating spectacle. A perfectly-aimed swift would hurtle towards a flying ant, and pass straight on with no apparent loss of speed or checking of its flight. It was as if the swift had never seen the flying ant, but simply hurtled through the space it occupied. I half expected to see the drifting speck still there as the swift shot past, but the space it left was empty. The impression was not of the insect being plucked from the air, but of it being instantaneously absorbed into the body of the speeding swift. A likely explanation is that the swift flies with a gaping bill and the ant gets lodged in a pocket of its throat, to be swallowed later.

Swifts

Another August, when the same nest swarmed, I watched a group of black-headed gulls flapping and circling over my garden, but no swifts came. It was easy to see the gulls pick the flying ants from the air, and they made a lovely sight as they flapped, veered and circled overhead. However, their performance was clumsy compared with that of the whirling, dashing, cleanly-aimed swifts that homed with such speed on their targets. In fact, as I stood by the nest I saw two gulls make for the same flying ant. Coming from opposite directions, the gulls almost crashed head-on, just veering at the last split-second, the one that missed the ant giving a sudden scream of frightened protest.

The queen ants that have somehow escaped the swifts, swallows, martins, gulls and starlings in the sky come fluttering down to earth, each with a small male clinging to her abdomen. Having landed, the queen ant pushes off the male, who has now finished mating with her. Then she runs a short distance, stops and with her legs starts scraping at the base of her wings, which break away and fall to the ground. Now she runs off to find a suitable hole or crevice, where she digs a small chamber and blocks the entrance with soil. She will spend the rest of her life underground. Her wing muscles disintegrate, and nourishment from these is fed through her mouth to her first small batch of grubs. When these have pupated and emerge as tiny adult workers they make their way out of the chamber, forage for honey-dew and other food, take over the care of eggs and grubs, and feed and groom the queen. Fresh chambers and connecting tunnels are excavated in the soil, and a new ant colony starts to expand.

Making a Garden Pond

The flourishing ant colony beside which I watched the swifts and gulls is under a large stone near my garden pond. A pond adds enormously to the interest of a garden nature reserve. So why not dig one? Ponds used to be an attractive feature of farmlands and villages, but now most of these have been drained and filled in, and of those still left, many are being poisoned by fertilisers and pesticides that seep in from the surrounding fields, orchards or market gardens. Thus your pond could help, in a small way, to remedy this sad loss. The pond could be rectangular or oval. It does not matter much about the shape, but make it at least half as wide as it is long. For a small pond, four feet by two or two and a half feet would be a suitable size, but it can be as big as you like. Decide on a situation where it gets a fair amount of sunshine, but make sure that it is not too near any tree, or the bottom will soon get clogged with leaves.

A suitable depth for a small pond would be one foot six inches to about two feet, but there is one important point to consider before digging it. This is that you should make one end slope very gradually to the top. It will provide a shallow area where birds can drink and splash in the water. It will also allow little froglets and toadlets to climb out of the water when their tadpole stage is finished. When your pond has been dug and smoothed over, and you have made sure that there are no sharp stones sticking out of the soil, you will be ready to line it with a waterproof material. A sheet of heavy polythene would be suitable for this, but make sure that it is big enough to overlap and spread for at least six inches round the edges. When you have pressed down the sheet as thoroughly as you can, lay flat stones round the overlapping edges to keep it in place—broken pieces of flagstone will do. Now your pond is ready to be filled and stocked with water-plants and creatures.

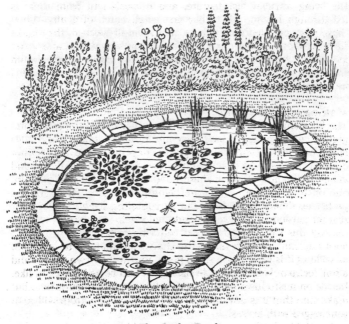

The Garden Pond

Collecting for the Garden Pond

Collecting for your pond will require an expedition into the country. You may find a suitable pond in a low-lying meadow, yellow with buttercups, but wherever your search takes you, make sure that you have a scribbling pad and pencil, so that you can record the various plants and animals you see. You could note down which plants are in flower, the situations where they grow, what insects are seen visiting them and what other creatures are doing—and of course, you should date your observations and record the weather.

I say 'scribbling pad and pencil' because these are rough notes to be made on the spot, and a pencil is quicker to write with than a pen, and useful for making sketches. The notes can be written out properly with a pen in your neat book when you get home; but never rely on memory, or important details of observation may be lost, and others will become distorted and inaccurate. I stress this point very strongly, because it is the most important thing I have ever learned to do in my studies of Natural History.

Now, supposing you discover a fair-sized pond in a meadow. As you approach the pond you will notice that many of the plants in the marshy ground around the pond are different from those in the rest of the meadow. You will see that the plants at the edge of the water are different from those farther back, that those standing in the shallow water are different still and that in deeper water there are plants with floating leaves and others that are completely submerged. This change in the flora from dry ground towards the centre of the pond is called 'zonation'. The plants are zoned according to the amount of water they require. You will notice, too, that there are some animals not seen farther out in the meadow. There may be a moorhen swimming jerkily on the water, a dragonfly cruising to and fro over the pond and some damselflies fluttering around its edges, and you may see some beetles on the leaves of waterside plants that are not found elsewhere.

Waterside Plants

Now let us consider some of the plants you are likely to see in the different zones. There may be scattered clumps of soft rush. It is easy to recognise the stiff, glossy stems, sharply pointed at the top and two or three feet high, each with a small tuft of tiny brown flowers sprouting from one side. You may also see the jointed

Marsh Horsetail

stems of marsh horsetail standing up from the wet grass, each
stem with a whorl of about six slender branches curving upwards
from the joints. You will probably find that some of the stems
have a brown cone at the tip. The cone contains spores, for
horsetails are not flowering plants, and like ferns and mosses,
they reproduce by spores, not seeds. A spore is an extremely
minute reproductive cell which is dispersed by air movement,
whereas a seed, which develops from a fertilised ovule, is
composed of very many cells, and contains a complete embryo plant
with a store of food to give it a start in life. Horsetails are the only
representatives left today of a very ancient group of plants. Some

Kingcups

of these were large trees that grew in the warm, steamy coal forests, a hundred million years before the first dinosaurs or the first flowering plants appeared on earth.

But back to the present and the marshy zone. If it is spring, the pale, four-petalled, lilac-tinted flowers of lady's smock or cuckoo flower will be in bloom. Its narrow fruit will dry as they ripen and suddenly explode, shooting the little seeds to a distance of four or five feet from the parent plant. In this manner the plants get scattered about the marsh and are saved from crowding each other. Nearer the water's edge some gaudy clumps of kingcups, with flowers like giant buttercups, are sure to catch your eye. Unlike buttercups, however, the flowers of kingcups have no petals, and it is the sepals, green in bud, that turn golden-yellow as they open above the glossy, heart-shaped leaves. If it is early summer you may see ragged robin, another plant requiring marshy ground. Its flowers somewhat resemble those of red campion, which belongs to the same plant family, only the petals appear to be torn or shredded—hence its name.

Closer to the margin of the pond, water forget-me-nots will be coming into bloom. The flowers, on slightly curling branches of the stem, are larger than those of the common forget-me-not, and heavenly blue but pink in bud, each open flower with a yellow eye-spot at its centre. Now, too, at the water's edge, the yellow flags will be showing their first big blooms, on stems that may be six feet tall, arising from thick stands of sword-like leaves.

In high summer, meadow-sweet will hold its frothy bunches of cream flowers three feet or so above the marshy ground. Despite its strong, sweet scent, the flowers of meadow-sweet are without nectar, but you may see little pollen-eating beetles crawling over them. Nearer the ground, the water mint will be showing its globular heads of little lilac flowers. Bend down and pinch one of its leaves, and your finger-tips will smell of peppermint.

Water Plants

Now we have come to the shallow-water zone. Here, at one end of the pond, encroaching inwards from its margin, are the tall ranks of reed-mace where a moorhen may be hiding, or sitting on a nest of broken reed stems. Between the spear-shaped leaves you will see dark green, cigar-shaped flower spikes. These are the densely-packed female flowers, and the portion of stem above them

Reed-mace

is yellow with the stamens of the male flowers. Soon the male flowers wither, and the spike turns chocolate brown as the female flowers start fruiting. Unlike the holly, where male and female flowers arise from separate trees, the male and female flowers of reed-mace are on the same plant. In this case the plant itself is hermaphrodite, but not the flowers. Another plant, not so common, but which I have rejoiced to see on two or three occas-

Flowering Rush

ions, is the flowering rush. Despite its name, this plant is not
a rush, and its tall stem ends in a bouquet of lovely, rose-pink
flowers. The flowers have three petals alternating with three sepals
of the same bright colour, and the flower stalks all arise from the
top of the stem. The flowering rush is, I think, the most beautiful
of all the shallow-water plants. Where the water is fairly open,
and the reed-mace has not encroached along its margin, you are
likely to see water plantains. Their large, plantain-like leaves rise
out of the water, and in summer they surround a flower stem
about two feet high. This bears loose clusters of small, three-
petalled flowers, pale pink or lilac in colour, which open only in
the afternoons.

Now look at the plants floating on the surface of the pond.
There is probably an area carpeted with bright green patches of
duckweed. The little floating discs of duckweed are really flattened
stems, and each bears a tiny root which hangs down in the water.
In summer new discs are continually being budded and breaking
off from the old ones. This is known as 'vegetative reproduction',
and it enables the plants to spread quickly over the surface. An-

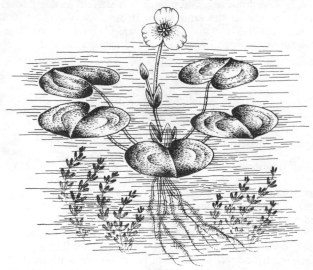

Frogbit

other floating plant with roots dangling in the water is frogbit. Its rounded floating leaves look like small waterlily leaves, and in summer you will see its white, three-petalled, male or female flowers raised on short stalks above the water. You are most likely to see frogbit if the pond is based on chalky soil. It spreads along the surface during summer by sending horizontal shoots, called runners, through the water. Each shoot has a bud at the tip, which develops into a new plant and becomes detached as the shoot withers—another case of vegetative reproduction.

Nearer the centre of the pond the gorgeous flowers of the white waterlily form many-petalled floating cups, with wide, polished leaves spread on the water around them. The floating leaves and flowers of the waterlily are carried upwards on long stalks from a thick, horizontal stem, called a rhizome, which is rooted in the mud. The leaves unfurl and the flower buds open only on reaching the water surface.

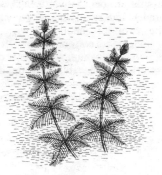

Water Milfoil

The submerged plants will not be so easy to see, and you may have to wade in and pull up a few specimens to identify them. But before doing so, test the mud with a stick, for what looks like the solid floor of the pond may be a covering of soft mud or silt, and your foot will sink straight through it.

Near the edge of the pond the surface may be studded with small rosettes of leaves like green stars. These are the upper leaves of starwort. The rest of the plant is submerged, with pairs of opposite leaves spaced along its stem. Only at the tip do the leaves grow close to form a floating star. A little farther out, in deeper water, you will see submerged feathery jungles of water milfoil. Pull up a plant, and you will notice that its feather-like leaves are arranged in whorls of four along the stem. In parts of the pond water milfoil may be replaced by even denser growths of Canadian pondweed, which has small leaves in groups of three along its stem. This plant was introduced from North America and has since spread in freshwater all over Britain.

Any of these submerged plants will do for your garden pond, but only put a few specimens in your polythene bags, for they will grow new shoots and spread quickly. Frogbit would be a good floating plant to take home, but not duckweed, for it will spread like a green carpet over the surface.

I have mentioned a few of the typical plants that you may find in and around the pond. There are many other kinds, but what you see depends to some extent on the soil and situation. For instance, in a heathland pond where the soil is peaty and slightly acid, you may find bladderwort in the water, and the beautiful bogbean growing from its shallows, with sphagnum moss, sundew, bog asphodel and cotton grass in the marshy ground around it. Bladderwort and sundew are both carnivorous plants. Bladderwort has little air-filled bladders on its feathery leaves. When minute trigger-hairs on one of the bladders are touched by a water flea or other tiny creature the bladder suddenly fills with water, sucking the creature in, where it is slowly digested. Sundew spreads a rosette of spoon-shaped leaves on the ground. The leaves are covered with long red hairs, each with a drop of sticky fluid at

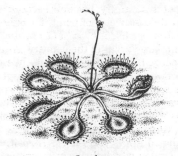

Sundew

the tip. A fly or other insect, attracted by these glistening globules, gets firmly stuck. The edges of the leaf curl inwards, and the hairs bend over like tentacles to draw the insect to its centre. Here, the soft parts of the insect are gradually digested and absorbed. A possible explanation of this unusual habit is that living, as they do, in places where the soil is poor in mineral salts, the plants evolved an ability to trap and digest animal food. Thus they compensate for deficiencies in the soil; but how the change in structure and behaviour came about is not explained at all, and remains a fascinating mystery.

The Common Frog
Now let us take a look at the animal life of the pond. For collecting the various creatures you will need some screw-top jars and a fine-mesh net with a strong frame. If you visit the pond in March

Common Frog

or early April you may see rounded masses of frog spawn floating in the shallow water at its edges. Pull off a little spawn to take home for your pond, and leave the rest—on no account take the whole mass of eggs. The common frog, which really *was* common in the early part of this century, has now become relatively scarce. Frogs depend on the still water of ponds for breeding, and along with the ponds that get filled in or built on, the frogs are being squeezed out from large areas of the country. Also, the toll taken for school and college Biology classes, where the frog is a standard animal for dissection, must have contributed to its decline. Thus, in taking a little spawn for your garden pond, you will be doing an important practical service in helping to ensure the common frog's survival as a species in this country. In summer, when the little frogs leave your pond, they will know it as their home and return there to breed a few years later. Then it will matter that much less if the pond in which they were spawned gets filled in.

A few days after hatching, the tadpole of the common frog develops external gills which show as little tufts on each side behind its head. A week later the external gills wither and internal gills start to form. For the next six weeks or so the tadpole breathes like a fish. Water, sucked in through its mouth, passes over the gills and out through a small opening called a spiracle on its left side. Limb-buds appear by the base of its tail, then, over the next few weeks, a great change occurs. The hind legs gradually take form and the tadpole develops lungs and swims to the surface at times to gulp air. The hind legs lengthen, become functional and assist in swimming, and the front legs break through the skin. Finally, the tail is slowly reabsorbed, and the little frog climbs out on land. This great change from the larval, tadpole form to the adult shape, is known as 'metamorphosis'.

Prehistoric Lobe-fins

Three hundred million years ago an ancient group of fishes known as lobe-fins, because their paired fins were attached to lobe-like, stumpy legs, lived in freshwater pools, swamps and shallow lakes among the coal-forest trees. These lobe-fins developed lungs to help them to breathe when the water became stagnant and poor in oxygen, owing to the rotting portions of tree-ferns, club-moss trees and giant horsetails that gradually littered the mud of their

Lobe-fin

watery world. Thus, whenever pools became clogged or dried up, the fishes were able to make their way overland, with the help of their lobed fins, to fresh bodies of water. Any modifications that made the overland trip easier would be strongly selected, so in the course of millions of years their limbs developed joints, and their bodies became more flexible. Among the ferns and mosses of the forest floor there were hordes of worms, millipedes, early insects and primitive spiders, so the lobe-fins' descendants learned to feed on these, and spent more of their time on land. Their encumbering fringe-fins disappeared, and fingered feet were formed to grip the soil. So, the first amphibians came into being. In the three months of its development in the pond, the common frog re-enacts this age-long evolutionary process.

Mudskippers

Even today there are small fish called mudskippers that spend most of their time on land. Mudskippers live in the mangrove marshes along tropical seashores. They have limb-like front or pectoral fins, by means of which they can lever themselves over the mud quite quickly, assisted by their tails, or climb up on exposed supporting-roots of mangrove trees. Mudskippers have not developed lungs, but they have large gill-chambers which they fill with water before coming on land. However, the water in their gill-chambers has to be renewed at frequent intervals, and they need to keep their skins moist, so they are not able to travel inland from the

Mudskipper

shore. Mudskippers feed on worms, small crustaceans and insects that they find on the mud flats and the mangrove roots. When disturbed, they go skittering over the mud into the sea.

Lungfish

There are three kinds of fish, however, that do have lungs as well as gills. These are the three kinds of lungfish living today, one in Australia, one in South America and one in Africa, of which there are four species. Lungfish are closely related in kind to the ancient lobe-fins, and are the only survivors of an equally ancient group. The living lungfish inhabit pools, streams or rivers that tend to become stagnant or dry up during the long dry season. They survive these critical periods because they can breathe air. The South American lungfish tunnels in the mud, leaving just a small breathing hole, when its stream dries up; and two species of African lungfish do likewise and secrete slime, which hardens in to a cocoon with a hole at the upper end. In this way they can survive for long periods in mud that has become baked by the sun. This resting state in hot weather is known as 'aestivation'.

African Lungfish

The Australian lungfish, which inhabits rivers in Queensland, and relies more on its gills for breathing, does not aestivate. An interesting point about the African and South American lungfish is that their eggs hatch into larvae with external gills. After a few months their external gill-tufts are absorbed and permanent internal gills develop—a similar change to that we saw in the young frog tadpole. Unlike the lobe-fins, the lungfish, despite their ability to breathe air, were never able to invade the land, and the paired fins of the present-day African and South American kinds are reduced to tentacles.

Development of Toads and Newts

We have travelled a long way in time and space—but now back to the pond. Toads and newts may have spawned in the pond, but their eggs will not be so easy to find. The eggs of the common toad will be in long strings of jelly, tangled round the stems of plants in the deeper water. Newts lay their eggs singly, and stick them on water plants, bending a small leaf round each egg to protect it. The development of toad tadpoles follows a similar pattern to that of frog tadpoles, but newt larvae, which are yellowish in colour, do not grow internal gills. They retain their tufts of external gills until they develop lungs and leave the pond. The front limbs appear first, and their feathery gills are not absorbed until all four legs are well developed.

Newt Larva

External and Internal Fertilisation

When frogs and toads reach the pond in early spring, each male mounts a female and clasps her tightly with his forelegs, so that his hands are pressed beneath her breast. The couple remain together, thus, until the female has laid her eggs. The male fertilises the eggs as soon as they emerge from the female's body, after which he releases his hold and they part to make their separate ways back to land. Fertilisation in frogs and toads is external, as it is in fishes and most other water creatures. By this, we mean that the male reproductive cells, called sperms, are shed into the water near the female reproductive cells, or eggs. Each sperm, which can only be seen through a powerful microscope, has a lashing tail, called a 'flagellum', by means of which it swims towards an egg and fuses with it. The fertile egg cell is then able to develop into a new individual creature. Fertilisation in mammals, birds, reptiles and insects is internal. That is to say, the sperms are shed directly into the female's body, where they fertilise the eggs before these are laid. Internal fertilisation is essentially an adaptation of life on land.

Fertilisation in Flowering Plants

Flowering plants overcome this problem of life on land by using insects or wind to carry pollen from the male organs, or stamens, of one flower, to the female organ, or pistil, of another. The pistil consists usually of three parts—the stigma, which is sticky or feathery to trap the pollen; the ovary, which contains the ovules; and the style, not present in all flowers, which is a stem or neck joining the stigma and ovary. After landing on a stigma, each pollen grain of the right kind germinates and sends a pollen-tube containing a male reproductive cell down through the style and into an ovule, where the male cell fuses with an egg cell, which can then develop into an embryo plant. This, however, is a much simplified account of the process, for flowering plants undergo what is known as 'double fertilisation'. That is to say the pollen tube contains a second male cell which fuses with two other cells in the ovule and causes a food store to develop. This food store, known as the 'endosperm', is used to nourish the embryo plant during its growth.

Hermaphrodites

Most flowering plants are hermaphrodite, that is to say each flower has stamens, and a pistil containing the ovules which, after fertilisation, become seeds. As the seeds develop, the ovary grows into a fruit, such as a berry, pod or capsule. However, some flowering plants, such as holly, are either male, having flowers with stamens but no pistil, or female, having flowers with a pistil but no stamens. Some animals, such as earthworms, slugs and garden snails, are hermaphrodite and contain both male and female organs. This means that each earthworm or snail will lay eggs after mating. Slugs and snails lay clusters of round eggs under stones or logs, but earthworms lay theirs in little oval cocoons which can be found in the soil.

Reproduction of Flowerless Plants

Ferns, horsetails and mosses, as mentioned earlier, are not flowering plants and reproduce by spores—but that is not the whole story. The spores of ferns are produced on the underside of the fronds, and those of horsetails on cones at the top of fertile stems. If, after being released in the air, a spore lands on suitable ground it germinates. However, it does not hatch into a baby fern or horsetail, but into a flat, green, tissue-thin, little plant called a 'prothallus', which lies on the surface and attaches itself by tiny root-like structures. I have seen fern prothalli, which are heart-shaped and about a centimetre long, growing on rotting logs in a wood, and at the base of damp shady walls. The fern prothallus forms minute male and female organs on its underside. Each female organ produces an egg and each male organ produces sperms. The sperms swim through wet soil to the female organs and fertilise the eggs. A fertile egg then develops into a minute embryo which is nourished by the prothallus. Soon the baby fern emerges, sending its own roots into the soil, and the prothallus withers.

Fern Prothalli

Alternation of Generations

Here we see a pattern of life that is in one way similar to that of amphibians, such as frogs and newts. Ferns and horsetails, like amphibians, live on land but depend on water for sexual reproduction. The big difference is that these plants reproduce by spores that do not require fertilisation, and it is their offspring, the prothalli, that produce sperms and eggs. This kind of double life-cycle is known as 'alternation of generations'. It occurs, also, in mosses, liverworts and most seaweeds, and in a few animals, such as jellyfish, aphids and certain gall-wasps.

Look at some cushions of moss growing on an old wall in spring. You will see little green or rust-red capsules at the top of slender, pin-sized stalks, rising from some of the moss plants. These stalked capsules are the spore-producing generation of the moss. The moss plant itself is the sexual generation which develops male and female organs, each in a little cup of leaves at the top of the stem. The sperms swim in rain water or dew to the female organs and fertilise the eggs; and the stalked capsules, which are really separate plants, arise from these. Spores are later shed from the ripe capsules, after which the stalk and capsule wither and fall away. Some of the spores will land on suitable ground and germinate, giving rise to new moss plants.

Moss with Capsules

Now compare this with the life-cycle of a fern, where the spore-producing generation is the fern plant, and the sexual generation is the tiny prothallus, which gives rise to a baby fern and soon withers. But meanwhile the little fern has formed roots in the soil and become independent. Thus the fern can grow to any size, according to its kind, and there are ferns in tropical rain forests that grow into tall trees. In mosses the situation is reversed. Here the sexual generation is the main plant, but it cannot grow big because it depends on rain water for reproduction. Its offspring is the stalked capsule which remains attached to the moss plant, so cannot grow big either. If only the little stalked capsule had learned to get down from its mother's knee and stand on its own feet, so to speak, by forming roots in the soil and growing leaves, then we might have had spore-producing generations of the moss plant as tall as trees.

Liverworts have a similar life-history to that of mosses. A common liverwort is pellia which can be found on the banks of streams and ditches. It has no leaves, and the plant body, called a

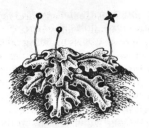

Liverwort with Capsules

thallus, is flat and frond-like with a forked tip and lobes at the sides. The male and female organs are on the upper-surface of the thallus and, in early spring, round black spore-capsules are produced on white stalks. Each capsule splits into four segments to release the spores; so what looked like a round-headed pin, opens out like a tiny four-petalled flower.

The Oak Apple Gall-wasp

An example of alternation of generations in animals is to be seen in the life-history of a little gall-wasp that causes the formation of oak apples on the twigs of oak trees. Oak apples swell rapidly in May, and at that time they are variedly coloured with pale green, yellow and rose pink. As they mature in late June, the galls, for that is what they are, become yellowish-brown suffused with rosy tints and spongy in texture. I collected one of these mature oak apples and placed the twig to which it was fixed in a jar. After covering the top of the jar with a piece of gauze, I placed it on the table in my study and waited. A few mornings later, when I got out of bed and went to my study, I found about three dozen tiny

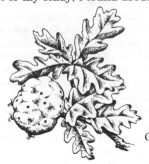

Oak Apple with
Gall-wasps emerging

gall-wasps flitting about in the jar, and I saw that the oak apple was pitted with their exit holes. In the evening I took the gall-wasps back to their oak tree and shook them from the jar on to one of its lower branches.

An oak apple develops from one of the buds on a twig, and after hatching from the eggs, the minute grubs set up some sort of irritation which causes the bud to produce the abnormal plant tissue of the gall. Each grub lives in a separate cell, feeding on sap produced by the tree, and when fully grown it pupates in the cell. In late June or July the little gall-wasps, which are either all brothers or all sisters—for the two sexes develop in separate oak apples—bite their way out. After a short rest they fly off, eventually meet others of the right sex, and start mating. The fertilised females then make their way into the soil at the base of an oak tree, and lay eggs singly in the tissues of young roots. This results in the formation of root galls, each with a single grub inside. The root galls are about a third of an inch wide when mature, and look like little brown nuts. They take about sixteen months to mature, and the adult gall-wasps emerge in the second winter.

Now comes the surprise. If you visit an oak tree that had oak apples on its twigs, and do so round about Christmas time, you may see a wingless insect that looks rather like a very plump ant, crawling up the trunk or along one of the branches. It is an oak apple gall-wasp, and it is a female, for there are no males in this alternate generation. Moreover, she is larger than the tiny winged forms that emerge from oak apples in summer, and different in appearance. If you are patient enough to watch her movements you will eventually see her start laying her unfertilised, virgin eggs in a bud at the end of one of the twigs. Next summer the bud will become an oak apple, and in it will be little grubs that had a mother but no father.

As in ferns and mosses, the alternate generations are dissimilar—the sexual generation of winged gall-wasps arising from oak apples, and the non-sexual generation of wingless forms arising from root galls. The difference is that in ferns and mosses the non-sexual generation produces spores, whereas in the gall-wasps it produces virgin eggs. These astonishing facts were not known to early naturalists, who called the insects from root galls by one name and those from oak apples by another.

Fertilisation in Newts

So—from my simplified account of reproduction in frogs and toads, the train of my thoughts has taken me to ferny woods, old walls, the banks of ditches and the branches of an oak tree. But now let us return to the pond in early spring. I pointed out that fertilisation in frogs and toads is external, but in the case of newts, despite the fact that they must reproduce in water, fertilisation is internal. Moreover, it is accomplished in an unusual manner, for the sperms from the male are not shed directly into the body of the female.

Smooth newts, being the commonest of the three British species, are the most likely to be found in the pond. You will see them swim to the surface with rapidly beating tails, let go a bubble of air, breathe in a fresh supply and return to the shady underwater jungle. It is easy to distinguish male newts at this season, for they are in full breeding dress. Catch one in a net and place him in a jar of water. You will see that he has a tall wavy crest along his back and tail, a similar crest along the lower edge of his tail and fringes of skin on his hind toes. He is olive brown with a brilliant orange belly, and his lower tail-crest has an orange margin with a stripe of bluish or mother-of-pearl iridescence above it. His body and tail are pat-

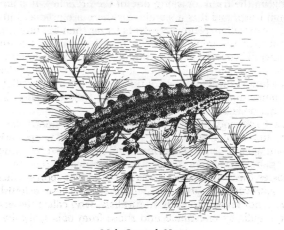

Male Smooth Newt

terned with black spots and there are black lines along his head. Now, having seen what a splendid creature he is, set him free in the pond, for the bright colours and adornments are there to be flaunted and displayed in courtship.

I have watched male newts courting females in ponds, and it is a charming spectacle. The male moves around the female waving his tail, undulating his crest, nudging her with his snout, and pressing or rubbing it gently along her sides. This may go on for hours, then finally he positions himself in front and, facing her, bends his tail double and vibrates it rapidly so that her body is stroked by the vibrations set up in the water. After repeating this performance a few times, the male newt emits a little capsule of sperms, called a 'spermatophore', on the floor of the pond. He then withdraws and the female newt, who has remained still and passive during the courtship, moves forward until the swollen cavity called the 'cloaca', which opens at the base of her tail, is directly over the spermatophore. She then presses her cloaca down on the spermatophore and takes it in. Once inside her body, the capsule dissolves and the released sperms fertilise her eggs. When the breeding season is over the newts climb out on land and move away. The crest and toe-fringes of the male are reabsorbed, and now he looks much like the female.

It will be nice to have a few newts for your garden pond, but it is better not to disturb them in the breeding season. Wait until the newt larvae have hatched and take home a few of these; then you will have the pleasure of watching them grow and develop until their metamorphosis is completed in August or September.

Warm-blooded and Cold-blooded Vertebrates

Newts, frogs, toads and other Amphibians are all backboned animals that have an internal skeleton. Such animals are called vertebrates. There are four other classes of vertebrates besides Amphibians. These are Fishes, Reptiles, Birds and Mammals. Birds and Mammals are said to be 'warm-blooded' vertebrates, which means that they have a constant body temperature. Fishes, Amphibians and Reptiles are said to be 'cold-blooded' vertebrates, which means that their body temperature varies with that of their surroundings. It does not mean that their blood is always cold, and a lizard will have warm blood if it is basking on a rock in full sunshine. Indeed, some reptiles maintain a fairly constant body

temperature, but it is controlled by their movements and behaviour, and not from inside, like that of birds and mammals.
Take, for instance, the crocodile. When I went on safari in East
Africa I saw crocodiles basking with their mouths wide open on
the banks of the Victoria Nile. They were not waiting for a meal
to walk in, but were regulating their body temperature.

Crocodiles spend the night swimming about and hunting for
food in the river. At sunrise they climb out of the water and flop
down on a gently sloping beach or a grassy area on top of the
bank. As the sun's heat strengthens, they open their mouths wide
so that evaporating moisture from the membranes lining the
inside of their jaws cools their blood. Around midday, when the
sun climbs overhead, they retire into the shade of trees or return
to the water, either submerging or lying half out of the water
with open mouths. Then for two or three hours in the late
afternoon they move back into the sun, and return to the river at
sundown. They stay in the water at night to conserve their body

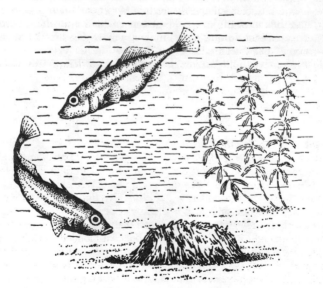

Male Stickleback guiding a female to his nest

heat, because water holds its heat much better than air. By following this sequence of alternating periods in sunshine, in shade and in water, crocodiles are able to maintain a body temperature that varies by only a few degrees.

Back again to our pond in the meadow—the only fish likely to be present is the three-spined stickleback. Take two or three for your garden pond, but do not take too many for they are very voracious. In spring the male three-spined stickleback develops a bright red throat and breast, and his eyes become brilliant blue-green. He scoops out a depression on the floor of the pond and piles bits of weed into this, forming them into a mound with sticky secretions from his body. He then bores a tunnel through the mound and induces females to lay their eggs in it, but drives away all male sticklebacks that enter his territory. He guards and aerates the eggs by fanning water through the nest with his fins, and protects the tiny young for their first few days after hatching.

The other vertebrate inhabiting the pond is the moorhen—a bird with a totally inappropriate name, for moors are one of the few habitats that it invariably avoids. Moorhens usually pair for life, and their nest of dead reeds will normally be on the mud or water, concealed among the stands of yellow flag or reed-mace. However, I have seen a moorhen incubating her eggs in a nest which she had built on the branch of a hawthorn tree over-

Moorhen and Chick

hanging a wide stream. Both parents incubate the eggs, which are whitish with brown speckles, and the black fluffy babies enter the water after hatching, but are fed by their parents for the first three weeks. It is charming to see the parent birds dip under water, emerge with a morsel of food in their beaks and deliver it gently to their chicks. Moorhens feed chiefly on water plants and insects, and there will only be one pair in the pond unless it is a very extensive one, for they are fiercely territorial.

Invertebrate Animals

The vast majority of animals in the world are invertebrates, and the same applies to the pond. Examples of invertebrate animals are insects, spiders, snails and worms. Vertebrate animals are generally big compared with invertebrates—but if you fill a barrel with apples and then pour peas into the barrel, shaking them down so that they lodge in all the spaces, there will be far more peas than apples in the barrel. If, after this, you pour sand into the barrel so that it is filled up with sand, peas and apples, you end up with far more grains of sand than all the peas and apples put together. So it is in any natural environment—there will be far more invertebrate animals than vertebrates, and far more tiny invertebrate animals than there are larger ones.

The peas in the barrel were able to occupy spaces that were not available to the apples, and the sand grains were able to occupy spaces that were not available to the peas. So it is with animals—the smaller they are, the more niches there are in the environment that they can occupy that are not available to larger creatures. The bigger an animal is, the more space it requires to move about in, and the more food it must consume to keep alive. For instance, an African elephant will eat about one and a half hundredweight of vegetation a day, and drink about fifty gallons of water, whereas some chalcid wasps can feed, grow up, pupate and complete their metamorphosis inside the eggs of moths. Thus, a batch of fifty moth eggs, occupying the space of a square centimetre, can supply enough food to nourish fifty chalcid wasps, not for a day but for the whole of their growing lives.

An Invertebrate Phylum

All vertebrate animals are included in one big group or phylum called the 'Chordata', but there are many phyla of invertebrates. I shall describe in brief just one of them which contain familiar animals. This is the phylum 'Arthropoda', which comprises all classes of animals that have segmented bodies, jointed legs and an external skeleton which covers the skin except at the joints and between the body segments. The five main classes of Anthropoda are as follows.

1. *The Crustacea*: With a few exceptions, this class contains all the marine anthropods, and includes crabs, lobsters, shrimps, sandhoppers and water-fleas. It also includes woodlice, which are said to be the only crustaceans able to spend the whole of their lives on land. However, when I was on holiday in Tenerife I found a species of sandhoppers under stones and leaf-litter in the banana plantations well away from the shore.

2. *The Insecta*: This is the only class of invertebrates that have evolved the power of flight. Apart from a few primitive kinds, insects have a larval stage and undergo metamorphosis. They have six legs, and usually two pairs of wings in the adult state.

3. *The Diplopoda*: This is the millipede class. Millipedes feed on fresh and decaying vegetable matter. They are usually long, often cylindrical, and have two pairs of legs on most of their body-segments. The pill-millipedes have short bodies and can curl into tight little balls. They should not be confused with pill-woodlice, which have only seven pairs of legs.

4. *The Chilopoda*: This is the centipede class. Centipedes are carnivorous, and have one pair of legs on most of their body segments, but the front pair take the form of poison-claws and curve round the head. These are used to capture and paralyse their prey. Centipedes are strictly nocturnal creatures, spending the day in hiding and, in some kinds, the mother guards her eggs and the young until they are able to look after themselves. One day in North Africa I turned over a stone, and there was a large centipede, about four inches long, curled round her clutch of nearly white babies. I touched her with a twig, and instead of retreating, she bit at it fiercely, still clutching her group of offspring. In centipedes there is an indirect method of fertilisation similar to that we saw in newts. The male deposits a spermatophore on the soil, which is taken up by the female.

5. *The Arachnida*: This class includes spiders, harvestmen, mites and scorpions. Arachnids have four pairs of legs and are without antennae. All spiders spin silk. Even hunting spiders that do not

spin webs, usually trail a line of silk behind them as they move about, and the females enclose their egg-batches in silk cocoons. Wolf spiders carry their egg-cocoons with them, attached to their spinnerets, and many other spiders guard their cocoons. I was able to testify to one instance of this when I was once in Majorca and found a European black-widow spider with her egg-cocoon under a stone on the waste ground behind my hotel. The egg-cocoon, attached by strong threads to some dry stems on the ground, was exposed to the blazing sunshine when I lifted the stone. To save her eggs, the black-widow started feverishly biting free the threads attaching the cocoon. Soon she had to retreat from the hot sun to cool down in the shadow of the lifted stone, but out she came again to sever a few more threads with frenzied haste before being forced back into the shadows by the heat. Out she came a third time, but I could not torment her any further, so I replaced the stone. The black-widow spider is not aggressive, but she can give an excruciatingly painful, and occasionally dangerous, bite when provoked. However, there is no doubt about her merit as a staunch and devoted guardian of her eggs.

Pond Invertebrates

Most of the invertebrate animals that you catch in the pond will belong to the phylum Anthropoda. But before you start collecting any for your garden pond, just stand or squat quietly at the edge of the water and watch the small creatures come and go. Pond skaters will skim over the surface with backward thrusts of their long middle pair of legs. If you move your arm, those nearest will leap away over the surface-film as if they were on a solid base. They do not even wet their feet, for these are covered with extremely minute, water-resistant hairs. There will also be sociable groups of whirligig beetles twisting, turning, swirling, revolving around each other on the surface. Wave your arm, and they will start gyrating at a frantic pace, yet without ever bumping each other. If you wade into the water they will all dive to the bottom, each with a small bubble of air attached to its rear. Return to the side and stand still for a few minutes—you will see them bob up to the surface, one after another, and twist, swivel and wind around each other as before. As the whirligig beetle swims, the under-surface is immersed, but the shiny upper-surface repels water and remains above it. The middle and hind legs of the whirligig are very short, broad and fringed, to form tiny paddles that are vibrated at speed in swimming. These two insects, the first a bug, the second a beetle, have become adapted to occupy a special niche in the pond community, as surface dwellers that feed on insects which fall into the water.

Pond Skater

Now gaze down into the water itself. Back-swimmer water-boatmen rest back downwards, suspended from the surface-film, or propel themselves with powerful strokes of their long oar-like hindlegs. Lesser water-boatmen swim in rapid jerks over the

Swimming Leech

muddy floor of the pond, and small water-beetles paddle vigorously above the mud, occasionally diving into it and kicking up little puffs of silt as they go by. Larger water-beetles, streamlined and neatly oval, swum up from the submerged jungles of pondweed, tilt themselves head-downwards to break the surface-film with the hind tip of their bodies, pause to renew the air supply beneath their wings, then row themselves smoothly down again. Bright vermilion water-mites, not more than two millimetres long, swim here and there through the water with a rapid running motion of their legs, and a leech swims past with graceful up-and-down undulations of its flattened body.

You will notice creatures moving on the floor of the pond. Water-snails and small black flatworms glide over the mud, and caddis-fly larvae shuffle along in their cases of cut plant stems, leaf sections, small snail-shells or little stones, according to the species. Water-lice crawl over the mud, and freshwater shrimps slither here and there on their sides, or leap up and glide swiftly through the water in a curve that lands them on the mud again. These two crustaceans are scavengers that eat whatever dead or decaying animal or plant material they find. The other pond crustaceans are minute. At the edge of the water milfoil jungle a swarm of water-fleas, or daphnia, floats in mid-water, each tiny unit engaged in a perpetual dance of upward jerks and downward drifts, and little pear-shaped copepods jump through the water with sudden back-whisks of their long antennae. These small crustaceans sift microscopic plant-life from the water. The myriads of microscopic plants form the base, or first link, of many food chains in the pond, for the water-fleas which eat them are eaten by water-mites, damsel-fly nymphs, sticklebacks, newt larvae and small water-beetles.

Now a piece of the mud bottom stirs, and you begin to perceive it for what it really is—the large-eyed head and stout cylindrical body, tapered at the rear, of a two-inch dragonfly nymph. You had not seen it as it rested, alert and watchful, on the mud, for its dingy colours merged with the surroundings. Suddenly the dragonfly nymph's hinged mouth-claw shoots, flash-quick, from beneath its head, and grabs a water-louse. The claw folds back and the nymph's jaws start to munch contentedly.

These are a few of the invertebrate animals that you might see in the pond. If you sweep your net gently to and fro through the

thickets of submerged water plants you will find many more that
were living among the stems and foliage. Damsel-fly nymphs,
mayfly nymphs, smaller caddis-fly larvae with cases of green
leaves that make them hard to distinguish among the plants, and
water-scorpions. The latter are not scorpions, but predatory water
bugs which capture prey with pincer-like front legs. A large,
perfectly dry brown spider might turn up in your net. This is the
water-spider which, so far as is known, has the distinction of
being the only spider in the world that swims and lives permanently under water. The water-spider spins a curved platform of
silk among the submerged plants. This is filled with bubbles of air
which the spider carries down from the surface and releases under
the web. Finally, a silk dome, filled with air, is formed—a diving-
bell-home in which the spider rests. When swimming below the
surface of the pond the water-spider appears as a living jewel of
glittering quicksilver, for its velvety body is enclosed in a sheath
of air.

Take home plenty of invertebrate animals for your garden pond,
but see that you have far more small invertebrates in your col-

Water-spider with Air-bell

lection than there are larger ones. If you have not already stocked
your pond with submergent water plants, fix the stem bases of
those you have in small tins of soil, and cover the soil with stones

to prevent it from floating out into the water when you lower the plants into your pond. Floating plants like frogbit can be placed straight on the water surface. Do not pour the water creatures from your jars or containers into the pond, but float them out by tilting each jar below the surface and pulling it gently backwards and up.

When the young frogs, toads or newts leave your pond they will find food and shelter in the wild strip of garden. Newts will hide under the large flat-bottomed stones in damp shady parts, and some flower-pots, well concealed and laid on their sides half-buried in the soil, will become permanent day-time shelters for toads throughout the summer months.

Classes and Families

A long, narrow wooden box placed in the shelter of a hedge or large bush in the wild strip, and covered with soil and moss, might tempt a hedgehog to set up home if you fill it loosely with dry grass or hay. Hedgehogs are mammals belonging to the order 'Insectivora', which include the mole and the four kinds of British shrews, one of which is confined to the Scilly Isles. Just as a phylum is split up into separate classes, each containing animals that are more similar to each other than they are to the rest, so each class is split up into separate orders. For instance, dogs, cats, weasels and other flesh-eating mammals that have sharp canine teeth and cutting molars, belong to the order 'Carnivora'. Rats, mice, beavers, squirrels and guinea-pigs belong to the order 'Rodentia', cloven-hoofed mammals such as cattle, sheep, deer, antelopes and giraffes belong to another order, the different kinds of bats to yet another and so on. In the same way, orders are split up into separate families, each containing animals with still closer resemblances. Thus, in the order Carnivora the dog family, 'Canidae', includes wolves, jackals and foxes; the cat family, 'Felidae', includes lions, tigers, leopards and lynxes; and the weasel family 'Mustelidae', includes otters, badgers, polecats and pine martens.

Try to sort out the other orders of mammals, then try to do the same with birds, and then with insects. When you have done your best at this, look them up in books and see how correct you were, and what mistakes you made. Later, try sorting out the orders into separate families. It is a fascinating game to play with a friend, and you will come to understand how different creatures are related to each other and how, in the far distant past, they evolved from common ancestors. Your imagination will be stirred, and you will come to see that by experimenting with different kinds of food, trying out different ways of life and exploring new areas of the environment, the animals were able to avoid competing with each other. Then you will feel an urge to discover all that is known about the processes and pressures, acting over millions of years, that caused the animals to diverge, adapted them to fill new areas of life and initiated the development of structures and behaviour that fitted them for different styles of living.

The Hedgehog

The hedgehog is one of the few wild mammals that most people see sooner or later, even if it is only as a squashed body on the road, for it has adapted well to living in parks and gardens. For millions of years, the hedgehog's one means of defence has been to roll up into a prickly ball and, apart from the motor car, its only enemies in Britain are the fox and the badger, both of which have learned how to force it open with their claws. Young hedgehogs are born in early summer and there are usually five to a litter. The babies are blind at birth and have soft white prickles. About five weeks later the mother starts taking them out on foraging expeditions. At dusk, on a mid-summer evening, you might see her leading a string of young ones from the nest.

Hedgehog

I very often hear a hedgehog before seeing it, for its search for insects, slugs, snails and other creatures is accompanied by snorts, soft grunts and snuffles. If I approach a hedgehog in the open it immediately stops in its tracks and lowers its snout so that the prickles on its neck and head stand upright. Should I come closer, the hedgehog curls into a ball, but if it is beside thick plant cover it usually makes a hasty retreat. One night in late spring I was woken up by a series of loud puffs, hisses and gurgling noises. I thought a hot-water pipe must have burst, so I got up and rushed downstairs; but not being able to find anything wrong inside the house, I went outside to investigate. My flashlight revealed two courting hedgehogs facing each other on the flower bed. After pausing for a moment they made off into the next garden, and I inwardly cursed myself for being so clumsy and missing the chance of watching their behaviour.

In autumn, hedgehogs accumulate layers of fat around the neck and shoulders to supply the small energy demands of hibernation when their bodies cool and their heart and breathing rates slow down to a life-supporting minimum. Then, towards the end of October, each hedgehog seeks out a dry, well-concealed hollow under a thick hedge, the cavity of an old wasp nest or a garden compost heap, and constructs a nest of leaves and moss which are carried home in its mouth. For the first month or two the hedgehog sleeps intermittently, and on mild evenings it may leave the nest or 'hibernaculum', and wander abroad; but by the new year its sleep has become very deep, and it will not stir until it wakes up in the spring.

Another ground-living mammal which uses spines as a means of protection is the echidna or spiny anteater, of which there are two species in Australia. The echidna looks rather like a hedgehog with a thin snout and large claws. Its snout ends in a tiny toothless mouth, and it feeds on termites and ants which are licked up on its long sticky tongue. The echidna's spines offer good protection against dingoes and other predators and, like a hedge-hog, it will roll itself into a ball when disturbed. If the ground is soft, however, the echidna can dig itself vertically down, keeping its spines erect until it disappears beneath the surface. Echidnas are egg-laying mammals belonging to the order 'Monotrema', which also contains the duck-billed platypus. Their single eggs are laid in a pouch; when the young hatches, it is carried in the pouch until its spines start to grow. From then on the mother leaves her baby in a safe hiding place returning at intervals to feed it until it has been weaned.

Echidna

Convergence

The echidna somewhat resembles a hedgehog because it lives a similar kind of life and has evolved the same means of protection. When two different kinds of animals have come to bear certain resemblances because they play similar roles in the living community we call this phenomenon 'convergence'. The echidna shows convergence not only with the hedgehog but with the true anteaters of South America which also have thin snouts, small toothless mouths, long sticky tongues and large claws for opening termite nests.

Adaptive Radiation

The mammals with which we are most familiar are known as 'placental' mammals. That is to say, their young develop in the womb or uterus and are nourished through an organ called the 'placenta', which makes extremely close contact with the mother's blood. However, the majority of Australasian mammals belong to the order 'Marsupialia', or pouched mammals. Many of these show convergence with placental mammals of other continents. The reason for this is that the marsupials entered Australia before it became separated from the Asiatic mainland, and before the more successful placental mammals had reached it. Thus the marsupials were able to branch out, diversify and exploit the various habitats and food resources without serious competition. Some became tree dwellers, some grass eaters, some carnivores, some insect eaters and so on.

This branching out process, where a group of related animals becomes variously changed and specialised for different modes of life, is called 'adaptive radiation'. By adaptive radiation the marsupials came to fill similar niches in the environment to those filled by placental mammals in other parts of the world. A 'niche' is the particular role an animal plays in the living community, and where animals fill similar niches they tend to show convergence. The marsupial mole looks remarkably like any other mole, the marsupial mice look like field mice or wood mice everywhere else, the rat kangaroos look like the jerboas of North Africa, the Australian native cat is similar to the civets of southern Asia, the wombat, which has rodent-like front teeth, looks like an oversized marmot, the tree-living possums are similar to lemurs, bush-babies and lorises, the flying phalangers or glider possums show remarkable convergence with flying squirrels, the thylacine or marsupial wolf, so tragically exterminated by the early sheep farmers of Tasmania—or probably so, for the last known wild specimen was shot in 1930—really looked like a wolf or hunting dog, and the kangaroos of the grassy plains have heads resembling those

Thylacine

of gazelles and antelopes that graze the African savannahs. They also have rather similar stomach structures, containing stomach bacteria and protozoans to aid the digestion of leaves and grasses.

Nest Boxes

Now back from the ends of the earth to your garden sanctuary. You have provided a home for a hedgehog, flower-pot shelters for toads and large flat-bottomed stones for newts and for insects and other invetebrates—one of the insects you are likely to shelter will be the handsome violet-bordered ground beetle, the largest of our common garden beetles. You have also established a self-contained habitat for freshwater creatures. The next job will be to put up two or three nest boxes for birds to breed in.

To garden birds, houses with gardens probably appear as inland cliffs and crags scattered among open woodland and scrub. Sparrows and starlings nest in crevices of these crags, and house martins fix their mud cups on the stone surface, in the shelter of eaves and gutters. Blackbirds, thrushes, finches and dunnocks will be happy to nest in the trees, bushes and hedges of this man-made, shrubby woodland, but robins, wrens, tits, nuthatches, wagtails and flycatchers will be ready to accept nest boxes, for there is always a housing problem for hole-nesting birds.

There are two types of nest boxes. One has an open front, boarded up half-way; and robins, flycatchers and wagtails prefer this type. The other is an enclosed box with a round entrance hole, which will suit tits and wrens, and nuthatches if you are fortunate enough to live near an oak wood. For tits and wrens, a hole the size of a ten-penny piece will prevent sparrows from entering and taking over. For nuthatches, the hole must be larger; but the exact size does not matter, for they will reduce it to their requirements by applying mud round the edges and working it in with their bills. Fix the nest boxes to trees, fences or garden sheds and see that they face in a northerly direction. If they face south, the nestlings may get over-heated and die. A little moss, spread on the floor of the boxes will make them more attractive when prospecting birds visit them in spring.

Helping Birds in Winter

You will help the birds through the hard winter months by putting out extra food for them. Net bags, such as those used by green-grocers for carrots or oranges, if filled with peanuts and hung from a branch, will be appreciated by tits and greenfinches. Strings of peanuts in their shells, lumps of fat or meaty bones, hung from branches, will attract tits, and it is delightful to watch these acrobatic little birds swinging upside-down as they peck away at the food. If you want a bird table, all you need is a wooden plat-form, twelve inches square, screwed down on a post about five feet high; but I prefer to feed the birds on the lawn where I can scatter the food widely. I collect all bread, cake and biscuit crumbs,

Blue Tit on Strung Peanuts

chopped leftovers of cheese, meat scraps, skins of roast chicken, bacon rinds and bread soaked in fat from the frying pan.

The sparrows come first, even before I have finished scattering the crumbs, then a couple of collared doves alight and walk to-wards the crumbs, one or two blackbirds join them and a song thrush appears in the background. Quickly some starlings arrive, and more flutter down from the sky. The sparrows and collared doves peck away at the bread and cheese, the starlings in a close milling flock gobble everything as rapidly as they can, a blackbird spends half his time chasing off a persistent rival, and this is the song thrush's chance until one of the blackbirds sees him and drives him off, but when the larger mistle thrush comes bounding over the lawn the blackbirds themselves must give way. A robin flies in, picks a morsel of cheese, then returns to a bush but comes back for another, and another, and a few chaffinches and dun-nocks feed round the fringes of the scattered crumbs. When all the other birds have cleared what they can find and flown away the dunnocks remain for quite a long time, hopping here and there and flicking their wings almost too rapidly to see, as they peck up the minutest bits of crumb that only their bills can gather.

Sometimes a magpie alights at the bottom of the lawn and walks and hops towards the scattered food, alert and wary, with pauses on his way, and head well up, feathers sleeked, and one eye on the window so that I have to stand back and keep quite still. On seeing him the sparrows and small birds scatter into trees and bushes, the blackbird flies up on to the fence and the starlings watch the magpie approach, then stand in a row a couple of yards away, looking very subdued as they wait for him to finish and fly off. On one occasion, however, a collared dove remained feeding, then puffed out its chest and went jumping towards the magpie, driving him off before he reached the crumbs. The magpie flew on to the fence, but came back, and the collared dove repeated its aggressive performance, then flew after him and really saw him off. This was a most surprising piece of behaviour that I should never have expected from a collared dove.

Collared Dove threatening a Magpie on the lawn

Occasionally some black-headed gulls come circling over the lawn, and then all the small birds scatter. The gulls fly round and round and swoop over the food, but dare not alight or swoop too low. At last one of them swoops down, picks up a piece of bacon rind or chicken skin, slapping the ground with his coral feet as he passes, and swallows the food in flight. The gulls continue to circle over the lawn and then another swoops and grabs some food, a third one follows suit, but none of them dares alight so near the house. Suddenly the gulls fly off, and all the small birds return and flutter down to peck the scattered crumbs.

For the naturalist in the world today, much that he holds most dear seems threatened from all sides. Just as an alpine slope would be bereaved and diminished without its blue gentians, its apollo butterflies, its whistling marmots and its flock of alpine choughs, or as a rock pool would be diminished without its green and scarlet seaweeds, its expanded sea anemones, its starfish and its glass-transparent prawns, so the human species will be bereaved and diminished if it can no longer experience the magic and the pulse of the universe in the clear, sweet trilling of tree-crickets on a warm Mediterranean night, or gasp at the fragile beauty of a wild flower. Natural History is concerned with the quality of life that cannot be registered on the balance sheet of material comforts, for it is about joy and wonder, and the saving and cherishing of this beautiful planet, with its fantastically varied life. In setting up a garden sanctuary, you will be doing something of incalculable value in the world, and come rain, hail or snow, so long as there is a window in your mind and in your house, you will never, never be bored.

Suggestions for Good Books

Rupert Barrington: *The Bird Gardener's Book* (Wolfe)

F. H. Brightman: *The Oxford Book of Flowerless Plants* (OUP)

Michael Chinery: *The Natural History of the Garden* (Collins)

John Clegg: *The Observer's Book of Pond Life* (F. Warne & Co. Ltd)

T. L. Jennings: *Studying Birds in the Garden* (Wheaton)

Arthur Jewell: *The Observer's Book of Mosses and Liverworts* (F. Warne & Co. Ltd)

Jean Mellanby: *Nature Detection and Conservation* (Carousel Books)

David Nichols & John Cooke: *The Oxford Book of Invertebrates* (OUP)

Marion Nixon: *The Oxford Book of Vertebrates* (OUP)
Tony Soper: *The Bird Table Book* (David & Charles Ltd)
Wildlife Begins At Home (David & Charles Ltd)
Hamlyn All-Colour Paperbacks
  Catherine Jarman: *Evolution of Life*
  Sali Money: *The Animal Kingdom*
  Tony Morrison: *Animal Migration*
  John Sparks: *Animals in Danger*
             Bird Behaviour
  Ian Tribe: *The Plant Kingdom*

Useful Addresses

XYZ Club, Zoological Society, Regent's Park, London NW1
British Naturalists' Association. Branches all over the country.
  Address of local secretary obtainable from Council for Nature,
  Zoological Gardens, Regent's Park, London, NW1
Children's Centre, Natural History Museum, Cromwell Road,
  London SW7
British Trust for Ornithology, The Nunnery, Nunnery Place,
  Thetford, Norfolk, 1P24 2PU
Field Studies Council, Preston Montford, Montford Bridge, Shrews-
  bury, SY4 1HW
Young Ornithologists' Club, The Lodge, Sandy, Beds., SG19 2DL

For details of the last three of these organisations, see *Something to Join*.

MISCELLANY

However you divide the contents of an encyclopaedia, there are always essential pieces of information left over that seem to go nowhere in particular. It is these that you will find in this final section of JUNIOR PEARS.

Lantern Clock 1688

TIME: CALENDARS AND CLOCKS

The Days of the Week

The names of the days—Sunday, Monday, Tuesday (Tiw—the God of War), Wednesday (Woden or Odin), Thursday (Thor), Friday (Frig—wife of Odin) and Saturday come from Old English translations of the Roman names (Sol, Luna, Mars, Mercurius, Jupiter, Venus and Saturnius).

How the Months Got Their Names

January   From Janus, a Roman god. The Anglo-Saxons called it *wulf-monath*—the month of the wolves.

February   From a Roman god, Februus. A.S.: *sprote-cal*—the month when the kale, a kind of cabbage, sprouted.

March   Originally the first month in the Roman calendar. From Mars, the god of war. A.S.: *hreth-monath*—the rough month.

April   From the Latin *Aprilis.* A.S.: *Easter-monath*—month of Easter.

May   From Maia, a goddess. A.S.: *tri-milchi*—the month when the cows were milked three times a day.

June   From Juno, mother of the gods. A.S.: *sere-monath*—the dry month.

July   Named after Julius Caesar. A.S.: *maed-monath*—meadow-month.

August Named after Augustus Caesar. A.S.: *weod-monath*—the month of vegetation.

September The seventh Roman month. From the Latin word meaning *seven*. A.S.: *haerfest-monath*—harvest month.

October The eighth Roman month. From Latin word meaning *eight*. A.S.: *win-monath*—the month of wine.

November The ninth Roman month. From Latin word meaning *nine*. A.S.: *wind-monath*—month of wind.

December The tenth Roman month. From Latin word meaning *ten*. A.S.: *mid-winter monath*—mid-winter month.

The Year

The Equinoctial or **Tropical Year** is the time the earth takes to go round the sun: 365·2422 solar days. The **Calendar Year** consists of 365 days, but a year of which the date can be divided by 4 without a remainder is called a **Leap Year**, with one day added to the month of February. The last year of a century is a Leap Year only if its number can be divided by 400 (e.g. 1900 was not a Leap Year, but 2000 will be one).

The Longest and Shortest Days The longest day is the day on which the Sun is at its greatest distance from the equator; this is called the **Summer Solstice**. It varies between June 21 and 22.

The shortest day is the day of the **Winter Solstice**, and in 1992 falls on December 21.

Dog Days These are the days about the rising of the Dog Star, the hottest period of the year in the Northern Hemisphere. Roughly they occur between July 3 and August 25.

St Luke's Summer is a warm period round about St Luke's Day (October 18).

St Martin's Summer is a warm period round about Martinmas (November 11).

The Christian Calendar Until 1582 the calendar used in all Christian countries was the Julian Calendar, in which the last year of all centuries was a Leap Year. By the sixteenth century this had caused a difference between the tropical and calendar years (see **The Year**) of 10 days. In 1582 Pope Gregory ordered that October 5 should be called October 15, and that of the years at the end of centuries only every fourth one should be a Leap

Year. This new calendar was called the Gregorian Calendar and was gradually adopted throughout the Christian world. In Great Britain and her Dominions it came into use in 1752; by then there was a difference of 11 days between tropical and calendar years, and September 3 of that year was reckoned as September 14.

Easter Day can be, at the earliest, March 22; at the latest, April 25.

Whit Sunday can be, at the earliest, May 10; at the latest, June 13.

The Jewish Calendar dates from October 7, 3761 B.C. In 1993 the Jewish New Year (5754) begins on September 16.

The Moslem Calendar dates from the Hejira, or the flight of Mohammed from Mecca to Medina (July 16, A.D. 622 in the Gregorian Calendar). In 1993 the Moslem New Year (1414) falls on June 21.

Summer Time

Summer time—the putting forward of the clock by one hour during the months of summer—was first introduced in the First World War. Its purpose then was to cut down on the use of power for lighting; but in peace-time it was continued so that people might enjoy longer summer evenings.

From February, 1968, summer time was established for a three-year trial period to conform with Central European time. The new title chosen for it was British Standard Time. This experiment was abandoned in October, 1971, when the United Kingdom reverted to Greenwich Mean Time.

Normally British Summer Time is from the day following the third Saturday in March until the day following the fourth Saturday in October.

Time all over the World

This table shows what the time is in the important cities of the world when it is 12 noon at Greenwich. Places in ordinary type are ahead of Greenwich; those in *italics* are behind Greenwich.

Accra, Ghana .	12 Noon	Ankara, Turkey .	2.00 p.m.
Adelaide, Australia .	9.30 p.m.	Athens, Greece .	2.00 p.m.
Algiers . . .	1.00 p.m.	Baghdad, Iraq .	3.00 p.m.
Amsterdam,		*Baltimore, USA* .	7.00 a.m.
Netherlands .	1.00 p.m.	Bangkok, Thailand .	7.00 p.m.

Belgrade,			Luxembourg	. . 1.00 p.m.
Yugoslavia .	.	1.00 p.m.	Madrid, Spain	. 1.00 p.m.
Berlin, Germany	.	1.00 p.m.	Mandalay, Burma	. 6.30 p.m.
Berne, Switzerland .		1.00 p.m.	Melbourne,	
Bombay, Inda .	.	5.30 p.m.	Australia	. 10.00 p.m.
Boston, USA .	.	7.00 a.m.	*Mexico City*	. 6.00 a.m.
Brisbane, Australia .		10.00 p.m.	*Montevideo, Uruguay*	9.00 a.m.
Brussels, Belgium	.	1.00 p.m.	*Montreal, Canada*	. 7.00 a.m.
Budapest, Hungary .		1.00 p.m.	Moscow, Russia	. 3.00 p.m.
Buenos Aires,			Nairobi, Kenya	. 3.00 p.m.
Argentina	.	9.00 a.m.	New Delhi, India	. 5.30 p.m.
Cairo, Egypt .	.	2.00 p.m.	*New York*	. 7.00 a.m.
Calcutta, India	.	5.30 p.m.	Nicosia, Cyprus	. 2.00 p.m.
Calgary, Canada	.	5.00 a.m.	Oslo, Norway .	. 1.00 p.m.
Canberra, Australia.		10.00 p.m.	*Ottawa, Canada*	. 7.00 a.m.
Cape Town, South			*Panama* .	. 7.00 a.m.
Africa .	.	2.00 p.m.	Paris .	. 1.00 p.m.
Chicago, USA .	.	6.00 a.m.	Beijing, China .	. 8.00 p.m.
Colombo, Ceylon	.	5.30 p.m.	Perth, Australia	. 8.00 p.m.
Copenhagen,			*Port of Spain,*	
Denmark .	.	1.00 p.m.	*Trinidad*	. 8.00 a.m.
Darwin, Australia .		9.30 p.m.	Prague,	
Detroit, USA .	.	7.00 a.m.	Czcchoslovakia	. 1.00 p.m.
Dublin, Ireland	.	12 Noon	*Quebec, Canada*	. 7.00 a.m.
Freetown, Sierra			*Quito, Ecuador* .	. 7.00 a.m.
Leone .	.	12 Noon	*Reykjavik, Iceland*	. 11.00 a.m.
Gibraltar.	.	1.00 p.m.	*Rio de Janeiro* .	. 9.00 a.m.
Halifax, Nova			Rome .	. 1.00 p.m.
Scotia .	.	8.00 a.m.	*St John's,*	
Hamilton, Bermuda .		8.00 a.m.	*Newfoundland*	. 8.30 a.m.
Harare, Zimbabwe	.	2.00 p.m.	*San Francisco, USA* .	4.00 a.m.
Havana, Cuba .	.	7.00 a.m.	*Santiago, Chile* .	. 8.00 a.m.
Helsinki, Finland	.	2.00 p.m.	Seoul, Korea .	. 8.30 p.m.
Hong Kong .	.	8.00 p.m.	Singapore	. 7.30 p.m.
Honolulu, Hawaii	.	2.00 a.m.	Stockholm, Sweden.	1.00 p.m.
Jerusalem .	.	2.00 p.m.	Sofia, Bulgaria	. 2.00 p.m.
Johannesburg,			Suva, Fiji .	. 12 Midnight
South Africa	.	2.00 p.m.	Sydney, Australia	. 10.00 p.m.
Karachi, Pakistan	.	5.00 p.m.	Teheran, Iran .	. 3.30 p.m.
Kingston, Jamaica	.	7.00 a.m.	Tirana, Albania	. 1.00 p.m.
Kuala Lumpur,			Tokyo, Japan .	. 9.00 p.m.
Malaya	.	7.30 p.m.	*Toronto, Canada*	. 7.00 a.m.
Lagos, Nigeria.	.	1.00 p.m.	*Vancouver, Canada*	. 4.00 a.m.
St. Petersburg,			Vienna, Austria	. 1.00 p.m.
Russia	.	3.00 p.m.	Warsaw, Poland	. 1.00 p.m.
Lima, Peru .	.	7.00 a.m.	Wellington, New	
Lisbon, Portugal	.	12 Noon	Zealand .	. 12 Midnight
Los Angeles, USA	.	4.00 a.m.	*Winnipeg, Canada*	. 6.00 a.m.

BRITISH FLAGS

The Union Jack* was adopted in 1606 following the Union of England and Scotland, and took its present form in 1801, when there was the further union with Ireland (see HISTORY). It consists of three heraldic crosses:

> the cross of St Andrew, which forms the blue and white basis;
> upon which lies the red and white cross of St Patrick;
> upon the whole rests the red and white cross of St George dividing the flag vertically and horizontally.

The Union Jack

The correct manner of flying the flag is with the larger strips of white next to the flagstaff uppermost.

The Royal Standard is the sovereign's personal flag, only to be flown above a building when she is actually present. It is divided into quarters, the 1st and 4th containing the three lions *passant* of England, the 2nd quarter containing the lion *rampant* of Scotland and the 3rd quarter containing the harp of Ireland. (*Passant* and *rampant* are terms in heraldry, see the section on Heraldry that follows.)

The White Ensign, the flag of the Royal Navy, is a white flag bearing the cross of St George, with a small Union Jack in the top corner next to the flagstaff.

---

* Although it has become usual to call this flag the Union Jack on all occasions, it is strictly correct to do so only when the flag is flown at the jackstaff of one of Her Majesty's ships. At all other times it should be called the Union Flag.

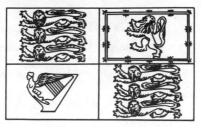

The Royal Standard

The Red Ensign (known as 'the red duster'), flag of the Mercantile
Marine. It is a plain red flag with the Union Jack in the top
corner next to the flagstaff.

The Blue Ensign (similar to the Red Ensign, but with blue background). flag of the Royal Naval Reserve (RNR).

A NOTE ON HERALDRY

Man has always used symbols to decorate his armour; but heraldry
as we know it started in Europe in the twelfth century. Knights
began to wear helmets which completely covered their wearers'
faces, making recognition difficult. So when they met together at
tournaments or went on crusades it was necessary that each
should have a personal badge. This became known as the knight's
coat-of-arms because it was worn on his sur-coat over his armour.
The most obvious place to put the arms was on the shield. On his
helmet a knight sometimes bore another distinguishing badge—
the **crest**—which rested on a band of twisted cloth—the **torse**. This
held in place a **mantling** to protect the metal from the hot sun.
When all these are brought together they form an **achievement of
arms** (Fig. 1). Once you have seen them together you are unlikely
to make the popular mistake of calling a coat-of-arms a crest.

Because heraldry was formulated so long ago, the language
used is a mixture of Norman-French and Latin and English. At
first this may seem difficult; but once a few terms are mastered it
can be seen to be a very practical language. Describing arms in
words is called **blazoning**, and the method is to name the colour
or colours of the **field** (the background), then to describe the main

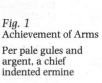

Fig. 1
Achievement of Arms

Per pale gules and
argent, a chief
indented ermine

13th century Knight

charge and its colour, and finally to name the subsidiary charges
with their colours. Only five **tinctures** are commonly used—red,
called **gules**: blue, called **azure**: green, called **vert**: purple, called
purpure: and black, called **sable**. There are two **metals**, gold (**or**)
and silver (**argent**), and these are usually represented by yellow
and white. In addition there are **furs**—**ermine**, **vaire** and
numerous variations. A basic rule of heraldry is that a coloured
charge should not be placed on a colour nor a metal one on a
metal.

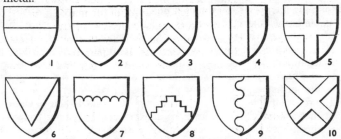

Fig. 2   Some ordinaries and lines of partition

1 Chief: 2 Fess: 3 Chevron: 4 Pale: 5 Cross: 6 Pile: 7 per fess invected:
8 per chevron indented: 9 per pale wavy: 10 Saltire

All items on a shield are known as **charges** and can be anything
and everything from ants to zebras. The main charges are known
as **ordinaries**. Sometimes the field is divided into more than one
colour (as in Fig. 1), and the ordinaries lend their names to these
divisions. The dividing lines can be straight or wavy-shaped or
angular; Fig. 2 shows some of these.

Fig. 3

It is possible to tell from a coat of arms to which member of a family it belongs. The head of the family bears plain arms, but his sons must carry a symbol to **difference** his arms from those of his father and his brothers (Fig. 3). Women bear their father's arms on a **lozenge** (a diamond shape), with no difference, and they cannot inherit arms if they have brothers. If a woman marries, her husband **impales** his wife's arms on the **sinister** side of his shield (Fig. 4). (In Latin **dexter** means right and **sinister** left, but in heraldry this refers to the left and right of the man carrying the shield.) If a lady has no brothers, she herself inherits the arms and her husband places them on his own arms on an **escutcheon of pretence**. Their children may **quarter** both parents' arms. Sometimes the quarterings may run into hundreds, but they are not all displayed.

Fig. 4

1 Per pale a chief indented impaling a bend: 2 Per pale a chief indented and on an escutcheon of pretence a bend: 3 Quarterly, 1st and 4th per pale a chief indented 2nd and 3rd a bend. (Note—Colours are omitted in these blazons.)

At first, no doubt, men chose their own symbols; but soon the monarch became the ultimate authority for granting arms. In England this authority is delegated to the Earl Marshal (at present the Duke of Norfolk), who is responsible for arranging great state occasions. To help him he has the College of Arms consisting of the Kings of Arms—Garter, Clarenceux and Norroy and Ulster— six Heralds and four Pursuivants. In Scotland the principal officer is Lord Lyon, who has three Heralds and three Pursuivants.

Heraldry is a living part of our history. Not only is it found in old manuscripts and in churches and castles, but it can be seen on town halls, banks, company offices and advertisements. Look at your school badge and those of your friends. Some are real arms and have been granted to the school; but most are badges based on the arms of the town or a famous man (Fig. 5). Some, alas, may even have been invented by someone with no knowledge of heraldry.

BBC
A gold band of communication surrounding the Earth

National Coal Board
An heraldic pictorial representation of a coal mine

UK Atomic Energy Authority
Pictorial representation of an atomic pile

Barrow Grammar School badge with a bee and arrow from the 'punning' arms of Barrow and the roses of Lancashire

Fig. 5

This is no more than an introduction to the subject and you may want to read more about it. The books listed below are not dry but lively, well-illustrated and in one instance very amusing. Your library may have them. If you want to take your study further, the Secretary of the Heraldry Society, 45 Museum Street, London, WC1, will be pleased to send you information.

Simple Heraldry, by Iain Moncreiffe and Don Pottinger.
Boutell's Heraldry, revised by C. W. Scott-Giles and J. P. Brooke-Little.

Shield and Crest, by Julian Franklyn.
Discovering Heraldry, by R. H. Wilmott.

NOTES ON COINS

Coins as Weights and Measures A penny weighs 3·564 grams, and has a diameter of 2·0320 cm. The diameter of the 50p coin is 3 cm: of the 20p coin, 2·14 cm. The £1 coin weighs 9·5 grams, and has a diameter of 2·25 cm.

British Coins Our coppers are really bronze (97 parts of copper, $2\frac{1}{2}$ parts of zinc and $\frac{1}{2}$ part of tin). The **farthing** (then of silver) was first struck in 1279 and withdrawn at the end of 1960. First **halfpenny** struck, in silver, in 1280: changed to bronze with penny and farthing in 1860: the old halfpenny ceased to exist on August 1, 1969. **Penny** introduced in 8th century: first copper pennies struck in 1797: demonetised on February 15, 1971, when Britain switched to decimal coinage and introduced also the new two pence piece. **Threepence** struck as silver coin in 1551; replaced in 1937 by a twelve-sided brass coin that was demonetised in 1971. The £1 coin was introduced on April 21, 1983.

Our **silver** in 1947 became cupro-nickel (75% copper, 25% nickel). The **shilling** (called then a testoon) was first struck as a silver coin by Henry VII: it is now the 5p piece. The **florin** (10p) appeared in 1849, the first step towards putting the English coinage on a decimal basis. (This earlier scheme was abandoned.) The **half-crown** was first struck in the reign of Edward VI: ceased to exist on January 1, 1970. The **sixpence** ceased to be legal tender on June 30, 1980. The **historical portraits** on all bank notes are: £5, Duke of Wellington; £10, Florence Nightingale; £20, William Shakespeare; £50, Sir Christopher Wren. A new series of notes was introduced in 1990: a new £5 (with a portrait of George Stephenson) was followed by a new £10 (with a portrait of Charles Dickens) and a new £20 (with a portrait of Michael Faraday).

Legal Tender Bank of England notes and gold dated 1838 onwards are legal tender for any sum. The £1 coin is legal tender to any amount. Silver (cupro-nickel) coins with values up to and including 10p are legal tender up to £5; 50p and 20p coins up to £10, and bronze up to 20p.

American Coins The word **dime** comes from the French dixième, a tenth part, and is the name given to the silver 10 cent coin, which is a tenth part of a dollar. **Nickel** is the popular name for the five-cent American coin, made of copper and nickel. The probable origin of the **dollar sign** ($) is that it is an adaptation of the old Spanish method of recording the peseta or piece of eight as a figure eight between sloping lines (/8/).

DISTANCE OF THE HORIZON

The distance to which you can see depends on the height at which you are standing.

At a height of		You can see	
5 ft	(1·52 m)	2·9 miles	(4·64 km)
20 ft	(6·1 m)	5·9 miles	(9·44 km)
50 ft	(15·24 m)	9·3 miles	(14·88 km)
100 ft	(30·48 m)	13·2 miles	(21·3 km)
500 ft	(152·4 m)	29·5 miles	(47·2 km)
1,000 ft	(304·8 m)	41·6 miles	(66·5 km)
2,000 ft	(609·6 m)	58·9 miles	(94·24 km)
3,000 ft	(914·4 m)	72·1 miles	(115·36 km)
4,000 ft	(1,219 m)	83·3 miles	(133·28 km)
5,000 ft	(1,524 m)	93·1 miles	(149 km)
20,000 ft	(6,096 m)	186·2 miles	(298 km)

THE SEVEN WONDERS OF THE ANCIENT WORLD

1. **The Pyramids of Egypt** The oldest is that of Zoser, at Saggara, built about 3000 B.C. The Great Pyramid of Cheops covers more than 4·9 hectares (12 acres) and was originally 146 m (481 ft) high and 230 m (756 ft) square at the base.
2. **The Hanging Gardens of Babylon** Adjoining Nebuchadnezzar's palace near Baghdad. Terraced gardens watered from storage tanks on the highest terrace.
3. **The Temple of Diana at Ephesus** A marble temple erected in honour of the goddess about 480 B.C.
4. **The Colossus of Rhodes** A bronze statue of Apollo (see A DICTIONARY OF MYTHOLOGY) with legs astride the harbour entrance of Rhodes. Set up about 280 B.C.
5. **The Tomb of Mausolus** At Halicarnassus, in Asia Minor. Built by the king's widow about 350 B.C. From it comes our word 'mausoleum'.

6. **The Statue of Olympian Zeus** At Olympia in Greece; made of
   marble inlaid with ivory and gold by the sculptor Phidias,
   about 430 B.C.
7. **The Pharos of Alexandria** Marble watch tower and lighthouse
   on the island of Pharos in Alexandria Harbour. Constructed
   about 250 B.C.

ROMAN NUMERALS

I	1	LX	60
II	2	LXX	70
III	3	LXXX	80
IV	4	XC	90
V	5	IC	99
VI	6	C	100
VII	7	CX	110
VIII	8	CXC	190
IX	9	CC	200
X	10	CCC	300
XI	11	CD	400
XII	12	D	500
XIII	13	DC	600
XIV	14	DCC	700
XV	15	DCCC	800
XVI	16	CM	900
XVII	17	XM	990
XVIII	18	M	1000
XIX	19	MLXVI	1066
XX	20	MD	1500
XXX	30	MDCCC	1800
XL	40	MCMXCIII	1993
L	50	MM	2000
LV	55		

SOME ALPHABETS

Greek

Name	Letter		English equivalent
Alpha	A	α	a
Beta	B	β	b
Gamma	Γ	γ	hard g

Name	Letter		English equivalent
Delta	Δ	δ	d
Epsilon	E	ε	short e (as in 'egg')
Zeta	Z	ζ	z, dz
Eta	H	η	long e (as in 'bee')
Theta	Θ	θ	th
Iota	I	ι	i
Kappa	K	κ	k or hard c
Lambda	Λ	λ	l
Mu	M	μ	m
Nu	N	ν	n
Xi	Ξ	ξ	x
Omicron	O	o	short o (as in 'box')
Pi	Π	π	p
Rho	P	ρ	r
Sigma	Σ	σ, s	s
Tau	T	τ	t
Upsilon	Y	υ	u or y
Phi	Φ	φ	ph, f
Chi	X	χ	kh or hard ch
Psi	Ψ	ψ	ps
Omega	Ω	ω	long o (as in 'dome')

Russian

Letter	English eq	Letter	English eq
А а	a	П п	p
Б б	b	Р р	r
В в	v	С с	s
Г г	g as in 'good'	Т т	t
Д д	d	У у	oo as in 'food'
Е е	yeh	Ф ф	f, ph
Ё ё	yo as in 'yonder'	Х х	kh as in 'loch'
Ж ж	zh	Ц ц	ts
З з	z	Ч ч	ch
И ий	ee as in 'deed'	Ш ш	sh
К к	k	Щ щ	shch
Л л	l	Ы ы	i as in 'did'
М м	m	Э э	e as in 'egg'
Н н	n	Ю ю	yu
О о	o	Я я	ya

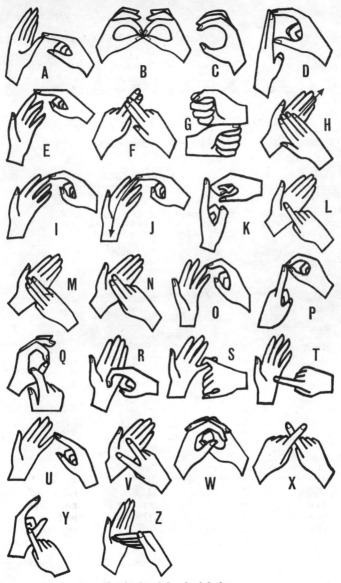

The deaf and dumb alphabet

LONGEST AND HIGHEST
Highest Buildings and Other Structures

	m	ft		m	ft
KTHI-TV mast, N. Dakota . . .	628	(2,063)	City Bank, NY . .	225	(740)
CN Tower, Metro Centre, Toronto	555	(1,822)	Toronto-Dominion Bank Tower, Toronto . . .	225	(740)
TV Tower, Toronto .	550	(1,805)	Terminal Tower, Cleveland . . .	215	(708)
TV Tower, Oklahoma City . .	479	(1,572)	Metropolitan Life, NY	213	(700)
Empire State, New York	448	(1,472)	TV Mast, Stuttgart .	213	(700)
Sears Tower, Chicago	443	(1,454)	500 Fifth Avenue, NY .	212	(697)
World Trade Center, New York . . .	417	(1,368)	Chanin, NY . .	207	(680)
			Lincoln, NY . .	205	(673)
ITA TV Masts, Emley Moor (Yorks), Belmont (Lincs) . .	385	(1,265)	Husky Tower, Calgary, Canada . .	190	(626)
Bank of China, Hong Kong . . .	368	(1,209)	Telecom Radio Tower, London . . .	176	(580)
			Chicago Temple . .	173	(569)
AMOCO Building, Chicago . . .	346	(1,136)	Ulm Cathedral, Germany	161	(529)
John Hancock Center, Chicago. . .	343	(1,127)	Bank of State, São Paulo, Brazil . .	158	(520)
			Blackpool Tower . .	157	(518)
TV Tower, Tokyo . .	329	(1,082)	Cologne Cathedral, Germany . .	156	(512)
Chrysler Building, NY	318	(1,046)	St John the Divine, NY .	152	(500)
C. & S. Plaza, Atlanta	312	(1,024)	Strasbourg Cathedral .	142	(468)
First Interstate World Center, Los Angeles	310	(1,017)	The Pyramid of Cheops, Egypt . .	137	(450)
			St Peter's, Rome . .	136	(448)
ITA TV Mast, Winter Hill (Lancs) . .	309	(1,015)	St Stephen's Cathedral, Vienna . . .	134	(441)
Texas Commercial Tower, Houston .	305	(1,002)	St Joseph's Oratory, Montreal . .	126	(414)
Allied Bank Plaza, Houston . .	302	992	Salisbury Cathedral .	123	(404)
Eiffel Tower, Paris .	299	(984½)	Antwerp Cathedral .	121	(397)
60 Wall Tower, NY	289	(950)	Torazzo of Cremona, Italy . . .	121	(397)
Bank of Manhattan, NY	282	(927)	The Tower Block, Millbank Development, London	118	(387)
Rockefeller Centre, NY . . .	259	(850)	Freiburg Cathedral, Germany . .	117	(385)
Woolworth Building, NY . . .	241	(792)			
Moscow State University . .	239	(787)	St Paul's Cathedral, London . .	111	(365)
Albert Hertzog Tower, Johannesburg . .	235	(772)			

Longest Tunnels

	km	Miles		km	Miles
Seikan, Tsugaru Channel, Japan	53·9	(33½)	Shimizu, Japan	9·6	(6)
Channel Tunnel	50·50	(31½)	Rimutaka, New Zealand	8·8	(5½)
Moscow Metro, Belyaevo–Medved Kovo, Moscow, USSR	30·7	(19)	Ricken, Switzerland	8·4	(5¼)
			Grenchenberg, Switzerland	8·4	(5¼)
East Finchley to Morden	28	(17½)	Tauern, Austria	8·4	(5¼)
Golders Green to South Wimbledon	25·6	(16)	Otira, New Zealand	8	(5)
			Ronco, Italy	8	(5)
Oshimuzu, Japan	22·2	(13¾)	Hauenstein, Switzerland	8	(5)
Simplon, Switzerland to Italy	20	(12½)	Colle di Tenda, Italy	8	(5)
			Connaught, Canada	8	(5)
Shin-kanmon, Japan	18·7	(11.6)	Hoosac, USA	7·2	(4½)
Apennine, Italy	18·4	(11½)	Sainte Marie-aux-Mines, France	7·2	(4½)
Rokko, Osaka–Kobe, Japan	16·9	(10)	Rove, France	7·2	(4½)
Furka base, Switzerland	15·4	(9½)	Severn, England	7·0	(4½)
St Gothard, Switzerland	14·8	(9¼)	Mont d'Or, Switzerland to France	6·4	(4)
Loetschberg, Switzerland	14·4	(9)	Albula, Switzerland	6·4	(4)
Mont Cenis, Italy	13·6	(8½)	Boughton to Cedera, S. Africa	6	(3¾)
Cascade, USA	12·4	(7¾)	Totley, England	5·9	(3½)
Arlberg, Austria	10	(6¼)	Standedge, England	4·8	(3)
Moffat, USA	9·6	(6)			

Longest Bridges

	Length of waterway			Length of waterway	
	m	in ft		m	in ft
Oosterscheide, Netherlands	5,021	(16,476)	Forth Road, Scotland	1,876	(6,156)
Lower Zambesi, Africa	3,450	(11,320)	Rio Dulce, Argentina	1,786	(5,860)
Storsstrom, Denmark	3,200	(10,500)	Hardinge, Bangladesh	1,639	(5,380)
Tay, Scotland	3,136	(10,290)	Victoria Jubilee, Montreal.	1,621	(5,320)
Upper Son, India	2,999	(9,840)	Moerdijk, Netherlands	1,432	(4,700)
Godavari, India	2,706	(8,880)	Humber, England.	1,370*(4,626)
Forth Railway, Scotland	2,526	(8,290)	Verazzano—Narrows, New York	1,298	(4,260)
Tay Road Scotland	2,294	(7,365)	Sydney Harbour, NSW	1,255	(4,120)
Rio Salado, Argentina	2,042	(6,700)	Jacques Cartier, Montreal.	1,185	(3,890)
Golden Gate, San Francisco	1,889	(6,200)			

* The longest single central span of any suspension bridge in the world.

Longest Ship Canals

	km	Miles		km	Miles
St Lawrence Seaway, Canada (including L. Ontario and Welland Canal)	604·8	(378)	Kiel	97·6	(61)
			Volga-Don USSR	96	(60)
			Panama	80	(50)
Gota, Sweden	184	(115)	Elbe-Trave, Germany	65·6	(41)
Suez	164·8	(103)	Manchester	56·8	(35½)
Volga-Moscow	128	(80)	Princess Juliana, Netherlands	32·8	(20½)
Albert (Antwerp-Liege)	128	(80)	Amsterdam	26·4	(16½)

A GUIDE TO SOME OF THE MOST IMPORTANT MUSEUMS IN GREAT BRITAIN

National Museums

The British Museum, Great Russell Street, London, WC1.
Victoria and Albert Museum, Cromwell Road, London, SW7.
Royal Scottish Museum, Chambers Street, Edinburgh, 1.
National Museum of Wales, Cathays Park, Cardiff.

Prehistory and Early Civilisation

British Museum, Great Russell Street, London, WC1.
Horniman Museum, London Road, Forest Hill, SE23.
National Museum of Welsh Antiquities, University College of North Wales, College Road, Bangor.
National Museum of Antiquities of Scotland, Queen Street, Edinburgh, 2.
Pitt Rivers Museum, Parks Road, Oxford.
Ashmolean Museum, Beaumont Street, Oxford.
Fitzwilliam Museum, Cambridge.
Yorkshire Museum, Museum Street, York.
Wells Museum, Cathedral Green, Wells, Somerset.
Museum of the Glastonbury Antiquarian Society, Glastonbury.
Verulamium Museum and Roman City, St Albans, Hertfordshire.
Viroconium Museum, Wroxeter, Shropshire.
Reading Municipal Museum, Blagrave Street, Reading.
Bath Roman Museum, Abbey Churchyard, Bath.
Roman Site and Museum, Corbridge, Northumberland.
Legionary Museum, Caerlon, Gwent, Wales.
Avebury Manor, Avebury, Wiltshire.
Segontium Roman Fort Museum, Beddgelert Road, Caernarvon, Gwynedd.
Museum of Sussex Archaeology, Barbican House, Lewes.
Colchester and Essex Museum. The Castle, Colchester.

Natural History and Geology

British Museum (Natural History), Cromwell Road, London, SW7.
National Museum of Wales, Cathays Park, Cardiff.

Royal Scottish Museum (Natural History Dept.), Chambers Street, Edinburgh, 1.

Zoological Museum, British Museum, Natural History Dept., Akeman Street, Tring, Hertfordshire.

Oxford University Museum, Parks Road, Oxford.

Cambridge University Museum of Zoology, Downing Street, Cambridge.

Geological Museum, Exhibition Road, London, SW7.

Horniman Museum, London Road, Forest Hill, SE23.

Brooke Museum, Brighton, Sussex.

Robertson Museum and Aquarium, Marine Station, Keppel Pier, Millport, Scotland.

Hancock Museum, Barras Bridge, Newcastle-upon-Tyne, 2.

Marine Biological Station, Aquarium and Fish Hatchery, Port Erin, Isle of Man.

Cannon Hill Museum, Pershore Road, Birmingham.

Royal Botanic Gardens, Kew, London.

Botanic Gardens, Oxford.

University Botanic Gardens, Cambridge.

Zoological Gardens, Regent's Park, London: also in Edinburgh, Manchester and other big cities.

Geography

British Museum (Ethnographical Dept.), Great Russell Street, London, WC1.

Imperial Institute, South Kensington, London, SW7. (For the countries of the Commonwealth.)

Horniman Museum, London Road, London, SE23.

Royal Geographical Society Museum, 1 Kensington Gore, London, W8.

Pitt Rivers Museum, Parks Road, Oxford.

Cambridge University Museum of Archaeology and Ethnology, Downing Street, Cambridge.

Pitt Rivers Museum, Farnham, Blandford, Dorset.

Science

Science Museum, Exhibition Road, South Kensington, London, SW7.

Museum of the History of Science, Broad Street, Oxford.

Whipple Museum of the History of Science, 14 Corn Exchange Street, Cambridge.

Science and Engineering Museum, Exhibition Park, Great North Road, Newcastle.

Wellcome Historical Medical Museum, 183 Euston Road, London, NW1. (Medical science.)

Anatomical Museum, University New Buildings, Teviot Row, Edinburgh, 1. (Medical science.)

Birmingham City Museum, Dept. of Science and Industry, Newhall Street, Birmingham, 3.

Agriculture

Agricultural Museum, Wye College, Wye, Kent.

Rothamsted Experimental Agricultural Institute, Harpenden, Hertfordshire.

Reading University Dept. of Agriculture Museum, Reading, Berks.

Cambridge Agricultural Institute, Cambridge.

The Curtis Museum, High Street, Alton, Hampshire.

West Yorkshire Folk Museum, Shibden Hall, Halifax, Yorkshire.

Transport

London Transport Museum, Covent Garden, London, WC2.

Motor Cars

Science Museum, Exhibition Road, South Kensington, London, SW7.

Museum of Carriages, Kent County Museum, Chillington, Manor House, Maidstone, Kent.

Museum of Motor Cars, Beaulieu Abbey, Brockenhurst, Hampshire.

Ships

Science Museum, Exhibition Road, London, SW7.

National Maritime Museum, Greenwich, London, SE10.

Royal United Service Museum, Whitehall, London, SW1.

Fisheries and Shipping Museum, Pickering Park, Hull.

Railways

National Railway Museum, Leeman Road, York.
Great Western Railway Museum, Swindon.

Aircraft

De Havilland Mosquito Museum, Salisbury Hall, London Colney,
Hertfordshire.
Science Museum, London, SW7.
Shuttleworth Collection, Old Warden Aerodrome, Old Warden,
Bedfordshire.

Photography, Film and Television

National Museum of Photography, Film and Television, Prince's
View, Bradford.

Theatre

Theatre Museum, Covent Garden, London, WC2.

Public Services

Imperial War Museum, Lambeth Road, London, SE1.
Scottish United Service Museum, Crown Square, Edinburgh Castle,
Edinburgh.
Royal Military Academy Sandhurst Museum, Camberley, Surrey.
The Armouries, Tower of London, EC3.
Wallace Collection, Hertford House, Manchester Square, London,
W1. (Armour.)
Glasgow Museum, Kelvingrove, Glasgow. (Armour.)
Airborne Forces Museum, Maida Barracks, Aldershot, Hampshire.
Chartered Insurance Institute Museum, 20, Aldermanbury, London,
EC2. (Firefighting.)
National Army Museum, Royal Hospital Road, SW3.
Royal Air Force Museum, Colindale, Hendon.

Social and Domestic History

Victoria and Albert Museum, Cromwell Road, South Kensington,
London, SW7.

Museum of London, Aldersgate Street, EC2.
Cambridge and County Folk Museum, Cambridge.
Welsh Folk Museum, St Fagan's, Glamorgan.
Stranger's Hall Folk Museum, Norwich.
York Castle Museum, Tower Street, York.
Bishop Hooper's Lodging Folk Museum, Gloucester.
Kent County Museum, Chillington Manor House, Maidstone, Kent.
Manx Village Folk Museum, Cregneash, Isle of Man.
Folk Museum, Kingussie, Inverness.

Furniture

Geffrye Museum, Kingsland, London, E2.
Old House, High Town, Hereford.
Georgian House, Great George Street, Bristol.
Ham House, Petersham, Surrey.
Temple Newsam, Leeds.
The Pavilion, Brighton.
Iveagh Bequest, Ken Wood, London, NW3.

Costume

Victoria and Albert Museum, Cromwell Road, London, SW7.
Bethnal Green Museum, Cambridge Heath Road, London, E2.
Gallery of English Costume, Platt Hall, Rusholme, Manchester, 14.
Museum of Costume, The Pavilion, Brighton, Sussex.

Children's Museums

Bethnal Green Museum, London, E2. (Dolls, dolls' houses, toys, model theatres, children's books.)
Tollcross Museum, Tollcross Park, Glasgow.
Museum of Childhood, 42 High Street, Edinburgh 1.

Cricket

Imperial Cricket Memorial Gallery, Lord's Cricket Ground, London, NW8.

The Arts

National Gallery, Trafalgar Square, London, WC2.
National Portrait Gallery, Trafalgar Square, London, WC2.
Tate Gallery, Millbank, London, SW1. (Modern art.)
Victoria and Albert Museum, Cromwell Road, London, SW7.
Wallace Collection, Hereford House, Manchester Square, London, W1.
Sir John Soane's Museum, 13 Lincoln's Inn Fields, London, WC2. (Architectural drawing.)
Dulwich College Picture Gallery, College Road, London, SE21. (Chiefly seventeenth and eighteenth centuries.)
National Gallery of Scotland, The Mound, Edinburgh, 1.
Scottish National Portrait Gallery, Queen Street, Edinburgh, 2.
National Museum of Wales, Cathays Park, Cardiff.
Fitzwilliam Museum, Cambridge.
Ashmolean Museum, Oxford.
Bowes Museum, Barnard Castle, County Durham.
Walker Art Gallery, Liverpool.
Whitworth Art Gallery, Oxford Road, Manchester.
Norwich Castle Museum, Norwich.
City Museum and Art Gallery, Birmingham.
Barber Institute of Fine Arts, The University, Birmingham, 15.
Graves Art Gallery, Sheffield, 1.
Museum of Eastern Art, Broad Street, Oxford.
Royal College of Music, Donaldson Museum, London, SW7. (Musical instruments.)

Museums Illustrating the Lives of Famous People

Jane Austen Jane Austen's House, Chawton, Hants.
J. M. Barrie The Birthplace, Kirriemuir, Angus, Scotland.
The Brontës Brontë Parsonage Museum, Haworth, nr. Keighley, Yorkshire.
John Bunyan Bedford Public Library, Bedford.
Robert Burns Alloway Cottage and Museum, Ayrshire.
Lord Byron Newstead Abbey, Nottinghamshire.
Thomas Carlyle Carlyle's House, 24 Cheyne Row, London, SW3.
Sir Winston Churchill Chartwell, Westerham, Kent.
S. T. Coleridge Coleridge's Cottage, Lime Street, Nether Stowey, Somerset.

James Cook Museum of Literary and Philosophical Society, Whitby, Yorkshire.

Charles Darwin Downe House, Downe, Kent.

Charles Dickens Dickens' House, 48 Doughty Street, London, WC1.
Dickens' Birthplace, 393 Commercial Road, Portsmouth.
Bleak House, Broadstairs, Kent.

Francis Drake Buckland Abbey, Plymouth.

Thomas Hardy Dorset County Museum, Dorchester.

Samuel Johnson Dr Johnson's House, Breadmarket Street, Lichfield.
Dr Johnson's House, 17 Gough Square, Fleet Street, London, EC4.

John Keats Keats Memorial House, Wentworth Place, Keats Grove, London, NW3.

David Livingstone Scottish National Memorial to David Livingstone, Blantyre, Scotland.

John Milton Milton's Cottage, Chalfont St Giles, Buckinghamshire.

Horatio Nelson Nelson Museum, New Market Hall, Priory Street, Monmouth.

Isaac Newton The Museum, Grantham.

Cecil Rhodes Rhodes Memorial Museum, Bishop's Stortford.

Capt. Scott Polar Research Institute, Cambridge.

Walter Scott Lady Stair's House, Lawnmarket, Edinburgh, 1.

William Shakespeare Shakespeare's Birthplace, Stratford-on-Avon.
New Place, Stratford-on-Avon.
Anne Hathaway's Cottage, Shottery, Warwickshire.
Mary Arden's House, Wilmcote, Warwickshire.

George Bernard Shaw Shaw's Corner, Ayot St Lawrence, Hertfordshire.

R. L. Stevenson Lady Stair's House, Lawnmarket, Edinburgh 1.

James Watt Watt Institution, 15 Kelly Street, Greenock, Scotland.

Duke of Wellington Wellington Museum, Apsley House, Hyde Park Corner, London, W1.

John Wesley Wesley's House, 47 City Road, London, EC1.

William Wilberforce Wilberforce House, Hull.

William Wordsworth Dove Cottage, Grasmere, Westmorland.
Wordsworth Museum, Grasmere, Westmorland.
Wordsworth's Birthplace, Cockermouth, Cumberland.